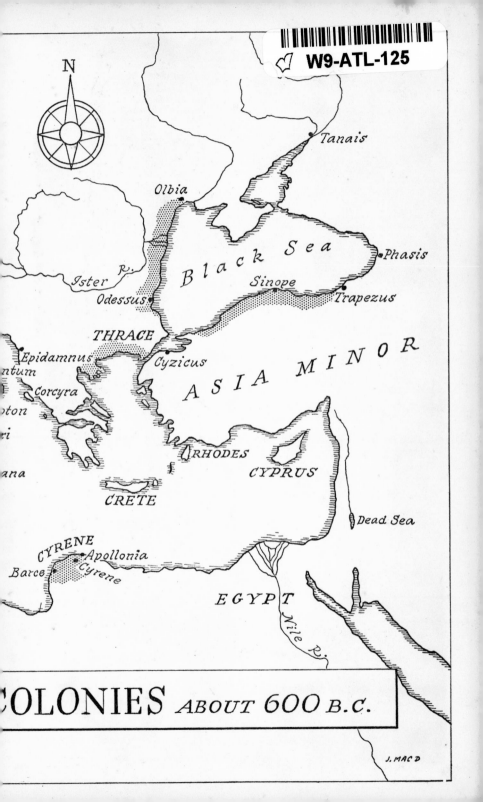

N

Tanais

Olbia

Black Sea

Phasis

Ister R.

Odessus

Sinope

Trapezus

THRACE

Epidamnus

ntum

Cyzicus

ASIA MINOR

Corcyra

oton

ri

RHODES

CYPRUS

ana

CRETE

Dead Sea

CYRENE

Apollonia

Barce

Cyrene

EGYPT

Nile R.

COLONIES ABOUT 600 B.C.

J. MAC D

Ancient Greece and the Near East

David McKay Company, Inc.

New York

ANCIENT GREECE

and the

NEAR EAST

BY **RICHARD MANSFIELD HAYWOOD**

Professor of Classics

New York University

Second Printing, September 1968

To

RICHARD

ANNE AND

MARY

"Haec sunt ornamenta mea"

FOREWORD

The size of this history of the Near East and Greece to the death of Alexander permits rather little discussion of debated facts or interpretations. I have mentioned some of the more interesting debates as to fact and have tried at least to raise some of the questions of interpretation or of the philosophy of history.

Several of my friends have graciously read parts of the manuscript and have helped me to improve it. William F. Albright, whom I knew as a colleague at Johns Hopkins, read Chapter 3; Saul Weinberg of the University of Missouri read Chapter 10; George Hanfmann of Harvard University read the parts dealing with Lydia; my colleague Harmon Chapman of University College read the parts dealing with philosophy; William Dunmore, my colleague in the Classics Department of University College, read almost all the manuscript. My wife read it all. I am grateful to them all for their help and encouragement; responsibility for what is said in the book remains with me.

University College   Richard M. Haywood
New York University

CONTENTS

ix

ILLUSTRATIONS

PHOTOGRAPHS
(*between pages 50 and 51*)

xi

Ancient Greece and the Near East

CHAPTER

1

THE SCOPE AND THE METHOD
OF ANCIENT HISTORY

From the primeval slime to Constantine is the facetious definition sometimes used to set the temporal limits of ancient history. The primeval slime is too early; our interest begins at the indefinite time when man began to act somewhat like Man and less like an aimless beast, that is, in the Old Stone Age. In the great revolution of the New Stone Age, the lord of creation began to assert his dominance. He improved his tools, learned to make plants grow according to his will, and used his intellectual advantage over the beasts to entice some of them into coming and living with him to be protected by him, to work for him, to yield him their milk, which Nature had intended for their own young, and, if it was his will, to be eaten by him. Man was beginning to act like Man.

Scholars used to disagree as to whether the area of prime importance in the next phase was the valley of the Nile or the region between the Tigris and Euphrates Rivers—Mesopotamia. With the better understanding of the Neolithic Age that archaeological researches have given us, we can see that the next stage of culture in these two regions, and in the valley of the Indus River in India as well, developed naturally out of the Neolithic culture. The ability to deal with metals and a system of writing were the two things most needed for

1

the next stage of civilization. These things were developed independently in Egypt, Mesopotamia, and India. By 3000 B.C. the new stage was well under way, both systems of writing and work in copper and copper alloys having appeared.

For more than two thousand years this civilization was centered in Mesopotamia, Asia Minor, Syria-Palestine, and Egypt. The development in India, which at first was close to the others, is not so important to the history of the West, nor are the other civilizations that developed in China and, later, in the Western hemisphere, which also lie outside our main cultural tradition.

From generation to generation and century to century, political dominance resided now here, now there. Kingdoms and empires rose and fell. Now one altar reeked with sacrifice while another was cold, and then the situation was reversed. Imperial languages at last were known only by priests and scholars, while humbler languages became for a time the *lingua franca*, only to disappear in their turn. But through all these vicissitudes, a common cultural property of all the inhabitants of these regions of the Near East was built up and disseminated. There was a certain common background of ideas and superstitions, practices in government and trade, and techniques, whether in agriculture, metalwork, or weaving. And far out on the periphery, where certain natural products were sought, in Greece or Sicily or Spain, around the tin mines of Bohemia or up on the Baltic end of the amber route, some faint reflection of this culture was known.

The next stage bears the stamp of Greece. That wonderful congeries of people of mixed blood who are known as the Greeks had the benefit of the cultural experience of the earlier peoples in the Near East. The style of everything that the Greeks did was different, however. It was the beginning of the modern Western style. For some reason they early acquired the habit of generalizing, of trying to see all experience as parts of a related whole that made some sense, and of trying to analyse everything that presented itself to them, from the appearance of the heavenly bodies to the fascinating behavior of man. The earlier peoples had not been so given to generalization and analysis. They had had cities, but nothing like the Greek type of city, as we shall see. The high intellectual tradition was the possession of a few among them, not of the many, as among the Greeks.

By the year 300 B.C. or shortly thereafter, it must have become plain to well-informed people in the Greek world (that is, in the eastern part of the Mediterranean lands) that, although culturally crude, the Romans and their federation of peoples in Italy were to be reckoned with as wielders of considerable military power. By the year 30 B.C., the Romans had learned a great deal culturally from the Greeks; and in that year, Octavian, the grandnephew of Julius Caesar, took from Cleopatra her kingdom of Egypt, completing Rome's conquest of all the great kingdoms of the Mediterranean world.

Two or three years later, this same Octavian was to assume the name Caesar Augustus. Under his guidance, as he preferred to call it, rather than his rule, the government of Rome became a monarchy, disguised at first, to be sure, but more and more plainly a monarchy under his successors. This great organization systematically moved outward in every direction until the natural boundaries were reached. The people of the West had learned much of the way of life of the Greeks who, as part of the great empire, still peopled the East. Now the world was as nearly one world under the control of one government as it has yet been, the result of "the boundless majesty of the Roman peace." The solid managerial ability of the Romans protected the Greek way of life.

In the end, the great empire was to be divided; the West was to fall gradually into the hands of Germanic kings, while the East, with its capital at Byzantium, was to go its separate way for a thousand years more. As the primeval slime is too early for the beginning of the ancient world, so the reign of the emperor Constantine, which lasted from A.D. 324 to 337, is too early for its ending or for the beginning of a new period.

It is true that by the end of Constantine's reign the organization of the empire, and especially of the court at its center, was more like that of later kingdoms than it was like that of the empire in the first and second century of our era and that Christianity had become the official religion. But the Middle Ages (if indeed it is right to speak of any 'time between") did not begin until well after Constantine. The latter part of the fifth century is early enough to set the beginning of a new age in the West; by then the West was clearly slipping out of the control of the Romans and into that of the German kings. In the sixth century, the Byzantine emperor Justinian made a great attempt to recover control of the West and had some success in North Africa and Italy, but only temporarily. For some time the eastern and western parts of the empire were to go their separate ways, both of which owed something to the older Roman style, and both of which had changed enough so that they really represented two new styles.

HOW ANCIENT HISTORY IS WRITTEN

The Scholarly Personnel

Scholars all over the world contribute to the development of our knowledge of ancient times, the chief contributions coming from Europe, the Near East, and the United States. The scholars who study the earlier peoples of the Western hemisphere add the elements of possible traces of emigration and cultural exportation.

Many working in the main stream of the operation study the history of their own areas. The archaeology of early and Roman Britain is done almost entirely by Englishmen. Some of these archaeologists (like the members of some other branches of scholarship) have no formal connections with universities. Some are part-time amateur scholars; some are members of museums and governmental organizations designed for the study and preservation of local antiquities. From Britain to India, from Scandinavia to the edges of the Sahara, the professor, the local enthusiast, the government expert, and the visiting scholar work together. But Greece, Italy, the Near East, and Egypt are the chief centers of interest. Occasionally there is friction between the interested parties, the result of the disputes of scholars, the supposed national interest of governments, or a lapse in good manners.

This field also attracts many scholars whose chief interest is in more modern studies. The sociologist may turn to Greek and Roman history to search for examples of personality types that, according to his theories, might have appeared in a certain kind of society. The historian of mechanical inventions will naturally master the ancient part of his field. The scholar in mathematics, in government, or in art will be imperfectly trained in his subject if he does not have some grasp of its ancient history, and in such fields as government or art, the richness of the ancient material may cause him to specialize there.

Fields of Specialization: Chronology

The establishment of a sound chronology is indispensable to the proper firmness of any history. Many scholars from time to time make contributions to the chronology of the ancient world in the course of other work; and a few make chronology their chief interest.

Naturally it is desirable to establish an absolute chronology wherever we can. If we cannot, it is something to have established a relative chronology between events that appear to have some connection. It is easier to fix dates absolutely in the later part of the period, where we have reliable written accounts. Sometimes our sources give us a day-by-day account of a series of events, as the letters of Cicero occasionally do. On the other hand, they are silent about such an event as the birth of Christ.

Sometimes a reliable author tells us that something happened in the same year as something else already firmly dated by another system of chronology. The historian Polybius tells us that the Gauls sacked Rome in the year of the Peace of Antalcidas, a date that is fixed as 387/6 B.C. in Greek history. But if the year does not start and end at the same time as ours, and if nothing is said about the month of the event, we are forced to give the date in such a form as 387/6, because the year covered parts of two of our years. The mention of an eclipse that includes a fairly close date may allow us to assign the eclipse to a precisely calculated date in our system.

Of course chronology was of interest to people in ancient times— to chancelleries, to priests, to scholars. In the ancient Near East, where it is almost impossible for us to get an absolute chronology, events and royal acts were still dated by the years of the reign. The officials of the chancellery had to have some sort of dating in their records of what had happened and what had been done. The obvious method was to date everything by the years of the king's reign. When a new king came to the throne, the officials began a new sequence of dates determined by the years of the new reign.

Calendars came early, especially in those countries that had large agricultural operations supported by irrigation systems. In Egypt and in Mesopotamia, for example, the development of a calendar of a sort was more of an agricultural necessity than it was elsewhere. In a large monarchy, on the other hand, the calendar also served the useful purpose of bringing about in regular sequence and in unison those holidays and observances that mold public opinion and patriotic emotion. Often the fragment of a chancellery record that we find— a decree, a proclamation, a letter to a fellow sovereign or to the governor of a province—has a date with a day and a month and the year of the king's reign.

Soon the idea of the era was developed. The kings of the region of Asia after Alexander the Great (generally referred to as the Seleucid Kingdom) made the beginning of the reign of Seleucus I, the founder of the dynasty, the beginning of an era. Many other states have done this; the United States of America still has two official dates, the year of Our Lord and the year of the independence of the United States, and even newer nations have likewise created their private eras to minister to the pride and sense of unity of their people.

A Greek of Elis, where the Olympic games were celebrated, originated the idea of dating by Olympiads, the four-year periods at the end of which the Olympic games were held. It was agreed that the first Olympic meeting should be dated in the year that we know as 776 B.C. The second Olympiad was then the period of four years that began in 772 B.C. One could locate a date as being, for instance, in the third year of the ninetieth Olympiad. This system came to be very commonly used among the Greeks. The Romans were to develop a comparable system, that of dating by years after the founding of the city (*ab urbe condita*). "The city" was Rome, and its founding was assigned to the year 753 B.C.

After the time when many cities among the Greeks regularly elected magistrates, they kept records of them, and one, called the eponymous magistrate, gave his name to the year. That is, a certain year at Athens could be referred to as "the archonship of ———." For a year in Roman history, one could speak of the consulship of two specified men, because there were two joint chief executives, called consuls, every year.

It was to the interest of the priests as well as the secular government to pay some attention to chronology. A priestly class appeared early, controllers of relations with the unseen powers and specialists in the intellectual life. They needed, of course, to have as good a calendar as possible to help control the sacrifices. In Babylonia, at least, they became interested in chronology in the broader sense as a result of their study of the heavenly bodies, which was first undertaken so that they might have some idea when to look for the new moon or even an eclipse, and which ended as austere astronomical work on the one hand and as a baneful astrology on the other.

Scholars, too, were interested in chronology. Some were interested only in getting the matter straight, as were those who fitted Greek dates into the system of Olympiads. Christian scholars of the third and fourth centuries of our era were interested in reconciling the different systems of chronology, because the Church embraced people who had used several different systems, whereas it traced its own antecedents back into the Hebrew system. An elaborate set of concordances of the main systems was worked out, so that one could tell what year of the Roman era corresponded to a given year of the Seleucid era or the system of Olympiads or the Hebrew system of reckoning from Abraham. Finally the Christian era was set up, reckoned from the epoch-making (in the original and literal sense of the term) event of Christ's birth, and tables were made to express all important dates as so many years before or after the birth of Christ.

Geography

The historian needs to have reliable maps of the regions he considers. These are supplied to him not only by professional geographers, but also by amateurs who contribute much detail. The excellence of the maps of Roman North Africa is due in the first place to the efforts of the officers of the French armies that occupied the region in the nineteenth century. They explored the region and made useful maps, noting the points at which archaeological discoveries were made. These maps, useful as they were, have been now brought up to the higher modern standard.

The most spectacular contribution of the army officers and the archaeologists in French North Africa was in the field of economic geography. In southern Tunis, near the coast, there were signs of ancient habitation everywhere, but the rainfall was so slight that it was difficult to see how agriculture had been possible in Roman times. It was even suggested that here was proof of a major change in climate since those times, for there simply must have been more rainfall then. The careful exploration of the French officers and archaeologists disclosed traces of innumerable small dams, cisterns, ducts, and olive presses, suggesting olive groves with equipment for catching and preserving all the scanty rainfall. Upon the publication of their report, some large agricultural firms were persuaded to try olive culture in this region with the same methods, and now it is virtually one large and beautiful olive orchard.

The historian does not find many systematic accounts of physical or economic geography among the works of the ancients. Scattered all through ancient writings, however, are useful remarks about temperature, rainfall, the location of places that we could not otherwise locate, the kind of products that grew best in one country or another, winds, ocean currents, and so on. A great deal of industry has gone into the careful collection and analysis of such data, and scholarly ingenuity still occasionally extracts from a casual remark of an ancient author some new fact of geography.

The Literary Sources

Historians analyze the literary remains of antiquity in every possible way. Not only are separate data on geography or religion or government carefully sifted out, but the general tenor of the writings is also analyzed as an index of the prevailing interests of the people of the time or the level of education assumed in them by the writer.

Sometimes it is hard to draw the line between belles lettres, or "literary" writing, and technical writing. In a way, the Sumerian or Babylonian epics seem to have been literary, yet it may well be that the priests promulgated these stories of the doings of the gods as a means of social control. The later story of the death and resurrection of the Egyptian god Osiris and other comparable tales have been shown to be the librettos for the great festivals of Osiris and other gods, when their adventures or sufferings were re-enacted for the populace.

If a Greek or Roman orator published his speeches, he often did so to make a political point of some sort rather than to give his countrymen an opportunity to study the elegances of his speech at leisure. As a result, they are not always useful. For example, the counter-speeches of the Athenians Aeschines and Demosthenes about Demosthenes' long campaign to get the Athenians to oppose King Philip of Macedonia obfuscate rather than enlighten our ideas of this part of the history of Greece in the fourth century before Christ.

Papyri

So many papyri have been uncovered by people poking around in the rubbish heaps of ancient Egypt that many scholars have made papyrology their chief interest. Every imaginable kind of writing was entrusted in ancient times to the paper made of the papyrus plant, which grew in and around the Nile. When this paper was thrown out onto a dump, the dry climate of Egypt preserved it, and there, as well as in a few other places, large finds of papyri have been made.

Some of the papyri come from the older days of Egypt, as far back as 2,000 B.C. Many were religious; some are formulae for passage into the other world. A few give specialized information of great interest; one shows that even in the days of the Middle Kingdom the country was carefully organized so as to yield the utmost income to the government through a planned economy. Another gives examples of how to do arithmetical processes. Others give us some idea of the state of medical knowledge.

A great many of the papyri come from the days after the death of Alexander the Great in 323 B.C., when Egypt was the kingdom of the Ptolemies, the descendants of Alexander's general Ptolemy. Even greater numbers come from the time of Roman dominion, after 30 B.C. From the Greek and Roman periods, we also get many fragments of the works of Greek authors, some several pages long. From such fragments, we can make, for example, passable reconstructions of several lost plays of the Greek dramatist Menander, who flourished in the third century B.C. But a good many fragments cannot be confidently assigned to any author, and some are bits of the works of authors whose work we already possess in full. Others offer a page or two that can be assigned to a lost work of some author.

The greater number of papyri from both the Ptolemaic period and the Roman period contain small pieces of information that are useful in reconstructing the practical side of the history of the times. They throw light on the system of planning the production of food from the land, overseeing the peasants in planting and harvesting, and delivering the amount due as tax to the government depots. Light is thrown on the government monopolies in manufactures and imports. We get a vivid picture of the despair of a town council during the troublous days of the third Christian century when it was faced with a new exaction from the Roman imperial government. We see a certificate issued during a persecution of the Christians showing that so-and-so has come before a magistrate and performed the acts of loyalty to the empire as a Christian would refuse to do because these acts seemed impious. We read a letter home from a lonely Egyptian youngster far away in Europe with a Roman legion. Most of the papyri are written in Greek, although some are in Latin, Aramaic, Coptic, and still other languages.

Collections of papyri are found in many museums, universities, and institutes. Scholars from all the Western countries who are interested in papyrology correspond with each other, meet at congresses, and support publications in which the results of their research are reported, and these results are eagerly used by other students of ancient history.

Cuneiform Tablets

Cuneiform tablets, made of clay, were used in the Near East. They are called cuneiform (*cuneus* being the Latin for wedge) because the wedge-shaped end of a stylus was used to impress wedge-shaped marks on them. The meaning of such writing resulted from the combinations of these marks. The tablets were often baked to harden and thus preserve them. Sometimes the tablet was wrapped in a clay envelope, which was marked with identifying signs, and both were baked together. The only way to refer to a document filed by this system was to break the clay envelope.

The cuneiform tablets of the Mesopotamian area are much like the papyri of Egypt in that the greater number of them contain data of various kinds, never intended as the material of formal history. They carry the records of business houses, the correspondence of chancelleries, private letters, lists of words to serve as partial dictionaries, or astronomical facts. They are written in several languages and date from a little before 3,000 B.C. to the first century of the Christian era. The decipherment and study of these tablets is so forbidding a task that the comparatively few scholars who choose this as their specialty have never been able to treat thoroughly the large number of tablets already available. Yet, as we shall see, the information that scholarship has gained from the cuneiform tablets has thrown floods of light onto parts of history that in the early nineteenth century were almost entirely dark.

Epigraphy and Numismatics

The inscriptions and the coins of the ancient world were meant to be seen and pondered. Some of them carry a message deliberately calculated to deceive, some of them carry governmental propaganda, and some pass on some message that a private citizen wished to be seen. The kings of Egypt, for example, ordered inscriptions, in the temples, to provide accounts of their military campaigns, with pictures to accompany parts of the story. Sometimes, as in the case of the Battle of Kadesh, the account was intended to deceive, or rather, if we wish to be charitable, the Egyptian Pharoah thought that the rather awkward story of his battle with the Hittites would be the better for a little editing. The great Babylonian law code of Hammurabi was inscribed on a stone stele (or column) to make it available to those who could read.

The Roman Empire was the heyday of the inscription, and scores of thousands of them from that period have been preserved. They testify to the pride and pleasure that men took in being Romans. They set up inscriptions recording the details of their official careers—their success stories—from which the epigrapher can deduce the typical course of many and different careers in the imperial service. Sometimes men presented town halls or theaters to their native towns in the provinces and recorded in an inscription across the portico exactly how much their munificence had cost them. Burial inscriptions sometimes record the achievements of the deceased, especially one who had risen from humble beginnings. Thousands upon thousands of funeral inscriptions make it possible to study the fascinating system of names or to get some idea of the elements of population in a given locality. As the scholar pores over the epitaphs, he sometimes finds something like the simple line, *Hic omnis dulcedo sita est,* "Here all sweetness is laid away," the cry of a broken heart from long ago.

The numismatist may regard his coins as work of art or as documents of economic history or as evidence of government propaganda. Able men designed and executed them, and they often are very beautiful, to be taken seriously as works of art. They show interesting developments of style, and sometimes their stylistic conventions throw light on other problems of artistic work. As documents of economic history, the coins well repay the arduous work of analyzing their metal content, establishing their dates and sequences of issue, and studying the extent of their circulation. As propagandists, the Romans especially used coins to convey ideas that the government wished to impress upon people—the government has everything under control, peace has been restored, the accession of a new emperor is officially proclaimed.

Fine Art

The almost numberless works of art left to us from the ancient world are the chief objects of study for another group of scholars. These men have to specialize within this already special field, because no one could possible acquire a working mastery of the art of the whole ancient world. From the gems and the gold jewelry of the Sumerians of three millennia before Christ to the great buildings or the gorgeous mosaics of the late Roman Empire, there is an untold wealth of beautiful and impressive objects, large or small, upon which man has put the stamp that makes them works of art. They are fascinating in themselves as things of beauty and fascinating, too, for their materials, the techniques they demonstrate, and the development of styles and of modes of regarding reality. Perhaps it is true that the art objects of the ancient world have more freedom from the history of their time than anything else that has survived; often they can stand alone and speak to us with independent and individual voices. Yet they are part of the material of the ancient historian, and sometimes he can make them speak in the chorus of voices to which they once belonged.

WRITING ANCIENT HISTORY NOWADAYS

But why is it that, with this wealth of material, ancient history was not completely written long ago, leaving nothing for the modern scholar to do? The first and obvious reason is that new material continually becomes available. Often it appears purely by accident. Perhaps the digging of an excavation for a new commercial garage in the city of Constantine, Algeria, discloses the remains of a cemetery of pre-Roman times, with gravestones bearing interesting names and religious symbols. Or a farmer in England discovers on his property a treasure of silver vessels buried in late Roman times. Then, too, during World War II, bombs, on the one hand, and aerial photography for reconnaissance, on the other, disclosed a good many traces of the ancient world.

Coins and other pieces of evidence occasionally appear in the hands of dealers. This material is less useful, because the dealer usually will not tell, even if he knows, the precise place and conditions of its finding.

But, in addition, the purposive search for new material goes on continually. Specialists in various lines are on the hunt for manuscripts. Nowadays new ones appear only rarely, yet two lost works of Archimedes, the mathematician and physicist, have been discovered in the twentieth century, one in a palimpsest in a collection in Istanbul and another in an Arabic translation that had not been recognized before as a translation of one of his works.

The most spectacular and popular method of getting new evidence from the ancient world is the archaeologist's: he organizes an excavation. He must have good judgment in choosing his site and show some diplomacy in getting official permission to excavate there. He must be a competent fund-raiser. He must be a good executive to manage the excavation well and a good archaeologist to interpret the results. Naturally these functions tend to be distributed among teams of people; now and then someone manages the whole process alone.

The public is impressed and excited by the recovery of important

things long lost to sight and does not stop to think of all the difficulties
of initiating an excavation and bringing it to a successful conclusion.
Little is ever written for popular consumption about the difficulties
and dangers of such a project: the personnel may get shot at; their
chances of suffering from the local diseases are excellent; much of
the work is boring, for there is a great deal of unavoidable routine
and many days when nothing happens; and the living conditions
are often uncomfortable, for these are usually primitive places, and
it is high summer.

Little is said, too, about the desk work of the archaeologist, the
long hours that he must spend studying materials that do not yield
their secrets at once. He must often restudy the context in which
things were found in the excavation. He must find and read the
reports of other excavations where comparable material was found.
Often he must find the money and the free time to travel in order to
see and handle other examples of the material he is working with.
Perhaps he has a great many fragments of pottery, which patient
work will show to be partly local products and partly importations
from two or three other places. Nothing in the lot is beautiful or
striking, but this mass of broken pottery can, with hard work, be
made to yield a story of manufacture and trade relations that will
be helpful in reconstructing one small part of ancient history.

In addition to the new material that accidentally comes to light
or is purposively brought to light, there are new ideas and new
energy involved in the writing of ancient history. Now scholars ask
questions that the scholars of two hundred years ago would not have
thought to ask—questions about economic motivations, for example,
and the location of power in a society. Furthermore, the appearance
of new material often leads to the reappraisal of old material. As
we know more about the people of the Near East, we make more
effort to see how their ideas and practices may have been transmitted
to the Greeks and Romans. And the number of active scholars is
greater than it used to be; the more minds at work on the subject,
the more shades of ideas will be explored.

The scholar may work on the isolated fact or on the sweep of the
whole field. He may publish in a learned journal a note that establishes how a disputed reading in a manuscript should be interpreted.
He may write an article reviewing the current state of the dispute

about chronology in Mesopotamia around 2,000 B.c. He may read a paper to the annual meeting of a learned society in which he describes the archaeological campaign (as a season's work in the field is called) of the preceding summer and then publish the paper in the annual transactions of the society.

The book that he writes is perhaps an examination of all the coins of a certain Greek city and an attempt to establish a new sequence of styles and new datings. It may review the gold objects of a period in Mesopotamia, or analyze the sociological implications of a Greek tragedy, or discuss the financial policies of the Roman emperors in the fourth century. All these are severely technical studies, aiming at the establishment of new sets of facts.

His book, on the other hand, may undertake to describe the whole course of history in such a unit as the Old Kingdom in Egypt, or the kingdom of Pergamum, or the Roman province of Britain. This book offers a good deal of well-known and accepted information, together with some original contributions by the author. He will perhaps attempt to give a better version of a number of parts of the history or argue that the whole matter has been misunderstood.

Ancient historians rarely, if ever, write universal histories or propose grand schemes of history. This lack is perhaps unfortunate, because ancient history must play a large part in any such scheme and to have the scheme rest upon an accurate knowledge of ancient history would be highly desirable.

CHAPTER

2

EARLY MAN AND THE NEOLITHIC
AND URBAN REVOLUTIONS

I t has taken us a long time, but we have come a long way. Our earliest ancestors, the early forms of man as he was over a million years ago, had very slender prospects of rising to be the lords of creation that the society of *homo sapiens sapiens* (to give him his full name) now considers its members to be. Those early men were, to put it simply, animals in their cultural life. They had no shelters, no fire, no tools. They wandered about gathering food as best they could, for they had no social or political organization, no agriculture, and no domesticated animals.

Man's Potentialities

Man's great secret lies in the fact that when he came down out of the trees, his lack of specialized physical equipment forced him to become the great improviser. For example, because he did not have a fine coat of fur, he learned to wear clothes. Now in our own time, his dullness of sight is compensated by lenses, his comparative lack of speed by devices that will carry him at great rates, his lack of offensive and defensive physical power by weapons with which no animal can cope.

Like the monkeys, man is a creature who uses his eyes and his sense

16

of touch. His eyes moved around to the front of his head and gave him stereoscopic vision. The areas of the brain that associate sight with muscle movements were forced to strengthen themselves, for he stopped going on all fours and used his hands, not as two more feet, but to handle and manipulate things as he saw them.

The parts of man's brain that retain and combine information are better developed than those in other animals' brains. This combination of memory and association gives man his real advantage over the rest of the animate world. The monkeys who still live in the trees are probably no more intelligent than their ancestors of millions of years ago, because nothing has happened to make them so. But man has been through a process that has built him up. He can remember things that are past and conceive things that will not exist until he has caused them to exist. Even the simple stone tools that the men of the Old Stone Age made, for example, imply a certain forethought; the man who starts to make one has to have some idea of an end result rather different from the piece of stone he first holds in his hand. Almost at the beginning of man's toolmaking activity he was making tools with which to make other tools—using a hammer stone to make a hand-ax, or a stone flake to shape a wooden spear.

THE OLD STONE AGE

About half a million years ago began the Paleolithic Age or the Old Stone Age. The name results from the fact that men had begun to make stone tools of a sort. The use of occasional improvised tools or weapons is within the powers of modern apes, but at the beginning of the Old Stone Age man was beginning to do better than that: he was making tools of stone in a purposive manner, or at least he was doing so now and then. From the many excavations or finds made in Europe, North Africa, and Asia, it is clear that certain simple kinds of knowledge about making tools of stone were widely diffused among the men who inhabited these three continents.

During that long period of half a million years, there were four glaciations. Although the cause is not entirely understood, the colder weather brought glaciers down over much of Northern Europe, Asia, and America. During the thousands of years that the glaciers persisted, great changes naturally occurred in the climate of the regions south of the actual glaciers; vegetation and animals alike underwent changes. Some of the most fascinating detective work of scholarship establishes the nature of life in various areas by the patient and ingenious study of minute evidences left from those long-ago ages. Even some pollens have persisted to yield evidence about the plants and trees. Remains of animals show us what animals were prevalent at certain periods, and we learn with what weapons men hunted them. We learn, too, that sometimes man was the hunted instead of the hunter.

Although the slowness of human progress during this long period is almost incredible, we must never lose sight of the difficulty of making some of the early steps that to us now seem very simple and easy. Man learned to manufacture and to use fire. There is evidence that he used it for warmth, for cooking, and occasionally for artificial light, apparently by burning animal fats in crude stone lamps. He learned to clothe himself with skins, which he could sew with a crude bone needle. He had tools of flint, horn, bone, and ivory. In the latter part of the Stone Age, not only had the tools become standardized in somewhat efficient forms, occurring in widely separated places, but they also had become specialized, whereas the early tools had been comparatively simple and meant for general use. Meager as these achievements may seem, they gain in luster if they are compared with the lack of achievement of such creatures as the apes, who apparently are unable to take the initial step of looking ahead to something not actually in sight and at the same time looking back to something no longer in sight.

The Cave Paintings

The truly startling achievement of the man of the late Old Stone Age is painting. In Spain, France, and Switzerland, caves have been found whose roofs were painted some 20,000 years ago, or a little less, with wonderful pictures of animals. Many are depicted pierced with lances, and the purpose of the pictures seems to have been to bring success in the hunt by sympathetic magic.

Surely no other works of art have ever been placed in such inaccessible spots. Even after the caves had been found, the pictures could be viewed only by heroic efforts. Some parts of them are in inaccessible regions of the caves, where it is almost impossible to get a look. They wander across irregularities in the cave surfaces or around corners. But the artists were true artists, like those later workers who lovingly finished off parts of their sculpture or woodwork that were not meant to be seen. The old craftsmen had an eye for the salient characteristics of each animal and for the representation of action, and they created pictures of extraordinary liveliness and charm.

The story of the discovery of some of the caves is full of excitement and romance. The combination of chance discovery with skilled, imaginative detective work on various kinds of evidence lends great interest to a number of well-written modern accounts of these earliest times of man. The first of the caves to come to light was that of Altamira in northern Spain, discovered in 1868 by a hunter whose dog had fallen through the small opening and could not get out. The Stone Age objects on the floor of the cave could readily be accepted as authentic— the bones and teeth of stag, horse, and bison, oyster shells, flint knives, bone awls, and needles — but it was some decades before everyone would accept the roof pictures as authentic Stone Age art. When the last opponents capitulated, a great search led to the discovery of many more caves with similar paintings. One of the best, that of Lascaux in France, was discovered by the same accident with a dog.

The paintings of the Altamira cave were done partly with the finger-tip, partly with a solid point dipped in paint, and partly with a brush such as might be made by chewing the end of a twig. Sometimes the outlines are filled in by daubing, as one might do with some moss or animal fur, and partly by spray painting, which could be done with the mouth. Iron and manganese oxide give red and black paint. In the Lascaux cave, there are blue-black and dark brown manganese oxides and soot for black. The pigments were ground with mortar and pestle, apparently with an aqueous medium more often than a fatty medium.

THE NEW STONE AGE

The Neolithic Age or the New Stone Age was so named because there is a noticeable difference between its stone tools and those of earlier times. We see at once that the tools of the New Stone Age are more carefully shaped, better smoothed, completely finished, and the comparative crudity of Old Stone Age tools leaps to the eye. Now the materials are more carefully chosen, and they are worked by a process of applying pressures at certain key points, causing small flakes to come off until the piece of stone is gradually brought down to the desired shape.

The stone knives and scrapers and other tools are really remarkable, considering that they are made of stone. We even have sickles of a usable size with small teeth in them. Our microscopes show tiny remains in the teeth of the grains that were cut with them long ago. The question may well be raised, however, whether these tools were so much better in use than the older type that their manufacture and use is the sign of a genuinely new age. It is possible that a man could manage comparably well with the older tools, even if the newer were somewhat superior.

It is, however, the further consideration of the achievements of this age, which probably began about 6000–5000 B.C., that has led to the use of the term "Neolithic Revolution." The domestication of plants and the domestication of animals seem to the historian far more revolutionary advances than the invention of a process for making superior stone stools. These two achievements did much to bring about a genuinely new way of life among mankind, comparable to the Industrial Revolution.

Recent finds seem to indicate a possibility that it was in the Near East that man first became a food-producer rather than a food-gatherer. The man of the Old Stone Age had killed such animals as he could and gathered such grains or vegetables or fruits as he could find. In the new order of things, wheat and barley were the first plants to be domesticated. Grains of these two types can be found in the excavations of early Neolithic sites in the Near East, so well preserved that the botanist can examine them as he would the grains of modern wheat or barley. With specimens found in the excavation of later sites, the palaeoethnobotanist (that is, the expert on the types of ancient plants) can trace the development of great numbers of new breeds.

The animals that man persuaded to come to live with him were those which in their wild state had had some sort of social life. That is, they were the ones who had customarily lived in groups and had a leader: the cow, the horse, the dog, the goat. It is interesting to speculate on how the arrangement was first made (and naturally we wonder at what stage the cat joined the movement), but we can be sure only of the general fact that those animals which naturally like a social way of life were brought into man's. Now man had new allies who would provide him with food and assist him with their strength or their speed or their keen senses and who were not quite bright enough to perceive how they were being exploited.

This was indeed a revolution in human life. The steady and systematic use of plants and animals must have led to some increase in the numbers of mankind. Life must have become somewhat easier and surer than it had been, although it can hardly have been very easy. But the new ways would tend to bring about psychological changes. Mankind must have developed a somewhat more aggressive attitude toward Nature, a feeling that it is possible not to accept things as they are but to change them. The study of how to make such change would be intensified by an increase in life expectancy. The average person of the Old Stone Age must have had a short life, but now, if more people lived to the age of, say, forty, there must have been more opportunity for fruitful observation and reflection and experimentation and for the handing on of the results.

It is tempting to suppose that new virtues now made their appearance. There were advantages to be had by the energetic man who planned ahead and was willing to drive himself to feats of labor. The scale of virtues must have been enlarged to include thrift and hard work, now that thrift could be practiced and it was not absolutely necessary to work so hard as before.

Now that it was possible for a man to produce a small surplus, a prudent person might well bethink himself of ways of getting hold of other people's surpluses. One of the best ways was to enslave other people and keep them in one place to produce under duress, allowing them only a bare subsistence. Probably we should ask ourselves whether men were any better as men after this revolution. In some ways, they probably were. If *homo sapiens* does not appear in the very best light when he is inventing the institution of slavery or shrewdly and indecently learning to appropriate from the cow the milk that Nature meant for her young, still, it is likely that the new way of life was in general somewhat less brutal.

THE URBAN REVOLUTION

Archaeology presents us with the fact that Neolithic man lived in villages rather than on single farms.* These villages somehow grew into cities in the next age. The villages were mere aggregations of people who all were making a living in the same way. The cities, representing the next stage of social organization, which seems to have begun about 3500 B.C., were social organisms whose members had differentiated functions. Ways had been found to use the many little surpluses to support some people who did not produce food at all, but rather performed some other functions that could be represented as being in the public interest.

We generally find a king and a college of priests at the head of these cities, whether in Egypt or the Near East or Greece. It has been suggested that the method of getting the organization started was to convert certain luxuries into necessities and to increase and concentrate the surplus. Copper tools, for instance, were luxuries; the ordinary man managed to get along without them. But by about 3500 B.C. the technique of making tools out of the alloys of copper that occur in nature was fairly well understood. A coppersmith could be brought into a community if there was enough of a surplus to pay such an expert for working full time at his trade. Perhaps the government of the town, which was still in its beginning stages, contracted for some weapons to get him started.

If the people could be persuaded that their relations with the gods were safe in the hands of the priest-king or of a team of king and priest, the ordinary man would probably be willing to part with his surplus in order to support a pair of high-powered specialists to take care of relations with the other powers, both seen and unseen. This expert service was another luxury that could be converted into a necessity.

As the organization grew, it could undertake large-scale irrigation works, another expert service that the ordinary man would never think of, even as a possible luxury, until it had been done, when it would soon come to seem a most pressing necessity. To do a little manual labor each year on the irrigation works and to part with a little sur-

---

*A conservative date for these simple early villages is about 5000 B.C. The excavators of Jericho, in Palestine, would have a settled community there by about 6000 or even 7000 B.C.; some archaeologists find this date too early.

plus to the specialists in charge would seem necessary, even if a little burdensome.

Perhaps the leaders in war (or in little contests between villages) were the ones who became kings. A vigorous man might well stand forth as leader in such struggles, get an extra share of loot, perhaps in the form of slaves to work for him, and find his way straight to kingship. Certainly kings are commonly found. In the story of Saul, we see the process by which a king was chosen among a people who had managed without one. Among the Hebrews, and later among the Greeks, we can see that kings could not always maintain the idea of their usefulness and could be ousted, as has been the case in the twentieth century. In early times, the combined role of king and priest was an excellent one, but it often proved advisable to divide the work because there was too much for one man to do.

Among the Sumerians, at the bottom of the Tigris-Euphrates Valley, we find this urban revolution, as it has been called, in progress between 3500 and 2500 B.C. At the same time, the same sort of revolution took place in Egypt and along the Indus River in India.

Thus, we find that the cities had kings, sometimes combining the functions of king and priest. There were temples with granaries, storerooms for other materials, and staffs of minor priests. Kings, gods, and priests took as much as they could of the scanty economic surplus. The contributions of grain to the god might be symbolically consumed by him; they would also nourish the corps of priests in a less symbolic way.

In the temple (or the palace) there was a group of specialist artisans. We find that bowmakers, bronze workers, and the like would be kept as slaves or servants. The building of the god's house, the daily or periodic services to the god—feeding him, washing him, entertaining him, adorning his house and his statue—were done by a corps of people. Not the least important were the scribes, those who could write. It may well be that writing was invented for the purpose of keeping track of all the various things in the possession of the king and the priests. Early specimens of writing are generally lists of stores; for example, the recently deciphered Linear B tablets from Mycenae, Pylos, and other sites of early Greece consist of such lists. This supremely useful invention of writing is properly regarded as the chief sign of the achievement of civilization by a people.

These cities had more capacities for growth than did the ordinary Neolithic village, which seems to have had only one or two hundred families, as far as we can judge from a goodly number of excavations. As has been said, the city was not a mere mechanical aggregate of persons, all of whom did very much the same thing, but an organic unit whose members, like the parts of the body, performed differentiated and complementary functions. Unfortunately this new organism also contained the seeds of trouble because it created economic classes with opposed interests.

The role of the priest deserves careful consideration. The priest may seem a charlatan, one who fattens himself on the credulity of the ignorant. Often also the wealth concentrated in the hands of the priesthoods and their sense of ancient prestige combined to make them enemies of necessary change, especially in Egypt.

From another point of view, these men were the first experts in social control. They and the kings together first devised the systems by which men could live in genuine social groups. The king and the priest are practically inseparable, too, if we think of the growth of formal codes of law to guide and regulate the life of these new social organizations. The priests, and with them the scribes, were freed from the arduous daily round of producing food and given an opportunity to reflect, to observe the general scene. It was they who shaped the presentation to the people of the gods and kingship; presumably they were responsible for many of the myths of the gods. They also took on the function of representing to the people what the people should think about themselves. They, too, were the pioneers of natural science, of the knowledge of arithmetic, geometry, astronomy, the calendar, and geography.

The Spreading of Towns and Cities

These new societies soon began to reach out for new materials. In Egypt, there early were two groupings that could properly be called kingdoms; about 3200 B.C. they were combined into one. This single kingdom could use the combined surpluses to reach outside for materials, as to the copper and turquoise deposits of the Sinai Peninsula, over toward Palestine. The drivers of the animals, the workmen, and the guards who went on the expedition could all be supported by the surplus at the king's disposal.

The search for raw materials inevitably spread the new and more complex forms of social organization. The Egyptian expeditions that went south to Libya and Nubia for gold spread a more complex form of society there than the people would otherwise have known, remote as they were from all the other centers of civilization of the ancient world. Such expeditions would naturally help the formations of organizations in the places to which they went or through which they passed, for the more energetic and ingenious local people would naturally seize the opportunity to organize their own people in such a way as to draw the most profit from the visits of the Egyptians. The need for an organized local effort to collect whatever the visitors wanted must have been apparent. In this case, the result was the gradual spread of some of the manners and beliefs of the Egyptians southward beyond the actual borders of Egypt, where they persisted.

Some of the records of the Sumerian businessmen of lower Mesopotamia that have been preserved on baked clay tablets show us explicitly that the caravans had to pay protection money here and there as they journeyed outward into the Arabian Desert or up into the hill country. In the simple early days, even the collection of protection money from passing merchants marked a new stage of organization. If the caravan carried such manufactured goods as tin or incense, to be traded for raw materials, the trading that was done at the source of the raw materials would add something to the surplus there and again contributed to the formation of a more complex social group.

We shall also see the spreading of culture in the case of the Egyptian influence on Crete and the Greek mainland. Egypt, in the days of her greatness, taught much to the Cretans and offered them the opportunity of prosperity by paying them for their raw materials—fruits, hides, meat, timber. The Cretans became steadily more prosperous and more sophisticated, modeling their civilization on the Egyptian, but in their best days producing works and a way of life unmistakably their own, in spite of their debt to Egypt. The Cretans in turn passed on much of what they knew to the Greeks of the mainland while trading with them; and these Greeks, as they became more sophisticated, in turn developed a way of life and a group of products from their workshops that were their own even as they showed a clear indebtedness to the Cretans.

Cultural traits seemed to spread more actively from their sites of origin in the Near East toward the west than toward the east. In the early days of the Sumerians, there seemed to be a connection with the nearer part of India, on the Indus River. During a great part of ancient history as we have defined it, there was almost no active and fruitful contact with India. Before the end of the Roman Empire, there was intercourse with both India and China, but not such as there was even in early times between the Near East and the West.

Obviously there was a great deal of contact between different areas that we cannot trace, contact that came earlier than what has just been described and that transformed men of the Old Stone Age into men of the New Stone Age. The great discoveries of the domestication of plants and animals apparently spread like wildfire and became known among a great many people in Asia, Africa, and Europe. It is thought that by 3000 B.C. some of these people had crossed Bering Strait and taken this new knowledge to the Americas.

It is an interesting fact that some of the peoples on the periphery of the great powers were drawn as groups into the high civilization of the ancient world, with its cities and other complex features, whereas other peoples sturdily resisted. The Scythians of South Russia, for instance, were organized as nomads. Some few of them, as individuals, were drawn into the high civilization of the Greeks and later into that of the Romans, but as a group, they resisted. Their simpler civilization was so stable and satisfactory that it could hold its members against what evidently was the very strong attraction of the Greeks and the Romans. The early Germans were organized in more sedentary groups than the Scythians, but they too were without city life. Many of their members, as individuals, went over to the Romans, but again the community refused to adopt the more complex and fragile way of life and generally managed to hold its members against the new attractions.

CHAPTER

3

EARLY BABYLONIA

The civilization of the Neolithic Age—the New Stone Age—developed more fully in western India, in Mesopotamia, and in Egypt. The new civilization in India, which had been much like the other two at first, lies outside our area here because it did not, as did the others, lead toward our modern Western civilization. In most ways, however, the development of the new type of civilization was roughly parallel in Mesopotamia and Egypt, because in both places it came from similar Neolithic beginnings. There is reason to believe, as some have, that in some respects the Mesopotamians were first and that the Egyptians learned from them—in the use of certain materials, for instance, or of certain types of decoration. This chapter will describe Mesopotamian civilization during its first two and half millennia, to about 1500 B.C.

THE LAND OF THE TWO RIVERS

Geography

Mesopotamia, "the region between the rivers," is the land lying between the Tigris and Euphrates Rivers. The upper part, Assyria, which developed later than the middle and lower parts, will be discussed in a later chapter. The middle part, including the city of Babylon, was called Akkad; the lower part was Sumer. Together we call them Babylonia. The two rivers, which rise in the mountains of Armenia, flow to the Persian Gulf. Geographically, it should be kept in mind that the new land that they have built up at their mouths over the last ten thousand years extends farther into the gulf than it did when the Sumerian city of Eridu was a seaport.

These rivers could never be entirely tamed by man so that they would not flood the plains around them when the melting snows of the highlands swelled their waters in March. In a number of places in southern Mesopotamia, it may be noted, archaeologists have found deposits, many feet deep, of pure water-borne silt above the earliest remains. These deposits seem to suggest that the Flood we read about in the Bible was a real event in Mesopotamia, an occurrence of such magnitude that it might well live on in tradition. Normally the water, when led into the plains by irrigation works, made the earth yield rich crops. The silt deposited by the water kept up the fertility of the soil along the courses of the rivers, in addition to creating new land at their mouths. The grains, vegetables, and fruits that are familiar in the United States can be grown successfully in this region, as can the domestic animals with which we are familiar. In summer the region is hot, but not very humid; in winter the climate is mild, with infrequent frosts. A year's rainfall is likely to be about six inches.

East of the two rivers were Media and Persia; their territory is mountainous and not infertile, but better suited to produce men than to provide a luxurious living for them. To the west lies the Arabian Desert, a vast region that is largely barren. In ancient times, its oases and sparse vegetation could support some nomads, who, like the inhabitants of the mountains to the eastward, often cast covetous eyes upon the fertile plains of Mesopotamia and invaded them.

Around the upper reaches of the rivers the land was higher and the climate cooler than further south. This territory was later to be the center of the Assyrian Empire, and at the earlier time we are now describing the future Assyrians were already living there.

To the west of the Arabian Desert lie Syria and Palestine. If less productive than Mesopotamia, they are much more fertile than Arabia. "The Fertile Crescent" describes this region of mostly fruitful

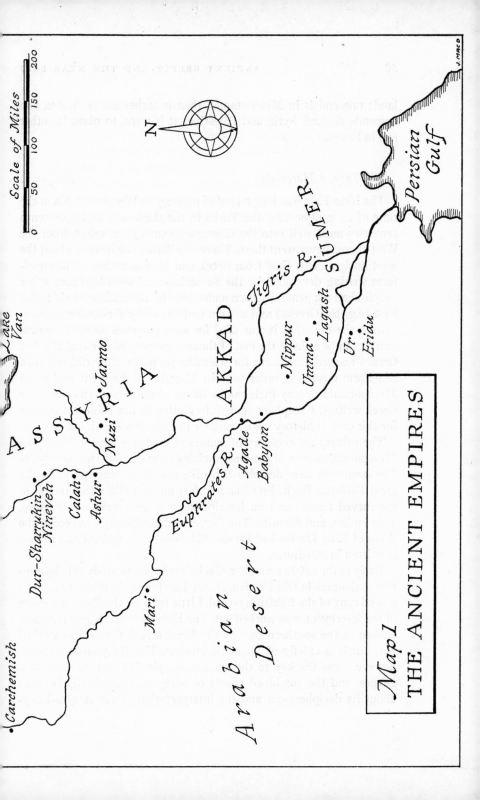

Map I
THE ANCIENT EMPIRES

land; one end is in Mesopotamia, then it arches above Arabia and descends through Syria and Palestine, at is were, to plant its other end in Egypt.

The Source Materials

The Near East was long a land of mystery to Westerners. From the time of its conquest by the Turks in the thirteenth and fourteenth centuries until well into the nineteenth century, travelers from the West almost never went there. There was little to be learned about the most ancient Near East from Greek and Roman authors. The cuneiform writing developed by the Sumerians and used by many other peoples had not generally been understood by the ancient world to the west (e.g., the Greeks) and was not understood by the moderns either, despite the fact that it was used for such purposes as astronomical writings until at least the end of the first century of our era. If a few Greeks learned cuneiform for scientific purposes, they did not read cuneiform records in order to write histories of the great nations of Mesopotamia. A very little can be learned from Herodotus and other Greek writers. Except for some information in the Bible, no sources for this part of history were available in early modern times.

The subsequent recovery of masses of evidence for the history of Mesopotamia is one of the most exciting feats of modern scholarship. The languages were deciphered by the use of the inscription on the great Behistun Rock. Five hundred feet up on a cliff in western Iran are carved figures and an inscription in three languages—Persian, Babylonian, and Elamite. The figures and the inscription record the deeds of King Darius I of Persia (521—486 B.C.), and the inscription is written in cuneiform.

Early in the 1800's a number of scholars began to study this inscription and others in Old Persian. Henry Rawlinson, in the 1840's, made a good copy of the Behistun record. Little by little the Persian version of the inscription was worked out. The Elamite version, in a language spoken in the southern part of the Persian realm, was also worked out, but it is chiefly of linguistic interest. The Babylonian version, however, was the key to the ancient Babylonian and Assyrian languages, and the combined efforts of many scholars finally brought about its decipherment and the interpretation of the Assyro-Babylonian language. This, in turn, led to the recovery of the ability to read Sumerian, which is written in the same cuneiform characters as Assyro-Babylonian (or Akkadian).

Remains of many other languages of the ancient Near East have been found. Some are now well understood; others still create puzzles for the scholar. The inscriptions found in the Hittite country of Asia Minor are in eight languages, for example, and are not yet entirely understood. The Sumerian language, however, has proved to be very important, and a good many tablets carrying various materials in this language have been discovered. The Sumerians were the first people of the region to come to a stage beyond the Neolithic and Urban Revolutions. Their language acquired such prestige that, long after it ceased to be politically important or generally spoken, it was used by other people of the region, especially by priests, as a universal learned tongue.

Since the 1840's, excavation has brought to light tens of thousands of clay tablets in cuneiform. The first excavators were adventurers indeed. Even to enter Mesopotamia was a fairly daring feat for a European, and to expose one's self to the uncertainties of the attitudes of the Arab inhabitants and the Turkish officials, as well as to the climate, while trying to unearth chapters of the past must have seemed mere foolhardiness to many outside this determined group.

The excavations disclosed the ruins of ancient cities under the mounds that dot the landscape. Many of these cities were first built on clay platforms to raise them above the high water of the river. The houses of unbaked brick would crumble and their remains would be tamped down so that new ones could be built above them. The excavators learned to deal with layer after layer of occupation; their grasp of fact and their precision of method grew with each new excavation. Archaeological institutes were organized. Governments became interested. Universities created professorships. Museums welcomed the new materials, and often new museums had to be founded to receive them. It has now become difficult to find space to store or display the great numbers of significant objects that have been found. Many useful materials, especially inscribed clay tablets, have to be put aside for years before they can receive serious attention from the small group of scholars qualified to study them.

CROWNS AND THRONES IN MESOPOTAMIA
(3500–1500 B. C.)

Signs of Progress

Filling in the steps by which man in Mesopotamia moved through the Neolithic and Urban Revolutions is one of the chief occupations of the mid-twentieth-century archaeologist. At such sites as Jarmo, in Iraq, which dates from before 5000 B.C., there were permanent habitations and Neolithic implements, but the pottery that was later to be ubiquitous had not yet been invented. There were stones for grinding grain, and hoes and sickles, so we know that grain had already been domesticated. Jarmo was very early; but similar finds have now been made at other sites in Mesopotamia as well as all over the Near and Middle East from Greece to Pakistan. This pre-pottery Neolithic stage is now dated between about 7000 and 5500 B.C. By the early fourth millennium, the people of the region had made such good progress toward the Urban stage that they were beginning to move into a new period that may simply be called the historical period from the fact that writing came into use.

The Sumerians

The people who are known as the Sumerians had no known relatives, and their prehistory is obscure. In the early fourth millennium, many of their famous cities were already occupied by a civilized population, and for two thousand years or so thereafter the lower part of the Land of the Two Rivers was to bear the stamp of the Sumerian way of doing things.

We know the names of many Sumerian cities, and we have written allusions to struggles between them and occasional combinations of them under a single overlord. In the early third millennium the Sumerians were generally dominant in lower Mesopotamia. Eridu, now far from the sea, was then a seaport on the Persian Gulf, and discoveries on the islands of the gulf suggest a lively commercial intercourse between them and the mainland, even in such early times. The city of Nippur, up the valley, has yielded rich treasures of cuneiform tablets.

Sometimes we get a closer, momentary view of the relations between these Sumerian cities. The records of an early king of Lagash, for example, tell of the raising of temples and the digging of canals. Those of his grandson tell of victories over several of the neighboring cities. This early imperialist was also celebrated on a famous work of art, "the Stele of the Vultures," a stone column (Greek *stele*) bearing a lively scene in which his phalanx is shown advancing, while vultures are already feasting on the warriors who have fallen before it.

A few generations later, a scribe of Lagash describes, in a work that has come down to us, an era of corruption when the hand of the tax-collector emptied every pocket. King Urukagina, who must have been an administrator of some talent, managed to reform this situation and give honest government. But Lagash fell shortly thereafter to an old rival, the city of Umma, whose King Lugalzaggisi was an able imperialist. We hear that under him Umma dominated Uruk and Ur (mentioned in the Bible as "Ur of the Chaldees," the old home of Abraham), and his armies even went as far as the shore of the Mediterranean.

The Early Akkadian Empire (ca. 2390–ca. 2180 B.C.)

But the Sumerians often had to bow to the energy of other people of Mesopotamia. Sargon the First came to power about 2360 B.C. in the city of Agade (i.e., biblical Akkad). He finally conquered Lugalzaggisi, ruled all Mesopotamia, and campaigned in other lands, even asserting his power in Syria and Anatolia.

Among the other kings of the hundred years or so of Akkadian domination of Mesopotamia, Naram-Sin, grandson of Sargon, is especially known because of his conquests and the discovery of the striking stele that portrays his victory in a mountain campaign : the troops are light armed and the king leads them in person up a mountain ; as in "the Stele of the Vultures" a number of fallen enemies are shown.

The Sumerian Revival (ca. 2070–ca. 1960 B. C.)

Between the Akkadian Empire of the descendants of Sargon the First and the revival of Sumerian culture, there was an interlude of about a century (2180–2070 B.C.) when Mesopotamia was dominated by the Guti, a people from the mountains to the eastward. We know little about them.

But then came the Sumerian revival. With it not only can we connect a man, Gudea by name, but we also have several statues of him. Although they are somewhat stylized, they seem to portray a calm and forceful person. He was only governor at Lagash, not king, but he administered his city well, advancing commerce and irrigation and gaining a great reputation as the shepherd of his people. After his time the seat of Sumerian power was at Ur for several generations.

Ur was then a city of perhaps 24,000 people, as has been calculated by counting the number of houses to an acre in the ruins and assuming six to ten people to a house. The ruins show that Ur covered 150 acres, and thus this calculation gives 160 people to the acre, which is about the same as the figure for modern Damascus. But the great excavator of Ur, Sir Leonard Woolley, believes that the suburbs around the inner town contained ten times as many people and that Ur had a quarter of a million inhabitants.

The great ziggurat, or stepped tower, dedicated to the moon god must have been the chief feature of the city. This is the greatest of the two dozen or so ziggurats excavated in Mesopotamia. Usually they were made of rammed clay. This one, however, which had a foundation 200 by 150 feet and is still about 70 feet high, is made entirely of brick. On the inside, the brick is unbaked, but on the outside it is baked and employs bitumen (asphalt) instead of mortar.

Excavations have disclosed that around the ziggurat there was an extensive area where state business, which was often managed by the priests, was carried on. Clay tablets found there show that imposts of various kinds were paid at this place and that the accounts of the bureau were carefully kept. All over Babylonia clay tablets from this period are found, some of them even employing double-entry bookkeeping. The law courts were also in the area around the ziggurat, and their records, too, were preserved on clay tablets, some of which have come down to us.

Industry, as well as the courts and the bureau for the collection of taxes, had a place in the great temple complex. It is a reasonable conjecture that at first all skilled workmen were controlled by the temples and that they only gradually became secularized. Weaving shops have been found, and records of cost and production have come to light. Other records show that the managers of the temple controlled several shops where jewelry was made. The temple supplied the materials and took the product to adorn the images of the gods or to bedeck the bodies of dead sovereigns and the followers who were still slain to accompany them to the other world. Gold, silver, and precious stones and certain designs worked in them were long thought to have religious efficacy. There was, of course, no difficulty about selling the products of the temple workmen in foreign trade or for secular use at home.

The Babylonians

After a century or so of Sumerian power centered at Ur, there was another period of confusion from which emerged a powerful state with its capital at Babylon. Some of the new people who had formed this state, called Amorites, or "Westerners," ranged as far as Palestine. The dynasty of kings at Babylon lasted from about 1830 to about 1530 B.C. It was then superseded by a dynasty founded by an Iranian people called Kassites. Kassites appear in Babylonian documents for some time before 1530 as ordinary working people; they rose to power, however, and for about four hundred years they dominated Mesopotamia. Under their rule, Babylonian culture continued to flourish.

The greatest of the Babylonian kings was Hammurabi. He seems to have been an organizing genius. A code of laws associated with his name was discovered at Susa in 1901, inscribed in the Akkadian language on a stone stele about six feet high. The question of the date of Hammurabi's reign illustrates the difficulty we still encounter in establishing some points of chronology. His reign used to be placed as early as 2300 B.C.; now it is generally dated about 1792–1750 or about 1728–1686 B.C. and the more recent date seems safer.

This reduction of chronology resulted from excavations at Mari, which was once a brilliant city on the Euphrates. The city had a great temple to Ishtar, the mother goddess, and a great palace area, which included the same sort of business offices that were found in the temple area at Ur. Twenty thousand clay tablets and fragments were found in the palace archives. Some of the letters are originals of the correspondence of the king of Mari with Hammurabi of Babylon. Others show that the king was contemporary with an Assyrian king, Shamshi-Adad, whose dates can be established by other lines of evidence. These provide the most definite and direct evidence yet found for the date of Hammurabi and have led to the acceptance by many scholars of what is called "the low chronology," a chronology that would put the date of Hammurabi's reign at 1728–1686 B.C., centuries later than formerly accepted dates. In addition, it is confirmed by the discovery of objects that can be independently dated by Egyptian archaeology.

Nuzi, which lies to the east of the middle Tigris, is another recently excavated city that, like Mari, has yielded fresh and interesting information. The Hurri or Hurrians, called Horites in the Bible, appeared in Mesopotamia late in the third millenium B.c. Nuzi was one of their cities, and many clay tablets have been found here, written in the Babylonian language with some Hurrian words. They belong to about the fifteenth century B.c. Touching many aspects of life, they add exactness in one detail or another to our picture of the culture that had by this time become general in Mesopotamia.

ACHIEVEMENT IN MESOPOTAMIA DOWN TO 1500 B. C.

The Management of Nature

The management of Nature consisted chiefly of the construction of dams, dikes, and canals for irrigation, and we are now very well informed about these ancient Babylonian irrigation systems. The whole course of the two rivers was never brought completely under control. In some periods, as, for example, under the rule of Ham-murabi, there was unified political control over a large area, and the irrigation system must have been better co-ordinated then than at other times when the country was divided and smaller political units maintained a precarious existence.

Another aspect of the management of Nature, not officially rec-ognized today, but not entirely strange to us, is the performance of "sympathetic" rites of various kinds—a kind of "white" magic. When on their New Year's Day the Babylonians heard, as part of the reli-gious ceremonies, a recital of the triumph of the god Marduk over primeval chaos in that primordial age when he formed the world from chaos, we may say, following our way of looking at things, that they were performing a magical ceremony to assure the survival of the world. We might similarly regard some of the ceremonies designed to insure the fertility of plants and animals as magical ceremonies.

Ours is the detached and analytic way of looking at man and the world that first became common among the Greek philosophers and has been the Western way ever since. To the ancients—before the Greek thinkers of the sixth century B.C.—man and the world did not seem so sharply separated. Rather, in their ceremonies they were offering a reminder to Nature, to a natural system of which they formed part, not standing off from it and trying to force it to behave.

Part of the literature of the Sumerians and Babylonians that has come down to us consists of hymns and prayers as well as "epics" describing the doings of the gods. The epics, which are quite short, were apparently part of the apparatus for dealing with the gods. In this literature, we find a recognized list of gods representing natural phenomena. The sky and the majesty of the cosmic system are felt as a god, Anu. The violence of the thunderstorm is in Enlil, who must execute the decrees of Anu, whether benevolent or destructive. Ishtar, the great mother and goddess of love and union, is in one sense a counterpart to Enlil. A later age might speak of these forces as attraction and repulsion, not as two deities. The Earth Mother is felt as something living, something that is fertilized and brings forth richly.

All this order of beings, which includes everything (for nothing, not even a rock, is thought of as entirely inanimate and outside the system of living beings) is arranged in a hierarchy of command, with man near the bottom. It behooves this rather low figure in the chain of existence to solicit the favor of beings above him. To this end there was developed a system of ritual and liturgy that might have astonished an intelligent man of 5000 B.C. If to us this way of describing and dealing with the universe and its powers seems unsophisticated, we must realize that it represents a pioneer attempt to handle a most important problem. Our own (sometimes unwarranted) confidence in our knowledge of natural science is such that we find it extremely difficult to realize how the problem of describing and dealing with the universe must have appeared to men who did not have our exact knowledge (and the precise scientific terminology to express it) and our aggressive attitude toward Nature. In actual practice, the views on this matter developed in early Mesopotamia gave satisfaction to Near Eastern man for thousands of years.

The role of the priest was thoroughly developed. We know that by 1500 B.C. there were many grades of priesthood. Religious buildings were often very elaborate. Not only had a tremendous religious liter-ature been collected and standardized, but music was also a familiar part of liturgical apparatus. We are only just learning how compli-cated Babylonian music had become.

The Management of People

The achievements of the Sumerians and the Babylonians in manag-ing people were remarkable, too, obvious as they may seem to us. The men whom we are discussing were often great innovators.

At the beginning of the history of Mesopotamia, social organization was very simple, but the Sumerians soon brought it to a stage of con-siderable complexity. Monarchy was the normal form of government. The records of early Sumerian times also mention government by elders, sometimes with the men capable of bearing arms called in as an assembly to consider important matters. There is also mention of occasions when leaders were chosen for emergencies, laying down their powers after the crisis was over, much as Roman dictators were to receive and lay down their office. But government by kings is mentioned most frequently in cuneiform sources.

The role of the king, like that of the priest, was early developed. The kings often spoke of themselves as the shepherds of their people and insisted on the diligence and vigilance with which they performed their duties. On other occasions, however, they called attention to their power. Titles and other symbols of kingship were devised. The obvious method of asserting importance by building an impressive royal res-idence must have been thought of early. Certain architectural features —the ceremonial stairway or large doors, perhaps—could be endowed with the symbolism of the king's power and majesty. The two steles showing kings in the act of winning victories, mentioned earlier in this chapter, are further examples of the arts in the service of the government.

The art of writing was an important by-product of the development of the art of government. As we have seen, one of the earliest moves was to persuade the mass of the people to give up a part of their sur-pluses to support certain other people who worked for the benefit of everyone and did not produce their own food. The king, priests, soldiers, and such technical specialists as coppersmiths probably were the first of these men thus supported by others. Writing apparently was invented for the purpose of keeping track of the assessment and payment of what the government demanded from the people. In later times we shall find writing used for such governmental records, but for no other purpose, at Cnossus in Crete and Mycenae in Greece. The Sumerians were using a well-evolved pictographic writing before the end of the fourth millennium. During the third millennium they transformed their system into conventional symbols representing sounds rather than pictures, so that they had a true phonetic writing. They used the wedge-shaped marks in various combinations made with the end of a stylus on soft clay that we call cuneiform writing. The Akkadians and Babylonians adopted this system to write their common language.

Remains have been found of the professional schools in which writing was taught to those who hoped to be professional scribes. The pupils were probably the sons of people in moderate circumstances. Their later status could range from that of a clerk without responsibilities to that of a major administrator, and the instructors in the schools were professional teachers of some standing. We have remarkable descriptions of schools and examinations from early times.

From tablets written by schoolboys it is plain that writing and the teaching of it stimulated reflective thought among the Sumerians and the Babylonians. Many lists have been found that were prepared for the use of the students. Some of them constitute a kind of classification of the language into groups of related words and phrases to help the students learn the rather difficult cuneiform system of writing. Other lists give a grammatical classification of the language. Still others contain arithmetical problems and their solutions. In later Babylonia there were dictionaries of Sumerian for Babylonians who knew it as a learned language no longer spoken.

It has been observed that in all the writings of the Sumerians we find almost no trace of the abstract and generalized way of thought that was to be the great contribution of the Greeks after 600 B.C. and that is so characteristic of our own modern culture. If in the schools of the scribes there were discussions of grammar, word forms, and usage, there seem to have been no statements of rules that applied generally. There are court records and codes of laws, but no rules or principles of law are found. The mathematical tablets give practical methods for the solution of problems that are sometimes surprisingly complex, but they never give axioms or theorems. Tablets telling of public events never attempt to link them together into what we should call meaningful history.

The kingdoms of early Mesopotamia developed bureaucracies, or responsible bodies of officials. Many of the clay tablets from all parts of the long period we are discussing convey administrative information and royal commands between different areas and different levels of the governmental system, allowing us to infer much of its structure and extent.

Organized armies were developed in our period. There are bas-reliefs showing soldiers in a tight phalanx, protected by helmets and shields and using swords, lances, and bows as offensive weapons. The corresponding arts of fortifying and capturing cities were well developed by the end of this era.

Beside the king, priest, soldier, and craftsman as specialists, we find the jurist. A great deal of information has been recovered about the legal systems of the period. Thousands of clay tablets, some Sumerian, but most Babylonian, give information on many kinds of official and private, commercial and domestic legal transactions. Some of these tablets are not originals, but copies made for the teaching of law students or of scribes. In a city of the Assyrian Empire that flourished a thousand years later was found an extended repertory of Sumerian and Babylonian legal forms, apparently used by Assyrian law students of about 650 B.C. or by scribes who might be asked to draw up documents. We also have a number of collections of officially published regulations, of which the so-called Code of Hammurabi, published just after 1700 B.C., is the largest. Two Sumerian collections have been found, one about 150 years older than Hammurabi's and one about 350 years older.

This mass of evidence for legal machinery shows that the combined efforts of kings, priests, and juristic specialists had brought imposing results. Although in the early days the priests played an important part in the management of the courts, the civil power gradually arrogated this function to itself almost completely, leaving only some minor jurisdiction to the ecclesiastical arm. The king made himself head of the civil system, and appeal to him was possible as a guarantee of impartial justice.

The legal information that we have provides many signs of well-developed social systems. One is the mere fact that there was a government which would take upon itself the management of a system of courts and the establishment of a body of rules to govern all sorts of relationships. We shall see systems—among the Hebrews and the Homeric Greeks, for example—that had not yet moved out of a much simpler stage, a stage that hardly grasped the idea of impartial justice. Another is the fact that we have no trace at all of men's being rebuffed by the court because they chose the wrong form of legal action with which to approach the court. In other words, we have a system that has gone beyond the rigid formalism which often characterizes the very early stages of legal systems. On the contrary side, there are signs of the growth of the notion of equity, that is, the idea that cerain legal adjustments and remedies may be desirable that cannot be provided for by definite rules. Yet the extreme severity of some penalties seems primitive to the modern jurist who considers these materials.

The provisions of the Babylonian laws throw a great deal of light on the society of the time. Agriculture was the basis of society, of course, and in that agriculture irrigation played a cardinal role. There are a number of provisions for penalties against the man who has failed to let the water through to his neighbor's field as he should or who has been so careless about his dikes and ditches that he has flooded his neighbor's land. There are precise rules, with prices, for the renting of oxen as draft animals and provisions for cases of goring by oxen. Stock-raising and grazing in general take a minor place.

We hear of royal property, temple properties, and private holdings. Apparently private real estate could be sold or rented and bequeathed freely. In Babylonia proper at this time, we seldom have the primitive arrangement by which an estate that supports people in common is inalienable, at least in theory. Society is at a much more advanced stage than that. One interesting provision, however, is that the soldier by profession holds land that he cannot alienate or even lose by his own folly or by being captured; the property and profession of soldiering are both hereditary.

Industry and trade were well developed. Some industries, like weaving, continued to be carried on by managers of temple properties as most industry had been in early times. It seems reasonable to suppose that temple manufactures were generally intended to supply the needs of temple personnel but inevitably overflowed into the open market.

We find mention in the codes of many kinds of free artisans, along with slave artisans and those attached to temples and probably slaves. There are free people who keep inns, act as tenant farmers, represent firms as commercial agents, and indeed perform most of the functions of a free economy of the type common before the Industrial Revolution. There is precise regulation of wages, commissions, rents, and damages either for nonperformance or for negligence. Every agreement that has to do with the exchange of goods or services, as well as those that deal with land, had to be written and witnessed, for the man who had no written instrument to show was without standing in the courts.

Business practices include partnerships and agencies, but not limited-liability corporations. The practice of lending at interest was common; gold, silver, copper, and bronze were the commodities lent, for money, in the strict sense of metal whose weight and fineness were guaranteed by a government stamp, did not yet exist. Our nonlegal sources make it possible to put together the whole story of the complex venture of financing and preparing a caravan to make a long journey, payment of the customs and bribes that were necessary on its journey, the sale of goods and purchasing of others, and the final accounting of the profit (or loss) on the venture. A merchant who was accustomed to engage in such ventures outside his own country must have been a skillful and resourceful man of business. He also spread abroad some knowledge of the business practices so clearly reflected in Babylonian law.

The code makes it clear that this was a stratified society. The noble at the top enjoyed privileges that came from his nobility; he also had to acknowledge that nobility entails duties. The commoner who struck a noble was severely punished, but less so for striking another commoner. A noble had to pay more for striking an equal than a commoner did. The physician received a lower fee, fixed by the code, for treating a commoner than for treating a noble and still less for treating a slave, and he was subject to a similar gradation of penalties for bungling the treatment of noble, commoner, or slave.

Slavery was taken for granted. Although kidnapping by slave dealers was frowned upon (unfortunately not always true in later times) slaves might come in as prisoners of war. Or the free commoner might be officially sold into slavery for nonperformance of his obligations. The slave enjoyed some protection under the law, if only as a piece of property that must be safeguarded.

A woman was expected to be under the control and protection of a man. Marriage was arranged on principles something like those that have prevailed abroad, which may seem unromantic and even mercenary to the American, but which are aimed at making marriage strong and stable, producing children and careful of their interests. Women could hold property and could even engage in business. It was assumed that the proprietors of wine shops would be women, and we find that they were liable to punishment if it could be shown that conspiracies against the king's peace were discussed or hatched over the winecups in their shops. Divorce was possible for good reasons, for example, flagrant misbehavior of the wife. Dowry and family property were watched carefully by the eye of the law.

The Use of Materials

Wood and stone were rare in Mesopotamia. It is probable that very little wood was used in ordinary building, but there are traces of skillful use of it for furniture, and in temples and palaces imported wood was used for roofing and trim. Now and then archaeologists find some indifferent stonework, as in the foundation of a building excavated at Mari, but in general the situation provides a definite contrast to the practice in Egypt, where great quantities of stone were skillfully used.

Most building employed mud-brick. In some cases, for example, the use of asphalt and mortar, we can see notable technical skill. Furthermore, the Sumerian builder was familiar with the arch and the vault, both of which used to be thought later inventions.

The artist manifested himself, too, in the cylinder seals that early came into use among the Sumerians. A design was cut into a little cylinder of hard stone, so that when the cylinder was rolled on moist clay the owner's seal came out in relief—a personal seal that could hardly be counterfeited. Many thousands of these seals have been found, and they form a vigorous and often charming branch of art exercised in the making of a useful possession for an individual.

A good many beautiful stone and metal vases are found in the ruins of temples, presumably used in the service of the gods. Here, too, we can see that the artistic impulse manifested itself in the shaping and decoration of otherwise prosaic containers for things to be offered to a deity.

In the use of metals we find both considerable technical skill in production and the artist's concern with the rightness of form. These artists cast copper and bronze, knew how to solder and rivet, and engraved and inlaid metals beautifully. Their managers had access to supplies of gold, silver, copper, and bronze (copper alloyed with tin).

Workmen in the period had many other talents. They had learned how to prepare leather. Not only could they weave cloth; they could also bleach it, dye it, and soften it. The idea and the use of cosmetics had been developed, as had perfumes and incense. It was understood that certain substances, which we now class as drugs, had specific effects on the human system. A number of wonderful tools had been invented. First and foremost was the plow. Others were the solid wheel, the sail, and the potter's wheel. The basic idea of standard measurements had appeared, leading to a definition of lengths and weights, standards for measuring them, and government insistence on their integrity. Another of the great inventions was a number system; this was sexagesimal and had a place notation, with an equivalent for our zero.

CHAPTER

4

EGYPT

The Nile

An early Greek historian felicitously spoke of Egypt as the gift of the Nile, a description that is often and deservedly repeated. The great river starts as the White Nile in the lake country of equatorial Africa and as the Blue Nile in the highlands of Abyssinia. After these two rivers join, they receive the waters of a third, the Atbara, and then run seventeen hundred miles northward to the Mediterranean Sea. There are no more tributaries, for during most of that journey there is no water to be added to the already great river.

In several places along the early course, the river runs across rock so hard that the water wears it down extremely slowly and runs in cataracts through narrow channels. After passing Assuan it runs through a wider channel which over countless years it has cut in a plateau of sandstone, then of limestone. Finally it runs through a goodly stretch of flatter country, much of which is composed of the rich alluvium washed down and deposited by the river.

The annual flooding of the Nile is caused by the spring rains and the melting snow from Abyssinia, which swells the Blue Nile. The process is a slow and majestic one, for the rise does not reach the main part of Egypt until July and does not come to its peak until the beginning of September. In modern times before the building of the dam at Assuan, a normal rise was about 25 feet. A rise of only 20 feet was not enough and meant a dangerous shortage of food for the next year. Twenty-two or 23 feet would mean an uncomfortable shortage. On the other hand, 30 feet meant damage to dams and dikes and perhaps some loss of soil rather than the usual increment of rich new soil from the settling of the silt brought down by the river. Presumably conditions in ancient times were more or less analogous.

Naturally the river was always present in the thoughts of the ancient Egyptians. The sun was equally present. The country does not have the cloudy and rainy weather that occurs normally in many parts of the world, and day after day is bright and cloudless. If the heat of the sun is oppressive in the warmer season, it is gratefully received in the cooler season. At the same time, however, the dryness of the atmosphere makes the higher temperatures of summer days less oppressive. To this same dryness and the virtual absence of rain, as well as to the hermetical sealing effect of the desert sands, we owe the preservation of many records of ancient Egypt written on papyrus (the paper made of the papyrus plant, which grows in moist places by the Nile), which would not have survived in a moister climate.

Egypt as a Geographical Entity

The Egyptians spoke of their country as "the Two Lands." It is both one land and two lands. It is one in that all its life is related to the river and all its usable territory lies close on either side of the river. Just beyond, on both sides is the desert. The dividing line is definite—a visible line where the effect of the water stops and where the cultivated soil marches with the dry unirrigated desert.

Egypt is also two lands. Upper Egypt, along the southern or upper course of the river, lies in a narrow valley, held in by cliffs on either side, with the desert beyond. Lower Egypt, the northern part of the country, widens out into the Delta, because there are no longer the restraining limestone cliffs. Here the flat, marshy land, much of which was created by the river, stretches farther on either side before it is bounded by the desert.

In early times the two parts were separate kingdoms. The people spoke different dialects and regarded themselves as having different

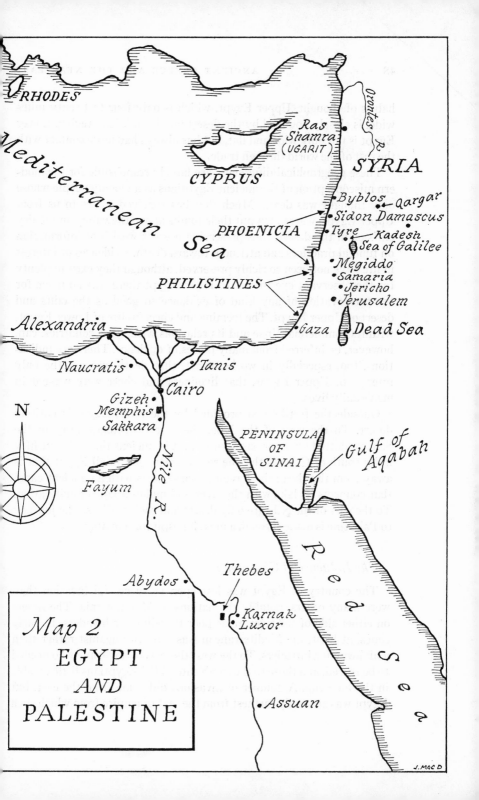

RHODES

Mediterranean Sea

Ras Shamra (UGARIT)

Orontes R.

SYRIA

CYPRUS

Byblos
Sidon
Qarqar
Damascus

PHOENICIA

Tyre
Kadesh
Sea of Galilee

Megiddo
Samaria
Jericho
Jerusalem

PHILISTINES

Alexandria

Gaza
Dead Sea

Naucratis

Tanis

Cairo

Gizeh
Memphis
Sakkara

Nile R.

PENINSULA OF SINAI

Gulf of Aqabah

N

Fayum

Red Sea

Abydos

Thebes

Karnak
Luxor

Assuan

Map 2
EGYPT
AND
PALESTINE

J. MAC D

habits of thought. Upper Egypt, which is only four to twenty miles wide, is closely bounded by the desert and is an inland region. Lower Egypt is not only wide and flat, but has always had more contact with the rest of the world through trade.

These geographical differences are largely responsible for the modern misconception of the ancient Egyptians as a gloomy people whose only thought was death. Much that has survived comes to us from Upper Egypt, where men put their tombs above the valley on the dry cliffs or in the desert, thus preserving a great wealth of information on funeral practices and attitudes toward death. Evidences of interest in life have not been so richly preserved, although they exist in plenty for the observant eye to see. In lower Egypt there was no place for the preservation of any kind of evidence so good as the cliffs and desert of Upper Egypt. The teeming and cheerful life of Lower Egypt, with its commercial tinge and its relations with other countries, can, however, be inferred from many pieces of evidence. There are indications, too, especially in works of art, that death was not the only interest of Upper Egypt, that liveliness and cheer were present in men's daily lives.

Outside the fertile area provided by the river, Egypt is entirely desert. To the west of the Nile, the desert stretches away to the Sahara, dotted by a few oases important in ancient times. About fifty miles south of Cairo is the one really green spot in all Egypt that is away from the river: the Fayum, a large oasis with an ancient canal that connects its lake with the river and makes a lane of cultivation. To the east of the Nile are only desert and rocky hills, so the journey to Palestine is made through a most inhospitable country.

The Influence of Geography

The country of Egypt was less open to successful invasion than were many others, notably the nations of Mesopotamia. The desert on either side of the river made poor traveling for invaders. In early times, at least, the Mediterranean was a barrier against rather than a highway for intruders. To the west there were no people who needed to be feared, and those to the south caused the Egyptians little trouble in the long run. A number of invasions did come from the east, but Egypt was generally farthest from the seat of empire from which such invasions were launched and was the last country to be conquered and the hardest to hold.

It is probably true, then, that it was Egypt's physical features and location that discouraged invaders. What meaning does this have in Egyptian history? It has been suggested that his comparative freedom from encroachment gave the early Egyptian a feeling of security and confidence. But the serious student of history may well feel that he can more easily establish the results of the invasions that did take place (that of the Hyksos, for instance, which will be described later) than of those that did not take place.

The relation of man and the river in Egypt has quite naturally given rise to other general pronouncements. It would seem very likely, for example, that the presence of the river and the need of a great common effort to make irrigation works had something to do with the rise of a highly organized society along its banks. The evidence at our disposal does not, however, allow us to follow step by step the rise of society along the river.

We do know, though, that in the Paleolithic Age, when northern Africa still had rainfall, the river was far wider than it is now and flowed at a much higher level. A series of terraces above the present level suggests that the river cut itself a somewhat narrower and deeper channel, then another and another, as over thousands of years the climate became drier. Early man moved about on the banks of the dwindling river, now and then absent-mindedly dropping some crude possession, which now serves as evidence that he had been there. Even in the historic age, beginning about 3200 B.C., there must have been enough moisture to produce a sort of jungle along parts of the river bank, for occasionally the early artists would depict it.

When northern Africa, first the southern part and then the whole area, began to dry up, the land on either side of the river became less and less hospitable; the Sahara Desert was created by the gradual cessation of rainfall. Some of the men who had lived there doubtless went elsewhere. Some descended to make the river valley their home, and they brought with them or enticed the most amenable animals, as the deposits of bones show.

In a rough way, distinctions can be made between the stages of this prehistoric culture of Neolithic man in the valley. The earliest villages seem to go back to about 5000 B.C. At Deir Tasa in Middle Egypt has been found a cemetery of this period. In the graves are the remains of food, as well as ornaments and Neolithic tools. Life was evidently simple, but already there was an idea of a life beyond the grave of the sort that persisted in Egypt.

A few hundred years later copper had been introduced, probably from Asia, so that the civilization should be called Chalcolithic, or "copper and stone." A typical spot is El Badari, in Middle Egypt, whose culture is known as Badarian. The people were agricultural and pastoral. They used amulets shaped like animal heads, presumably to gain the strength or swiftness of the animal. They made good pottery, the even firing of which shows that they had kilns. They had ivory ornaments and needles and awls of bone. They had a taste for jewelry, some of which was made by boring and shaping rather hard stones. They did not live in isolation, for their ivory came from the South, their shells from the coast of the Red Sea, and their turquoise from Sinai. The cultural traits of the Badarian period seem to have been fairly widespread in Upper Egypt.

In the next period there was a sudden flowering of the ability and inclination to draw. Slate palettes for the grinding of cosmetics also appeared and were to persist. On such a slate one would grind a little malachite with a pebble and make green eye-paint of a sort still used in Africa; it is germicidal, very helpful in keeping flies away from the eyes, and probably useful in lessening the glare of the sun. These palettes were often carefully shaped, and their ornamentation became increasingly elaborate as time went on. Often the palette, the grinding pebble, and the little lump of malachite were put in the grave near the head of the deceased.

Even in prehistoric times, Lower Egypt, to the north, seems to have had more contacts with other parts of the world than the southern region did. The style of some of its clay jars suggests a Palestinian origin. Lapis lazuli came from Mesopotamia and obsidian from Abyssinia, Arabia, or the islands of the Aegean. The idea of molds for making mud bricks probably came from Mesopotamia.

There is archaeological evidence from the end of the prehistoric period of a sizable and continued immigration of new people of Mesopotamian origins. The discovery of new physical types in graves of this time is striking, as is the sudden appearance of a number of cultural traits that are new in Egypt and have Mesopotamian affin-

Bison and wild boar, from the cave of Altamira, Spain.

The American Museum of Natural History.

Panel of enameled brick from the Procession Street of the Babylon of Nebuchadnezzar II (605–562 B.C.).

The Metropolitan Museum of Art.

The ziggurat at Ur.   Courtesy of The British Museum—University Museum Expedition to Ur.

Relief from the palace of Ashur-nasir-pal II, 9th Century B.C.
Courtesy of the Bowdoin College Museum of Art.

Old Akkadian cuneiform inscription, c. 2200 B.C. Contract for the purchase of a house.
The Metropolitan Museum of Art.

Akkadian seal, 24–2200 B.C. RIGHT : Impression of the seal.
The Metropolitan Museum of Art.

Assyrian ivory inlay for furniture, c. 710 B.C.
The Metropolitan Museum of Art.

The Sphinx, Gizeh.

Courtesy of Trans World Airlines, Inc.

The royal official Methethy,
late 5th dynasty, about 2420 B.C.
The Brooklyn Museum.

Egyptian mirror (New Kingdom).
The Brooklyn Museum.

Queen Hatshepshut, c. 1490–80 B.C.
The Metropolitan Museum of Art.

Model of an Egyptian fishing and
fowling boat, c. 2000 B.C.;
found in a royal tomb.
The Metropolitan Museum of Art.

Temple of Deir-el-Bahari at Luxor; reign of Queen Hatshepshut.

Courtesy of the Tourist Office of the United Arab Republic.

ities. Pretty examples of cylinder seals appear. In architecture, decorative panels of brickwork appear; and there are new artistic motifs: balanced groups in composition, sometimes strange animals, sometimes a hero or divinity with two flanking animals.

The historic period begins here with the formation of two kingdoms, the kingdom of Upper Egypt and the kingdom of Lower Egypt. It is possible that a considerable number of people arrived from Mesopotamia and were able to organize the two kingdoms somewhere around 3400 B.C. For three centuries the two lived more or less peaceably. Then, about 3100, Menes, king of the southern kingdom, was able to spread his power over all the northern region, and a union of Egypt was effected (which essentially was to last to the present day). A capital city was built at Memphis, just south of the Delta at the natural junction of the two parts of Egypt.

Although it is possible thus to lay down the outlines of the history of Egypt from the earliest times to the union of the two kingdoms, we have no evidence to tell us how these people, so simple and crude in their ways when we first meet them, made their great adjustment to the river. Although Egyptians seem to have been a very strenuous people, because they did develop a large national unit and did achieve such mighty works as harnessing the Nile and building the pyramids, the fact remains that we cannot trace the steps by which they arrived at such capabilities. We do not even know whether the large kingdoms arose before the large-scale irrigation efforts or after.*

THE EARLY HISTORICAL PERIOD
3100–2686

Sources and Systems of Dynasties

Although the dates of Egyptian history can be and are expressed by our ordinary system of dating, it is the custom among scholars to use as well the system of dynasties that we owe to Manetho, a Greek-speaking Egyptian priest of the third century before Christ. There is

---

*See J. W. Wilson, *The Burden of Egypt*, chap. 2, for a careful analysis of the evidence and a sensible discussion of Toynbee's "challenge and response," Childe's "urban revolution," and Redfield's "folk society" in relation to early Egypt.

some reason to believe that his history of Egypt was written in the popular style of the time and that he was influenced by a desire to remind the Greeks who then ruled Egypt of the ancient glories of his people. He had access to the native source materials, could read them, and might have written a scientific history, if he had so wished. Unfortunately his work survives only in the form of more or less extensive quotations by Greek and Roman authors interested in chronology, for Manetho had tried to make his book manageable and digestible by arranging his material according to families of kings, or dynasties.

Even today it often is convenient to use his middle-sized temporal units. Thus, the early historical period (3100–2686 B.C.) may also be referred to as "the first two dynasties." There will be other periods when the use of the dynastic system seems to make references more meaningful; the Eighteenth Dynasty, a golden period from 1567 to 1320 B.C., is one. Such a method of reference is also valuable because dating by our modern absolute system is subject to some uncertainty, especially in the earlier parts of Egyptian history, and when scholarly work, from time to time, leads to the general acceptance of a new absolute dating (say 1502 B.C.), we can still speak of events as having occurred in a certain year of a certain dynasty without rewriting all our histories.

There are lists of kings and events other than Manetho's, but the sources are scanty until the later periods. The "Turin Papyrus," written in the Nineteenth Dynasty, contains the remains of a complete list of all the kings from Menes in 3100 B.C. down to the time when it was written. The "Palermo Stone," so called because it is in the museum of Palermo, Sicily, is one of the many pieces of evidence that unfortunately have been partly spoiled by careless handling. It offers what seem to be authentic records of Egypt up to the Fifth Dynasty, not wars or conquests, but the height of the Nile from year to year, the consecration of temples, the arrival of 49 ships with cedar wood from Lebanon, the return of an expedition to the South bringing back gold and incense. A rather small amount of material, difficult to use as historical data, comes from the excavations of the tombs of the first two dynasties at Sakkara—such things as cylinder seals, tags and labels, and now and then a tombstone or a statue with an inscription on it.

The Language and its Decipherment

The Egyptians early developed a language worthy of respect as an instrument of communication. Its structure has some resemblance to that common among the Semitic languages of nearer Asia; in other ways it is like the languages of Africa that are called Hamitic. The language has a large vocabulary and is careful in expression and strict in word order.

Although the system of writing may seem to appear suddenly at the beginning of the historical period, it is possible to see anticipations of it in the centuries before. When it developed, the language could be written in the pictorial signs that are known as hieroglyphs or with cursive forms of the signs in the style known as hieratic. Then a system was devised to write it as an alphabetic language, with at least one character understood as expressing each of its twenty-four consonantal sounds. The vowels, which were not written, can sometimes be guessed from a comparison with the way in which Egyptian words are written in Babylonian or Greek and especially in Coptic, the later popular form of the early Egyptian language.

Our ability to read these writings depends upon the devoted labors of many scholars and the fortunate chance that brought to light the so-called Rosetta Stone, named for the place in Egypt where it was found in 1799 by a member of Napoleon's expedition. This stone slab contained a decree of the priests of Memphis in honor of Ptolemy the Fifth, one of the Macedonian kings of later Egypt, written in hieroglyphic characters in one section, in the very rapid form of hieratic known as demotic in another, and in Greek characters in the third.

Although scholars were already attempting to read Egyptian writing and collections of materials were being made, even the discovery of the Rosetta Stone did not lead to an immediate solution of the problem. The Frenchman Champollion was the most devoted student of the subject. Had it not been for his untimely death in 1832, he probably would have made it possible to read most Egyptian texts, but as it was, the labors of other European scholars achieved this end in a few decades. Champollion gathered more examples of the different kinds of Egyptian writing than other scholars did and pursued his researches by methods closer to those that seem proper today. Although comparison of the triple text on the Rosetta Stone was helpful, he made progress also from comparison of other hieroglyphic and hieratic texts.

The Achievement of the First Two Dynasties (3100–2686 B. C.)

The four hundred years of the first two dynasties were a time of great progress in Egypt.* It is surprising, therefore, that we can lay our hands on so little detailed evidence for the events and the political accomplishments of this great period, but we can at least point to the results that we know were achieved before the early stages of the Old Kingdom (the name generally applied to the next five hundred years).

The most important achievement of the first two dynasties was the establishment of the unified monarchy of Upper and Lower Egypt as a powerful central government, although the details of the process are largely unknown to us. We see references only to such governmental activities as a voyage to Lebanon for cedar or the building of a number of ships. There is evidence, too, of the exploitation of Sinai and of the securing of the southern frontier. Nevertheless, by the end of the Second Dynasty, the unified government of the Two Lands was definitely established.

The idea that the one kingdom was composed of two kingdoms had such vitality that the king had to wear a double crown to symbolize it, and because he was buried in Lower Egypt, there had to be a cenotaph in Upper Egypt to symbolize his burial there. The government was an absolute monarchy based on the idea that the king was a living god. We do not know how this useful and practical belief was imposed on the people; we do know that at the end of this period the idea was so generally accepted that service to the king, in this life and in the next one, was the most important of all activities. The general structure of the government had been established: the royal court was fully organized and the army and the civil service fully responsive to the will of the monarch. The irrigation system and the cultivation of the

---

*W. B. Emery's *Archaic Egypt* has a clear and interesting discussion of the problems of establishing early Egyptian dates.

disposable land were well advanced, even though some pictures belonging to the next period show hunting scenes in uncultivated areas along the river bank.

Within the borders of the kingdom, the movement of goods can be partially traced by today's archaeologists. For example, the materials found at Sakkara—alabaster, basalt, diorite, and other stones—come from nearby, from the eastern desert, from the western desert, from the Fayum, and from Nubia, south of Egypt. Finds of pottery show that the products of certain shops were widely distributed. The river was the one great highway, while heavy loads traveling on land went by sledge, since the wheel was not suited to the sandy soil.

Sinai sent turquoise (as in the Badarian period), malachite, and copper. The woods of Lebanon were imported in some quantity. Ebony came from the south, far up the river, as did ivory and resin. As for export, Egyptian stone vessels have been discovered in Palestine, at the wood-exporting city of Byblos below the hills of Lebanon, on the island of Cyprus, and even on the Greek mainland.

The Egyptians of the first two dynasties were as enterprising in their handling of materials as they were in the development of government. Their tools were chiefly of copper. Examples of very fine work in wood have been preserved—furniture and coffins—as have ivory fittings—feet for tables—made with imagination and skill. The people of this period began to use the potter's wheel, but after making some excellent pottery, they apparently lost interest somewhat and gave their attention and best efforts to the making of elegant stone vessels. Although they continued to make a great deal of pottery, it was of an ordinary and routine type. They learned to make jewelry of gold and to shape hard and precious stones. After a good many rather unimpressive efforts, they began to produce free-standing sculptures of some merit.

The architecture of the first two dynasties is represented first by the remains of some early houses, rather simple, made of sun-dried brick with few beams (because wood was scarce) and with a considerable amount of such flimsy materials as reeds, especially the papyrus reed. When the Egyptians learned to work in stone, and stone masonry of the First Dynasty has been found, they often reproduced the designs appropriate to these earlier materials and sometimes even the appearance of them; for example, stone walls were carved to look like walls of reed matting. (This procedure was followed by the Greeks, too, when they began to use stone and has often been repeated with many new building materials introduced in our own time.)

Some stone was used in the public buildings of this early period. Cut stone slabs are found as facing in some of the great tombs, and a few temples are known to have had at least some elements of stone. Sun-dried brick, however, was the chief material in such structures as the royal tombs at Sakkara, on the Nile near Memphis, and not far south of modern Cairo. It is now believed by some scholars that these are the real burial places of the royalty of the period and that the simpler tombs found at Abydos in Upper Egypt are the cenotaphs, or empty tombs, built on the principle that a king of the Two Lands should have a tomb in each.

These tombs could be as large as 200 by 100 feet. Around the central chamber, where the king was buried, were many rooms. Some few have been found unplundered in the twentieth century, and they yield a complete supply of all the things needed to reconstruct this earthly life for the kings beyond the grave. The structure itself is thought to imitate the palaces. In the storerooms are food and drink, of course, in impressive variety and quantity. There is furniture of wood inlaid with ivory, and plates and cups to set on it. There are tools and weapons of every kind. In a pit beside each royal tomb was buried a boat, in which the spirit of the monarch was to travel with the sun god on his daily trip.

Another great achievement of the age is the calendar year of 365 days, which was in use at the beginning of the Old Kingdom. It is to be presumed that during the first two dynasties, a considerable amount of thought and work had led up to this achievement. The year consisted of three seasons, each of four thirty-day months, and at the end of the third season were five days to fill out the number of 365. The first season was that of the flood of the Nile, and was so called. It began toward the end of July and was associated with the heliacal rising of Sothis, or Sirius, the Dog-Star. This is the rising at which the star can be seen in the sky at dawn, and the day of this rising came to be called the first day of the year. The second season was named for the growth of the crops, and the third for the harvest.

The Egyptians cannot have failed to note the phases of the moon and to connect various kinds of lore with them. Their months, however, were not lunar months of 28 or 29 days, but were fixed at 30 days each. Since 365 days is not the true length of the year, the calendar would gradually get out of order and, after four years, be wrong by one day, as it is with us, but the Egyptians did not correct the calendar as we do in Leap Year. At the end of a hundred years it would be 25 days off, and at the end of 4 times 365, or 1460 years, it would have come full circle and be correct again for one year. Apparently the Egyptians felt able to manage with a calendar of this sort, although some scholars believe that there was always a corrected calendar in use.

THE OLD KINGDOM

The period of Egyptian history known as the Old Kingdom lasted from 2686 to 2181 B.C. and included the Third, Fourth, Fifth, and Sixth Dynasties. What used to be the last centuries of the Old Kingdom are now regarded as the First Intermediate Period and include Dynasties Seven through Ten, from 2181 to about 2040 B.C. The distinction between these periods is based on the firmness of the power of the central government at Memphis during the Old Kingdom, the inability of the dynasties at Thebes and Herakleopolis to do more than exercise a very limited control over the rulers of the nomes (the smaller governmental units) during the First Intermediate Period, and the restoration of control over all Egypt by the Theban rulers, which marks the beginning of the Middle Kingdom about 2040 B.C.

The Royal Government

The society of the Old Kingdom was admirably organized. At its head was the absolute monarch, the king who was also a god. He was regarded as the source of all law and the owner of all land and other material property in the country. His contact with affairs and with the common people was managed through a class of nobles. The most important offices of the realm were filled by members of his family. The vizier, or vice-king, administered justice, the grain supply, the treasury, the army, public works, and the priesthoods of the state gods. The king had managed to gain enough power to be able to appoint rotating governors for the forty-odd nomes, which formerly had been independent. On some of the borders, however, he seems to have tolerated permanent wardens of the marches, especially in the South.

The king's divinity was such an awful thing as to make him untouchable and unapproachable. It lent authority to his will, supported his assertion of ownership of all Egypt, and, perhaps most important, was thought to continue after death and improve the chances of his subjects' survival after the close of this life. Yet a time was to come when the king had to struggle for power with the priests of the great state cults and with the governors of the nomes, who succeeded in exacting permanent and hereditary standing from him. Even without enough evidence to follow the process in detail, we can see that power relations shifted from time to time and that they depended, not on arrangements once made or on written formulas, but on the people involved in them and the forces operative at a given time.

Complaints about the administration of justice tended to come when the royal power was weak rather than when it was strong. The kings were able enough students of human affairs to realize that an autocratic government must dispense even-handed justice. Yet the king was still the source of all law, and there was no written code to be set beside the magnificent published codes of the Sumerian and Babylonian kings as a sign that justice was the same for all and the same at all times. The courts over which the vizier presided used a customary and unwritten law.

Although undoubtedly there was a great deal of small-scale barter between individuals, all formal trade seems to have been conducted by the king and his officials. Certainly it was the king's expeditions that went to Byblos on the coast of Palestine to get the cedar and other woods of the mountains behind, woods which are generally spoken of simply as "the cedar of Lebanon." Evidence of an Egyptian temple at Byblos suggests that Egyptians resided there and that perhaps there was a small colony to arrange for the trade in wood and in goods coming from the interior of Asia to be forwarded to Egypt, but there is no evidence of economic imperialism in Asia or elsewhere.

The exploitation of the turquoise and copper mines of Sinai was managed by royal officials and guarded by detachments of the army against attempted raids. The tomb of a First Dynasty king at Sakkara has yielded a rich collection of copper tools and weapons, together with a great reserve supply of copper that might be worked up into tools or weapons as needed for replacements in the next world. Copper, then, was plentiful at this time, but probably much of it was imported from Asia.

The royal government regularly conducted a census of the resources of the country and exacted taxes in kind. Those holding some of the grain-bearing land paid in grain. Those holding pasture land paid by sending animals or their hides. Because there was no money in the strict sense, these exchanges of goods were done on the basis of the "piece," a unit of value based on weights of metal. The actual transactions were generally made by bartering things that had comparable values in "pieces" without any use of precious metal as a medium of exchange.

Public Works: The Pyramids

The king could also exact labor as his due. Although it is to be presumed that forced labor was used on irrigation projects and other public works, its most interesting and spectacular use was for the building of the pyramids. If a hundred thousand men worked for twenty years to build the Great Pyramid, we obviously must admire the administrative ability that assembled, fed, and housed the great throng and planned their work. Perhaps a smaller corps of men, chiefly the expert workers in stone, was on duty all the year, and the many unskilled peasants were gathered to furnish the power of their muscles during the season of high Nile, when the farm work would be at a virtual standstill and the blocks of cut stone could be floated to the site and hauled into position to be dressed.

The suggestion has been made that this work was offered by the king to take care of a populace that had suddenly outgrown the available land as peace and prosperity made the population increase sharply. Tempting as it may be to see an analogy to modern governmental schemes for the relief of the unemployed, we should rather regard these projects as expressing the belief of the time that the continuance of the king's life and divinity beyond death was the most important concern of the whole people.

The great efforts expended on these tombs were expected to benefit everyone. The king himself was to continue to rule in the next world. The exact manner of his continued existence was expressed in many ways that to us seem inconsistent. It was a very important characteristic of Egyptian thought, however, to be able to view some aspect of life and the world in several different ways at once. The writings put in the chambers of the pyramids and known today as Pyramid Texts offer an astounding variety of religious and ritual and magic attempts to ensure eternal life and promote the eternal status of the dead king. Possibly the most inconsistent feature of this mixture, from the modern point of view, is that it represents the king both as the humble servant and the irresistible lord of the gods.

To the noblemen of the Old Kingdom, it seemed highly desirable to have their tombs around the pyramid of their sovereign. If they had no thoughts of so exalted an existence as that of the king's, they still could hope that in the next world they would be around him and serve him and have an existence better than that in this world. Little as we know about the beliefs of the common people, there is reason to suppose that they, too, thought of themselves as grouped about the nobles in the next world and, less directly, about the king, with an eternal existence somewhat better than this life.

The pyramids thus show us something of the physical effort that could be exerted in the Old Kingdom and something of the system of belief that could be translated into this physical effort. They also represent the maturing of art in Egypt.

During the First and Second Dynasties the kings had been buried in mud-brick structures known as mastabas (the word that the modern peasant applies to them). Their function was double: they must protect the body from disturbance or destruction and they must protect the things put with the body to provide for its material needs— food, tools, weapons, and other articles of daily life. The first king known to have a pyramid is Djoser, founder of the Third Dynasty, who began his rule about 2686 B.C. This forceful man had a talented second-in-command, I-em-hotep, one of whose many gifts was architectural ability.

I-em-hotep planned and built an elaborate mortuary complex at Sakkara. Everything was made of white limestone, which was quarried nearby. The chief structure was a pyramid that rose in six unequal stages to a height of about 200 feet. Around this structure were tombs for nobles, altars, shrines, and storehouses, with elaborate gates and courtyards. It is noteworthy that this gifted architect made these stone structures imitate the appearance of earlier structures of light wood, reed, and brick in spite of his great originality in designing the individual structures and combining them into a unified group.

The Fourth Dynasty was the great age of pyramid building. The first king, Snefru, was an energetic administrator who built a pair of pyramids, only one of which was of true pyramidal shape. The second, third, and fourth rulers of this dynasty built the best known of the pyramids at Gizeh, by the river, a few miles below modern Cairo. Khuf-wy, whom the Greeks were later to call Cheops, built the Great Pyramid around the year 2590 B.C.

The Great Pyramid is the largest single building ever constructed. Its base covers 13 acres and is virtually square, the longest side, 756.08 feet, being only 7.9 inches longer than the shortest. The sides almost exactly face the points of the compass, and the corners are almost exact right angles. It was 481.4 feet high, but the top 31 feet are now missing, for in a later age the Arab conquerors of Egypt stripped off the white limestone blocks that formed the outer surface and the peak. The core of the pyramid consists of about 2,300,000 large blocks of a less fine yellow limestone. Inside is a set of corridors and chambers. Nearby there are three small pyramids for the king's three queens and a systematic group of mastabas for other members of the family and noble officials. The complex includes a mortuary temple, where prayers for the king were to be said, a processional causeway that leads almost to the edge of the river, and a relatively modest temple at the end of the causeway. This arrangement came to be standard.

Here, design and execution alike are mature. The Great Pyramid is built with great skill, and the accompanying structures are individually well designed and harmoniously grouped. A great many statues formed part of the equipment of the complex. In addition, the tomb of Queen Hetep-hras, Cheops' mother, found unviolated, has yielded furniture that is classic in design and perfectly executed.

As a group, however, the pyramids are suggestive of still another aspect of the life of ancient Egypt: the gradual decline of the power of the kings. Never again was a king to build his tomb with the expenditure of the incredible effort that went into the pyramid of Khuf-wy. The pyramids of his son Kha-ef-Re (Chephren) and of his grandson Men-ku-Re (Mycerinus) are smaller, and thereafter the size of the pyramids declined steadily. The last one of classic dimensions was built by Pepy II at the end of the Sixth Dynasty, about 2180 B.C.

Difficulties of the Central Government

The maintenance of power in the central government is one of those persistent problems of government that can never be permanently solved, but must be worked on persistently, just as the great irrigation system of Egypt had to be kept in order by unending work from generation to generation. Here we must not allow ourselves to forget that we are dealing with vast stretches of time, vast at least in comparison with the temporal units into which Greek or Roman or yet more modern history is divided. The supremacy of the kings over all Egypt went back to the beginning of the First Dynasty, about 3100 B.C., and persisted, although sometimes with difficulty, until about 2181 B.C., when the First Intermediate Period began. Truly it was a tremendous achievement for a government to maintain itself in essentially the same form and to discharge its duties with consistent success for so long a time.

It has been noted that the power of the god Re increased greatly during the Fourth Dynasty and after it. Re had at first belonged to the city of Heliopolis as its local deity, but the fact that he was conceived as the sun eventually brought him more than local worship. The kings acted very shrewdly in adopting his cult, which was admirably suited to be associated with and to support the royal power. In the early Fifth Dynasty, the pyramids began to be accompanied by an obelisk and temple, both belonging to Re and both tending to increase in size and elaborateness. Although this change may suggest that the priests of Re had achieved a position that enabled them to challenge the power of king or at least to exert a quiet control over him, as the priests of Amun were to do somewhat later, the evidence hardly supports the conclusion.

There is another possibility: the kings may have felt it advisable to strengthen their power by intensifying their connection with Re.

Even in conservative societies, the ideas and ideals that serve to unite society will occasionally need to be varied or refurbished to regain their appeal. There is some evidence that the superiority of the king over the nobles was waning somewhat in the Fourth and Fifth Dynasties; we cannot know exactly why. The kings had weakened the power of the throne by granting lands to many of the nobles in order to provide the services of food and prayer for the royal tombs; and at some time in the Fourth Dynasty, they had conceded the permanent tenure of the governorships of the nomes, which until then had been held by nobles in turn at the king's pleasure. Perhaps Re and his priests seemed useful allies for the kings.

Not until the Sixth Dynasty, however, about 2181 B.C., did the central government become unable to exert control over all the land. Only then did the First Intermediate Period—two centuries or so of control by local rulers—begin. It is impossible to specify the direct cause of these later events in the tendencies toward division that began in the Fourth Dynasty.

Religion

Re was only one of a bewildering number of Egyptian gods. Each locality and district had early developed its own deities, which represented the forces of Nature. They were thought to have a variety of forms, especially the forms of plants and animals, and might be conceived as the friendly, useful cow, the fearsome lion, or the jackal or snake of a still lower order of creatures—although the modern mind may have even more difficulty comprehending a tree or plant divinity. Since these were nature gods, they often were thought to die and to be reborn with the cycle of the year, a cycle accompanied by ceremonies, prayers, and festivals.

As people did, the god had a house, and generally some object in an inner place represented the essence of his god's power. The divine image was served by the priests, as it was in Mesopotamia. They fed it, bathed it, amused it, took it for promenades, and displayed it to the people on certain occasions.

Some gods were widely recognized from an early time because they were thought of as cosmic forces. Re was the sun, Ya'h the moon, Nut the sky, and Geb the earth. Osiris, originally a local god of the type who died and was reborn, achieved national status as a dying and returning god because the story of his vicissitudes had great appeal for all classes of society, apparently because the priests of his cult polished up his story; other dying and returning gods remained local divinities.

Some attained national recognition because as their worshipers became prominent, they pushed the divinity forward with them. The god Horus, for example, was first the local god of a small place who became the god of the nome, then of his part of the Delta, then of the whole kingdom of Lower Egypt, then of both kingdoms, and then, when Menes united the two kingdoms, of the united kingdom of the Two Lands. Much later, with the rise of the Thebans in the Middle Kingdom and in the Eighteenth Dynasty, the god Amun of Thebes was carried up in power with the new rulers to such a position as no Egyptian god had ever before enjoyed.

THE MIDDLE KINGDOM

After the Old Kingdom came the First Intermediate Period, in which the power of the central government was so in eclipse that many of the nomes felt themselves independent. The restoration of unity and the effective power of the central government about 2040 B.C. marks the beginning of a new period, the Middle Kingdom, which continued until about 1780 B.C. Then we find a group of Asiatics called the Hyksos in control of Egypt, and we may say that the Second Intermediate Period had begun, a period of difficulties that were too much for the government to cope with, as had been the case in the First Intermediate Period. With the restoration of Egyptian control over the country about 1570 B.C. came the beginning of what is sometimes called the New Kingdom and sometimes the Empire.

Our sources do not allow us to see clearly what mistakes or weaknesses brought about the gradual inability of the government of the Old Kingdom to control the country. Nor can we explain why the rulers of Thebes—in fact, no great city—were able after eighty or so years of struggle to establish their superiority over their chief rivals, the rulers of Herakleopolis, and reunify the country about 2040 B.C. But clearly the very stable government of the Old Kingdom was capable of losing its control of the country as a whole, and, equally clearly, after more than two hundred ensuing years of rivalry between local powers, it was possible to re-establish a strong and stable central government.

The Government of the Middle Kingdom

The new regime of the Middle Kingdom resumed the activities that had been beyond the reach of local governments. There is recorded an expedition that went across to the Red Sea, built ships, and sailed down to Punt, the land of myrrh. This was the land at the bottom of the Red Sea, probably including both shores, the African and the Arabian. Another expedition renewed the exploitation of the mines of the Sinai Peninsula, and still another reopened Nubia to commerce in the stone that was desirable for the royal statues. Trade with Byblos and the interior of the Near East also was resumed.

The monarchs of the Middle Kingdom acquired a firm control over their realm, although local power and interests could command their respect. Like the rulers of the Old Kingdom, they were regarded as gods. To give proper divine support to their enterprises, they brought forward Amun, the local god of Thebes, to take a leading place in the pantheon with Ptah of Memphis, Re of Heliopolis, and Osiris of Abydos.

The name Amun means "the hidden one," an excellent conception of a god who was to be used to support the power of the throne. Furthermore, he was combined with the sun-god Re, the great god of the Egyptian nation. Under the Empire, the most massive of all Egyptian temples was built for him at Karnak, his wealth was unrivaled, and his high priest was a political power who might shake the power of the king himself.

The royal burial places cast light upon the period, as the pyramids do upon the Old Kingdom. The tombs of the kings became grander and those of the nobles less ambitious, reversing the tendency of the later days of the Old Kingdom. Apparently the relative sizes of the tombs of kings and nobles corresponded to their relative power.

It has been noted, too, that other evidence shows the kings of the Middle Kingdom managing to assert their power and authority against the influence of the nobles, although in the local sphere the nobles and nomarchs, or district leaders, did not yield entirely the power that they had acquired and exercised during the First Intermediate Period. For example, people sometimes provided accounts of themselves in the form of instructions to their descendants, and it is worth noting that in the First Intermediate Period such accounts could sometimes breathe a strong spirit of self-reliance and independence, whereas in the Middle Kingdom they came rather to suggest the necessity of reliance on the king for worldly advancement.

Yet the nobles did retain another advance achieved in the late Old Kingdom and the First Intermediate Period: they had laid claim to the same kind of life after death that had previously been the exclusive privilege of the king, and they did not give up this claim. We do not know how far down the social scale these new claims went, but it is plain that the nobles at least could use the same magic spells and the same prayers and the same ritual as the king to achieve beatitude in the next world. Perhaps it should be noted, however, that the expression "Book of the Dead," an expression that has been applied to the whole known body of formulas used to help in the afterworld, is misleading, for these formulas were never assembled in any one book or in any one place.

Since the Egyptians felt that some material form was required to house the personality in the life after death, they had developed, probably as early as the Second Dynasty, the process of mummification to preserve bodies. But because it was still possible that the body might be destroyed or decay, figures of stone and wood, wall paintings and reliefs were made for the tomb to be substitutes for the actual body. Careful mummification was expensive enough to be for the noble rather than for the ordinary man, who at best could afford only a simple version, perhaps backed up by a very simple image of himself.

A New Time of Troubles: The Second Intermediate Period

After nearly three hundred years of successful operation, the kings of the Middle Kingdom lost control of the realm; and for a few generations, Egypt suffered from the internal struggles that gave the Hyksos their opportunity to gain control of the country. These people were part of one of the movements that brought people from outside the civilized world to enter it and join in its life. They probably came from Asia; and they infiltrated Egypt rather than invaded it. By about 1720 B.C. they were in control of the Delta, that is, Lower Egypt, and there, for over a hundred years more, they lived in great fortress-camps. They dominated Lower Egypt and compelled Upper Egypt to accept their leadership. The Egyptian word "Hyksos," which formerly was thought to mean "shepherd kings," is now understood to mean "kings of foreign countries." It is not a precise ethnic designation, for some known names of individual Hyksos are Semitic and others are Hurrian. Some of the Hurrians, a people whom we met earlier in Mesopotamia, are known to have moved on as far as Syria and Palestine, and now we find some in Egypt among the Hyksos.

Although the Hyksos "ruled without Re," as the Egyptians put it, and were not at all respectful of Egyptian culture, they were not utter barbarians. They did bring in some distinctive cultural traits: the use of the horse and the battle-chariot, the compound bow, which was more powerful than the simple bow, body armor, and some elements of design in clothes and jewelry. Perhaps their greatest influence on Egyptian life lay in the fact that they toughened the Egyptians and changed their attitudes, as those who practice continued coercion of other people sometimes do. The Egyptians finally pulled themselves together and drove out the Hyksos about 1570 B.C.

EGYPTIAN CIVILIZATION

Agriculture

The management of the river began far to the south. There the government set up the Nilometer, a gauge that gave some indication of what the year's rise would be early enough to allow for any necessary special preparations. The chief of such preparations presumably was to strengthen the dikes that kept villages and gardens from flooding and to make sure of the strength of the artificial basins that were designed to hold the flood water for a while before releasing it to provide a new dosage of water. In addition to the dikes and basins, there were systems of canals for the efficient distribution of the water, and in many places enough water remained in the subsoil to create good wells.

The all-important cereal crop—wheat, barley, and emmer—was planted as soon as the water subsided and the land was dry enough to be worked, probably sometime in late September or early October. Harvest came in what is spring in Europe (and the United States). Thus, later, when the cereals of Egypt were a great source of supply for imperial Rome, the spring harvest allowed the grain to be gathered at Alexandria and sent off to Rome during the season when navigation was safe.

It is plain that the government's system of taxing land distinguished between pieces on the basis of their irrigability and consequent productiveness. A piece of land that could be watered by the normal flood was most reliable. If it could be irrigated by raising water, if it contained good subsoil water, or if it lay beside a canal, it had a relative and corresponding value. A system of surveying was developed that made it possible for the government to keep account of all land by such categories, and boundary marks were replaced if the high water removed them.

The real use of such a description of the land, of course, was for the assessment and collection of taxes, which were still necessarily levied in kind and took the form of specified numbers of sacks of grain from the harvest. A system of weights and measures had been developed, and it served well for the regulation of this process. In the Hellenistic Age, after the death of Alexander the Great in 323 B.C., the Greek Ptolemies who ruled Egypt had a wonderfully arranged system of taxation that relieved the peasant of everything except bare subsistence. It was also in operation under the Egyptian Empire and may have been well developed under the Old and Middle Kingdoms. The king could collect part of the yield of the soil, he could collect cattle and hides, and he could also claim a certain amount of labor from his subjects for the irrigation works or the royal building programs. The effort that in another country he might have allocated to roads was well spent on the river, Egypt's one great highway.

Cereals were always the most important crop. There were many vegetables: onions, radishes, beans, lentils, and others. The soil and climate were good for all kinds of melons, and the date palm and other fruit trees were highly prized. Although the olive tree does not grow well in Egypt and olive oil had to be largely imported from

Palestine, other sources of oil were found for food, lighting, and the basis of medicines and toilet preparations. The castor-oil plant, sesame, and saffron yielded oil, as did the seeds of a number of other plants. The vine can be grown in Egypt, and grapes are mentioned as important and desirable. In addition to wine the Egyptians had a brewed drink like beer.

Flax and papyrus plant were important products of the marshier ground. The Egyptians prepared their flax well, wove it with great skill, and had some attractive dyes for it, as is shown by the few pieces of linen cloth that have survived to modern times. They early learned to make writing paper from the papyrus plant by preparing thin strips that could be pounded together in a lengthwise and cross-wise pattern. They wrote with reed pens and with ink which remains legible today. Papyrus had many other uses, as in sails for river boats or hangings in houses.

The well-attested love of the Egyptians for flowers, as for many other aspects of Nature, is part of the ample proof that they loved and enjoyed this world; their thoughts were not all of defeat, death, and a different life. They relished this life and firmly believed that it continued beyond the grave. We get glimpses and hear echoes of pleasure in an Egyptian garden where there are a pool, flowers, fruit trees, and now and then the refreshing breeze from the north. Music and a dainty foreign maid who pours the wine are part of the picture.

Flowers were used at private feasts and public festivals. The floral motif appeared in such architectural forms as stone columns imitating the stems of plants, with capitals representing the flowering heads. Their successful use of the motif in ornamentation of many kinds had an influence on Syrian, Assyrian, and Persian art, and then on the art of the Ionian and the mainland Greeks. Perhaps it was the source of the flower motifs of Minoan art in Crete.

In the economy, animals were important, the ox and the cow being the chief large ones. There was little place for the horse in Egypt except to draw the war chariots that were used after the Hyksos had introduced them. Apparently one or two attempts to introduce the camel did not succeed. The donkey remained the animal for trading expeditions, whether to bring goods from Nubia and the Sudan or merely to the next farm. The goat, as everywhere, was the poor man's animal. Sheep were raised, and in the Delta, where the soil is generally moister, pigs were kept. Fowl were part of every household, both earthbound fowl and doves and pigeons, and the wild waterfowl were often caught and fattened in coops.

Materials and Craftsmanship

Egyptian craftsmanship with flax and with papyrus was, as has been said, excellent. They were also superb handlers of wood, even though their native woods were scarce and of an inferior sort. The local ones could be used for such rough work as the building of rafts or for the few beams and supports necessary for houses made of reeds or mud-brick or for the many simple boats used as ferries on the river or cargo carriers on the canals of the Delta.

Large pieces of wood with a good grain had to be obtained from Asia Minor through Byblos and other ports. In the Old and Middle Kingdoms, the cedar of Lebanon was the chief import. In the later days, when Egypt had an empire in Asia, oak, ash, and other good woods became available. The more exotic, like ebony and the fragrant woods, came from the lands south of Egypt. There was elaborate woodwork inside the pyramids and the temples of the Old Kingdom. Wood was desirable for ships, coffins, and furniture. The Egyptian cabinetmaker was a master; the best furniture was well designed and executed with exemplary skill. Rare and fine woods were often used, and inlaying with wood or ivory was common.

Egypt was better supplied with gold (from the mines of the South) than were the nations of the Near East. Some silver, in the form of a gold-silver alloy, came from Egyptian mines, and some was brought from other nations. The Egyptian craftsman worked these metals with sure taste. In addition, the desert east of Egypt yielded a variety of stones that were made into attractive jewelry: garnet, onyx, chalcedony, jasper. The blue of turquoise and the dull red of carnelian were popular; both came from the desert. The blue lapis lazuli had been brought from Asia even in very early times, and the purple amethyst came from Nubia. All these difficult materials were skillfully worked.

Copper was the important working metal of the Old Kingdom. Some of it came from the mines of Sinai, and some was imported from Asia. There are samples of true bronze (copper alloyed with tin) from the Middle Kingdom, although the source of the tin is not known. Tools were mostly of copper. It is conjectured that long copper saws and abrasive powdered stone were used to cut stone for building.

Many kinds of stone were used. Some of no great beauty was good enough to form the core of pyramids. But there were good limestones for the outer surfaces of buildings; for example, the limestone from nearby quarries that covered the Great Pyramid. A good deal of granite of various colors was used, and the most famous quarry was at Assuan, in the South. Alabaster was used for statues and parts of buildings as well as for small ointment jars or other little vessels, and one great quarry can still be seen. Another quarry produced the very hard dark yellow quartzite much used for the sarcophagi of the kings. Two blocks from this quarry are known to weigh over a hundred tons apiece.

Some of the highly expert work in all these materials was done to clothe, adorn, house, or bury important people. Most of it was produced in the service of the government, for the service of the king and his family was part of government service, and such work aimed to express the majesty of the god-king and support his beneficial reign. Many of the products of Egyptian workmen that have come down to us so satisfy our aesthetic sense that we refer to them as works of art.

Egyptian art has its champions who insist that the art of the fifth century before Christ in Greece is not the only classic art, as is often asserted or implied. Egypt, they say, had more than one period of truly classical art and in more than one department of art. From beads to pyramids, Egyptian objects often show a fine sense of the relation of means to ends and a truly classical beauty. We need not condemn the Egyptian refusal to accept perspective as the only method of representation. Those who are not historians of art must regard these differences of opinion with some detachment and try to make their own judgments.

The Handling of Ideas

In the main, ideas were handled in a strictly utilitarian spirit. Although the Egyptians made careful astronomical observations and devised a superior calendar, they did not work out any body of theory on such matters. Although they were competent in the practical geometry of surveying land and building large structures, they showed little interest in exploring geometry as a theoretical system. But such statements are made from the point of view of modern Western civilization, which admires the Greeks for their pioneering in abstract and generalized thought. If it is true that the Egyptians, like the other peoples before the Greeks, did not excel in this area, it does not detract from the most important thing about their work in science. They did a great deal of basic work that enabled the Greeks and after them the modern world to start farther ahead than might otherwise have been the case. Much of it probably was never put into writing; and none of it, so far as we know, was cast in the theoretical form characteristic of the Greeks. From the small amount of surviving writing about their handling of arithmetical, geometrical, and medical problems, it is clear that they had made some of the difficult first steps and deserve to be regarded as real contributors in these fields.

In the ideas of government, too, they made progress, although it is probable that no Egyptian ever wrote a treatise on the subject. They devised a method of managing the large and complex region of the Nile, which endowed the government with the prestige it needed and armed it with a detailed system of controlling everything and keeping track of everything.

It seems possible to discern what in their religion was spontaneous religious sentiment and what was the product of priestly agents of the government. The determination to use every means of prayer, ritual, and magic to make this life continue after death seems spontaneous, even if the means may have been partly devised by priestly managers. The early worship of local nature gods in every region seems the natural product of people in general, as does the strong feeling for the sun as the source of all good things. On the other hand, we can see that the priests did some effective work on the elaboration of cult and ritual, on the shaping of the stories about the gods and their relations, and on the more worldly interests of their gods and themselves.

Literature

In the Middle Kingdom, as in the Old Kingdom, a rather modest amount of literature expressed the ideas and feelings of the Egyptians. In the more difficult days at the end of the Old Kingdom and during the early Middle Kingdom, a number of pieces were put into writing (for there may have been an oral literature of court singers of which we know nothing) that express concern and pessimism. One is "The Dispute with His Soul of One Who Is Tired of Life," which has some fine poetic touches.

A much brisker piece is the three-hundred-line "Tale of Sinuhe," the story of a noble of the Middle Kingdom who, having an uneasy conscience, discreetly fled from the jurisdiction at the accession of a new king. He lived his whole adult life in the service of a Palestinian princelet until, when his years grew heavy upon him, he sued for a return to Egypt. He was graciously made welcome by a slightly amused monarch, and he settled down for his old age in the only country the Egyptian could love, full of gratitude for the benevolence of the king. Another document that shows the temperament of docility toward Pharaoh in the Middle Kingdom is the instruction of an official to his son, a testament of advice, which urges the son to guide his life by studying what will please the king and gain his favor.

CHAPTER

5

THE EGYPTIAN EMPIRE

(1570-1085 B.C.)

The period of Egyptian history that is sometimes called the Empire and sometimes the New Kingdom followed the period of domination by the Hyksos. It is tempting to suppose that subjugation to foreigners of a rather distasteful type and the gradual gathering of strength to expel them made the Egyptians more energetic and more aggressive and that their new spirit encouraged them to the conquest of the nearer part of Asia. In actual fact, however, the restoration of the country to a proper state of efficiency engrossed the energies of three generations after the expulsion of the Hyksos in 1567 B.C. Imperialistic conquest began only in 1469 with the first great campaign of Thutmose III in Asia. To reconstruct the psychology of the Egyptians at every point during the course of that hundred years would be to outrun the evidence.

REBUILDING AND BUILDING: THE NEW EGYPT

Thebes was the center of resistance to the Hyksos, just as it had been the locus of the central power that gained strength and brought the Middle Kingdom into being out of an age of self-assertion by local powers. Ahmose I of Thebes, the founder of the great Eighteenth Dynasty, assumed dominance in 1570, drove the Hyksos from their main camp at Avaris in northern Egypt in 1567, pursued them from the country, and captured their chief fort in southern Palestine.

Ahmose I then turned to the reconquest of Nubia, which was necessary for the restoration of the well-being of Egypt and fairly easily accomplished. At home, he had to do some fighting against the minor leaders who were not entirely ready to acknowledge the establishment of a national government. Much of his effort went into the task of re-establishing the details of the national government, in the course of which a corps of officials that acknowledged the domination of the king was built up. As a result, during the three hundred years or so that the Empire was most successful, we hear nothing of centrifugal tendencies of power; that is, the national government was firmly in control of local governors and other officials.

Amenhotep I, the son of Ahmose I, ruled from 1546 to 1526 B.C., spending most of his time on the internal affairs of the kingdom. One index of return to a healthy condition was the work of the artists of his reign and those that followed it, once again up to the old standards. These were the standards first aimed at in every field of activity. The inscriptions in which the king commemorated his great deeds, for example, were composed in correct and standard Middle Egyptian, the style of language brought to perfection during the Middle Kingdom.

Next Thutmose I (1526–1508) drove farther to the south, extending his sway as far as the Fourth Cataract of the Nile, where the river turns to go southwest a while before resuming its northward course. In Asia Minor, his army went as far into northern Syria as the great bend of the Euphrates, and Thutmose I set up a triumphal column on the river's bank. Apparently no attempt was made at this time to establish firm Egyptian rule through this region, although such a parade of military strength would do much to establish prestige and make peaceable trade possible, and there is evidence that trade was and continued to be active.

The next king, Thutmose II, was perhaps not physically strong, for he died in his early thirties. He and his half sister Hatshepsut, who had more than her share of the unusual energy of this line, had been married for eighteen years when he died, about 1504 B.C. He had already proclaimed as his successor Thutmose III, his son by a concubine, perhaps because he was aware that his wife was an extremely forceful person. The little boy's claim to the throne had also been reinforced by his marriage to his half sister, his father's daughter by Hatshepsut.

For a year or so Hatshepsut seemed to content herself with exerting the usual influence of a dowager queen. Then, presumably knowing that she could rely on her subordinates, she caused herself to be proclaimed king, claiming all the other royal titles. We can have some understanding of how she gained and held this power, so anomalous for a woman. In the first place, she granted extraordinary favors to her officials. Her vizier was also high priest of Amun, a useful combination. Her chief steward was granted a number of offices that presumably enriched him and, in addition, was given the privilege of building himself a tomb more royal than a commoner's. Second, her publicity stressed the purity of her royal blood, in contrast to young Thutmose's. Third, the boy was too young to assert himself successfully against such opposition. Fourth, the representations of her suggest that she was one of those small, dainty, and beautiful women who often are more truly formidable in affairs than their more bulky sisters, and it would be easy to indulge in romantic speculations about the use she made of her feminine charm. It must be noted, however, that she did not kill the young king, as many in their part of the world have done in similar situations. Instead, she allowed him some share in the government until he became sole ruler in 1482 B.C. It is not known whether he rid himself of her by violence.

Hatshepsut's reign was one of peace and internal development. There was no campaigning in Asia, perhaps because the young king would soon have been old enough to command the army and might have seized such an opportunity to assert himself. Hatshepsut was very proud that she was one of the few rulers who had sent an expedition down the Red Sea to Punt, one that had carried Egyptian manufactured products to trade for incense, ivory, and rare woods. Trade with the regions to the south by means of the river was a matter of royal concern, for gold and fine woods were especially desired. The Sinai mines also received due attention. There was a brisk program of building, especially to the greater glory of Amun, which suited popular opinion and so was politic.

When Thutmose III became sole ruler, he marked the completeness of concentration of power and his personal resentment against Hatshepsut by removing her name from a good many places where it had appeared and by having a number of her monuments destroyed. Much of our evidence for this *damnatio memoriae* (as the Roman emperors were later to call it when they did it) takes the form of otherwise undamaged monuments with her name chiseled out and, contrariwise, fragments of monuments in dumps with her name remaining.

He also marked the completeness of the change by starting out almost at once on a great compaign in Asia. It was high time: already there was a gathering of force against Egypt. The prince of Kadesh, which was on the Orontes River, in Syria, had gathered at Megiddo in Palestine a formidable host of three hundred and thirty princes. Their very number shows how individually insignificant they must have been. Thutmose marched rapidly to Palestine and then moved more cautiously to the Carmel Range and the Pass of Megiddo, which is the crucial point of a journey from Egypt to Syria and the north. He won a great victory before Megiddo and took the town after a siege of several months. The account of the booty suggests that the petty princes of the region were wealthy and able to command the services of fine artisans; and the new influences apparent in Egyptian art in the next century or so seem to reflect the fine craftsmanship of nearer Asia.

During the rest of his long reign, which did not end until 1450 B.C., Thutmose could be sure of Palestine and Syria, although his army occasionally showed itself there for psychological effect. His fighting was done north of Palestine, against Kadesh and against the kingdom of Mitanni, which was across the Euphrates in the great bend of the river that is nearest to Syria. His governor of Palestine was domiciled at Gaza, with subordinates here and there to watch the local princes. The time soon came when almost no military strength was needed, and the army was reduced to a police and an intelligence force. The swift and inexorable descents of the full army on any resistance to Egyptian rule were not readily forgotten.

Thutmose III was succeeded by two able but unspectacular rulers, who for nearly half a century preserved and extended Egypt's power.

With the accession of Amenhotep III in 1417 B.C., however, we reach a time when Egypt's power was perhaps less solid, but more glamorous.

THE WORLD OF AMENHOTEP III (1417-1379 B.C.)

The glory of the Egyptian Empire reached its height during the reign of Amenhotep III; this was Egypt's Golden Age, when her domestic strength and prosperity and her sway over other lands were at a high point. As we shall see, imperial problems received less attention from Amenhotep III's successor, Amenhotep IV (1379–1362 B.C.), the great monotheist who changed his name to Akh-en-Aten (or Ikhnaton). Egypt lost some of her power in regions where such inattention was costly, and furthermore in the following generations, new movements of people in the outside world lessened Egyptian power and superiority. So too did the rising use of iron, which Egypt did not have.

Looking Out from Egypt in the Early Fourteenth Century

The power of Egypt extended southward as far as the Fourth Cataract. The southernmost town, Napata, was the point where the caravans—of donkeys, rather than camels, which were introduced later—came in from the Sudan and Central Africa, bringing gold dust, ostrich plumes and eggs, and slaves. If Egyptians sometimes went to the other end of the caravan routes, we have no account of what they saw there. From the reign of Hatshepsut on, there were regular expeditions to Punt for its incense and other products. The people of Punt, as they are represented on reliefs in the queen's tomb-temple, were simple folk.

To the west there was mostly desert, although the oases there today existed then. Near the coast of the Mediterranean lived uncultivated people who rarely made the Egyptians any trouble and had nothing to offer them. In this age, the people of Africa were not in the main stream of affairs. The Near East was the focus of civilized life.

Palestine and Syria were well under Egyptian control. The Hebrews had not yet arrived in Palestine. The Canaanites had come out of the desert, however, and the Aramaeans (still another people whom we shall discuss later) had come to northern Palestine. There were groups of the Hyksos here and there. These people lived in fairly small groups, because any kind of union had always seemed impossible in this area. Yet the petty principalities were often prosperous and able to offer the Egyptians desirable products made by their craftsmen, especially chariots and furniture of wood with inlays and other decorations, and rich stuffs for clothes.

From the other side of the Euphrates, three peoples of Mesopotamia looked respectfully (and often greedily) toward the Egyptians. The old kingdom of Babylonia had been under the control of the Kassites for some time, as we have seen. Farther north in Mesopotamia were the Assyrians, who were later to be the most important people of the Near East. In the great bend of the Euphrates, which is nearest Syria, was the kingdom of Mitanni. The people of Mitanni were a part of the Hurrians, the Biblical Horites, who were also found in other parts of the Near East, but who were less powerfully organized elsewhere.

The rulers of these three kingdoms appear in what we know today as the Amarna Letters, a cache of clay tablets found at Amarna, a city built just after the time of Amenhotep III by Amenhotep IV, or Akh-en-Aten. The tablets were a part of the royal correspondence of the time, and the situation they portray may certainly be projected back into the reign of Amenhotep III or even earlier. The letters are in cuneiform writing, and most are in Akkadian, the language of the former rulers of the Mesopotamian region and now the language of diplomacy, too.

Although the rulers of all three countries generally affected an air of equality with the Egyptian ruler, they had no hesitation about repeatedly requesting gifts of gold. We get the impression that Egypt was rich in gold beyond what other countries could hope for. They in turn sent the Egyptians expensive gifts of furniture, clothes, and jewels. Not only do we hear of requests for gold; there are also negotiations for royal marriages and occasionally talk of treaties and of the other matters that normally constitute diplomatic exchanges.

In addition, the correspondence found at Amarna illustrates the relations of Egypt with still a fourth power, found north of Syria, in what is now Turkish territory—the Hittite kingdom. Before the Hittites reached out in conquest, they occupied the middle and south-eastern parts of Asia Minor. Their kingdom was formed shortly after

2000 B.C. and was to last until its destruction in the great migratory movement of about 1200 B.C.

Our present knowledge of the Hittites is another of the triumphs of modern research. The excavation of their former capital, near an otherwise unimportant place in Turkey called Boghaz-Keui, disclosed remains of buildings and brought to light about 10,000 cuneiform tablets. Some threw light on matters known already from the Amarna Letters. Although some were written in Akkadian, as were so many at Amarna, the Hittite language itself is most commonly represented on the tablets, and it has proved possible to decipher it. (Actually six other languages beside Hittite and Akkadian were identified.)

Somewhere around 1600 B.C. the Hittites had a period of strength during which they temporarily conquered Babylon. But the ambitions of other people, troubles with the succession to the throne, and the general difficulties of maintaining an empire caused the Hittites to retire to their original territory. For a long time they had to be content to stay there, for the power of Mitanni was dominant in western Asia in the latter part of the 1400's. A new era in Hittite history began with the rise of Suppiluliumas, about 1380 B.C. He ruled during the period of Egypt's greatest weakness, when Akh-en-Aten was neglecting everything but his program of religious changes. Little by little the Hittites moved into northern Syria. They scored some successes in their struggles with Mitanni, across the Euphrates, but were not able to conquer it. Yet they were able to dominate northern Syria for about a hundred years, until they fell about 1200 B.C.

The records of the great age, 1600–1200 B.C., which were found at the site of the Hittite capital, show us a hard-working king who was head of the civil, military, and religious life of the kingdom. The queen was unusually important. The Hittites were more precise and consistent in their thinking than the Egyptians. We find traces, for instance, of a system of law that developed slowly from age to age. If their religious system was much like those of others of their time, it had, perhaps, fewer inconsistencies. In their later centuries, the Iron Age had begun; and their iron deposits, which they knew how to use, were very helpful to them. They seem to have been a conquering people holding themselves apart from the conquered.

In the following centuries, although the great Hittite Empire had fallen, the records of Assyria refer to Hittite kings in this region. We also have very imperfect knowledge of a later Hittite kingdom in Palestine, whose hieroglyphic records we cannot read. These were the Hittites of the Bible.

In another direction, Egyptian influence extended to the islands of Cyprus and Crete. Cyprus had long been a source of copper and timber ; its name means "Copper-land." Crete, as we shall see, had slowly developed a brilliant civilization, largely under Egyptian influence, and at the time of Amenhotep III it was enjoying its greatest period. Crete had great influence on the mainland of southern Greece, where the great days were just beginning.

Beyond these islands lay other, less civilized places, sources of raw materials for the great empires, which were reached by land and by sea. Presumably Egyptian ships went no farther than Crete, but the Mycenaean sea rovers may well have gone as far as England. The land routes made a connection with the amber regions of the Baltic and the tin mines of Bohemia. Probably the Egyptian man of business was hardly conscious of the people at the far ends of the trade routes which served him.

Internal Affairs under Amenhotep III

The Egyptians liked to say that tribute came to Pharaoh * from all the world around Egypt. The fact seems to be, however, that tribute or imposts came only from Palestine or Syria and that the rich things sent by other kings were balanced by gifts of Egyptian gold. But Nubia and the Sudan, now part of Egypt, yielded no mean amount of gold, the fertility of the soil remained, and trade with other lands was lively, so that Egypt was now richer than any country had ever been. The power of the king was the greatest that the world had seen. The centrifugal tendencies of the officials and the local grandees had yielded to the power of the central government.

Thutmose III (1504–1450 B.C.), the great general and administrator, was probably the most able of all the kings of Egypt. Amenhotep II (1450–1425 B.C.) and Thutmose IV (1425–1417) seem to have been

---

*The word "Pharaoh" means "the great house," as in our expression, "the White House announces . . ." The first certain use of it known to us occurs in a letter to the king Akh-en-Aten, a little later in the Eighteenth Dynasty.

competent rulers. Amenhotep III (1417–1379), however, apparently had the flair for magnificence and for personal publicity that makes it natural to use his name as the symbol of the entire period of grandeur, actually beginning with Thutmose III and continuing through the seventy-six years of the three succeeding reigns.

An unfortunate aspect of Amenhotep III's brilliant reign was that the king simply ignored the fact that the forces of opposition in Asia could be held down only by steady effort. The letters of the Amarna collection betray the fact that appeals from governors or minor potentates of the region were not even answered, much less heeded. By the end of the reign, the situation in nearer Asia was desperate; and during the succeeding reign, when even less attention was paid to foreign affairs, there were serious losses of territory. Yet other affairs seem to have been competently administered. The impression of some tension between the great priesthoods and the civil officials survives in our records, but such a situation is only what might be expected.

The Art of the Golden Age

These years included the third classical period of Egyptian art, following the first at the time of the great pyramids in the Old Kingdom and the second in the Twelfth Dynasty, during the Middle Kingdom. The abundant materials preserved to us reveal that the workmen of the time handled everything from the planning and construction of huge temples to the execution of jewelry with a sure and fine touch.

It is interesting that in all ages the royal architects had little hesitation about plundering the constructions of earlier times for materials in spite of the wealth and plentiful labor supply that usually characterized Egypt. The architects of this age were no exception. They took apart some earlier buildings to furnish dressed stone for their buildings, and their buildings were in turn plundered on a large scale by the architects of Rameses II, a hundred years or so later.

The palace of Amenhotep III in Thebes, excavated in modern times, was built largely of mud-brick, with some few components of painted wood and only an occasional slab of stone. When discovered the walls had remained about waist-high, and a surprising number of objects had survived the plundering of many generations. Although it was not the habit of the kings to build dwellings of stone for themselves, as they did for the gods, they made their mud-brick palaces fit for kings. Traces have been found of painted walls and ceilings whose gaiety and grace suggest the attractive paintings found in Crete. There were fayence tiles set into the walls, and friezes of fayence ran around the rooms.

Another interesting feature of Amenhotep III's reign is that the king caused several series of commemorative scarabs (small clay seals) to be prepared and sent all around the realm. They carried hieroglyphic inscriptions. The first series let it be known that he had married the commoner Teye, who was to be a strong partner to him in all respects. We may perhaps suppose that this was a warning to the whole world that the lady was to be regarded with respect, in spite of her birth. Another series tells of his exploits in a wild bull hunt, and another of his exploits in shooting lions. From another series we learn of his marrying a princess of Mitanni who arrived in unparalleled splendor with a retinue of 317 ladies. Teye, however, remained First Lady. These scarabs are generally oval, a little over three inches long, and finely made. (Later, we shall find the Roman emperors using coins for the same purpose of emphasizing certain events and ideas.)

In the cemetery at Thebes there are some ninety private chapels that belong to the golden time of the fifteenth and fourteenth centuries. The paintings on the walls display a number of clear and fresh colors—blue, yellow, pink, brick-red—and have a richness of composition and execution that shows a sophisticated taste. On other walls there are reliefs of the same classical perfection. Fine reliefs are also found on many *stelae*, or columns. The papyri, which also form part of the funerary equipment, often are adorned with colored vignettes.

It is especially interesting to find that sometimes we can see the practice and trial work of these artists of so long ago. Around the workmen's villages that are attached to the great cemeteries of the kings and their entourages can be found potsherds and pieces of lime-stone bearing sketches and trial portraits, some of which are recognizable as preliminary versions of official stone portraits of major kings. Even these remains share the high quality of the other work that has survived.

The skill of the Egyptian artist and the corresponding good taste of the ordinary person showed itself in innumerable small items and practical things. Not only was the jewelry of the noble lady beautiful;

so too were things for the table that cannot have been very expensive. Vases or bowls or spoons are generally well designed. The decoration is inspired by the plants or flowers of the Nile Valley or by the animals and birds that could be seen there. For some reason pottery-making was never as highly developed as it was in other countries, but glass was made by the Egyptians from early ages. In the Eighteenth Dynasty, the manufacture of fayence reached its high point of all time. The shapes of the vessels and the designs on the tiles are highly pleasing, and the colors of the applied glaze are astonishingly bright.

Literature

The spells meant to benefit the dead form a large part of the literature of the New Kingdom, as had been the case in the earlier periods. Those of the Old Kingdom, found in the pyramids, are called "Pyramid Texts." In the Middle Kingdom prominent private persons arrogated to themselves the use of these charms, which had formerly been reserved for the kings. Now we call them "Coffin Texts," since they were written on coffins. In the New Kingdom the spells were written on papyrus rolls and are somewhat misleadingly called "The Book of the Dead," since there was no one book or place where all the known spells were collected. Some of these writings may be called spells, and some may not; all were thought to be useful for insuring survival.

In another style and somewhat more to modern taste is the victory hymn addressed to Thutmose III. The god Amun-Re is represented as praising the king for his great victories and expressing his satisfaction at the king's devoutness, his temples, and his offerings. The hymn has many fine passages of an appropriately elevated sort, and parts of it were used for hymns to Amenhotep III and other kings.

From the reign of Amenhotep III, just before his son's promotion of Aten as the one god, comes a hymn to the sun that has a certain spirit of monotheism and shows an inspiring uplifting of the spirit. The sun is addressed in a tone of worship and from a number of aspects, not only as the great life-giving orb that daily speeds across the sky, but also as a god who is everything, sees everything, and does everything. From one of the tombs at Amarna comes the greatest of all hymns to Aten, a majestic address that differs from the earlier hymn to Aten in being better poetry and having a more consistent tone of monotheism. Although comparison of this hymn to Psalm 104 is not unjust, it is not at all probable that there is any direct connection between the two poems. Two excellent lyric poems come from another tomb dating from the Eighteenth Dynasty. On one wall of the tomb a fine "Praise of Death" was found; on the other wall was "The Harper's Song," a sweetly melancholy exhortation to a pleasant indulgence during this brief existence.

From the New Kingdom also come tales of marvelous adventure— one, for example, of a younger son forced to leave home by the advances of his older brother's wife—which suggest *The Arabian Nights*. Another such tale is about the capture of Joppa by an ingenious ruse that introduced Egyptian soldiers into the city in baskets said to be full of booty. The Greek historian Herodotus later recounted stories of the kings of Egypt that have this same flavor, which to us suggests the Near East.

New Influences

The ease and frequency of communication and the fact that Egypt naturally drew able people from other countries was bound to affect the character of the country in spite of the static and conservative quality of Egyptian culture. New people, new products, and new ideas came in such quantities that they affected Egyptian life. More foreigners were used as common soldiers than before; and some of them rose to responsible military positions. The surviving works of art show that the craftsman and his patron were often pleased to admit influences from other countries. If the civilization of Egypt now took on a more cosmopolitan cast, however, there is no reason why we should regard a change as a cause of the troubles that were to come.

THE MONOTHEISTIC INTERLUDE

Amenhotep IV, "Amun-is-content," son of the great king, who was made his father's colleague about 1370, was a religious fanatic in a hereditary position that required a broad-minded and energetic administrator. His mind seems to have been almost entirely devoted to religion, and especially to the worship of Aten, the sun's disk, to the exclusion of all the older gods.

The worship of Aten seems to have begun, perhaps as a result of the new cosmopolitan spirit, during the reign of Amenhotep II. The old worship of Re as the god of the sun was intensified and specialized as the worship of Aten, the visible form of the sun's disk, the universal god, for the sun is a universal manifestation. The young king embraced the worship of Aten with such fervor that he refused to believe in or patronize any other of the gods that were so involved with his country's history and with the *arcana* of its present government.

He changed his own name, "Amun-is-content," to Akh-en-Aten, "he-who-is-serviceable-to-Aten" (often given as "Ikhnaton"), and built himself a new city, Akh-et-Aten, "Horizon of Aten." Here he retired with his family and a group of courtiers who had supported him in the quarrel with the priests of Amun that had arisen from his advocacy of Aten. He went so far as to forbid the worship of all the old divinities. In the new worship only he and his family worshipped Aten directly. The king was regarded as the embodiment of Aten, and the nobility were expected to worship him directly. The people apparently were expected to acquiesce in the disappearance of such religious support as they had previously known.

Akh-en-Aten is said to have sworn never to leave his new city, which was a spacious and beautiful place on the river about halfway between Memphis and Thebes. The modern name of the place is Tell el Amarna (the location of the Amarna Letters). The king paid little attention to the appeals of his governors and allies in Asia, although one frantic cry for help was followed by another. Instead, his time was spent in meditation, in thinking about the building of his city, or in religious duties.

It is a curious fact that despite his other-worldly interests, the king exerted a great influence on both language and art in the direction of naturalism. The formality of the written language tended to be replaced by the informality of spoken language. The formality of art was replaced by a naturalism that represented exactly what the artist saw. The language of royal decrees and the art of the palace and the city were both highly distinctive because of this naturalistic tendency.

Akh-en Aten presently appointed one of the younger members of his family as coregent. After a few years he seems to have made overtures through this coregent toward a reconciliation with the priests by permitting the re-establishment of the worship of Amun at Thebes.

But he died in 1362 B.C., and the coregent died soon after, leaving the throne to his younger brother, Tut-ankh-Aten, who ruled at Amarna only for a short time. Thereafter the exclusive worship of Aten was apparently abandoned, and the king moved to Thebes, changing his name to Tut-ankh-Amun. The excavation of his tomb in 1922 caused great excitement because of the extraordinary wealth of its furnishings, which had not been plundered.

Although there were times when the authority of the central government was at a low ebb and it was doubtful whether the king could make his writ run or indeed who was king, there are few examples in Egyptian history of struggles over the throne on the death of a legitimate and established king. To be sure, Queen Hatshepsut had boldly upset the usual rules of succession. Now, in 1352 B.C., on the death of the young Tut-ankh-Amun, who left no male heir in the Thutmosid line, his queen made an attempt to hold the power by writing to the great Hittite king Suppiluliumas, asking for a prince to marry her and be king of Egypt.

The Hittite king had taken advantage of the inertia of the Egyptian kings to make himself master of their allies in Mitanni and Assyria and of their subjects in northern Syria and Phoenicia. He moved cautiously, and the queen sent a second letter; both were found in the Hittite archives. But others were fishing in these troubled waters, and the Hittite prince was murdered on the way to Egypt.

Probably the most powerful man in Egypt was Horemheb, commander of the army and a man who had served the pharaoh well for a long time. Very likely it was he who intercepted the Hittite prince. Then what power the queen had was neutralized by marrying her to her aged grandfather Ay, a high official of long service, one whose blood was obviously good enough for the royal position. The old gentleman died soon, and Horemheb took the throne. He probably had arranged the queen's marriage to her grandfather and had then quietly worked to replace her influence with his own. Our sources for this period are full enough to tell us in some detail what happened, but naturally they do not tell us what happened behind the scenes.

When Horemheb came to the throne, he completely restored the worship of Amun, returned the priests to their posts, gave back the confiscated endowments, and repaired temples everywhere. He laid a heavy hand on the civil government, punishing many men who had taken advantage of the inattention of former rulers to abuse the powers of their offices. He tried to efface every reminder of the Atenist pharaohs by destroying the city of Amarna and chiseling their names off monuments elsewhere. In the official records no trace of them remained. The succession was reckoned from Amenhotep III to Horemheb.

It is difficult to see what good there can have been in the Atenist movement. It was not a forerunner of Judaism and Christianity. It had no ethical content and promised no benefits to anyone. On the other hand, it woefully damaged the Egyptian government, both at home and abroad. The harm done to the Empire in Asia was irreparable. Probably the damage to the Empire at home was more successfully repaired.

It has been conjectured that Akh-en-Aten was attempting to shake off the influence of the priests of Amun. We know that the god's wealth in land, animals, stores of grain, slaves, and gold was immense. Amun was the senior partner in all the imperial ventures of Egypt and received the better share of the yield. At about this time he was getting several hundred pounds of gold a year from the mines of Nubia and the Sudan. Yet it was within the king's power to dismiss the priests and confiscate their endowments, and he did so. A more resolute and worldly king might have permanently reduced or broken the power of Amun. It is not clear, however, that the priests were a hindrance to the civil government or that the concentration of real property and gold in their hands was harmful to society. The temple estates may well have served a useful purpose as minor units of social organization.

THE LATER CENTURIES

The Nineteenth Dynasty (1320–1200 B. C.)

Presumably it was because Horemheb had no son that the throne again had to pass to someone of a different family. He made a succession arrangement that was a slight variation on that by which he had come to the throne, choosing his old friend Pa-Rameses (who is known as Rameses I). This elderly man had a long and honorable career behind him and a grown son who was already vizier of Upper Egypt. Their joint prestige, together with Horemheb's, assured the succession without trouble. Rameses I died after a little more than a year, and his son Sethi succeeded him.

Sethi (1318–1304 B.C.), an experienced and vigorous soldier, immediately began a campaign in Asia. After a number of successful minor operations in southern Palestine, which reminded the inhabitants of what Egypt could do, he won a victory over the Hittites and checked their expansion for the moment. He also took the practical step of moving the administrative and military center of Egypt to a place near Tanis in the Delta, building a whole new government city.

Rameses II (1304–1237 B.C.), coming to the throne at the age of twenty, was soon tested by a full-scale movement of the Hittites against the Egyptian possessions near them. In 1300 he took the field and met the enemy at Kadesh, where he rashly walked into an ambush. Probably by his great personal courage he redeemed a disaster, was able to hold off the Hittites, and maintained Egyptian supremacy in Palestine. But our knowledge of the affair has to be gained by discounting the version inscribed in text and pictures on his mortuary temple at Thebes, at Karnak, farther south at Abydos, and even in the great temple that he had cut out of the rock of the valley wall far down in Nubia at Abu Simbel.

In 1284 the relationship between Egypt and the Hittites was established for the rest of the century by a treaty said to have been engraved on silver. Chance has preserved both a Hittite version in cuneiform, found in the excavations of the Hittite capital, and an Egyptian version in hieroglyphics. The treaty made a definite division of territory, giving northern Syria to the Hittites and southern Syria and Palestine to the Egyptians. The two powers agreed to substitute a defensive alliance for their former attitude of aggression. This is the only agreement of nonaggression known in the ancient Eastern world. Then as so often happened, the pact was solidified by a marriage: the daughter of the Hittite king was married to the pharaoh.

The buildings and monuments of Rameses II are to be found everywhere in Egypt. Early in his career he attended to the completion and beautification of the new official city in the eastern Delta, and a great many fine ornamental pieces have been recovered from what was apparently the palace. The chief feature of his building at Karnak is a hall so vast that it could contain the Cathedral of Notre Dame in

Paris. He seems never to have lost the taste for covering wall surfaces or columns with partly spurious accounts of his prowess.

Critics of art find the work done in Rameses' long reign disappointing. To some, the grandiose architecture seems slightly dishonest in that the foundations are not well and truly laid. The sculpture and painting and smaller work are criticized as being uninspired and executed in a mechanical and slovenly manner. Tempting as it is to theorize about a possible connection between the lackadaisical character of this king in his later years and the character of art, we are probably going far enough if we record the impression of a falling off in artistic performance.

As the thirteenth century drew toward its close, a great movement was afoot among peoples who had not been much heard of in the civilized world. Some moved by land, and some had learned to be rovers of the sea. More than one group of the sea people had established bases in Africa west of Egypt. In 1232 they invaded the Delta and there were struck down by the Egyptians, although this was not to be the end of their attacks. It is difficult to be precise about these migrant and troublesome people, for we have references to the strangers only when they attacked the established peoples.

The Twentieth Dynasty (1195–1080 B. C.)

The Nineteenth Dynasty ended with a confused and difficult period. Finally the orderly succession to the throne was re-established with the accession of the vigorous Rameses III (1198–1166 B.C.). The great crisis of Egypt in this dynasty began with a new joint attack by the Libyans and the sea peoples, who were again defeated. There was no other great attack from the west, but from the east came a great wave of people migrating by land, whom Rameses III defeated as they reached the boundary of Egypt. These migrants had already overcome the Empire of the Hittites, which dissolved into separate kingdoms, never again to be of great weight internationally. The Egyptians also won a great naval victory against the sea peoples who moved against them at the same time—not in mere raids, but in serious attempts to take and keep Egypt. One group of sea people settled on the nearby Asian coast after their defeat by Pharaoh and were to be known later as Philistines; from them, Palestine got its name.

Egypt was not to end its history by being so conquered. Through the more than one hundred years of the Twentieth Dynasty it remained powerful enough to discourage attacks from outside, although the Asiatic possessions had been lost in the great invasion that had been repelled at the border. The domestic agricultural wealth of the nation remained unimpaired, as did the supply of gold from the south.

The chief difficulty of the twelfth century seems to have been the failure of the royal management, for which we have no ready explanation. In general, the authority of the central government was not well maintained. Not only some local officials, but the priests of Amun, too, seem to have been able now and then to challenge the authority of the king. The priesthoods, especially Amun's, by now had such enormous endowments that they constituted very considerable nuclei of power and might even be compared to the local powers that opposed the central government toward the end of the Old Kingdom. Furthermore, the army was composed largely of foreign mercenaries and often proved very difficult to control.

The end of the Egyptian Empire (or New Kingdom) may be said to have come about 1085, when the kingdom was separated into the familiar North and South, with the priests playing a very important part. The great days were over, and for the next four hundred years there was little worthy of remark. Egypt had not fallen, in one sense. Yet in another sense she had, for the dynasties of Nubians and Ethiopians seem foreign. Life went on at a lower level of intensity. What was lacking was not a government or a way of life, but the intensity and efficiency and extra achievement, the artistic and literary successes, that in the past had raised Egypt above the level of commonplace and routine social organization.

CHAPTER

6

THE COCKPIT OF THE NEAR EAST

As the Balkans have been called "the cockpit of Europe," so we may refer to Syria, Phoenicia, and Palestine as "the cockpit of the Near East," the place, that is, where diplomatic and military struggles between the great powers repeatedly took place. Its invasions by the Amorites, the Hyksos, the Egyptians, and the Hittites and the struggles that occurred at Kadesh, Megiddo, and other places on its soil have already been mentioned, but only as part of the history of the great powers. Now we need to consider the early history of the region in a more systematic way.

The older name of the whole region was Canaan, a name found in the Bible, in the records of Egypt, and in the Amarna Letters. The name of Palestine for the southern part of it, which made up the kingdom of the Israelites, comes to us from the Philistines, who settled on the coast in the twelfth century before Christ. In Greek history and later periods, we shall find other examples of regional names that come from one people in one part of the area. We shall reserve the word "Palestine," then, for the time after the arrival of the Philistines. Part of the Canaanites, who lived about halfway up the coast, more or less in modern Lebanon, came to be known as Phoenicians and their territory as Phoenicia. The northern part of Canaan was known in ancient times as Syria, as it still is.

The first important fact about the geography of this whole region is that its location laid it open both to invasion and to peaceful infiltration by new peoples, with the resulting introduction of new ideas and practices that might come from Egypt or Mesopotamia or the desert. Furthermore, the broken and uneven character of the area made it difficult to build up political units of any size; indeed, as we have seen, the prince of Kadesh gathered three hundred and thirty princelets to oppose the Egyptians.

In a rough way the land is divided into four strips, which run north and south. The western strip is the plain that runs along the shore of the Mediterranean. Next comes a series of rugged hills. The third zone is that of the Jordan Valley, where the Jordan River, which is amply fed, flows through a lower and lower channel until it goes through the Lake of Galilee, about 700 feet below sea level, and ends in the Dead Sea, about 1300 feet below sea level. The fourth strip is a range of barren hills beyond the valley of the Jordan. Then comes the desert.

EARLIER HISTORY

Archaeology has brought a startling increase in our knowledge of this region, as it has for other parts of the Near East. Often we find that the account in the Bible is confirmed and made more intelligible, although in literally thousands of passages our old translations have had to be slightly revised as a result of new archaeological knowledge. In addition, a wealth of detail has been added to some parts of history that could be understood only in a broad way from our Egyptian sources or from remarks in the Greek and Roman writers.

Much of the archaeological advance has occurred in the branch of the subject that ordinarily is least publicized—the interpretation of the results of the excavations. They rarely yield a spectacular building or relief or piece of jewelry, but many of the great mounds that are excavated have produced stratified remains of successive cities on the same site. The pottery of the different strata has at last and after a great deal of work and discussion been classified, and little by little dates have been firmly established for the successive destructions and rebuildings of many of the cities. For example, it seems possible, as we shall see, to date some remains of destroyed towns to the time of the campaigns of Joshua and others to the time of the campaigns of the Chaldaean king Nebuchadnezzar, thus giving corroborative evidence to our scanty accounts of the two campaigns. Not only has the chronology of the region been established, but the patient work done on the unspectacular objects found in the excavations has also added depth to such other aspects of our knowledge as religious practices, craftsmanship, and trade routes.*

Early Inhabitants

Long before it was known as Canaan, well back into the Old Stone Age, this region had inhabitants. By about 8000 B.C., some of them were in a Middle Stone period in which they had learned to grow wheat and were burying their dead. Then other features beside the domestication of grain that are generally considered characteristic of the Neolithic Age appeared—not only stone implements of the new type, but also the domestication of animals and the beginning of community life. The excavation of Jericho has revealed a pre-pottery Neolithic stage, which is dated at about 6800 B.C. by the radiocarbon test, and a pottery stage, which is dated at about 5850 B.C.** Here we seem to see "civilized" man in a very early stage.

Commonly used as the radiocarbon test is, we may well take a moment to describe it. The action of solar radiation creates in the atmosphere carbon fourteen (C_{14}), an isotope of carbon, now thought to have been always present in the atmosphere in constant amounts (in spite of some attempts to prove that its amount was different before about the time of Christ). Taken by photosynthesis into plant organisms and thence by eating and digestion into animal organisms, it is believed to remain in a live organism in the same proportion and condition as it was in the atmosphere. At the death of the organism, radioactive decay begins; that is, particles of carbon fourteen begin to disappear. Its half-life, or the point at which there remain half the particles capable of departing, is 5688 years plus or minus 30. The conditions surrounding the dead plant or tree or human or animal

---

*W. F. Albright's *The Archaeology of Palestine* explains clearly and in detail how the pottery is dated, how the general chronology is worked out, and how the objects found in excavations are made to yield information.

**Some scholars believe that these dates must be too early for a place so elaborately built up, in spite of the radiocarbon test.

body make no difference in the rate of the departure of the particles. By an analysis of the proportion of these particles that has already disappeared, it is possible to gain an idea, accurate to plus or minus 200 years, of the age of organic matter several thousand years old, whether it is a wheat seed, a wooden dam, a piece of fabric, or an animal frozen in a glacier.

In the region that later became Canaan, the Chalcolithic Period, or the time when both stone and copper were used, seems to have begun at about 4500 B.C., and the Early Bronze Age began just before 3000 B.C. and lasted for perhaps a thousand years. At this point, the archaeologists feel that they have their chronology well in hand as a result of the study and discussion of the stratified sites that have been excavated. Some of the inhabitants gave their towns Semitic names; we begin to have a more definite idea of the people who were there.

The period from 2000 to 1500 B.C. is called the Middle Bronze Age, and one of its chief features was the arrival of the Hyksos in the land and their domination of it. From perhaps 1750 to 1500 they were in control, and it was a prosperous time. Yet there is the suggestion, too, that it was a time of violence. Although many towns were built as places of very strong defense, there is evidence that they were sometimes taken and destroyed.

The migration of Abraham from Ur, in southern Mesopotamia, to Canaan also falls in this period. During his time, the Bible speaks of Amorites and Hittites as being in the region that later became Palestine. Even though the chief political success of the Amorites was in Babylon and the empire of the Hittites lay north and west of Syria, we need not be surprised at encountering other groups bearing those names.

The Late Bronze Age in this region is reckoned at about 1500 to 1200 B.C.—the time of the greatest power of the Egyptian Empire and a time when the people of Palestine were thoroughly exploited by the Egyptians. But the Hittites still preserved the monopoly of iron. That those deposits of ancient materials in which iron is found are not earlier in date than the ending of the Hittite Empire, about 1200, is one result of the modern effort expended on establishing the chronology.

After about 1200 B.C. comes the Iron Age and with it the phenomenon of most interest to us in this region—ancient Israel. Let us note that it was also a time when the great powers ceased troubling the area. The Hittites and the Egyptians were no longer in position to disturb each other or the people in between. Some of the migrating people who had brought down the Hittites, especially the Philistines, had settled in Palestine. Assyria was not yet strong enough to make herself felt here, although toward the end of the period she played a very important part in the history of Israel.

THE HEBREWS AND THE ORIGIN OF JUDAISM

Between the twentieth and the twelfth centuries before Christ, a period of constant shifting of peoples in the Near East, documents of Mesopotamia, Asia Minor, Syria, Palestine, and Egypt mention groups whom they call Habiru. These people wandered about, sometimes living off animals in the nomad style and sometimes working as musicians or smiths or practitioners of other crafts. They also appear as brigands, mercenary soldiers, and slaves. It may well be that some of the people referred to in these documents were the biblical Hebrews, because many of the names and localities and activities of the two are similar.

The Hebrews of the Bible, as a probable part of the Habiru, were many separate groups. There came a time, however, when some groups of the Habiru, the biblical ones among them, became associated with certain territories by conquering them or being absorbed into their people. In such cases they took on national names. The Hebrews of the Bible settled in Canaan and became known as Israelites, whereas other groups of the Habiru became Moabites, Ammonites, Edomites, and Midianites. At this point both the Bible and the other documents cease to speak of any group as Habiru or Hebrews.

Life in Canaan

Abraham and his group came to the hilly strip of the land of Canaan that lies between the coastal plain and the Jordan Valley. In these hills, which are hardly fit for agriculture, they lived the life of seminomads with their sheep and goats. The biblical account of their life gives a fine picture of the tribal and family organization of a society.

Now that we know something of the earlier literature of Mesopotamia we can see that the cosmogony (that is, the view of the origin of the world) of these people was that of the people of Mesopotamia. The Creation, the Garden of Eden and the Fall, the Flood, the Ark, and the Tower of Babel were all Mesopotamian stories of the world. Stories of this sort naturally became the common possession of the shifting population of the Near East and appear, for example, in the literature of the Hittites as well.

The religion of the Hebrews in these earlier days, however, was not the polytheism common in the ancient world, but a working monotheism. The patriarch, the head of the tribe, would make an agreement that he and his people would worship one god exclusively. It was understood that the god, in turn, was to take this one tribe under his protection. The covenant was understood to be a bilateral affair that was to be binding on both parties forever. But these people did not deny the existence of other gods. To have done so would have been a strange idea, one that would not have occurred to anyone at this time.

The Egyptian Period

Soon a considerable group of Hebrews went down into Egypt. People occasionally went to Egypt in times of scarcity, but it is possible that this group went in company with the Hyksos. If so, it would make more plausible the story of the Hebrews' rising to positions of power in Egypt, and it would explain the silence of the Egyptians about any such episode and the enslavement in Egypt of the group after the expulsion of the Hyksos. We can readily imagine that the Hebrews who went to Egypt multiplied in a situation that was for some generations favorable and that among a good many other foreign groups in a strange land they acquired a sense of their own unity as a religious group.

If the captivity in Egypt described in the Bible began when the Hyksos were expelled, it lasted a long time, for it was probably in the thirteenth century that Moses, of the tribe of Levi, led the group of state slaves who made the break for freedom. There must have been considerable cohesiveness among the Hebrews to have preserved some sense of identity as a group during all this time, and this feeling probably furnished the unity necessary to the organization of the exodus from Egypt. Possibly many captives who were brought from Palestine during Egypt's great period became members in spirit of the earlier Hebrew group among the state slaves. Furthermore, many non-Hebrews also were in the exodus, as the Bible tells us.

The traditional forty years of wandering ascribed to this group may be regarded as one generation or a little more. The fugitives made their way into the Peninsula of Sinai, where they avoided the Egyptian strongholds and went through the remarkable experience of being forged into an enduring nation. This feat was accomplished by the leadership of Moses, who worked with such sentiment of unity as they had to begin with.

Moses naturally had to contend with other men's claims to lead and with the jealousy of minor groups. Life in the wilderness was hard, and many remembered the fleshpots of Egypt with longing, but the physical obstacles were overcome. Most important of all, a new covenant was made in the name of the whole group, which was far larger than any of those family groups who in earlier times had made their covenants through the patriarchs. Now Israel came into being as a nation by virtue of the covenant that it made as a whole, and the god of Moses and of Israel came to be known as Yahweh or Jehovah.

Although it has often been suggested that the monotheism of Akh-en-Aten was the source of the monotheism of Moses, this theory is neither necessary nor sound. It is not necessary because the particularistic and practical monotheism of the earlier patriarchs was source enough for the later monotheism. It is not sound because we cannot possibly establish a connection between the views of Akh-en-Aten and those of Moses.

Israel in Canaan

During the period of the conquest of Canaan, the newly forged group came to be commonly known as the Israelites, and the term "Hebrew" is rarely found. After the Babylonian Exile of the sixth century, they came to be known as "Judeans" and "Jews", but in the late thirteenth century, it was Israel, or the Children of Israel, who came out of the wilderness to the land of Canaan. That is, they came up from the desert of Sinai to the coastal strip of Canaan, which was then inhabited by a mixed people who may be called the Canaanites.

Moses died before the Promised Land was reached, and Joshua led the people into Canaan. The biblical story seems to give two versions of what followed, and both are probably true, although they seem inconsistent. One version is the swift conquest of Canaan by Joshua in a single campaign. Combining swift marches, hammerlike blows, and clever stratagems, and, when it seemed necessary, commanding the sun or the moon to stand still, he took many strong places of the Canaanites and defeated their armies in the field; the land of Canaan was now in his power. The other version, which is also found in the Book of Joshua and at the beginning of Judges, represents the taking of Canaan as a long and laborious process that included some reverses. The probable fact is that Joshua won some brilliant victories—and recent excavations seem to show traces of the destruction and rebuilding of some of the cities in question at about this time—and that a lengthy process of Israelite conquest, Canaanite recapture, reconquest, and, in fact, disunion among the Israelites themselves lasted long beyond the death of Joshua.

The Civilization of Canaan

Naturally the Israelites, who had for a long time been slaves in Egypt and had then been wanderers in the wilderness for a generation, were not abreast of the ideas and techniques of their day. The Canaanites were. Their pottery, for instance, was far superior to that of their conquerors, and they also built far better towns and fortifications. A number of them were literate. There were people who could write Akkadian cuneiform or Egyptian hieroglyphs or their own alphabet, which was to give rise to the Phoenician alphabet, which in turn gave rise to the Greek alphabet and eventually to ours.

The Canaanites had also achieved the other aspect of literacy—a literature. It was especially strong in religious and mythological pieces. Some of their best came from those stories about the gods composed to be recited at the great festivals and intended to give universal validity to the ritual that portrayed what the community wanted. Baal, the god of the Canaanites who in the Bible got the worst of it in a contest with Yahweh, was a god of rain, the god who made everything happen in the agricultural world. He was represented as being killed every year by Mot, who represented drought and thus the death of vegetation and of all life. The festival of Baal's coming to life with the autumnal rains not only celebrated the arrival of the rains, but was also a great effort of the community to make sure that they would come. Stories of divine matings gave support to sexual intercourse between a priest and a priestess or between others for the purpose of ensuring the increase of the flocks and of the people, a ceremony evoking none of the attitudes that a city-dwelling and nonpastoral people might read into it.

Centrifugal Forces

To hold Israel together, once it had been made a nation by the leadership of Moses and the shared experiences of the wilderness, was extremely difficult. Some of those who had participated in the exodus from Egypt, comfortably settled in Canaan, found it hard to keep up the austere ideals and the devotion to the interests of the whole that had seemed necessary in those earlier days. Others who had never been to Egypt or whose ancestors had never been to Egypt had lived for some time according to the customs of Canaan and were reluctant to commit themselves to all that being an Israelite implied. The enticements of Canaanite comfort and Canaanite beliefs made it very difficult for Israel to maintain that united devotion to Yahweh, that strict adherence to the covenant, so necessary to solidarity as a nation.

There was no central capital or shrine for Israel in this period, no national government as we know it. Each tribe had complete autonomy. Because the Canaanites were not united and there was no military threat from outside, nothing forced political and military unity on Israel. The military emergencies of the twelfth and eleventh centuries often seemed to call forth local leaders, who were known as judges, but interestingly no one of them ever succeeded in becoming a king.

It was during these first two centuries in Canaan that the legal codes of Israel began to take shape. Some of the laws were straightforward statements of major principles: "Thou shalt————" or "Thou shalt not————." Others are of the type called casuistic (that is dependent on certain situations): "If such a thing happens, the rule shall be so-and-so." As far as we know, there was no need of a legal system so refined and complex as that set forth in the Code of Hammurabi, because the social and economic system was far less complex. There was a certain amount of farming and a considerable amount of raising of cattle, sheep, and goats. Even the few necessary trades that not everyone involved in a small farming operation would want to handle for himself, like smithing and potterymaking, and those that went with the common type of farming, like the trade of the tanner, were practiced on a modest scale.

The Kingdom of Saul, David, and Solomon

The great movement of the Sea Peoples and of the migrants on land which was turned back from Egypt by Rameses III left the Peleset, or Philistines, on the coastal plain of southern Canaan. It is ironic that their name has come to be used to signify people of little cultivation or understanding, for they were more cultivated than the people of Israel. They also had a tight political organization that gave them a practical advantage, and somewhere along the way they had picked up the secret of making iron, which they managed for some time to keep out of the hands of their neighbors. Furthermore, they were acquainted with commercial practices.

All these factors led them to attempt to expand. Israel lay in their path and here at last was a force sufficient to drive Israel to the creation of a central authority of a sort. Saul, of the tribe of Benjamin, was the man who was chosen to be king and lead the opposition to the Philistines. Samuel, a priest and prophet, led a movement of opposition to Saul and to kingship in general that suggests to us why none of the earlier military leaders had become king. Samuel insisted, in effect, that if Saul became king he would infringe the rights of the citizens, commandeer their property, and, in addition, infringe the rights of God with regard to Israel. Nevertheless Saul was chosen king by the people of Israel in 1020 B.C.

Saul's career was a stormy one. He was able to organize some victories against the enemies of his people, but he always had to contend with the opposition of the conservative element at home, led by Samuel. His own nature was unfortunate. He found it hard to give due credit to his helpers, he was subject to fits of dark depression, he sometimes flew into horrible rages, and he was too pleased with minor soothsayers and witches.

A famous and, for him, unfortunate incident in the career of Saul gave a political start to David, the son of Jesse. Saul had been dismayed by the Philistine army, which was led by the great Goliath, but the young David slew the giant adversary and gained a reputation for the deed that time has still not tarnished. The king made David one of his assistants and his own musician as well, to exorcise with his playing and singing the dreaded dark moods that came all too often.

Now David rose and Saul declined. David was the darling of the people. Saul, mad with jealousy, tried a number of times to procure the death of the younger man. Finally he ended his tortured life after his troops had been badly defeated by the Philistines in 1005 B.C.

David, meanwhile, had fled into exile among the Philistines in fear for his life after Saul's repeated attempts to get rid of him. Now he came back and was made king, though not without a number of incidents of violence. Some historians feel that David had a remarkable talent for appropriating the results of his followers' violence while allowing the onus of the deeds to fall on the doers. But in any event, he now led Israel to a new unity of action and to a series of military successes that made her the leading power of western Asia. He took Jerusalem from the Jebusites, so punished the Philistines in a number of engagements that they never threatened Israel again, made Israel's force respected beyond the Jordan, and overcame some of the Aramaeans of Palestine. Israel now controlled the territories lying between Kadesh in the north and the head of the Gulf of Aqabah in the south. This military effort did a great deal to unite the nation in spirit. It must be remembered, of course, that temporarily this region was not the cockpit of the Near East; when the great powers revived from their eclipse of two or three centuries and once again fought back and forth across Palestine, Israel was not strong enough to hold her own with them.

David, having brought the kingdom to new power and new unity, expended a great deal of effort in equipping it with some of the necessary psychological and political appurtenances of a nation. Jerusalem was made the political and religious capital; there had been no capital city up to this time. The new city, often called "The City of David," was not within the jurisdiction of any tribe and was thus more effective as a symbol of national government. Plans were made, too, for the building of the temple that should be the center of the worship of the God of Israel, and David appointed priests from among his adherents.

The Bible describes a good many other measures taken to make an efficient national government out of the simple and loose organization that had hitherto existed. The boundaries of some of the tribes were altered, apparently for the purpose of weakening the tribes. Royal officials instead of the heads of the families and tribes were appointed to represent the new units at the capital. Not only was the force taken out of the political organization of the tribes, but their military strength was lessened by making the army into a professional and national group rather than a tribal militia. The new army was directly under the authority of the king rather than the several tribes. Naturally plans for national taxation were made, and a civil service was built up, many of whose members were not Israelites, but had been trained elsewhere.

The Bible also gives a vivid picture of the colorful personality of David, apart from his role as king. He was surely the composer of many of the Psalms, although others that were not his became attached to his name. His friendship with Jonathan has become proverbial, as has his grief for his son Absalom, who lost his life in a rebellion against his father's authority. We learn, too, of his taking women from their husbands, either slyly or brutally—probably only minor episodes in the life of a king of those days. We see the local way of doing things in the struggles for succession that began even before the death of David. His favorite wife, Bath-Sheba, pushed her son Solomon, although the legal heir was the older son Adonijah. David finally gave in. Solomon became king, and of course Adonijah lost his life.

Solomon became king in 965 B.C. and ruled until 925. One of his tasks was the completion of the organization that David had so well begun. Another, especially important, was the building of the temple. From the accounts of this building process we learn much about the relation of the kings of Israel to the Phoenicians. One group of the inhabitants of Canaan had settled in the area known as Phoenicia, about halfway up the coast. The good ports of Tyre, Sidon, and Byblos were theirs, and behind were the hills that yielded the various excellent woods that the Egyptians described as the cedar of Lebanon. By this time the Phoenicians were beginning to be known as seafaring merchants. Their political power was never great, and now they found it politic to do whatever they could for the kings of Israel.

To Solomon they furnished both craftsmen and materials for the great temple. It was built in the Canaanite style, with vestibule, holy place, and holy of holies. The excavations in Palestine have disclosed that at the Solomonic level (that is, the early Iron Age), there was much Phoenician influence in the walls and gates of the towns as well as in the small material remains. Solomon's subjects felt the weight of these projects. Taxation was increased, and there were heavy demands for forced labor.

Solomon increased his wealth by shrewd trading. The horse-and-chariot trade was one of his specialties. There is evidence that his commercial agents were busy all around western Asia, but the most spectacular of all his enterprises was the great copper refinery at the head of the Gulf of Aqabah, evidently planned and built as a unit to smelt the copper of Sinai and of Edom. Part of the project was a port. Solomon's ships could deal with all parts of the Red Sea and with places even farther away, and it has been suggested that the Queen of Sheba really did make the long trip from southwest Arabia to Jerusalem for the purpose of making a trade treaty with him.

Inevitably foreign influence crept in. Israel could not possibly live entirely to herself in these circumstances. Her people needed to travel for commercial and diplomatic reasons. Strangers likewise came into the kingdom. Intermarriage with foreigners was not unknown. The king himself added a number of outsiders to his harem and even built chapels to their foreign gods for them. Although there seems to have been no change in the basic religion of Israel in spite of the introduction of so many foreign religious elements, later historians were to feel that Solomon was responsible for weakening the religion of Israel.

Another natural result of the exchange with other peoples was some rise in the general level of culture. Both the poetry and the prose of the period, as we see them in the Bible, were elegant and effective. The Psalms are fine poetry, and the account of the kings is fine historical writing. The literary materials that were to form the Pentateuch (Genesis, Exodus, Leviticus, Numbers, and Deuteronomy) were beginning to take shape, although they were not to be put in their canonical written form until after the Babylonian Exile.

The Division of the Kingdom

The prosperity of the regime of Solomon was not shared by all its people. Taxes were high, drafts of labor for government's projects were frequent, and there was corruption in government. Furthermore, the northern tribes were galled by Judah's assumption of superiority. Under Solomon's son, the kingdom could not hold together. The leaders in the northern part apparently wanted to throw off what seemed to them the domination of the south, and they wished to continue religious life as it had been. At the time, there was no objection to monarchy, if that monarchy did not seem to favor the southern regions of the kingdom. But with the violent refusal of the people of the north to pay taxes, the kingdom was permanently divided. The northern kingdom was to be known as Israel and the southern as Judah, and in the next chapter we shall discuss their later history against the background of the Assyrian Empire.

THE PHOENICIANS

The Phoenicians had a far wider outlook on the world than did most of the smaller peoples with whom Israel came into contact. They were that part of the mixed Semitic people of Canaan who lived on the coastal plain below the mountains, where grew the woods of Lebanon, and who based their ships in the ports of Tyre, Sidon, and Byblos. Inhabitants of this region had long since learned to look to the sea. Even in the Old Kingdom, the ships of Egypt had come here, and the local people must have been mariners themselves, at least in a modest way.

For some time the Egyptians dominated the nearby sea, but later, from perhaps 2200 B.C. to about 1400, the ships of the great commercial people of Crete patrolled the waters to put down piracy and were very likely to destroy the vessels of rival traders. During the last two centuries or so of great Cretan power, the ships of the Mycenaeans, from southern Greece, must have ranged widely through both the eastern and the western Mediterranean. Even though the impressive palace of Cnossus, in Crete, was destroyed in a great raid about 1400 B.C., the ships of Crete need not necessarily have been swept from the sea entirely. On the other hand, the fall of the power of the Mycenaeans around 1100 B.C. probably did mean that the Greeks disappeared from the sea for some time.

The Phoenicians took advantage of the great weakening or total disappearance of the maritime peoples. Little by little their ships began to venture farther through the waters of the Mediterranean. To go to Greece through the islands was no great feat of navigation, a voyage that others had made many a time, as they knew. The visits of the Phoenician traders during the dark age that followed the fall of the Mycenaeans were (we shall see later) useful in bringing the Greeks some knowledge of Near Eastern culture. Perhaps the most important cultural item thus transferred from east to west was the alphabet, toward 800 B.C.

We know that the Phoenicians were not powerful enough politically and militarily to contend with the kingdom of Israel, nor did they wish to contend for such predominance. Instead, they were content to let others strive and to accept their protection. (We shall see this same attitude continued in connection with the Phoenicians under the Assyrian Empire.)

At the time, however, adventures other than military awaited the keener spirits among the Phoenicians. We do not know when they pushed into the western Mediterranean, perhaps as late as the 700's. Just before 800 B.C. they founded Carthage, on virtually the same site as modern Tunis. This dating is traditional, for studies of pottery would put it nearer 700, and Utica, near Carthage, claimed that it was an earlier foundation. The Carthaginians founded colonies and trading posts all along the coasts of what are now Tunisia, Algeria, and Morocco. The places seem generally to have been twenty-odd miles apart, or about a day's sail. The early ships were not well pitched and calked. It was well to draw them out of the water every night to give their hulls a chance to dry. For this purpose, as well as for trading with the natives, a series of stations was established on the African coast. Phoenician colonies and stations were to be established in western Sicily, too, in the Balearic Islands, and in southern Spain, and their ships are thought to have gone down the Atlantic coast for some distance and up as far as Cornwall.

Then around 800 B.C. the Greeks began to come out of their dark age, and before long their ships were seen in many places. They managed to drive the Phoenicians from the trade along the northern shores of the Mediterranean. Then, too, Greek settlements were made in eastern and central Sicily, destined to struggle for centuries with the Phoenicians. Carthage became the leader of all the Phoenicians of the West and the mistress of no inconsiderable empire. It was she who led the Phoenician contests with the Greeks. But finally, in the third and second centuries before Christ, she fought a series of three wars with the Romans and was destroyed by them in the third. This was to be the end, far away in the West and far in the future, of the expansion of the Phoenicians upon the sea that was well under way in the days of David and Solomon.

THE ARAMAEANS

The Aramaeans deserve special mention among the numerous smaller peoples of the Near East who are known to us at least by name. During the reign of David, they were getting a kingdom organized in upper Transjordan, and in the reign of Solomon, they were prospering. Presently they established a strong kingdom at Damascus, of which we shall have more to say in connection with the next historical period, when we find them even farther north, on the edges of Assyrian territory.

The Aramaeans played a role in inland trade analogous to the Phoenicians on the sea, although they never built up an empire like that of Carthage. They were the managers of the caravans that traveled about the Near East, sometimes making connections with overseas trade at the ports. The Aramaean language came to be very widely used. Probably in the time of Christ more people in Palestine spoke it than Hebrew, and Christ himself was probably a user of Aramaic. At one time it was the language of diplomacy throughout western Asia. A number of our historical source materials were written in this language.

CHAPTER

7

ASSYRIA

Assyria was located on the upper Tigris in a territory about three hundred and fifty miles long and nearly three hundred miles wide, about the area of a fair-sized American state. The western part, a little too dry for agriculture, was suitable for grazing, whereas the eastern part was more fertile. Even today the climate can be very hot in the summer, although the nearness of the mountains is a help; in winter it is occasionally cold enough for snow. The country was fairly well supplied with building stone, and many interesting stone remains have survived.

The names of the chief god, the principal city of the early period, and the nation as a whole were the same—Ashur. It often appeared as part of the name of the king, too, for example, Ashur-uballit, "Ashur-has-given-life." In the same way, we have seen "Amun" or "Aton" or "Re" included in the names of Egyptian kings.

The Assyrians were somewhere on the scene as an organized nation during most of the historical period that we have been considering. By the middle of the third millenium Ashur was a city and under Sumerian influence. The nation became more powerful very slowly. It played some part in the history of the Akkadian and Amorite and Kassite regions down the river. The Assyrians deserve credit for having saved much of the Sumerian and Babylonian culture by adopting, protecting, and spreading it. On their western side, they were often either friendly toward or in conflict with the Hittites, with Mitanni, with the people of Syria, and with Egypt. Finally Assyria became the greatest nation of the ancient world, dominating the whole Fertile Crescent and Egypt, but its power lasted only about two hundred years. Just before 600 B.C. Assyria fell before a coalition of hostile neighbors. The nation and the people disappeared.

EARLY ASSYRIA

We know very little about the condition of Assyria in the early part of the third millennium except that there was a city and modest nation of that name which was somewhat under the influence of the Sumerians. Then when Sargon founded his great Akkadian Empire, Assyria was a part of it and shared in the combined Sumerian and Babylonian civilization. When the Sumerians later regained control of Mesopotamia, Assyria was subject to them.

We do know, however, that Assyria was able to continue as a recognizable entity, in spite of foreign domination and strong foreign influence, for a very long time after the beginnings early in the third millenium. The nation was over a thousand years old when we find her king Shamshi-Adad appearing in the documents from Mari (discussed in Chapter 3). He apparently was strong enough to decree that his son should rule in Mari. But then the power of Assyria seemed to decline; and it is reasonable to suppose that the genius of Shamshi-Adad's contemporary, Hammurabi of Babylon, who captured Mari, led to the lessening of the power of Assyria or to its conquest.

If the Assyrians were sometimes independent and powerful and sometimes compelled to acknowledge the sway of other nations, they nevertheless steadily absorbed the culture of the Sumerians and Babylonians. For example, the Babylonian code of law, based on the Sumerian, was in use in Assyria. The laws discovered at Ashur show that the Assyrians were capable of making sensible adaptations of or additions to these laws to suit local conditions. Assyrian art, at first derived from the Sumerians and Babylonians, early began to show its own vigorous nature, which in the end was to produce a spirited classical art that excelled especially in lively animal scenes.

Thutmose III of Egypt seems to have had Assyria as an ally in the rear of Mitanni during his Asiatic campaigns and parades. He speaks of "tribute" from Assyria—lapis lazuli, horses, wagons, and valuable woods—although probably it would have been more accurate to speak of reciprocal gifts. In the time of Amenhotep III, however, Assyria apparently fell under the power of Mitanni, then enjoying its strongest period. Very shortly afterward, Ashur-uballit was able to throw off its domination. This king appears in the Amarna Letters, asking his brother monarch of Egypt to send him gold.

The Assyrians felt the force of the migrations that occurred about 1200, but were able to survive and remain a nation. As we have said before, the power situation changed greatly at this time. The Hittites were so battered by the invasion that they remained thereafter a group of small and weak kingdoms and were never again an empire. Egypt was no longer consistently able to make her power felt beyond her own borders. This state of affairs was to give the Hebrews an opportunity to dominate Palestine for a while, as it was to allow the Assyrians to build up slowly toward their great imperial period. For the time being, however, they made no spectacular advances. It can hardly be said that there was a power vacuum for them to rush into; it would be more accurate to say that for some time there was no serious rival to any nation that made itself moderately powerful.

Tiglath-Pileser I

The reign of Tiglath-Pileser I, who ruled from about 1114 to about 1076 B.C., is probably typical of Assyria in the centuries just after the great migrations and before her real rise to power. We happen to have the annals of this reign, from which we learn that hostile peoples who otherwise play no part in history had taken over part of the Assyrian territory to the northwest and that Tiglath-Pileser I drove them out with great slaughter. In the next year he campaigned around Lake Van, to the north, and so firmly established his power that a confederacy of twenty-three princes (whom we should probably call leaders of tribes) was forced to give hostages and pay a yearly tribute of horses and cattle.

Furthermore, the king reported that he was the first of Assyrian monarchs to see the Mediterranean, as the annals of a later year tell us in describing a campaign across the Euphrates and into Phoenicia. There is interesting testimony to Phoenician familiarity with the sea in the party that they organized for the sporting monarch, whose earlier annals had boasted of his hunting elephants and wild bulls. This time he met a great fish and killed it, and as our imagination reconstructs the scene, the experience and confidence of his hosts stand out. The Phoenician cities of the coast paid him tribute, partly in the prized woods of Lebanon.

We hear, too, of repeated invasions of Aramaeans. Here we are less well informed, but we may conclude that one group of them settled where Mitanni had been, in the bend of the Euphrates. Most were to settle on less desirable land in northern Palestine. We also learn that the Babylonians invaded Assyria with some success and that the invasion was later avenged conclusively.

These annals show the god Ashur as senior partner in the activities of the king, as Amun was in Egypt. He commanded the king to smite those not yet subject to him. The conquered were subject to him, tribute was paid to him, and the conquered gods were brought home to be dominated by him. We see, too, that there are only hints of the efficient system of imperial control that was to exist in later times. Now the conquered were merely to give hostages and pay a regular yearly tribute, although when the king led the royal army through their territories, they had to make an extraordinary contribution.

THE ASSYRIAN EMPIRE

The date at which Assyria's imperial period began cannot be easily fixed. We can see some slight beginnings of empire under Tiglath-Pileser I, but a period of comparative weakness followed. Adad-nirari II (911–890 B.C.) strove with a multitude of peoples, his annals reminding us how many peoples who are not important to history as we know it could seem significant enemies of the Assyrians. But neither reign marks a conclusive step toward empire.

Ashur-nasir-pal II (885–860 B.C.)

Ashur-nasir-pal II may be called a mixture of high-powered bandit and empire builder. The bas-reliefs of the palace in his new city of

Calah show us something of his army and its exploits. By now this army had weapons of iron—strictly speaking, wrought steel. The native Assyrians made up a heavy infantry, and the allies furnished the cavalry (as was later to be the case among the Romans). One of the bas-reliefs suggests that the camps of the Assyrian army (like those of the Romans) were very carefully and thoroughly made. We can also see battering rams, sheds to protect the sappers as they tried to undermine the walls, towers from which to shoot at the defenders on the walls, and a technique of concerted action in assaulting fortified places. Probably these military improvements had been made gradually.

The king campaigned in the rough country east of Assyria, reduced a number of minor peoples, but found the Haldians of Urartu far more of a problem and, leaving them for the time being, turned to easier conquests in the West. This we learn from the bas-reliefs and from the annals, which were cut in the pavement of the entrance to a temple in the new city.

The kingdom of Urartu was to be for some time an occasional adversary of the Assyrians, but it never played a major part in the affairs of the Near East. During the 19th century, there were a few excavations in their territory, and renewed excavations in the middle of the present century have shown that the workmen of Urartu were competent and original in both the major and the minor arts. Their temples were planned differently from those of the Assyrians. Fine masonry has been found in the remains, and mosiac inlays in stones of contrasting colors, as well as wall paintings, sculptures, and good small pieces worked from ivory and metal.

The Aramaeans, of course, played a larger historical role than Urartu. Their involvement with the Assyrians is attested by a list of the booty exacted from one of their minor kings whose city Ashurnasir-pal took. First were the animals—horses with chariots, cattle, and sheep. Although only two talents of gold and two of silver (a talent having a weight roughly equivalent to sixty pounds) were on the list, there were a hundred talents of lead, two hundred of bronze, and three hundred of iron. Evidently the Aramaeans were already settling down to being a manufacturing people, for they were also required to give a great many bronze vessels and gold and ivory couches. Those Aramaeans who were conquered by the Assyrians established themselves within the Assyrian territory and, as time went on, became the trading class of Assyria.

Ashur-nasir-pal also reduced another Aramaean kingdom in the great bend of the Euphrates and later he crossed the river into Syria. Here he demanded booty from the city of Carchemish, a great trading city at the chief crossing of the river. The list that we have is richer than the other, including such additional items as furniture of ebony, which must have come from the Sudan, and woven goods, like mantles.

The Phoenicians, who saw the prospect of good trading in a region organized by this energetic king, sent him rich and unusual gifts. There were things made of the precious metals, cloths of Tyrian purple, and furniture of boxwood, ebony, and ivory. Most picturesque of all was a collection of rare or fierce wild animals from gazelles to lions, which the king put in his zoological collection in Calah.

Today the king's palace in Calah is one of the most famous spots in the annals of historical research in the Near East, for here the Englishman Layard began his pioneer excavations in 1845. He found that the new city of Calah had been surrounded by walls and moats and had an ample water supply brought from the Tigris. The palace and the adjacent temples were partly of mud-brick and partly of stone, and figures of winged animals, often with human faces, were prominent. The wall reliefs are precious documentation of the civilization of the time as well as major works of art, showing us, for example, the weapons and the techniques of the army.

Ashur-nasir-pal himself was a master hand at what has come to be known as "calculated frightfulness," and his annals contain vivid boasts that he made great piles of heads of the conquered or impaled their bodies or, especially, flayed them alive. This latter practice consisted of beating a man until his skin was loosened, whereupon a skilled operative could remove it from a living man so that it could be carried away and hung up to the greater glory of the conqueror.

Shalmaneser III (858–824 b.c.), Ashur-nasir-pal's son, continued the imperialistic policy in Syria and Palestine. In 853 b.c., his forces met a coalition of twelve Syrian kings at Qarqar on the Orontes River. The Assyrians claimed a great victory; if their claim was false, as it may be, the fact remains that they were in control of practically all of Syria and Palestine within a few years and that they retained control for over two centuries, that is, until the downfall of their nation.

In the Assyrian inscription that describes this battle as one of the military activities of the first six years of Shalmaneser's reign, we find Hadadezer of Damascus named first among the enemy leaders. Damascus (sometimes called Aram Damascus) was one of the most important of the several Aramaic principalities in Palestine. Third was Ahab of Israel, in these days ruling a prosperous kingdom from the new capital, Samaria, although apparently the prosperity was for the few rather than for the many. The king was in close association with the Phoenicians and had married Jezebel, a Phoenician princess. This was the Jezebel who won herself an immortality of dishonor by procuring the death of Naboth, the neighbor who would not sell his ancestral vineyard to the king. Ahab must have been a powerful king for his time and place, because the Assyrian inscription ascribes 2,000 chariots and 10,000 men to him at the great battle (which is not mentioned in the Bible).

In later years, some Greek and Latin authors told tales of a queen of Assyria, Semiramis, who lived in this period. Born of a goddess, so the tale went, she was nourished by doves who brought her food until she was found and reared by the king's chief shepherd. She first married a great general and, when he died, became the wife of King Ninus, reigning by herself long after his death and producing marvels in war and building. Ultimately people ascribed every great engineering feat of the Near East (the building of Babylon, for example) to her. Her cruelty and lust were also spoken of. In more modern times she has been the subject of both poetry and opera. Modern scholarship can now identify her with Sammuramat, a king's widow who ruled efficiently for five years during her son's minority and retired to the position of queen mother when he assumed power in 810 B.C.

Tiglath Pileser III (744–727 B. C.)

After a long period during which the Assyrians had had little success with their imperialistic policies, the great warrior and statesman, Tiglath Pileser III, usurped the throne of Assyria and reasserted her claims to the economic surplus of her neighbors. Because Assyria had often been able to dominate Babylon, this king proclaimed himself king over Babylon as well. It probably was typical of the times that the kings of Israel and Damascus tried to revolt and tried to force the king of Judah to join, but he appealed to the Assyrians and brought Tiglath Pileser down upon the two nations. The deportation of many of the inhabitants of Israel is described in the Assyrian annals. This shifting of population was one of the basic practices of Assyrian government in conquered territories. The nobles were likely to be sent to one place and the people to another, agricultural people were often sent to pastoral regions and vice versa, and the result was to break up whatever loyalties or constellations of power existed and to allow people bare subsistence at great effort rather than prosperity. Another result was a new cosmopolitanism among those who were moved about and met of necessity new people.

For a long time the Assyrians had been in the habit of making their new territories into provinces in charge of governors (somewhat as the Romans were to do later). The custom of other nations had generally been to regard the conquered territory as the same nation or area that it had been before, only asserting that the conquering king was king of the new as well as the old. Tiglath Pileser III made a significant change in the old Assyrian provincial system by breaking up the provinces, some of which were very large, into units so small that their governors could not possibly muster the economic or military resources to oppose the king or revolt. The governors were rotated, closely watched, and compelled to submit frequent reports. Such a system made it much easier for the central government to control not only the conquered territory, but also the possible ambitions of the nobles who served as governors.

The deportation policy was continued under the new system, and in 722 B.C., a rebellion against the son of Tiglath Pileser brought about the destruction of Samaria, the capital of Israel, and the dispersal of the inhabitants. The city was then rebuilt and furnished with an adequate number of new residents brought from elsewhere. This move marked the end of ancient Israel as a sovereign nation.

Assyria at Its Height ((721–633 B. C.)

Sargon II (721–705 B.C.) established a standing army in the place of the occasional levies that had been the rule. Although many of the soldiers were foreigners, we do not hear that he had any great difficulty with revolts in the army or with military attempts to play a part in the government. In addition, the king made great efforts to restore the canals, which had been neglected.

He established a new capital city, Dur-Sharrukin or Sargonsburg. The palace dominated it, the rest being only a setting for the royal buildings, not a real city. It did, however, have a regular plan; its streets were straight and crossed at right angles. In the style still common in that region, there were blank walls on the streets, and the houses really faced on the courtyards within. Before the excavations in the middle of the nineteenth century, the name of Sargon was known only from the reference in the Bible to his taking the city of Ashdod. This excavation disclosed many remains of the palace and gave a fair idea of the rest of the town. Thus, instead of a single biblical reference, we now have knowledge of Sargon from letters discussing the building of the palace and the town, from the remains of the palace, which contain representations of the king and his court at their various activities, and from the royal annals, which were inscribed on stone slabs and displayed in the palace.

The fine bas-reliefs that show us the king were colored in parts to bring out the detail. Furthermore, there was a great deal of beautiful tiling in the palace, a form of art that has always been a specialty of the Near East. Blue, yellow, and white are the favorite colors, although red and green appear. The tiles are used for the surfaces of gates, for friezes, and on wall surfaces. Some have conventional ornamentation, whereas others are used for good-sized scenes of the king's exploits or pictures of daily life.

Sennacherib (704–681 B.C.) is best known for the mysterious misfortune of his army before Jerusalem. Perhaps, as the Bible says, the soldiers were sorely smitten with the plague (which was assumed to be sent by God) as they were besieging the city. The annals of the king claim no more than that he shut up Hezekiah, the rebellious king of Judah, in his city and reduced the other places of his kingdom. Both kingdoms of the Hebrews had at times acknowledged the power of Assyria and had often sought to throw it off, believing the nation to be distant and weak. Although the capital of Israel, Samaria, had been destroyed in 722, the end was yet to come for Judah. We hear much of Assyria in the Bible, for we have the warnings of the prophets about relations with Assyria as well as accounts of political and military conditions.

Sennacherib's troubles in other quarters foreshadowed the downfall of Assyria that was to occur a century later. To the east and northeast, the frontier was under pressure from the Medes, Cimmerians, and Scythians, pastoral or nomadic peoples of Indo-European stock. We learn something about this danger from the surviving records of the king's consultations of the sun god and the answers to his questions given by the priests from their inspection of the livers of the sacrificial victims (a kind of divination that we shall find in use among the Etruscans in Italy).

Babylon, in spite of the fact that its culture was so important to the Assyrians, was also a thorn in their side. From about the year 1000, it had been full of Aramaeans, who at times were rebellious and troublesome and at other times were actually able to assert their independence. Finally, Sennacherib lost his patience and destroyed the city of Babylon.

With such pressures on the kingdom from the eastern peoples, it was folly for Sennacherib's son Esarhaddon (680–669 B.C.) to make the effort to conquer Egypt, which for several hundred years had been under the domination of dynasties from the south, Libya and Nubia, and often had been unable to hold herself together as a unified nation. Her products had appeared in the trading records or in the tribute lists of the Assyrians, and now, in 670, Assyria took the country, but held it only until 662. The Egyptians were able to drive out the Assyrians as they had driven out the Hyksos long before, but much more quickly. Psamtik, or Psammetichus, used Greek mercenaries as part of the forces with which he recovered Egypt's freedom.

Ashur-bani-pal (668–633 B.C.) was the last of the great kings of Assyria. Although he scored no spectacular success either in politics or in warfare, he was successful in maintaining the power and prosperity of his country, a task that never allowed any room for slackness or complacency. His real distinction was that he was a learned prince, with a touch of the antiquarian about him. He learned the dead Babylonian language of a thousand years before his time and the Sumerian of two thousand years before. There were helps for students, of course, just as today there are beginners' books and grammars and dictionaries for every important language.

As king he formed a great royal library at Nineveh, much of which survived to be found by the excavators. His agents searched every likely place in Assyria proper, where there were already some libraries, and elsewhere in the region, especially in Babylonia. Some of the tablets they brought in contained magic formulas for various occasions; others told the old legends of the region of the two rivers. Many provided historical information, sometimes sober, sometimes a purple patchwork, sometimes edited to bring out official truth. The mathematical and astronomical knowledge of Babylon was inscribed on others; indeed, it has been seriously stated that we possess so many tablets with scientific content from Assyria that it would take the scholars now competent in the subject several centuries to deal with them. The great library also contained dispatches and archives of the royal government.

Enough scholarly work has been done on these tablets to establish that the Assyrians of this period understood the works that they gathered and copied, for we find repeatedly that they edited them or commented on them or combined them. We also discover from the tablets that there was a sound system of instruction in the necessary languages for those who were to be scribes and that, as was so often the case at the time, the post of scribe offered opportunity for both a certain worldly advancement and the mastery of the intellectual content of the culture.

Assyrian art, too, was at its height, as the reliefs in the king's palace show. Scenes of the king's lion hunts were especially favored. One large hall still shows a hunt something like a modern rodeo. In the first scene, a wooden enclosure is about to be opened, with a great square of soldiers around it. From it issues, not a calf to be pursued and roped, but a group of lions, which the king pursues in his chariot and kills. There have been no finer representations of animals than these. The artist must have studied many lions in motion, and his technique was adequate to portray what he saw.

The Fall of Assyria

Occasionally during the reign of Ashur-bani-pal and even oftener in the two decades after his death, the Assyrian Empire was having difficulty performing all the tasks involved in warding off the enemy on the outside and keeping a firm hand on the restless elements within. And then the Chaldaeans of Babylon decided to make an alliance with the Medes. Nabopolassar of Babylon and Cyaxares the Mede joined to assault Nineveh in the year 612. They took and destroyed the city. A group of the Assyrians escaped and maintained a minor Assyrian kingdom until 608, but with no real effect. As we shall see in the next chapter, Assyria was now divided between the Chaldaeans and the Medes.

In spite of the rejoicings of the Hebrew prophets, we are not entitled to conclude that Assyria fell because her imperialism and her cruelty had earned her the bitter hatred of mankind. Her conduct had been no better and no worse than that of most imperialist nations throughout history. In fact, keeping the peace over large areas, she had earned a certain gratitude from many people. The attack of the Chaldaeans and Medes should be regarded as a normal piece of international business.

Nor is it possible to draw up a scheme of events that led Assyria inevitably to her fall. As Carthage, wealthy and spirited, was to be utterly cut off by the Romans in 146 B.C., so Assyria fell when she might conceivably have prospered for centuries more. The serious student of history must recognize the fact that there have been declines without falls and falls without declines and thus fortify himself against the meretricious persuasiveness of the phrase "decline and fall."

CHAPTER

THE CULTURE OF EGYPT AND
THE NEAR EAST: A SUMMARY

The time had now come for Persia's emergence as a great imperial power, in control of all the regions that we have been considering. The confrontation of Persia and Greece will have a large role in the chapters that follow, as will the development of the culture of the Greeks. A summary here of the culture of Egypt and the Near East will provide a useful preliminary to the description of Greek culture.

GOVERNMENT

As we have seen, the important techniques of governing had already been developed by the time of Persia's rise. Both domestic and imperial government were expertly conducted. Psychological methods of supporting the government were understood. The person and the office of the king were supported by such dignities and attributed characteristics as the aura of divinity and the role of the shepherd of his people. Statesmen had a sense for ensuring the loyalty of the people, perhaps partly by refined terrorism, partly by the connection of religion and government, partly by supplying just and impartial courts as a service of government.

120

Those in power knew how to organize and manage a large staff to get the work done. Egypt, especially, had learned to manage its closed and unified territory so as to extract all possible revenue from agriculture, industry, and commerce. Incidentally, but usefully for us, there was a remarkable amount of governmental record-keeping.

The conduct of foreign affairs, too, was refined and ingenious. The use of armies, an obvious device in this field, had been carefully developed. Statesmen knew a fair amount about such matters as treaties, dynastic alliances, and the use of money, whether it should be called tribute or aid to friendly nations. The Amarna Letters, for example, are full of information about such devices.

If we consider the conduct of government from another side, that of the troubles afflicting governments, we find ourselves rather scantily informed except for certain recurrent patterns. It was always difficult for those in power in Egypt and the Near East to avoid murder by their nearest and dearest. Again and again the rulers of the ancient states in this region were assassinated by members of their own families who hoped to usurp the throne. Attacks by foreign powers were always a danger, too. Predatory imperialism was accepted and even honorable, for kings were expected to retain the respect of restless elements by successful campaigns.

We seldom learn much of domestic stresses and strains, but we do know that Egypt for some time at the end of the Old Kingdom could not exert the necessary control over the great lords until at length the central government was able to reassert its predominance in the land. We have seen declines without falls, as in the case of the Old Kingdom, and falls without declines, as in the case of Assyria. It is seldom that we can tell exactly how successful any ancient government was in functioning over a significant period of time.

During these early centuries, an enormous amount of thought and energy must have gone into the development of formal religion. We should probably be justified in saying that church and state were intimately connected all through the period and that it would never have occurred to anyone that the two should be separate. The condition of society and the religious attitudes that could lead a man to think of his religion as something intimate and personal still lay far in the future. The enterprising characters who first offered themselves as governmental managers, their necessities of life contributed by other people, would undoubtedly have offered to handle the group's relationship to the unseen powers of the universe as well as to earthly enemies and the food supply. It is plain enough that government had this function in the early societies that we can study.

In this area there was much to be done. A system of gods had to be set up to give meaning and direction to the work of the priests. Part of this involved the establishment of a cosmogony, or theory of the creation of the universe. The stories of the creation that have come down to us from the Sumerians, Babylonians, Assyrians, and Hebrews show that one of the earliest attempts gave universal satisfaction.

The nature of the several gods and of their relations among themselves showed certain similarities in the various systems. The sky god or father of the gods, the storm god, the god of the sea and the god of the underworld, the goddess of love—all are known in many places. All seem to have been suggested by the powers of Nature, and the common conception of a god who dies and is reborn seems to have grown out of her cycles. The god of the Hebrews, however, even before their religion attained the austere elevation of its later period, was the lord of Nature rather than merely a part of it. The idea of a single god above the others, a national god, served, as did the festivals, to cement society. The principle that it is useful for all the citizens to have some ideal in common was well understood, and the national character of Amun or Ashur or Marduk helped to keep the nation a united and going concern.

The festivals that the priests devised may well have served more than one need. The ceremony that took place near our Christmastime was a struggle by the whole community to help the sun to stop waning and begin to wax again so that it could provide them with life through the crops. The myth of the dying and returning god, which goes with this ceremony, was probably meant to lift the ritual acts into the realm of the permanent. In other cases, too, the performance symbolized whatever was wished for, and the myth that accompanied it was meant to lift these acts to a dimly apprehended higher plane of permanence. Although some of these myths later received highly sophisticated literary treatment, we must not let this fact make us forget their very serious original purpose. In the chapters on the Greeks, we shall see the need to keep in mind the distinction between the myth in its original serious use, the myth as part of literature, and the legend arising from the deeds of men.

It may well be that in the course of the long period that we have already studied the more intelligent men acquired some confidence in human efforts and felt a little less urgency in such rites as that to bring back the sun from his December weakness. These men could also see that festivals are very useful in giving a comforting rhythm to life, in relieving the boredom of toil and sameness, and in assuring the faithful in an indirect way that all their interests are being taken care of by the government.

Nevertheless, it is all too easy to picture the priesthood as a set of fat and cynical parasites. We should do better to regard them as a set of typical government officials, sometimes lazy and inert, sometimes alert and ingenious. The priest, like the scribe, was freed from arduous physical toil and given an opportunity to lead the intellectual life. If some used their freedom for riotous living—and even in those days the good eating of priests was notorious—others used it for better purposes. There are, for example, the astronomical observations of the Babylonian priests, who wished to know the courses of the heavenly bodies, which they regarded as divinities, partly in order to know when the new month was to begin. But there is also the Assyrian lore of divination by the liver of the sacrificial victim. Like divination were the omens of various kinds used in attempts to predict the future, at first for kings and governments and then for the common man. The astronomical observations, which we approve, and the study of divination and omens, which we find it difficult to accept, were presently to join in astrology, a pseudo-science that still is popular.

TECHNOLOGICAL ACHIEVEMENT

Building Materials

The peoples of lower Mesopotamia made the best of the fact that stone was not readily available by working out techniques for making clay bricks, which when reinforced with bitumen became extremely strong. The scanty remains of buildings constructed from these bricks show that a good sense of design had already developed. The Assyrians, however, had stone at their command. Their monumental

stone figures and such engineering works as the great stone canal of
Sennacherib demonstrate their mastery of the material. The Egyptians
at the beginning of the Pyramid Age overcame the problem of working in stone with great suddenness and skill. They learned to quarry
and dress it, and they worked out means of transporting huge pieces
on the Nile. Although their early stone work showed too much influence of other materials they had been used to, the designers soon
learned to think in terms of the stone they were now using. Probably
it is correct to think of the magnificent stone structures at Mycenae,
in Greece, as in the Egyptian tradition, and the same may be true of
Stonehenge, in England.

Wood seems never to have been used for buildings of any importance, but the examples of furniture preserved by the dry climate
of Egypt show how skillful the ancient artisans were in dealing with
this excellent material. They used hammers, saws, chisels, drills, awls,
files, and rasps. They were fond of inlays of fine woods or ivory, a
material that they handled with skill and assurance, and they also
used inlays of glass or sometimes semiprecious stones. Their adhesive
was a casein glue much like the modern form.

Painting of all kinds was known. Wood was sometimes painted,
and paint has been found applied to many other materials—pottery,
plaster, canvas, papyrus, and ivory. Some of the paints can be analyzed, like the crimson cochineal, which comes from an insect, or
madder (red) from a root and henna from a conifer, yellow from
saffron or turmeric, and blue from indigo. There is evidence that easel
painting was done. Wall plaster was known and sometimes paint was
applied to it, but frescoing (that is, the application of paint to fresh
wet plaster) seems to have been practiced only in Crete.

Clothing

Clothing was made chiefly of wool and linen. Although cotton was
known in India, it was rare or unknown in the West, and silk was not
yet being imported from China. Time has spared not only some of the
fabrics, but also pictures of the looms, the nature of which is readily
intelligible to the modern expert.

The most striking finds of fabrics were in the tomb of King

Tutankhamun. Some linen cloth from there was so fine as to have 280 x 80 threads to the inch, and certain pieces were woven as tapestry with fine colored designs.

Food

Man by this time, had come a long way from being a mere gatherer of food. It is possible to tell by the study of seeds found on ancient sites (as well as by mention in documents) what vegetables and fruits had been taught to live with man, do his bidding, and finally be devoured by him as the animals were. Wheat, millet, and other cereals were of prime importance, and rye would push its way into this company wherever conditions were difficult for wheat. Ovens were developed early; an Egyptian papyrus has recipes for over thirty forms of bread and cake. There were peas and beans, artichokes, cucumbers, leeks, onions, garlic, beets, lettuce, and radishes. Among the fruits were dates, figs, pomegranates, and watermelons. Wine was common. Oil was made from olives and many other materials such as almonds, linseed, radish seed, and sesame. Honey served for sweetening, and there were flavorings of almond, aniseed, cinnamon, and ginger. Beef, veal, lamb, pork, fowl, and fish were eaten, although at certain times and places there were prohibitions against one or another. Milk was drunk or made into cheese, and butter was used in the form of butterfat.

There was, in addition, considerable knowledge of the industrial uses of plants. Dyes were made from saffron, madder, woad, and indigo. The fibers of flax and hemp were used. Gourds were used as vessels. Unfortunately, men have learned only recently to be producers of wood rather than merely gatherers of it. These early peoples, like so many after them, plundered their resources of wood and paid the same penalties for the deforestation of their lands and hills.

Transportation

The wheel, the greatest of all inventions in transportation, was apparently invented in the period that we have just studied. There were, however, only the simplest beginnings of the complementary invention—the paved road for the wheel to run on—although we hear of an engineering corps in the Assyrian army that cleared roads for the army, and the Persians were soon to have a system of royal roads that seem to have been partly paved. Yoked oxen were first used to pull wheeled vehicles. The shoulders of the horse and others of his kind are not shaped properly for yokes, and the ancient world never developed a harness that allowed a horse to exert his full strength.

Boats of every kind had been developed. On rivers and lakes there were small affairs of skin and reed; on the Nile there were also boats or rafts that could carry huge blocks of stone. Boats were propelled by sails, generally square-rigged, and by oars. Navigation on the sea was generally confined to the less stormy months from spring to autumn. The ancient mariners ranged to Britain and beyond, and it is plain that on some runs, for example, from Egypt to Crete, they must have gone well out of sight of land.

Metallurgy

The development of metallurgy was a long and complicated process. Although it is easy to imagine some man seeing beads of copper shining where he had built a fire on copper-bearing rock, the actual situation was far more difficult. Somehow the idea had to be grasped that certain raw materials could be made to yield metals, and then appropriate means of applying heat had to be devised for each metal. For instance, the simplest class of copper ores—carbonates and oxides—can be reduced to copper by heating them in a crucible with charcoal. Here, with the use of small crucibles, true metallurgy may be said to begin.

Iron ores—compounds of iron and sulphur—must be put through a more complicated process of roastings and smeltings. Iron is much more difficult to handle than copper, and the processes that bring success are not obvious even to the man who has learned to handle copper. Iron must be smelted with a good heat, and the bloom, or mass, which comes from the smelting, must be hammered to remove some of the impurities and produce wrought iron. This is only the first product, the second and final being wrought steel. The old-fashioned production of wrought steel from wrought iron had two parts. First, the metal was heated in contact with charcoal, then hammered, a process that added a carbon content to the metal and began its transformation to steel. The second part involved heating and hammering the metal, then cooling it suddenly by immersion in water ("quenching") to maintain the desirable inner structure that the metal had when it was hot. The smith could, if he wished, heat his metal slowly and cool it slowly to make it tougher and less brittle, although he sacrificed some of its hardness by doing so.

Little by little, over a number of centuries, this art was learned. By perhaps 1500 B.C., there were smiths who were masters of it all and who could with fair consistency combine these techniques to produce usable steel weapons and tools. For many an age thereafter, the smith was one of the most respected of all workmen. His product, both cheaper and better than copper or bronze, was of great value in clearing and cultivating land and also, unfortunately, in furthering man's inhumanity to man.

NONMATERIAL ACHIEVEMENTS

Writing, which began as a device for governmental record-keeping, obviously had tremendous influence. The governments learned to use it as a device for enhancing their prestige—for example, by publishing highly tendentious accounts of military successes as inscriptions on stone on temple or palace walls or floors. The use of writing for belles lettres was not nearly so extensive as it was to be in Greek and Roman times and later.

The two earliest writing systems, the Egyptian and the Sumerian, both developed from pictographs. The Egyptian was ordinarily written with pen and ink on papyrus, the Sumerian and its successors in Mesopotamia on clay tablets with a stylus. Syria and Palestine were the scene of the liveliest inventiveness in this field. Some people there could write Akkadian, the international language of 1500–1200 B.C. or thereabouts, in cuneiform. A well-trained man could also handle Egyptian hieroglyphics and demotic and the cuneiform alphabet of Ugarit, which has become known to us through the excavations at Ras Shamra, on the coast of Syria. More important, after 1500 B.C. some people knew a linear alphabet from which Hebrew, Syriac, Arabic, and other oriental languages developed their forms of writing. From this linear alphabet, too, the Phoenicians developed the system that they were later to teach the Greeks and that eventually became the alphabet of the Western world.

Cuneiform writing gradually gave way to alphabetic writing in antiquity; the latest known cuneiform tablet can be dated A.D. 75. Well before this time people in general had switched to the use of the alphabet. Not only did the form change, but the material changed also. People had written on everything—stone, wood, leather, cloth, gold and silver, pottery—but papyrus and the clay tablet were used most. Parchment appeared during the reign of Tiglath Pileser III. It was the combination of the alphabet, papyrus, and parchment to which cuneiform and the clay tablet finally yielded near the beginning of the Christian era. The cuneiform system of writing was soon forgotten and not recovered until modern times.

To assess the literary achievement of this period is difficult. The most important generalization that can be made is that the humanism of the Greeks was yet to come. Now the epics concern only gods, and gods who are not humanized. Only occasionally the humanistic note sounds clearly, as in the Egyptian "Harper's Song." Probably the work of the Hebrew writers is best in this respect; the history of the kingdom under Saul and David is good work, and the poetic quality of the Psalms is universally recognized. Even though the literature of this period was to be overshadowed by the incomparably richer achievement of the Greeks, the tremendously important technique of putting thoughts into permanent form by writing had been worked out.

Another outstanding accomplishment of these centuries was the development of the processes of business. The remains of laws and of business documents show us that much useful work had been done in this field. Techniques of measuring had been worked out (which of course were useful in other ways, too), and standards of measurement for areas of land and for volume and weight of all kinds of products had been adopted. The idea that the government could serve its citizens by regulating and guaranteeing such measures had arisen. An important branch of the law regulated all the arrangements having to do with the use of land and the production and exchange of goods. From the records of law and of business transactions that have survived, we can see that sensible practices had been set up for the ownership, acquisition, alienation, lease, use, and inheritance of land.

For industry and commerce, principles of contract had been devised, and partnerships were known. Indeed, the principles of financing industrial and commercial transactions were far beyond a primitive stage.

The achievements of these ancients in what we should call science are far less impressive. Nevertheless, if we add to them the mathematical and astronomical work of the Babylonians in the next few centuries—say between 400 B.C. and 100 A.D.—a very respectable start was made in the abstract sciences by the peoples of the Near East. The Babylonians developed a useful sexagesimal system of numeration, one aspect of which was to consider the circle as an abstract figure capable of being divided into 360 degrees. Perhaps the easiest (but, of course, oversimplified) way to describe the sexagesimal system is to say that we use it when we say 1:23 instead of twenty-three minutes past one, for the "one" represents an hour, a unit with sixty parts, and the "twenty-three" the twenty-three parts of a second unit of sixty parts that have elapsed. The figures used had varying values according to their places (what is called "positional notation"), just as they do in the decimal system.

Some of the Babylonian clay tablets that have been found give tables for such arithmetical operations as squaring and cubing. Many tablets include problems and their simple algebraic solutions. Geometric problems were also dealt with. These tablets show that among the Babylonians there was an interest in mathematics in the proper sense of the word. Their mathematics and astronomy were closely connected, and if we again go a little beyond our period, we find them going beyond the observations of the heavenly bodies made for religious purposes by the priests and beginning true astronomy with attempts to theorize.

In another scientific field, a professional class of physicians had arisen in both Mesopotamia and Egypt. Part of their ideas and practices depended on the supernatural, for it was felt that disease might be sent by the gods and could be removed by them. As a result, spells and incantations were freely used. They had, however, some genuine knowledge of drugs, although other substances that they administered seem to us to be without efficacy. The scanty records of medical practice make it plain that the physician had learned to examine his patient by questions, by ocular examination, and by palpation, and to record and compare symptoms. The Edwin Smith Papyrus shows that the Egyptians had attempted to consolidate their knowledge of the treatment of wounds resulting from war and accident. The Ebers Papyrus is a discussion of physiological matters, which in spite of its rational attitude, naturally suffers from the lack of exact physiological knowledge. But however far the medicine of this early period falls short of modern knowledge, it represents great advances in both attitude and knowledge.

Conclusion

The purpose of this summary of the culture of the Near East and Egypt to about 600 B.C. has been to emphasize the enormous progress made by the peoples of that region. Not only the brilliance of the Greeks, but also the congeniality of the Greek style and ours have tended to obscure somewhat the achievement of those who came before. In the twentieth century, the people of Egypt and the Near East have frankly acknowledged the superiority of the West in power and technical matters, and Westerners have as frankly thought of them as backward. Such attitudes are sometimes carried over and applied to earlier times in such a way as to cause an unduly high estimate of the contributions of the Greeks to Western civilization and an unduly low estimate of the contributions of their predecessors. The fact is that the Greeks and Romans made very few improvements upon the technology of Egypt and the Near East; here and there they even regressed. Although it is not the primary task of the historian to make judgments, in this case it seems that the comparison must be made for the sake of counteracting a somewhat unfair and widely disseminated opinion.

CHAPTER

9

THE NEAR EAST IN THE SIXTH CENTURY AND THE PERSIAN EMPIRE

By the sixth century B.C., the Greeks had already become a people and were involved in relations with Egypt and the Near East. In the next chapter, we shall move backward in time to the Minoan civilization of Crete and the early civilization of Greece. This Mycenaean civilization, as it was called, was followed by a dark age among the Greeks, from which they began to emerge in the ninth century B.C. In the meantime, some of them had emigrated to Asia Minor and settled along the coast. Thus, they form a part of the sixth-century scene. But before turning our full attention to them, we must consider the situation in Egypt after the fall of Assyria, the situation in Asia Minor after the fall of the Hittites, and the brief history of the Chaldaean or New Babylonian Empire, which controlled Mesopotamia after the fall of Assyria. All three of these regions came under the control of the empire of the Persians, which suddenly rose to power late in the sixth century.

Any intensive description of the Greeks, the first of the moderns of the West, must include their conflicts with the Persians and ultimately the conquests of Alexander the Great, which ended the Persian Empire. Thereafter, the Near East appears in our history as subject to the kings who succeeded Alexander or as provinces of the Romans,

131

who now and then had to reckon briefly with the Parthians and their successors, the New Persian Empire, on their eastern frontier.

It must be remembered that during a large part of the most brilliant history of Greece, many of the most civilized Greeks, those of Asia Minor, were under Persian control, and that the Persians dominated the rest of the Near East, a region of old and intense civilization. Although later these regions were not able to resist the Roman armies, they still were populous, rich, and civilized. Indeed, the Roman West probably never equalled the part of the Empire to the east in wealth and civilization. And when in the fifth century of the Christian era, the West finally slipped away into the hands of the Germans, the peoples of the East were able to maintain themselves as Romans. While the West was struggling through a long attempt to recover civilization, the peoples of the Near East, under the leadership of Byzantium, perpetuated their brilliant culture. Even though our emphasis falls first on the Greeks and still later on the Romans (with a brief mention of India and China in connection with the Roman Empire), we must not allow ourselves to forget how important the Near East has been during a large part of man's history.

EGYPT IN THE SIXTH CENTURY

The Assyrian Esarhaddon's conquest of Egypt in 669 B.C. did not last out the decade. By 662 the Egyptian Psamtik I (663–610 B.C.), whom the Greeks called Psammetichus, had so consolidated the power that he had gained over other aspiring lords that he was able to declare himself king. Presumably the Assyrians, who had demands on their energies in Babylonia, were glad enough to give up their claim to dominion in Egypt and tolerate a king who would be friendly to them.

Psamtik had been much helped in his rise by Greek mercenaries from the Ionian Greek cities of Asia Minor. In 650 B.C. or even earlier, a group of Greeks had established a trading place on one of the branches of the Nile in the Delta of Egypt, calling it "The Fort of the Milesians," Miletus being perhaps the most active and enterprising of all the cities on the coast of Asia Minor. The question of how much these early Greeks learned from the Egyptians in the intercourse that now became frequent is a difficult and disputed one.

It seems that we must believe that they learned something, yet it is very hard to establish that either the mechanic arts or the fine arts of Greece owed much to Egypt. Certainly the intellectual life of the Egyptians was too magic-ridden and too confused by their inability to discard anything once believed to have had any great appeal to the Greeks or taught them much.

After Psamtik's death, Necho II (609–595 b.c.) tried to repay the support (or tolerance) of the Assyrians by coming to their rescue against the Babylonian and Median alliance. In spite of a demonstration by Egyptian troops in Mesopotamia, Nineveh had already fallen. Now Necho tried to help the remnant of the Assyrians, but without success. He did manage to assert Egyptian dominion over part of Syria. But in 605 he was defeated at Carchemish, at the great upper bend of the Euphrates, by Nebuchadnezzar, the crown prince of Babylon, whose father's death then took him home to assume the throne. This defeat ended any hopes of Egyptian power in the region.

Although the political and military strength of Egypt no longer sufficed for empire, she was still able to prosper by virtue of her production of wheat and oil, her manufactures, and the gold from the regions of the south. Necho built (or repaired) a canal from the Nile to the Red Sea. He sent an expedition of Phoenician sailors to go down the Red Sea and keep on going to see if they could circumnavigate Africa. The brief account of their voyage that survives makes it seem that they really succeeded in doing so. He encouraged Greek merchants, who by now had superseded the Phoenicians in the waters of the Aegean and the Black Sea, although the Phoenicians may have been more active in the western Mediterranean.

The archaizing movement of this period is a fascinating and puzzling phenomenon. In art, for example, the style of the Old Kingdom was revived, sometimes illogically, as when an old funerary motif was copied on a small box having nothing to do with matters funerary. The "new" style was seen in many branches of art, from scarabs to larger achitectural decorations and statuary.

Further, the state officially sponsored the movement. Old Kingdom priesthoods, titles, and ranks were revived. All this, of course, went back to a far distant past, far beyond the glories of a Rameses who had flourished only six hundred years before. Perhaps this movement was a conscious attempt to provide a new set of ideals and aims and thus a new source of energy for a society bruised in spirit by the Assyrian conquest and conscious also that it had been through a period of some weakness and disorganization under the Nubian and Libyan dynasties. Every society must have some sort of image of itself or some ideal goal at which it aims. Occasionally a shrewd government succeeds in enlivening a people by creating completely new aspirations. More often, probably, there is a nominal return to a glorious earlier period while a practical-minded government is fully in touch with everything that is new and useful. In the Roman Empire, we shall see some interesting examples of manipulation of ideal goals, partly to speed recovery in times of stress and partly perhaps just because the old ideals had become a little tarnished and in need of refurbishing.

Amasis, who ruled Egypt from 569 to 527 b.c., began in a politic manner as the opponent of the Greeks in Egypt, for general feeling was strong against all foreigners. Gradually, however, he turned to the practical course of using the Greeks. He had a garrison of Greek mercenaries at Memphis to protect the capital. About 565 he gathered all the resident Greek merchants into a new extraterritorial city at Naucratis, in the Delta, presumably to keep them from being too much in the public eye in several places. Their trading brought wealth to Egypt, they helped him to keep in touch with affairs in the world outside, and they also kept in touch with sources of mercenary soldiers. It is interesting that he sent gifts to the Delphic Oracle, in Greece, of which we shall hear more later, presumably on the grounds that the priests of Delphi had already become extremely well informed about international affairs by learning what they could from the many people who came there for consultation.

When Amasis became king, the New Babylonian Empire under Nebuchadnezzar probably seemed the chief power of the world and a real threat to Egypt, because it claimed all the domain of Assyria. But the vigorous Nebuchadnezzar died in 562 and was replaced by a less aggressive king. Before long, however, Cyrus the Persian gained control of the Medes and showed the world that he was an active imperialist. The Egyptians, Babylonians, and Lydians made an alliance against him. In 547, however, Croesus of Lydia was conquered by Cyrus, and in 539 Babylon fell to him. Then Cyrus was succeeded by Cambyses, who conquered Egypt in 525 b.c.

Egypt was to be under the control of the Persians until its conquest by Alexander the Great in 332 B.C., although she more than once threw off Persian control temporarily. After the death of Alexander, his general, Ptolemy, gained control of Egypt. The Ptolemies governed the country with some success until 30 B.C., when the Ptolemaic queen Cleopatra died and her kingdom was taken by the Roman Octavian, soon to be known as Caesar Augustus. The Romans ruled Egypt until the end of the ancient world. In the seventh century, the Moslems took Egypt as they moved across North Africa toward Spain, and ancient Egypt gave place to medieval Egypt.

THE NEW BABYLONIAN (CHALDAEAN) EMPIRE

After Cyaxares the Mede and Nabopolassar, the Chaldaean king of Babylonia, had defeated the Assyrians, Babylonia's share of the territories of Assyria was Mesopotamia, Syria, and theoretically Egypt, while the Medes took the part lying north and east of the Tigris. Nabopolassar was succeeded in 605 B.C. by his son Nebuchadnezzar, a very able soldier and administrator, who was to rule until 562.

The colleges of priests were very powerful in Babylonia at this time, forming rich and privileged corporations. The fact that they could even challenge the power of the king is well worth the attention of the student of history. The methods by which such a group can exercise power are fairly obvious in general, although the particulars may vary from one age to another. Nebuchadnezzar took care not to offend the priests, acknowledged the power of the gods, and made rich gifts to them. After his death, the priests were able to take a hand in making and unmaking kings. When Babylon fell to Cyrus the Persian in 539, Cyrus did not attempt to upset the privileges of the priests, presumably feeling that his regime could avoid trouble by using their support. These same priests were still making astronomical observations and cultivating the pseudo-sciences of omens and astrology. Astrology presently was to have a huge growth.

The excavations of Babylon show that under Nebuchadnezzar it was a large city and had many brilliant features. We also have an enthusiastic description of it by the Greek historian Herodotus, a native of Halicarnassus on the coast of Asia Minor, who visited

Babylon about the middle of the fifth century. The walls of mud-brick were often covered with brilliantly colored tiles. One entered the city through the great double gate named for Ishtar, the goddess of love, and decorated with fine representations of dragons and bulls in colored enamel. From the gate one could go down the great processional street whose name reflected the fact that it was the route of the annual procession in honor of the god Marduk. The walls flanking the street were brilliantly decorated with enamelled pictures of lions. Of all the marvels of Babylon, however, the most famous was the Hanging Gardens, one of the seven wonders of the world, which Nebuchadnezzar built for his Median queen. The spirit of this child of the hill country grew weary at the everlasting flatness of the countryside of Babylon, and he built her a high place.

In the year 600 B.C., Nebuchadnezzar marched to take possession of Egypt, theoretically his after the defeat of the Assyrians, but he was turned back by the Egyptian army in a battle near the border and returned to Babylon. Perhaps this repulse encouraged Jehoiachim, king of Judah, to declare his freedom from Babylon. In any event, the kings of Israel or Judah had often before refused to bear the mild yoke of the great powers. This time, the frantic warnings of the prophet Jeremiah went unheeded, and the Babylonian king returned in 598 to besiege Jerusalem and take it in March, 597. The new king, Jehoiachin, was taken off to Babylon with great numbers of his people, and a puppet king, Zedekiah, was put on the throne. A find of tablets at Babylon shows that Jehoiachin was treated there as a lawful king who was being detained, and the writers of the Bible likewise continued to date events by the years of his reign, because he was still living and still regarded as king. Unfortunately, however, the Jewish people were led into revolt again shortly afterward. In 586 Jerusalem fell, and Nebuchadnezzar, determined to have done with such annoyances, ravaged the land. All over the region, archaeologists have found signs of fierce destruction that can be dated to this period.

The Babylonian Captivity

Presumably some of the humbler Jews who were taken off to Babylon with Jehoiachin were so weighed down by their grueling life of slavery that they had no energy left to think about the old country. Others who were not enslaved adapted themselves to the new situation and became Babylonians of whatever station was possible for them, often a reasonably comfortable one. There was, however, a group of the more important and intelligent people, able to live very well in Babylon and always in touch with one another, who were resolved to keep alive their faith and practices and who looked forward to the day of their restoration. The writings of the prophet Ezekiel and of the other prophet known as Deutero-Isaiah or Second Isaiah belong to this group and period. They exhort the people to take their misfortunes as the just retribution for the sinful ways of their nation, to stand by one another and their religion, and to await the day of their return. As such things go, the day of their deliverance was not long in coming—a mere forty-odd years.

After the death of King Nebuchadnezzar, the throne was held for short periods by two poorly qualified men and then by an amiable man favored by the priests, one Nabonidus. At this time, signs point to an antiquarian movement in Babylon, but one less clearly marked than in Egypt. Whether it was due to the priests or to the royal government is hard to tell. Our information about Nabonidus is somewhat ambiguous at best: it is not plain whether he was an ineffectual antiquarian or a man of some parts and a lively freethinker, but it is certain that he was not so buried in thoughts of the past as scholars once supposed. Before the end of his reign, he associated his son Belshazzar with him, and it was Belshazzar who was actually in charge in Babylon on that famous occasion when the handwriting was said to have appeared on the wall to announce to him that he had been weighed in the balance and found wanting—on the night in 539 B.C. when the troops of Cyrus the Persian entered the city.

Cyrus soon issued an edict of toleration that made it possible for the Jews to return to Judea, as their territory should now be called. A rather small number did go back. Restoration was a slow business, for many people preferred not to undertake the difficult task of restoring the old ways, and there was opposition from those who had taken up the land left vacant by those carried off into exile. After some painful vicissitudes, the faithful few succeeded, about 516 B.C., in rebuilding the Temple. This was only a minimum of achievement, however. The Jewish community was still small and could not draw to itself many of those who should have been its members.

The scribe Ezra and the administrator Nehemiah succeeded in reinvigorating their people somewhere around the last half of the fifth century and the beginning of the fourth (the closest that we can come to their dates). The Persian king had authorized Ezra, an important man among the Jews of Babylon, to return to Judea and reorganize his people there, a task that he accomplished with remarkable success. He brought back the early sacred writings that were to be formed into the Pentateuch (the first five books of the Bible) and expounded them to the people. There was a great revival of religious feeling and a wave of desire for the restoration of the old ways. Feeling was so strong that Ezra finally ordered every marriage of a Jew with a non-Jewish woman to be dissolved. Although it was a logical move for the restoration of a strong Jewish people, there was great opposition, but Ezra persisted. These new religious tendencies included no proselyting; the Jews were content to hold their own people together without campaigning for new members.

Nehemiah, who also figured in this restoration, was a cup-bearer of the Persian king. He asked to be sent to Jerusalem with extraordinary powers, chiefly because a movement to rebuild the walls had been denounced to the king as a preliminary to rebellion. Nehemiah, although he defended the reconstruction, was, like Ezra, appreciative of the sober and tolerant Persian government and intended to be loyal to it. His achievement was to set up, with some difficulty, a theocratic administration in Judea under the Persian government that was to last until the Hellenistic period, which followed the death of Alexander the Great in 323 B.C. The High Priest governed under the Persian government and under the Law of Moses. Below him were both a civil administration and a temple administration. Naturally the two branches were jealous of each other and managed to create trouble, but not enough to keep the government from functioning successfully.

Thus, Ezra supplied a new devotion to an old way of life, and Nehemiah supplied an administrative system that worked. These two, with the group who had stayed loyal to the faith of their fathers, may be said to have saved the Jewish people as a society from the real danger of disintegration, in the exact sense of that word.

THE PHRYGIANS

Until this time, the only people of Asia Minor to merit our attention were the Hittites. They were to be succeeded in central Asia Minor by the Phrygians, who apparently came from Thrace and northern Macedonia and seem to have formed part of the great movement of peoples who destroyed the Hittite Empire and swept on toward Egypt around 1200 B.C. The Phrygians cannot be said to have appropriated all that the Hittites had had, for much of the country remained in the hands of smaller Hittite kingdoms, and the high culture of the Hittites was apparently too complex for the Phrygians to assimilate quickly. They settled in the middle of Asia Minor, little by little consolidating a powerful kingdom and learning the more civilized ways of people in this part of the world.

The Phrygian capital was Gordium (or Gordion, to spell it more nearly in the Greek than in the Latinized style), about seventy miles southwest of the modern Ankara. A number of their kings seem to have been named Midas, as in the familiar tale of the Midas to whom the god granted that everything he touched should turn to gold. In the legend, he finally asks the god's permission to rid himself of his embarrassing power by washing his hands in the headwaters of a river, which becomes golden when he does so. Perhaps some of the rivers did carry gold dust, but the real source of Phrygian gold was their mines. In addition, this part of Asia Minor is good for agriculture, and in those days it was strategically situated for trade. The Phrygians prospered mightily.

In recent decades, the city of Gordium, like so many sites of Asia Minor, has been explored by the archaeologists, whose discoveries show that for about fifty years the Phrygian kingdom enjoyed a golden age. But there are plain traces, too, of the disaster that then overwhelmed Gordium and presumably the whole kingdom. The Phrygians were overrun in 696 B.C. by the Cimmerians, a people of the rough and ready type that they themselves had been more than five hundred years before. Although we shall hear again of Cimmerian incursions into Asia Minor, it is impossible to say with any definiteness who they were and where they were generally settled.

The relation of the Greek cities of the coast to the old civilizations of Mesopotamia and the Hittites is a difficult and elusive subject.

The Greeks seem to have been rather slow in learning what the peoples of the interior had to teach them. The excavations in Phrygia yield little evidence of intercourse between Phrygians and Greek coastal cities, and we may perhaps assume that until their fall, the Phrygians barred the Greeks from intercourse with the people farther east.

THE LYDIANS

After the great disaster of the Phrygians, the ascendancy in Asia Minor passed to the Lydians, whose capital was at Sardis, not far from the coast. By now we are concerned with a part of history recorded by Herodotus, the fascinating Greek of Halicarnassus, who tells us a great deal about early events in Asia Minor as a preliminary to his account of the great struggle between the Persians and the Greeks of the mainland. Gyges was the first of the line of Lydian kings described by Herodotus; he acquired the throne about 685 B.C. by a more than dubious piece of dealing, and it is interesting that he sent to Greece to consult the Delphic Oracle about the whole matter.

The kingdom of Lydia grew rapidly in wealth and power in spite of one or two very damaging raids by the Cimmerians. It controlled the gold and silver deposits, the rich agricultural country, and trade routes from the coast into Asia Minor. The first kings only raided the Greek cities periodically. Later arrangements brought the cities more or less contentedly under Lydian control. Trade was good in the seaport cities; they had access to the wool and woven goods and the other and varied manufactures of the interior, and they sent their ships to the territories that produced grain, fish, timber, and wrought steel on the shores of the Black Sea, to Egypt, and to Greece proper.

Croesus of Lydia, like Midas of Phrygia, still symbolizes the wealthy king. But he was the fifth of the Lydian royal line, counting from Gyges, and as Herodotus tells the story, the Delphic Oracle had predicted that the fifth of the line would meet with disaster because of the violent manner in which Gyges had seized the throne. Croesus could see Cyrus the Persian as a menace far off on the horizon of his political thinking. After some thought and inquiry, including, according to Herodotus, several consultations with the Delphic

Oracle, he decided to move across the Halys River toward Cyrus. Nearly fifty years earlier, in 585 B.C., the Medes and the Lydians had decided to terminate their territorial dispute by putting their common boundary at the Halys, which flows northward through Asia Minor into the Black Sea. As we shall see, Cyrus learned that Croesus had crossed the river and was trying to establish a hold on that part of Median land, which the Persian now believed to be his. The Persians conquered the Lydians in 547 B.C., and Asia Minor, including the Greek cities of the coast, was to remain in their possession until the conquests of Alexander, a little more than two hundred years later. There is every indication that it was a time of reasonable, although not unbroken, peace and great prosperity for the whole region.

THE RISE OF PERSIA

Early Times

The peoples from whom the Persian Empire was to develop probably drifted in from farther east about 1500 B.C., occupying the Iranian plateau, which stretches eastward from Mesopotamia to the Indus River. They called themselves Aryans and their language Aryan; the country was called "Land of the Aryans," or Iran, as it is nowadays.

The Medes and the Persians were the most important of these new peoples. For a long time the Medes played the largest role, and their king ruled over a loose federation of other groups from his capital in the north, which was later to be known as Ecbatana, one of the capitals of the Persian Empire. The Persians were settled in the south, near where the kingdom of Elam had been, to the east of lower Mesopotamia. Elam appears often in the history of Assyria, for her kings often incited the Babylonians to resist the Assyrians. For one or two short periods, Elam had enjoyed considerable power, but finally, in the seventh century B.C. the Assyrians had destroyed the country and left it unpopulated. The Persians had taken advantage of the opportunity to occupy some former Elamite territory.

The Medes and the Persians lived a simple life, largely pastoral, because the agricultural possibilities of their country were limited.

They had no important cities. In the ninth century, both peoples appear in the Assyrian annals in connection with the Assyrian campaigns against the peoples along their eastern frontier.

It was Cyaxares the Mede who joined with Nabopolassar of Babylon to take Nineveh in 612 B.C. and thus end the empire of the Assyrians. The Medes took the Assyrian territory on their side of the Tigris, while the spoil of the Babylonians was the Assyrian territory in Mesopotamia and a claim on Egypt. At this time, the Medes still enjoyed the leadership of the whole group, but that situation was changed by the energy of Cyrus the Persian. About 559 B.C., he became king of the Persians, owing fealty to the king of the Medes. Two years later he had reversed their positions; Persia was now the suzerain of the Medes. People still spoke, however, of the Medes and the Persians.

The Medes and Persians belong to a large and loose group of people whom we call Indo-Europeans. The basic resemblance between their languages points to a common origin or at least to residence near one another at an early stage in the formation of language. We can be sure of the affinity of the languages; we cannot be sure of the affinity of the people. Such common words as "father" and "mother," all belonging to an early stage of civilization, tend to be alike in these languages. One group of Indo-European languages belongs to India and others to peoples found in the Near East: Hittites, Medes, and Persians. The branches of the Greek language form another group in this linguistic system, as do the Italic, Slavic, Germanic, and Celtic.

Existing alongside the Indo-European languages of the Near East are the Semitic languages; here, too, are a number of distinguishable languages with strong similarities. The Akkadians and Assyrians were the great Semitic peoples of Mesopotamia. In Syria and Palestine, the Hebrews and the Canaanites and Aramaeans, their neighbors and rivals, represent this group. The Egyptians belonged to another category, the Hamites.

Persia Becomes an Empire

Cyrus, having learned that Croesus of Lydia had crossed the Halys River into the territory that once belonged to Media, set out from his Median capital of Ecbatana in 547 B.C. on a great tour of conquest and organization in the northwest. He secured the territory of Assyria proper, which had recently been under the dominion of the Medes, and moved westward into Asia Minor. The kingdoms of Cilicia and Cappadocia prudently put themselves under his protection, and, as we have seen, he conquered Croesus in 547 B.C. and annexed the kingdom of Lydia. At the same time, the Armenians decided to acknowledge the power of Persia and were made into a satrapy, or province.

The Greeks who had settled the good harbor sites along the coast of Asia Minor had long profited by their trade in the kingdom of Lydia despite the fact that nominally they were not free, but under the domination of King Croesus. Cyrus offered them a reasonable arrangement, which they refused as not being up to their expectations. Finally he decided that he would have to take them by force. His task was made easier by their failure to combine for resistance. The people of Miletus had made their peace with him at the outset. Those of Phocaea, on the other hand, decided to emigrate and one night sailed away to the West. Some of this group lost their nerve and returned to be Persian subjects, but the rest at last settled in Italy, and there we shall meet them again among the forerunners of the Romans.

The rest of the Greek cities were either destroyed or subjugated. In what was to become typical Greek fashion, they not only failed to unite but also produced a crop of traitors who sold out to the Persians either for money or for a position of some advantage in the new regime. The change of masters was to prove no great disadvantage to these Greek cities, however, for the new empire offered them a field for profitable trading. Under the Persians, they were generally governed by "tyrants," members of the commercial class unhampered by the ideas of patriotism or status that kept the old aristocracy from accepting such appointments from the Persians.

Now Cyrus turned to the conquest of his Iranian relatives to the east and made a swing through lands of Asia which still have a romantic sound to Western ears. Sogdia lay between the Oxus and Jaxartes Rivers, and its capital, Maracanda, was later to be the golden storied city, Samarkand. Cyrus moved across the plateaus and the rivers and the rich oases of this region as far as the boundary of India.

Bactria was the easternmost province; it was to be a notable outpost of Western influence after Alexander the Great took over the Persian Empire and brought many Greeks into it.

At this time, Babylon was the greatest fortress of the world, and Cyrus had hitherto passed it by. Now he began to feel that his affairs were in order elsewhere and that he could turn to the subjection of this great city and its region. There is room for suspicion that it was the priests of Babylon who really saw the handwriting on the wall and read it as meaning that Cyrus was certain to be the king of Babylon soon. His armies were able to enter the city without striking a blow. The priests were confirmed in all their properties and privileges, possibly as a reward for disloyalty rather than as a result of religious tolerance. Such tolerance was the Persian policy, however, strikingly manifested in connection with the Jews. In the year 538 B.C., an edict was published in Aramaean (the official language of the Persians for business in the western satrapies) decreeing that the Temple in Jerusalem should be re-established. But despite this policy, as we have seen, the restoration of the Jewish people was to be a long and arduous task rather than the immediate result of a Persian royal decree.

In 530 B.C., Cambyses succeeded his father on the throne. His great project was to conquer Egypt; by 525 the conquest was complete. Furthermore, the Greeks of Cyrene, to the west on the African coast, submitted to his power. Cambyses thought of moving still farther westward to conquer the North African empire of Carthage. The Phoenicians, who had yielded to the Persians with their usual indifference to the notion of sovereignty and their usual interest in possibilities for commerce, were to transport the troops in their ships. But they now showed another side, an extreme stubbornness about unreasonable demands from the great powers whose protection they were already paying for. They refused to move against their fellow Phoenicians in Carthage.

THE RELIGION OF ZOROASTER

The religion of the Persians was based on recognizing and placating the forces of Nature, as was customary among ancient peoples. As usual, there was a chief god, called Ahurah. Mithras, who was conceived as the sun, was worshipped for a long time and was still a religious factor much later when Christianity was about to triumph.

Against this not uncommon background the great mystic and religious teacher Zoroaster worked. He cannot be said to have transformed it. Although his *Gathas,* the verses that contain his visions and his teaching, came to form part of the *Avesta,* the sacred book of the Persians, Zoroaster himself was never universally honored as a prophet, as for example Mohammed was, and his teachings never met with either popular or official acceptance. Nevertheless, his thought was to have a great influence, one that is still active in the twentieth century.

Zoroaster refused to recognize the manifold divinities of Nature, asserting that there is only the lord Ahurah-Mazda, god of all the universe, who represents the principle of light and Goodness. This god had an entourage of ten vaguely conceived attributes, including Righteousness, Good Thought, Piety, Salvation, Obedience, and Fire. This grouping of abstractions often occurred in religions of the Near East and was to continue even in early Christianity. For example, in Irenaeus' *Against the Heresies,* an authoritative Christian work of the second cenutry of our era, fanciful groupings of just this sort appear, which heretics had proposed as Christian theology.

Zoroaster dismissed the other gods of common belief as *daevas,* or demons. Naturally he could not claim that they did not exist. The Christians were to have the same difficulty later with their assertion of monotheism. Any suggestion that nature gods of the Persians or the gods worshipped when the Romans came to power did not exist was countered by the believer with the simple answer that everyone knew that there was evidence that they did. Easier than denying them was asserting that what seemed to be gods were demons, or spirits, who had no powers comparable to the powers of God, yet could be active for evil.

The Devil is a necessary part of a sound theology. Zoroaster apparently was the first to assert that there is a principle of evil that makes itself felt in the world. He called it Ahriman. It had nothing in common with the lord Ahurah-Mazda; in fact, between the two there was a fight to the finish. In this theology, that finish was fore-shadowed: the victory of Light over Darkness. Zoroaster believed that no man can escape making the great moral choice, that he must march under one banner or the other and in the end suffer judgment for his life and receive his reward or his punishment.

Zoroaster may have lived as early as 1000 B.C. or as late as about 600 B.C. Whenever he lived, he left his thought as a legacy that was to be appropriated in different ways by different people at different times, as is generally the case with any creative and really significant intellectual contribution. In the main, the Persians themselves seem to have been most influenced by the idea of the great dualism. For the rest, their working religion remained much as it had been.

There is reason to believe that Persian religious ideas led to certain developments within Judaism and thus to some of the conditions that gave rise to Christianity. Again, these ideas seem to have had some influence on Islam. Even now there are some few followers of Zoroaster in Persia and India.

DARIUS THE GREAT AND HIS EMPIRE

His Rise

The spectacular story of the rise of Darius the Great offers examples of the difficulties of orderly government in the ancient Near East. As has been said, the persistent problem of regulating the succession to the throne was very difficult for these people. When Cambyses died in 522 B.C. on his way home from his conquest of Egypt, there had undoubtedly been foul play. We cannot be sure now whether Cambyses had secretly killed his brother Bardiya before he left for Egypt, as one tradition has it, and whether it was a pretender who now, in the spring of 522, proclaimed his rule as Bardiya or Bardiya himself. Whoever the man was, he gathered enough support to make himself king in fact in Media and Persia. We are told that he gained great favor by letting it be known that he would be less tyrannical than Cambyses had been and by remitting tribute and military levies for the next three years, thus making a contrast with Cambyses' exactions for his campaign in Egypt.

Darius was twenty-eight years old at this time and had been in the entourage of Cambyses in Egypt. Although his family belonged to the nonruling branch of the royal house, in the most practical sense he was born to rule, for he was the sort of person who by nature manages other people and administers affairs. Within a few months and with the aid of six noble Persians, he had slain the usurper of Cambyses' throne and gained control of the government of Persia. Then he had to face a series of revolts in the eastern part of the empire; before he was through he even had to face a revolt in Persia itself. Fortunately he was able to handle these outbreaks in succession and did not have to struggle with any combination of those who opposed him. The personal ambitions of the satraps may have had much to do with the revolts, but they were not the only cause. There was a feeling in Media, for example, that the old supremacy of the Medes should be re-established. The Armenians may have been aiming at complete independence. The Babylonians seem to have wished to set up a king of their old line and be independent. The Lydians and the Egyptians, however, made no attempt to throw off their new yoke, and to the Phoenicians it probably seemed a good protective arrangement rather than a burden. In any event, the next year, 521, Darius had the whole Persian Empire in hand again. It was he who put on the Behistun Rock the story of his rise to power which was discussed in Chapter Three.

THE ORGANIZATION OF THE PERSIAN EMPIRE

Darius was to rule from 521 until 486 B.C. In this time, he perfected an organization that was already well begun. At the head was the king, a hereditary monarch who ruled by the grace of Ahurah-Mazda or, in other lands, Amun, Marduk, or whatever divinity was thought to dispense grace to monarchs. The king's word was law, but only within the framework of what his men of law told him was "the law of the Medes and Persians, which changeth not," or the custom of the country, or the law or the custom of one of the countries that had been made a part of the Persian Empire.

The new empire had a choice between attempting a program that would direct all men's loyalties toward one set of goals and one that would allow them various goals under the protection of one government. The Persians preferred to be tolerant of differences of every kind except those which might break the peace or lead to rebellion. In religion they were entirely tolerant. Furthermore, they were willing to have justice administered according to local custom. They did not, however, allow the local rulers to continue as client kings. Deposed sovereigns were treated with the respect due their station, as Nebuchadnezzar of Babylon had treated Jehoiachin of Judah, but they were firmly cut off from their people. We must not attribute too much mildness and humanity to the Persians, however; punishment was inhumane in the extreme, whether inflicted on rebellious satraps or common criminals or political enemies. Mutilation and impalement, for instance, were common.

Persia stood firmly at the center of the whole governmental organization. She was not taxable. Efforts were made to preserve the rugged breed of citizen soldiers who, with the Medes, still made up the solid part of the army. Many of the soldiers whom the subject peoples had to provide were of good quality, but many others were mere rabble. There was an attempt, too, to preserve the slightly unsophisticated virtues of the nobility, on whom the government had to rely to staff important positions in the army and the civil service. Herodotus tells us that the essentials of their education were learning to ride, to shoot with the bow, and to speak the truth.

The royal roads were an essential part of imperial management, although how much work was done on grading or surfacing is not known. About every twelve or thirteen miles there was an imperial station, sometimes with an inn. There were horses at each station, and messages could be passed along just as they were by the pony-express system of Wells, Fargo & Co. Whereas the ordinary traveler might take ninety days to get from the coast at Ephesus to the royal city of Susa, the imperial post could probably do it in a week.

There were twenty subdivisions of the government, called satrapies and governed by satraps, a word which means "protector of the realm." The twenty satraps were at first chosen from the noble Persians, but eventually their office seems to have become hereditary, as did the office of nomarch in Egypt. Nonetheless, the central government was able to exert sufficient control over the satraps to keep the Empire together, even though it sometimes allowed them great freedom—to the point of making war on one another.

The satrap was almost independent. His state was elevated, and he might revel in pomp. Always, however, he must have been conscious that he had a secretary and a local military commander who were independent of him and whose duty it was to make regular reports to the king. He also received periodic visits from the king's "eyes and ears," traveling inspectors whom presumably the satrap could not coerce or bribe. The satrap's duty was to keep the peace, administer justice, and get the taxes in. He could use his discretion, but was expected not to outrage local feelings or customs and not to oppress the people financially or otherwise.

CHAPTER

10

THE BEGINNINGS OF THE GREEKS

THE GEOGRAPHICAL BACKGROUND

If Greece proper can be called the chief home of the ancient people whom we know as the Greeks, there were also many other places in which they were the leading inhabitants. They were in the islands of the Aegaean and on the coast of Asia Minor, in the islands to the west of Greece around the entrance to the Adriatic Sea, in southern Italy and in Sicily, and in southern France (where Marseilles now is), and in other smaller settlements. In all these places there was a certain similarity of living conditions because all were strongly influenced by their nearness to the Mediterranean. The Greeks, like the Phoenicians, tended to expand into those places where they could find the climate and agricultural conditions to which they were accustomed.

The climate of Greece is subtropical. Although there is much snow in the mountains, it is not common down at sea level. The summers can be hot, but they are often tempered by grateful breezes and are never so hot as in some other places inhabited by the ancient peoples, like Mesopotamia. All around the Mediterranean the climate is suitable for those great gifts of Nature, the olive tree and the vine. In the flatter areas, the cereals can be grown, often with a rainfall that to Americans would seem very scanty.

The weather is generally brighter than that in continental Europe and the United States, especially during the winter. The appeal of sunshine after the fogs and damps of winter, which nowadays draws so many vacationists toward the Mediterranean, may well have attracted the northern people of that day, who often migrated en masse to invade Greece or Italy. Those from damper and greener lands are likely to find the clearer air and the sharper outlines of the landscape around the Mediterranean beautiful and stimulating.

Even though Greece proper and the islands offered only a fair living, they seem to have provided good breeding conditions in antiquity. The Greeks spread far and wide around the shores of their sea. In the dark days after the fall of Mycenae, as we shall see, there was an emigration to Asia Minor. Again in the eighth and seventh centuries B.C., there was a great movement of colonization to Sicily and South Italy, and the Greeks of Asia Minor sent out settlers to the shores of the Black Sea. Before Alexander the Great conquered the Persian Empire in the late 300's, there were a good many Greek mercenaries and traders in the Persian territory; and after Alexander's conquest there were fine opportunities for a great many Greeks in the army, the administration, and commerce all through his realm in the Near East. Again, when Rome became the mistress of the world and the city of Rome became the world's greatest city, Greeks from all over the Mediterranian world came there in great numbers. When Rome's western territories slowly slipped away into the hands of the Germans toward 500 A.D., knowledge of the Greek language slowly faded in the West; but in the East, civilization was carried on by the Greek and Christian Byzantine Empire.

THE GREEK CHARACTER

It is difficult to assign precise traits of character to the Greek people in such circumstances—if indeed one can ever generalize about national characteristics. The ancient Greeks lived in a wide variety of places and over many centuries. They did great things in many widely differing fields and rather unfortunate things in a few ways. Probably no people has ever scored so many triumphs of the intellect, but the Greeks also had their intellectual slums where astrology and cheap literature and quack philosophers were to be found. The

Greek city state could sometimes be a brilliant example of how well men can manage their political affairs. In it, on the other hand, the mob could also commit political crimes, and traitors could betray their fellow citizens for money, position, or revenge.

We shall therefore avoid sweeping statements about the Greek character. As the tale of their activities is unfolded, it will be possible to make some limited and cautious generalizations. There are many aspects and many nuances to the long story of this fascinating people. The Greeks are more interesting if we do not insist on disregarding their variety and their genuine inconsistencies and contradictions.

THE DRIFT TO THE WEST

We return now to about 3000 B.C., a time when civilization had made good progress in Sumeria and Egypt, when the rest of the Near East was well advanced in the Neolithic Age and about to enter upon the use of copper. We shall examine the progress of civilization in the area of the Aegaean Sea, where the Greeks developed under the influence of the great peoples whom we already have studied. This influence was also being exerted in other directions, of course— southward from Egypt and up into the highlands from Mesopotamia.

The archaeologists, whose investigations in this area constantly spread into new areas and search for evidences of the prehistoric as well as the historic, have found that about 3000 B.C. men in the early bronze stage from Asia Minor, Syria, and Palestine drifted westward to the smaller islands of the Aegaean, to the larger island of Crete, and to the mainland of Greece. Some of the finds suggest that there were later waves of immigration into the islands. Archaeology also establishes tentatively that around 1900 B.C. a new wave of people arrived in Greece proper from somewhere in the East. These were the Greeks. A completely new type of pottery, known as Minyan ware, appeared in Greece at about that time. Similar ware is found in the remains of Troy and farther east. A good case has been made out for the movement of a group of people toward the west from somewhere around Asia Minor, for the settlement of some of them at what we know as Troy, and for the settlement of a certain number of others in northern Greece. It is probable that this was the last considerable movement of new peoples into the circle of the Aegaean world.

Formerly it was supposed that all the people of Greece entered it from the north and by land. Some scholars believe that the evidence of the excavations, although equivocal, leaves a possibility that important elements in the population came from the basin of the Danube. Other scholars hold that there is no evidence for such an immigration, especially if it be assumed that the people came from the region of the Danube.

THE GREAT CENTERS

Cnossus

The story of three centers, Cnossus, Mycenae, and Troy, will illustrate the history of this period between 3000 and 1200 B.C. Cnossus was on the north shore of Crete, Mycenae in the Peloponnesus, or southern part of Greece, and Troy in Asia Minor, commanding the entrance to the Hellespont (the modern Dardanelles). Mycenae and Troy were strongly fortified; no remains of fortifications for the brilliant palace at Cnossus have been found. There are a great many other centers of the same kind, but not so large and rich and without the suggestion of power radiating from them to some distance. Essentially each of these three was the residence and office building of the head of the people, surrounded by houses for military aides and merchants.

Sir Arthur Evans' excavations at the begining of this century at Cnossus, on the north shore of Crete, were among the most spectacular of archaeological operations. The clearing and partial restoration of the great palace gave a new picture of a large building other than a temple. The palace, which belonged to the fifteenth century B.C. was very different from those of Mesopotamia, and, of course, quite unlike the mud-brick palace of Amenhotep III at Thebes, the only one to have been found in Egypt. At Cnossus, the wall frescoes and the small objects that were found gave a new picture, too, a picture of a civilization that resembled the Egyptian in its refined cheerfulness, but had marked differences. Of course, many other sites on Crete have been and are being excavated.

It will be well to remind ourselves before we go further with the history of Crete that the establishment of historical periods in the Aegaean area is a complex task. It is done chiefly by the stratigraphic study of pottery, as is the case in Palestine. The first step is to excavate and find pottery and other objects on Aegaean sites. This process goes on from year to year, of course, and new finds are continually being added to our collections even while the old materials are being studied, restudied, and debated.

The next step is to attempt to establish a sequence for the pottery and other objects uncovered in a given limited area. Stratigraphy is very important; that is, indications of relative age come from the fact that different strata of the excavation yield different objects, those buried deepest being oldest. Careful reporting makes it possible to know in what context each object was found. Little by little archaeologists have taught themselves to work out sequences of styles, following the slow and conservative changes of styles of ancient peoples. This is easier if some pottery is found unbroken, but much can be done even though all is in fragments. The pottery from the many sites of Crete may be taken as a whole for this purpose, and by now there is fair agrement on the sequence in which the different kinds found in Crete were made. The pottery found on the mainland of Greece has proved susceptible to arrangement in such a sequence, as has the special class of pottery found at Mycenae.

The next step is to attempt to establish some relation between the local sequences. For instance, we shall see that the kind of Mycenaean pottery present in Homer's Troy when it was destroyed was present in a Mycenae that was flourishing and powerful. Whenever possible, a great deal of work is done to establish correspondences between the local sequences. A man who engages in this work must have tremendous knowledge of the excavation reports and be able to remember, for instance, that Cretan ware of a certain type is found in Egypt in conjunction with certain Egyptian objects and at perhaps twenty-five minor spots around the Aegaean in conjunction with Mycenaean ware of a certain type and perhaps now and then in conjunction with Phoenician things.

The styles on Crete are divided into Early, Middle, and Late Minoan, each of which comes to be referred to as a period of time. "Minoan" comes from Minos, the name of the kings of Crete. In the Cyclades Islands of the Aegaean, the styles are called Cycladic. On the Greek mainland, they are called Helladic, with Mycenaean as a special group. We may refer, for instance, to Late Helladic II to

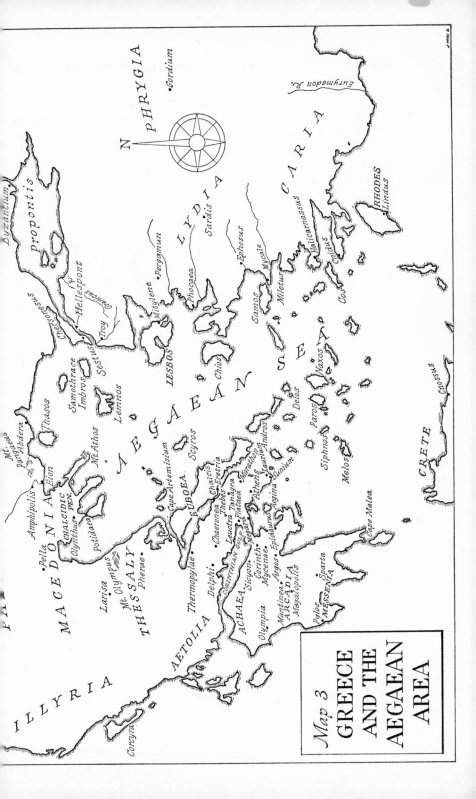

Map 3

GREECE AND THE AEGAEAN AREA

specify a style of pottery and therefore a time period. It has been possible to assign approximate dates to all these periods according to our system of years before the birth of Christ, always with the understanding that these dates are approximations, even when for convenience they are given as exact dates. Our ability to tie all these periods, based on sequences of pottery styles, to our absolute chronology results from a modicum of certainty about some Egyptian dates, at least when we get down as late as 1500 B.C., and more certainty when we get below 1000 B.C.

From about 2100 on (to return to our story) trade was lively about the Aegaean Sea. Thereafter, the influence of Egypt in Crete became increasingly important, as we can see from Egyptian objects of art, chiefly jewelry, that have been found in Crete, and from the Egyptian note in Cretan work. Doubtless the Middle Kingdom had ideas as well as goods to export to the Cretans; this sort of influence is much harder to trace.

As the period of strong Egyptian impact continued, the Cretan civilization reached its own maturity. Objects of art show that the Cretan workmen developed a style of their own. Apparently, too, the merchants learned to sail the sea in ships of their own, even to Egypt, and began to carry on trade with Byblos and Ugarit, on the Syrian coast. The wealth and power of the Cretans increased. A shift to the north coast of the zone of most extensive building suggests that trade with the region north of them, which later was very important, may have begun. At this time certain peculiar features of the culture—for example, the great palaces, the Cretan style of pictographic writing, and their own style of clothes and implements—made their appearance. We can see, too, that the culture of Cnossus became more advanced as compared with that of the rest of Crete.

The height of the Minoan civilization, as the civilization of Crete is called, was reached between 1600 and 1400 B.C. The most striking evidence of Cretan wealth and power at that time is what remains of the palace at Cnossus. It was located a few miles from the sea, and there are no traces of fortifications and none at the port around it. Scholars (with some dissenters) have generally concluded from the facts that the Cretans did rule the waves at this time, as later Greeks believed that they had done. That is, their navy made their cities safe without fortifications. The palace was set on a small hill in a valley where the larger hills slope toward the sea. Such a site is suited to a fortress, for one may expect to dig a well down through the hill and find underground water. Indeed, the palace at Cnossus was well supplied with water, even to having bathrooms with drains.

The building was large, complex, and well constructed. The masonry is excellent. There are dwelling apartments, rooms of state, a throne room, and a great many service rooms and storerooms. Later Greek legend told of a labyrinth in Crete where one could readily get lost; it is easy to see that such a story could have grown up from simple people's having seen the palace of Cnossus.

Today, there are remains of other dwellings, and representations of houses on fayence tiles have been found. Apparently two- and three-story dwellings were not uncommon. Even in some of the smaller towns (which had no fortifications either) there were comfortable houses of more than one story. Some of these towns must have looked much as the little island villages of the Aegaean still look, with houses close together and rising in tiers from the edge of the water.

The frescoes, reliefs, statuettes, and jewelry give us a picture of a luxurious and gay life. There are representations of people gathered about a small sports arena, where the women apparently joined the men. They were slim, long-legged people, who wore their hair long and gave it some attention. They did not have the strong sense of modesty about their bodies that was common in the Near East. The men wore light and short clothes. The women wore skirts that are suggestive of the modern skirt and bodices cut low enough to show off the breasts. Another set of scenes shows the revels when the harvest is in. There are scenes of boxing matches and of group dances. Most unusual are the representations of male and female athletes who meet a charging bull, grasp his horns, and vault over to the bull's back as he throws up his head.

The symbolism of the bull in Minoan civilization is pervasive and not entirely clear. According to legend, the Athenian Theseus went to Crete when the annual group of seven youths and seven maidens was sent to be sacrificed to the Minotaur, who was a creature half man and half bull, the result of the unnatural lust of the Minoan queen for a bull. Theseus is said to have gone into the labyrinth where the creature lived and slain it. The story may go back to a time when mainland centers owed dues of some sort to the Cretans, and perhaps a group of youngsters to be trained for the dangerous bull-leaping was sent every year. Theseus' slaying the Minotaur may symbolize the mainland's freeing itself from the domination of Crete. We do know that the bull played a role in the Minoan religion. If, as has been suggested, the monarch wore a bull mask in some ceremonies, perhaps those of sacrifice, we can see how a legend might have grown up about a creature who was half man and half bull and destroyed the young people sent to Crete.

The religion of the Minoans was more a matter of awe and worship than of fear and propitiation. Their good cheer and love of beauty is manifest in the material remains of their religion. We have several statuettes of the female divinity who seems to have been the chief object of worship. Nothing could be less forbidding, for she is often represented as a most gracious and winsome lady in the dress of a fashionable Minoan. Often, snakes are shown with her ; one of the most attractive statuettes shows her holding a pair. The bull and the dove also appear with her. Not uncommonly, she is shown against an attractive background of trees and birds, and she has the youthful male consort whom great female divinities often have. Possibly the king was regarded as divine and the name Minos was not an individual name, but the cult-name of every king. In the Greek tradition, at least, this name is always given to the ruler of Crete.

For a long time the Cretan workmen had been learning from those of Egypt. At the height of Minoan civilization they had become extremely skillful. The builders did beautiful work. Large as the palace of Cnossus is, however, we cannot call it monumental; in fact, no trace remains of anything anywhere in Crete that can be called monumental. There are no great temples, but there are small shrines in palaces and houses. There was no tendency to bigness in statues or pictures. Everything was to be enjoyed on an intimate scale, not as a public display or as a symbol of royal power. The workmen whom we should call artists did felicitous work in all the minor fields and were especially happy in drawing themes from Nature—flowers and trees, animals and fish—and in giving them a curious light and delicate quality.

We must assume that trade was the chief source of the wealth of the kings of Crete. The period of Minoan bloom was the same as that of imperial greatness in Egypt. There must have been a steady trade in both directions. Two frescoes in Egyptian tombs show what seem to be people in Minoan clothes carrying goods of Minoan workmanship. The almost total absence of Minoan pottery from the excavations in Egypt seems to constitute a fairly good argument from silence that Crete did not ship oil or wine in pots to Egypt, for even if pots break, the fragments still are almost indestructible and turn up somewhere. But Crete was capable of shipping timber, hides, meat, and fruit to Egypt.

We can only guess at the extent of the carrying trade. It may be that the Cretan mariners touched the ends of land routes down which came Bohemian tin or other products. They may have carried such raw materials as timber from different places to Egypt. The fact that the place-name Minoa has survived to modern times in a number of Aegaean sites suggests that they had commercial stations here and there. In addition, they must have done a good deal of carrying goods to places other than Egypt, for example to Byblos and Ugarit.

As they themselves had been influenced by Egypt, so they exerted an influence on others, especially on the people of the Greek mainland. Mycenae in the Peloponnesus (that part of Greece which is below the Gulf of Corinth) was the most important of the places in Greece to feel the Minoan influence.

For a short time at the end of the great period of Crete, from about 1450 to 1400 B.C., it is plain that a somewhat different culture flourished at Cnossus, one that now had many marked points of difference from that of the rest of Crete and many signs of contact with the culture that had developed at Mycenae. A suggestion made some years ago that the Mycenaeans managed to gain control of Cnossus and a little territory around it at this time has recently been confirmed by the decipherment of the so-called Linear B script.

A script had been developed in Crete out of pictographs for use in keeping the records of the imperial stores in the palace at Cnossus. It is still not known what language was used, although there are indications that it was akin to Akkadian or some other much-used language. A second script was developed from the first one. Sir Arthur Evans called them "Linear A" and "Linear B." Linear B seemed to be an adaptation of Linear A for use with a different language. Linear A was found at several places in Crete; Linear B was found only at Cnossus.

In 1939, tablets inscribed with Linear B were found at Pylos, in the southwest Peloponnesus. Other such tablets have come to light in Greece at Mycenae and nearby Tiryns, at Eleusis in Attica (the territory of Athens), and at Thebes and Orchomenus, a little to the north of Attica. Numerous attempts have been made to decipher both Linear A and Linear B. Linear A is still a mystery. Many hypotheses as to the nature of the language of Linear B had been offered and had failed to win general acceptance. Naturally, one possibility was that the language was Greek, and this suggestion seemed most likely to Michael Ventris and his collaborator, John Chadwick, who finally solved the puzzle. Ventris had had the decipherment of Linear B as a goal ever since, as a schoolboy, he had heard Evans speak on the subject. The method he used to decipher Linear B may be described as a rigorous application of modern cryptographic methods. When all the data of the writing on the tablets had been analyzed and arranged by these methods, and the Greek language was set beside the mass of data as a language that it might represent, Greek it proved to be.

Presumably the Greeks of the mainland had been in control of Cnossus for some time before the great destruction of the palace around 1400 B.C., a destruction that can be deduced from the remains. The Greeks had had time to adapt the Linear A script, which was in use there, to meet their need to write records in Greek, changing it into Linear B for that purpose. This new form of writing spread to the mainland of Greece; there is no evidence that it spread around the rest of Crete.

If Greeks were in control of Cnossus at the time of its destruction, it does not seem reasonable to suppose that a surge of Greeks from the mainland destroyed it. Who, then, did destroy the palace? Here archaeology cannot give us an answer. Perhaps the native Cretans rose against the foreign power that was controlling their chief city, or perhaps a great raid from the sea looted and destroyed Cnossus without touching the rest of Crete.

Mycenae and Mainland Greece

Mycenae apparently inherited the leading position of Cnossus after the great disaster that occurred about 1400 B.C. Probably life in Crete went on much as before, except that the brilliant center was never built up again. Now the center of Mycenae entered on its period of greatest wealth. By this time the workmen of Mycenae had so matured their style that their products, chiefly the pottery, can be readily recognized by their stylistic traits. Thus, for example, we know that the trade of Mycenae ranged as far as Egypt. Much of their pottery was found in the ruins of Amarna. Strangely enough, far more Mycenaean pottery than Cretan dating to the period just before the fall of Cnossus is found in Egypt.

In the West, the Mycenaeans traded with Sicily and South Italy and made some settlements there. In the other direction, they traded with Troy, which commanded the entrance to the Dardanelles and thereafter to the Black Sea. Possibly the old story of Jason and the golden fleece and the wild princess Medea comes from the tale of an attempt to explore the trading potentialities of the Black Sea region.

People as well as goods were exported to Cyprus and Rhodes. Rhodes may well have been the center of a minor kingdom mentioned in the Hittite records of the fourteenth and early thirteenth century B.C. as being centered on a nearby island. The Hittites called these people by a name that may be identified with "Achaeans," as the Greeks sometimes called themselves.

Mycenaean goods also went to the ports of Syria and Palestine and from there into the interior. The Aegaean must have been a lively place, for it carried the ships of the Egyptians, who from 1400 to 1200 B.C. enjoyed the last of their great days and slowly lost in power, those of the Mycenaeans, and those of the Phoenicians, who were about to enter on their greatest commercial days. If the evidence of the remains can be trusted, the Mycenaeans slowly lost many of their markets to the Phoenicians from about 1300 on. In other cases, the rise of local industries or local merchants may have lessened the opportunities of the Mycenaeans. Their prosperity slowly declined during the thirteenth and twelfth centuries, and about 1100 B.C. they suffered some mysterious military disasters that are generally attributed to the movement of the Greek people known as the Dorians, the ancestors of the Spartans and others. There was to be a period of poverty and weakness (which we shall discuss in the next chapter), lasting until roughly 800 B.C.

Greece had centers other than Mycenae in the days of Mycenaean greatness. Thebes was a place of some importance. It was perhaps richest of all the Greek cities in gripping stories of the adventures, the struggles, and the grisly deeds of its royalty. Here the vigorous Oedipus made his mistakes, killing his father and marrying his widowed mother. Here his daughter Antigone defied the king at the bidding of conscience and died, and her lover, the king's son, killed himself beside her body. These events were the stuff of legend, transmitted in the popular memory and by the bards until the time when the great Athenian writers of tragedy used them as raw material for their plays.

Athens, too, was a noteworthy center. Already there were a palace and a citadel on the high place, the Acropolis. It was from Athens that Theseus went to vanquish the Minotaur, the Cretan monster. Elsewhere at Tiryns, near Mycenae, on the southwestern coast of Greece, the excavations also show a palace on a hill. And the palace excavated at Pylos may well be that palace of the old Nestor where, in the *Odyssey*, Telemachus the son of Odysseus was well entertained.

The style of the mainland palaces is not that of the Minoan palaces. They were rather of the so-called megaron type, simpler than the Cretan type and based on a set of large main rooms. Apparently the mainland builder, when called on to construct a palace, did not think in terms of a large and complex building, but rather multiplied a simpler form. On the other hand, the architect of the tholos tombs, known also as beehive tombs, was a fine engineer (we shall later find the word *tholos* used in its primary sense of a circular building). Cnossus is the only place in Crete where these tombs are found. They seem to have been a mainland product. They are constructed of dressed stones, which weigh many tons and are built up into corbelled arches in the shape of a beehive. The engineer could perfectly well have visited Egypt and learned there how large stones are handled, but he could not have got there the conception of a tomb of this shape. It has been suggested that some Mycenaean may have found his way to England, since Mycenaean ships ranged far, and may have showed the people there how to quarry, transport, and erect the huge stones that make up the complex of Stonehenge.

Cnossus again is the only place in Crete where we find a throne room, which on the mainland was a regular feature of palaces. The vases that are said to be in the Palace Style when they are found in the ruins of Cnossus seem originally to have been a mainland style. In dress and armor, the mainlanders, although they made some borrowings from the Minoans, had a good many types that were independent of Minoan influence. They were, of course, in touch by sea with a number of places outside the Minoan cultural sphere.

The culture of these early Greeks, then, should be regarded as the earliest stage of Greek civilization rather than a colonial version of the Minoan civilization, which died out and had no relation to the later Greeks. There was an age of great weakness and disorganization after the destruction of the chief centers of Greece around 1100 B.C., with the result that we can find few material remains to use in interpreting this intermediate period, but there was nevertheless a certain continuity from the great older days of Greece to the beginnings of the new Greece of the classical period.

Let us return now to Mycenae itself. The city of these early days is not the classical city of Greece, the *polis*, as it is usually called. It is not a city in any proper sense, but represents an early stage in the process of the formation of cities that was described in Chapter Two. The king lived in the citadel with the people who ministered to him and guarded him and helped him to manage affairs. There were storehouses for some of the surplus of which he relieved his subjects. On the slopes below the citadel there was a modest settlement. In Mycenae, the remains of some of the houses below the citadel suggest that their owners were either important merchants (for example, in oil) or were among the king's commercial managers. Perhaps the two were the same. The people in general lived as agriculturists all about the territory. There were hamlets here and there. We deduce the radiation of power outward from this citadel from the striking wealth that we know to have come in to it, from the persistent legends of power and wealth, from the evidences of trade with many places, and from the clear remains of roads for pack animals and bridges that show some organization at work for a good many miles about Mycenae. The citadel itself is but a few miles inland from the excellent harbor of modern Nauplia; to have commanded only the harbor and the plain back to Mycenae would have provided sufficient foundation for some prosperity in those days.

The archaeological investigations of the site of Mycenae have turned up pots and sherds that can be assigned to the Early Bronze

Age. This corresponds to the age that is called Early Helladic (about 2500–1900 B.C.) by the scholars whose interest is in classifying the objects found in Greek lands. Other pots and sherds are assigned to the Middle Bronze Age or Middle Helladic (about 2000–1600 B.C.). No signs of dwellings from so early a time have been found.

The remains indicate that the prosperity and importance of Mycenae increased greatly in Late Helladic I; we now have a parallel classification, Mycenaean I, which is 1600–1500 B.C. Now there was a palace on the hilltop and royal graves. These were the graves found in 1876 by Heinrich Schliemann, who had just aroused great interest by his excavations at Troy. The present-day visitor, as he comes through the Lion Gate, the chief gate of the citadel, sees the round hole where the graves were and he can see the rich finds from them in the National Museum at Athens.

The wealth of these graves was fabulous. The bodies of the men had gold masks for the faces and gold breastplates. The bodies of two small children were wrapped in thin sheets of gold. By the men were lying daggers, swords, drinking cups of gold and silver, and other equipment. The women had toilet boxes of gold and dress pins of precious materials. Their clothes were ornamented with gold discs figured with bees, cuttlefish, leaves, rosettes, and spirals. In some of the graves were large vessels of bronze and vases of clay, fayence, and alabaster. There were inlaid daggers and elaborate gold and silver vessels made to imitate the forms of the heads of animals.

In Late Helladic II or Mycenaean II (1500–1400 B.C.), the remains indicate increasing prosperity and show a greater elaborateness in the structure of the citadel and the buildings. This is the age when the Mycenaeans seem to have controlled Cnossus. The greatest age was Mycenaean III (1400–1100 B.C.). This period began with Mycenae's appropriation of the leading position that had been held by Cnossus, and it ended with the gradual falling off of Mycenaean trade, which we have described, and the ruin, about 1100 B.C., of all the chief centers of Greece.

Shortly after 1400 the citadel was enlarged and strengthened with new walls. The famous Lion Gate was built, and the palace reached a new stage of size and richness. One goes up to the Lion Gate along a comfortably wide approach between two powerful walls.

The two jambs of the gate, the threshold, and the lintel are four huge pieces of local stone, each weighing many tons. The remains of arrangements for a double door can be seen. Above the lintel is a huge slab, which gives the gate its name. Two lionesses stand on their hind feet, almost upright, resting their front feet on a plinth, which in turn rests on two altars. From the plinth a column rises between the two lionesses, whose heads are missing.

This heraldic-appearing device is the more interesting because in Crete and early Greece there is so little royal symbolism compared to the great amount known to have existed in Egypt and the Near East. This palace at Mycenae and those in Crete are not to be compared to those of Assyria for devices advertising the power and majesty of the king. The tholos tombs from the Mycenaean domination are the only suggestions of monumental constructions in Crete, and those were covered with earth so that they looked like little hills rather than symbols of the royal power.

A number of explanations of the symbolism of the Lion Gate have been offered. One is that the column symbolizes the great mother-goddess, who is to add her divine strength to that of the fortifications. Another is that the column symbolizes the shrine of Mycenae, guarded by the lions. An attractive view is that the column symbolizes the palace, which in turn symbolizes the kings. As the column seems to grow from the altars, so the power of the kings comes from the gods. The lions are the heraldic symbol of Mycenae, and the whole is a symbol of royal power of the sort that we have seen before and shall see again in the Roman Empire.

The new palace was large, well built, and attractively decorated. Military scenes were prominent in its gay frescoes. It had a spacious hall of state, a throne room, a shrine, a bathroom fully deserving the name, a set of guest rooms, and many smaller apartments.

Down outside the walls the great tholos, or beehive, tombs were built. They had already been rifled in classical Greek times. Magnificent as they are, they were apparently meant to be opened only for burials, then to have the entrance sealed again. Furthermore, the top was covered with soil. Nowadays the great tomb that has been known as the Treasury of Atreus or the Tomb of Agamemnon seems to be only a little hill when one looks down at it from the citadel, giving no hint of how impressive the structure can be when one approaches and enters. The fine tomb known as Clytemnestra's was so well hidden that its existence was forgotten and a theater was built above it just before the Christian era.

As we have seen, the discovery that the language of the Linear B tablets is Greek led to the interesting conclusion that Cnossus was in the hands of Greeks when it fell. The new knowledge that comes from the reading of the Linear B tablets found at Mycenae, Pylos, and elsewhere has engaged the attention of many scholars and led to some interesting new conceptions of life at this time. Actually, we have only tablets that were baked in fires, and these fires were caused by hostile attacks on the buildings where tablets were stored. The ordinary one was not baked to preserve it; and naturally unbaked clay would not remain intact long. Although the number of tablets preserved by such accidents is limited, it still suggests that there was a considerable amount of record-keeping. The kingdoms of Greece seem in this respect to have been much like the earlier kingdoms of Mesopotamia. Another conclusion to be drawn from the presence and contents of these tablets is that the poet Homer did not know how highly organized the life of Mycenae was—or the life of Pylos and the other kingdoms. Presumably the memory of a good many details of Mycenaean life had faded, even though we may believe that certain traits of the earlier time were preserved by the bards until the time of Homer.

We do not know whether the kings and nobles of Mycenae were entertained by singers of Homer's type, illiterate men who learned their trade and practiced it without the aid of writing. Possibly they were, and possibly the memory of the great deeds of men was kept green by being so celebrated. The Linear B tablets give us no hint that writing was used for any purpose other than the highly practical keeping of records.

There are records of stores of food and weapons. Craftsmen are mentioned: carpenters, masons, bronze workers, bowmakers, and others. Whether they were free workmen or slaves we cannot tell. Possibly they were organized as part of the palace staff, whether free or slave, and produced only for the king. There is reason to suppose that the scribes themselves were trained in an official school and remained a closed group with rigid traditions. Presumably, however, the society would have had to advance to a more sophisticated stage before it arrived at such glorification of the work and status of the scribe as was common in both Mesopotamia and Egypt.

The records suggest, too, that there was some formal division of land with consequent responsibilities in the way of taxes. We learn that the gods had lands and slaves and offerings. We also learn that the gods of later times—Zeus, Poseidon, and others—were worshiped at this early time, and we learn that Dionysus was already among the Greek gods at this early date instead of being imported some hundreds of years later, as had generally been thought. This divine organization, like the temporal, was to become more simple in the age that followed the destruction of Mycenae and other cities.

It is impossible for us to know in detail how this brilliant civilization came to an end. The archaeological evidence indicates that sometime in the 1100's there were attacks on it that presently brought it down. The palace at Mycenae was captured, looted, and then burned. Greek legend speaks of a Dorian invasion, a movement of one group of Greeks southward from their earlier home in northern Greece, as coming about 1100 B.C. As we have already seen, however, the trade and prosperity of the Mycenaeans had fallen off before this time. The general disturbances that came around 1200 B.C., in some of which the Greeks themselves may have participated, may have had something to do with the lessening of some kinds of trade. The weakness of Egypt may have been involved. Whatever the causes were, the combination of the loss of position in world trade and occasional violence made the Greeks of the next few centuries less prosperous, so that the archaeological evidence is scanty and hard to interpret.

Troy

Troy was in the northwest corner of Asia Minor, on a ridge about four miles from the Aegaean Sea and four miles from the Dardanelles, the strait that leads to the Sea of Marmora, the narrow passage of the Bosporus, and the Black Sea. The city could control the entrance to the Dardanelles and was in position to control the crossing of the Dardanelles by those who wished to come or go by land between places in Asia Minor and those on the European side.

The German archaeologist Schliemann excavated here and announced in 1872 that he had found Homer's Troy, the city of the *Iliad*. The modern archaeologist tells us that all this part of Asia Minor has been explored since Schliemann's day and that no other place could have been Homer's Troy. The modern archaeologist also tells us, however, in his precise way, that there are nine layers and forty-six strata on the site and that what Schliemann thought was Homer's Troy was a city at an earlier and deeper level. The fact that the ancients saw no need of scraping down to bedrock before rebuilding a city after a great fire or earthquake has preserved for us a record of both the major and the minor changes during the history of Troy, as it has in so many places.

The first layer—the bottom layer, the oldest layer—at Troy represents life there in the first half of the third millennium, or roughly from 3000 to 2500 B.C. There was a very small fortress set up, only about three hundred feet across, but it had a strong stone wall with towers at the gates. The age of copper had begun, but stone tools were still in use. There are no signs of trade with the other peoples we know, unless the use of copper is a sign. This period ended with a great fire.

The second layer, which brings us down two or three hundred years nearer to 2000 B.C., apparently was Schliemann's Troy. Because Schliemann did not report on his work with the exactness customary nowadays, the modern archaeologist cannot be entirely sure what he was doing. Schliemann found considerable wealth and signs of a great fire. People had fled and left things lying about—vessels of gold, copper, and bronze, jewelry, bronze weapons. The source of this wealth may have been the control of the strait of the Dardanelles. The third, fourth, and fifth levels all continue the culture of the earlier inhabitants of the place. They carry us to about 1900 B.C. It must be understood that Schliemann did not lay bare the whole area, but dug down in a limited region. The upper levels (the later levels) did not interest him much, for he was seeking what seemed to him to be the Troy of Homer.

The sixth layer, which the historian calls Troy VI, has a new interest. The remains found at this level seem to indicate the arrival of a new group. Some of the people in this movement settled at Troy, and some went on to Greece and introduced a new note there, as we saw earlier in this chapter. As we also know, the grey pottery called Minyan ware, which was new in Greece at this time, is found at Troy. At first the Trojan kind was exactly like the Greek, although in later centuries the styles diverged.

This Troy existed from about 1900 to about 1300 B.C. and was overthrown by a great earthquake without a fire. The settlement was by now considerably larger than the modest citadel of the early days. It traded with the Mycenaeans, for several hundred Mycenaean vases have been found at this level. What it exported to them we do not know. Troy may have been a textile center, because the grazing was good, and the presence of loom weights in the ruins is evidence of a sort. The Trojans also bred horses, which would make a good export to kings and nobles of a land too steep and rocky for horses to flourish there naturally. Perhaps the Trojans also had an invisible export in their power to control the Dardanelles. There is no evidence that they traded with the Hittites, who were in their great days and ought to have been accessible. Yet there is evidence that they did trade with Cyprus.

If the Troy of song and story did exist, Troy VIIa was it. Lasting only a generation or two, it was destroyed by a devastating fire. The later Greeks put the date of the great affair described by Homer anywhere from the fourteenth century to 1184 B.C. The modern archaeologist would put it between 1250 and 1200. The calculation of the date depends on the dating of the Mycenaean pottery that was present in the city when it fell. If this pottery could be dated more closely, we could date the fall of Troy more closely. But at least we know that Mycenae was still at its height, for the same type of pottery is found there in a setting of power and prosperity. There is no direct proof that this Troy was destroyed by a group of Greeks led by Agamemnon of Mycenae, but it is perfectly possible. No writing of any sort has been found at Troy to help us.

The survivors of this disaster built Troy VIIb and went on for a generation or so, then fell before the onslaught of a people much simpler than they were, to judge by the remains of the culture of the invaders. Perhaps this new assault on Troy came as part of the great movement of peoples around 1200 B.C. It is probable that the Trojans had been able to be some hindrance to attempts to cross the strait from the European side. Without their resistance, the movement of people from Europe into Asia Minor must have been easier.

The further history of Troy does not concern us now. The site was not to be left unoccupied, but Troy (or Ilium) never seemed as important again as had this earlier Troy. Alexander the Great remarked enviously that Achilles was fortunate to have Homer to sing his praises. Troy, like Achilles, still lives in the minds of men because Homer was its poet.

CHAPTER

11

THE TIME BETWEEN

The time between the ending of the Mycenaean civilization and the beginning of the classical civilization of the Greeks lasted about three hundred years, from about 1100 B.C. to about 800 B.C. The historian must be especially careful in describing what appears to be a period of a lower quality of culture, and such is the case here.

First, we know that in the century after about 1200 B.C. the Mycenaean peoples of Greece and the islands traded less intensively with other peoples. The reason is not clear. One result was that there was less wealth in many places among the Mycenaean peoples. Another result, which comes out clearly in the archaeological evidence, is that a certain artistic unity and continuity that had existed among the Mycenaean peoples ceased and was followed by the growth of many local styles and, as time went on, by what seems to have been increasing poverty both in material things and in artistic ability. In summary, it may be said that the exchange of information and goods plainly became less active, that as a result styles of manufacture became local rather than international, that the lessening of communications seems responsible for a material and artistic impoverishment in some places, and that possibly in

171

this more localized world there was a general lessening of strenuousness and inventiveness.

Secondly, the great centers were gone. Nothing comparable to Cnossus had grown up in Crete, although there are signs that a modest prosperity continued there after its fall. It may well be that the weakness of Egypt harmed the prosperity of Crete and that the lessened economic power of both Egypt and Crete was reflected in the falling off of Mycenaean trade. Mycenae, Pylos, Tiryns, Thebes, and other Mycenaean centers had been stormed and destroyed in the movement of the Dorians and their allies around 1100 B.C. Those of the original people who remained in the territories of these great centers had probably been made slaves or serfs or were living quietly in backwaters, and most of the new population were now Dorians and others who were not equipped to carry on manufactures and trade. Troy, too, was gone, and even the disappearance of a center on the other side of the Aegaean must have made a difference to the Greek people in the islands, if not to those on the mainland of Greece. If none of these centers had been a really large city, like the later Athens, nevertheless all of them had been centers of more strenuous and concentrated commercial and artistic activity than was possible for mere villages. Their disappearance must have done something to cause life around the Aegaean to be lived in a quieter and more parochial style.

The later Athenians liked to assert that their city was the only one that had been continuously inhabited from the beginning, and, in fact, the archaeological researches that seem to show that all the other centers suffered disasters at the end of the Mycenaean period do not show evidence of such a disaster at Athens. The quality of the pottery fell off gradually at Athens, as it did elsewhere. The archaeologists have given the expressive name "Sub-Mycenaean" to the somewhat listless local styles that developed. At Athens, however, there presently came a change. A local style with a certain keenness and good taste appeared, a style that presently was to emerge in the finest form of what is known as Geometric Pottery, because its ornaments are geometric figures rather than plants, beasts, or men.

A third feature of the period, the movements of peoples, is better known from Greek tradition than from archaeology. If there is always some question about trusting a tradition that was purely oral until it found its way into written works, and then not until the sixth and fifth centuries for the most part, there is also the consideration that great events tend to be handed down with some degree of accuracy among peoples who are accustomed to rely on their memories. In some cases, local pride may have shaped the tradition a little—a city wishing to improve on its history during this time, or perhaps a leading family wishing to manufacture prominent ancestors. But it is likely that much was handed down accurately. Perhaps we should note that Greeks were always very careful about genealogies, a habit that makes it seem that the names of great men, even those of the Mycenaean period, were probably handed down with care. The chances are that it really was Oedipus who killed his father and married his mother and that the man who returned from the war at Troy to be killed by his wife and her paramour was Agamemnon.

We shall speak of two chief phases of those movements of peoples known from tradition: first, the arrival of the Dorians, which brought down the old centers around the year 1100 B.C. and carried the Dorians widely around the Aegaean; and second, the movement of the Ionians and others, which created a number of Greek cities along the coast of Asia Minor. To the Greek tradition a great many of these tribes or peoples were interesting, but we must simplify the story by telling only of the most important and typical groups.

The Dorians and their allies had been in northern Greece for some centuries. We do not know why they decided to move. They destroyed some centers near their own region and went in force into the southern part of Greece, below the Gulf of Corinth. It was probably then (because the word does not occur in Homer) that the southern part received the name of "Peloponnesus," or "island of Pelops," which is still applied to it. At this time, too, the terms "Hellas" for all Greece and "Hellenes" for all the Greek people, terms that are still in use, seem to have originated. As so often happens, the name of a small place and a small group of people somehow came to be applied to a whole country and to all its people.

The invaders destroyed Mycenae, Pylos, and other centers and made themselves masters of all the Peloponnesus. From now on, it was to be a Dorian territory, and the Spartans, who lived there, were to be the most prominent of the Dorians. But the Dorians spread farther. They went to Crete, to many of the islands, even as far as Rhodes, and to a few places on the mainland of Asia Minor. By the classical age of Greece, they were still thought of as a recognizable group and as the most powerful one among the Greeks.

The other large movement in this period was that of the many people generally known as Ionians, who went from Greece to the coast of Asia Minor, probably in an irregular way and over an extended period of time. By the sixth century, the Ionians of Asia Minor were to emerge as the intellectual and artistic leaders of all the Greeks. This fact adds special interest to the difficult task of tracing their early history. In the main, the migrations took place between 1000 and 900 B.C., to judge from the scanty and difficult archaeological evidence. Therefore, the Ionians could not have migrated before the end of the Mycenaean period, carrying the high Mycenaean culture with them, as one small body of evidence was formerly thought to suggest. Nor did they migrate late enough to carry with them the new culture that by 800 or 750 B.C. was beginning to appear in several parts of mainland Greece.

The Greeks who went to Asia Minor were able to take or gain possession of a number of good locations for cities on the coast. Samos and Chios were two excellent island sites near the coast. All through their history, however, the Greeks found the people of the interior difficult neighbors. None of the cities was ever able to expand inland to a great extent or establish a powerful realm for itself on the land. The converse of this fact is that many of them later became active on the sea and in founding colonies.

Thus the whole circuit of the Aegaean Sea—mainland Greece, Crete and the smaller islands, Rhodes, the coast of Asia Minor, and the islands near it—all except Thrace, which constituted the northern coast of that sea, had come to be inhabited by Greeks who felt some degree of likeness to one another; and through the rest of the history of the ancient world, this was to be a Greek region. We must not, of course, exaggerate the degree to which their kinship was consciously felt; we may be sure that it was not consciously cultivated by any interested party or group.

The Greek language came to be spoken through this entire area. The few and evanescent traces of non-Greek languages confirm our natural supposition that there were groups of non-Greek people here and there, but their languages and their other cultural traits gradually disappeared. There were a number of different dialects of Greek, differing in pronunciation more than in vocabulary, so that most Greeks could make themselves understood by other Greeks.

We cannot find evidence of much contact between these people and the cultivated parts of their world during the three centuries or so of this period. It is plain that they still knew how to build some sort of craft in which to get over the water. It is not plain why they did not sail more often to the old places and why the other people did not come often to them. We might conjecture again that the weakness of Egypt in this period had something to do with it.

It was formerly supposed, because the Ionians were nearer than the other Greeks to the older seats of civilization and because they were so brilliant in the sixth century, that they were in direct contact by land with the older culture in Asia Minor. But archaeology offers us no materials from the Greek cities to prove such early influences. There is no known trace of a land route. The recent work at Gordium, in Phrygia, which would have been a logical intermediate point, has disclosed only slight evidence of contact with the Greeks of the coast of Asia Minor. There is good evidence, however, that the later resumption of fruitful interaction between the Greeks and the people of the Near East was by water, that the Greeks of the eastern islands and of the mainland were early in responding to these contacts, and that the Ionians, coming into the movement a little late, presently found themselves at home in it and advanced to the leadership of it. (The emergence of the Greeks from the time between will be the subject of the next chapter.)

THE HOMERIC POEMS

Iliad, Odyssey, Epic Cycle

The Homeric poems are the greatest single monument of the time between. Two great epic poems, the *Iliad* and the *Odyssey*, are ascribed to Homer. The *Iliad* is some sixteen thousand lines long and would take several long sessions (over thirty hours) to recite. The *Odyssey* is somewhat shorter. These poems represent memories of the

Mycenaean Age and of the time between that were handed down by professional singers without the use of writing. With due care we may use them as historical sources.

It is generally believed that Homer's poems—or at least the *Iliad*—belong to the Ionian community of Asia Minor and date from somewhere between 850 and 750 B.C. The *Iliad* describes an intense incident of the war at Troy and suggests the interests of Greece and the Aegaean. The *Odyssey* tells of the wandering and adventures of the Greek Odysseus on his way home from the war, suggests the sea in all its moods, tells of adventure in far places, and describes the life of Odysseus' island kingdom, Ithaca. Not only do the two poems seem different enough to be the products of two men (although this is a dangerous argument); they also have internal inconsistencies that have suggested that each was built up out of a combination of other poems. In the *Iliad,* for example, a man is killed at one point and soon after appears in good health. The two great Greek champions, Achilles and Diomedes, are never on the scene together, as if the two stories of heroic valor, one of Achilles and one of Diomedes, had been mechanically combined. Because we know nothing definite of the man Homer, questions have naturally been raised and long discussed: Was there any such man? Or are the poems compilations made by some ingenious person or by a group rather than the work of one poet? Do the two poems form a pair or were they produced at different times and in different places by different people? The sum of all these doubts is called the Homeric Question.

The *Iliad* is the story of the wrath of Achilles, not of the fall of Troy. It is assumed that the Greek host had been trying for almost nine years to take Troy and had meanwhile been making raids on other places in the vicinity. Agamemnon of Mycenae, the great king in command of the Greeks, took from Achilles a girl who had been assigned to him as part of his share of the booty from one of these raids. This intolerable infringement of custom led Achilles to sulk in his tent and refuse to fight. Agamemnon was persuaded by the other chiefs to offer full and honorable restitution, which was refused by the enraged Achilles. Now, according to the code of the time, Achilles had put himself in the wrong.

While he continued to sulk in his tent, the Trojans, under the leadership of Hector, the king's son and their greatest fighter, fiercely attacked the Greek encampment on the shore. Patroclus, the best friend of Achilles, went out against them in Achilles' armor and was killed by Hector. This brought Achilles back into the fray at last; but he sinned again against the code by mistreating the dead body of Hector, whom he had killed in revenge for the death of Patroclus. Finally the gods themselves commanded Achilles to yield up the body to Hector's father, King Priam of Troy, for burial. The poem ends with the funeral of Hector.

The *Odyssey* is a tale of adventure. Odysseus, the hero, was a stout warrior, but a man of more depth of character and resourcefulness in varied situations than many of the other Greek chiefs of the *Iliad,* where he also appears. The poem opens with a council of the gods on Mount Olympus during which the goddess Athena, his especial protectress, persuaded Zeus to free Odysseus from the nymph Calypso and let him start home again. As he and his contingent had been sailing home after sharing the capture of Troy, they had been blown from their course and into a long series of adventures in the little-known seas and islands of the West. Finally all his men were lost, and Odysseus found himself on an idyllic island inhabited by a good-natured minor divinity, Calypso, who wished to impart immortality to him and keep him there forever as her lover. Unfortunately Odysseus had incurred the wrath of Poseidon, the sea god, and as he set out from Calypso's island on the raft he had built, freed by Athena's intervention, he was blown off course and almost lost his life, getting ashore finally in the land of Phaeacia. Here he was hospitably entertained, and in a long flashback he told the Phaeacian court the story of the adventures that had at last destroyed all his comrades and left him alone and cast away on the island of Calypso. Here are the famous stories of the Cyclops, of the enchantress Circe, who turned Odysseus' men into swine, of the Sirens, of Scylla and Charybdis.

After Odysseus had told his story, the Phaeacians sent him home to his own island of Ithaca in one of their ships. The last half of the poem tells of his arrival in Ithaca, disguised as a beggar, and of the plans and preparations that led up to his killing the lords of Ithaca who had been feasting in his hall and trying to persuade his wife, Penelope, to admit that Odysseus must be dead, marry one of them, and thus enable the successful suitor to take the throne of Ithaca in Odysseus' place.

His son, Telemachus, was near the age of manhood. Although he had not felt able to oppose the crowd of suitors alone, he played a man's part beside his father in the great scene where Odysseus had his reckoning with those who had made free of his house and tried to take his wife and throne.

The poems of the so-called Epic Cycle told all the story of the Trojan War, from the earliest events that led to the abduction of Queen Helen by the Trojan prince, through all the details of the war, including the device of the wooden horse and the actual taking of Troy, and through the homecomings of all the heroes. All the old stories of the Mycenaean age—for example, the grim tale of Oedipus, King of Thebes—were also told by the bards. They were finally put into written form by the authors of the Epic Cycle, but practically all of them failed to be copied in the later ages of Greece; had they been, it might have enabled them to survive to modern times. Yet we know their contents, as has been said, because they are referred to often by other writers of Greece and Rome whose work has survived. The tale of Oedipus, for instance, was treated in a great play of Sophocles, while Aeschylus made a magnificent trilogy (a set of three tragedies) from Agamemnon's homecoming and murder by his queen and the revenge of his son Orestes and his daughter Electra on their mother and her lover.

The Oral Poet

The most recent development in Homeric scholarship has thrown a great deal of light on the development of the poems and on their form. It has long been known that the Greeks had "rhapsodes" (the word means "stitchers of songs") who sang for the entertainment of the great, as troubadours did later. Although the usual English word has been "bard," it is probably better to call these singers "oral poets," the term that has become common among scholars of the subject.

A small group of modern scholars have investigated the methods of oral poets, especially those of the South Slavic peoples. These oral poets are illiterate. They sing in metrical lines, as Homer did, although their meter is not his. They rely on memory to an extent that we can hardly imagine, although we know that, like them, the Greeks and Romans generally worked their memories harder than we do.

Columns of the temple of Amun at Karnak, 14th Century B.C.

Courtesy of Trans World Airlines, Inc.

Palace at Persepolis; north stairway of the audience hall begun by Darius I (521–486 B.C.).

Courtesy of Erich F. Schmidt, Oriental Institute, University of Chicago.

Gold cup from Mycenae; in the National Museum, Athens.
Courtesy of the Royal Consulate General of Greece.

Cretan seal ring of jasper, 15–1100 B.C.; women approaching seated divinity. Shown twice actual size.

The Metropolitan Museum of Art.

The Palace at Cnossus. South Propylon (restored).

Mycenae, the Lion Gate. *Courtesy of the Royal Consulate General of Greece.*

Mycenae, a royal grave circle. *Photograph by Luis-Yves Loirat.*
Courtesy of the Royal Consulate General of Greece.

Athenian geometric vase,
9–8th century B.C.
*The Metropolitan Museum
of Art.*

LEFT: Athenian black-figured amphora, c. 525 B.C.
RIGHT: Athenian red-figured amphora, 5–4th century B.C.

The Metropolitan Museum of Art.

Archaic marble head of a youth,
2nd quarter of 6th century B.C.
The Metropolitan Museum of Art.

Athenian grave monument, c. 400 B.C.
The Metropolitan Museum of Art.

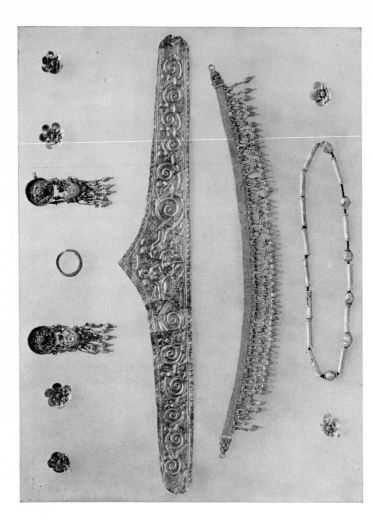

Greek gold jewelry, soon after 350 B.C.
Diadem, necklace, beads, earrings, rosettes in form of flowers.

The Metropolitan Museum of Art.

The South Slavic oral poet begins as a youngster to imitate the oral poets whom he hears. He learns a huge armory of "formulaic lines," useful lines which he can bring out in exactly the same form as he builds up a song. He also builds up an armory of "formulaic themes," such units of narrative as banquet scenes, scenes of heroes arming themselves for battle, challenges, fights, stripping the arms from a fallen enemy, departures, arrivals, and storms. He gradually builds up a repertory of these basic materials, constantly practicing the combination of the materials for the production of songs for which there is, of course, no written text. Originality is not prized. He frankly draws on traditional heroic material, which he may change and adapt as he pleases. The greatest performers are those who can lend the most life and the highest finish to songs that are in general very like those of the other performers.

The oral poets of ancient Greece worked this way, if we may judge by the *Iliad* and the *Odyssey*. The main characters have standing epithets, such as "Achilles swift of foot" or "flashing-eyed Athena," which occur again and again. Many lines occur several times in exactly the same form; for example, "And Odysseus, ready in counsel, answered him, saying . . ." Sometimes a group of several lines recurs in the same form, as does one that describes the hospitable offering of food to a newly-arrived stranger. When Agamemnon, in the *Iliad,* is ready to offer restitution to Achilles for his affront, he gives a long description of the gifts that he would make. This description is repeated word for word by the envoys whom he sends to Achilles. This repetition of phrases, lines, and passages, which would seem strange in other Greek works, apparently is a sign that the poem was composed in the tradition of the oral poets and offered to audiences familiar with their manner. There are other signs: again and again there are swift recapitulations of earlier action or repeated explanations of the same fact, as if the poem were meant to be intelligible when presented in parts or on several different occasions.

If we assume that the *Iliad* and the *Odyssey* were the product of a man, or two men, trained in the tradition of the oral poets, we shall be less concerned with the Homeric Question as it has been stated and discussed in the last few generations. If the man was so trained, naturally he drew on a mass of traditional material for his story, and it is not surprising that the joints are discernible here and there. If he made a slip here and there, killing off a minor character, perhaps, and having him appear in battle soon afterward, the slip weighs nothing against the great unities of the poem—the fine structure that discloses itself to careful examination, the unity of tone, the unity of characterization of the major figures. The poem, with its manifold excellences, would be within the powers of a very great practitioner in the tradition of the oral poets.

How did it come to written form? We do not know. Probably it was dictated. Scholars have persuaded the modern South Slavic oral poets to present their best songs slowly, so that they can be written down or recorded on tape. The singers have generally felt that the version of the song produced in this way is superior to what they regularly do, singing at normal speed to an audience. The Greek text of the poems that we have is thought to rest on a version made in Athens in the middle 500's by order of Peisistratus, the tyrant of Athens, who wanted to have readings from Homer as a new attraction for a festival.

The activity of the oral poets for many generations before Homer will explain why works of such excellence as the *Iliad* and the *Odyssey* appeared at the very beginning of Greek literature. They were not produced from nothing by a miracle. Homer inherited the results of the careful practice and performance that had gone on for probably four or five hundred years.

Homer as Evidence

What, then, are we to think of the Homeric poems and the poems of the Epic Cycle as we learn of them in the works of later authors as historical sources? When we can check Homer's references to an earlier time, he is often accurate. The new knowledge from the Linear B tablets about the complexity of the organization of the palace and kingdom of Mycenae makes it seem that much had been forgotten by Homer's time. But even so, the simple kingdom of Odysseus in Homer probably represents faithfully a minor kingdom both of Mycenaean times and of Homer's own time.

Homer does know a catalogue of Greek chiefs and their contingents that fits the great Mycenaean Age and no later age. It must have been passed down in the same form through all the time between. He and the poets of the Epic Cycle knew stories of great and dreadful events from all the chief Mycenaean centers. The story of Oedipus the Theban, the stories of Hercules, which have Tiryns as a center, the basing of the legend of the Argonauts at Orchomenus, and the great stories of Mycenae itself suggest that all the great and lasting tales arose in Mycenaean times.

The elements of other dialects that are mixed with the Ionic of Homer suggest a Mycenaean origin for many of the phrases. More important in the matter of language, however, is that a large part of the vocabulary and phrasing may well have been traditional and thus preserve the usage of an earlier age. If the weapons are said to be of bronze, it is because the phrasing handed down by the oral poets called them bronze, phrasing that consisted of metrical patterns that were passed on in formulaic phrases or lines or blocks of lines in which one could not readily substitute *iron* for *bronze* even though one sang in the Iron Age, as Homer did. The later singer might not know how a battle of chariots was conducted, however, and therefore he might use the traditional language to get his heroes onto the battlefield in their chariots but have them fight on foot.

We may conclude, then, that the Homeric poems are good evidence that a great assault on and capture of Troy did take place. We may accept the names of the great men, because a people very interested in genealogies probably would not have accepted a mere tale with fictitious heroes in the first place—or at any time. We may suppose that most of the details of material things and their uses, whether in the home or in battle, are accurate. We may further suppose that Homer has left us a good picture of kingdoms and of the relations between people in an earlier time.

Homeric Society

Older descriptions of Homeric society used to consist mainly of catalogues of weapons and methods of warfare, houses, food, clothing, marriage customs, and the like. The weakness of this procedure is that it gives no picture of the society in action. It does not show us men's chief aims, their system of loyalties, or the mainsprings of their morality. Modern classical scholars have drawn on the methods of the sociologists and anthropologists to restudy Homeric society in order to present it as a working model rather than a collection of dismantled parts laid out on a bench for inspection and discussion.

Homeric society is that of a heroic age. This does not mean that the men of that age were bigger or braver than their descendants, even if Homer speaks of their hurling rocks which two men "of the present day" could hardly lift. It means rather that it was a society that glorified the hero, or the leading man of warlike qualities. The idea of a heroic age is also the reflection of a tendency to think that the great figures of an earlier age must have been typical rather than exceptional, as we are inclined now to think of the time of the Founding Fathers as a heroic age.

At the top of the society was the king, either a great king like Agamemnon, whose position reflected the power of Mycenae, or a minor king like Odysseus, who was hardly more than the first among equals on a remote and rather poor island. His power was hereditary, but had to be maintained by his own ability. While Odysseus was away, his son Telemachus grew to the verge of manhood. His right to succeed to the throne was recognized, but he had not yet been able to assert it by his own ability, so that the suitors of his mother could still hope that one of them could marry her and make himself king.

Kingship was not a comfortable and assured position. Some of the most famous stories from the old times were about struggles for royal power. Dreadful deeds made the best plots for the oral poets in days when romantic love was not yet used as a subject and few other human activities except warfare had much dramatic quality. The oral poets kept the stories alive from generation to generation. Later men, and especially the Athenian writers of tragedy, reworked them to bring out their deeper significance.

Warfare was the best sphere for the assertion of royal leadership. The routine problems of government that are dealt with by the government of a modern state hardly existed in so simple and highly traditional a society. Even the administration of justice hardly existed. Either the weight of tradition prevented the rise of problems of justice, or those that did arise were dealt with by the heads of families or clans or, in extreme cases, by a meeting of all the men who could bear arms. We shall see that as the bonds of custom and tradition and rule by family groups gradually relaxed, allowing men to feel that they had more choice in their actions, more and more attention was paid to the idea of justice and the difficult art of practicing it privately and publicly.

The nobles were below the king and were linked to him by bonds of obligation something like those of the Middle Ages. Naturally the duty to support him in war was most important. Both the king and the nobles had land, which was the chief source of wealth. Homer does not speak of the complexities of Mycenaean society as we glimpse them through the Linear B tablets. He says nothing of the holding of land by individuals and gods with precise limits and tenures. Yet there is nothing in Homer to exclude precise landholding; Agamemnon could propose to present to Achilles a number of villages that were under his control.

There was a real gap between the landowning king and nobles and those who had no land or had only tiny subsistence plots. It was not possible to make money in other ways and buy land with it, nor was there any free land on the frontier to be taken up and cultivated by individuals, as in the American West. It was possible, however, for a group of people to migrate as a community, fully organized, with government and gods. The Ionian Greeks who crossed to Asia Minor and found new land did so in this manner, as did the Greeks of another great colonizing movement in the eighth and seventh centuries B.C. Probably no Greek would ever have thought of separating himself from his community to go out alone and face both the dangers and the isolation involved in starting a new frontier farm.

Among the humble people were some itinerant laborers—carpenters, metalworkers, or soothsayers. Such men must have made a very precarious living, because each estate had its own men to do all the ordinary woodwork or metalwork about the place. The workmen mentioned in the Linear B tablets of Mycenae may have been either free men or slaves.

The oral poets should probably be classed with the itinerant workmen. They had a skill, however, that was less likely to be cultivated on each estate. They may well have been the first men who moved from one place to another to offer their services. The average man would not have thought of moving to another place or even visiting one.

Probably the slaves were mostly women, because in warfare the men of the losing side were likely to be butchered. There was plenty of work for these captive women to do. Their owners expected to make mistresses of them at their pleasure. It was assumed in general in the ancient world that more children were a good thing, for the difficulty was more in replenishing the population than in keeping it from being excessive. A large household would have room for as many children as could be produced. The offspring of slave women might be second-class citizens without bearing a painful stigma of illegitimacy.

Slaves could have a better life than some free men. Hard work was the rule for all ordinary people, but the slave could count on food, shelter, and clothing, and the same treatment that would be given to a free person of humble status. If he was not free to go away, there was little loss, as no ordinary person, slave or free, thought of going anywhere.

The lowest class were the thetes, men who had no land or only a tiny plot and who could achieve only the barest subsistence. They would offer themselves to do odd jobs or to help with the harvest and were all too likely to be cheated of the coat or other recompense promised them for their work, since they had no group to back them up. Such men could have no hope of more than the barest hand-to-mouth existence, and they were also denied the comforting sense of belonging to some household or community.

Even in the most prosperous days of Mycenae, when trade brought in considerable wealth, agriculture and stockraising (cattle, pigs, and goats) were the basis of the economy. The basic economic unit was the *oikos,* or household, which might be so large that we should call it a manor or, as in the case of Odysseus, a kingdom. Everyone worked at the common task of producing food and clothing, laboring for the whole group rather than for themselves. The head of the *oikos* saw to it that everyone was fed and clothed. Although clothes or weapons were individually owned, there was little idea of private property as we know it. Certainly the head of the *oikos* could not regard the land as his private property in the sense that he could sell some or all of it or bestow parts of it on others or bequeath it to whom he pleased. It is interesting to note that the lords and ladies knew how to do the work of the place. Penelope could weave. Odysseus was proud of his carpentry and of his skill and strength at plowing or reaping.

Bronze, and later iron, were the chief resources lacking for self-sufficiency. They might be got by exchange or by raiding. The self-sufficient *oikos* felt no need to export; its problem was to import the metal that it could not produce for itself. If it were near the seacoast, it might develop skill in semiprofessional piracy, but trading ships must have appeared only rarely. Otherwise it might raid its neighbors. All this led to a strange but consistent code that glorified piracy, encouraged large-scale robbery, and frowned on petty theft. The merchant, the professional arranger of exchanges, appears only rarely in Homer, and then he is generally a Phoenician. We still do not know whether the houses just below the citadel in Mycenae whose remains suggest trade in oil and other commodities were the homes of private merchants or royal agents.

The primitive character of the economic organization is shown by the fact that gifts played a number of properly economic roles. These were not real gifts in our sense, because they were not freely given. Something was always expected in return, as in our economic transactions. Sometimes the gift was a payment for services, past or future. Sometimes it was a bribe. Sometimes it represented the payment of dues or the fulfillment of a vassal's obligation. The gifts given during courtships were balanced by the giving of the woman in marriage and by her dowry. The processes of foreign relations and diplomacy also entailed the giving of gifts. The chief materials were metals. Very often they were in the form of tripods or caldrons, not intended for use but stored away like money to be used again as gifts. In Homer, such articles are often spoken of as untouched by the fire, and their pedigree is given. The value of the gift was enhanced by having the names of several important persons attached to it.

Among the great lords, class status and loyalty to class came first as principles of social organization; presumably, those at the top of society are always banded together to preserve their common position. The family group in the larger sense, or the clan, was another rallying point for loyalties and another source of status. Family connections mattered in relation to status and loyalty to a degree which we can hardly imagine today. The group authority of the family or clan also determined and restrained the actions of the individual member to an extent that is strange to us. In fact, it is likely that the member of such a family group did not think of himself as an individual with aims and preferences and problems, as a man of the twentieth-century United States does.

These groups gave their members a complete and fixed code of behavior. The individual had no doubts and probably even no thoughts as to where he belonged in society, and likewise he had neither doubts nor thoughts about his code of behavior, which he had acquired without realizing that he was doing so. Later we shall attempt to describe the process of the loosening of these social bonds and the growth of individualism. Some of the best things in later Greek literature came from the attempts of the Greeks to work out a rational way of living to replace the traditional way that had prevailed in the earlier ages.

The behavior of Achilles in the *Iliad* shows the working of the code of the warrior leader. It was fixed and needed no discussion. The only question was whether a man lived up to it. Achilles felt responsible only to himself and to his desire to achieve honor and glory in his position of warrior king. When he refused to fight, no one spoke of his responsibility to the state, for there was no state to which he should have felt responsible. He was honor-bound to fight, because he had come in response to a proper claim on his services. Yet Agamemnon's insult of taking the captive girl from him raised another point of honor as important as the conduct of the war. By his indignant refusal to accept the full satisfaction that Agamemnon offered him, Achilles violated the code, and he did so again by outraging the dead body of Hector. Finally he yielded to the command of the gods and made proper amends; his return to the accepted pattern of behavior completes the story.

The competition among the Greek warriors for honor and glory is unlike anything that we have seen in earlier history. This lack may have resulted in part because the monarchs of Egypt and the Near East must have learned early to discourage such sentiments among their nobility. The Homeric hero was very conscious of his competitors for glory and wished to have trophies as visible reminders of his triumphs. Hence the pauses in the action of the *Iliad* while armor is wrenched from some warm corpse.

This same spirit of competition persisted in later Greek life. A victory in the Olympics or the other games was a triumph that would remain glorious for a lifetime, even though the simple wreath given as the visible reward would have seemed a poor prize to a Homeric warrior. At the Athenian festivals of later centuries, there were to be competitions of choruses, prizes for the best tragedy and the best comedy and for the best tragic actor and the best comic actor.

Religion in Homer

The practice of telling stories about the doings of the gods as if they were extremely powerful people was common in the ancient world. Both the Egyptians and the Near Eastern peoples had used this symbolic method of presenting their conceptions of the unseen powers of the universe. Their accounts had also included monsters and earthly forces analogous to the chthonic powers worshiped by the Greeks. Behind the gods of Homer we can readily see the unseen powers that the mind of man would naturally deduce from his observation of the world and mankind.

Homer practically ignores the chthonic gods—the gods of the Earth—of whose worship clear traces are found elsewhere in our sources for early Greece. It is difficult to be precise about the chthonic gods, for they were worshiped by the simpler people and did not ordinarily receive the tribute of temples or statues or clear literary treatment. Such a religion is bound to be much concerned with fertility on the one hand and with the uncanny and the monstrous and the formidable powers of the underworld on the other. There was a real division in Greece between the worship of the chthonic powers and the worship of the other gods, who have come to be known as the Olympians from the fact that Homer placed their home and their councils on Mount Olympus.

Homer's gods were dissociated both from the grosser and more terrible aspects of religion and from the crudities and imperfections of other divinities. Zeus and his entourage of divinities had come to power by hard fighting against earlier divinities who were gross and crude. The struggle is rarely mentioned in Homer; his emphasis is on the refinement and excellence of the gods who now reign. So elsewhere Homer calls attention to the fine qualities of horses or spears or ships. Apparently excellence and fitness and fine workmanship of every sort were a great joy to the people for whom Homer sang.

The behavior of this company of humanized natural forces was that of a company of aristocrats, far removed from the uncouth banging about of which we hear in the Mesopotamian tales of the gods. Zeus presided over a court of gods who were powerful, but who had to acknowledge that he was most powerful. The gods feasted in ritual style. They had their alliances, intrigues, loyalties, jealousies, and love affairs. One measure of Homer's success in giving a humanistic description of the powers of the universe is that although these gods lost their power to inspire fear or awe even in Greek times, they did not lose their power to inspire the literary man and the plastic artist and they have not yet lost it.

Zeus was the great king of the Olympian gods. Hera was the wife who resented his marital infidelities and manipulated him as best she could, although trembling at his anger and his power. Poseidon, one of the younger brothers of Zeus, was ruler of the sea, and Pluto or Hades, the other, ruled the world below. Pallas Athena, the patroness of the civilized arts and the especial goddess of Athens, was the virgin goddess who sprang from the forehead of Zeus. Aphrodite, the goddess of love, was known to every ancient people under some name, for she symbolized all the forces of attraction and union in human affairs. Ares, the god of war, was the universal symbol of the contrary tendency—strife and division. These two, with their close and necessary relation, are represented by Homer as lovers.

Apollo, in the first book of the *Iliad,* rained his disease-bringing arrows on the Greeks for their insult to his priest. He was logically also the god of medicine. In later ages, he gained greatly in importance, largely through the activity of his oracle at Delphi, which consistently stood for everything sane and moderate and for the higher aspects of religion. He was also god of the sun, while his twin sister Artemis was goddess of the moon and figured in many a later tale as a virgin goddess devoted to the forests and to hunting. Hermes was the messenger of the gods, carrying the decrees of Zeus. It was he who went to Calypso's island to tell her that she must allow Odysseus to go home. Hestia was the goddess of the hearth, the center of the home. Demeter represented the kindly earth, which puts forth her fruits for man. Last of all came the grimy one who could handle metals, Hephaestus, the smith of the gods. His skill was of that exalted nature appropriate to a divinity. Nevertheless his unaristocratic function was symbolized by his walking stiffly and by his smith-like appearance and manner. The symbolism of his being the husband of the glorious Aphrodite is not altogether clear.

The gods did not represent justice. Zeus apportioned the good and the bad to man according to his whim. But even though a man was helpless before the occasional flagrant injustices visited on him by the gods as a poor man might be before his lord, he still had one compensation: he could laugh at the gods as the poor man might laugh among his friends at the spectacle of the lord lording it. The gods, however, did not laugh at men. They were more likely to regard men with such wondering pity as a man might feel contemplating the ants running about a disrupted anthill. But they would crush men as a man might crush an ant. Troy had to be destroyed, for example, to satisfy the outraged feelings of Hera and Athena, as we see at the beginning of the fourth book of the *Iliad*. Still, the gods always treated men with careful courtesy when they addressed them directly.

Men did not offer the gods reverence, worship, or love. They made offerings as one would send off dues to a very remote feudal lord, and they hoped for the best in return. If they did not expect justice from the gods, they never had any sense of having sinned against them and felt no need to atone for wrong conduct. If a man did wrong, it was against the custom of his group, not against the gods. But if a man swore an oath by a god and broke it, he had done that god an injury and must make amends, as we might offer an apology or pay for damage done.

The relation of Homer's people to the gods gives us an idea of the psychology of the time. With all their spirit of competition and personal honor, the Homeric people had not the clear sense of self that we do. They do not speak of the mind. If a striking idea came to a man, he was likely to assume that it was sent by a power outside himself. That is, he did not have the idea of the self as something with attitudes and ideas. Again and again, we find that a company of gods is hovering over the actors of Homer's poems and that all the decisions are attributed to the gods. Athena is represented as standing behind Achilles and telling him to control his anger against King Agamemnon. This decision, like most in the poems, was one that Achilles could have made for himself according to our way of thinking, and the gods seem like quaint and useless machinery unless we can make the effort of imagination necessary to realize that Homer used them because he did not have the later conception of the fully developed individual and his psychological processes.

The Influence of Homer

Homer is the fountainhead of European literature. Through all of earlier Greek history, down to the last days of Byzantium, he was regarded as the greatest of Greek authors, and he enjoys that position in modern Greece. To the Romans, too, he was the greatest of authors; and in Latin writings, he was often quoted, echoed, or referred to. In the centuries when little Greek was known in the West, Homer continued to be known through the Latin writers. In more modern times, he was read in the West in his original Greek, and many translations into the modern languages were made. Nowadays a new English version appears every few years.

If there is any one secret of Homer's lasting popularity, it is that his vision of life has given satisfaction to generation after generation. We need not forget the great skill of his narrative or the charm of his language or the rich flexibility of his meters; these are qualities that add to his greatness, but do not constitute the essence of it. The essence of his greatness is that his characters and their relation to one another appeal to one generation after another as a satisfactory statement of human life. Even though his people prove on close examination not to have our way of speaking of the individual, yet to us as to past ages they have seemed true and good examples of man and the world.

That later Greeks and Romans found Homer's view of life satisfying is a fact about them worth recording. We do not know how much of his attitude is traditional or how much of it represents the purely Ionian attitude in the cities of Asia Minor. We do have the two poems, and we do know that the vision of life in them was influential from Homer's time on. Even the dissent is significant. If the Greek philosophers wished to argue a new view of the powers of the universe, they were inclined to say that the Homeric point of view—not merely the human point of view in general—was wrong. The Athenian Plato, who wished to construct a carefully controlled society, stated emphatically and specifically that there would be no place in it for Homer or other poets of his kind.

If indeed the *Iliad* and the *Odyssey* were written by different men at different times, both poems portray people of frank and generous natures, people who know a code that men could live by reasonably, without mean struggles with each other or attempts to impose on each other. Their values are largely internalized; that is, the code has become so much a part of them that the force of it seems to be inside them rather than outside. They respect themselves and other people; their contests are more for the purpose of following the code or gaining honor than scoring a point by a small tactical triumph over some other person.

There is a great variety among these men. To us, who live in an unrestrained society, the realization comes hard that in a highly conventional society with a set code of manners and behavior genuine individualism of many kinds, even eccentricity, can flourish better than it does in our own society. Thus, while Homer's people show widely differing traits, all are of a general type that the Greeks found satisfying, as the moderns do.

Achilles might have been a mere ruffian without the influence of the heroic code, for he was a young man of great physical prowess and not much given to reflection. The essence of his story is that he found it difficult to keep within the boundaries of behavior set by the code, for his vigor and hot temper pressed him hard. The story of his struggles with himself is a most appealing one.

Agamemnon, the great king, is portrayed as a man of unfailing tactlessness. As he went the rounds of his captains to encourage them, he unerringly said to each man what would please him least. But he was a man and a king and one who intended to do what was right by the light that was granted him.

Odysseus, on the other hand, is the adventurer, ready for any situation, whether courage or guile is needed. He was a great spinner of false tales when he landed in strange places, but we do not find him spinning tales to gain a mean advantage. Surely no one was ever so perfect a narrator of his own adventures as Odysseus at the court of the Phaeacian king.

The swineherd Eumaeus, to whose hut Odysseus went on his return to Ithaca, was a slave and a responsible, hardworking man, loyal to the memory of his master and ready to fight for him on his unexpected return. Against this admirable man are set a loudmouthed beggar and some of the house servants who had not been faithful.

Two young people appear. Telemachus, the son of Odysseus, is appealingly shown as, ready for manhood, he attempts to find and assert his identity, as we should say today. With the return of his father, the growth of a plan, and finally the destruction of the suitors he stands forth as a man grown, free at last of his doubts and uncertainties as to what kind of person he is. The other person is Nausicaa, the daughter of the Phaeacian king, the only well-bred young girl who appears in Greek literature. Her hopes and doubts, her courage and proper courtesy are well portrayed, but we do not see her become a woman as we see Telemachus become a man.

There is a fascinating gallery of women. The incomparable Helen appears as a grave woman, no longer young, living soberly with her husband, speaking frankly when necessary of that past which had caused so much trouble, and no less charming than she had been before. The nymph Calypso is the good-natured woman who asks only to make a man happy in a quiet way. Circe, the lovely witch who turns men to swine, had suffered a wound the nature of which we are not told, but the man who would not wish for the opportunity and take the risk of trying to soothe her bruised spirit would be a clod indeed. At home Penelope is waiting, the faithful wife who for endless years has believed that her husband is not lost, until at last she has him back and, hardly able to believe that he is really home, finally makes his homecoming perfect.

The greatest single scene in the two poems is that in which the Trojan Hector says good-bye to his wife and his little son as he goes forth to fight Achilles, a scene that cannot and must not be paraphrased. According to the taste of the West from Homer's day to ours, this is the true substance of life. The continuing satisfaction with Homer's view of life is not the least of the cultural traits which constitute the continuity of the West from then to now.

CHAPTER

12

THE NEW AGE OF GREECE

About 800 B.C. the Greeks began to be more in touch with the other civilized peoples of their end of the Mediterranean and to live in a more active and prosperous way. This new age was to last until about 500 B.C., at which time we may say that the classical age of Greece began, to last about two hundred years. We can see that between 800 and 500 many characteristically Greek activities appeared and were advanced close to their high point. The analysis of Nature and Man was one such activity, issuing in philosophical studies and literary treatments of great problems, as well as in what we now should call pure science. Greek literature made great advances during the new age, as did the whole complex of the practical and the fine arts. Forms of government appeared that were unlike those which we have studied so far.

We shall devote six chapters, this and the next five, to the description of this period. In this chapter the scanty information about the restoration of contact with other peoples will be presented and an account given of the great movement of Greek colonization that soon followed. The following chapters describe the formation of the *polis*, or city-state, and the rise of tyrannies, two important phenomena of government. A chapter will be given to the development of Sparta and one to the development of Athens; then the intellectual, artistic, and religious life of the time will be described in Chapters Sixteen and Seventeen.

THE RESTORATION OF CONTACT

We do not know why life among the Greeks became somewhat livelier around 800 B.C. The scanty archaeological evidence seems to suggest that there was a little more trade between the Greeks and that their pottery and other material possessions, as far as we can judge them, began to be of a finer and more spirited type. There was a significant and fruitful increase of trade by sea with Phoenicia, Palestine, and Egypt. Although the matter is not settled, it may well be that it was the Greeks themselves rather than the Phoenicians who carried the things that now serve us as evidence for this trade.

The study of the articles that are found suggests that the restoration of contact between the Greeks and the other people was well under way by 800. Rhodes and Crete were important in this movement; Cyprus was apparently a useful station along the way. Corinth, which is located in an excellent position for a sea power, was apparently involved in this trade by 800. A group of Greeks—apparently from Rhodes and other eastern Greek islands—founded a trading station in Syria at about this time. The place, now called Al Mina, is at the mouth of the Orontes River. Pottery was the chief thing that the Greeks had to offer in return for fine woven goods with gay patterns and brilliant dyes, articles of ivory and bronze, and jewelry.

By about the year 750 B.C., the Greeks of the mainland and the islands were fully in touch with the peoples of Egypt, Phoenicia, Syria, and the Hittite country of southeast Asia. There was soon to be some slight contact even with Urartu, north of Assyria, whose ware was sometimes carried to the Black Sea and shipped. The impact of the decorative style that was introduced to the Greeks by Near Eastern wares after about 750 was such that Greek artisans responded strongly, gradually abandoning the somewhat austere decoration of Geometric Pottery for new types that, by comparison, were riotous in line and color. The archaeologist can trace this influence as it made itself felt in Crete first, in Corinth and Laconia (the Spartan territory), then in Athens, and then among the Ionians of Asia Minor.

It is worth noting that the Ionians of Asia Minor were late in feeling the influence of these renewed contacts. By 700 their ships were voyaging to Cyprus and northern Syria, yet it was toward 650 before they suddenly surged forward with an appropriation of the techniques that the other Greeks had known for some time, rapidly outstripped them, and took the lead in both intellectual and artistic life.

What was different from the preceding age? We may say that the great migrations had already taken place and that there had been a chance to recover from the extensive violence, destruction, and dislocation that these migrations had caused around 1100 B.C. Many people had begun to prosper somewhat in their new situations. Some found the energy to sail over the horizon and re-establish contact with the great world, and the effect was the general quickening of the Greeks around the Aegaean. We can hardly say more, and probably there is no need to attempt to describe the change further.

One early and important result of the new contacts was the adoption of the Phoenician alphabet among the Greeks, probably by the year 800. The Phoenician alphabet could be readily used for Greek if certain letters were invented: *phi* (ph), *chi* (ch), *psi* (ps), and *xi* (x). The Phoenician language had no need for these letters, not having the sounds. It is interesting to note that at first there was no uniformity in supplying this lack; several different devices were used for the missing letters in different places. But in the end there was an all-Greek alphabet, based on the Phoenician.

Another important feature of the new age, but not a borrowing from other people, was the beginning of what is known as the *polis*, or city-state. Later we shall give a great deal of attention to the interesting mechanism of the *polis*; here we may simply point to its rise as one of the interesting features of this age of rapid change. It may readily be supposed that the Ionians early felt a need for a governmental unit that was small and efficient and had a fortified center, because their life was long that of frontiersmen facing the vigorous inland people of Asia Minor. It would seem natural, too, that the inhabitants of a rather small island should have a single stronghold. These fortified places, however, are different from those of the Mycenaean time in that some became the nuclei of real cities. These *poleis* (the plural of *polis*) were also sovereign states of very modest size, sometimes incredibly tiny by our standards. Historians have generally spoken of them as city-states. Lately the useful custom has grown up of using the word *polis* without translating it.

COLONIZATION

The great movement of colonization began so soon after the full resumption of Greek communications and trade with the rest of the eastern Mediterranean that it suggests a certain new vigor among the Greeks, already expressed in a rise in the population and now ready to express itself in the formal sending out of colonies from a good many places and to a good many places. The great movement of colonization began around 750 B.C. and continued actively until after 650 B.C. The migrations of the age before, especially that of the Ionians to Asia Minor, may be regarded as the first Greek colonizing movement. This was the second, and there were to be others later.

The Greek mariners of Mycenaean times had known their way around the whole Mediterranean and perhaps out into the Atlantic. Probably much of this knowledge had been lost to the Greeks in the intervening period. Geographical and nautical information was not freely shared in those days, but was the precious secret of those who acquired it expensively and dangerously. The Phoenicians, who were the great navigators of the period from 1000 B.C. on, were notoriously secretive about their voyages.

When the Greeks began to resume their old trade with Egypt and the Near East, they presumably began to venture again toward the West as well. By 750 they may well have been getting around the whole Mediterranean. Here a vexed question of scholarship raises itself. Did the Phoenicians make settlements in the far West shortly after 1000 B.C., or was it nearer to 700 B.C.? The position taken in Chapter Six and here—that the Phoenicians did not make settlements in the West until nearly 700 B.C.—rests on recent analysis of the pottery of Carthage and some other Phoenician settlements in the West. It has proved possible to arrange that pottery in sequence, as has been done with many other collections excavated in a limited region. New excavations have seemed to get to bedrock in the cemeteries of Carthage, excluding the possibility of earlier burials with pottery and other datable objects in them waiting to be found. The conclusion is that there is no real evidence that the Phoenicians were frequent visitors to the West or made settlements there until nearly 700 B.C. This is not quite the dry-as-dust argument that it may seem, for imagination has spun a long story of the Phoenicians in the West before 700 B.C.

Neither individuals nor very small groups of people went out to colonize under their own auspices, as so many did in the early days of the United States. It would have been very dangerous to do so, and it was not in the spirit of the times. The Greek colonists went as communities, ready to set themselves up in working order. This does not mean that a whole community would arise and depart, leaving its former habitation empty (although this happened two or three times that we know of), but a group of people large enough to form a complete social organism and defend themselves met, established their form as a community, and then went out together and settled.

The project was always under the auspices of some *polis*, which was called the metropolis or mother city. The colony was likely to retain a sentimental tie with the *polis* that had founded it. Only occasionally did a closer bond persist, one that might perhaps lead the colony to support the metropolis in a war. At the outset, the founding city would choose an oecist to be in charge. The site was chosen on the basis of reports from merchants about sites offering agricultural or commercial advantages and having a reasonable climate and neighbors who would probably be friendly. The oecist generally made a trip to Delphi, a picturesque place a few miles from the north shore of the Corinthian Gulf, in Greece, where the oracle of Apollo was already gaining in popularity and influence by the year 750. There he consulted the priestess who represented the god about the form of worship of the new colony. He was likely to get a rather conventional answer that the worship should be of Apollo and the greater Olympians.

He might also get a suggestion as to where the new colony should be. The priests of Apollo were great collectors of information from their visitors and were as well informed as any chancellery about the affairs of the Mediterranean world. We have seen that King Amasis of Egypt cultivated the Oracle in the late 500's and that his reason may well have been to get a source of general information. There were many stories about the Oracle's suggestions. For instance, it is said to have urged the foundation of Byzantium on its magnificent commercial and military site by suggesting to an oecist that he found his city across from the city of the blind. After prolonged thought, he decided that the people of Chalcedon, who had settled across the strait, must have been blind to pass up the solid advantages of the site of Byzantium. The story was probably invented later, for the priests had a habit of circulating stories about the good things that the Oracle had made possible at earlier times.

No detail on the gathering and dispatching of the colonists has been preserved. It is plain, however, that some cities acted as agents for the founding of colonies. Megara, a city of modest size at the northern end of the Isthmus of Corinth, sent out a great many, but surely she herself did not have enough population to furnish that many colonists. If overpopulation of Megara was not the reason for the sending out of these groups, the overpopulation of other places whose citizens were sent to Megara or came there of their own will might be the cause. In addition, there is evidence that now and then a group, perhaps a tenth, was picked out of an established community and told to go elsewhere. Presumably the least desirable element was selected. It probably became known that Megara was in the business of organizing colonies, and people who were ready to make a move may have flocked there to join the current venture.

The Range of Colonization: The East

Let us begin our consideration of colonies with those at the eastern end of the Mediterranean, even though they were far from being first. As we have seen, the Ionians were slow in joining the generally more active style of Greek life after 800 B.C. It was only after 700 B.C. that they joined the colonizing movement. Their slowness in this matter is all the more marked because for a long time their efforts to extend their territories inland had no success and their first colonies seem to have been founded with the idea of getting more agricultural territory rather than more trade. They began by trying to establish agricultural colonies in eastern Thrace (which is now Turkey in Europe) and in the Propontis (which is now the Gallipoli Peninsula). In Thrace, they were successful with only three colonies. Perhaps the colonies were undermanned. One of them, Abdera, was twice wiped out by its neighbors. Such devastation occurred only rarely; more often the neighbors found the Greeks stimulating and worthy of imitation. The third foundation of Abdera was one of the rare instances where a whole city moved. The people of Teus packed up and went to Abdera to get away from the Persians after the Persians conquered Lydia in 547 B.C.

The future of Thrace was to be that of a strategic region of considerable natural wealth, not a great home of Hellenism. Its good soil, its timber, its minerals, and its location made it an object of interest to the Persians, who made it a part of their empire in the late 500's. Later the Macedonian king, Philip II, saw its value when he was trying to build up his own weak country in the fourth century B.C. and went to some pains to acquire and hold it. Yet Abdera, in this rural and somewhat remote territory, could remain a Greek city and could point with pride to the philosopher Democritus and to others only slightly less distinguished as her sons.

A number of colonies were founded on both the north and the south shores of the Propontis, both as agricultural communities and also as way stations for the Black Sea trade. The Greeks had found trade with the Black Sea difficult because of the problem of getting through the Bosporus, the strait through which one finally enters the Black Sea after going through the Dardanelles and the Sea of Marmora and past Istanbul (the modern city on the site of Byzantium). During the summer, when most of the sailing was done, the ship heading for the Black Sea would have to sail into the prevailing northeast winds and in addition fight the current coming from the Black Sea through the strait. But the sailors of Miletus, one of the leading Ionian cities, discovered that in the spring one could catch southwesterly winds, that a good skipper might learn to use more favorable currents near the shore, and that at night in the summer one might even get a favorable wind.

Miletus was said to have founded some ninety colonies in this region. This figure suggests that Miletus, like Megara, did some organizing of people from other places who wished to try a new life, for she could not have supplied all the colonists herself. Because the number is so very large, it also suggests that some were mere trading posts rather than real colonies. There are not enough known Greek cities on the Black Sea to make up the roster of Milesian colonies, if there were ninety real ones, however small. Megara, too, had colonies in the Black Sea region, and some of the Ionian cities other than Miletus had sent colonies there.

This region was a magnificent source of raw materials. There was some gold. From inner Asia Minor, south of the Black Sea coast, came wrought steel. Flax and hemp were both produced. The waters were rich in fish. Perhaps the prize product was the rich cereal yield of the lands on the north shore. Many of these cities prospered. None of them ever became a famous city or produced a famous man unless, as in one or two cases, he went to Greece itself, made his contribution there, and stayed there. Yet it would be a mistake to shape our ideas of the Greeks so narrowly on the later Athenian—and, it sometimes seems, a somewhat idealized and ethereal Athenian, too— that we assert that these energetic people were not typical Greeks. As we said, there is room for a great deal of variety and even of inconsistency among the Greeks of different places and of different centuries whom we shall discuss.

These Greeks of the shores of the Black Sea were real Greeks who lived in an area which was colder and less sunny than most Greek sites around the Mediterranean, who rubbed elbows with people who often were rough and wild, who often intermarried with the local people and took on many of the rough ways of the frontier, and who were not distinguished for artistic achievements or fascinating experiments in government or the establishment of new intellectual systems. It is doubtful whether they had the lofty attitude toward "barbarians" that was expressed by some of the Greeks. It is more likely that the majority of the Greeks had frequently been in contact with peoples of a very different stamp without thinking overmuch of any distinction between them and the typical Greek.

The interchange of ideas between the Greeks and the others was not as lively as the interchange of goods; if the local people were glad to use some Greek pottery and other manufactured goods, they did not rush to make themselves entirely like the Greeks. Beyond the first tribes (people of no great interest) whom the trader met as he trudged inland or went up the great rivers was the great nomad people of the Scythians. We have already mentioned them as a people who resisted the allure of "civilization" in these early days, in the time of the later Greeks, and in the days of the high empire of the Romans, continuing for several hundred years in the simple and stable way of life which they had when we first learn of them.

Naturally, as the waves of influence outward from the central groups of Greeks became more and more complex, there was less and less impulse for the Greeks in the colonies to borrow intangibles from the peoples around them. Nevertheless the Thracians seem to have inspired a wave of what we may call shamanism. Some of the earlier philosophers of Greece seem very like the shamans, or ecstatic religious leaders, of Thrace.

Eretria and Chalcis in Euboea specialized in the colonizing of the three-pronged peninsula of Chalcidice and the region around it in western Thrace. Later this was to seem a strongly Greek region, although there were cities only on the coast and they had little hold on any territory inland. Another colony that may be regarded as being in the eastern part of the Mediterranean was Cyrene, in North Africa, in that well-watered and fertile coastal section between Egypt and Tripolitania that is still known as Cyrenaica. The priests of the Delphic Oracle had a story to tell about this piece of colonizing, too, claiming that the first settlement, founded in the wrong place because of the oecist's obtuseness, had suffered much hardship. Of course the colony had begun to prosper as soon as it was removed to the location that the Oracle, in its typically indirect way, had tried to point out to the oecist. Life in Cyrene was good. The people were known for their addiction to pleasure, which was possible in a land noted for its grain, its wine, its roses, its horses, and a peculiar plant called *silphium*, which has been equated with asafetida and was very much in demand for seasoning and for medicinal purposes, so much so that the plant is even beautifully portrayed on coins of Cyrene.

There were many places in the eastern Mediterranean where it was not possible for the Greeks to found colonies because the inhabitants were ready and able to drive them off. They did, however, manage to establish one or two trading-posts in difficult regions. That at Al Mina, at the mouth of the Orontes River in Syria, may have been established by 800 B.C. Around 650, as we have seen, the merchants of Miletus seem to have been allowed to make a settlement on one of the branches of the Nile, near the sea. Other Greeks were welcomed in Egypt as mercenary soldiers and as resident traders. We have already discussed Amasis, ruler of Egypt from 569 to 527, who used a garrison of Greek mercenaries at his capital at Memphis and also gathered all the Greek traders at an extra-territorial settlement in the Delta that they called Naucratis.

The Range of Colonization: The West

Corinth held the position in western colonization that Miletus did in the eastern Mediterranean. Her position on her isthmus gave her a peculiar advantage in trade, for she could ship or receive goods either at her harbor on the eastern side of the isthmus for the Aegean trade or at her other harbor, three miles away on the western side of the isthmus, for the trade to the West. Sending goods through the Gulf of Corinth was advantageous in two ways: it was a short route to western Greece, South Italy, and Sicily, and it avoided the difficult and dangerous rounding of Cape Malea, the southern tip of Greece. It was well worth while to have the goods carted across the Isthmus of Corinth to another ship.

Corinth had colonies on the west coast of Greece, the chief of which was Corcyra. She also began the colonization farther west and was always most important there. The first colony was apparently on the island of Ischia, off the Bay of Naples. The most important was Syracuse, in Sicily, founded in 735, where the fine harbor and rich hinterland made an excellent combination. From the beginning, Syracuse prospered; and a time was to come, shortly after 400 B.C., when she probably was the most powerful city in the world. Practically all the colonies in Sicily were on the seacoast. The people of the interior were vigorous and warlike and often made difficulties for the Greeks, but never to the extent of driving them away. After some time, many of them were brought to terms, in some cases because Greek ways appealed to them.

The colonial foundations in Italy avoided the coast closer to Greece, the east coast, which is made inhospitable by the fact that the central mountains of Italy come much nearer to the sea here than in the west. Cities were founded on the coast at the bottom of Italy and on the western coast up as far as the north shore of the Bay of Naples.

Sicily and southern Italy may be called the America of Greece, the richer and more open place in the West where the Greeks went in search of new opportunities. Because there was no nation there to claim their allegiance, they remained Greeks in thought and feeling and were regarded as still eligible to compete in the Olympic Games, which were open only to Greeks. Acragas in Sicily and Poseidonia in Italy will serve as examples of these colonies.

Acragas (later called Agrigentum by the Romans) was on the southern coast of Sicily, a little more than halfway toward the western end of the island. The *polis* prospered greatly on agriculture and trade. We hear of the luxury of its citizens, their artificial lake, and their enjoyment of their festivals. They built temples that would be large by any standard and are surprising as the products of a city of this size. Their remains are still a great attraction for visitors to Sicily. The city had one famous son, as did so many: Empedocles, one of those philosophers who seemed to resemble the shamans of Thrace. The coins of the city that have been preserved are beautiful work, and their excellence suggests strong local pride.

Poseidonia was on the west coast of Italy, some sixty miles south of Naples. This site, like Acragas, attracts visitors by the magnificence of the temples that still remain, in good enough condition to give an adequate idea of how they were meant to look. One may stand in the doorway of the great temple that has often been associated with Poseidon, but is now thought to be the temple of Hera, see the glint of the sea a few miles away, and then turn and look through the temple and across a fertile plain to the hills. The place was good for both trade and agriculture and was pleasant. The temples were built in the fifth century, a little earlier than the Parthenon at Athens, and show all the refinements, such as the subtle curves to correct optical illusions, that are so admired in the

Parthenon. The people of this town knew what was the latest thing and how to get it.

Poseidonia, like Acragas, has a Roman name: Paestum. But before it became Roman, it was destined to be conquered by the neighboring Lucanian people and to be subject to them for over a hundred years. When the Romans moved southward in Italy, Paestum received their colonists in 273 B.C. and became part of the Roman commonwealth, as did all the other Greek settlements of South Italy and, later in the third century, of Sicily.

We saw that there was not a great deal of cultural exchange between those Greeks who settled at the eastern end of the Mediterranean and "the natives," the people they found there. Here in the West the Greeks probably learned little from the local peoples, but it is of the greatest importance that the Greeks of South Italy and Sicily taught much to the people they found there. Finally the great Roman appropriation of Greek culture in all its forms came to pass and resulted in the combined Greco-Roman culture that has formed a most important part of the culture of modern Europe and the United States.

The most civilized peoples whom the Greeks met in the West were the Carthaginians and the Etruscans. If one adopts the later date for the foundation of Carthage, as we do here, the Phoenicians and the Greeks moved into the western waters at about the same time, and the foundations of Carthage, the city that was to lead the western Phoenicians until it was destroyed by the Romans in 146 B.C., took place toward 700, at a time when the Greeks were busily colonizing South Italy and Sicily. Carthage was on a site that is now a suburb of modern Tunis. It established trading posts all along the coast of North Africa, from Cyrene to Morocco, and in southern Spain. The Carthaginians settled in the western end of Sicily and were not far from some Greek cities, Acragas, for example.

The Etruscans lived in Italy north of Rome. According to one story, they came there by sea from somewhere in the Aegaean not long after the fall of Troy. There was also another story about some of the Trojans who sailed away to the West after their city fell, which was to be picked up by the Roman poet Vergil and made part of his account of the founding of Rome. We need not debate the Etruscans' origins here. The important point is that by the time of the arrival of the Greeks they were fairly well established on the more northern coast of western Italy.

Both the Carthaginians and the Etruscans taught the Greeks a few things of no great importance. The Greeks taught the Carthaginians little. Much Greek ware has been found at Carthage, but it does not seem to have influenced the local product. On the other hand the Greeks taught the Etruscans many details of the manufacture of both pottery and metal goods, as well as giving them some Greek ideas. The Etruscans had ideas of their own in these fields and were able to absorb some Greek culture without being overpowered by it. Because they controlled the city of Rome, later to be the center of the Roman realm, the Etruscans were the first great teachers of civilization to the Romans. Their indirect Greek influence on the Romans came earlier, then, than the direct Greek influence of South Italy and Sicily on the Romans. But these were long-term results of the Greek migration to the West; we must return to the Greeks themselves during the period of colonization.

With the roles of the Carthaginians and Etruscans explained, we may appreciate better the feats of the Phocaeans, the Greeks who had the honor of going farthest west. Theirs was a small *polis* in Asia Minor, but they were daring sailors, even for that age. About 600 B.C., they worked up a route to Tartessus in Spain, where silver and tin were to be had. They used penteconters, or fifty-oared fighting ships. The Phoenicians, who tried to dominate by force the seas to the West, might well shrink from attacking a pack of these fast oared warships. Such ships, on the other hand, could not carry a heavy load and could be used only on a run where precious metals formed a cargo that was valuable without being bulky. The Phocaeans had planted a string of colonies along their route—on the island of Ischia near Naples, in the Balearic Islands over toward Spain, and on the east coast of Spain—where their ships could refit and provision. Perhaps their most important achievement was the founding of Massilia (the modern Marseilles), through which a steady stream of Greek and, later, Greco-Roman influence was to pass to the people of Gaul (the modern France), who were very susceptible to such influences.

In their typically daring and decided manner the people of Phocaea decided to move en masse when the Lydian kingdom fell in 547 B.C. and they realized that they were face to face with the Persians. One night they simply sailed away. In a few hours some lost their nerve and returned. The majority went on and settled in Corsica, which was so good a place for settlement that the Carthaginians and Etruscans felt that they must combine to drive the Phocaeans out of it. The Phocaeans finally yielded to their joint aggression by moving to the mainland below Naples.

The Carthaginians pressed their attacks on the Phocaeans and other Greeks, and little by little the situation evolved that in essentials was to endure until the Romans became masters of the West. Carthage controlled the Strait of Gibraltar and the metal trade from Spain, the whole coast of North Africa from Cyrene to Morocco, the Balearic Islands, Sardinia and Corsica, and the western end of Sicily. The Greeks controlled the coasts of South Italy, a large part of Sicily, and the northern shores of the Mediterranean in eastern Spain, France, and the Italian Riviera.

The Effects of Colonization

It seems, although it cannot be proved, that the movement of colonization must have greatly increased the total number of the Greeks. The removal of many people to new lands that were far more fertile than the old and the removal of others to fine sites for commerce, combined with the new and energetic spirit of the time, were the sort of thing that we should expect to promote a growth of numbers. The spreading out and the increase in numbers of a people of such marked characteristics is worth the attention of the historian.

The colonizing movement must also have promoted changes in the social alignment of the Greeks. Many a man must have improved his position in agriculture by moving to the better soil of a colony and found himself a more weighty member of the community than he had been as the fourth son of a small farmer at home. The increased amount of commerce, which came from the increase in numbers and prosperity of many people who had made the great move, naturally was a stimulant to manufactures. Many shrewd people must have improved their status by making their way into industry and trade instead of remaining in marginal agriculture. We must

remember, of course, that not all the trading was done by the poor
or those of no standing. Many an aristocrat perceived the opportunities here for him.

The new distribution of the Greek people, which was one effect
of the colonization, was to endure for several centuries. When the
intense culture of Athens is described in some of the following
chapters, or the struggles of Athens with Sparta, we shall do well to
remember that at that same time countless thousands of Greeks
were going their own way all over the Mediterranean world without
doing anything distinctive enough to be mentioned. Nevertheless,
if these Greeks never achieved the intensity of Athens, they spread
to other people at scores of points a little something of a culture
more intense than any these people would otherwise have known.

COMMERCE AND INDUSTRY

The Ships

Our knowledge of the Greek merchant ships that traveled the
ways of the sea during this period is gained from a few pictures
on early Greek vases. They were small vessels, capable of being
drawn up on shore. They were rigged with a single square sail, not
so well equipped for handling as a modern sail would be, and with
oars for use at certain times, as in rounding difficult headlands,
where a little auxiliary power would be of great use. They were very
like the ships of the Phoenicians except for one thing: instead of
their being mere tubs, their design was effective and graceful.

But these ships could not always go their way in peace; even the
Greek states did not always live in peace with one another. Early
in this period—probably by 800 b.c.—the ship of war was invented.
That is, some ships were fitted with bronze rams at the waterline.
Thus, a ship could punch a hole through the side of another ship
if she could get into position, deliver the blow smartly, and back
off to clear the ram. This change implied a whole new style of
shipbuilding. The warship must have plenty of power from the oars
to be independent of the wind in maneuvering. Her men must be
trained to deliver the blow crisply and quickly. The shipbuilders of
Corinth led in making slimmer and trimmer hulls for more speed

and in devising ways to pack more rowers into the ship without making her too large. In the final design, there were three banks of oarsmen. One would sit with his legs almost touching the back of the men just before and below him. The lower man's head would be about on the level of the upper man's stomach, and the bottom man would be in the same relative position. The upper men would pull slightly longer oars. At the end of this period the chief warship was the penteconter, the fifty-oared ship. These were the warships that the Phocaeans sent in packs to Tartessus to bring back the valuable silver and tin through a sea that the Phoenicians were trying to close to other people's ships.

The sea traffic of the Greeks had to contend with pirates, some of them Greek, almost anywhere that it moved. Historians believe that certain colonies were founded with the express purpose of preying on traffic in certain waters. No power except the Carthaginians made any effort to suppress piracy, and in the West, the Greeks might have to fight the Carthaginians as well as the pirates. As we have seen, the shores of the western sea were gradually and informally partitioned between Greeks and Carthaginians. On the other hand, as time went on, the Phoenicians did less trading in the ports of the Greeks at the eastern end of the Mediterranean.

Cities, Routes, and Materials

Miletus was probably the greatest of the Greek commercial cities at the eastern end of the Mediterranean, although Phocaea and the island cities of Samos and Chios were close behind her. Many communities developed special products of their own. The woollen products of Miletus and the wine of Chios became famous, for example. Miletus was strong in the Black Sea trade where many of the colonies were of her founding. A part of her business was certainly the carrying of goods for others. Many cargoes of steel, wheat, fish, furs, timber, flax, and hemp went from their sources around the Black Sea to Greek cities whose merchants had asked to have the goods brought to them. When the later kings of Lydia brought the Greeks of the coast under their control and opened the trade routes of Lydia to them, Miletus especially was able to combine her sea routes with her new trade in the interior of Lydia and became very busy and wealthy.

From the middle 600's on, Egypt was receptive to Greek merchants and mercenary soldiers. The services sold by the mercenaries should not be overlooked when we consider Greek trade. Some such men left their bones on foreign fields, to be sure, but others returned to Greece with fortunes made from their generous pay and their booty. They, like the merchants, must have brought home many interesting ideas from Egypt or from the service of other powers in this long-civilized area.

The merchants tended at first to be from Ionia and the eastern islands—an assertion that rests on the belief that each city dealt in its own pottery rather than in everyone's. Thus, the pottery found at Naucratis, the trading city in Egypt, can be used to prove that different cities were active there at different periods; and the pottery indicates that the Ionians and eastern islanders were there first and that the merchants of Athens, Corinth, and the Spartan territory were active there in later years. The trade route from Greece proper probably ran from southern Greece down to Cyrene and along the coast to Egypt.

The Greeks were very impressed by the antiquity and the different-ness of Egyptian culture. They not only learned many things about the techniques of handling materials from the Egyptians—although it is hard to be precise about what they learned—but they were also moved by Egyptian customs to some speculation that was not highly useful. They probably borrowed from the Egyptians the practice of making temples of stone. But the houses that the Greeks built in stone for their gods followed the design of the homes that their kings and great men had been used to building, long houses with columned porches.

Corinth was probably more powerful and wealthy even than Miletus. Trade between East and West tended to come to the Isthmus of Corinth, whether it came from the East across the Aegaean or from the West and through the Gulf of Corinth. The long-haul traffic was so lively that it finally seemed worth the expense to make a ship railroad across the isthmus, linking her two harbors. It was about three miles long and paved with marble slabs in which grooves had been cut. The ships were drawn out of the water in a wheeled cradle and hauled along this railway by oxen.

Corinth prospered from the possession of her two harbors. Her shipwrights gained a great reputation for merchant ships and ships of war, which led to profits from building both kinds for other cities. Her merchants profited from being at the crossing of a water route from east to west and a land route that went south into Laconia and north into central Greece either by land or first by water through the Gulf of Corinth to the north shore of the gulf and thence by land. The chief manufacture of Corinth was a fine pottery of what is known as the orientalizing style, the more lively style that under Eastern influence replaced the austere Geometric after about 750 B.C. This pottery was very popular everywhere and often was sold as a container already filled with another product. Perfume, from the East, for example, packaged in such containers, must have been very popular in the West. Corinthian bronze work, especially armor, was also very acceptable everywhere.

Syracuse was the chief colony of the many that Corinth founded in the West. Goods carried there would often be redistributed, going to other cities of Sicily, up the west coast of Italy to Greek cities and to the Etruscans farther north, or even southward to Carthage (where the many Corinthian vases have been very helpful in establishing the dates of the strata of the excavations). The return cargoes from the West were generally raw materials, as they were from the Black Sea region. The Etruscans controlled iron deposits on the mainland and on the island of Elba, and they were good smiths. Their iron and wrought steel must have been important in trade.

Toward 550 B.C., the pottery of Athens became far more important in trade than it had been and was sent almost everywhere that Greek trade went, even to the places where Corinthian ware had formerly dominated. The merchants of Corinth were willing to carry Athenian ware if it was what their customers wanted. A great many beautiful Athenian pieces of every type are found in the modern museums that contain the finds from Etruscan sites. The Etruscans presumably paid for their imports from Athens in iron or wrought steel.

Many other cities prospered on the lively trade around the Isthmus of Corinth. The island of Aegina, just below Athens, had a prosperity and an importance that testify that the people of so small a place must have been very energetic and shrewd. Megara, like Corinth, was on the Isthmus of Corinth and had a harbor on either side, but the isthmus was wider and harder to cross at this point, and Megara had no products of her own attractive enough to compete with those of Corinth except as an obvious second best. Sicyon, on the southern coast of the Gulf or Corinth, also shared in the trade and was regarded as a leading city in this period.

In the East, the most prosperous colonial foundations were Byzantium and Chalcedon. Potidaea was the chief of those founded on the Chalcidic Peninsula in the neighborhood of the modern Saloniki. Corcyra was the chief of the colonies on the west side of Greece, dominating with her island city the trade that went up the Adriatic Sea to a region inhabited by intractable people with whom it was possible to trade if due precautions were taken, but who remained outside civilization. Syracuse was undoubtedly the greatest colony in the West. Massilia, or Marseilles, had no near rivals for the trade with the rich territory of Gaul. There were a great many less important *poleis* where people could live comfortably and well, as in Acragas and Paestum.

The Commerce in Ideas: Coinage

This was a period of new circulation of ideas as well as new circulation of material goods. The Greeks were now in position to learn many of the useful traditional techniques of Egypt and of the Near East and to consider the frequent differences in customs. They themselves passed on a certain amount of their own culture to the peoples whom they met around their colonies. The use of the alphabet and the use of coinage stand out as two definite and useful new practices that the Greeks learned, the alphabet at the beginning of the period, just before 800 B.C., and coinage about the middle of the period, around 650 B.C.

Coinage, as we have seen, was an invention of the Lydians. It passed from them to the Ionian cities. Miletus and Ephesus were very active in coining, producing handsome coins of electrum, a natural mixture of gold and silver found in Lydia. Other Ionian cities produced their own, some of them of silver. Two other Greek systems of coinage soon joined the Ionian. Aegina further showed its enterprising spirit by devising a system of coinage that soon became known as the Aeginetan standard and was used in Athens for some time, in Megara, in the Peloponnesus, and in some of the southern and eastern islands as far away as Rhodes. The third system, the Euboic, began in Euboea and had Corinth as its most influential user. In 593, Athens changed from the Aeginetan system to the Euboic.

King Croesus of Lydia minted some coins of pure gold; the Persians were to follow with a famous gold coin, the daric; and much later King Philip II of Macedon minted very beautiful gold coins, the first gold coinage of Europe. Gold coinage was unusual, however, and except for the electrum in some early Ionian coinage, the Greek coins were of silver.

The three Greek systems of coinage, the Ionian, the Aeginetan, and the Euboic, the coins of which contained only moderately differing amounts of silver, were used in three constellations of commercial cities. The systems were highly competitive, and the defection of Athens from the Aeginetan standard to the Euboic was a notable event. The production and sale of silver bullion became much more important than it had been when silver was used only for jewelry. Silver from Spain was used by a number of Sicilian states. Athens had mines from which she could supply a fair amount of silver.

Naturally the introduction of coinage, beside facilitating the exchange of goods in intercity trade, had effects on the life of those cities which adopted it. It was likely to enliven their trade somewhat and intensify the effects that came from having a trading economy instead of a static agricultural economy. It now became possible to have a new form of capital and a new flexibility in commercial enter-prises. The Cretans and the Spartans and the Byzantines, however, resisted the introduction of coinage, being conservative people who were a little worried by the social changes that they could see going on in other states and, perhaps, beginning in their own.

13

THE RISE OF THE POLIS

The new age of Greece, from about 800 B.C. to about 500 B.C., which is our present concern, began with most of the Greek people still living under the system of families, clans, and tribes that had persisted since the end of the Mycenaean Age, although the *polis* had probably begun to appear among the Ionians of Asia Minor and the Dorians of Crete and the Peloponnesus. During the new age some hundreds of *poleis* appeared in the Greek world, although many people continued to live as before under the system of families, clans, and tribes and under the leadership of kings.

The *polis* is not easy to define. It was not uniform. Generally the kings had disappeared. There was usually a fortified center. In most cases, this center developed into a true city, where there was a purposive specialization of function. Yet Sparta was a *polis*, retained monarchy, had no fortified center, and did not develop into a true city. Always, however, the *polis* was more like what we should call a state than the older system had been. There was a government in the *polis* that had acquired power at the expense of the clans and the tribes. There was a physical place in the territory where buildings and people and activity tended to concentrate, even though other people might be scattered all through the territory, most of which was agricultural land. This focal point made life more intense. Although the government was not necessarily democratic, some *poleis,* notably Athens, were interesting examples of democracy carried to some length. The citizens of every *polis,* whether it was a democracy or not, were likely to have a very strong sense of being banded together for common purposes and often an equally strong sense that their interests were inconsistent with those of the neighboring *poleis.* This sense of separatism was an important feature of Greek life, along with an intensification of intellectual and artistic life and a sensitivity to the problems of human relations.

In a way, the rest of this book is a description of life in the *polis,* for this was the most significant of the forms of life in Greece down to the end of the fourth century before Christ. We may begin with its development from the earlier forms and thus come a little closer to a working knowledge of the *polis* by observing its divergence from other forms. The scarcity of evidence on this development is regrettable, but we can be sure what the situation was at the beginning of the new age and at its end and we can catch a number of glimpses of the process of change.

EARLY DEVELOPMENTS

The Ionians of Asia Minor

The Ionian cities of the seacoast of Asia Minor seem to have made the change from the old ways during the time between. Insofar as we can determine their form at the beginning of the new age, around 800 B.C., they no longer had kings and had begun to replace the system of clans and tribes under the kings by a tighter system of attachment to a state of a sort, which had a visible center with temples, other buildings, and some ceremonies to symbolize the state or *polis.* This amounts to saying that among the Ionians the essentials of the process were complete when we first catch sight of them as they emerged from the time between. It is not plain why they ceased to have kings. We must understand that in the ancient world there was no feeling whatsoever that there is a logical progression from monarchy to what we consider the superior form, democracy. Indeed, the process of migrating to Asia Minor might have been expected to call for firm leadership by one man for each group. The process of settling and repelling the attacks of the people of the neighborhood might also be expected to have encouraged or perpetuated monarchy. Yet no kings survived among the Ionians and the others who migrated to Asia Minor.

Although we cannot be sure that the cohesiveness of family, clan, and tribe had declined very much among the Greeks in Asia Minor, we can be sure that there had been some growth of a sense of union as a group or a nation or a *polis,* a development certain to subtract something from the practical strength of the earlier bonds. So far as we know, there had been nothing like a nation or a *polis* in earlier Greece. Now something of the sort had appeared and must necessarily take something away from earlier loyalties. To say that the difficulties of dealing with the natives in Asia Minor required this new and tighter organization does not fully explain the change, for there surely had been need of cohesiveness against enemies in earlier times.

As we cannot find an adequate, complete explanation for the disappearance of many of the kings, so we find it hard to explain why the nobles who headed the clans should have tolerated or even furthered a more general kind of government, one that could get started only by taking away from the clans such powers as the celebration of some major religious rites and the direction of military operations. It is not mere mysticism to say that the growth of the *polis* was in the spirit of the times and that we do not completely understand the causation.

The change was invariably made in an orderly manner, as far as we know. If the king lost his position, his head did not roll. There are no stories of the violent deposition of kings. The king, who had normally been first among equals, now became one among equals, a member of the upper class or nobility. Sometimes he retained the hereditary position of high priest because the king had traditionally dealt with the gods on behalf of the people. Sometimes the man chosen to do this priestly work was called "king" because this seemed the proper title.

If the nobles saw some of the power of their class transferred to the new *polis,* they did not suffer a disastrous diminution of power. In political matters, tradition was so strong and the leverage of the ordinary man so slight that we must assume that the change was acceptable to the leading people rather than forced on them. Possibly they did not foresee that radical concessions would have to be made to the mass of the citizens in some of the *poleis*. In others, of course, such concessions never had to be made; many remained under the firm control of the minority of leading citizens throughout their whole history, first as independent entities, then under the control of the Macedonian and other kingdoms, and then under the control of the Romans. The early stages of the growth of the *polis* did not involve any notable loss of power for those used to having the direction of affairs. The power was merely exercised in a different framework. There was no loss of status either for the king or for the nobles. The king's family lost an office that must often have been very onerous, yet they kept about as much distinction as they had had before. The nobles continued to be the leading people throughout the change, for, it must be remembered, their power within family, clan, and tribe was only lessened, not removed, and at the same time they gained a certain amount of authority within the new organization. The transfer of a fair amount of the power to the *polis* cost the leading people neither practical power nor status.

The Cretans and Spartans

The formation of the *polis* among the Dorians of Crete and the Peloponnesus took a slightly different course. According to tradition, the Spartan system, which came to dominate the Peloponnesus, owed much to Cretan Dorians. The Dorians, who had conquered Crete at the time of the great Dorian migration, around 1100 B.C., had been ruled by kings and organized by clans and tribes. As time went on, the kings and the large tribal organizations quietly disappeared, and the people found themselves living in separate agricultural villages of modest size. They had made serfs of the original inhabitants. Groups of a few villages, perhaps four or five, then combined into a *polis*, which probably did not have much of a visible center or a defensible place. It was neither a city nor a state in any modern sense. But the new arrangement was genuinely useful in that it combined the forces of the dominant Dorians into groups strong enough to assure their control of the people whom they had subjected—reason enough to make the change. In the case of the Ionians and others, there were doubtless similar reasons, which are not so clear to us.

The change in the system corresponded to the need to hold down the conquered people. The essence of the new Dorian *polis* was that it could produce an efficient body of men trained and toughened in the practice of arms and raised in the tradition of an aristocracy that expected to maintain its privileged position by force whenever need arose. Family life amounted to little, for the men lived a soldier's and sportman's life. The clans and tribes persisted as a way of keeping track of people, but without their former significance as groups that could command primary loyalty or initiate action.

Sparta was to be the most important Dorian *polis*. The process of formation was like that in Crete, although the kingship did not disappear, changing instead into the curious phenomenon of a double kingship. Five villages were combined into the *polis*. As in Crete, there was no urban center comparable to those of other outstanding *poleis*. The Athenian historian Thucydides was to remark at the end of the fifth century that no one in some later time, seeing the ruins of Sparta, would think them appropriate to the power of the Sparta of his time. Here, as in Crete, the essence of the change was that it created a solidly cemented group of people, who could thereby hold down a conquered people. The importance and interest of Sparta is such that all of the following chapter will be devoted to a detailed description of it.

Other Cities of Greece

Like the Spartans, the Corinthians were Dorians, but their *polis* was to be the greatest commercial city of Greece—and of the world—during most of this period and therefore had a busy and built-up focus. North of Corinth on the isthmus was Megara, which early in the same period was also an important commercial state, a rival of Corinth. Megara, too, had harbors on both sides of the Isthmus of Corinth, but soon the Corinthians conquered some of her territory, and thenceforth Corinth was to be clearly the stronger of the two *poleis*.

Athens claimed to be the only city of Greece that had been inhabited during the Mycenaean Age and continuously thereafter. The Athenians thought of themselves as Ionians, although ordinarily the term is used of those Ionians who had gone to colonize the coast of Asia Minor. According to an Athenian tradition, their kingship had lapsed

when King Codrus gave his life to save his country. In fact, most of
the kingships of the Greek world probably were surrendered so peaceably that people hardly noticed when the kings technically ceased to
be kings. Although the kingship did persist in some places among the
Greeks throughout this period and those following, it seems that
among most of the Greeks kings had somehow gone out of fashion,
for they were not retained even in the many places where vigorous
one-man leadership was desirable, as we have seen in Ionian Asia
Minor.

THE ARISTOCRACY

The life of the Greek and Roman world was to be dominated by the
aristocracies, in spite of the fact that the democracy of Athens is in the
foreground of much recent writing. If, in fact, we look at the whole
course of history up to modern times, the occasional appearance of
democracies may seem to be no more than an interesting eccentricity.

In the period from 800 to 500 B.C., the aristocrats gained in power,
wealth, and spirit at the expense of both the kings and the common
people. In most cases, the king and all his clan were absorbed into
the general system of clans. Naturally, the leaders of these clans had
been important during the monarchies, for through the clans the
society was organized and in a practical sense managed. Their leaders
were, as a matter of course, in frequent communication with the king;
they were his advisers and the channels through which the royal
power, such as it was, was exerted on people in general and through
which the energies of the people flowed toward the king. If there
ceased to be occasions that called for royal leadership, or if, as we
have suggested, there was a change of fashion or attitude, the leaders
of the clans could probably with some ease force the king to retire to
the position of head of one of the clans.

In many cases, an official was created to hold the title of king and
take charge of sacrifices and relations with the gods in general, often
for one year at a time, although at the beginning it might be for life
or for ten years. At Athens, at Megara, in the Megarian colonies, and
in several other places, there is clear evidence of the existence of such
a titular king, chosen for a short time to perform these necessary royal

functions and having no claim to the position except as the result of having been chosen by the group.

In a number of places, there is evidence that the aristocrats chose some of the older men to sit on a council. They were likely to be past military age, which might mean either forty-five or sixty, to be chosen for life, which meant that vacancies came from deaths, and to be accountable to no one for their acts in office. There is also evidence that there were magistrates to preside over the rudimentary business of the *polis*, sometimes for a term of one year and sometimes for ten. These men were likely to be held accountable; that is, they had to undergo a formal review of their acts at the end of their term of office and answer for what they had done. They were, of course, aristocrats chosen by their peers, not by the people at large.

If this is a dim and faraway beginning of what we think of as democracy, it still is a beginning. For a fairly tight group of aristocrats to elect one of their number every year to be a chairman and handle routine business in a simple *polis* was a new idea. Presently there was to be a group of such officers with more work to do; and the time was to come, at least in Athens and some other *poleis*, when a goodly number of citizens were to have a voice in the choice of officers and it can be said that there were democratic elections.

The Bacchiadae of Corinth, a powerful clan, are said to have ousted the king in 747 B.C. and ruled as a clan for ninety years. Earlier there had been a notable king of Corinth named Bacchis; and the Bacchiadae were the clan who claimed descent from him. It has been estimated that there were over two hundred men more than fifty years old in the clan. Because no firm rule of succession among the descendants of the king had been worked out, there were some struggles among those who claimed to be in the proper relation to succeed to the throne, leading at least once to murder and usurpation. Finally the whole clan took control of the situation. They deposed the men who then claimed kingship, made a formal council the chief body, began to elect one of their number each year as magistrate to preside and made him eponymous, and occasionally called an assembly of those who could fight in the armed forces to inform them of matters that needed to be widely known or to ask for their ratification of some proposal for action. We may assume that by 747 Corinth was well into the new surge of commerce and that the chief people were resolved not to be interfered with either by useless struggles for power or by any king who did not understand that the times were changing or who might try to pre-empt for himself all the profit from the new opportunities.

The rise and the sway of the Bacchiadae will serve to illustrate the tight exclusiveness of aristocratic rule and the process by which kings might be superseded. Other *poleis,* too, were dominated by one powerful clan rather than by the whole aristocracy. The Aleuadae dominated Larissa in the rich plains of Thessaly, the Penthilidae controlled the island of Mitylene in the Aegaean, and the Neleidae were the chief clan of Miletus. The Alcmaeonidae, or Alcmaeonids, were the most important clan of Athens. All these names end in -*dae*, a Greek patronymic meaning "the children of" or "the descendants of." It was common for clans thus to choose a distinguished earlier member and group themselves around his memory by calling themselves his descendants.

The aristocracies gained in power and wealth at the expense of the common people as well as at the expense of the kings. Probably, however, neither the aristocrat nor the common man of that day would have understood what we mean when we speak of aristocrats gaining at the expense of the common man. Both would have taken it for granted that the more powerful does what he can and the less powerful suffers what he must. The conception of a powerful central government that sometimes protects the many from injustice at the hands of the more able and better organized few had not arisen. The only organizations known to the common man were monarchy and this newer form, aristocracy.

In that day the common man had a sense of dependence on and obligation to the aristocrat that does not correspond to anything in our modern life. The aristocracy organized and led the colonial enterprises that often gave a new opportunity to the common man. Its trading enterprises likewise could sometimes benefit him. These benefits were, of course, only incidental to the main purpose and arose only from the fact that the aristocrats needed manpower for their trading and colonial ventures. If at home they ruled with an iron hand and often took advantage of the common man, they also had that sense of responsibility which is the proper mark of an aristocracy and often does not exist in the upper classes of the modern world. This responsibility manifested itself chiefly in the fact that the aristocracy bore the brunt of any warfare and for this the common man must have been very grateful. In many *poleis*, there was a class of slaves or serfs or dispossessed people to be reckoned with. The poor citizen as well as the rich one had an interest in preserving a strong and firm front against any uprising among them. In the colonies, there were neighbors to whom a firm front must be presented. Furthermore, the leadership of the aristocracy was useful in drainage projects or other enterprises involving a fair amount of land, and the general preservation of the peace in each minor locality was the responsibility of the aristocratic families there. Strong and competent leadership in every field was important in the early stages of every colony. The common man must often have felt that the privileges of the aristocracy were fairly earned.

The power of the aristocracy rested on both a practical and an ideal basis. In spite of the growing importance of trade, land was the chief source of wealth, as it continued to be true through all the history of the ancient world. The people who had the best land in Greece tended thereby to become the richer, more powerful, and more aristocratic class—even more than in many of the colonies or in many other places, for in Greece the land on the plains was much superior to the land on the slopes (and it still is). Even before the deforestation of classical times had caused fairly rapid erosion on the hills to the benefit of the areas below, the earlier slow process of washing down soil and nutritive elements had benefited the plains. In Greece proper, it was clearly understood that the farmer of the plain had an advantage over the man who tried to work the poorer soil of the hills.

Meagerly informed as we are, we can see that the holding of land in the older parts of Greece went back to arrangements made at some unknown time which gave definite holdings of land to individuals and forbade their alienation. As we saw in the case of the *oikos* described by Homer, a piece of land on which a number of people lived, to which they all contributed their efforts, and from which they all drew their living under the presidency of the head of the group could not logically be the property of the head of the group in our sense of property, so that he could mortgage, sell, or bequeath it as something in which no one else had an interest.

The aristocrat might, however, multiply in trade the advantage that he had over the common man because of his better land. Also, even if land was inalienable, he might find ways to extend his control, if not his ownership, over the land of some of his poorer neighbors. There is evidence enough of resentment against the encroachments of the aristocracy. In the chapter on Athens we shall be able to marshal enough evidence to show that the misery of the common people and their resentment could become such that there was fear of revolution and how the matter was adjusted.

The aristocrats could also base their power on their claim to be the repositories of all knowledge of how to deal with the gods. This was a matter of prime moment: the Greek of that day knew no other way of avoiding the wrath of powers that at best were only dimly understood. No one would have thought, at least in the early part of our period, of challenging the necessity and the efficacy of the customary addresses and gifts to the gods.

The aristocrats could also claim a monopoly of the rudimentary courts, which were really only sessions of arbitration, for the *polis* had not as yet claimed and made good its claim to the establishment and execution of a complete set of laws. The poet Hesiod, whom we shall discuss in more detail later, complained bitterly of the rapacity and venality of those who sat to arbitrate the claims of others. There was at first no written law. A body of precedents for the handling of simple disagreements could easily be manipulated by the aristocrat who undertook to arbitrate the dispute. In the end, the advantage of the aristocratic side was likely to be served.

Early Law Codes

Zaleucus of Locris, a rich colony in southern Italy, is said to have published the first of the Greek law codes in 663 B.C. and to have based his code largely on the customary rules of Crete, Sparta, and Athens. In this code, we see the tendency for the *polis* to arrogate powers to itself. Vengeance for murder and other deeds of violence had been the duty of the clan and had resulted in feuds, of course. Now Zaleucus and other legislators in other places declared that the *polis* would protect its interests, especially its interest in avoiding repeated pollution from bloodshed, by acting against the guilty party. We can readily imagine the outraged feelings of the old-fashioned people who saw this change as an unwarranted intrusion of the government into what were essentially the private affairs of citizens and clans. Without doubt some of them asked where this intrusion of the government and assumption of new functions was going to stop if no one could make a stand against it. To us it seems no great assertion of the powers of the *polis* to curb the feuding of the clans, whether from fear of continued pollution through bloodshed or from the feeling of the clearer thinkers of the new age that some settlement other than repeated acts of blind force was needed when murder had been committed.

Another object of the legislators was to protect the noble families, who to them were the essence of the *polis*, by protecting their estates. The alienation of the estate, already tacitly forbidden, was specifically forbidden in the code. (Nineteenth-century literature is rich in sermons on the woes that follow the loss of the family property by a weak or foolish man in a single generation.) The Greek lawgiver also provided that a man without sons might adopt sons and threw safeguards around heiresses so that their property might not somehow be lost for want of a protecting man. Because civil rights and property were connected, the loss of an estate, beside weakening the family in general, cost the chief of the family his citizenship and thereby cost the *polis* a citizen.

A third object of the legislators was to establish courts other than those courts of arbitration, if they can be called courts, that were generally held informally by the nobles, and were likely to be part of the simple machinery of the clan. To bring disputes before the magistrate who presided over the whole *polis* or in some cases to bring them to the council or the assembly of all full citizens might insure fairer settlements and thus avoid resentments that might prove too hard for the *polis* to control.

A generation or so after Zaleucus, one Charondas drew up a code for Catania, in Sicily, which like that of Zaleucus was based on customary rules and likewise aimed at extending the powers of the *polis* somewhat so as to check internal strife and injury. This code, too, asserted that the *polis* would deal with acts of violence and that it would try to assure the property of a family and watch over heiresses or orphans to protect the family if its usual adult male protector had died. Charondas framed his code in verse for ready memorization. It was widely copied throughout the Greek world.

In Mesopotamia, the publication of codes of law had been achieved long before. The Egyptians, who must have known the Mesopotamian codes, preferred to continue with their system of the dispensation of a customary and unpublished law under the control of the vizier. Perhaps the new familiarity of the Greeks with the ways of the Near East caused them to desire such published codes, which were still, of course, far simpler than the well-developed Mesopotamian codes of a thousand years earlier. The Greeks were to develop laws rather than the law in the next few centuries. This was one field in which their passion for analysis and system did not operate strongly. The Romans, who were the chief appropriators of Greek culture, adopted many Greek laws as part of their great legal system, which is one of their bequests to the modern world. There were other peoples who came in contact with the Greeks or the Romans who preferred to operate with only customary and unwritten law, as did the Scythians, or with very simple systems of law which were finally put into writing, as did the Germans.

New Members and New Ways

Tight as the control of the aristocrats was, it was possible now and then for new people to rise. The chances, of course, were best in the areas where there was some movement, in the sending out of colonies and the expanding activity in trade. For the man who stayed on a small farm, surrounded by more powerful neighbors, there was little prospect other than hard work and steady pressure on all his activities. But the man of wit and energy who seized an opportunity in trade or in a move to a colony might occasionally rise to wealth and power. Those who had been accustomed to control might well look askance at him and criticize the vigorous methods by which he had risen. A sensible aristocracy, however, married the new man into itself and kept his energy and ability on its side. The fact that the new man could provide himself with the metal armor that was necessary for the chief combatants in battle made refusal to recognize him more difficult, and the ability to equip one's self for the heavy infantry, as well as the possession of other movable wealth, was added to the possession of real property as a qualification for full citizenship.

The beginnings of the *polis,* the great colonizing movement, and the expansion of trade must be regarded as achievements of the aristocracy. They were lively people, not merely tough and tenacious holders of agricultural estates. During this period, they developed a new style of living in Greece, one that took advantage of the products of the Near East and of Egypt, encouraged the development of fine craftsmanship among the Greeks in the material sphere, that soon developed some brilliant new ideas among the Greeks themselves, and set the social tone of aristocracy for the Greeks, the Romans, and to some extent for later Europe.

If there was never the wealth among the Greeks that there sometimes was in the Near East and later among the Romans, there was a freedom of outlook and a frankness in social relationships that is congenial to modern taste. Country life, hunting, and an interest in horses and dogs were characteristic of this aristocracy as they have been of many later aristocracies. In our time, when the horse is seldom anything but an expensive toy or a status symbol of dubious value, it is difficult to realize its usefulness in the assertion of social superiority and the maintenance of the ascendancy of the few over the many.

For all their amiable and advanced traits, these aristocrats held down the masses with resolution and skill. The many, in their turn, were sometimes resigned, because they were not always hungry or miserable or insecure and they were used to hard work. Others, however, were either goaded to resentment by their treatment or were inspired to resentment by those of their number who somehow —perhaps by making the most of some opportunity to leave the land and go into trade—had advanced themselves in the world and still had not been absorbed into the aristocracy. The details of this social conflict must mostly be conjectured. There is proof of occasional outbreaks of violence, when the masses rose and tried to overthrow their masters and were again subdued. One interesting piece of evidence is the fragments of the poems of Theognis of Megara, an aristocrat who had been dispossessed, along with his fellows, by a popular uprising. Many of the lines from his poems, which have come down to us by being quoted by later authors, speak of his burning desire for revenge and his contempt for those people who not long ago lived like beasts and now hold the land that was his. "When the bird of spring sings and tells us that it is time for the plowing, I am sick at heart to think that others hold my good land."

THE PHYSICAL STRUCTURE OF THE POLIS

Some idea of the appearance of a typical *polis* at this early stage is possible. Perhaps the territory around it consisted of fifty to a hundred square miles, although Athens had a thousand, and many had less than fifty. The *poleis* outside Greece proper, which had been founded as colonies, naturally had more room. The arable land was all taken up except in those places that had more room and could spare land for grazing. There was ordinarily a citadel, a high and defensible place with a water supply. Houses were tightly packed inside its defenses. Below the citadel was an open place for meetings, whether an assembly of the people, a market, or the informal gathering that is a necessary ingredient of life around the Mediterranean. Then, as the town grew, more houses were built in the lower town outside the defenses, and in time there might be a new wall enclosing much additional space. At first there were no imposing marble structures. Houses and temples and (if any) palaces were likely to be of timber and mud-brick in a style something like that of the modern house of timber and stucco.

THE TYRANTS

In the century from about 650 B.C. to about 550 B.C., a great many tyrants arose in all parts of the Greek world. The word is applied to a man who achieved sole power in his *polis* by illegal means, not by inheritance or general demand, as a proper king would. The tyrants all arose at more or less the same period, the late seventh and early sixth centuries. They were usually aristocrats; often they used high office as means to gain sole control of the *polis*. None of them was able to establish an enduring monarchy, although in one or two cases the family stayed in power for a hundred years. Most frequently the sons of the tyrant lost power after a period of oppressive and unpopular rule.

The tyrants had in common the fact that they arose in cities of a commercial cast, where it was easier for factions to exist. Conversely, the places that never had tyrants were those, like Sparta, that were out of the stream of commercial life and had carefully planned aristocratic regimes. The tyrants differed, however, in their reasons for aspiring to power and in the character of the support they commanded. Although some seem to have supported the desires and claims of the common people, we should probably be cautious about supposing that any of them were genuine champions of the downtrodden.

The chief tyrants of Greece in this period were those of Corinth, Sicyon, Megara, and Epidaurus. (The slightly later tyranny of Peisistratus at Athens will be discussed in Chapter Fifteen.)

In Corinth, the tyrant Cypselus seized power just before 650 B.C., using his position as commander of the army. He drove out the ruling clan of the Bacchiadae. His son, Periander, was tyrant from about 627 to 586. While Periander maintained his own power with an iron hand, he did his best to encourage the general prosperity, partly because such a policy would lessen discontent with his rule and partly because he needed money to support his position. He made rich offerings at Delphi and Olympia and organized the Isthmian Games, which were among the most important, although they were never so brilliant as those at Olympia. The duties on trade gave him adequate revenue. He sensibly cared for the landowners by prohibiting the movement of people from the country to the city and for the common people by prohibiting the purchase of slaves, who would have furnished competition for the free poor man on the farm and in the shop. It was he who made the ship railway across the isthmus and he even spoke of cutting a canal. In his later years, he became most odiously tyrannical, in the modern sense of the word. Although in some other places the downfall of tyrants was followed by the slow rise of democracy, this was not the case everywhere, for tyrants did not necessarily give real assistance to the many. In Corinth, an oligarchy followed the fall of the tyranny when the successor of Periander was murdered about 582.

Orthagoras became tyrant of Sicyon about 650 B.C. and founded a dynasty that lasted for a century. These tyrants, too, became oppressive to all, but like those of Corinth, they encouraged trade, attracted competent artists, and built distinguished buildings to beautify their city. Cleisthenes, who ruled from about 600 to 570, was an oppressive and a brilliant ruler. He made a ruling that serfs could not even come into the city; the masses were to be kept down strictly. On the other hand, it was he who was chiefly responsible for attracting artists to Sicyon. In addition, his horses won at the games at Olympia and at Delphi, and he founded a set of games of his own. After the Olympics of 576, he invited suitors for his daughter to come to Sicyon, where he spent a year entertaining them and assaying them. Finally he chose an Athenian, Megacles. Cleisthenes, a notable statesman, was the son of this marriage, and the great Pericles was a great-grandson.

If the tyrants sometimes confiscated the lands of aristocrats and gave them to landless men, they were trying not to help the masses, but to remove the power of their opponents by taking their land and bestowing it upon people who would thereby be made adherents of the tyrant, knowing that he could revoke the gift. Another method used by the tyrants to increase their own power and lessen that of their opponents was to force reorganization of tribes or other social units so as to break up old sentiments of solidarity and build up new settlements more favorable to the regime. Still another was to replace old cults with new gods, with friends of the tyrant as priests and with observances and festivals that would support the popularity and influence of the regime.

14

SPARTA

$\mathcal{S}$parta early became an impressive phenomenon to the other Greeks. Greek literature is full of allusions to the manners, the sayings, and the deeds of the Spartans. The Romans, too, wondered at the Spartans and admired them, as people in later ages have found much to wonder at and admire—and other traits, too, of which to disapprove. Today the words "Spartan" and "laconic" remain with us as reminders of this ancient influence. In this chapter we shall describe the history and organization of Sparta and attempt to explain their impact on the imagination of other peoples.

THE EARLY HISTORY OF SPARTA

The Spartans were among the Dorians who moved into the Peloponnesus to end the Mycenaean Age. While many others went on, this group settled in the Peloponnesus. There they combined five villages to make a *polis,* as many of their Dorian brethren had formed *poleis* in Crete. At the outset, the new *polis* was plagued with strife arising from the former rivalries of the tribes and clans and from the social and economic pretensions of some of the more powerful citizens. This situation was cut through by the reform attributed to Lycurgus, the first notable event in the history of the Spartan state and perhaps the greatest.

The reform of Lycurgus probably came between 825 and 800 B.C., although the evidence is contradictory and scholars have urged widely differing dates. We cannot even be sure that there was a man named Lycurgus who pushed through the reform, although in this simpler polity it was easy for a single man to conceive and actuate a major change in government, as we shall see in later cases. The essential thing is that somewhere in the earlier history of Sparta, before the days of her greatness and preparatory to them, there was made a new arrangement of her people and government that removed the old causes of internal strife and made a true *polis* of a people who had not yet learned to work together.

The three old tribes found almost everywhere among Dorians were superseded by five new tribes, one for each of the villages. The power of the clans was neutralized, as was that of the old tribes; they remained, but only as framework for the registry of citizens and for the performance of some religious duties, not as centers of loyalty or power. The two kings traditional in Sparta were left the duties of Greek kings: to command in military operations and to perform religious duties. Henceforth their political role consisted of holding two of the thirty seats in the council. After this reform, the kingship of Sparta, like the presidency of the United States, was to be what the incumbents made it. Some later kings of Sparta were nonentities and some were great leaders. They could not command except on the battlefield; in politics they had to lead by personality, persuasion, and pressures.

Presumably the heads of the kinship groups had been the counsellors of the king as being representatives of effective groups in the population. The reform now provided that the twenty-eight regular members of the council, of which the two kings were *ex officio* members, should be elected from the men over the age of sixty by vote of all the men who had achieved citizenship. They were to hold office for life. The council was generally called the Gerousia, or Council of Elders. This reform also helped to neutralize the power of the kinship groups. The members of the Gerousia now represented the whole people, and if one of them felt his own kinship group to be highly important, he would be unlikely to find support among the others for settling anything on such a basis.

The men who had full citizen's rights—the Equals—made up the Assembly. We shall discuss presently the strenuous system for molding the males in the form that this society wished; the Equals were those who passed the final test. Although not every male could achieve this status, as we shall see later, we may say that the system had a strong democratic tinge as it concerned those who had the full status. They met at certain times for the purpose of hearing the proposals that had been framed for them by the Gerousia. The system was not democratic enough to allow the Assembly the initiative in legislation.

The *polis* had triumphed, too, in the fact that among the Equals there were no distinctions arising from the old racial division of the tribes and from kinship divisions of family and clan or from differences in economic ability. Every man who could achieve the grade of Equal was to fight in the army and participate in the Assembly. No basis was left for struggles arising from racial, kinship, and economic groupings. Other *poleis* were stirred and riven by problems caused by these loyalties and, as a result, often found themselves in the hands of tyrants. Sparta never had a tyrant. The loyalty of her citizens was so strongly directed toward the *polis* that there was no issue by which an aspirant to tyranny could attract support and no disaffected group to which he could appeal. The final support of the rights and interests of the citizenry was the board of Ephors, or overseers, five men who were elected by the Assembly for one-year terms. They were also to supervise the working of the system that molded the people; two specific functions within that framework were to watch over the condition of the boys and to judge cases of disobedience. A time was to come when the power of the Ephors grew so that they were almost a presiding group in the *polis*.

In the three generations or so following the organization of Sparta attributed to Lycurgus, the Spartans conquered the Dorian villages around them in the district of the Peloponnesus that is called Laconia. Hence the word "laconic," which we generally reserve to describe the brief Spartan form of speech. Lacedaemon is another name for the region about Sparta, which is a pleasant and fertile one. The modest *polis* of the five villages added a goodly territory to itself by its conquests in Laconia. The people, to whom the Spartans referred as *perioeci,* or "dwellers around," now acknowledged the suzerainty of Sparta by accepting resident Spartan agents to watch over their self-government of their villages, by paying some dues to the Spartans, and by allowing themselves to be conscripted for military service with the Spartans. They had no political rights at Sparta. In the long run, however, they seem to have found their relationship reasonably comfortable.

The Spartans, having surrounded themselves with related people who were willing to follow their lead, now turned to the conquest of the rich territory of Messenia, the country lying to the west, which they subdued between about 740 and 720 B.C. The Messenians were made serfs and left to cultivate the land for half the produce, paying the other half to whatever Spartan was now master of that piece of land. The serfs were known as Helots. Villages of *perioeci* were established in a number of places in Messenia. When the Spartans had completed the work of organizing Laconia and Messenia, they had greater resources in land and peoples than any other *polis* in all Greece of the eighth century.

The conquest of Messenia took place at a time when other *poleis* were sending out colonies, and it was made, at least partly, in response to the same rising pressure of population that caused the colonizing movement. The Spartans founded only one colony, Taras (the Latin Tarentum and the Italian Taranto), in the instep of Italy. A story was told that the Spartan women raised a crop of illegitimate children while their husbands were absent on the conquest of Messenia and these were sent off to Taras. The story is probably true at least to the extent that some dissident element was sent to Taras. Both ancient and modern communities have often been glad to ship discordant elements off across the sea.

The culture of Sparta in the late eighth century and the first half of the seventh century was not what we think of today as Spartan. It was neither grim nor austere. The Spartans were a landed aristocracy supported by the toil of serfs on deep-soiled fields. They themselves were free of menial duties, confident in their superior position and their equality with the other full citizens, owing no more than a proper respect to the Gerousia and the kings. They took great pleasure in their sports and their hunting and their race horses, as would be expected of landed aristocrats trained to the practice of arms. Their entries in the Olympic Games always did well. They also took pleasure in handsome and spirited girls and women. The girls were not secluded, but were trained to a vigorous health, as were the boys, and to a modest and becoming frankness and freedom.

We have some fragments of the poetry of Alcman, a Spartan of this early time, that is hardly the product of a man crushed by a boorish system. One is the earliest known example of the pleasant poetic theme of nighttime quiet. "Still are the mountain tops and the ravines, the shoulders of the mountains and the vales, the race of creeping things which the dark earth bears, the mountain creatures and the race of the bees, the monsters in the depths of the dark-gleaming sea; the tribes of the wide-winged birds are still." Another is a lament for old age, a theme commoner in Greek poetry than in ours. Alcman does not confine himself, as some Greek poets do, to complaining that his years are heavy upon him, but turns his thoughts to something better. "Sweet-voiced maidens with your lovely song, my limbs can no longer carry me in the dance. Oh, I wish, I wish that I were a kingfisher, the holy purple bird, fearless of heart to fly at the blossom of the wave with my mate."

The archaeological evidence for the Sparta of this period does not suggest an austere way of life. People did not have luxurious houses, to be sure. Sparta was an unwalled country town of free-standing wooden houses built only with axe and saw, as a minor rule of Lycurgus had suggested, and therefore looking something like the American log cabin. There were trees between the houses and none of the fearful crowding characteristic of those places where all the population lived inside a fortification. The Spartans did, however, have some luxurious personal possessions. They were friends with the people of Samos, who were great traders and must have called often at Spartan ports on their way to the West with the products of the East. The Spartan lady could have things of ivory or bronze made either abroad or by workmen in Sparta, and in either case they showed the fashionable orientalizing motifs. Sparta had its own makers and painters of pottery, who developed a style of their own that was still recognizably in the orientalizing stream, as was the work, too, of the Corinthian and Athenian craftsmen.

In governmental affairs, an interesting modification of the constitution took place about the middle of the eighth century. The Gerousia, or Council of Elders, was given the power to dismiss a meeting of the Assembly if it balked at ratifying what the Gerousia had proposed. This might seem a lessening of such democracy as there was. We find, however, that the Ephors, who were elected annually by the Assembly, now became entitled to attend meetings of the Gerousia. This change suggests a practical deal in which the Gerousia was granted the power to maneuver a little when it could not carry the Assembly with it at once, and the representatives of the people were allowed to watch as responsible intermediaries the process of the formation of decisions in the Gerousia. Democracy gained more than it lost, for another part of the change was to transfer from the kings to the Ephors judicial powers, as well as summary power to control some lesser magistrates and to discipline the citizens.

The Spartans occasionally had differences with the other peoples of the Peloponnesus. Sparta and Corinth were consistently on friendly terms, but Argos more than once defied or defeated the Spartans. The Arcadians, who were in the north central Peloponnesus, were able to discourage any Spartan interference with members of their group. Sparta's greatest difficulty was caused by the great revolt of the Messenians, which lasted from about 640 to 620 B.C. and was supported by some of the other peoples. Twenty years of struggle for what seemed her very existence must have made Sparta feel that stricter measures for security must be taken.

One measure was the creation of a system of alliances to insure the safety of Sparta against her serfs or outside attack. She made one or two minor conquests in the Peloponnesus and quite a number of judicious alliances. As the largest and most stable of the *poleis,* she was generally able to take the lead, and in time her system of alliances became solid and influential. In a number of cases, the Spartans gave others assistance in getting rid of their tyrants, so often indeed that their hostility to tyrants came to be taken for granted. In these cases, the end of the tyranny meant the resumption of rule by an aristocratic minority, a situation very acceptable to the Spartans.

The other measure for security was a heightening of her own conservatism. The lack of precise evidence for dates leaves us uncertain as to whether the changes in the constitution—the power of the Gerousia to dismiss the Assembly and the new power of the Ephors—belongs to the middle of the eighth century or perhaps here in the late seventh century, although the former date seems more likely. But in any event, after the suppression of the revolt of Messenia, all the provisions of the system seem to have become more rigid. Although the system was admirably calculated before to produce the specialized Spartan type, it was now made more difficult for a Spartiate, or full citizen, to have any thought of business and trade or for a middle class to grow up. The best way to gain this end was officially to reject the new invention of coinage. The Spartans were to have no gold and silver coinage. The old iron money was to be used, money that could serve for nothing except a few simple internal transactions and that was of no value in the new world of silver coinage and fairly large denominations, for use in international trade.

The suspicion arises that the Spartans were worried about far more than the rebellion of the Messenians. They were in touch enough with the world to form an estimate of the new forces abroad. New possibilities, new horizons, and a new spirit had combined with the old loyalties and animosities based on race and kinship to give the more enterprising of the downtrodden a hope that they might rise, to give the group in general a new sense of opportunity for those who were bold and vigorous, and to cause bitter factional struggles and the rise of tyrannies in many *poleis*. To the Spartans none of this seemed good. They had committed themselves to an economy based on agriculture and realized how upsetting it might be to their system to have a lively trade develop. They had no desire to allow a strong commercial class like that of Corinth to arise, to allow the downtrodden to improve their position, or to reintroduce any of the causes of factional or class struggle or tyranny that they had forestalled by devising their conservative constitution. Presently democracy was to arise in many places, notably in Athens—a full democracy, not the limited democracy of the Spartan Equals. This, too, appeared dangerous to the Spartans and intensified their conservatism.

The Dorians of Crete and those of Byzantium, a *polis* on the Bosporus, likewise rejected the use of the new coinage and tried to avoid the influence of the new ways. In recent times, a number of peoples have tried to avoid contact with Western ways because they feared that to adopt any major trait of Western culture would finally bring about the end of their own traditional cultures. Other peoples have not been able to resist the influence of the major Western peoples and have either completely disintegrated (some African tribes, for example) or have seen modifications of their structure that amount almost to disintegration (American Indians).

The Spartans periodically ejected foreigners from their territory, not wishing to allow outside influence to steal in. They themselves did not travel. We have no evidence that at this time they intensified the rigors of the traditional preparation for citizenship; we do have evidence to the contrary: they allowed some of the Helots and *perioeci* to attain a qualified citizenship.

Sparta's desire to stand apart from the international trade of the day was made easier of fulfillment because she had a certain amount of iron in her territory and had learned how to handle it. As in the earlier Homeric days, metals were the one thing not usually available for self-sufficiency. Iron and wrought steel had long been important items of international trade, and now silver bullion and silver coinage were important. If the Spartans could get along without silver and could produce enough wrought steel for weapons and for tools, they could have much better success with their program of living largely to themselves and avoiding such involvements with other people as might cause breaches in their unity.

Our observations of some peoples, the Zuni Indians, for example, who have achieved a way of life harmonious with their natural surroundings has taught us that in some contexts the modern Western notion of progress has no relevance. So it was with the Spartans. We are pleased with the fact that the Athenians developed a democracy that is an ancestor of our democracy. We may equate the Athenian system with "progress" and label the Spartans as unprogressive; we are not entitled to pass an adverse value judgment on them for attempting to achieve a static system in which people were not equal.

THE SPARTAN SYSTEM

The Training of the Individual

The interference of the state in the affairs of the Spartan began at his birth. He was presented for approval, not to his father alone, as with the other Greeks, but also to a board of elders, who had the power to order that a deformed or sickly baby be exposed out in the mountains to die. Once through this exacting *rite de passage,* the Spartan boy had seven years of living with his mother, and the idea of the stern mother is part of the legend of Sparta.

At the age of seven he was called by his draft board. From then until he was thirty, he lived in barracks, and all his training looked toward his attachment to the larger unit of the state rather than to any such small units as the immediate family or a larger kinship group. The little boys were organized into troops that were led by older boys and supervised by men. The responsibility of training the young was taken very seriously by all the men. The boy went barefoot winter and summer and wore one simple garment. His bed was of rushes, which he pulled with his own hands along the banks of the Eurotas River. His food was simple and well spiced with appetite.

The boys were hardened by physical and military exercises as well as by this cheerless way of living. Discipline was strict. The spirit of competition was fostered by games of various kinds, including those involving the ball, which as an instrument of games had by now made its appearance. At the age of eighteen, the youngster became what might be called a junior member of the armed forces for two years. He received intensive military training and was also employed in the force, known as *Crypteia,* or secret police, that was charged with watching the Helots. From twenty to thirty, he lived the life of the soldier under the strictest discipline.

At thirty, a man's education was over. His final examination came with his nomination to one of the messes, or dining societies. One blackball kept him out. If he was elected, he became an Equal; if he was blackballed, he became an Inferior, a definite position that left him without a vote in the Assembly and without full civil rights. It is hard to imagine a better way of forcing a man to shape himself to the standards and ideals current in his society. The average Spartan probably could read only a little; he was not musically or artistically trained. He had little idea of the amenities of life as they came to exist among the other peoples of Greece, notably the Athenians. He might readily be called uneducated, and the word would apply if our system or that of the Athenians were a universal model. Education, however, is (or should be) what a society wants the young to learn. Probably few societies have had so good a system as the Spartans for teaching the young what they wanted the grown man to know. He was trained to put the state, or the whole society, before any part of it in his affections and loyalties. He was given the attitude that it was the right of the Spartan to be master and live on other people's work and that it was his duty to protect and support this system in every way and at any cost. He was taught to be a skilled soldier and to feel himself one with his comrades at home and in the field. He was protected from the distractions of knowing overmuch about the pains and pleasures of other ways of living.

Comment on the training of the boy has tended to emphasize the brutal side. Not only was he taken from his mother at a tender age and made to live a rough life under stern discipline, but there were other occasional high points that shocked outsiders. At one festival, the older boys underwent hard whippings. Cakes were set out on the altar, and the successful boy was the one who approached the most times through a gantlet of men (those who laid on the whips), took a cake, and withdrew through another gantlet. It was not unknown for a boy to die of bruises and loss of blood. (We may remember that a good many boys of our own time have faced injury for life on the football field to avoid the imputation of cowardice.) The boys were taught to steal, too. This idea should be regarded with some common sense. It is hard to believe that they were encouraged to roam up and down alleys and try to raid backyard gardens. Much more probably, as part of their work in the secret police who watched the Helots, they received careful training in slipping unseen through the farming country. In such situations, they would need to live off the country without being noticed. Anyone who called attention to himself had bungled and was punished.

The more positive side of the training of the young has been less noticed. The Spartan boy was taught good manners. The men made it their business to watch the young at their exercises and games and to encourage them by commending honorable and brave conduct. They also taught them to take part in serious and agreeable conversation. The boy was not allowed to be a boor who paid no attention to his elders or to people whom he did not know well. He was taught to pay respect to age; other people noticed Spartan superiority in this respect. He was taught also to speak up when something was to be said or when he was asked a civil question. The Spartan was no tongue-tied oaf, nor did he yield to the temptation that beset the Athenian in later days, to deliver a well-rounded oration if ever an opportunity presented itself. The Spartan way was to be able to engage in general conversation, as we express it. His tendency was always to be brief—laconic. If the Spartans did have a weakness comparable to the cleverness of the Athenians in speech, it was that they loved to deliver themselves of epigrams at times when they saw that the audience was ready. "They say that the Persians are so many that their arrows darken the sun!" cried a faint-hearted ally as the Greek force waited at Thermopylae. "Very well," said the Spartan Dieneces after a suitable pause, "we shall fight in the shade, then."

The man of thirty who had succeeded in winning full acceptance into society by being elected a member of a mess and thus becoming an Equal expected to be a member of the army until he was sixty. Now that he was an Equal, he was a full voting member of the Assembly. He was allowed to marry at twenty, but for the ten years between twenty and thirty he was expected to live strictly in barracks and visit his wife only by stealth. It has been suggested that the brief notices on this custom refer to a secret trial marriage that did not become fully effective unless and until it turned out that the couple were capable of producing the children who were so important. After he reached thirty, he could set up a household, but had to take one meal a day with his mess. The Helot who worked his land supplied him with a certain amount of plain fare for his meals at home and in the mess. Legally he could alienate the plot of land which the *polis* assigned to the upkeep of himself and his family, but it was regarded as dishonorable to do so, and the man who could no longer make his contribution to his mess could no longer belong to it. We are not properly informed either about those who were blackballed and failed of election to the company of Equals or about those who somehow lost their land. It is possible that both were treated with the same condescension that in some modern European countries the gentry has felt for the merchant class. It is also possible that they found many practical consolations for not being able to take part in the narrow and strenuous life of the full citizens.

The Perioeci and the Helots

The *perioeci*, although they were of the Dorian blood like the Spartans, were kept in an inferior position. Yet they were not so discontented as to rise against their masters. They had their land, their dues were moderate, they enjoyed the protection of the Spartans. Many a time they distinguished themselves on the battle-field as part of the Spartan army. Villages of *perioeci* had been put in the hillier country around the city of Messene, presumably to help in the surveillance of the conquered Messenians. The *perioeci* were free to engage in trade, but the trade cannot have amounted to much. Yet some of them were well-to-do. By Greek standards their life was not very hard, and they cannot have cared a great deal about being forbidden to marry Spartan women or hold parcels of the land that was meant to support the Spartan Equals.

For the Helots life was grimmer; their name is another word from Spartan life that has passed into general usage in the Western world. The Helot was not a slave, one who had lost every freedom, but a serf, one who had lost the right to move. He was attached to the holding of a full Spartan citizen and obliged to pay him half the produce of the land. It was good land, and a man could live well on half the produce of it. The owner could not raise the rate.

Helots campaigned with the army both to fight and in menial capacities. Now and then one would strike a blow with such courage that he would find himself rewarded with promotion to a second-class citizenship, and as time went on it became possible to have a regular section of the army composed of these "new people," as they were called. But in general there was war between the Spartans and the Helots, not only in the loose sense of the basic opposition of their interests, but in the strict sense that every year the Ephors formally declared war on them so that it was legal to attack them at any time. The *Crypteia*, or secret police, snooped incessantly, and the youngsters in their cadet years, participating in the *Crypteia*, were encouraged to murder any Helot whose activities were suspect or who seemed to be a leader. Even though some of the Helots gave good service with the army, more than once the army had to return home for fear of a revolution among the less devoted.

The Organs of Government

The kingship of Sparta is a good example of the decay of royal power and the transfer of the reality of power to the heads of the clans and then to a larger group. The two kings, belonging to two royal houses, were still hereditary monarchs. They kept the role of mediators between the *polis* and the gods, a role that lasted longer than any other function of Greek kings. They kept judicial functions of the sort that the head of a kingship system would have; they settled matters of adoption or arranged marriages for those whose legal protectors had all died. They were commanders of the army when it took the field. Although the practical power of the kings was far less than that of the Gerousia, strong kings could often exert a great deal of influence. There are instances in Spartan history of a king's pushing an enlightened policy that did not appeal to the elderly and often decrepit members of the Gerousia.

The Assembly had no initiative in government. It met only to approve or reject the proposals prepared for it by the Gerousia. Its influence was comparable to that of conservative public opinion today. We should hardly expect this limited company of men, trained in a static society to obedience and conformity, to produce a great deal of grass-roots sentiment for novelties in government. If the actions of other *poleis* made it necessary to stir up the thinking of the elderly Gerousia, the Ephors, not the Assembly, were the ones to do it.

THE SYMBOLISM OF SPARTA

Sparta has served wonderfully as a source of symbols in history. Spartan simplicity, Spartan courage, and the Spartan mother are ideas that have long been useful to the orator and the statesman who wished to put certain ideals of communal life in concrete terms. There are other and more complex ways, however, in which Sparta has been used as a symbol of historical ideas.

One of these is to make Sparta symbolize the excessively militaristic nation that has abandoned higher values in its pursuit of power and that pays the penalty in the end by allowing its citizens to become so brutalized that, in addition to losing the higher things, they can no longer perform their civic and military duties properly.

This sort of symbolism fits well into the argument that one's own nation is pursuing a more enlightened, more cultivated, and ultimately more efficient and profitable policy than is some other contemporary nation. It is not, however, a sound piece of historical reasoning so far as Sparta is concerned. Life in Sparta may have become less gay and more austere after she decided to stand apart from the stream of Greek life. The Spartan may have come to seem a little rustic by comparison with the Athenians and some others. It is not true, however, that the Spartans brutalized themselves, that they banished all higher values, or that they ruined themselves.

A variation on this symbolism is to make Sparta represent a society that has chosen so extremely difficult a way of life that it has no energy left with which to progress. To suggest that Sparta is the symbol of such a process is to import into Greek history what is merely a local idea in the West—the idea of progress. The idea of progress has no relevance to Sparta or to any society that has found a way of life suited to its people and its physical environment, and to demand that Sparta should have progressed seems an impertinence.

The Greeks themselves were very interested in Sparta, and most of all as the great example of a *polis* with a stable constitution. Sparta had avoided factional struggles after she got her constitution, had avoided tyranny in the age when tyrants were to be found everywhere, and had avoided the struggle of the few and the many— the oligarchs and the democrats—of which we have yet to hear a great deal. Many theorists offered explanations of how it was done and tried to show that Sparta was the great example of one thing or another. Perhaps the most influential of all these theories was that Sparta was the great example of the mixed constitution, or the threefold form of government.

In this scheme, the king represented monarchy, of course, the Gerousia represented aristocracy, and the Assembly represented democracy. No one was troubled by the unmentioned presence of the unprivileged slaves, serfs, and inferior citizens. The fact that there were three elements rather than two (oligarchs and democrats) was thought to encourage compromises and second thoughts instead of resort to force in civil disagreements. From another point of view, the kings were made to represent the executive, the Gerousia the legislative, and the people the judicial, because the people were the fount of authority and the court of last resort.

This symbolic view of Sparta was widely discussed among the Greeks, was taken up and discussed by the Romans, was known to the Italian Machiavelli and the Frenchman Montesquieu, and was a part of the intellectual equipment of the men who framed our own constitution. As a result, the theory of the mixed form of government, the tripartite form, in which Sparta was made to symbolize the ideal, had a definite influence on the formation of our constitution and other constitutions that have been devised more recently. Although it is easy to find valid criticisms of this theory as it is applied to Sparta, it has had a sound practical influence.

CHAPTER

15

ATHENS IN THE NEW AGE

During the new age, from about 800 to about 500 B.C., Athens, like Sparta, went through some striking changes. At an early date, the kings of Athens unified the territory of Attica, some thousand square miles, to form the first stage of a new *polis*. Thereafter, as elsewhere, the nobles grew in power and reduced the kingship to a religious office. There was the same ascendancy of the nobles and despair of the poor. But unlike the Spartans, the Athenians, led by Solon, accepted the implications of the age of commerce and exchange with other peoples and, indeed, put themselves in the front of the movement. At the same time, they accepted Solon's grant of more power to the people. Then they had a tyrant, Peisistratus, one of the most brilliant of all Greek tyrants. By 500 B.C., the tyranny had been ended and another Athenian statesman, Cleisthenes, had made the government yet more democratic, preparing the way for the complete and radical democracy of the fifth century. In the eyes of the Greeks, Athens was the champion of democracy, and inevitably she was set against conservative Sparta in their thinking. The restless and forward-looking and bold Athenian was frequently contrasted with the steady and sober Spartan.

244

ATHENS BEFORE SOLON

The Unification of Attica

Although the Athenians had survived the shocks of the Dark Age after the fall of Mycenae and the other centers of that time, they were slow to unfold their capabilities and gain in intensity of living and performance in the new age. Perhaps the reason is that they were relatively long in developing their *polis*. We do not know exactly when it was that they unified Attica by bringing the dozen or so little kingdoms in that region into alliance with Athens. They were slow, however, to take the next step, that of concentrating many of their people in a center where the stimuli of life together and of exchange with other lively centers could act upon them. Athens, the great sea power of the future, was behind Corinth or Megara or Aegina on the sea and behind the Spartans in the development of a heavy infantry. She had not sent out colonies when the others did and had not developed industries at home.

Very little is known about the early period. There were no *perioeci* or Helots, however, and from their absence we may conclude that the unification was a relatively peaceful one that did not involve the forceful subjugation of the other people in Attica. There is no evidence at our disposal about the power of the central government. Neither is there evidence of great resentment or of attempts to break away from the new union. Because there was no great concentration of people and energy in Athens itself during the early centuries of the union, we may conclude that the leading families of the country districts retained a great deal of influence. When we come to a period for which there is more evidence, around 600 B.C., we find that Athens was securely in the hands of the great families whose holdings were partly in the city and nearby, partly scattered all through Attica.

The Period of Aristocratic Supremacy

The aristocrats of Athens, like those of the other *poleis*, took the king's power from him early. As was usual, too, one of the aristocracy was given the title of king for the purpose of attending to religious affairs; this title for this purpose persisted even in the days of the full democracy in Athens. Our evidence gives us glimpses of this "king" sitting in judgment on cases of impiety, presiding over the council when it dealt with murder (which was regarded as essentially a matter of pollution and therefore a religious matter), and performing a rite that we heard of in the Near East, the sexual intercourse of priest and priestess, in this case his wife, as a symbolic act to bring fertility to their people.

The first new official was known as the archon. This word is the counterpart of our "regent," which is derived from Latin. The Greek word and the Latin word from which each is derived are both participles used as nouns and mean "the holder of the power" or "the person who is in charge." The archon was at first an officer for life, it seems, although the office was not hereditary, then for a term of ten years, then for a term of one year. This last arrangement may have begun in 683; at least the listing of one-year archons began at that time. They were eponymous; that is, the year was named by the name of the archon. At first the archon always came from the great clan of the Medontidae, just as the great clan of the Bacchiadae long supplied the leaders of Corinth. Presently the other aristocrats asserted their claim to the office; as at Corinth, the aristocracy in general rather than a single clan guided the state once the tyrants were out of power. The office of archon naturally came to carry prestige for both individual and family. This is why it became an annual office; that is, if the office were annual, more people could enjoy the prestige of holding it. It was now no longer possible for one family or a small group of families to assert that only they had a claim to this office. (In the Roman Republic and the early Empire the consulship had a similar history and significance.)

A polemarch, or general, was created sometime after the development of the new-style king and the archon. In times when Athens had more wars to fight, it would not perhaps have been so easy thus to isolate the king's function of leadership in war and hand it over to one of the aristocracy. Then a group of six lesser archons, known as the *thesmothetae*, who were concerned with the law was created. This probably happened at some time in the seventh century when there had begun to be enough specific problems to make it necessary to deal systematically with the law.

It is difficult for us to realize how little government the *polis* needed at this time. The religious functions of the man called the king can hardly have occupied him for more than some part of a dozen days a year. The archon was not like the head of a nation or even the mayor of a city, for there were almost no functions of a government to occupy him. His chief task was to watch over property, for (even though the Athenians were not much in trade) the new age was bringing a sense at Athens as at other places that land, like other forms of property, might be regarded as a private possession and alienable. The aristocrats of Athens, too, thought it well to protect families from the loss of their land if possible, at least to the extent of not allowing orphan minors to lose it. The archon took orphans as his wards, and orphan heiresses were married off as soon as they were fourteen to their nearest male relative (excluding brothers) so as to keep the property in the family. Furthermore, as fate would have it, that other new official, the polemarch, found few occasions to lead the army in the field.

Somewhere and at some time in early Greece was devised the idea of elections, which we did not find in the Near East. In *poleis* ruled by aristocrats, the governing council was likely at first to be made up of the heads of the clans, the men who controlled the effective groups in the *polis*. Here and there we get evidence of a change to an elected council, as at Sparta, and of elected officials, like the Ephors. At Athens the board of nine archons—that is, the king, the archon, the polemarch, and the six *thesmothetae*—was chosen by the council. There was an election of a sort, but we do not know how it was managed. The procedure of counting votes, so familiar to us, must have grown up at about this time, too. Some elections were handled by acclamation, as was said to be the case with the Gerousia at Sparta, but some were certainly done by counting of votes. Thus we may suppose that when the members of the council at Athens got together to decide who would hold the offices for the coming year, the maneuvering and trading among the great families was settled and sealed by a counting of votes. This system was truly a closed one, for the council that chose the archons was composed of ex-archons, who were members for life.

The conspiracy of Cylon in 632 B.C. was the most exciting single event of these early centuries. This young man is known to have done himself credit by winning the dash at Olympia—the 200-yard race for one length of the stadium. It was rather more useful to him, as a prospective tyrant, that he had married the daughter of the tyrant of Megara. Cylon had some soldiers from Megara to assist the people on whom he could count because of his family connections, some of them relatives and some retainers, when he seized the Acropolis in Athens. Megacles, the archon, who was of the great Alcmaeonid family, sent around Attica and soon had a force of men to blockade the Acropolis. Ordinary men supported the archon, because they were not ready to desert the loose government of the great families to which they were accustomed for anything that they might be led to expect from the promises of a tyrant. Cylon escaped. Although his supporters took sanctuary, they were massacred by order of Megacles. Such ruthlessness among citizens shocked everyone, and the conviction grew that the *polis* had been so polluted by this shedding of blood that some purification was necessary. The details of the story are not quite convincing, yet it seems that, as a result of Megacles' actions, a special court of aristocrats did pass some sentence on the whole clan of the Alcmaeonids, who were exiled for a long time thereafter. We shall see how in later times this charge against them was exploited for political purposes.

About 620 B.C., the laws were published by a specially appointed commissioner named Draco, whose name has become synonymous with severity. This publication of the laws was not necessarily the result of popular demand to know what the laws really were, for popular demand, at least in our sense of the expression, would not have been regarded at this time. They may rather have been published as a maneuver in the rivalries of the great families or for the same reason that prompted the publication of such other codes as those of Zaleucus and Charondas (mentioned in Chapter Thirteen). The little we know of the code as set forth by Draco shows us that it was possible to sell an insolvent debtor and his dependents into slavery. The fragment that we have of the code also tells us something of homicide trials. The court, aristocratic in nature, decided whether the killing was intentional. If it was not intentional, the offender had to go into exile for life, unless he was unanimously pardoned by the kin of the slain man. This looks not so much like ridding the *polis* of the pollution of bloodshed as like getting a guarantee that the kin of the slain man will not repay unintentional bloodshed with intentional bloodshed.

THE REFORMS OF SOLON

Solon was chosen archon for the year 594 B.C. with the idea that he would devise some changes to remedy an unhappy situation. He was chosen, as the archons were at that time, by the aristocrats of the council, the governing body of the *polis*. Athens was still very much under the control of the clans, although in other *poleis* the central government had taken away much of their power. Even though industry and commerce were undeveloped, the foremost people had acquired a taste for the luxuries that could be bought abroad, and the rivalry among the great clans had extended itself to movable wealth. In their greed many people had taken too great advantage of the weakness of the poor.

Probably the leading men realized that they had pushed the common people to the point of revolution. In the beginning, the possessors of the best land were the leading people. There was a considerable difference between the good land of the plains and the land of the hills. The small farmer on the poorer land was always at a disadvantage and often must have had to appeal to his more powerful neighbor for help. The beginning of the use of money made this situation worse, because the management of money, even in a simple way, is done better by some people than by others. Many poorer men had got into debt, and some of them had been seized for debt and sold into slavery with their families. Some were probably managing their own farms as agents for people to whom they were hopelessly in debt.

Naturally the individual could not be expected to refrain from attempts to add to his holdings, and the less energetic man might seem to have paid the natural penalty for his own lack of ability. Yet the time came when the aristocracy collectively stood back and decided that it must find a way to protect the weaker men. Very likely there was also some sentiment for giving the middle class more voice in government and for putting Athens more in touch with the modern world of industry and trade. Solon would hardly have dared to make the changes that he did, nor would he have thought of them, had they not been favorably discussed beforehand by some of his contemporaries.

Solon himself was of one of the lesser families of the Athenian aristocracy. He had been engaged in trade and had traveled widely. He had proved his leadership by stirring up the Athenians to drive the Megarians out of the island of Salamis, which lies very close to the coast and very near to Athens. We have the remains of some well-expressed poems of his on the political and economic situation, which would surely have been cast as essays in prose if he had lived two hundred years later. In his day, however, no one wrote in prose on any formal or serious subject. In a sense, Solon was to be a one-man constitutional convention. Yet the matters he dealt with must all have been discussed again and again. If the aristocracy had the political wisdom to propose a change, it must have had some collective wisdom to offer him on the nature of the change.

The Problem of Debt and Slavery

As is natural with a good, careful balancing of interests, no one was thoroughly pleased by Solon's reforms. But the council and the assembly of the arms-bearing men had sworn to accept what he offered, and they did. He disappointed the hopes of the poor by not redistributing the land. He disappointed the rich by canceling all debts that involved land or persons. In addition, he forbade any further enslavement for debt and the use of one's person as security for a debt. The *polis* now sought out and ransomed many citizens who were in slavery at home or who had been sold into slavery abroad. Thus Solon restored to Athens many of her poorer citizens who had lost their rights and become slaves. Even in the later days of Greece, the principle that the citizen can be cast aside if he cannot keep up his property qualification was in operation. In this case, Solon provided for a bill of amnesty that restored citizenship to those who had lost it, except those who had been guilty of violence against individuals or the *polis*. We shall meet wise acts of amnesty at Athens later.

A New Attitude toward Industry and Commerce

Solon went to the root of the troubles of the poorer citizens by his measures to change Attic agriculture from cereal-growing to a preponderance of olive-growing and to encourage industry and commerce. These moves were the beginning, after centuries of quiet agricultural life, of the brilliance of Athens as an industrial and commercial city, the intellectual as well as the commercial center of the Mediterranean world.

First he prohibited the export of cereals. The soil of Attica is not well suited to their growth. For olives, however, the composition of the soil is good. Beside, olives can be grown on little patches of ground here and there on slanting hillside ground that is hardly suitable for cereals. The roots of the olive strike deep and tap moisture well below the ground. Olive trees take a few years to mature and begin to bear, however, and are thus better for the man who has a little capital or does not need an immediate return because he has other products. They also repay some thought and ingenuity. The olives may be eaten as olives, fresh or pickled. The first pressing may be sold in a fine container as choice oil, and the further pressing may be sold with less care in presentation as oil for ordinary eating, then as plain oil for lighting or for cleaning the body, as we use soap. From every point of view the promotion of olive culture was a good thing for the Athenians.

Although some cereals were always to be grown in Attica, a good part of the required cereals was henceforth to be imported. Solon boldly aimed at the conversion of Athens to an olive-growing, cereal-importing, and industrial and commercial *polis*. The whole plan succeeded. He provided that every father was to see to it that his son was equipped with a trade. He also provided that grants of citizenship be possible for skilled workmen who would come to Athens with their families and plan to stay. This measure may well have attracted some good workmen from Corinth and other Dorian communities that offered them no hope of citizenship.

Another aspect of his sweeping economic policy was to desert the Aeginetan system of coinage and shift to the Euboic system. This meant that the silver content and the weight of the coinage of Athens was changed slightly and the effect was to make it readily acceptable in a different set of places, although a soundly-based coinage could pass anywhere with some calculations and adjustments.

The landowning class suffered somewhat from his measures, for many of them must have had heavy losses from the cancellation of debts. But they also were the chief producers of olives and had some capital for trading. Probably a few people had already engaged a little in trade, as had Solon himself. These people and the land-owning class must have been the first and the chief beneficiaries from the upsurge of trade in Athens. Benefits to many poorer people followed naturally. Those Athenians who had trades or who learned trades and those skilled workmen who were attracted to Athens would be among the first to profit by the new activity as they played their rather important part in it.

Our great emphasis thus far on the importance of finds of pottery for establishing dates has perhaps somewhat obscured the fact that finds of pottery are also very useful for establishing routes of trade. Pottery came to be one of the great specialties of the Athenians. Not long after Solon's enactments, Athens was again at the front of the industry as she had been in the days of Geometric ware. Now her ware was made of a fine local clay with a little imported red color added to it to make a product that looked much like the reddish soil of Attica. These vessels were painted with black designs and are referred to today as "black-figured ware." Presently it became the style to use the black paint for the background, leaving the red to show through as the pictures. This style is called "red-figured." Here, as so often, we must stop and reflect that what we speak of as "Greek art" is the product of men who were straightforwardly work-ing for the commercial market and produced very fine work. Greek vases were meant to be used. Today they appeal to us for their grace of line and for the clean and lively drawing of the pictures on them, often scenes from Greek myth and legend. When they were made, they appealed to people all over the Greek world. Their remains help us to learn that Athens now developed a lively trade with the West, with Etruscans and Carthaginians as well as with Western Greeks. The Corinthian ware had become a little mechanical and careless and did not stand up well to the competition of the new Athenian product.

Solon's Political Measures

Although in later days at Athens, when there was much argument about political origins, Solon was claimed as the founder of Greek democracy, he probably would have rejected the idea himself. He would have been more likely to describe himself as giving recognition in government to all elements of the citizen body. His government seemed conservative in practice even to those who claimed him as the founder of democracy; they did no more than claim him as having taken first steps.

Solon divided the free citizens into four classes according to income in terms of farm produce. The produce apparently had to come from one's own land. Those of the first class were known as pentacosiomedimnoi, or five-hundred-bushel men. The second class were known as hippeis, or knights, or three-hundred-bushel men. The name of the third class was the zeugitae; there is no English equivalent, but we do know that they were two-hundred-bushel men. The fourth class, the thetes, were laborers who had no land and no specified income. If a man made some profits from trade and wished to be reckoned in one of the three upper classes, perhaps he had to find someone willing to sell him land—not, of course, always easy, because land and status went together. Possibly his money income could be calculated as income in kind.

The assembly of the people was now open to citizens of all four classes. They had the privilege of electing the archon, and all four classes could vote. The situation now came closer to our idea of an election than anything we have yet seen. The use of the new classification becomes clear when we see that only the first two classes were eligible for the archonship, as doubtless seemed right and proper to the two lower classes, little as we might like it nowadays. But this principle can be turned around. That is, the archonship was for the first time open to people who had the property qualification of the first two classes whether or not they belonged to the class of the Eupatrids, or nobles, another way of saying the people who had owned the good land for several generations. This modification may well have given a chance at the archonship to a few people who had risen in the social scale and could now show the proper amount of income—a real and useful innovation. Possibly it even promised more opportunity for some strong clans who came from the outskirts of Attica and had never been able to gain admission to that inner group which passed around among its members the archonship and the consequent membership in the council.

The highest class were distinguished by alone being eligible for the office of state treasurer. Perhaps it was felt that the men of most wealth had the most financial ability and also the most property to assure their responsibility. Other rules based on the classes were that members of the third class were eligible for certain minor offices and that members of the fourth class were not eligible for any.

It is as well to remind ourselves that in modern terms the assets of all four classifications represent only a very modest property. The distinctions between them seem correspondingly modest. One of the second class could theoretically get his income out of about seven acres of good land, although he would be likely to have more land than that, some of it in wheat, some in vines or olive trees. If most of his income was in wine or oil of fair quality, the amount would probably make him more prosperous than if it were all in wheat. His total property would be something more than seven acres of good wheat land, then, or more acres if it were poorer land or planted with trees or vines. There would be a house of mud and timber, perhaps a small wood lot, a yoke of oxen, some sheep and goats, poultry, and a horse for the head of the family.

Under the new arrangement, the archons passed into the council, as before, after their term of office. The council remained, but a new, second council was introduced. From now on the old one was known as the Council of the Areopagus, from the place where it met. This council, like those of most of the Greek *poleis*, had general supervisory powers of a vaguely defined nature. Being composed usually of the heads of important families, it wielded a certain amount of practical power and controlled the *polis* in much the same way that the clan heads did their own little areas by dealing sensibly and firmly with anything or anyone who threatened to disturb the peace or upset the existing order. These powers and the jurisdiction of homicide cases were left to the Council of the Areopagus, but the development of other organs of government seemed to leave the council less room for the exercise of its general powers of supervision.

The new council was to be known as the *Boule* (pronounced boo-lay'), or simply the Council; it is often spoken of, too, as the Senate of Athens. Its composition could hardly have been more different from that of the Council of Areopagus. It had four hundred members, a hundred from each of the four tribes that were traditional among the Ionians (to whom Athens belonged), chosen by lot from those who came forward, and serving for only a year. We shall hear more of the practice of choosing men by lot; to the Athenians it seemed the democratic way. These four hundred probably included some men of the greatest families, but most were ordinary, well-to-do citizens. Working up a party to dominate the Council of a given year was difficult or impossible because the falling of the lot was, of course, unpredictable. Once one was chosen, it would be hard to gather a party, because the term was only for one year. The function of the *Boule* was to keep a general watch on the affairs of Athens and to prepare proposals for any meeting of the Assembly. It plainly took something away from the power of those who had been used to directing the state, for the old council had been able to manage the Assembly, assuming administrative authority themselves and only occasionally offering the Assembly a carefully timed and carefully phrased proposal for its approval. If the new *Boule* could guide the Assembly, it would be expected to do so less factionally and more in the interest of the whole *polis*. (It must be noted that some modern scholars do not believe that the *Boule* was created by Solon and date it a hundred years later.)

The Assembly was given another power by Solon, one that was inherent in general Greek thought. Those of the people who qualified for the Assembly were generally felt to be the final source of justice, and thus it was not uncommon to regard them as the judicial element among the constitutional powers and to bring cases before them as a court. When the Assembly constituted itself a court, it was called the *Heliaea*. This court had one piece of business not common among the other Greeks—the examination of the accounts and the acts of the outgoing magistrates, for the ex-magistrate did not get his place in the Council of the Areopagus unless he passed this scrutiny. The Assembly did not wield so much power over the magistrates by its power of review as we might think. The power of tradition and the economic power of the leading men were always to be reckoned with, even if one of these men had been guilty of some act deserving of criticism. The *Heliaea* could also sit as a court in other matters. In such cases, it often divided itself into panels of about 500.

From the foregoing account it might seem that we are well informed about the reforms of Solon. Such is not the case. We can put together an outline of them that is fairly well attested and seems to make good sense. For the motives we have little evidence and are driven to conjecture and analogy from what we know of other *poleis*. We also are scantily informed about the results of Solon's reforms. It is supposed that his program was the great event in the Athenian move from a tribal state, dominated by the heads of the old clans and rather behind the other *poleis*, and that after Solon's time more power was in the hands of the smaller farmers and the men like himself who had branched out into trade. For the latter supposition there is the evidence only that Athenian pottery spread more widely through the Mediterranean to indicate an upswing of trade and a new alertness in manufacture. Probably the lot of the man who tried to farm in a small way was still very hard, although he was protected from slavery for debt.

THE TYRANNY OF PEISISTRATUS

The sworn agreement to observe the laws of Solon for ten years was kept, although he was besieged with complaints and abuse from every side. Perhaps, however, we should discount his story of the general dissatisfaction, for even temperate statements of discontent might soon become tiresome and loom large. In any case, there was no explosion when the ten years were over, but there was an unsuccessful attempt at tyranny by one Damasias, who had been elected archon and would not lay down his power until he was dislodged from it by force. After Damasias was removed, a group of ten archons was elected for the rest of the year. Five were Eupatrids, or nobles, three were small farmers, and two were craftsmen from the town. We may be sure that before Solon the small farmers and the craftsmen would not have been able to gain such recognition. There were also two occasions during these ten years when the strife of factions was such that it was not possible to choose an archon.

Slowly the two chief interests in the *polis* crystallized into two political parties. The main group of the Eupatrids, who were great landowners, came to be known as the party of the Plain, because their holdings were chiefly in the flatter land of Attica. Their opponents were largely the group who had given most support to Solon's reform in the first place and were unwilling to allow reaction against it and nullification of it now. This other party was known as that of the Coast or Shore. It is tempting to suppose because of the name that they may have been largely business men, but the business men of this time probably were not influential enough to constitute a real party. The rise after some time of a third party, that of the Hills, is connected with the great name of Peisistratus, who was soon to be tyrant. If the third party can be assigned a program at all, it may be said to have favored a stronger central government with more control over the local grandees, which would have been what the Athenians saw in other *poleis,* and the encouragement of a large class of holders of moderate-sized farms who could be relied on as heavy infantry, which again was what the Athenians saw elsewhere. The three parties were combinations of local groupings and class groupings and groups supporting the interests of the great families. Their actions cannot be so analyzed as to be ascribed in each case to specific and isolated motives.

The strife of these parties did much to make possible the tyranny of Peisistratus. Athens was not one of the few states that avoided faction and had no tyrants. Peisistratus had distinguished himself as a general in some engagements against the Megarians. Then he appeared one day with wounds streaming blood and asked the Assembly for a bodyguard on the ground that his enemies had tried to murder him (his enemies, of course, could tell no other story than that he had wounded himself). The Assembly found his story convincing and provided the bodyguard. Fifty citizens armed with clubs were thought enough, for these were the local machinations of local great men in a *polis* of moderate size. In 561 B.C., then, he was able to seize the Acropolis and make himself tyrant. Soon the parties of the Plain and the Shore, which could have prevented him had they combined initially, did unite against him. Their show of force was enough to make him give in and leave town. Presently they fell out again, and the leader of the party of the Plain, Megacles the Alcmaeonid, made a plan with Peisistratus that brought him back to the city as tyrant. He married the daughter of Megacles. But he also held out a little. Because he already had sons, he did not consummate the marriage, not wishing to complicate his plans with further children. After a while the bride went home, and her father, thoroughly alienated from Peisistratus, forced him to withdraw again.

Peisistratus now entered on a long period of preparation. He and his supporters moved to the north shore of the Aegaean, where they made a settlement and in ten years had acquired both money and allies, the money from the timber and precious metals of the region and the allies from the neighbors of Athens who were not friendly to her, chiefly Eretria and Thebes. He was able to hire a thousand mercenaries from Argos. In 546 B.C., he marched on Athens and once again made himself tyrant, this time with little trouble. To use mercenaries and foreign support to gain a tyranny was a new method. Even this would probably not have worked if Athens had had a strong and united government.

Between his first usurpation in 561 and his death in 527 Peisistratus was in power for nineteen years and out of power for fourteen. Once firmly established by force in 546 he settled down to a marked and consistent policy. He was firmly in control until his death and was able to bequeath his power to his sons Hippias and Hipparchus. Although he confiscated the estates of a few of his enemies, notably the Alcmaeonids, he preserved the estates of others who withdrew to exile. Several of his measures had two aspects, that of helping to build a class of small farmers and that of reducing the power of the Eupatrids. To this purpose, he distributed some of the confiscated estates. He sent traveling justices of the peace around Attica to hear cases for two reasons: to undermine the traditional jurisdiction of the chiefs of the clans and to help the farmers by not taking them away from their work for court sittings in the city. Probably even an enlightened tyrant would prefer not to have the country people more in touch with politics by visits to the city. With his income from his mines in Thrace, he could make loans to farmers on easy terms for improvements and equipment. He made himself accessible and agreeable to all; the tyranny was much lightened by the fact that a reasonable complaint could be made directly to the tyrant. By this means he probably also prevented his subordinates from feeling that they could do as they pleased without his ever knowing about it.

Peisistratus maintained the constitution as it had been. But his men were elected or appointed to every post. As ex-archons they little by little filled the Council of Areopagus. The *Heliaea* was composed of the people in general, who were favorable to him. In a trial of naked force he had all the advantage. He had disarmed the citizens and had his own mercenary force. All the formal and official organs of government were in his hands and the hands of his supporters. He controlled the official revenues and the unofficial ones that he had developed for himself in Thrace. He held the Acropolis. Meanwhile, the Alcmaeonids had settled at Delphi and made themselves respected and influential. More than once they tried to return to Athens by force, but were foiled each time.

One Eupatrid, Miltiades, seized a strange opportunity to leave the country, although he had not felt the need to go when Peisistratus came into power. He accepted the invitation of the Dolonci, a tribe in the Chersonesus, or Gallipoli Peninsula, to become their king. They are said to have sent a delegation to consult the Delphic Oracle. Their ambassadors were told to choose the first man who invited them in as they traveled from Delphi toward home. Peisistratus was glad to see a formidable Eupatrid go and glad to think that this part of the approaches to the Black Sea wheat region would be in the hands of an Athenian.

The tyrant maintained friendship with other tyrants in the islands of the Aegaean, especially Lygdamis of Naxos. The chief of them, Polycrates of Samos, was a large-handed pirate chief who kept a hundred galleys and preyed on trade while ruling as tyrant at home, constructing great public works, and entertaining poets at his court. Although not a formal ally, he maintained a friendly attitude to Athens. After the Persians conquered Lydia in 547 B.C., they cast their shadow over every other power in the Aegaean and Asia Minor. The Greek cities of the coast of Asia Minor were now under Persian control. Presently a Persian satrap betrayed and overcame Polycrates. King Darius moved across the Hellespont in 514 and secured for Persia the nearer part of Europe.

In Greece itself Peisistratus had friends, but the great influence of Sparta was against him as it was against all other tyrants. The Alcmaeonids did not fail to make representations to the Spartans that it would be better to have a reliable nobility in power at Athens than a tyrant who was all too inclined to make concessions to the ordinary man. The Delphic Oracle, especially when consulted by Sparta, began to throw out hints that could be interpreted to mean that it was Sparta's duty to overthrow the tyrant of Athens.

Besides favoring the common man against the nobles at home and making such alliances as he could for Athens abroad, Peisistratus pursued an enlightened commercial and cultural policy like that of other tyrants. Although we cannot point to specific measures to help trade, we do know that the Attic pottery, the reliable evidence of Athenian commerce, spread as far as Spain in the West and all over the Aegaean and up to southern Russia on the Black Sea. Peisistratus had the good sense to pay for such popular public works as a water supply. It was a sensible move, too, for a tyrant to institute the great Panathenaic festival to celebrate the unification of Attica. Probably a number of Ionians migrated to Athens now from distaste for the Persian rule in their cities. Such new members would be likely to have an effect on Athenian life, for Ionia had been feeling the stirrings of great new ideas for two or three generations, as we shall see. The most important innovation was the beginning, about 535, of the performance of plays at the festival of Dionysus. From this came Attic tragedy, the great literary glory of Athens. The festival began to be built up as an occasion for visitors to the city— the first example of the glorification of a local festival for economic purposes and to stimulate local pride.

The Expulsion of the Tyrants

Peisistratus died in 527 B.C., the tyranny passing smoothly to his sons, who were well trained in governing and continued all his policies. The family was driven out in 510 by the power of the Spartans, but in 514 there occurred a curious event that according to popular song and legend was to be the cause of their fall. Two young men, Harmodius and Aristogeiton, assassinated Hipparchus, one of the sons of Peisistratus, because of a personal grievance having nothing to do with the government and not intended to end the tyranny. Nevertheless these two came to be known as "the tyrannicides." Statues of them with daggers raised to strike were made, and drinking songs honoring them as the authors of freedom became popular. The popular version of the story did much to obscure the truth.

The expulsion of the tyrants actually came about through the assistance that the Spartans gave. They had more than once shown themselves ready to interfere in the affairs of other *poleis* by helping to depose tyrants. For a long time their assistance had been sought by the exiled Alcmaeonids, and they had received veiled encouragement from the pronouncements of the oracle at Delphi as well. Although the rule of Hippias in Athens had become much harsher after the assassination of his brother Hipparchus, he was still in full control of the situation. He repelled the first attack of the Spartans. Soon came another attack in greater force, which drove its way into Athens and blockaded the tyrant and his mercenaries on the Acropolis. As fate would have it, the Spartans captured the children of the family as Hippias tried to smuggle them out, and terms were made under which he and the others of the family of Peisistratus withdrew from Athens. Hippias went to Sigeum, near Troy, and trusted in his son-in-law, one of the tyrants under the Persians, to introduce him to the protection of the Great King, as the Greeks called the king of Persia.

THE REFORM OF CLEISTHENES

The Spartans had hardly withdrawn from Athens when the Eupatrids began a violent struggle for primacy in the new government. Cleisthenes, the current leader of the Alcmaeonids, had been the moving spirit in persuading the Spartans to move at last and in organizing the exiles to do their part in their own restoration. Nevertheless, his rival Isagoras was elected archon in 508 B.C. Cleisthenes, unwilling to accept the election, let the word get around that he would welcome the support of the humbler people and those who were not fully recognized in the clan system, just as Peisistratus had done. Isagoras attempted to nip this movement in the bud by requesting the help of the Spartans. The Spartan king sent a herald ordering the Alcmaeonids to withdraw from Athens because of the

old pollution that they had caused by the massacre of Cylon's supporters when Cylon had tried to become tyrant in 632 B.C. Cleisthenes
had as yet no force to oppose the Spartans, so he withdrew. Then the
Spartan king came to Athens with troops and began to banish those
people who seemed dangerous to Isagoras. He ordered the dissolution
of the Council of the Areopagus, planning to replace it with an
oligarchy picked by Isagoras. Now the Council gathered the citizenry
and blockaded the king and Isagoras on the Acropolis, although
finally it allowed them to withdraw. Cleisthenes and the others came
back, and he was given the opportunity to make the changes that
he had promised.

The aim of Cleisthenes' reform was the creation of a new basis
of participation in the affairs of the *polis* that would leave no free
citizen under a disability as a newcomer or as a descendant of a
poor and unprivileged family and that would make it impossible in
the future for the leading citizens to gather support for such struggles
as the one he had just had with Isagoras. There is a certain improb-
ability about the whole reform; it is hard to believe that a reformer
could so remake a working system and get acceptance of his new
system and that it would then operate successfully for many
generations.

The basic unit of the new system was the deme, which was somewhat analogous to the little settlements about Attica or to the neigh-
borhoods into which even a great modern city tends to divide itself in
the sentiment of the inhabitants. In the city of Athens itself, there
were several demes. It is possible that there were as many as 170 in
all Attica. They were to be the practical working units at the lowest
level. Each citizen belonged to one and kept his membership even if
he moved his residence to another, so that a strong sentiment was
attached to membership in the deme. Each deme had its deme hall,
its records, and its demarch, or official leader, as well as its modest
finances and its religious observances as a single entity. The demes
served as the basic units in elections. In the registration of new members there were none of the old distinctions, such as the lack of full
membership in the religious observances, that had bothered some of
the old poor and the new craftsmen. The new equality, which we might
be tempted to call democracy, was called *isonomia*, or "equality before
the law." The demes had enough functions to seem real units of the

polis. They were small enough to recapture some of the intimacy of earlier days, which must have added to their effectiveness. Casual references to them in later literature all assume that membership in the demes was a real bond.

Another division below the level of the whole *polis* seemed advisable, and because people were thoroughly used to being organized into the four Ionian tribes, which had both a religious and a racial basis, Cleisthenes took advantage of their acceptance. He boldly created ten new tribes and succeeded in breathing life into them, borrowing the idea of a tribe but making no further use of the four old ones. His method was ingenious. He used an old category called a *trittys,* or third. Each of the ten tribes had three of these thirds; each of the thirds was made up of a little group of demes from one of the three working divisions at Attica: the city and its suburbs, the coastal region, and the agricultural interior. Thus each tribe had elements from each of the three main elements of the *polis,* and no tribe was so solidly constituted that any clan or group or economic interest or social interest could dominate it. The tribe, like the deme, was endowed with such functions and such emotional components that it worked. It served as a unit for electoral purposes. It had its own finances and its religious observances. The fact that the tribe was the basis of military organization and that each elected its own general must have added to the significance of the tribes.

All the old organizations remained, just as the Council of the Areopagus remained when Solon created the new council, the *Boule.* The old organization of the four tribes, the clans, and the old priesthoods retained religious functions for the most part. In modern life we hardly notice that we, too, have such survivals of institutions. For example, in heavily populated areas the county has largely been superseded, yet the courts are still likely to be organized by counties.

The new system was made to work very neatly in the matter of forming the *Boule.* The demes elected a goodly number of men who were over thirty and at least of the third class in property. Then each tribe chose fifty men from those its demes had proposed. This choice was made by lot from people already guaranteed, as it were, by election. The five hundred members of the *Boule* were separated by tribes into ten prytanies of fifty men each. The prytanies took turns being on full duty for a tenth of the year, living in the council-hall and being on call twenty-four hours a day. A chairman was elected by lot for each day. Thus one man every day had the experience of being at the head of the group that was guiding the *polis*. Because a man could be on the council only twice and be chairman only once, a very large part of the eligible citizens must have served on the council and so acquired an intimate knowledge of how the affairs of the *polis* were managed.

Ostracism

The procedure of ostracism was perhaps devised by Cleisthenes, although it seems more likely that someone else invented it about the time it was first used, in 487 B.C. The essence of the procedure was that the assembly was asked whether it wished to have an ostracism. If it voted in favor, another meeting was held at which, without discussion, the voter could write on a piece of broken pottery, an *ostracon,* the name of anyone whom he wished to see sent for ten years into honorable exile, his property being publicly preserved inviolate. Whoever received most votes (presumably with some minimum number necessary) had to retire for ten years.

It has been suggested that the procedure was devised to protect Athens against an incipient tyrant, since the memory of the Peisistratids was green. In a way, this theory may be true, for the group of several men who were ostracized during the 480's were either of the Peisistratids or closely connected with them. There was a war with Persia in the offing, and it is possible that there was a party in favor of submission to Persia, perhaps with the thought that the Persians would be glad to re-establish a tyranny at Athens and that the Peisistratids would be the most likely candidates. It may be said that the people chose Themistocles to lead the ever-nearer struggle with the Persians by removing the other men from the scene. At the last moment, in 480, an amnesty was declared, and all those who had been sent away were brought back to play their parts in a conflict the policy of which they could not now influence.

Excavations have uncovered many *ostraca* scratched with names. One find had the same name written in the same hand on each fragment. Apparently someone's chief opponent intended to come to the vote prepared to furnish anyone who wished it an *ostracon* ready to use against him.

Whether or not ostracism is attributable to Cleisthenes, two other events do characterize the beginnings of his system. First, the Spartans tried again in 506 to reduce the Athenians and force them to make their government acceptable to the Spartans. But the Athenians defeated the Spartans, and the Thebans and the Chalcidians from the nearby island of Euboea as well. Second, having defended their freedom, they embarked upon an imperialism that was to become very marked during the fifth century. They sent cleruchs, or holders of assigned lands, to Chalcis, thus expanding into a good farming area and increasing the number of men of the third class or higher who could be required to serve as hoplites, or heavy-armed infantrymen.

It is worth while now and then to reflect on whether the customary division of history into periods is justified. The reform of Cleisthenes may be said to end the period of the remaking of the *polis* of Athens. This period had begun with Athens as a tribal state that had quietly deposed its king, remained under the domination of the clans for a rather longer time than the other *poleis,* and then slowly began to acquire a centralized government, which took on one by one the powers of a competent government. The reforms of Solon did much to allow participation by the citizenry on a broader base. The reform of Cleisthenes did not change Athens into a democracy, for the influence of wealth and old family was still strong and likely to influence the Assembly to choose men from such backgrounds as archons. The Council of the Areopagus was still highly influential. However, the clans could no longer stir the state with factional quarrels, and the new elements as well as the old poor now had some rights. With the reform of Cleisthenes, the *polis* had become a genuine state, and the conditions were present for the great experiment in radical democracy that occurred in the fifth and fourth centuries.

CHAPTER

16

RELIGION AND PHILOSOPHY

P robably the major change in religion during the period from 800 to 500 B.C. was that caused by the rise of the *polis*. Those people who promoted the *polis*, whoever they were and whatever their reason for doing so, as a matter of course urged the right and duty of the new government to represent its members in religious matters. The *polis* as a whole began to address itself officially to divinities who were thought to give it protection and prosperity. Naturally all the older forms of religion persevered to some extent, as did the simpler and more superstitious rules and taboos. It is impossible in a few pages to do justice to the evidence that we have of the recognition of the Unseen in Greek life, from the most elevated form to the simplest.

The Cults of the Poleis

In general the *poleis* established cults of the major gods whom we met in Homer. Zeus was worshiped everywhere. Some other god, however, was more likely to be the favorite of a *polis*, as Athena was thought to be especially devoted to the interests of Athens. Hera was a favorite, perhaps because she was thought to care for the interests of women and be a present help in childbirth. One of the fine temples still standing at Paestum, in southern Italy, was dedicated to her. Probably Apollo was most popular of all; his temples were everywhere from Asia Minor to Italy. There was not, now or ever, a precise and unified body of dogma about the nature of the gods. Each one was likely to have several aspects, as Apollo was god of the sun, of disease and medicine, of music, of prophecy, and also had a connection with vegetation and cattle. A god was often worshiped in different aspects in different places and had different names. Pythian Apollo of Delphi was a god of prophecy, while Delian Apollo was patron and protector of the island of Delos, his birthplace. Naturally the *polis* kept under its control the holy place and its temple or other structure, the appointment of priests, and the management of festivals unless some family or other group had long since established itself in the priesthood of some very old cult.

The cult of the hero is strange to us. These were local cults, centered on the graves of great men of earlier times. Some notable force was thought to be exerted by their remains. The cult was generally an official one of the *polis* and often emphasized the *polis*. In some colonies, for instance, rites and sacrifices were offered at the grave of the oecist who had led out a colony. Such hero cults were common all over the Greek world.

The Variety of Religion

Before the rise of the *polis*, the family groups had necessarily had their own religious observances, because the Unseen must somehow be dealt with. Even though the strength of family bonds was loosened by the transfer of loyalty to the *polis*, the cults of the family groups were not so weakened as to disappear. In Athens at the height of the enlightenment of the fifth century, a citizen could not become a member of the council unless he could prove his active adherence to such a cult.

Religious feeling became connected with many places. It was thought that in some spots the gods spoke to men (we shall later discuss the most famous, the oracle of Apollo at Delphi). There were many such and in all parts of the Greek world. In innumerable minor places, too, the power of some god was believed to have manifested itself. Offerings were brought there and prayers were said. Votive offerings, sometimes tiny clay statues, were brought in great numbers to every holy place. Blood sacrifices were often made; that is, animals were killed and offered to the divinity.

The temple itself might be called an afterthought. The holiness of the place was established first, and the rites and observances did not require a temple. Someone—a tyrant or the *polis*— would decide to build one. The temple was always located in the holy place, for the Greeks would have seen no point in choosing any available site and building on it, as we do with our churches. Furthermore, the temple was for the god, not for the people. The interior usually contained a room for the cult statue and perhaps a storeroom or treasury. Admission might even be forbidden to all except priests and attendants on the ground that the temple was too holy a place for others. The adjective "profane" originally applied (in Latin) to those ordinary citizens whose entering the temple or approaching the ceremony too closely violated this taboo. The time was far in the future, in the fourth Christian century, when Christianity, having become legal, began to use the Roman knowledge of constructing big buildings for crowds of people and made large, permanent churches, no longer afraid of their being destroyed. The great interiors of ancient churches, like the Church of the Holy Wisdom (Hagia Sophia) in Istanbul, which we can imagine as thronged with many thousands of people, are in striking contrast to the small and divided interiors of the Greek temples, which were not meant for gatherings of worshipers.

There is no evidence that the Greek priests served the god as did the Near Eastern and Egyptian ones by feeding, washing, and entertaining him. Prayers and offerings could be made either by individuals or by priests. There were festivals of every sort. Probably all through Greek history the people closest to the soil have been most serious about festivals meant to ensure the yield of the field and the flock. Many other festivals were deliberately shaped to increase civic pride and unity and became great occasions designed to attract visitors, as is the case with many festivals nowadays.

The Great Games

The most famous of all Greek festivals was the Olympic Games, closely followed by the great festival of Dionysus at Athens (which we shall describe later). Athletic festivals were common in Greece. When the heroes of the *Iliad* and the *Odyssey* gathered for a funeral or, indeed, for almost any purpose, they liked to have athletic contests, not only as an amusement, but also as an opportunity to exercise their personal prowess and love of personal glory. We find no trace of contests of this sort among the earlier peoples whom we have considered. Hunting was always a favorite sport of the kings and nobles of the earlier peoples, and they seem to have found that danger spiced their enjoyment, but contests between man and man did not suit them.

The athletic competitions of the Greeks were likely to be connected with regular religious gatherings. A few of the games came to be widely known and attracted visitors in such numbers that they could be called national rather than local in character. An accessible site and shrewd local management caused these games to stand out above others as an attraction for athletes and for visitors. The Olympic Games were the first to become national rather than local, and the other three leading sets of games were founded in the early sixth century in frank imitation of them. The Isthmian Games were at Corinth, the Nemean near Argos, and the Pythian at Delphi. All were in honor of divinities.

Olympia (which is not to be confused with Mount Olympus) is in the western Peloponnesus in pleasant agricultural country. The festival there was in honor of Zeus, and the accepted date for the first meeting was 776 B.C. The period of four years from one meeting to another came to be known as an Olympiad, and dating by Olympiads and intermediate years ("in the second year of the fifty-first Olympiad") became an accepted system of dating. The last meeting was 1168 years later, in 393 A.D. The games retained their religious character to the last, and they were shut down for this reason under the edict of the Christian emperor Theodosius I forbidding public worship of pagan divinities. An interval of 1,503 years followed until the modern Olympics began at Athens in 1896.

The original games took place at the August full moon, a time when the grain was in and there was a lull before the harvest of the grapes and olives. Heralds went far and wide through the Greek world to announce the sacred truce that protected the occasion. Freeborn Greeks were eligible to compete. The athletes and the spectators came from all over the Greek world. The Greeks of the region of the Black

Sea or of Asia Minor and the islands came by water, not in passenger ships, for there were none, but in fishing smacks or freight ships. The Greeks of Greece walked. It was a hundred and twenty-odd miles from Athens, not an unreasonable walk for a Greek of those days. Most people traveled in parties. The émigrés of the prosperous *poleis* of South Italy and Sicily, who were still Greeks and eligible to compete, came by ship. On more than one occasion some resentment was aroused by the rich pavilions and other signs of the wealth of the tyrants of this Western region.

Olympia itself was not a *polis*, but a place for the sanctuary of Zeus and the celebration of the games. The festival was managed in early times by the people of nearby Pisa, and control passed later to the people of nearby Elis. They had no place to shelter the visitors, but the season was mild, there were fields and woods, and anyone who objected to sleeping out in a pine grove could stay at home. No formal amusements were provided for the visitors in the evening as is done by the cities where the modern Olympics are held. This crowd was content with itself. Merchants might well summon their agents to a meeting. Friends and relatives from different *poleis* could meet. Many a man must have recognized a smiling face that he had last seen scowling at him over the rim of a shield in the front lines of a battle. All sorts of people came in the hope of some gain—jugglers and tight-rope walkers, men who had fine and portable merchandise to sell, or orators who wished to air a theory at a great gathering. The historian Herodotus is said to have introduced his history of the Persian wars to the public by giving readings from it at the Olympics.

The Elean officials worked out a schedule of events that began with the taking of the oath. The contestants, who had done the last month of their training at Elis, stood before the altar of Zeus with their trainers and fathers and swore to compete fairly. Then they paraded to the stadium, where the heralds introduced each man by proclaiming his name, his father's name, and his *polis*.

The games began with races of four-horse chariots and riding horses. The contests of the athletes began with the pentathlon, the five parts of which were the dash, the broad jump, the discus, the javelin, and wrestling. Great importance was attached to good form in the jumping and throwing events, and they were customarily performed to the music of the flute. The winner was nevertheless picked on distance, not on form. The distance was not measured, as it is now, and there was no mania for keeping records and seeing them broken. It was enough to determine who had won the contest. The jumper used weights that looked like dumbbells. He would swing them forward sharply as he left the takeoff, then swing them back sharply and let them go. These weights have been found in excavations, and they are represented in pictures on pottery. Similar ones were used in the early meetings of the modern Olympics.

The day of the full moon had no contests. It was the day of the sacrifice to Zeus, the original cause of the meeting at Olympia. Perhaps fifty or sixty thousand people would gather around the great altar of Zeus. There was a parade of the officials, the athletes, the horses, and the delegates from the *poleis* bringing their offerings to the god. Because the best artists worked on these gifts of the cities to the god and on the victory offerings as well, Olympia little by little became a great repository of art. The description by Pausanias, the Greek Baedeker, who lived in the second century of our era, makes Olympia seem one gorgeous collection of art.

The next morning there were three races. The stadium did not have an oval track, but twenty-one straight lanes that were almost two hundred meters long. The starting line was a marble slab with double grooves into which the runners could set their bare feet for the start. One cannot set a foot very firmly into the grooves, and they are a little close together for the modern idea of starting holes. The Greek word for them was *gramma,* or "scratch," whence the modern word "scratch" for the starting line. The runners were set off by the word *"Apite!"* or "Go!" The first race was one length of the stadium. The second race was the double dash, down and back. Twenty runners ran in the twenty-one lanes, and each man turned round a post set in the marble slab at the far end and came back in the lane to the left of the one he went down in. Obviously the race was slower than a straightaway or one around a curve, but the race was the thing, not an attempt to get the time down. The third race was about three miles. This time a single post was set in the middle of the slab at each end, and the runners turned around it as they went up and down the track.

In the afternoon were the boxing, wrestling, and *pancration,* or general contest. The boxers wore strips of soft leather around their hands, there were no rounds, and the fight ended when one man signified that he had had enough. In the wrestling, it was not necessary to pin the opponent's shoulders to the ground, but only to make some part of his body above the knee touch the ground, and two out of three falls gave the victory. The *pancration* may seem brutal to modern taste because, along with wrestling holds and striking with the fists, choking and kicking were allowed. This does not mean kicking with boots on, however, but kicking with the bare foot, which requires much skill and is open to disastrous countermoves, as is choking. Nevertheless, the story is told of one pair in this event who lay locked on the ground, when suddenly one rolled over dead. As the shout went up for the victory of the other, he, too, rolled over dead.

The winner of each event was called to the judges' table of ivory and gold, itself a famous work of art, and given a simple wreath of olive leaves as the herald announced his name. On the evening of the day after the meet, as the crowd was on its way home on its fishing smacks or trudging over the hills and far away, the managers of the games gave a banquet for the victors. Sometimes statues were commissioned in honor of a victory and set up at Olympia. Famous poets, of whom Pindar's name is best known, were commissioned by tyrants or nobles to write victory odes. The *polis,* too, honored the victor on his return home. So much attention was perhaps an overemphasis on athletic glory. Even then philosophers were not lacking to offer scornful criticism of the cult of athletic glory. As we have said, there were many sides to Greek life and many basic inconsistencies.

It is customary to say that Greek unity was promoted by the Olympics and by the other great games as well as by the common language and religion. We cannot be sure, of course, how much the games did to promote a genuine unity of the Greeks. Surely going every summer (for some set of games was held every year) to a large meeting of people did much to leaven their intellectual life. Ideas as well as news could thus circulate among a people who had no other regular means of communication. It is open to doubt whether the games did anything to promote political unity except as they provided a place in which many disputes were arbitrated and many treaties made. Perhaps it was helpful for members of the little Greek *poleis* to remind themselves that the inhabitants of the other *poleis* were much the same kind of people, but presumably they knew that. The interminable wars of the Greeks were due not to pure xenophobia or ignorance of what kind of people their neighbors were, but to conflicts of interest. Possibly the yearly gatherings did something to lessen these conflicts.

The Delphic Oracle

The story of Pythian Apollo, the god of prophecy at Delphi, begins with the combat in which he vanquished the great serpent Python. Zeus himself had a similar combat against the monster Typhon, and the myths of the ancient world are full of these great struggles in which gods and heroes destroy giants, demons, and monsters. Because the priests of Apollo at Delphi early endeared themselves to the Dorians who were on the warpath, all the Dorians gave the Pythian Apollo a high place in their religious thought. The Spartans, who believed that the advice of Apollo had guided them well in such important matters as the establishment of the dual kingship, even had two officials to consult the oracle and record the responses. When the age of colonization began, the oracle of Apollo for some reason began to be consulted about the proper forms of religious observance in the prospective colonies. The priests were shrewd about learning whatever could be learned from their patrons, who generally had to stay in Delphi a little while awaiting the days when the priestess was sitting. These men of religion learned so much about the geography of outlying regions that they could give good advice on possible sites for new colonies. In addition, they were not above asserting in retrospect that they had given advice when they had not or that their advice had been better than was really the case. Be that as it may, Pythian Apollo acquired great prestige and influence as an adviser on colonization.

The Greeks were much concerned about pollution. A whole clan might become polluted, as the Alcmaeonids did by the massacre of the supporters of Cylon. A whole community could be polluted by a murder or even by an accidental homicide. Many a delegation was sent to Delphi to inquire what could be done about such pollution, and the answers were always sane and moderate. The Oracle rendered a great service to the Greeks during an age of change by exerting a steadying and comforting influence on those in doubt about what to do to be in right relation to the gods. These doubts ran through every phase of life. That emerging organization, the *polis,* often needed religious guidance in matters of observance as well as in frequent matters of catharsis, or cleansing from some miasma, or source of pollution. Many an individual had doubts and fears to which the Oracle could minister. Some, for instance, believing that they lay under an ancestral curse, were willing to pay for ceremonies of exorcism. Colonists went on their way confident in the advice of the Oracle. New hero cults were thought to be established properly.

The beautiful site of Delphi is in an accessible position just north of the Gulf of Corinth, a few miles from the north shore. Thus, some visitors could come by ship. Others tramped up through the hills and stayed in Delphi until the next day on which the priestess received questions for the god. The post of priestess was held by a succession of local women, and the idea of a sort of second sight among them is accepted by each modern man according to his own attitude in such matters. They are said to have raved when possessed by the god; a board of priests reduced what was said to respectable verse, for no one used prose for serious matters, and gave it in writing to the inquirer. A once held theory that the priestess was influenced by gases arising from a chasm has been given up for lack of evidence.

Dionysus

The idea of the division of life into the Apollonian—the sober, steady, and orderly way—and Dionysiac—the impulsive and emotional—is suggestive if used with care. We have seen that the priests of Delphic Apollo performed a useful function by helping the Greeks of the new age to bear the weight of their new individuality and to live in a steady and orderly way. These same priests were friendly, too, to the cult of Dionysus.

The mention of Dionysus in Homer, suggesting his worship in early times, is now supported by mention in the Linear B tablets. There is one persistent tradition, however, that the worship of Dionysus came from Thrace, and another tradition would have it come from Asia Minor, in both cases in the new age. It may well be that all are true and that one function of Dionysus, as a god of vegetation, was worshiped in early Greece, whereas the aspect of him most familiar to us was a later importation from both Thrace and Asia Minor.

Dionysus was readily received in Greece, whatever his origin. The people were ready for a religion that offered joy and ecstasy. The word *ekstasis* means "a standing apart from," and one benefit that the god offered was the faculty of standing apart from one's self, away from that lately somewhat more individualistic self that must have seemed to many tiresome to have always around. In the older days, one could lose oneself in the clan, with no need to be so conscious of the individual self and new, individual responsibilities. Under the influence of the wine that went with the festivals of Dionysus and as one of an excited crowd, one might occasionally give one's self the slip, so to speak, and have a few minutes of freedom from individuality.

But more is involved in doing justice to Dionysus. He was concerned with vegetation and the wine. He must somehow have been connected with fertility, for a model of a phallus—often a huge one—was invariably carried in his processions. The Greeks were not self-conscious as we are about human reproduction. To exalt and promote the powers of reproduction by carrying model phalluses in parades seemed only logical. If there was a decided emphasis on the phallus in the comedies played at Dionysus' great festival, it was in clean fun, not in obscene fun.

Finally, and partly under the influence of Apollo's priests, the orgies of Dionysus were regularized, and a remarkable combination of Apollonian and Dionysiac was achieved. The orgies of Dionysus, which appealed chiefly to women, were channeled into somewhat tamer observances. Every other year there was a supervised festival in which the women roamed on the hills and allowed themselves a freedom from ordinary inhibitions that culminated in the catching of a wild animal, tearing it apart, and eating it raw.

The Eleusinian Mysteries

The Eleusinian Mysteries developed from the cult of Demeter and Persephone at Eleusis, near Athens. The story of these two goddesses is another that falls in the category of the dying and reviving god. The pretty tale is that Persephone, daughter of Demeter, the goddess of the grain, was carried off below by Pluto, or Hades, the god of the Underworld. Her mother sought her, finally found her there, and got Zeus's permission to take her back, but because Persephone had eaten something while in Hades, there had to be a compromise that allowed her to spend half her time on earth and half in the world below. All this is described in a beautiful poem of the seventh century, the *Hymn to Demeter*.

There were two transformations in the cult attached to the Mysteries. In the earlier one, the performance of the ritual that symbolized the idea of the death and the return of the vegetation somehow developed into a mystery play, accompanied by the belief that there ought to be certain initiated people who would be able to see this play and thereby gain immortality, while all others were barred. The second transformation occurred when Eleusis became part of Athens and the whole cult was subjected to the Athenian flair for dramatizing and publicizing everything Athenian. There are many references in ancient literature to the Mysteries, but the performance was secret, and we can only guess that it repeated the chief story of the cult. It is certain, however, that a great many people gained a hope of immortality by their membership. At first, apparently, only the immortality of the family in general was hoped for, but with the growth of individualism the idea of possible personal immortality arose.

There were a number of other mysteries that we know very little about, the existence of which is revealed to us by casual evidence. The island of Samothrace, for example, was the seat of another considerable cult. Recent excavations have shown us much about the cult and the buildings. After the end of the fourth century, the famous Winged Victory stood in the basin of a fountain on the hillside overlooking the precinct where these Mysteries were celebrated.

SCIENCE AND PHILOSOPHY

In science, as in many other fields, the Greeks are the first of the moderns. They stood upon the shoulders of the Egyptians and the Mesopotamian peoples, whose first steps in science are coming to be rated more and more highly by scholars. But if we cannot give the Greeks credit for starting from nothing, as they were thought to have done when our knowledge of the earlier peoples was still scanty and vague, we can give them credit for cultivating scientific studies more intensively, organizing the knowledge into systems of general laws in the modern style, and trying to explain everything without ascribing it to the caprice of divinities. The style of Greek science, as of almost everything the Greeks did, is the beginning of the modern Western style and is in contrast to the ancient and Near Eastern style.

Science and philosophy were one and the same thing at their beginning, which took place somewhere around the year 600 B.C. among those Greeks who were known as the Ionians and who lived on the coast of Asia Minor. Until about that time, the ancient mythological and religious explanations of the nature of the world had suffered no serious challenge. The attempts that were made by a number of men in the city of Miletus and elsewhere in Ionia to gain a reasoned view of the world, Nature, and man were philosophical in that these men wished to understand how the whole system worked and make their way back to first causes. But these attempts were scientific, too, in that these men attempted to observe a wide range of data and draw strict conclusions on the assumption that the world works according to regular laws that are not capriciously altered by divine will.

It would not have occurred to these Ionian Greeks to call themselves either scientists or philosophers; probably neither of these words had yet been invented. After a century or so, the word "philosophy" (*philosophia*) came into use. It is important to understand that it was applied to the whole process of understanding what life and the world are and that what we call science was a major part of it. As more and more men (but never more than a few at a time by our standards) became interested in this systematic and rigorous kind of thought, some became more interested in one field than another and began to specialize, perhaps in astronomy or in medicine. In this way, certain bodies of knowledge, which we should call sciences, broke off from philosophy and acquired names of their own, just as in our day new fields of knowledge claim standing and names—geriatrics, for example.

Thales of Miletus

Thales is the first man to whose name we can attach any definite philosophical ideas. His lifetime fell somewhere between about 640 and 545 B.C.; he is said to have lived beyond the age of ninety. Some of our data about him suggest that he was the vigorous, practical sort of whom the lively commercial city of Miletus must have had many. He is said to have forecast a fine olive crop and made a financial killing by cornering all the presses. He is also said to have been a good astronomer and especially interested in navigation.

It is not known whether Thales wrote anything. He is thought to have learned something of astronomy from the Babylonians and geometry from the Egyptians. The assertion of later Greeks that he was the first philosopher may rest upon their knowing that he introduced a certain amount of order, rational arrangement, and theorizing into astronomical and geometrical data that the Babylonians and Egyptians had gathered for purely practical purposes. This to the Greeks would have seemed philosophical activity.

Thales said that water is the primary substance, or substrate, from which all other substances are derived. Whatever one may think of this statement as a piece of science, it clearly took a new frame of mind to raise the point at all. Thales was a modern. He was probably influenced by the fact that we can see water in three states, liquid, solid, and vaporous, and can follow its changes between states. It would seem a reasonable conjecture that water might undergo many other changes not so easily followed. Possibly he was influenced by the traditional idea of Babylonian mythology (which would have been known at Miletus) that in the beginning everything was water, from which other things were derived as the world was created.

The startling effect that rainwater can have on semidesert soil would also tend to exalt the role of water in Nature. The sudden appearance of vegetable life from dry soil when it is moistened or the revivification of thirsty vegetable matter can dramatize the part played by water in plant growth. In addition, the idea of spontaneous generation, which was common in antiquity, arose from the fact that people thought they had seen it happen when insect life appeared in pools of water.

The Ionian School

The Greeks who later wrote about these early philosophers obviously knew little about them. They did know the name of Anaximander, the most prominent thinker in Miletus in the generation after Thales, and the name of Anaximenes, the leader in the next generation. Probably a number of people were interested in this sort of study and speculation, but there is no need to suppose that they spent all their time this way. They were more likely to be merchants who were lively minded. Although they were—and are—people of considerable importance in intellectual history, genuine information about them must have been hard to get a mere two or three hundred years later, when attempts were made to describe the beginnings of philosophy.

Anaximander of Miletus is called the pupil of Thales; but to be "a pupil" means only that he was a younger man who profited by discussions with Thales. He was in the prime of life about 560 B.C. It is probable that he wrote a book on philosophy. He was one who struggled manfully with the problem of the primary element, or substrate. In the place of water, which Thales had put forward, Anaximander spoke of the *apeiron,* or the Unlimited. Earth, air, fire, and water seemed to him to be the most handy gross classifications of matter, as they did to many other Greeks. He divided these four elements into pairs of opposite qualities, hot-cold and wet-dry. It seemed inappropriate that water, only one of these elements, should be primary. The more generalized conception of the Unlimited allowed these four to be derived from it and to be mixed together in it. The Unlimited itself was neutral in quality, not limited (that is, limited by definite qualities) and was not itself subject to changes, as water is. Presumably Anaximander felt more comfortable for having added these logical refinements to the conception of the primary element.

His description of the creation of definite matter is vague and metaphorical. The opposites "separated out" from the Unlimited because of the "everlasting motion." This might mean that when a piece of the Unlimited breaks off, the opposites are no longer held neutralized and so can form matter. It could also mean that the process takes place a universe at a time. He believed that the Unlimited was not limited in amount any more than it was limited by having definite qualities. From it an infinite number of universes could be formed. A piece of the proper size might break off from the Unlimited, thus becoming capable of generating the opposites hot and cold and later the opposites dry and wet. He conjectured an ingenious sequence of further events in the process of creation.

The third leader of this sort of activity in Miletus was Anaximenes, who was said by later writers to have been a pupil of Anaximander and to have flourished about a generation later. For us the noteworthy part of his scantily recorded contribution is his assertion that air is the primary element. From air, he said, all things are created by condensation and rarefaction.

Heracleitus of Ephesus was the last of the great philosophers of the Ionian school. He was probably in the prime of life about 500 B.C., a date that puts him about a generation later than Anaximenes. Heracleitus, like the others, was deeply interested in the constitution of the physical world. He nominated fire to be the substrate and tried to work out a cycle of change from fire to air and earth and water and back to fire. He was much impressed by the prevalence and importance of change, for him best represented by the nature of fire, which is constantly moving and shifting, yet continues to be fire even as it changes. We are to imagine that beside the fascinating visible movement of fire there are two other movements: the struggle within it of the opposites hot-cold and the larger movement in the cycle of change into air, earth, and water. The river, too, is a convenient symbol of sameness with change. One cannot step twice into the same river, as Heracleitus put it. The water is different the second time, yet in the commonest sense it remains the same river. Its form as a river persists through the change of the water. "Everything is in flux," he said, by which he meant that behind the apparent sameness of solid things there is a change like that of the water in the river.

None of these men intended to allow his philosophy to end in nihilism; Heracleitus found a basic principle, an unchanging reality that could be relied upon, in what he called the Logos. This difficult word means a law or principle; in an orderly way it unites the substrate and the process that changes it. The Logos is not a material thing, and Heracleitus does not try to explain where it comes from. It simply exists and is knowable.

In this system we have the paradox that things change while remaining the same, as fire and the river do. The tension between opposites, hot-cold, wet-dry, and so on, serves to maintain a state in objects that is the same to outward view while a deeper change is steadily proceeding. This is a measured and controlled change that goes on according to the Logos. Here we have come upon a more abstract way of thought than we found among the early Ionians, and we can see the development of a contrast between a Form, which in itself is something and has existence, and the Matter that fills in that form.

Heracleitus was suffused with a consciousness of his own intellectual superiority. Among the fragments of his works that later Greeks preserved for us by quoting him, there are a number expressing a lofty contempt for the stupidity of people in general. He declares Homer, Hesiod, and other authors to be inadequate as guides to life. He sourly disapproves of all emotional forms of religion. He is so completely the intellectual that the revels of Dionysus would seem shameful to him, were they not in honor of a god. In human affairs, he says, one's own character is one's destiny. Such a statement shows that individualism and consciousness of self were advancing.

The Pythagoreans

Pythagoras of Samos flourished in the latter part of the sixth century; possibly he lived from about 560 to 480 B.C. He left Samos in early life, perhaps because he could not endure the dictatorship of Polycrates. Going to Croton, in southern Italy, he founded an order or brotherhood of which the chief purpose was the purification of the soul and its eventual release by the usual methods of mystic ritual acts, abstinences that we should call taboos, and ceremonial purgations.

There is no plain reason why the Pythagoreans were interested in science. Their spiritual aims came first, and no clue exists to any way in which their scientific activity furthered these aims. Probably Pythagoras himself originated their two great concepts: number as the first principle and the importance of groups of opposites. If the Pythagoreans had committed more of their thought to writing, we might have more information about their numerical studies. Their discoveries in the realm of musical tones as related to the length of the vibrating string seem straightforward enough. We are less satisfied when we try to understand the mystic properties of numbers, but nevertheless this idea had vitality until the time of Dante and beyond.

The Pythagoreans asserted that all things have number. A constellation, for example, is noted both as an arrangement of stars and as a number of stars. Number is one of the qualities of the constellation and, less obviously, of everything in the universe. They further asserted that not only does everything *have* number, but everything also *is* number. If we now return to the vibrating string and the note it gives off, the idea seems less simple. Perhaps the note that the string produces has number and is number. Perhaps number, not water or air, is the primary element, or substrate. The Pythagoreans even suggested that number is the basis of relations—of justice, for example—and of the soul and the mind.

They studied numbers with great ingenuity. They spoke of perfect numbers, which are equal to the sum of their factors, including one, as six equals one plus two plus three. Ten also was called perfect, but for different reasons. Aristotle reports that they found void, proportion, and other qualities in ten. Another writer speaks of ten as containing the linear, plane, and solid types, for one is a dot, two is a line, three is a triangle, and four is a pyramid, and all add up to ten.

One of their most brilliant ideas was that of incommensurable numbers, those which cannot be expressed as the quotients of integers. This arises from the so-called Pythagorean theorem that the square on the hypotenuse of a right triangle is equal to the sum of the squares on the other two sides. If the other two sides are one, the square of each is one, and the sum of their squares is two, and the square of the hypotenuse is two, so that the hypotenuse is equal to the square root of two. To recognize this as a numerical entity expressible only as the square root of two was an advance in mathematics.

The brotherhood of the Pythagoreans gained political control of Croton during the lifetime of the founder. But a powerful opposition developed and caused Pythagoras to go elsewhere. At a later time, the opposing party staged a massacre of the chief Pythagoreans, according to tradition, by burning them all in a house where they were having a meeting. The political power of the Pythagoreans was ended, but the brotherhood did not die out, nor did the teachings. Many men and a few women are mentioned in later times as Pythagoreans.

Xenophanes

Xenophanes of Colophon should not be called an Ionian, even though Colophon was in Ionia, because he left Ionia for exile early in life and was an exile for sixty-seven years, and because his interests were not those of the early Ionians whom we have discussed. He did take an intelligent interest in such matters as the formation of the earth; he noticed somewhere in his travels that there were marine fossils to be seen well above sea level. Social questions and morality were, however, of deeper concern. He attacked the representation of the gods in Homer and Hesiod. Their gods, he said, who displayed the less amiable characteristics of men, were an insult to the divine nature. Unlike many critics, he made an honest attempt to do better. God is one, he said, and sees, hears, and thinks as a whole. His power is such that by mere thought he achieves what he will. He does not move about, for changes of position are not appropriate to his importance. Probably we should not take these ideas to mean that Xenophanes was a monotheist in the modern sense. It is more likely that to him "God" meant the world as a whole.

By about 500 B.C., a number of the keener minds had freed themselves from the older religious and mythological attitudes toward the world and life. We cannot tell how widely such views were spread or how much the sharper thinkers influenced one another (although the influence of Xenophanes on Pindar, Plato, and Euripides can be traced through remarks of theirs that echo him), but it is plain that there were some advanced ideas in circulation and at least a small group of people who supported them, even if the great majority of people still lived according to the old ideas and had no interest in this new kind of thinking.

CHAPTER

17

ART AND LITERATURE
IN THE NEW AGE

$\mathbb{M}$uch of what we call art among the Greeks consisted of articles for use: coins, pottery, buildings, and the like. There were also, to be sure, artistic articles purely for pleasure and display: jewelry, and painting and statues for houses or public places. In addition, a good deal of art was produced for religious purposes.

Even in the dull time that followed the fall of the Mycenaean kingdoms, the artistic impulse did not disappear. Although the style of pottery so degenerated as to deserve the name of Sub-Mycenaean, artistic intention was still visible in its making. Athens developed her own style of Geometric Ware during this period, and by about 800 B.C., the beginning of the new age, respectable Geometric pottery was being produced in a number of places in Greece, especially at Athens and Corinth.

The Restoration of Contact

When significant contact was restored between Greece and the Near East, the workmen of certain places were more alert than others to study products from overseas. We have already noted that the Ionians were slow to accept the new influences, then suddenly bounded to the fore in both intellectual and artistic life. A very obvious change in the Geometric pottery and one that may symbolize the new influence was that the straight lines of the Geometric decoration were replaced by curving lines in the patterns and by flower designs borrowed from the older civilization. The Geometric had had schematized and somewhat angular figures of men and animals. Now these figures were filled out with curves, and a whole zoo of monsters and imaginary creatures was brought from the East to join them. The Greek was soon joyously adding interesting fauna of his own devising to the traditional creatures of the East on his pottery. Modern archaeologists have also found bronze bowls, shields, and small figurines that show the same spread of influence to the Greeks, and there are little ivory reliefs that tell the same story. Doubtless the same would prove true of fabrics if specimens survived.

The period of local styles during the time between and the period of the new age characterized by borrowing of Near Eastern techniques now was succeeded by a time when Greek workmen of every kind knew what was being done in the world and were able to do what pleased them and their patrons, with inspiration from, but without undue dependence on, others and without shortcomings in their own technique. It sometimes seems that statues and buildings of stone were the chief product of these fine workmen who lived in lands that are virtual rock piles compared with the green lushness of Italy and more northern European countries. The surviving temples and statues and gravestones impress us with their beauty and show us stone work everywhere. Yet study corrects this limited impression. A great deal of fine small work was done in jewelry and little figures. Many Greek coins are masterpieces. Pottery reveals a great deal about what the painter could do, and some idea about other painting can be gained from descriptions and fragments. Figures of bronze ranged from small ones suitable for decorations in houses to large statues of divinities.

Jewelry and Coinage

The technique of making jewelry and other small, fine objects was developed early among the Sumerians and continued to flourish thereafter. Those few scholars who have worked comprehensively with the great number of such objects preserved from ancient times are inclined to believe that there is little fluctuation in this type of art. After the great early surge that brought it to a high level of excellence, it went on and on with little change in quality and with few new discoveries. The Greeks in the new age became competent in this field and continued to be so throughout their history.

We can put together the stories of some of the great artists in this field during the age from 800 to 500 B.C. By the third of these three centuries, the industry—or the art, if we should call it that— was firmly established throughout the Greek world, and certain men had founded businesses that became dynasties. We know of such enterprises in Asia Minor, in the islands, in Athens, and in Laconia. The master did small pieces himself and handled larger pieces with the assistance of his sons and others whom he was training. The references to such establishments are reminiscent of what Benvenuto Cellini tells us about his work first in the service of older masters and then as an independent producer.

Such masters and the men with whom they surrounded themselves produced a great variety of things in gold, silver, bronze, hard stone, ivory, the combination of gold and ivory known as chryselephantine, marble, and wood. They made jewelry of every imaginable sort, ornamental fittings for daggers or for the bridles and bits of horses, and small things for use in houses: gold bowls, bronze figurines, plaques of gold and silver and bronze ornamented with everything from geometric designs to sphinxes and griffins. There was almost nothing for which they could not design some small and beautiful part. The person of refined and imaginative taste was able to surround himself with some very beautiful things.

Sculpture

In the latter part of the seventh century, the Greeks began to make sizable statues of limestone and marble. Although it is generally supposed that they got the idea from their contacts with Egypt, it is agreed that the surviving statues from the earliest period are decidedly not imitations of those which they could have seen in Egypt. Probably the cost of statues was moderate, whether they were in limestone, which was easy to work, or in marble, which was more difficult to work, but could be given a very satisfactory texture of surface and clearness of line. These statues should be considered as fine commercial products in order to avoid the mysticism so often attached to discussions of art.

Statuary was very desirable for religious purposes. The Greeks were so far from the Hebrew idea of not making "graven images" as to feel that a god would be pleased at having himself represented in a statue. Because religion was the affair of the *polis*, it was presumably the *polis* that commissioned the statues.

An establishment might take an order from a *polis* for the construction of a bronze statue of a god to be put in a temple or a holy place and send a team to the site to stay there for some weeks, build a little foundry, cast the statue on the spot from a design made by the master of the whole enterprise, then dismantle the foundry and depart. It is possible that some stone statues were made in somewhat the same way; that is, a fairly skilled cutter of stone would shape a block of good stone according to a design made by the head of the firm. There is evidence that successful statues were often reproduced many times by the work of such assistants.

Bronze was used for many statues, as the Greeks had learned to cast figures of some size before the end of the sixth century. The choicest of all statues were the chryselephantine ones, made of ivory and gold.

In addition to the statue of the divinity for the inside of the temple and perhaps another for the temple precinct, there was a call for ornamental reliefs when, also toward the end of the sixth century, the stone temple became common. Gravestones, too, with representations of the deceased came to be very desirable, and many are preserved from the end of the sixth century and early fifth. They are works of fine and restrained feeling.

Many examples have been preserved of male figures called *kouroi*, or young men, and female figures called *korai*, or girls. Both males and females followed a closely defined type. It was not until after 500 B.C. that the conventions of the type were relaxed and there came to be real freedom and variety in these statues. The *kouros* is naked, stands with his left leg slightly advanced, is upright, and looks straight ahead. The female figure is clothed, but follows the same rigid pattern as the male. There is a certain disagreement among historians of art as to why this highly stylized and somewhat archaic-appearing type persisted for so long among the Greeks. There are those who feel that the sculptors were slow to learn and that what we see in these figures is an early stage of development of taste and skill. The other point of view is that the stiff, conventional, and unchanging quality of the *kouroi* and *korai* is due to the strength of convention, not to the artist's inability to do what he wished to do. The other works of art of this period—relief sculptures, for instance—show that the artist was equipped with sufficient technique for other demands. Those who believe that many of the fine masters who did the small work also designed statues, using their assistants to execute them, naturally cannot believe that these masters were unable to design any kind of statue they wished. Convention must explain their seeming limitations.

Two ideas are especially unpalatable to those who take this side: they resist the idea that there is a cycle in the arts that entails many generations of apprenticeship before the ripe period can arrive, and they resist the idea that the highest excellence in art is the ability to make photographically realistic representations of things actually seen. The corollary of the argument that the characteristics of the *kouros-kore* type are due to a strong convention is that after about 480 B.C. the conventions changed and the free and varied poses of sculptured figures thereafter are due to this change, not to a sudden rise in the ability of sculptors.

Another contested point is the use of color on Greek statues and buildings. Many people long refused to believe the plain evidence of the traces of paint remaining on many stone statues and on many buildings. The Greeks did use color. Bright red, blue, brown, and gold were favorites. Garments were gaily painted, flesh was painted red or red-brown, and sometimes the details of faces were brought out by emphasizing eyes and lips and hair with an effect like that of modern women's make-up. Scholars now all agree that paint was used.

Painting

Painting progressed rapidly during the new age. Because so much of it has been lost, a somewhat wrong impression is created by the fact that what has survived is the painting done on pottery, which offers a restricted and curved surface. There is evidence, however, that painting was done on larger surfaces as well, as in the public porticoes. The interesting frescoes in the tombs of the Etruscans in Italy give some idea of what the Greeks could do on walls. The influence of Greek painting is plain in Etruria, and perhaps some of the tombs were done by Greek workmen. Innumerable finds of excellent Athenian vases show how enthusiastic the Etruscans were in the sixth and fifth centuries about Greek wares; the many museums in Italy north of Rome, where the Etruscans lived, are very rich in Athenian pottery.

Painted pottery was produced in Ionia, the islands, Laconia, Corinth, and Athens. The Corinthian ware of the eighth and seventh centuries was attractive, popular, and widely used in the *poleis* of the West where Corinthian merchants went and even in Carthage and other non-Greek places. By the later years of the seventh century, the Athenians were improving their product, and by the middle of the sixth century they had almost achieved a monopoly of the export trade in pottery. Their product is found in Naucratis in Egypt, in the Black Sea region in the East, and in many places in the West.

A natural distinction is made between the early "black on red" pottery, where a design in black is painted on the reddish clay background, and the "red on black" style that arose in Athens about 530 B.C. Now the red of the clay was the picture, and the black paint made a black background outlining it. Shadings of black could be put in, producing a more varied and subtle effect than had been possible before. The varied shapes of Athenian vases are pleasing. During the sixth century, the painters ceased to fill all the space with ornamentation, as they had done on Geometric ware, and replaced the formal friezes or groups of animals of the Geometric style with free and informal pictures. The painters cheerfully launched out on pictures that told a story, often one from myth or legend, and helpfully labeled their characters in many pictures. Quite ordinary people appear, too. There are city and country scenes of every sort, the rich man, the poor man, the slave, and the strange-looking foreigner. If one is to take pleasure in the work of these artists, he must not insist on photographic realism. The pictures are full of keen observation, liveliness, humor, and emotion.

Architecture

Greek architecture, as we see it fragmentarily and far away, was a very specialized activity. The temples of the Greeks were their most important buildings. Their houses usually looked in on a courtyard and were not interesting to look at from the outside. They probably were cramped and uncomfortable, as one would expect in a country where people live mostly outdoors or in a courtyard or in public places. There were no large buildings for business like ours or like those which the Romans built, and the government buildings did not amount to much. In Egypt and the Near East, there had been palaces for the kings and temples for the gods. In Crete and Mycenae, there were no temples; the gods lived in the king's house or in outdoor holy places. Now, in the Greece of the new age, there were no kings and no palaces, but it began to seem a good idea to build houses for the gods as the Egyptians and others had done. The first attempts were fairly crude affairs of wood and mud-brick, perhaps not even so large and imposing as the houses of some of the leading citizens.

With the rise of the idea of building in stone, however, a new interest appeared. Two chief styles developed, the Doric in mainland Greece and among the Greeks of Italy and Sicily, and the Ionic among the more eastern Greeks and in Attica, which was the only place where both Doric and Ionic seemed at home. The two styles were the subject of a great deal of thought and experiment and even theoretical discussion, most of which is lost to us. There are remains of some of the buildings of the sixth century, but it is better to reserve description of specific buildings until Chapter Nineteen, where we shall be able to describe some that are better preserved. There is evidence, however, that a good many people were giving thought to the problem of developing the two styles into something that would give satisfaction as a theoretically and practically satisfactory manner of constructing buildings. Emphasis was more on refinement than on variation. Presently it was felt that sound canons of elements and proportions were being agreed on and that it was possible to speak of a Doric order and an Ionic order.

The Doric and Ionic orders differ chiefly in the columns and the friezes and in the lighter general effect of the Ionic. The Doric column has no base; the Ionic has a round base. The Doric column seems sturdier, the Ionic more slender. The Doric capital is square, whereas the Ionic is turned over into volutes. The Doric frieze is an alternation of metopes, or squares sculptured in relief (or sometimes left plain), and triglyphs, or squares marked with two deep vertical grooves. The Ionic is a running frieze, an uninterrupted series of relief sculptures. The Parthenon is the perfect embodiment of the Doric order, and the Temple of Nike on the Acropolis of Athens is a good example of the Ionic. Both are discussed in Chapter Twenty-two. In the Corinthian order, which was not popular until after the classical age of Greece, the capitals of the columns are ornately carved with acanthus leaves. Otherwise this order is essentially Ionic.

LITERATURE

Hesiod

The earliest of the Greek authors of the new age was Hesiod, who lived at about the end of the eighth century. He was the first of those authors who developed new literary styles and who reflected the life of their own time. Hesiod tells us that he was a son of a Greek of Asia Minor who had emigrated in the reverse direction and come to the little town of Ascra, in Boeotia, to become a small farmer. Hesiod himself evidently knew the farmer's life. Yet he must somehow have learned the art of the oral poet, for his language is a stiffer and less gifted version of the language of Homer. He tells us that he once won a prize in a singing contest. It is probable that his works first gained fame among the oral poets and were spread by them.

His manner and his matter are different from those of Homer. The manner may be described as middle-class. His interest is in the way of life of his own time and especially in how a man of the small farming class can get along in the world. In his *Works and Days* he discusses the difficulties of the farmer's life on a small and not very fertile farm.

He gives many homely precepts for farming. In contrast, he discusses the life of the seagoing merchant, a life from which he shrinks as difficult, dangerous, and dishonest. Another part of the work lets us know briefly that when he and his brother disagreed about the division of his father's farm, his brother had corrupted the arbitrator, one of those local grandees whose legal jurisdiction the rising *polis* was to supersede, and had thus cheated Hesiod out of his share. The *Works and Days* is not a narrative, although its language is that of the oral poets, with some quaint and homely touches that would seem out of place in Homer. It might be called an essay on life in the new age, an essay that examines the conditions of life instead of taking them for granted, as Homer does, and assumes that a man may have a choice of how to make a living. Hesiod's loud cry for justice for the common man also belongs to the new age.

In *Theogony*, or *The Family History of the Gods*, he struggles to expound a larger conception of justice. It is a struggle for both poet and reader, for the language of the oral poets was not adequate for the discussion of such conceptions, and much of what we now should put as abstract argument had to be couched in the form of what looks like a rather simple-minded mythology. He went back to the early days of the gods, before Zeus became master on Olympus. Homer had taken the supremacy of Zeus for granted and made it plain that no justice is to be expected from Zeus unless it be his caprice to grant it. Hesiod wills it to be otherwise. He tells of the crude early generations of the gods and makes Zeus a great improvement upon his predecessors in refinement and justice, but one with room for much more improvement. Hesiod's Olympus is to be remade as he would remake the world of men, with justice respected and cultivated.

That later Greeks had a very high opinion of Hesiod is puzzling if one thinks of him only as a purveyor of tales about the family trees of the gods or a chronicler of the life of the small farmer, but intelligible if he is regarded as one of the earliest of Greek reflective thinkers. He was apparently the originator of what is sometimes called "the moral education of Zeus," the process of refining Greek thought about the divine nature. He not only knew the tradition about the early generations of the gods (which actually goes back to Hittite and Ugaritic tales), but he was also able to compose another work, of which some part survives, called *The Catalogue of Women*, about the genealogies of famous families. With appropriate seasonings, it provided genealogies back to the point at which they traditionally began, when some lady of the family had submitted to the embrace of a god and produced heroic offspring to shed divine luster down the long roll of generations.

Elegy and Iambic

By about 700 B.C., the development of more personal forms of poetry had begun. Hesiod had used the language and meter of the oral poets to express new ideas, but, although he was greatly admired, he had found no followers. After him men turned to new forms. Their poems were shorter, not narratives, but exhortations to valor, songs of sorrow, reflections upon life, songs of love, and expressions of personality.

The language of elegy still borrowed much from epic, however, despite the changes in form and content. The old expressions and turns of phrase were ready at hand, and the workers in the new field naturally used some of them. The meter was modified by changing every second line. The epic had had a succession of dactylic hexameters, with no setting off of stanzas or strophes. Now the hexameter was followed by a pentameter—as it were, by a hexameter that had had a piece dropped out of its middle and another piece dropped off its end, so that it was a little shorter and the rhythm was changed in an agreeable way. A hexameter followed by a pentameter was called an elegiac couplet; an elegy was composed of a succession of elegiac couplets. Elegy was sung to the accompaniment of the flute.

Elegy began in Ionia, but we know little of its earliest practitioners. The first distinguishable figure is Tyrtaeus, who worked in Sparta. There was a story that in the Second Messenian War, in the latter 600's, an oracle bade the Spartans ask the Athenians for a general, upon which the Athenians mockingly sent the lame schoolmaster Tyrtaeus, who thereupon composed fiery martial elegies that inspired the Spartans to fight and prevail over their enemies. Perhaps the story reflects the existence of an Ionian and then Athenian tradition of elegy which inspired Tyrtaeus at Sparta. What little we have of his elegies is fine, straightforward martial poetry, urging the Spartans to reflect on the great disadvantages of being worsted, as practical-minded Greeks would, and then to stand bravely and fight for all that was dearest to them. The Spartan spirit is also to be found in his elegy called *Eunomia*, a word that to the Spartan described the well-ordered condition of his state. The martial elegies were learned and sung by the Spartans for hundreds of years afterward. Athenians, too, thought highly of them, and for a long time Athenian boys were also made to learn them by heart.

Mimnermus of Colophon, an Ionian, lived at about the same time as Tyrtaeus, in the late 600's. In contrast to the martial note of Tyrtaeus, he sang of love and of the fleeting quality of youth, striking a note that might seem characteristic of the more polished and less virile life of the Greeks of the coast of Asia Minor. He could not sing the joys of youth without adding a note of terror at the imminent onset of old age.

What living, what delight is there without Aphrodite the golden? May I die off when these things no longer can move me—love taken in secret, sweet gifts, the bed—the things that are the bright flower of youth for both men and women. But when painful old age comes on, age which takes away a man's attractiveness and strength, unpleasant worries wear continually upon his mind. He can take no pleasure in regarding the light of the sun; he is disagreeable to boys, unhonored by women. Thus have the gods laid evil old age on us.

And again Mimnermus says, "Handsome as he may have been, when once his prime of life has been passed, a father is not honored or loved by his own children."

Another Colophonian, four hundred years later, wrote that Mimnermus passionately loved the flute girl Nanno and wrote of her. Some of the fragments of his work are said to have come from one book entitled *Nanno*. Since he is the first poet who wrote of love, it is unfortunate that the few lines quoted from *Nanno* tell us almost nothing. They are in the same bittersweet vein as the others and do not mention Nanno by name.

On the basis of the little that we have of his work, we can only say that Mimnermus was a poet of two simple ideas, the sweets of love in earlier life and the bitterness of having to pass on to the later stages of life. It is hard to imagine any society forcing the young to memorize his elegies as an aid to the formation of character, as the martial elegies of Tyrtaeus were memorized and sung by generations of Spartan and Athenian boys. On the other hand, it is probable that the elegies of Mimnermus were popular as solo pieces to be sung to languorous melodies and accompanied by the flute.

Elegy was used rather differently by the statesman Solon (639–559 B.C.), the first literary man of Athens (even though Tyrtaeus came from Athens, his poetry should properly be called Spartan). Elegy was essentially a personal address to other people. The addresses of Solon, whether to his fellow Athenians or to the world in general, reflect his varied interests. One of his liveliest elegies, that on the recovery of the island of Salamis from the Megarians, was delivered in the agora as an address to the people, presumably because the formal presentation of proposals about Salamis had been forbidden. The poem is said to have stirred the Athenians to effective action. Others have to do with the unhappy state of affairs that led to his being elected archon for the year 594, and describe and defend the remedial measures that he devised.

These elegies show some poetic quality. In addition, they illustrate the fact that elegy was used for a variety of subjects on which the poet wanted to expound his views. But most forcibly they illustrate the fact that prose writing did not grow up among the Greeks until after men had written in verse for a long time. We think of Solon's subject matter as essentially prosaic, and so it would have been, had the idea of writing in prose been conceived.

Archilochus of Paros, who probably flourished just before the middle of the seventh century, was said by the Greeks to have invented the iambic meter, meaning that he was the first man who wrote polished and effective iambic lines. The iamb consists of a short syllable followed by a long syllable, an obvious sort of metrical unit that occurs naturally in speech. The normal line had six iambs, but the Greek poet tended to treat them in pairs; if he had a line of six iambs, which was common, he would call it a trimeter, or line of three measures. A series of eight iambs would be a tetrameter, or line of four measures. The iambic trimeter came to be the normal line of the speeches in Greek and Latin tragedy and comedy; its easy conversational quality, as well as tradition, recommended it to the earlier writers of plays in the modern languages.

With Archilochus, purely personal expression makes a dramatic appearance on a literary scene peopled only with Homer and some lesser men who were producing the Epic Cycle, Hesiod (who did not found a school), and the elegiac writers, who were also launching a new type. Archilochus was the son of a Parian aristocrat and a slave woman. Possibly the fact that he was without a settled place in society, although he was a man of force and ability, caused him to take the unusual step of writing frankly and vividly about his own situation, adventures, and feelings. In any age the settled aristocrat rarely writes; had Archilochus had a place like his father's in that highly conservative society, he might well not have been impelled to write himself, thus setting the precedent of personal expression in poetry. As it was, he attached to iambic poetry its connotation of bitter attacks on Fate and persons.

As a young man he had an opportunity to make a new start by going out as a member of a colony that the Parians sent to the island of Thasos. The colonists' prosaic occupation was the mining of gold and silver. The young man complained in his verses of the dullness of the place, which had not a single pleasant spot. But when life was enlivened by some military action, he wrote of this, too, in his cross-grained manner, telling how he had thrown away his shield and run. But he had saved himself, he said, and he could get another shield better than that one. Presumably this is scoffing at the standards of society by one who resented the fact that he did not have a proper place in society; cowardice in battle was of necessity very seriously regarded.

In the imperfect accounts of him that have come down from antiquity, there are a number of mentions of his love for Neobule and her father's unwillingness to have the poet as son-in-law. His sour wrath was turned on father and daughter alike; one story is that he drove both to suicide. Finally he became a mercenary soldier, as many a disgruntled man has done, and met his death in battle in early middle age.

The ancients regarded Archilochus very highly. He was a poet of great ability in spite of his continual disappointment with life. He also wrote elegy well; his verses on a death by drowning, one of the poems that we happen to have, show a good technique and a pleasanter side of his feelings, apparent in other fragments as well. In his iambics he was a master of form and had wit and spirit that raised his critical and satirical observations on life far above the level of mere dreary complaining.

Lyric Poetry

Alcaeus and Sappho, two poets of Mytilene, the chief city of the island of Lesbos, both lived in the latter part of the seventh century and the early part of the sixth. Both wrote lyric poetry in the truest sense, poetry meant to be sung to the accompaniment of the *barbitos*, the local type of lyre.

The poetry of Alcaeus has many reflections of the political struggles of his age, attempts by the clans of the nobility to take away the ascendancy of a single clan that had ruled since the bygone days of the kings. Alcaeus many times gave voice to the high feeling engendered by this struggle. He apparently was the first to use in poetry the figure of the ship of state; the Roman Horace, a student of Alcaeus' work, used this figure effectively, and in modern times it has become a common figure. Many of his poems speak of his strong hostility to Pittacus, one of the leading figures of the time. Pittacus finally was chosen by all to be *aesymnetes,* a sort of dictator; the result was exile for Alcaeus. The performance of Pittacus in the ten years of his office was shrewd and efficient beyond what anyone had imagined possible. His former opponent returned to the reorganized community and lived out his days in peace.

Alcaeus wrote hymns to the gods—to Apollo, Hermes, Hephaestus, Artemis, Eros—that appear to have been intended not for public presentation at festivals but for presentation at social gatherings. Pleasant in tone, they seem more the expression of a poetic gift than an uplifting of the spirit toward the gods. He often sang the pleasures of wine and sociability. Sometimes the wine helps to dull the pain of exile; sometimes pure rejoicing at the company of friends and the pleasure of conviviality is the dominant note. In one short extant passage, he speaks of trying to make tolerable the blazing heat of midsummer; in another, later echoed by Horace, he gives a charming picture of indoor joys about the fire in winter.

Sappho is one of the small circle of lyric poets of the first rank whom the West has produced. Hers is personal poetry indeed, a compelling statement of the ecstasy and the pain that can come from the fierce attraction of one human being to another. The beauty, power, and charm of her verses need not be lessened by the frank recognition that the objects of her passion and desire were women. Mere respectability has had its revenge by destroying perhaps ninety-five per cent of her bequest to us.

Deathless Aphrodite, gorgeously enthroned, Zeus' child, contriver of wiles: Lady, I pray you not to crush my spirit with heartaches and with anguish,

but come to me if ever in the past you have heard my cries and your heart was moved and you left your father's house and came,

yoking your golden chariot. Your pretty swift swallows brought you from heaven through the middle air and over the dark earth with many a quick stroke of their wings,

coming promptly to me. And you, blessed lady, with a smile on your divine face, asked me what my sufferings were this time and why I called on you this time,

and what my mad heart most desired to have. "Whom am I to persuade this time to be your dearest one? Sappho, who is treating you badly?

For if she flees now, she soon shall pursue you. If she disdains your gifts, she yet shall give. And if she does not love, soon she shall, and even against her will."

Come to me this time, too, and free me from my bitter pangs. Do all the things my heart would do. Fight, you yourself, on my side.

The form of this famous poem is essentially that of a prayer, an appeal to the goddess in a formal way for help. Yet the earnestness of Sappho's plea is relieved by the suggestion that all this has happened before. The language is simple and straightforward and full of charm. Another famous poem of Sappho—this, too, preserved for us only by the accident of being quoted by a critic—is a straightforward statement of the feeling of the pangs of love and jealousy, unrelieved by any note of detachment or humor.

That man seems to me to be equal to the gods, the man who sits opposite you and hears your sweet voice

and your gracious laughter; this, I swear, has smitten the heart in my breast, for when I steal a glance at you, words will not come,

but my tongue keeps silence, a dart of fire has slid along at once beneath my flesh, there is no sight in my eyes, my ears are ringing,

a chilly sweat holds me, a trembling seizes me all over, I am paler than grass, and I seem to be on the brink of death.

Anacreon, who came from the Ionian city of Teus on the coast of Asia Minor, lived perhaps a generation later than Alcaeus and Sappho.

Like them, he sang of the pleasures of love and wine and sociability, but always in a lighter vein than theirs. He was invited to the court of Polycrates, the brilliant tyrant of the island of Samos. After Polycrates' unhappy end, the poet was invited to the court of Hippias and Hipparchus, the sons of Peisistratus. After the murder of Hipparchus, the grimmer atmosphere became uncongenial to him, and he seems to have spent his last years at the court of the Aleuadae in Thessaly, a decidedly minor circle for one of his past experience.

The poetry of Anacreon is pleasant and light. No strong feeling is expressed; the manner is that of the perfect courtier. In later times, perhaps in the late pre-Christian and early Christian era, a number of poems were written in his manner; they were collected and came to be known as Anacreontics. These poems, published in the sixteenth century, passed for some time as the work of Anacreon. Whoever their unknown authors, they have pleased many moderns.

Simonides of Ceos (556–467 B.C.) was another Ionian who made the rounds of the courts of the tyrants. Finally he settled in Athens, by then a democracy, and sang her glories and the especial glory of the great resistance to the Persians. His *threnoi,* or laments, were highly esteemed; they were meant to be sung to the flute at funeral ceremonies. He also gained many commissions for the *epinikion,* or triumphal ode for a victor in one of the great games. Simonides seems to have been a business man as well as a poet. Apparently realizing that there was a market for the funeral lament and the victory song, he turned out such superior performances in both fields that the lament and the song of victory were raised to the status of literary types.

The Choral Lyric

Probably the choral singing of modern times does not give us an adequate idea of the setting and effect of choral singing among the Greeks. We have religious hymns, as they did, but their hymns were sung by citizen groups rather than specialized choirs and addressed to the deities whom the whole city worshiped rather than in a church belonging to the people of only one parish. Here, as always, we must make the effort to imagine Greek activities on a small scale; almost the whole population of a city is present at the singing of a hymn in a religious ceremony. A small city welcomes home a victor in the Olympic games with a sense of civic unity impossible today. A fighting men's song is sung by a whole army, but with no more voices than there are in the massive choirs of mutual strangers brought together nowadays for special occasions.

Alcman, who worked at Sparta around the middle of the seventh century or shortly thereafter, is the first great name in the history of the choral lyric. He wrote felicitous hymns to the gods for choruses of girls as well as songs for men. Distinguished for his charm, he suggests an aristocratic Sparta full of grace and gaiety that accords with our other evidence about earlier Sparta.

The Sicilian "Stesichorus," a generation later, gained his nickname, "the setter of the chorus," from his work in this line; his real name was Teisias. The fragments of his work and the remarks of ancient authors about him show that he was in the habit of building his poems on Homeric themes. He treated the old stories with freedom and did much to turn the choruses from a somewhat rude song in praise of the gods to a polished literary form.

One type of choral song to the gods, the dithyramb, generally told of the deeds of a divinity. The dithyramb was sung especially in honor of Dionysus, a god said to have had many almost human adventures. At Athens the spring festival of Dionysus, the Great Dionysia, was steadily increased in splendor from the time of Peisistratus on, and the dithyrambs were composed as highly conscious literary pieces and sung by carefully trained and elaborately costumed choruses. Somehow, too, a new literary form—tragedy—evolved from the ceremonies of the festival of Dionysus. Perhaps the leader of the chorus carried on a sort of conversation with the chorus, thus adding life to the story of the god's exploits that was the substance of their song. Thespis, who lived at Athens under Peisistratus, is said to have made the decisive change that turned the choral song in honor of Dionysus into the first phase of Attic tragedy. We cannot be sure what Thespis did. Some small innovation would have started the process that led to fully-developed tragedy in two or three generations.

CHAPTER

18

GREECE'S GREAT CRISIS

Little as we know about the combinations of factors that produce peoples of great intellectual and cultural achievement, we are safe in believing that the Western world is better off because the communities of Greeks were not seriously attacked until they had had time to absorb the cultures of more advanced peoples and to form themselves along their own lines. But such attacks finally came, beginning about 550 B.C. The Lydians of Asia Minor and then the Persians laid their heavy hands upon the Asiatic Greeks. Later the Persians were moved to attack Greece itself, and they did so at the very time that the Greeks of the West had to fight against the Carthaginians and, less dangerously, against the Etruscans.

The high tide of Persian attack was rolled back at Salamis in 480, as was the Carthaginian at Himera in Sicily in the same year (one tradition said on the same day); and after the Persian defeat at Plataea in 479, the Persian forces withdrew from Greece. In 474 a great naval battle in Italian waters broke the sea power of the Etruscans. The immediate onslaught was ended, yet Greeks and Persians were to struggle intermittently, and Persia was sometimes to be a dominant influence in Greek affairs until her conquest by Alexander the Great. Greek and Carthaginian were also to fight from time to time in Sicily until in 241 B.C. the Romans took control of the whole island at the end of their long war with Carthage, the First Punic War. A hundred years later Greece itself became part of the Roman possessions. Up to that time the danger of the Persians and the Carthaginians in the early fifth century was the greatest that the Greeks had to face.

THE LYDIANS AND THE GREEKS

Before 700 B.C., the inland kingdom of Phrygia had controlled much of the territory of Asia Minor. The relations of the Greeks with it seem, from the archaeological evidence, to have been slight. Shortly after 700, the invasion of a people known as the Cimmerians broke the power of Phrygia. A generation later the kingdom of Lydia, which apparently had been under Phrygian control, seems to have been fairly well established as an independent power. Gyges, its king, appealed in 668–667 and again in 652 to the Assyrians for help against the Cimmerians; later he sent Cimmerian captives and other gifts to the Assyrian Ashur-bani-pal.

The Lydians continued to be in touch with Assyria by land. They also had diplomatic relations with Egypt, which implied communication by sea. Occasionally they raided the Greek cities of the coast, but they also traded with them in a modest way. They did not make the Greek cities tributary until the time of Croesus, he who was conquered by Cyrus the Persian in 547 B.C. The relation of the Greeks with the Lydians was a comfortable one; under the sway of the philhellenic Croesus they prospered on their trade with Lydia and with the world around the borders of the Aegaean and the Black Sea.

THE PERSIANS AND THE GREEKS

Those Greek cities which in 547 B.C. had refused the suggestion of Cyrus that they desert the Lydians were subjected by the Persians soon after Croesus fell. Two were simply abandoned at the advance of the Persians: the Phocaeans sailed away to Corsica, and the people of Teus to Thrace, where they refounded Abdera, a site on which two previous colonies had been destroyed by the natives.

The relation of the Greeks to the Persian Empire offers a problem in the exercise of historical judgment. Two questions especially obtrude themselves: Were the Greeks deeply unhappy and resentful under Persian rule, after 547? And did their falling under Persian rule blight their intellectual and artistic development?

The Persians required tribute and soldiers from the Greeks, as they did from everyone. They did not try to enforce cultural uniformity. There was no pressure on the Greeks to speak the Persian language or adopt Persian customs and the Persian religion. Did their membership in the Persian Empire help them? It is difficult to imagine any great danger from which the Persians protected them. Was it helpful economically? Only moderately so, at the most. Their routes of trade were so well established and so free from damaging interference (except the far western ones in waters claimed by Carthage) that they had little to gain economically from being included in the outer reaches of a huge empire. They naturally had some trade with the interior of Asia Minor, but they had had it before the coming of the Persians, and any sea-borne trade that went to the vital centers of the empire in Persia and Babylonia was likely to be carried, not by Greeks, but by the sailors of Cyprus and Phoenicia to the ports of the Phoenician coast, whence it went overland. The Persian satraps of Asia Minor were not oriented toward the Greeks as Croesus had been, nor did Persian rule in Egypt favor the Greeks as had that of Kings Psamtik and Amasis.

Did the Greeks resent the political situation? The Persians appointed a local grandee (or tyrant, as the Greeks chose to call him) as governor of each city. This move should have been thoroughly distasteful to the Greeks; we have no explicit evidence that it was. Indeed, the local tyrants may well have comported themselves acceptably to the more prosperous and influential people in their cities.

The loyalty of the Greeks to Persia was tested when in the year 513 Darius the Persian attacked the Scythians. His army crossed the Bosporus on a pontoon bridge, marched to the Danube and crossed that, too, on a pontoon bridge built by the Greeks of his fleet and guarded by them in his absence. He pursued the Scythians, who retreated before him, having no cities to defend, until he decided that it was not possible to bring them to an engagement. The Greeks who were guarding the bridge were urged by the Scythians to break it down, but they refused to do so. In general, the Greeks acted as loyal subjects, although some living in the region of the Bosporus tried ineffectually to prevent the return crossing there. Although Darius had failed to win the submission of the Scythians, whom he thought of as causing pressures on his northern boundaries, he left an army in Thrace that subdued the Thracians as far west as the Strymon River and induced the Macedonian king Amyntas to submit to the Persians.

Yet the Ionian Greeks did revolt from the Persians in 499, forty-odd years after they had first become subjects of the Persian Empire. The historian Herodotus in his fifth and sixth books cites the personal ambitions of certain Milesians as the cause of the revolt. Such reasons can hardly explain the rising of these people against a power that was far superior to them on the land and about their equal on the sea and against whom they had no burning grievance. The upper classes proclaimed *isonomia*, or equality of rights, to win the adherence of the lower classes. This suggests that the lower classes needed strong inducement. From our evidence, we can find no better motive for this unpromising and dangerous revolt than a (conjectured) sense among the Greeks of their own common character and a willingness to run great risks in the hope of re-establishing their independence of foreign domination.

The Ionian Greeks, the leaders of the revolt, petitioned Sparta for aid. The Spartans, correctly reasoning that their army would be at a great disadvantage in the open spaces of Asia, refused. The Athenians, who had already refused Persia's demand that they reinstate the Athenian tyrant Hippias, decided to send twenty ships, and Eretria, on the island of Euboea, sent five. In 498 the Ionians, thus reinforced, took their troops by sea to Ephesus and marched to Sardis. They could not capture the citadel, but the city was burned. This feat moved many other cities along the Bosporus and the Hellespont to join the revolt.

Perhaps the best that the Greeks could have hoped for was Persian recognition of them as a group of free and friendly states at the edge of the empire. If they had worked together extremely well and had made the most of the possibilities of their naval power (which had hitherto been in the service of Persia), it is possible that they might have been able to gain such recognition and freedom. At times during this war, they did co-operate better than Greeks usually did. But

Athens and Eretria soon withdrew their forces. Perhaps there was a pro-Persian party at Athens, or at least a party of prudence toward Persia, able to exert some influence. The other cities carried on the war, the Persians having the advantage by land and the Greeks by sea until the naval battle of Lade in 495. Some of the Greeks fled the battle, and the Persian victory was decisive. By 493 the Persians had reduced the last rebellious city.

The Milesians were severely punished. Their city was destroyed, their men killed, and their women and children enslaved. The Persians were not unduly severe on others. Indeed, they reviewed the taxes to make sure that they were not provocatively harsh, made the cities enter into mutual nonaggression treaties, and replaced the tyrants with democracies. The modern scholar living in a democracy is tempted to see in this last move a hint of enlightenment or concession to the democratic spirit. It is more probable, however, that the Persians felt that democratic governments in the Greek cities would be less able to agree on any move against Persia than the aristocratic governments had been.

Probably the answer to our first question, whether the Greeks were unhappy and resentful, is that the Greek sense of nationality or race, even in the second generation, could lend strong support to a struggle for independence, even though there was no deep sense of specific grievances against the Persians.

In answer to our second question, whether Ionian Greek life was blighted by the Persians, it has been suggested that the establishment of Persian control was an important factor in the cessation of the activity of the lyric poets and the philosophers. It is true that the activity of both lyric poets and philosophers in Ionia seemed to trail off at about this time. It is not true, however, that intellectual activities do not flourish under imperial control. Poetry and philosophy are highly individual enterprises, not massive joint efforts. In both poetry and philosophy, the succession of interested and gifted individuals in Ionia might simply have failed. In both, the time had perhaps come for interest to slacken. It is difficult, in any case, to see how a connection can be established between the form of government and the highly personal literary or scientific efforts of a small number of men.

THE PERSIANS INVADE GREECE

The Persians now moved to strengthen their hold on their other Western possessions. In 492 B.C., an expedition to the Thracian satrapy soundly defeated one tribe that showed fight. It reasserted Persian sovereignty over all the peoples, including the Macedonians, who had submitted to the Persians before the Ionian revolt. The fact that the accompanying Persian fleet suffered a disaster when attempting to round the promontory of Mt. Athos in rough weather did not make the expedition a failure.

The next move was against the Greeks. Herodotus has a story that King Darius, enraged by the burning of Sardis, had a slave say to him at dinner every day, "Master, remember the Athenians." Doubtless he felt a special annoyance against the Athenians and the Eretrians. The main consideration in attacking Greece, however, was that it seemed to offer a natural frontier. If Greece were subdued, the whole complex of western Asia Minor, the Bosporus, Propontis, and Chersonesus, Thrace, and Macedonia would be quiet. The first expedition was probably sent out to secure the islands, to punish Athens and Eretria, and to lead up to the subjugation of all Greece.

In the summer of 491, Darius gave orders to his maritime subjects to prepare warships and transports. Envoys demanded tokens of submission in the usual form, "earth and water," from the islanders of the Aegean and the mainland states of Greece. Most of the islanders submitted.

Aegina, which was in a state of undeclared war with Athens, gave the Persians the tokens of submission. Although the Athenians were not on the best of terms with the Spartans, they expected Spartan support in defending themselves and they now complained that Aegina was deserting her obligations to the Spartan Alliance and acting against the common interest. The Spartan king Cleomenes gave an example of Spartan control of her alliance by arresting the oligarchic leaders of Aegina, who had favored medizing, or taking the Persian side.

Demaratus, the other Spartan king, was himself inclined to medize. Indeed, he was at odds with Cleomenes on almost every issue. Cleomenes claimed that Demaratus was illegitimate and at last succeeded in causing him to leave the country, an illustration of the

Delphi, temple of Apollo.

Photograph by the author.

Epidaurus (Peloponnesus), the theater.

Olympia, temple of Hera.

Photograph by the author.

Paestum, 5th century temple (Doric Order).   *Photograph by the author.*

Taormina (Tauromenium), Sicily, the theater.

The Porch of the Maidens (Caryatid Porch) of the Erechtheum, on the
Acropolis of Athens. *Photograph by the author.*

The temple of Nike (Victory), on the Acropolis of Athens (Ionic Order).

Photograph by the author.

fact that even in Sparta, the stablest of Greek *poleis*, there could be surprising irregularities in government. Demaratus went to the Persian king, who received him. He later (in 480) accompanied the next king, Xerxes, on his invasion of Greece, and some of the best passages in Herodotus' account of the war are those in which Xerxes asks Demaratus from time to time what to expect next from the Spartans and Demaratus tries to explain to an oriental despot what Westerners will probably do.

Darius' Expedition to Greece: Marathon

In the early summer of 490, the Persian fleet set sail and made easy progress through the smaller Greek islands, where there was no opposition. It began its real operations at the southern tip of the large island of Euboea, where the people of Carystus defied the invader, but were soon overcome. Then it proceeded to the city of Eretria, which defended itself for a week, but then was betrayed to the besiegers by two of its own citizens.

The Persians now crossed to the mainland and landed at Marathon, perhaps advised by Hippias, the expelled Athenian tyrant whom they had brought with them, planning to reinstate him at Athens. Hippias could tell them that the relatively undeveloped beach at Phalerum, below Athens, was not a good place for a landing operation, even though it was unfortified, for he had long ago defeated a Spartan force trying to land there. On the other hand, his father had made a successful beginning of his return from exile by making his landing at Marathon.

The Athenians had no thought of anything but fighting. They sent a runner, Pheidippides, to Sparta with a request for help. He covered about a hundred and forty miles in about two days. The Spartans answered that they were in the midst of a festival and could not go out to war until the full moon, six days away; apparently such religious scruples were genuine. The Athenian assembly decided to send their 10,000 hoplites out to Marathon to meet the enemy. The cavalry and light-armed troops, who would have been of little use against their superior Persian counterparts, stayed at home.

At this point in this gallant operation of the Athenian people a single man exerted a decisive influence. He was Miltiades, the third of his family and third of the same name to have exerted power, although still citizens of Athens, in the Thracian Chersonesus (just north of the Dardanelles) and to have had firsthand experience of the military methods of the Persians. Herodotus tells an interesting story of the choice of the first Miltiades by the embassy of the Thracian Dolonci who had come to ask the Delphic Oracle to give them a ruler. The Oracle told them to choose the first man who offered them hospitality. Miltiades invited them in as they passed his house on their way homeward. This was in the time of Peisistratus. The second Miltiades received official Athenian support on the occasion of his attempt to extend the territory of the kingdom of the Dolonci. The third Miltiades had returned to Athens after Persia had so extended her power north of the Dardanelles. He was at the time one of the ten generals who commanded the contingents of the ten tribes, and he had been instrumental in persuading the Assembly to send the troops out to Marathon. Now, when the generals were evenly divided as to whether to fight or return to defend the city, he influenced Callimachus, the polemarch, to vote for fighting. The generals customarily commanded the whole force in turn, but now the influential Aristides and three other generals temporarily yielded their days of command to Miltiades.

As luck would have it, the great day was his own day of command in the regular rotation. The Athenian forces had stayed out of the plain (where the Persians would have all the advantage because of their cavalry) and had built a barricade round their position on the rising ground inland. Now they got word in the night that the Persian cavalry was away—why and where, we do not know.

As dawn was breaking, the Greeks moved across the plain, their line thinned out in the center to strengthen the wings. The Persians broke through the center and pursued, but the Greek wings wheeled to encircle. At last it became a Persian retreat to the shore and a battle around the ships that they were trying to board in order to get away. The Persians, who may well have planned to embark that day anyway, left six thousand dead on the field to the Athenian hundred and ninety-two and sailed away with the loss of seven ships. As the defeated enemy departed, late in the morning, the Athenians saw a signal from some point near Athens as the sunlight was reflected from a polished shield.

What the signal meant has never been established. Knowing all too well, however, that treachery was possible, the army set out on the march of eight or nine hours to the city. When the Persian forces sailed up to the beach at Phalerum next morning, they saw that the Athenian army had arrived and was ready to defend the city. Further, the approach by sea was now formidable, thanks to the foresight of Themistocles, who as archon in 493 had persuaded the *polis* to begin the fortification of Peiraeus, which was a complex of three harbors. Without further ado, the Persians gave up their attempt on Athens and began their journey home. That day the Spartan advance guard of two thousand men arrived. Hearing of the victory, they went on to Marathon, where they studied the field and the Persian weapons. They then returned to Athens, congratulated the Athenians, and set out to march another hundred and forty miles home.

The victory at Marathon did not permanently prevent the great invasion of Greece that Darius had planned. It was important in building up the confidence of the Athenians, however, and it stirred them to a more vigorous spirit of resistance. It gave the Spartans and other Greeks a more realistic idea of the Persian heavy infantry and therefore a stronger spirit of resistance to the Persians. Perhaps without this victory it would have been impossible to arouse the opposition that with great difficulty did eventually repel the full-scale Persian invasion.

A BREATHING SPACE

Persian Preparations

Darius himself was not able to launch the further invasion that he had planned. For three years he prepared for the gathering and provisioning of a great force that would combine land and sea operations. But in the year 487, Egypt revolted, giving a check to the preparations, and in the next year he died. His son Xerxes succeeded him.

In 485, Xerxes completed the reduction of Egypt. He then turned his full attention to the preparations for the invasion of Greece, one of the most spectacular of which was the cutting by forced labor of a mile-and-a-half canal across the peninsula of Mt. Athos. Some scholars of the nineteenth century doubted Herodotus' statement that the canal was dug, but the place where it was, now filled in, shows up in airplane photographs.

Preparations in Greece

Miltiades apparently had the idea of taking the offensive against the island states that had submitted to Persia in 491 and 490. He persuaded the assembly of the people to vote him naval and land forces for an undisclosed objective. Sailing to Paros, he attempted to extort money from the Parians on the ground that they had helped the Persians. He then applied force. The attempt failed, and he returned home severely wounded. Prosecuted for "deceiving the people," that is, failing to achieve what he had proposed to do, he was condemned to a huge fine of fifty talents rather than to death, since his days were plainly numbered. He died soon after.

The trial and condemnation of Miltiades were part of the struggle between rival elements among the Athenians. In Athens and later in Rome, prosecution of prominent men or their supporters, sometimes on political charges, sometimes on more personal grounds, was a regular method of carrying on the contest of groups or factions. In the prosecution of Miltiades we see the great clan of the Alcmaeonids trying to discredit the head of the clan of the Philaids and the political ally of Themistocles, who was likely to represent the rising merchant class in any difference as to policy.

During the decade of the 480's, there was a lively struggle over policies, about which we are partly informed. Themistocles was the leading figure. He advocated an active policy of building up naval power to resist the inevitable attack by Persia. During the decade, a number of men were ostracized. We have already suggested that the procedure of ostracism was more probably invented at this time than during the time of Cleisthenes, two decades before. The men who were ostracized were of the Alcmaeonids, and their ostracism seems to mean that Themistocles and the group who favored breaking the power of the great clans, on the one hand, and preparing actively for the war with Persia, on the other, were in the ascendant. Themistocles' policy gave Athens great naval strength and led her into the naval league, which became the Athenian Empire, which in its turn was to give the common man employment and political significance, thus furthering democracy at Athens. The historian Thucydides later praised Themistocles as one who, better than any man of his time, could foresee developments likely to result from a policy. Prescient as Themistocles was, he can hardly have foreseen all these results.

In 487, another change was made that lessened the power of the great clans and favored the new men: the archons were henceforth to be chosen by lot out of a panel of five hundred elected by the demes. They were still to be drawn from the first two classes in the state. They still had to be able to command votes in the first stage of the process. But if they were chosen by lot in the second stage, the influence of the clans or any other group was undermined, and the system was thereby made more democratic. It followed naturally that the archonship became less important politically and that the generalship, which remained entirely elective, became more important politically, because a general gained his office only by being able to command votes. Another effect was that the Council of the Areopagus, composed as it was of ex-archons, began slowly to lose its influence, for soon its members were men who had not necessarily demonstrated unusual influence at any time.

In 483, the discovery of an excellent new vein of silver in the state mines gave rise to a high political controversy. Instead of distributing it among the citizens as a windfall, as had been done before, Themistocles wished to use it for new warships. He had begun his policy of naval strength ten years before, when he urged the fortification of Peiraeus. Aristides, who opposed Themistocles in the controversy over the new vein of silver, was ostracized. It is interesting that he retired to Aegina, that great enemy of Athens, where the upper classes dominated. Class lines could thus be more important than national lines. If full democracy was yet to come to Athens, the events of this decade represent a strengthening of the *polis* in general as against the clans and a definite move toward democracy. The new Athens was clearly emerging.

The two hundred new ships that the Athenians provided for their navy were triremes, the type of ship first devised about half a century before, perhaps by the Corinthians. An ingenious outrigger arrangement made it possible to add an additional set of oars. It was not a bank of oars. The middle group of rowers sat each just behind one of the lower group, their waists about even with the heads of the lower group, and the third group sat just behind and just above the middle group in the same way. The vertical space required for all three groups was not three times that required for one man. Although there were now a hundred and seventy rowers, the ship itself was no longer than when there were only two groups of oarsmen.

The trireme was perhaps 120 feet long and less than 20 in the beam. It had 170 oarsmen, a small group of officers and petty officers, and an armed group of 14 spearmen and four archers. It had a square sail that was generally left ashore when battle was imminent. The ship was used chiefly to ram opposing warships; the armed personnel were to cover this operation and prevent boarding. Ramming was a skilled operation and required a highly trained crew. For the 200 triremes, 34,000 oarsmen were needed. Obviously a *polis* that wished to be a naval power had to have some money at its disposal and a large pool of freeborn citizens and allies; this was not work for slaves. Such a *polis* was also bound to feel some immediate political effect from this active participation of the populace.

The New League

By late 481, Xerxes was at Sardis and making ready to move his vast forces toward Greece. Heralds came to demand the submission of all the Greek states except Athens and Sparta. About a third of the Greeks gave their submission, chiefly the islanders and the people of northern Greece, all of whom felt farthest from any protection that Sparta and Athens might give. The Delphic Oracle, which had been known before to show a rather distressing worldly practicality, counseled against resisting the might of the Mede.

The *poleis* who were willing to resist sent representatives to a meeting in Sparta late in 480. A new league was formed, called simply "The Greeks" (although modern scholars generally call it the "Hellenic League"); it included the members of Sparta's league but was distinct from it. The leadership was Sparta's, but by decision of the members rather than because it was taken for granted. There was to be a congress with wide powers in every field. Sparta's leadership consisted of the right to appoint the military and naval commanders.

The Greeks were at least capable of imagining a federal organization and of making it work for a short time; to make it work over a long period proved impossible.

THE WAR

The ponderous forces of the Persians, which may well have numbered 500,000, although Herodotus would make them number 1,700,000 active combatants, crossed the Hellespont on a pontoon bridge and made their way across Thrace and Macedonia, drinking the rivers dry and eating the country bare, as it seemed to those inhabitants who were ordered to contribute to their supplies. They made their way down through Thessaly, whose people had no strength to oppose them and who joined them of necessity.

The first Greek resistance was offered at Thermopylae, where the road for the Persian land forces was narrow, flanked by the sea and by steep cliffs, and where the supporting fleet had to come through the narrow waters at the northern tip of Euboea if it was to land troops in the rear of the Greeks without making the long trip around Euboea. The prayers of the Greeks to Poseidon and the winds were answered by gales that first damaged the main Persian fleet, then wrecked a detachment that had been sent around Euboea to close the southern entrance to the strait and bottle up the part of the Greek fleet that was between the island and the mainland.

On the shore was enacted one of the classic scenes of human history as the best troops of the Persians, in this narrow space where it was a fair fight of man against man, were repulsed again and again by a small band, the core of which was three hundred Spartans under King Leonidas. As so often happened, a traitor appeared, one Ephialtes, whose contemptible deed deserves to be kept especially green in memory because it was done in conjunction with the immortal bravery of the Spartans. He led the Persians around by a mountain path to take the Spartans in the rear. The Spartans died there, obedient to their orders.

Probably the desire for money caused Ephialtes' treacherous deed. The motive of those Eretrians who betrayed their city to the Persians in the invasion of 490 was perhaps different, for they may have thought that they could thus escape the dire fate that awaited all the citizens when the city was taken. From now on in Greek history, treason was frequent. Perhaps in the earlier days there had been less because there had been less opportunity. Perhaps, too, in the earlier days it was less easy to imagine one's self as separate from the rest of the community and capable of profiting individually from treason. In the earlier days, there would have been no place for the traitor to live during his remaining years. But in the classical age of Greece, treason was frequent, not only the treason of individuals, but the treason of a faction in the *polis*—whether the rich or the poor—willing to betray the whole *polis* in the hope of getting the advantage over the other faction. On the other hand, treason was almost unknown among the Spartans.

The Battle of Salamis

A newly discovered inscription (published in 1960) shows that several weeks before the battle at Thermopylae the Athenians had decreed that they would send their women and children to Troezen in the northern Peloponnesus and their older men to Salamis. It had also been decreed that their two hundred ships were to be manned, half to go to Artemisium, at the northern tip of Euboea, while the other half patrolled the waters off Peiraeus and Salamis. This inscription makes it clear that from the early stages of the war Athens and Sparta worked together and that it was early planned to abandon Athens and make the real defense at Salamis and then, if necessary, at the Isthmus of Corinth. Because only half the fleet was to be sent to Artemisium, it seems that the ships there and the infantry at Thermopylae were fighting only a delaying action. In Herodotus' version of the events, the plan to abandon Athens came at the last moment and only after Themistocles had persuaded the Delphic Oracle to emit some ambiguous remarks about wooden walls and a battle at Salamis that could be used to support the withdrawal from the city. Perhaps the story was refashioned after the event so as to shed more luster on Themistocles, the hero of the war, and emphasize the difficulty he had in carrying his proposed measures.

After the battle at Thermopylae, the Persians came down to Athens and burned the city. According to the plan, the Greek fleet was to make a stand as the Persians came down toward the Isthmus and the

Peloponnesus, but now the Peloponnesian naval forces wished to retire without a struggle, intending instead to fortify the Isthmus in defiance of the plain fact that the Persian fleet, if not opposed, could land men anywhere it wished behind the fortifications. Themistocles was able to prevent his colleagues from withdrawing before the Persians. In a stormy session, he threatened that the Athenians would use their ships to migrate en masse to the West. He also sent a message to the Persian king telling him that the Greek fleet was about to retire and could be bottled up in the Bay of Salamis by prompt action. Such action would both keep the other Greeks from retiring and draw the Persians into an engagement in an unfavorable place.

The Persians took the bait, for such apparently treasonable behavior among the Greeks had come to seem normal to them. They sent a force that closed the western entrance to the bay. On the morning of September 23, 480, they advanced in line into the eastern entrance. The Greeks let them get a little way in, then appeared in formation and backed water until the head of the Persian line was opposite them and directly beneath the hill where Xerxes had stationed himself to watch the destruction of the Greeks. When the morning onshore breeze sprang up (as the Greeks had expected) and made a quartering swell that rocked the Persians out of formation and spoiled their co-ordination, the Greeks attacked. The maneuver, like the modern one of "crossing the enemy's T," brought the full Athenian force to bear on the head of the enemy line, with the rear unable to help. The Persians lost about two hundred ships out of perhaps a thousand. The rest withdrew from the bay.

The Persian fleet was not destroyed, but this defeat was severe enough to make Xerxes change his plans. The ships returned to Asia, with the Greeks following, but at a respectful distance, not in hot pursuit. The Persian army withdrew to northern Greece, whence part was sent home to Asia and part left to continue the war.

The Battle of Plataea

In the spring of 479, the Persian commander shrewdly undertook to separate the Greek forces that might be opposed to him. He offered the Athenians their independence and an alliance with Persia if they would desert the League and cease to resist. But the Athenians had

their eyes fixed on the risen star of their destiny and refused him.
Again he occupied Athens, and again they withdrew from their city.
Again he made his offer, and again they rejected it. The Athenians
now sent a furious protest to the Peloponnesians, who had done
nothing, and at last the loyal forces of Greece moved. A hundred
thousand men took the field to engage the Persians in Boeotia. This
unusually large army showed cohesion and steadiness for the few
weeks needed to defeat the enemy. The final battle was fought in
479 near Plataea, after the armies had been for some time in each
other's presence. The bravery and skill of the Spartan hoplites was
the deciding factor. Only a remnant of the Persian army survived.

The Ionian Greeks, meanwhile, seeing an opportunity to be free
of Persia, had offered to join the Greek naval forces. The Greek fleet
had crossed the Aegaean and sought out the Persian fleet. In a
decisive battle at Mycale, near Miletus, the Greeks defeated the
Persians on land and destroyed their beached ships. The battle, which
was fought on the same day in September as that at Plataea, induced
many more of the Greeks to revolt from the Persians.

Although the League's fleet now went home, the Athenian commanders remained and conducted a siege of Sestus, the Persian naval
base in the Chersonesus. In the early spring of 478, they took it, then
sailed home. Herodotus ends his history at this point. It was a logical
point to stop, if one reflects that much of his story revolves around
the adventures of Xerxes. It was not the end of the war, however.
For another ten years or so, the Persians maintained garrisons on
the European side of the Hellespont. Naval warfare went on, always
with the possibility of a new Persian naval offensive against Greece,
until 448. In 478, the threat from Persia still seemed real, and for
this reason some of the Greek states took the fateful step of making
a new organization for naval warfare in the Aegaean, the Delian
League.

THE WESTERN GREEKS

The Greeks of the West fought off a great attack by the Carthaginians at the very time when the mother country was being invaded
by the Persians. Probably it is not true that the victory of the Sicilian
Greeks over the Carthaginian invaders in the great land battle of

Himera occurred on the same day as the victory at Salamis, but the conjunction of the two events has symbolic, if not literal, truth.

The age of tyrants lasted longer in Sicily than among the other Greeks. In the early fifth century, the leading ones were Hippocrates of Gela and Theron of Acragas. On the death of Hippocrates, a brilliant officer named Gelon at first acted as regent for the tyrant's sons, then set them aside and became tyrant himself. At a time when the people of Syracuse had ousted most of the aristocracy, Gelon saw his opportunity. He attacked the city with the aid of the exiled aristocrats, but made himself tyrant instead of returning the government to them. He left his brother Hieron to rule Gela and made Syracuse his own center of operations. There he brought some people from Gela and the upper classes from some other towns that he conquered. So far was he from being a champion of the oppressed or caring about the harmony of the few and the many that he sold the lower classes of these conquered *poleis* into slavery. He improved the fortifications of Syracuse until it was probably the best fortified city in the world, and he developed an army of some 20,000 hoplites with a fine cavalry force and a navy of 200 ships. By marriage, he allied himself with Theron, the tyrant of Acragas.

Gelon was visited by envoys of the Greek League who asked him to help against the Persians. He felt strong enough to offer some troops, but on condition that he have the supreme command. Because the Spartans would not agree, he asked for the command of the fleet, but now the Athenians were not willing. Gelon therefore remained prudently outside this conflict, taking only the practical step of sending an envoy to Delphi to wait there and give the Persians, if they were victorious, some money as well as the earth and water that signified submission.

The Carthaginians probably saw that the alliance of Gelon with Theron of Acragas would cause them trouble in the western part of Sicily, which they considered their own. The Persians were said to have urged the Carthaginians to move, in order to keep the western Greeks busy during the invasion of Greece, but the Carthaginians would have had little enthusiasm for helping to put Persia in control of Greece and well on her way to the West. They had their own reasons for attacking Sicily. Having made elaborate preparations, they descended on the Greeks in 480, intending to conquer the whole island of Sicily. The Carthaginian commander began with the siege of Himera, on the north coast of Sicily, which was held by troops of Theron. Gelon came to the rescue with a strong Syracusan force, thinking it best not to wait until the Carthaginians arrived before Syracuse, which would have to be reduced sometime if they were to conquer all Sicily. The great battle fought at Himera was a glorious victory for the Greeks. The Carthaginian losses were such that they even feared a Greek attempt at invasion of the Punic territory in Africa and gladly made a treaty to end hostilities. It was seventy years before the Carthaginians again tried to get control of the whole island.

Syracuse and the other cities prospered greatly during those seventy years. The alliances and the common action of the tyrants made them too strong for Carthaginian attack and fostered a prosperous trade. Syracuse took the lead in all respects. She adopted the Attic standard of coinage, which became common all through Sicily. During this new prosperity, the tyrants often tried to promote culture in the old tradition.

In another region of the West, the Greeks of South Italy preserved the Greek spirit of separatism in their dealings with one another and with their Italian or Etruscan neighbors. Some of them were overcome by their neighbors, and none of them ever grew very strong. Their pressure on the Etruscans, however, helped the Romans to expel the Etruscan kings in 509 B.C., and in 474 the people of Cumae, having called the Syracusan fleet to their aid against the Etruscan fleet, defeated it so thoroughly off Cumae that the Etruscans never counted again as a naval power.

CHAPTER

19

GREEK CULTURE IN THE
EARLY FIFTH CENTURY

Undoubtedly the double victory over the Persians and the Carthaginians was the great event among the Greeks of the early fifth century. They must have gained a great deal of confidence from repelling these two formidable enemies. Probably they also gained a good deal of booty. The Greeks of Sicily, for example, acquired and parceled out among their cities a good many Carthaginian slaves, who were very useful to them.

Architecture

This increase in confidence and prosperity was reflected in the fine arts and in literature. A number of the many works of art produced in the early fifth century have come down to us. In Sicily and southern Italy, some grandiose temples were built. For example, Theron, the tyrant of Acragas, used part of the spoils from the Carthaginians to build in his rather modest *polis* a huge (173 x 361 feet) temple to Olympian Zeus. The temple of Zeus at Selinus, in Sicily, was almost as large. The fine temples of Poseidonia, the Roman Paestum, in southern Italy, were built not long after the Persian Wars. This was a part of the Greek world where the Doric order was ordinarily

319

used. The builders of both Sicily and Italy were at a disadvantage in not having supplies of good marble within a reasonable distance. They therefore worked with the local stone, a respectable but not a fine building stone.

Because the canons of the Doric order were probably fixed well before the end of the sixth century, we may take the temple of Zeus at Olympia, which probably was built between 470 and 460, as a typical if not early Doric temple. Although little of it remains standing, we know a great deal about it from careful excavations and from ancient descriptions. It was a rectangular building, 91 x 210 feet, made of rather poor local stone, since the expense of transporting marble to this out-of-the-way place would have been tremendous. It stood on a stone platform. A row of columns ran across each end and along each side, six on the ends and thirteen on the sides. There was a little space between the columns and the inner structure, making a porch on each end and a sort of side aisle down each length. The columns were of the style that characterizes the Doric order.

The Doric column stands on the platform and is not raised on a base. It has a slight *entasis*, or convexity, near its middle. This is to correct the optical illusion of concavity that would be given by a row of straight columns. There are vertical grooves in the column, called flutings. The column is made of fair-sized drums of stone piled one on another. Each drum has a hole in the middle of the bottom and top surfaces. A plug of wood, often reinforced with an iron rod, fits down into the top hole of the drum below and up into the bottom hole of the drum above. After the column has been all built up, the flutings are cut; they help to emphasize the vertical lift of the column. At the top is a swelling called the *echinus*, above which is a square capital.

A plain beam, called the architrave, rests on the capitals of the columns. Above the architrave is the frieze, a band of alternating triglyphs and metopes. The triglyph, a square piece with two deep vertical grooves, is above the head of a column and represents the end of a crossbeam in the older wooden structures that these stone temples suggest (we have already seen in Egypt this reproduction of wood when stone began to be used). The metopes are square pieces in between, which merely filled spaces, and they were usually ornamented. Above the frieze begins a pitched roof (tiled, in most examples of this style). At the ends of it are triangular spaces, called pediments. It was becoming the custom to fill them with figures at the time when the temple of Zeus was built; a problem in composition was set by the triangularity of the working surface. Inside was the *cella*, or chamber, which in the Olympian temple contained the greatest of all chryselephantine statues, the Zeus of the great sculptor Phidias. It stood forty feet high and was viewed from a gallery inside the temple.

The architect of the temple of Zeus at Olympia was a local man who did a good conservative job and produced a standard Doric temple. The sculptor Phidias was an Athenian. Two of his associates did the pediments, one of which represented the beginnings of a legendary chariot race, the other the fight of the Centaurs and the Thessalian tribe of the Lapithae, a wild, swirling composition. The metopes along the sides were plain, but those at the ends were carved to depict the labors of Hercules.

Sculpture and Painting

During the fifth century, there was a movement in sculpture away from the conventionality typified by the *kouroi* to a more literal and perhaps more prosaic art, which was nevertheless executed with wonderful skill and imagination. Here again we meet a difference of opinion among the experts. There is none to deny the excellence of the sculpture of the late fifth century according to its kind, but some feel that art portraying faithfully what everyone can see is a little inferior in kind to art in which the artist expresses what he himself sees according to a poetic convention. For the layman, the profit of such discussions probably lies in the suggestion that he look with care and sympathy at the more conventional, late archaic art of Greece as he encounters it in pictures or in museums or, if fortunate enough, in Greece.

A number of *kouroi* of the early fifth century suggest the change, for it is plain that their makers had been doing very careful studies in anatomy and had often changed toward representing the body with its real structure. Our perception tends to be pleased by this change, yet it is not necessarily a real artistic advance. Rather it is the beginning of a shift in the attitude of the artists of the time, which culminated in the production of many statues full of action, like the well-known discus-thrower of Myron. Certainly the idea of sculpture representing bodies in action was not new. An archaic sculpture in the Acropolis Museum at Athens shows a man carrying a calf on his shoulders, and another shows a man riding a horse.

The famous discus-thrower, the Discobolus, so familiar in modern photographs, is a marble copy of Myron's bronze original. Bronze statues were very popular at this time. The discus-thrower is a study in composition and a good example of the realism of the artist of the fifth century after the passing of the late archaic period, that is, after about 480. The statue is sometimes criticized on the ground that the calmness of the face does not suit the action—but sometime watch the expression of a modern shotputter or discus-thrower at the moment before the final drive starts. It is also fashionable to criticize by suggesting that all copies of Greek statues were made for vulgar Romans in later ages. The fact is that the Greeks themselves often bought copies of mass-produced statues, and it is fair to speak of mass production in a marble-cutting shop where the model of a figure was reproduced by assistants a good many times.

The ancients thought of Polygnotus, a painter of this period, as a distinguished early painter. Pausanias, who wrote a Baedeker-like handbook in the second century of our era, gave a carefully detailed description of the pictures, now no longer extant, with which Polygnotus decorated the treasury of the Cnidians at Delphi. He made large murals, so large that they allowed many figures of nearly life size. "After the Fall of Troy" was a subject that permitted him to concentrate on character and emotion rather than on action. "Odysseus in the Underworld" likewise allowed a careful study of the shades in Hades reacting to a visit from a living man. Polygnotus was regarded as highly successful in giving his characters expressiveness.

LITERATURE

Lyric Poetry

Pindar (521–441 B.C.) of Thebes was the greatest of the writers of choral lyric. He came of good family and was conservative in his outlook. He learned the art of the choral lyric in Athens, where it flourished in his younger years. His first commission to write a victory ode is said to have come when he was only twenty years old, a commission to celebrate the victory of a young Thessalian noble in the footrace in the Pythian Games at Delphi. In later years, he spent some time at the courts of Syracuse and Acragas, brilliant centers of the cultivated life. He received commissions from other tyrants and kings—those of Cyrene and Macedonia, for instance.

We have forty-four victory odes, or *epinicia*, that Pindar wrote for victories in the four great sets of games. We know that he also wrote all the other kinds of lyric, the *threnos*, or lament, the hymn to the gods, the processional song, the dithyramb for the gods. But only fragments of this other work remain. His *epinicia* are the culmination of the Greek choral lyric. The handling of language and meters combines with splendor and elevation of thought to make these poems masterpieces of their kind.

The construction of such an ode offered something of a problem. All one had to start with was the fact that one's patron, or his horses, or his son or nephew, had won a victory at one of the great meetings. The poet could not, however, merely string together phrases of flattery and call them an ode. Simonides, who was in his prime in Pindar's early years, had written victory odes that perhaps served as examples. In any case, Pindar is said to have been advised by an older poet to make free use of mythology; this he did. He found it not too difficult to establish some sort of relation between a myth and the victory he was to extol. Then he built up the poem with an intricate antiphonal structure, so far from appealing to modern taste that to follow it in detail is arduous even for the scholar. Such a structure, with an element here balancing an element there in a highly formalized pattern, did, however, appeal to Greek taste of the time.

The language used of the myth and the victory was bold, elevated, and brilliant. Pindar uses metaphors constantly, and they are daring as well as frequent. Like Homer, he speaks of the nobler and more elevated aspects of everything he mentions. His own inclination, as well as the tastes of his patrons, led him to glorify all that was old-fashioned, conservative, and aristocratic, in strong opposition to the newer attitude prevalent during his lifetime and characterized by sharp criticism of the older ideas of the gods, as well as criticism of the aristocracies and the idea of personal glory won in athletics.

The Beginnings of the Tragic Drama

The history of the early drama is not clear. We do know that the Greeks of Greece proper, of South Italy, and of Sicily had developed the choral lyric to a real art form by the middle of the sixth century. We know also that tragedy was always connected with the worship of Dionysus, the god of fertility, wine, and those emotional states of which joy in the arrival of spring is typical. Somehow the choral lyrics in honor of the god developed into a series of exchanges between the chorus and its leader. It is easy to imagine that the leader asked questions about the legendary life and exploits of Dionysus and that he was answered by the chorus. By about 500 B.C., the choral lyric had developed into a series of exchanges between the chorus, its leader, the *tragodos,* and another man who was known as "the answerer," or *hypokrites,* the word from which comes "hypocrite," "one who plays a part." *Hypokrites* came to be the Greek word for actor.

The developed tragedy of the fifth century was always presented as a religious ceremony in honor of Dionysus. In Athens it was presented at three different festivals. One was the Lenaea, which came in January. After the purely religious observances, both tragedies and comedies were presented, probably in the Agora at first, then in the Theater of Dionysus. The Rural Dionysia were celebrated in December in the demes of Attica. Many of the demes came to have modest theaters of their own. First came the religious ceremonies, meant to honor Dionysus as god of fertility and thus ensure the success of the autumn sowing and the rebirth of the land that seems to die in the dying days of December; then tragedies and comedies were played in honor of the god. The plays of the greatest poets sometimes appeared at those local festivals. Because they were held on different days and there was no great distance to go, people often went to several such festivals.

The Great Dionysia, also called the City Dionysia, held in March, was the greatest of the festivals. This festival became more important in the sixth century, probably as one of the results of Peisistratus' genius for organization. In the fifth century, the time we are discussing, the Great Dionysia gained in fame as the fortunes of Athens rose and the dramatic part of the program developed. By March the sea was open again after the dangerous storms of winter, and visitors from all parts of the Greek world came to Athens, often to combine attendance at this most brilliant festival with business or diplomatic affairs. This was the occasion for the proclamation of honors to citizens or other men who had deserved well of Athens. It was a natural time for the arrival of ambassadors, and after Athens had turned the Delian League into the Athenian Empire, it was the time for the members to make their monetary contributions. The celebration served as an advertisement to the Hellenic world of the wealth and power and public spirit of Athens and her artistic and literary leadership as well.

First came a ceremonial re-entry of the god into Athens, escorted by a torchlight procession. The next morning there was a great parade, which took sacrifices and gifts to his temple. That afternoon there was a choral contest among the entries of the ten tribes, who had been carefully trained for some time beforehand. That night there was a *komos,* or revel, at which there was a good deal of drinking and gaiety that often became riotous.

The other days were given over to the performance of tragedies and comedies in the Theater of Dionysus. The priest of Dionysus, flanked by other priests, sat in the front row. The performances, which lasted all day, were taken with high seriousness. Even the comedies, gay and bawdy as they generally were, were far from being mere frothy amusement, for they commented on serious matters in the comic spirit. Afterward an assembly of people considered all the problems that had arisen during the festival, for example, misconduct in the theater. We have only fragmentary information about such festivals elsewhere or about dramatic performances other than those at Athens. In this field, as in others, Athens seemed to stand naturally at the front in the Greek world. To the natural flair of the Athenians was added the talent of others who came to the city because of its leadership.

Authors who wished to present tragedies submitted them to an official chosen to select the plays. After due deliberation, three of these writers were told that this official would "give them a chorus." The expense of the chorus (costumes, for example) was borne by some rich man as a liturgy.* The author would train the chorus himself,

---

* For the liturgies, see Chapter Twenty-one.

at least in the early days; later there were professional trainers. The writer himself in these early times took the part of *tragodos*, the person who talked with the chorus and led it.

Aeschylus

Aeschylus, of the deme Eleusis, was born in 525 B.C. and died in 456. His deme was the home of the Mysteries, and he himself seems to have been a religious man. He had a vein of poetry and a sense of the spectacular; he was not a deep or original thinker. Of the eighty or more tragedies that he wrote, we have seven. The impressiveness (and sometimes the obscurity) of the plays that survive should not make us forget that he was a highly successful playwright, one in close touch with his public and one who knew how to write for the stage.

Aeschylus was a tremendous innovator. It was he who introduced the first actor, the *hypokrites*, or "answerer," who with the *tragodos*, or leader of the chorus, carried on the first truly dramatic conversations. Soon he added another "answerer," who completed the canonical number of three on the stage who had speaking parts. He made the corresponding innovation of cutting down the lines spoken by the chorus so that the dialogue might have first importance. Even in the few plays that we have, we can see a development in his power of handling dialogue and inventing characterizations that support the acts of the persons in the plays. He is said to have given great attention to every detail of the production of his works, from the music and dances of the chorus to the masks and costumes and background. It has been suggested that the realism of European drama—as contrasted with the quality of Sanskrit or Chinese drama, for example—is essentially due to the influence exercised by Aeschylus on both the matter and the staging of incipient Greek tragedy.

Each playwright customarily presented a group of three tragedies, called a trilogy, and a satyr-play. The satyr-play was usually a light and farcical piece. One such play, the *Cyclops* of Euripides, is a travesty of Odysseus' famous adventure with the Cyclops Polyphemus. The group of four plays is referred to as a tetralogy. Sometimes the three tragedies formed something like one play in three acts; more often, perhaps, they were on separate themes and had little relationship.

Aeschylus' *Oresteia* is the one surviving trilogy. Its three plays are entitled *Agamemnon, Choephoroe* (Libation-Bearers), and *Eumenides* (The Kindly Ones). The story of the House of Pelops was a famous one that had descended from the days of Mycenaean greatness and earlier. The atrocious crimes of the house began with Tantalus, Agamemnon's great-grandfather. Generation after generation did deeds so violent and so treacherous that they made good telling and lived on in oral tradition.

The scene of the first play, *Agamemnon,* is laid at Argos. Agamemnon was in fact king of Mycenae; the palace whose ruins may still be seen there on the hill was presumably the scene of real deeds of horror like those in the play. But about 468, Argos had taken little Mycenae, and now in 458 Argos was complimented by a friendly Athenian by being made the home of the great king of other days. Aeschylus started the play with the news of the fall of Troy, followed by the return of the king. In his absence, his queen, Clytemnestra, had brooded long and bitterly over his sacrifice of their daughter, Iphigeneia, to obtain a fair wind for the fleet to sail to Troy. She had also taken as lover her husband's cousin and bitter enemy, Aegisthus. When Agamemnon returned in triumph from the war, he brought with him as part of his share of the booty the Trojan princess Cassandra to be his mistress. Clytemnestra welcomed her lord and persuaded him to enter the palace walking on the crimson carpet which she had spread for him. Cassandra, left outside, gave the first mad scene in European literature, telling in the prophetic frenzy sent on her by Apollo of the past wickedness of this house and foretelling her own imminent death and Agamemnon's by the hand of Clytemnestra.

The play ends with the queen and her lover in control, in spite of the resentment of the citizens at the murder of their king. The character of Clytemnestra is carefully built up to make it plausible that a woman should do such a deed. Her deep resentment and the essential forcefulness of her character are brought out by a skillful use of all the means known then or now to portray character in the drama except carefully differentiated language; all the characters use more or less the same language. But the other devices are well used: her character in action; direct description by other characters; and the disclosure of her character by what she herself says, sometimes to one and sometimes to another of the other personages, in order to show different sides of her nature and provide effective contrasts with others.

Between this play and the second of the trilogy, *Choephoroe*, there is a dramatic interval of some years. The so-called unity of time applied to each separate play, not to all three plays of a trilogy. The unities of time and place (in spite of the "rules" of European critics) were not binding rules even within the individual play and were not invariably observed. It can easily be seen, however, that to keep all the action in one place and within a short compass of time added intensity and avoided awkwardness. The normal play was fairly short and had no intermissions; a chorus of twelve (increased by Sophocles to fifteen) was assumed to be present and participating in the whole action. To keep the action generally in one place and within one day's time was only good sense.

The essence of *Choephoroe* is that Orestes, the son of Agamemnon and Clytemnestra, who is not at home when his father is killed by his mother, finally returns to kill his mother in obedience to the command of Apollo and kills both her and her lover Aegisthus. Impartial criticism can find genuine faults in this play, faults that serve to set off the skill and success of *Agamemnon*. Even this late in his career Aeschylus could occasionally be a little stiff and archaic in his manner and slightly awkward in some of his dramatic devices.

The third play of the trilogy is *Eumenides*. At the end of the second play, Orestes sees the dread figures of the *Erinyes*, or Furies, the old spirits of vengeance for the shedding of blood, rising to pursue him for the killing of his mother. The third play opens with Orestes at Delphi, where he has taken refuge from the Furies at the altar of Apollo, the god, who commanded him to kill his mother. The Furies, who are ingeniously used as a chorus in the play, are asleep around him. Apollo spirits Orestes off to Athens, where as a suppliant he asks Athena to defend him and extricate him from his miserable condition. The Furies pursue him to Athens, and the Court (or Council) of the Areopagus is set up to hear this as its first case. Apollo and the Furies present their rival claims. The jury's vote is tied, and Athena casts the vote that frees Orestes.

Now the Furies, enraged at this flaunting of their ancient function by the newly established Areopagus, threaten to blight Athens in retaliation. Athena urges them to put off their gory ancient nature, become goddesses of Athens, honored by the greatest city of the world, and assume a kindlier nature suitable to the new age and the brilliant enlightenment of Athens. Finally they are persuaded by her talk—as fine a piece of nationalistic glorification as was ever written—and agree to become the kindly modern spirits of the modern city. Now their name changes to *Eumenides*, the kindly ones, in accord with the change in their character. A second chorus, this one representing Athenian citizens, suddenly rises and at Athena's bidding escorts the *Eumenides* around the flank of the Acropolis to the cave that is henceforth to be their home.

The management of the chorus in these three plays is most instructive about this part of the dramatic equipment, a part that to the modern dramatist might seem very awkward. The chorus was part of the ceremony of Dionysus out of which the tragedies grew; the playwright had it on his hands as something inherited that he had to keep and use. Probably writers all took it for granted and did not even think of dropping it.

In *Agamemnon* the chorus of Argive elders has a great deal to say about the former crimes of the House of Pelops, about the circumstances in which the Greek fleet went off to Troy, and especially about the death of Iphigeneia. The effect is to impress the spectator or reader strongly with the crimes of the wicked house. In *Choephoroe* the members of the chorus are maidens of the palace who have come with Electra, daughter of Agamemnon, to bring libations to his tomb. They are allotted about the usual amount of space in the play and comment on what is happening as the choruses of other plays generally do. But they also engage in a brisk three-cornered argument with Electra and her brother, stirring him up to obey Apollo's command and kill his mother. Then, at a crucial moment, they take part in the action by suggesting that Aegisthus be summoned without his bodyguard and so be exposed unprotected to Orestes. In *Eumenides* the pursuing Furies are the chorus—a very neat device, since there was necessarily a group of them pursuing Orestes. The supplementary chorus of Athenians that rises up at the end of the play to conduct the Furies to their new home is an unusual and striking dramatic device.

This trilogy illustrates the fact that these plays were good theater in their own time, even as they treated subjects of enough universality to make them appeal to people of other times and other places. The idea of the replacement of feuding, the repayment of crime with crime, by courts that at once do final justice is a high and worthy idea. For us the story as a whole may be lacking in dramatic appeal; what there is we find chiefly in the vivid presentation of the crime in *Agamemnon*, where the dramatist so wonderfully makes his first point: the folly and wrongness of trying to make two wrongs add up to one right.

For the Athenian spectator, the dramatic impact of the whole trilogy must have been tremendous. He would have felt the effect of *Agamemnon* more than we do; in the second play, the revenge of Orestes under Apollo's orders would have seemed more plausible and therefore more dramatic than it does now. The third play is one of the great examples of the praise of Athens. The Athenian who went to the plays that March day in 458 B.C. and saw this trilogy must have felt that being an Athenian was good.

The playwright Phrynichus, a contemporary of Aeschylus, wrote a play (not extant) on the sack of Miletus by the Persians toward the end of the Ionian revolt. For reminding them of the misfortune of their kinsmen, the Athenians are said to have fined him at the assembly held at the end of the festival. Next, probably in 476, Phrynichus, who was capable of being taught by adversity, offered a play (not extant either) on the Battle of Salamis that was accepted and produced with no less a person than the hero of Salamis, Themistocles, as the *choregus*, or furnisher of the chorus. Aeschylus' *Persians*, also about this battle, was produced in 472, with Pericles, who was to become so famous as a statesman, as *choregus*. These three plays are the only ventures into contemporary subjects on the Athenian tragic stage of which we have any word.

Aeschylus' play, which has come down to us, is an Athenian glorification of the Battle of Salamis. The possible consequences (from the gods) of open and straightforward gloating are avoided by placing the action at the Persian court and making the play rather a story of Persian defeat, the consequence of Persian *hubris*. The play gains in grandeur from the pomp of the Persian court, from its remoteness from Athens, and from the rolling, sonorous lists of Persian names. There is little or no dramatic conflict; the play comes close to being an elevated and interesting tale of how Persian power became *hubris* and how the *nemesis* that naturally followed brought the Persians low at Salamis.

Aeschylus' *Prometheus Bound* was one of a trilogy of which the others, *Prometheus Unbound* and *Prometheus the Fire-Bringer*, have been lost. The Titan Prometheus had helped Zeus to gain the mastery among the gods. Zeus represented the triumph of intelligence over the older powers, which were only brute force, and one of the first reforms planned by him was the eradication of man, a brutish creature. Prometheus disobeyed Zeus by giving man fire and thus, by implication, all the mechanic arts, which first raised him above the beasts.

The play begins with the arrival of Hephaestus, the smith of the gods, and two repulsive creatures, Force and Violence, at a lonely crag in the Caucasus, to which they shackle Prometheus. Our hero is thus rendered immobile. The playwright has him visited by a procession of people and divinities whose conversation with him brings out various aspects of his situation. The fact that Zeus's power is new is strongly emphasized. Zeus is a little uncertain, Zeus tends to be hasty and cruel, Zeus forgets what is due to older ideas of propriety and right. Above all, Zeus is wroth at the disobedience of Prometheus, one of his own group.

The insistence on the attitudes of one whose power is new could perhaps have some reference to the fact that the power of the Athenian democracy was relatively new, although it is rash to be too ready to see parallels and allusions of this sort. Zeus has his problem, too. Any executive faced with an utterly reckless rebel within his organization is likely to find it difficult to assert his own authority and maintain order and efficiency without destroying good feeling.

Apparently the trilogy ended in a reconciliation, Zeus abating his tyrannical wrath and Prometheus his stubbornly disobedient spirit. The action of this play is helped by the suspense provided by Prometheus' assertion that he knows a secret of extreme importance to Zeus, the secret of an oracle that threatens Zeus's overthrow.

Some of the dialogue consists of speeches overlong for modern taste. Some of it, however, is very effective in character portrayal.

In spite of the fact that often we cannot say precisely what problem, or what contemporary interest a Greek play was meant to deal with, still we can be sure that Aeschylus and after him Sophocles and Euripides were dealing with matters of intense concern to their audiences. The work of other men has not been preserved. If we had even a quarter of the two thousand or so tragedies (the estimated number written), we could make interesting comparisons of the subjects that were handled. We know, generally speaking, that in the fifth century there was furious discussion of all sorts of human relations that in earlier times had been governed by strict tradition and had not been suitable subjects of discussion. The fact that the Greeks discussed those matters that present themselves to people coming out of a closed and traditional society into a more open society, where decisions are made on many social and moral matters after thought and discussion, has made them interesting to Europeans going through the same process during the last few centuries. It has even been said that the Theater of Dionysus was a great philosophical forum. Yet to discuss these matters only on the tragic stage seems a little strange. Still the problems, the interested audience, and a potential art form were there, and men of genius brought that art form to its height as they offered treatments of the problems of their fellow Athenians. Then, at the end of the fifth century, tragedy suddenly went into eclipse just as a new form of discussion, the philosophical discussion in prose, sprang suddenly to vigorous life.

CHAPTER

20

BETWEEN THE WARS: 479-445 B.C.

The period between the end of the Persian invasions (479 B.C.) and the outbreak of the Peloponnesian War (431) is sometimes known as the *Pentakontaetia*, or "The Fifty Years." This name is also applied to that part of Thucydides' history of the Peloponnesian War which discusses this period. The present chapter deals with the first part of the same time, from 479 to 445, during which Athenian power led to conflicts between Athens and Sparta that ceased temporarily under a truce, the Thirty Years' Peace, made in the year 445. Full-scale war between the two powers, what we know as the Peloponnesian War, broke out nevertheless in 431.

Athenian energy, exuberance, and achievement are the greatest phenomena of all the first part of the fifth century. If we look farther back, we can see that Athens had been shaping herself for greatness during the preceding century. The policies associated with the names of Solon, Peisistratus, and Cleisthenes gave the masses of the Athenian people more dignity and freedom and prosperity and sense of participation in the commonwealth than the common people of other Greek states could have. The small farmer, the small tradesman, and the workman enjoyed a feeling of worth and responsibility as they participated in the work of the Assembly or of the *Heliaea*.

The genius of Peisistratus had done much to give the citizens a sense of being members of no mean city; the development of the festival of Dionysus, for example, had helped to spread the idea of the brilliance and the intellectual preeminence of Athens. The political reorganization of Cleisthenes had helped to create a sense that men were members of Athens more than of clans or of sectional groupings. Although Athens was not free from factional feeling or struggles, she wasted less energy on them than most *poleis* did. The glorious success of the city in the wars with the Persians had added to the feeling that Athens and the Athenians were a *polis* of special ability and of a great future.

A NEW PHASE IN THE STRUGGLE WITH PERSIA

The New Position of Athens

The Greek defense against the Persian invasions had been conducted by the Hellenic League under the formal leadership of Sparta, with Athens occasionally furnishing the actual leadership. The victory of Mycale in 479 B.C. was the last operation conducted by the Hellenic League with the membership that it had during the invasions and almost the last conducted under Spartan leadership. After the victory at Salamis, the Ionians wanted to join the League, a measure that would have meant that they must be defended. Sparta was not willing to accept them or the obligations that their membership would create. Therefore, after Mycale, the forces of the League formally returned to Greece. But the Athenians stayed, and they and some of the Eastern Greeks besieged Sestus, the Persian base in the Chersonesus. They took it early in 478, and the Athenians then returned to Athens. Here it was that Herodotus ended his history. Plainly the struggle between East and West was not finished, but the part that interested him most, the invasion of Greece by Xerxes, was over. Here at this same point Thucydides begins his sketch of the rise of Athenian power.

While the Athenian forces were trying to reduce Sestus, the government at home began to reconstruct the fortifications and the people as individuals began to rebuild their homes and reconstitute their farms. But an embassy arrived from Sparta to urge that neither Athens nor any city outside the Peloponnesus be fortified, lest the Persians, returning, find such cities useful as secure bases of operations.

This was flattering testimony to the new respect and apprehension that the Athenians could inspire in the Spartans. The Athenians took it as such and resolved not to be balked by the Spartans in preparing for the career of their new city. Themistocles, who generally could express the feeling of Athens, urged that the ambassadors be sent home at once with the message that Athenian ambassadors would follow them soon to discuss the matter. He himself went to Sparta as the forerunner of the embassy. At home the whole population—men, women, and children—worked furiously on the walls. Meanwhile, with flattery and promises, Themistocles led the Spartans along from day to day. Hearing that the walls were rising, the Spartans protested, whereupon Themistocles urged them to send another embassy to Athens and sent secret instructions that the embassy was to be detained there.

At last the dramatic moment came. Athens had her walls, he was informed, walls high enough to be defended. He came out openly and told the Spartans that Athens had fortified herself adequately and was no longer receptive to Spartan suggestions that did not suit her own interests. It is plain that to the Athenians this was a great moment; they were so used to accepting the leadership of Sparta that they felt this to be a bold move, to be surrounded with every sort of precaution, even to deceiving the Spartans, and every sort of countermeasure, even to getting the Spartans' second embassy into the position of hostages. When Themistocles proposed to improve and further fortify the harbor of Peiraeus, a year or so later, he was able to persuade the Spartans beforehand that the new fortification was necessary to secure Peiraeus as a naval base against further naval action by the Persians.

The Escapades of Pausanias

Athens was soon to have further recognition of her new spirit and her new position. In the summer of 478, the Hellenic League sent out another expedition, under the command of the Spartan Pausanias, who captured most of Cyprus, one of the Persian naval bases, and then captured Byzantium from the Persians. The latter was an important achievement; the grain route from the Black Sea was now open and the best Persian route to Europe was closed. Pausanias behaved in such an arbitrary and dictatorial manner, however, that some of the Greeks of Asia proposed to the Athenians that the representatives of Athens should assume command of the enterprise.

Pausanias' government had already become very sensitive about un-Spartan behavior by its commanders in the field. Further, Pausanias was said to have engaged in treasonable correspondence with the Persians. He was recalled, put on trial, and relieved of his command, although no severer measures were taken against him. Meanwhile all the naval forces of the League except the Spartans had placed themselves under the command of the Athenians. The officer whom the Spartans sent out found that the forces were unwilling to accept him as their new commander and withdrew.

His government did not insist that he return and be recognized by the others. Too often they had seen that their commanders could acquire abroad a taste for luxury and the unrestrained exercise of power. They felt that they were not needed for the prosecution of the present type of operation against Persia. Further, it seemed likely to involve more than had originally been planned, because the Greeks of Asia Minor were seeking to assert their freedom from Persia. The Spartans felt, therefore, that they preferred to withdraw and might properly do so. They were not without a grudging and apprehensive feeling toward the energetic and enterprising Athenians. The other people involved wished the Athenians to lead them; the Athenians were willing. A new league was therefore formed.

The First Phase of the Athenian Alliance

As the new league, known in its early phase as the Confederacy of Delos or the Delian League, changed its character, it came to be known as the Athenian Alliance or the Athenian Empire. The reasons for its founding were two: most of the Greeks not subject to Persia wished to continue their preventive action against her; those Greeks who were still subject to her or had recently been so wished to assert and make secure their freedom. Athens, with her traditional Ionian connections, naturally was more interested than Sparta. The new confidence and the new feeling for sea power in Athens also disposed her to throw herself into this enterprise.

The new organization did not supersede the league that had fought the Persians in Greece. The need that had given rise to that league was not felt to be past, and Athens and the rest had committed themselves to the alliance. It was by the terms of the old league that some years later Sparta called on Athens and others for help in her serious domestic troubles.

Who the original members of the new alliance were cannot be completely established. Many of the islanders of the Aegaean, but not all, were included. Perhaps part of the Thracian coast had already been freed from the Persians; but certainly the new league was soon to do rather well in freeing the Greeks of this region. Although many Ionian *poleis* joined, some were still firmly under Persian control and could not; the same was true of the Greek cities in the region of the Hellespont. But as the energetic campaigns of the League freed many of the Greek cities from Persia, it brought them in as new members.

The detailed arrangement of the new alliance apparently was never set down in a single document. The Ionian Greeks were used to the idea of alliances that might be described as partly federal. In the new league, Athens supplied cohesion and firm direction. Athens by herself was named as one partner; all the others were the other partner.

The purpose was apparently both defensive and offensive, looking to the freedom of all the Greeks from Persia. The arrangement was planned to be permanent and was sworn to by all parties with great ceremony and solemnity. The problem of withdrawal of members, which was soon to be very important, seems to have been left untouched in the original agreement. The council had two parts, the Athenians on the one side and the synod of the other members on the other side. Whatever the relation between them was originally intended to be, it was inevitable that the locus of power should soon be in Athens. The treasury was at Delos, the island sacred to Apollo and his sister Artemis and thus under divine protection. The synod met at Delos, as well; hence the new organization was known as the Delian League.

It was agreed that some members should furnish ships and men for the campaigns and that others should furnish money. Aristides happened to be in command of the Athenian fleet in 478, when the new league was set up. He may have laid down the form of the alliance; he certainly fixed the amounts that were to be contributed and, in the process, added to his reputation for fair and equitable dealing, acquiring his nickname "the Just."

During the first ten years, the new league freed many Eastern Greeks from Persia. We are not well informed on the details. But clearly the Athenians exercised their leadership as might have been expected. They provided a great deal of energy and direction, and in so doing they made such desirable acquisitions for themselves as Eion on the Strymon River in Thrace and the pirate island of Scyros, whose troublesome inhabitants they sold into slavery, taking their land for distribution among Athenian cleruchs, or colonists whose land was given to them by the drawing of lots.

Carystus, in Euboea, was forced to join the alliance. Naxos, which had seceded, was forced to return to it. We do not know the details of these operations. If such an organization was to persist, it had to be held together by force when secession was attempted, despite the fact that nothing may have been said about withdrawal in the original agreement.

On the other hand, the League had good success in drawing in new members along the coast of Asia Minor. The climax of operations in this theater was a brilliant victory over the Persians at the Eurymedon River in 467. The enemy had gathered a sizable fleet, evidently intending to take strong action against the Greeks. Cimon, the brilliant Athenian aristocrat who commanded the joint fleet, and a son of Miltiades, boldly took his ships into the river mouth on the shore of which the Persian base was situated. There they had room for a formal naval action. The Athenians drove the Persian ships ashore and followed with a sharp attack on the Persian soldiers who came to cover the landing of the survivors. The camp was taken. Then Cimon surprised and destroyed the other coastal squadron of the enemy. For the present, the League, with Athens furnishing both leadership and more than her share of the men, had driven the Persians out of Europe and had freed a good many of the Greeks in Asia Minor.

Sparta's Troubles

The struggles with Persia had for a time caused Sparta to live inconsistently with her system of collectivism and conservatism. Her men had had to be away from home and in contact with other people far more frequently than was thought desirable. It had been especially unfortunate for the *perioeci* and the Helots in the armed forces to see so much of other Greeks and above all to catch the new mood of the Athenians. There had been booty to divide, which had put new strains on the Spartan system. The captains and the kings had great difficulty in retaining their virtue when faced with the temptations of the great world outside Sparta. The holding of high commands away from the constant inspection and repression of the Spartan elders could cause a certain wildness of spirit, far removed from the Spartan ideal of service to the state and repression of individualism.

To retire to their old quiet ways as soon as possible was an obvious choice for the Spartans to make. This they did in the year 478, when they refused to go farther with the admission of the Ionians to the Hellenic League that had fought the Persians and would not take the responsibility for freeing the Greeks of Asia from Persian control. They made no objection, however, to Athens' organizing the new Delian League. At home they conscientiously moved to return to their former quietness of life, repression of individualism, and avoidance of contacts with the world around them. It may be that the plainly observable appearance of a new spirit of change in Athens toward democracy intensified the feeling of the Spartans that they had better take measures in defense of the style of society that they preferred. The supervision of the Ephors and the Gerousia was tightened. The archaeological evidence indicates that life became more austere.

The successes of the new league under the control of Athens were such, however, that a few years later, possibly in 475, a debate took place among the Spartans as to whether they should wage a preventive war against Athens and assume her place as leader of the Greeks on the sea. In the account of the debate that we have, one of the Spartans is said to have settled the matter by rehearsing vividly everything that was implied, both for the present and for the future, in Sparta's attempting to become a sea power adequate to inflict such a check upon the Athenians. The Spartans seem to have decided that the whole project was undesirable and probably impossible. At this point, then, the Spartans were aware that the Athenians had become too strong and vigorous for Sparta to be able to maintain her old attitude that she could dictate to Athens and keep her in a subordinate position. For the time being, the old Spartan Alliance, the Hellenic League formed to fight the Persians (to which Athens still belonged), and the new Athenian Alliance, or Delian League, formed a sort of balance of power.

In 469, the Messenians revolted from Sparta. They were not reconquered until 460. The fact that Sparta was deeply involved with the suppression of this revolt and then in addition shaken by earthquakes caused restlessness among the Peloponnesian members of Sparta's alliance, and a certain amount of force had to be used to keep the unruly members from withdrawing. The maintenance of the Spartan system in the Peloponnesus was a fairly difficult job, and Sparta probably chose wisely in not challenging Athenian leadership on the sea.

THE ATHENIAN EMPIRE

Policies and Personalities at Athens

Athens had moved so far from the style and manner of the days before Cleisthenes that a return to them was impossible, even though the ultraconservatives kept a watch and late in the fifth century attempted a revolution that aimed at a restoration of the pre-Solonian constitution. The new rights for the masses and their active participation in the fleet had given Athens a dashing spirit and a sense of unity that would have made any effective retrograde movement impossible. The more affluent had distinguished themselves as hoplites at Marathon and Plataea and even in the naval operations, especially at the Eurymedon River in 467 B.C. But Salamis and Mycale were the great names for the poorer men who served in the fleet to remember.

Yet it is possible to see the personalities and the policies of individuals exerting some influence upon the affairs of Athens at this time. Cimon, the son of Miltiades, was an aristocrat by birth and inclination. He was a handsome, straightforward, soldierly man. He believed in war with Persia and co-operation with Sparta, both of which policies he pressed frankly. As commander of the fleet, he was efficient and popular. The great success at the Eurymedon brought him to the peak of his career.

Themistocles, too, had had his great naval success: Salamis was his masterpiece. His talent for assessing a situation and for making tenable decisions showed best in the wide and difficult field of state policy. The development of the Athenian navy and of the policy of strength on the sea was due to him. It was a difficult policy, but one that was in accord with the times and with the temper of Athens and one that, if directed with wisdom and skill, promised prosperity and greatness to Athens for a long time.

The great admiration that the Athenians felt for Themistocles was mixed with uneasiness occasioned by his moral slipperiness. Again and again he had given rise to suspicions that he was trying to be a member of both sides at once. Yet we do not know exactly why he was ostracized, somewhere around 472. Perhaps it was in a trial of strength as to whether his aggressive policy toward Sparta should be followed to the extreme or a more friendly policy adopted.

True to himself, he was compromised again just after his ostracism. He was believed to have been in sympathetic correspondence with the Spartan king Pausanias. In 478, Pausanias had had to be recalled from his command of the fleet of the Hellenic League in Asiatic waters. A little later, incredible as it seems, he went to Byzantium, somehow set himself up as tyrant there, and renewed his overtures to the Persian king. Again, probably about 470, he was called back to Sparta. The Ephors finally got definite proof of what he had been doing. He fled to a temple for sanctuary, and there they let him starve, only allowing him to come out to die.

The agents of both Sparta and Athens, intending to arrest Themistocles, descended on Argos, where he had settled down for his period of ostracism. He did the conventional thing and headed for the Persian court. A series of adventures and escapades marked his irregular progress thither. Finally he contrived to have himself presented to the king, who was inclined to allow him to explain himself. Themistocles asked for a year, learned the Persian language, and so impressed the king by his account of himself that he was allowed to settle down at Magnesia as the king's pensioner. More than ten years later, when the Athenians had encouraged Egypt to revolt, the king is said to have demanded that he contrive some measure to damage and check the Athenians. Then, as the account goes, Themistocles decided that he had lived long enough.

Further Democratization

The leadership of the progressive group earlier exercised by Themistocles and Aristides (about whose career after his organization of the Delian League hardly anything is known) passed after 470 to Ephialtes and to that Pericles who was soon to become the great leader of Athens. Ephialtes apparently was the stronger of the two men at first and was regarded as more important.

By the middle of the decade of the 460's, the naval league was in complete control of the Aegaean, although the Persians were still not to be despised as a naval power, even after their great defeat of 467 at the Eurymedon River. The League, which was largely under Athenian control, dominated and policed the Aegaean. Cimon had persuaded some of the weaker and less strenuous members to contribute money instead of ships and men. The Athenians took this money, built ships in their own yards, and manned them with their own men, thus steadily increasing their own power relatively to the other members.

In the year 465, Athens sent a group of citizens and allies, ten thousand in all, to colonize a place in Thrace called Nine Roads. Plainly an attempt at control of some large part of the rich natural resources of Thrace, this move raised up a concerted effort of the Thracians in the next year, which inflicted a great disaster on the colony and prevented it from continuing.

In the same year, 465, the rich island of Thasos had withdrawn from the League. The Athenians defeated the thirty-odd ships that Thasos could muster and began a siege of the city. Here again the Athenians made it clear that they would tolerate no withdrawals. The people of Thasos in desperation asked Sparta to help them raise the siege, and it later came out that Sparta had intended to answer the call by invading Attica. But to these elements of power politics was added a pure historical contingency—a major earthquake that destroyed the town of Sparta and killed more than 20,000 people. Many of the Helots now rose in revolt to join the Messenian rebels who had been holding out since 469.

The Spartans turned to Athens for help in their extremity. Ephi- altes, the leader of the democratic forces, urged that Sparta be al- lowed to fall. Cimon, in his straightforward way, urged her support as the partner and yokefellow of Athens. The more generous policy prevailed, and he was sent at the head of the Athenian troops. Other states, too, rallied around, and Sparta was able to fight off this most critical danger and presently to take the offensive against the rebels.

From Sparta, Cimon returned to the siege of Thasos, which ca- pitulated in the summer of 462. Its fleet was confiscated and its walls torn down. Its gold mines were ceded to Athens and its contributions to the League were henceforth to be in money, for it was to have no armed forces. In other words, Thasos was to be a dependent of Athens. But when Cimon returned from Thasos, he was prosecuted by Pericles for mishandling of funds, for the democratic faction regarded him as an obstacle. But he, like Pericles, was notoriously incorrupt- ible, and he was acquitted. Then another appeal for help came from Sparta, which was besieging the rebels in their stronghold and hoping to crush them. Again he was sent to Sparta with troops.

While Cimon was away with a good-sized force of hoplites, prop- ertied men of conservative political views, Ephialtes and Pericles brought forward a measure that they had been planning for some time, a measure to limit the powers of the Council of the Areopagus, which were thought to stand in the way of a properly democratic government. They carried their measure, which may properly be called revolutionary in that it contracted the aristocratic element in the government and widened the democratic. The bitterness aroused by the move is shown by the fact that the conservatives soon pro- cured the murder of Ephialtes.

Perhaps the Spartans heard of this. Perhaps they grew mistrustful of the Athenians or of their influence among the other peoples as- sembled for the siege of the rebel stronghold. At any rate, they brusquely invited the Athenians to go home again. Cimon did so and there tried to have the vote that had been taken when he and the hoplites were absent reconsidered. But the people at home were in- furiated by the Spartan slight; in the end, the legislation stood, and in the spring of 461, Cimon was ostracized. This was the end of good feeling between Athens and Sparta.

The Council of the Areopagus, composed of ex-archons, had had wide powers, both of a general supervisory kind and of a definitely judicial nature. Some of the democrats claimed that many of these powers had been usurped, as power can be by a strong organ of government. Although the Council had probably lost in vigor since the introduction of the lot for archons in 487, it still numbered a good many men of notable families and still had its traditions. As ex-archons, the members were still of the two highest property classes.

The Areopagus was now stripped of all its authority except that of hearing prosecutions involving a religious element (for example, cases of murder or of damage to the sacred olive trees). Its political powers gone, it could not serve as the check upon the people as a whole that it had been before. The people was now fully sovereign.

The Council of Five Hundred (the *Boule*) was given the power to hold the magistrates accountable and the power to make arrests, judge, and execute judgment in certain cases that had belonged to the Areopagus. The summary exercise of such powers by a body not responsible to the people had not been consistent with democracy. Indeed, the exercise of similar powers by the Board of Ephors at Sparta was of cardinal importance in the maintenance of conservative society. In the next century, the Athenian teacher and essayist Isocrates, in his *Areopagiticus,* was to call for a restoration of the power of the Areopagus to deal in a general way with the health of the body politic. John Milton chose to call an essay arguing against similar authority *Areopagitica* in order to challenge Isocrates by his very title. Such far-reaching and unspecified powers are hardly imaginable to those who live in democracies of long-standing and Anglo-Saxon traditions.

ATHENS FIGHTS TWO WARS

Now for two or three generations not only did the Athenians wage wars; they also produced immortal works in the spheres of art and the intellect. Their bounteous energy cannot have been entirely due to the new opportunity of the people as a whole to exercise sovereignty; some of it seems to have been communicated to everyone, even to foreigners who came to Athens to live. The sense that great new things were possible and were coming to pass must have made itself felt in almost all classes.

The naval alliance, which Athens completely controlled by now, continued its war against the Persians. The policy around 460 B.C. was to attempt to complete the conquest of Cyprus, the base of the Persian fleet. But a new possiblity presented itself. Inaros, a Libyan king, raised a revolt in Lower Egypt, apparently not without Athenian encouragement, and promised extravagant rewards to the Athenians for assistance. The fleet left Cyprus, sailed up the Nile, and won a victory. But it was not a decisive victory. The Persians and the loyal Egyptians held out, and for several years this overambitious operation was to divert Athenian power from other theaters.

War with Sparta

It was not only the slight given to Cimon and his soldiers in the year 462 that ended good feeling between Athens and Sparta. The Athenians learned that Sparta had been planning to intervene on behalf of Thasos. Probably they also knew that the Spartans had discussed the possibility of a preventive war against them round the year 475, when it became plain that Athens was very much in the ascendant. If Athens was to continue her imperialistic ways, lording it over the other members of her alliance and deriving good profits from trade, it would be necessary, according to the natural Athenian calculation, to prevent Spartan interference by inflicting some harm on Sparta to check her. It would also be necessary to build up Athenian strength in Greece proper if possible.

Athens seems formally to have ended her membership in the Hellenic League, which had been formed to fight the Persians. When the rebels in Messenia capitulated to Sparta in 460, their right to leave the country was one article of the agreement. Athens received them and finally settled them at Naupactus, a good site on the north shore of the Gulf of Corinth. This was a move in rivalry of Corinth and her trade to the West. In 459, Megara, on the Isthmus of Cornith, left the Spartan Alliance and made a treaty with Athens, because she found the pressure of Corinth hard to bear. As a result, the Athenians helped the people of Megara to build walls from their city to their port of Nisaea, on the Gulf of Corinth. They also sent a garrison to the city. These actions were an affront to both Sparta and Corinth. They gave Athens a port on the route to the West and a strong point on the Isthmus to oppose Spartan marches into northern Greece.

In 458, these Athenian advances led to war with Corinth. At the same time, war broke out with the old rival, Aegina. The Athenians defeated the Aeginetans in a naval battle and laid siege to their city. Corinth sent help to Aegina, but she sent her main forces to attack the Athenians at Megara. The Athenians nevertheless continued the siege of Aegina and defended Megara with reserve troops, the old and the young men. In the next year, 457, the Spartans entered the fray in a curiously indirect way. They sent an army of their alliance, with a modest number of heavy-armed Spartans and some ten thousand allies, to Boeotia to settle a dispute between Doris and Phocis. This army went north without incident. But while it was in Boeotia, the Athenians sent out a naval force to dominate the Gulf of Corinth and prevent the Spartan forces from being ferried across the gulf on their return. They also put troops in position to contest a return by land.

As the Spartan commander weighed the situation, he was approached by members of the oligarchic faction at Athens, which did not slumber all through this century, no matter how outnumbered it was or how hopeless a return to a conservative form of society might seem. These men hoped that the Spartan might be induced to use his army to overthrow the democratic government at Athens. Now was an especially good time to strike, if ever, for Aegina might soon fall and free some Athenian troops, and the long walls from Athens to Peiraeus would soon be completed, making Athens, Peiraeus, and the space between the walls all one great fortress.

The Athenians had prepared themselves for a possible Spartan attack by gathering a respectable army of their own hoplites and of troops from their allies, although the members of the naval alliance felt no little irritation at being required to co-operate in such operations as this. A battle was fought at Tanagra in Boeotia. The Spartans won, with losses far heavier than they could afford; losses were also heavy on the Athenian side. The Spartan army, too depleted by the battle to remain an effective instrument of policy against Athens, went home.

About two months later, another Athenian army went to Boeotia, defeated the army of the Boeotian League, expelled the oligarchic leaders whose position Sparta favored, and set up democracies in the cities. Athens was now in control of central Greece. Before the end of 457, the long walls were finished, making her position slightly stronger, and Aegina gave in. Athens took away Aegina's fleet, razed her walls and forced her to join the naval alliance as a dependent of Athens.

In the next few years, Athenian power in Greece was supported by constant demonstrations of sea power. On land Athens was influential in Greece because she had forced the establishment of democracies in many places, supporting them with the threat of armed intervention. The point at issue in the constant tension between the few and the many in the Greek *poleis* was who or how many men should have full voting rights so as to control the essential policies of the *polis*. Naturally Sparta favored conservative governments in other *poleis* and Athens favored democratic governments, and each expected that in a great contest the *poleis* of its own general stamp would give it support.

A New Phase: After 454 B.C.

In 454, the Athenians and their allies who had been participating for several years in the revolt of Inaros and trying to free Egypt from the Persians suffered a disastrous defeat that put an end to all their ambitions in that direction. In this same year and probably because of this reverse, the Athenians took all the money of the naval alliance, which was deposited at Delos, and transferred it to the protection of Athena at Athens. This was a forthright declaration, if one was needed, that Athens regarded herself as mistress of the alliance and regarded all its resources as being at her disposal.

For some years now Pericles had been the leading man in Athens. He was elected general of his tribe every year, but it was his character and his abilities rather than his office that made him the most important person in the city. In 457, he had asked the people to rescind the ostracism of Cimon, who had returned and resumed command of the naval forces. Even though Cimon was not active in politics, he was the natural head of the conservative element that wished to co-operate with Sparta. There is no record of any great activity in the rivalry between Sparta and Athens during the three or four years after the disaster of 454 in Egypt, and in 451 Cimon brought about a truce between them that was to last for five years. He also conducted successful operations against the Persian fleet in the Aegaean that brought about a peace between Athens and Persia, although he died without seeing it. The peace, concluded in 448 and known as the Peace of Callias, provided that the Greek cities in Asia should be autonomous and settled the long quarrel between the Greeks and Persia with a reasonable definition of the sphere of each and a guarantee of peaceful trading on the sea.

To free the East Greeks from Persia was the purpose for which the Athenians and the other Greeks had combined thirty years before. Possibly Themistocles had foreseen that these Greeks, free of Persia, would come under the sway of Athens. Athens now had an empire. By 448 the only states that still contributed ships were Chios, Lesbos, and Samos. The rest had been persuaded to make their contributions in money, which came to be regarded forthrightly as tribute, instead of in ships. They now had no means of asserting themselves against Athens. At one time or another, many had attempted to secede from the alliance and had been forced to remain. Garrisons were placed in the *poleis* that had attempted to withdraw, and Athens chose the personnel of their governments.

All mints belonging to the allies were closed, and the use of Athenian coinage and standards was imposed on them. Although the automony of the allies was disregarded, it was at least an economic benefit to the whole alliance and even to people outside it to have this honest coinage in common use. Another infringement of the rights of the allies was the confiscation of land for the planting of Athenian military colonies, called cleruchies. This system (which the Romans were to follow later) was excellent for keeping an eye on people of doubtful loyalty. The Athenians, having taken charge of all the money of the League in 454, thereafter spent it as they pleased, and after that year the synod of the League ceased to convene.

The Thirty Years' Truce

Late in the year 447, the tide suddenly began to turn against the Athenians. The oligarchs whom the Athenians had driven out of

Boeotia returned and managed to gain control of several of the cities. A small force of Athenians, backed by troops of the allies, went to Boeotia, captured Chaeronea, and placed a garrison there, sending off the men of the city to be sold into slavery. A strong force of the oligarchic exiles then attacked the Athenians and defeated them, inflicting heavy losses. The Athenians evacuated Boeotia to gain the release of those of their number who were captured. The oligarchs at once regained complete control.

Now Euboea revolted, and in the other direction Megara revolted with the assistance of Corinth. The word came that the Peloponnesian forces were on the march. The Spartan king invaded Attica with a strong army. Suddenly he withdrew, and the word went around that Pericles had bribed him. Then Pericles took a strong force to Euboea and brought the whole island back under Athenian control.

Negotiations with Sparta during the winter resulted, early in 445, in the conclusion of the Thirty Years' Peace. Peace between the two powers and their allies was now to rest upon an explicit agreement, backed by necessity rather than good will. It was agreed that neither party would attack the other for thirty years. Because the question of influence was important, it was provided that any state not allied at the time of the treaty to one or the other might make an alliance with one or the other. This arrangement at least allowed a respite from warfare.

CHAPTER

21

PERICLEAN DEMOCRACY

The Thirty Years' Peace of the year 445 B.C. was observed by both sides until 431; it gave them both a respite from the losses and waste of their struggle, a respite that made them more powerful and prosperous than they had been before. The Athenian Empire was now at its height, and its guiding spirit was Pericles.

PERICLES AS LEADER OF ATHENS

Pericles, like Themistocles, was an extraordinarily clear thinker who could assess the factors in a given situation with such exactness that he could foresee the consequences of a policy better than other men could. It was an advantage to him that his family was one of the most distinguished in Athens; on his mother's side he was of the great Alcmaeonid clan, and his father's family was also prominent. The democratic Athenian voter consistently preferred the genuine aristocrat. Xanthippus, his father, was a wealthy man and had commanded the Athenian contingent at Mycale, where in 479 the combined Greek forces had successfully opened their campaign in Asia Minor against the Persians. Agariste, his mother, was the niece of Cleisthenes, an Alcmaeonid and the author of the liberalizing constitution that is generally called by his name. Pericles' attitudes were so thoroughly favorable to democracy that no one could accuse him of oligarchic sympathies because of his family connections. His character was also helpful to his career, for he was above any suspicion of peculation, or of shaping his policies for his personal advantage, whereas the plain odor of corruption had attended many an act of Themistocles.

Pericles and Ephialtes had come to the fore together in the late '60's as the leaders of the democratic element. When Ephialtes was assassinated, the sole leadership was left to Pericles. The manner in which he guided the Athenian *polis* during the next thirty years is worthy of study. During that time, he was regularly elected general of his tribe. The office of general, which by now was the position of military leader of one of Cleisthenes' ten tribes, was the only important office to which a man could be elected. Archons could not be voted into power, for even though his deme put a man up for the archonship, the lot would not necessarily fall on him in the second stage of the process. The attempts of scholars to find some way in which Pericles as general enjoyed a constitutional position superior to that of the other nine generals have not been successful; there was no such recognized position. Further, the board of the ten generals did not constitute a government or an informal ruling group. There was no tradition of their banding together to promote policies.

Pericles was able to commend his views and measures to the Assembly over this long period because of his character and dependablity, his incorruptibility, his sound ability as military man, his skill as an orator and political manager, the essential harmony of his views with the wishes and temper of the people, and his great skill in analyzing and predicting in the sphere of government. Of course he was not always in the forefront of affairs. Most of the speeches and proposals came from his friends and lieutenants while Pericles saved himself for the more important occasions when strong influence was necessary. The Athenian people was a great, restless, wrathful beast, which might at any time turn on its leaders and rend them. Pericles led it, shaped it, and controlled it. It turned on him once at the end of his career, just after the beginning of the great Peloponnesian War in 431. Even so, the people repented and restored him to favor and office before his death in 429.

Thucydides, in his history of the Peloponnesian War, gives an account of the funeral speech that Pericles had been chosen to deliver over the Athenian dead in the first year of that war. Their cremated bones lay in state for three days, during which time relatives made offerings to their dead. Then the bones were put into ten cypress coffins, one for each tribe, and carried on wagons to the place where they were given the honor of a public burial and where Pericles spoke from a platform built for the occasion. The speech is interesting as a demonstration of the persuasiveness of Pericles and as the first known attempt to convey to a people a picture of their ideal type (something the Romans of the Republic were later to do with great skill in their presentation of the portrait of the old Roman).

Pericles began, not with the bereavement and the grief of his hearers, but with the valor and constancy of earlier Athenians who had made Athens the only Greek city free and continuously inhabited from the earliest times, especially the valor and constancy of the last generation, their fathers, who had built the empire which they now enjoyed. Then he turned to the praise of the Athenian system, under which men were equal before the law and every man, no matter how obscure, might have his chance to serve the state.

Here he was plainly referring to the Spartan system, in which the poor might easily find themselves excluded from participation. Much of what followed was also meant to contrast the Athenians favorably with their rivals and present opponents, the Spartans, for the Spartan system could well symbolize the background of conservative governments against which Athens stood as the democratic exception. The Athenians, said Pericles, do not object to other people's doing as they please; that is, they do not insist on a rigid uniformity of thought and manners. At Athens men live in pleasant homes and enjoy pleasures organized by the *polis*. Athens is not closed to strangers for fear they might learn some secret of Athenian life or of the military system, for the Athenians rely on their courage and discipline rather than on secret maneuvers or devices. Whereas the Spartans toil all their lives to be ready for warfare, the Athenians live in an easier and pleasanter manner and still are able to do better than hold their own against equal numbers of Spartans.

We, he said, cultivate the beautiful with moderate expenditure and cultivate the things of the spirit without becoming soft. Wealth with us is for use rather than a symbol of status. The Athenian is expected to take part in public affairs. We regard the man as of no account who applies himself only to his personal affairs, and we feel that we are best governed by general knowledge and general discus-sion of what measures are before us in the Assembly. Our citizens know what they are about when they face dangers, for we do not train them to act with blind obedience nor do we fear that knowledge of the dangers they face will lessen their courage to act. We are gen-erous in spirit beyond other peoples, for it is our pleasure to confer benefits freely upon others and not to calculate the cost too closely. Our city, then, shows the Greeks what a *polis* can be, and the in-dividual Athenian can show himself the complete man, ready to present whatever facet of himself the occasion demands. The proof of this is the glory that Athens has won, a glory that shall last for-ever, with no need of Homer as its poet. Such is the city for which these dead have died.

Here Pericles turned to words of direct consolation to the be-reaved, having skillfully drawn the picture of the unrivaled worth of the *polis* for which the sacrifice was made. Not only must his hearers have gone home feeling a sober joy at the sacrifice, but they must also have felt themselves reinforced in the idea that Athens herself was the supreme value in life and that to be an Athenian was worth every effort.

EVENTS OF THE PERIOD

Pericles' Struggle with Thucydides

Pericles had carried through a number of measures that to the con-servatives seemed reprehensible. He had arranged that the state should pay jurors for their days of attendance in court. To the Athe-nian courts came the business of the allies in the Delian League as well as the Athenians'. The original purpose of this provision had doubtless been to make sure that the courts of the other *poleis* of the League should not be the means of constant attacks on the pro-Athenian element everywhere, for the Greeks early realized that formal prosecutions were an effective way of discrediting or removing political opponents. Now, however, the trial of these cases in Athens gave an opportunity to spread some of the profits of empire (at least in many instances), especially among elderly men who were past rowing in the fleet or similar active occupations and who could use the sum paid for jury duty, even though no man with a family could live on this as a daily wage.

Pericles had begun to use the funds of the naval alliance to rebuild temples in Athens and to build new ones. Here was more work. He continued the system of sending out cleruchies, or military colonies. Some of them went to places where land had been confiscated because of opposition to Athens. Such was the case with Euboea in 445, as a result of the struggle that led to the treaty of peace in that year. Many other cleruchies were placed on land the right to which had been peaceably acquired, for during all the fourteen years of the peace, from 445 to 431, the Athenians were always on the watch for new alliances with which to strengthen themselves or for new points of economic contact in such places as Thrace or the region of the Black Sea. There was good farm land here and there for two or three hundred men who would undertake the obligation of being on call for military service.

Thucydides, the son of Melesias (not the historian of the Peloponnesian War, who was a generation younger and was the son of Olorus), was a relative of Cimon and expressed the conservative view with the same straightforward honesty that Cimon had shown. He surrounded himself in the Assembly with a group of sober and influential men who signified by their presence around him their approval of his able speeches against the measures of Pericles, which to him seemed bribery of the people, dishonest use of the funds of the Delian League, and likely to corrupt the *polis*. It was he who compared the building of the beautiful structures on the Acropolis out of the funds of the League to a prostitute's decking herself out in expensive finery.

The conservatives were easily able to point out the less admirable side of the democratic system, just as a democrat could have pointed out the less admirable side of the conservative systems of the day, and neither party would have been willing to admit the force of the points made by the other. Pericles answered that the tribute money belonged to Athens because she furnished the security for which the others were paying. The furnishing of employment to the citizens or the granting of lands to them as cleruchs, the beautification of the city and the new splendor of the festivals were the rewards of their efforts and dangers. The real question was which of the two men could command more support, for there was no way of their coming to any compromise or accommodation of their views. The conservatives tried once to ostracize Pericles and failed. Then in 443, Thucydides was ostracized.

The Revolt of Samos

Samos and Miletus came to blows over a territorial question. Miletus, worsted, appealed to Athens. Athens had no right to interfere, for by the treaty that had made the alliance in 478, the members were declared to be autonomous with the right to make war among themselves. But Athens had no intention of allowing them to go their way in such matters. She ordered Samos to cease her hostile action and to submit the question to Athens for arbitration. Samos refused, knowing that Athens as arbiter would not be impartial. This was in the year 440.

Pericles at once sailed to Samos with an adequate force, took the Samians unawares, set up a garrison and a democratic government, imposed a fine and carried off hostages, and withdrew. But some of the Samian conservatives who had escaped to the mainland enlisted the aid of the Persians, recaptured Samos, and liberated the hostages, who had been left at Lemnos. This move encouraged Byzantium to revolt from the Athenian alliance.

Again Pericles acted with decision, but found it necessary to besiege Samos for nine months before she finally yielded. The Samians suffered the usual treatment: they had to destroy their walls and surrender their fleet, thus making themselves entirely dependent on Athens. Byzantium now returned to the fold. The effect of this incident was to make the allies all the more conscious that they really were subjects of Athens.

Athenian Colonization

Shortly after the making of the Thirty Years' Peace, the people of Sybaris, in southern Italy, asked the Athenians and Spartans to help them in refounding their city, which had been destroyed by the neighboring city of Croton. The Spartans refused; the Athenians accepted and supervised the gathering of volunteers from the Peloponnesus as well as from Athens. Before long there was friction; the original Sybarites were driven out and in 443 there was a new formal founding with a new name, Thurii, under the auspices of Athens. This was Athens' first colonial foundation (cleruchies were not new *poleis*), and it was done in the grand style. Hippodamus of Miletus, the eminent city-planner, laid out the new city. Lampon of Athens, an expert on religious matters, was one of the two official founders. Protagoras of Abdera, a leading sophist (whom we shall discuss later), devised a new and doubtless very up-to-date code of laws. The colonists were drawn from all over Greece. The direct leadership of Athens, however, and the protection of Athena were soon specifically rejected by the people of Thurii, and the city was put under the protection of Delphic Apollo. Thereafter the city was undistinguished among the Greek *poleis* of southern Italy.

The chief attempts of the Athenians to extend their influence without contravening the Thirty Years' Peace and to gain access to more of the resources useful to a naval power took place in Sicily, where treaties were made with some of the Greek cities, and at Amphipolis in Thrace, and in the Black Sea region. In 436, they drove away a native people and founded the city of Amphipolis on the Strymon River in Thrace, up river from Eion, where they had a naval base. It was useful for them to have another outpost in this country, which produced minerals and cereals and above all timber for ships. The new city soon flourished. Although the Athenians in it were a minority, Athens controlled it by her general power and the proximity of the naval station down the river.

Pericles himself led a naval parade around the Black Sea with a fine fleet. He made commercial arrangements with a native ruler on the north shore who could influence the flow of wheat from southern Russia, made plans for sending colonists to two or three important points, and assured the Greek cities of the region that the Athenians stood ready to protect Greek interests.

THE PERICLEAN SYSTEM

Citizenship

The citizenship of Athens, like that of every other ancient body politic, was a precious possession, which was not at all taken for granted. It carried with it privileges, perquisites, immunities, and also obligations. The modern citizen of the United States may lose sight of the value and the obligations of his citizenship, but in early days it was not easy to do so. Most Greek states did not readily bestow their citizenship on outsiders. Although Sparta sometimes granted her citizenship to *perioeci* and to Helots, she almost never granted it to real outsiders. The Athenians, too, were very slow to bestow citizenship on outsiders. They even took it away from some who had been thought to have it when, in the time of Pericles (451 B.C.), they passed a law that no one should be an Athenian citizen except those whose parents were both Athenian citizens. This disfranchised some of the children of Athenian fathers and non-Athenian mothers; a selfish unwillingness to share the profits of empire made men willing to inflict this blow on some few of their number. Naturally the children of noncitizens did not acquire citizenship merely by being born in Attica.

The Athenians were ingenious in using the great value of citizenship as a lever by making the entire or partial loss of citizenship the penalty for various offenses, both civil and criminal. They were like us in making it possible for the state to confiscate property to pay fines or judgments or to make good embezzled public moneys, but in Athens, if the citizen thus lost his property, he also lost his civil rights. There was a long list of offenses for which a man might lose such a privilege as speaking in the Assembly or bringing actions in the courts. For some heinous offenses he might lose all his civil rights; such offenses were the avoidance of military service or cowardice when on military service, embezzlement, bribery, or mistreatment of parents.

The Demes

Athenian citizenship was based on membership in the demes. The new father enrolled his new son in his own deme, and later the youngster was received into manhood as a member of that deme. A man's official name was a single name, the name of his father, and the name of his deme. The great orator of the next century, for example, was Demosthenes, son of Demosthenes, of the deme Paianea. The list of the deme's members was kept by its clerk. If it became necessary to prove citizenship, however, as was the case when one was chosen for the *Boule*, this list would not suffice, and witnesses had to appear to swear to the fact of citizenship. Membership in the deme was hereditary; if a man moved to another part of Attica, he kept his membership in his old deme and enrolled his children there, not where he now lived.

Not all demes were the same size or contained the same number of citizens. It is a fair guess, however, that the average deme had in it several hundred families of citizens. It was a genuine social unit, as well as a political unit, and capable of evoking loyalty. The Athenian could, in fact, feel loyalty to deme, tribe, and *polis* just as the American can feel loyalty to city, state, and nation.

The deme had a definite territory and generally a modest official building. It had a demarch, or mayor, and the citizens occasionally met in an assembly. One of their functions when assembled was the election of candidates for the *Boule*. By some sort of proportional representation the demes elected their men, who then went through a process of drawing lots (now little understood), the result of the two processes being that each tribe had fifty members in the *Boule*. Presumably, whenever lists of citizens were needed for such a purpose as making up panels of jurors, the making of the lists began with the citizen rolls kept in the demes. The deme also had financial and religious functions. Presumably each deme had a religious cult with regular observances. To us, the most interesting part of the religious aspect of the deme is the celebration of the Rural Dionysia, or the festival of Dionysus, which, as we have seen, was celebrated in the demes in the dark days of December.

The Tribes

That large group of Greeks who called themselves Ionians and to whom the Athenians belonged had traditionally divided themselves into four tribes, as the group known as Dorians had divided themselves into three. These tribes were a significant part of the early organization of both peoples. Although the ten new Athenian tribes devised by Cleisthenes sound artificial in their combination of three different elements of the people into each one, they proved to be a useful part of the new constitution, capable of performing worthwhile functions and evoking a minor loyalty.

Membership in the new tribes was hereditary, as in the demes. The tribe, although it had no specific territory, did have a place where its records were kept, for it had to keep lists of its members and records of its formal acts. Like the deme, it also had to have a place for the performance of the religious acts that were necessary for such organizations. It had officers, and its members assembled at certain times to transact business. One important piece of business for the tribe or its officers was the selection for the *Boule* of fifty men by lot from the lists sent up by the demes. The tribe's important electoral function was the election of its general, one of the ten who commanded the ten tribal contingents of the army.

Cleisthenes' creation of the tribes was a stroke of genius, for a unit of government was needed at about this level. He succeeded in relegating the old tribes to the background, where they continued to perform religious functions hallowed by time and custom. The new tribes had the great advantage of not representing the interest of any middle-sized or intermediate group in the state, while they performed a function intermediate between those of deme and *polis*. They could evoke loyalty and spirit in more than one way. Because the army was organized by tribes, the men served together in the field. They also worked together in organizing and training the army, which involved a good deal of common effort and time. And when for a tenth of each year its representatives in the *Boule* were the responsible government on full-time duty, the tribe must have watched their performance attentively. Other activities, too, promoted tribal spirit; for example, at the City Dionysia each tribe entered a chorus to sing in a formal contest.

The Assembly

Every young man who had reached his eighteenth birthday and was in possession of full citizen rights was entitled to participate in the work of the *Ecclesia,* or Assembly. After the time of Cleisthenes, he did not need to own land. In the time of Pericles, the Assembly had four regular meetings in each prytany—a word that can be used to mean both the period of time (one tenth of the year) and the group of members of the *Boule* who were on full-time duty during the time. At the end of the fifth century, pay for attendance at the Assembly was to be introduced, as pay for jury duty was introduced by Pericles; at this time, however, any citizen whose income depended on his own day-to-day efforts had to resign himself to losing a day's work and income if he chose to attend a meeting of the Assembly.

The Assembly was sovereign in Athens, not only in theory but in fact. No official or group could dictate to it, check it, or revise its actions, as the Areopagus had been able to do before 462 B.C. There was no unofficial group that by shrewdness and experience could manage it behind the scenes, although the career of Pericles shows that an exceptional man might openly lead it, but not dominate it. The career of Pericles also shows that the Assembly could gain genuine and forceful continuity only through the efforts of forceful individuals, although naturally a certain mechanical continuity was readily achieved. There were no powers of finance or aristocratic privilege that could dictate policies or quietly exert decisive influence on the Assembly. There was no written constitution that might have been difficult to change. The locus of power was in the people meeting in their assembly.

One of the four scheduled meetings in each prytany was a major meeting at which certain standing questions had to be raised. The conduct of the magistrates had to be reviewed and approved or condemned. The matter of the food supply had to be reviewed. In this time of naval supremacy, the food supply was not a very difficult problem, but the accounts of the meetings of the Assembly in the fourth century contain many references to anxiety about the flow of essential cereals to the city at a time when Athens did not have control of the sea lanes. The general state of the army and navy was another standing question.

Other matters were to be brought up at a specified meeting once a year. Aristotle, who wrote late in the fourth century, testifies that at the appointed meeting the question was put to the Assembly whether it wanted a session devoted to voting on ostracism, in spite of the fact that no one had been ostracized for nearly a hundred years. In the sixth prytany, the *Boule* was expected to schedule the presentation to the Assembly of the names of citizens who had failed to fulfill promises that they had formally made to the people.

Business other than that prescribed for certain meetings was brought before the Assembly only by the *Boule*. It was unconstitutional to propose a new subject of discussion in the Assembly; the proposal must be drafted and presented by the *Boule*. This provision offered some check on hasty action. If the Assembly did not like the preliminary proposal, it could reject it, amend it, send it back to be amended, or even offer a new one. All that was needed was that the *Boule* should have initiated the discussion of the subject.

The sovereign people attended to all the government of Athens and her empire. The officials, whom we shall discuss, were regarded as agents of the people and not sufficiently independent to initiate policies. They certainly were not legislative leaders, as the President of the United States or the governor of a state is expected to be. The Assembly scrutinized their actions ten times a year, and they had to render account on leaving office. There were many administrative boards, too, as closely watched and controlled as the officials were. Although some of the major priesthoods were allowed to remain in the hands of the old noble families in which they had been passed down from time immemorial, the Assembly controlled the creation of any new religious observance or priesthood or the construction of any religious edifice or the expenditure of any money for religious purposes. It controlled all Athens' relations to her allies, those of the naval league and the other allies. It had jurisdiction over such high crimes as treason, a jurisdiction taken away from the Council of the Areopagus; thus it had tried Miltiades, the hero of Marathon, for an attack on Paros in 489 that had laid him open to suspicion of using the naval forces for devious personal ends.

The judiciary, as we shall see, was not the separate and independent arm of the government that we like to think it in the United States. Among the Greeks, to judge was thought of as the prerogative and duty of the whole people, and the Athenians who sat as juries should be thought of as committees of the whole people presided over by officials but not controlled by judges as our juries are.

It is not certain how many people were usually present at meetings of the Assembly. A quorum for the major meetings of each prytany seems to have been 6,000. Presumably the people of more means were more regular in their attendance. A man naturally acquired a certain sense for the conduct of the affairs of the Assembly after attending a few meetings and afterward hearing some discussions about them. As a result, much business could be dispatched efficiently without much inept discussion or other waste of time.

Although theoretically every citizen had a right to address the Assembly, in practice the people were not readily approachable. The unpracticed orator who ventured to address them, the man who had no weight of personality, or one who seemed to be wasting their time might even be hooted down. Naturally a group of men arose, often known simply as "the rhetors" or "the speakers," who customarily took part in the debates in the Assembly and were listened to out of respect for the proven worth of their judgments. A man who had some property to support him might make a career out of being such an unofficial adviser of the people. Having made himself a real authority on the affairs of Athens, domestic or foreign, he would spend much time in discussion or in the execution of tasks delegated to him by the people, perhaps serving on some of the many boards and commissions, embassies, or military and naval commands. He was likely to find his income augmented by allied states or foreigners who wished to gain influence with the Assembly. By custom these payments were regarded as gifts rather than bribes.

The Offices

In 487, a generation after Cleisthenes, a change was made in the method of choosing archons that left the generals the only important officers who were elected. Not all who sought to be leaders of the Assembly sought election to the generalship, as Pericles did. Some may have mistrusted their military ability or preferred not to be burdened with the duties of the office. The generals could approach the *Boule* directly and ask it to make proposals to the Assembly. As high elected officials of their tribes, they had a certain prestige. Yet the office of general was not usually combined with great political influence; Pericles was an exception.

After the reform of 487, the archons were chosen by lot from a list sent up by the demes. By the time of Pericles, both the third and the fourth property classes were eligible for the archonship, in practice if not in law. Although the functions of the archons did not perhaps require so much ability as those of the generals, still they were not so simple that any ordinary man could perform them offhand. We find that a good many Greek (and Roman) officials availed themselves of assessors in such situations. Literally, the word means people who sat by them. That is, one could ask a more experienced friend to help. There are evidences that the friend sometimes helped so thoroughly that he, too, was prosecuted for the embezzlement of public monies. Many an official must have got help and comfort from the slender permanent staff, who generally were slaves and who naturally knew the details of the ordinary work.

There is some doubt as to the functions at this time of "the" archon (he had no further title), who had originally been in charge of the government. We do know, however, that he had jurisdiction over legal cases that involved family relations. The archon *basileus*, or king archon, still performed the religious functions that at the creation of his office had been transferred to him from the vanishing king. He presided over all trials for impiety or for homicide, because homicide was still thought of as bringing pollution and being a religious matter. He was the general supervisor of religion and was in charge of all the cults of the *polis*.

The polemarch had by this period yielded his military jurisdiction to the generals, and his chief function no longer had anything to do with war. Rather, he was in charge of all legal dealings between citizens and noncitizens. The *thesmothetae*, the six junior archons, were still in charge of the whole body of the laws. The nine archons had never formed a college that worked as one and exerted influence as a group. Now they were people of less influence than they had been before, and the fact was bound to be reflected in the Council of the Areopagus, which was formed of all the ex-archons, who became members for life.

There were about seven hundred officials in all, and virtually all of them were selected by lot. All the officials were paid, as was the *Boule*. There were more boards and committees of officials than seem necessary to get the work done; perhaps the idea was partly to distribute responsibility and partly to reduce opportunities for peculation. In naval matters, for example, the assembly decided whether

any new triremes were to be built during a year and settled on th
number. The *Boule* was in charge of the building of the ships, bu
worked through a board of ten. Another board of ten was in charg
of the yards.

An interesting feature of the Athenian system was the *leitourgiae*
or liturgies, services requisitioned by the *polis* from the richer citi
zens. In some modern states, the richer citizen is required to pa
heavier taxes than the poorer one. In Athens, he was required t
give his money, but he was also in charge of the spending of it. On
such requisition or liturgy was the trierarchy. The trierarchs wer
each responsible for outfitting a trireme, for outfitting and trainin
the crew, and for commanding the ship at sea, even in time of war
Perhaps some wealthy citizens of modern countries would find such
service more gratifying than merely paying a large income tax.

Another satisfying liturgy was the providing of the choruses fo
the singing contest of the tribes and the choruses for the tragedie
and comedies at the great festival of the City Dionysia. Here, as ir
naval affairs, the Athenians were keen and expert. The rich man wh
undertook to train a chorus, like the one who undertook to manage
ship, could find a great many good performers of every kind an
men who were expert at coaching them for a splendid performance
There were prizes for the best plays, as there were for the best ships
Modern Athens still has some of the "choregic" monuments erected
by the men who provided choruses for prize-winning plays. Bu
there was other work to do to make the great festival a success, and
more than one board was active. At the end, when the excitemen
was over, a review of the whole course of the festival was a part o
the regular order of business in the Assembly.

There was a surprising array of magistrates and boards to manage
the financial affairs of the *polis*. The income of the *polis* was from
taxes, rents, and fines, in addition to which there was the money of
the naval league. At every stage, there were two or three boards or
commissions through whose hands the money had to pass, each
watching the others and signing receipts for one another.

The Two Councils

In 462 B.C., there occurred a decisive change in the Athenian constitution comparable to the changes made by Solon and Cleisthenes

Although Cleisthenes had reorganized the *Boule* instituted by Solon and had given it the function of preparing all the business to be dealt with by the Assembly, he had not taken anything away from the older Council of the Areopagus. The Areopagus retained powers that evidently were enough to make the friends of democracy feel that the people were not yet in control of their own affairs. The whole matter is very tantalizing, however, for later writers seem not to have known precisely what authority the Areopagus had before and after the change of 462. They knew only that Ephialtes, the democratic leader, took away some powers of the Areopagus and was assassinated, probably in revenge by the conservatives, before he could do more.

Apparently the Areopagus lost some of its power to try religious cases, but kept cases of deliberate homicide, which must have been almost the first crime over which the *polis* asserted its jurisdiction. The courts took the cases that the Areopagus relinquished. Other jurisdiction, such as that over magistrates derelict in their duty, went to the *Boule*. The third power, and by far the most important, was that of general supervision. Seemingly the Areopagus had been able to inflict fines and to take other punitive or repressive action without even stating a reason. Such authority is the kind that the heads of the clans had probably been used to exercising in the old days, the kind most natural and useful to an oligarch, and the kind most distasteful to a democrat. This power was not transferred to the *Boule* or the courts, but dropped. The people could indeed exercise a comparable power of supervision, but only in full view and according to rules.

The *Boule* was extremely useful in that it served to link all other agencies of the *polis*. Any event of significance was reported to it and all agencies of the government reported to it. It proposed action to the Assembly when action seemed indicated. If the members of the *Boule* had served for life (as Roman senators did), they would have been in practical control of the government because of their monopoly of detailed information and their increasing skill in making judgments and handling affairs. Because they were chosen by lot from the demes' lists, it was hardly possible to plan on becoming a member. In addition, they held office for only one year and could not count on being chosen again, either in the following year or in any other.

The Courts

Cleisthenes did not alter the *Heliaea*, the single court of the people that had been instituted by Solon. At some time toward the middle of the fifth century, the court was broken into a number of divisions called dicasteries, usually of 201 or 501 jurors, or dicasts. These juries, so large according to our notions, were thought of as divisions of the whole people. They were presided over by a magistrate, who acted only as chairman. He had none of the powers of the modern judge except that of directing the whole course of the trial. Since the 201 or 501 jurors represented the whole people, their decision was final; there was no other power or agency to which appeal might properly be made. Nor was there a professional expert, like our judge, to give rulings during the trial and instruct the representatives of the people as to how they should reach a verdict. Every year the *thesmothetae*, the six junior archons, chose a group of 6,000 for jurors from those who volunteered for the task. They administered the oath to them, divided them into panels of 201 for civil cases and 501 for criminal cases, and attended to their pay. The daily pay for jurors was instituted by Pericles to make jury service possible for those of limited means, or, as the conservatives put it, as another way of using the people's money to bribe the people.

At this period, then, we find that the Areopagus still retained jurisdiction over homicide cases, that jurisdiction over cases involving family relations is one of the few functions that we can confidently assign to "the" archon, and that the archon *basileus* had jurisdiction in religious matters and the polemarch in cases involving Athenians and noncitizens. All other cases came before the people sitting as a court.

In civil matters, only the injured party or those in fairly close relationship could bring suit. In criminal matters, Solon had ruled that anyone could prosecute, a rule that, among other effects, made it possible for a powerful patron to act on behalf of a humble man who had been injured and who did not himself dare to bring suit. A prosecution was begun by summoning the defendant before the magistrate in charge. A simple preliminary procedure served to establish the issue and to put both parties on oath to support their allegations. The calendars of all the courts were crowded.

When the case came on, it was handled simply. Both parties had to represent themselves. They could interrogate each other and each other's witnesses. They could appeal to the feelings of the jury with the *argumentum ad hominem,* or frank appeal to prejudice, the successful use of which would cause a case to be retried today. The jury was flattered to have a defendant appeal to it for mercy. To bring in one's wife and small children was a standard piece of stage-setting, or to bare one's breast and show the scars received in the defense of the *polis.* Exchanging personal abuse of the most indecent kind was customary.

It was a recognized practice to try to injure one's personal enemies or political opponents by prosecuting them for any slips they made, such as the lapses in bookkeeping that seem to have been regrettably common among the officials. When Ephialtes was leading up to the removal of powers from the Areopagus in 462, he prosecuted several of its members. We cannot be sure what the charge was, but it seems to have been a matter of accounts. Many of the friends and associates of Pericles were subjected to politically motivated prosecutions. It was a necessary rule that the prosecutor who failed to obtain one-fifth of the votes incurred a severe penalty.

The *graphe paranomon,* or writ of unconstitutionality, often served as the basis for a purely political prosecution. Once the *Boule* had introduced a subject to the Assembly, any citizen could offer a new law or measure or proposal for action as a means of dealing with it. If what he offered was adopted by the Assembly, any other citizen could prosecute him by this writ, alleging that the new measure was improper or was in conflict with existing law. Any active statesman continually made proposals that the Assembly accepted. Because any one of them might lead to prosecution, an active man might face several such suits in a year.

The so-called sycophants also made use of the courts for their own advantage. Because anyone was allowed to initiate a criminal prosecution, these men brought suits against the wealthy, hoping to be able to extort money in return for dropping the prosecution. We can

see that there might be two points of view about this activity: th
wealthy man detected in some small irregularity might regard a pros
ecution as a form of blackmail, whereas others might regard it as th
performance of a patriotic duty. It seems established, however, tha
there was a class of those who prosecuted only as a kind of black
mail. As a result, apparently, it became customary for prosecutors t
protest their personal enmity to the defendant in order to avoid th
suggestion of sycophancy. Forthright and professed attempts to injur
one's personal enemies were a recognized part of Greek life.

Still another activity of the courts, strange to us, was the contin
ued scrutiny of officials. Those men to whom the sovereign peop
delegated power were closely watched. The new members of th
Boule and the new archons were tested and approved by the *Boul*
before they took office, but all other officials underwent their exami
nation, or *dokimasia*, in the courts. Certain persons were exclude
from office; those, for example, who had suffered partial or complet
loss of citizenship or those who had not yet rendered account fo
some other office. The man who had no such disabilities had to prov
before the *Boule* or the court that he was of the third generation o
citizens, that he had performed all his filial and military duties, tha
he had a family tomb, and that he performed his duties to certain re
ligious cults, those of "ancestral Apollo" and "Zeus of the family.
If no one successfully cast doubts upon his character, he was the
certified to hold the office to which he had been elected or chosen b
lot. As we know, once in every prytany the performance of the offi
cials was reviewed by the Assembly, if the *Boule* saw fit to raise
question, and, in addition, each official had to undergo a scrutiny be
fore a court at the end of his term. All this must have taken a grea
deal of time, even if jurymen experienced in the process did i
efficiently.

The Essentials of Radical Democracy

We have spoken of Solon, Cleisthenes, and Ephialtes as the au
thors of significant changes in the Athenian constitution. There wa
no one time at which the further changes were made that turne
Athens into the radical democracy of the age of Pericles. But we ca

st them here and say that they were made sometime between the ork of Ephialtes in 462 and the death of Pericles in 429.

The offices were made more democratic by the reduction of the property qualifications. They became open to members of the third nd even the fourth class rather than to the members of the first two lasses only. The *polis* began to pay its officials rather than expect hem to be wealthy enough to devote themselves to public affairs without compensation. There were two extensions of this principle generation or so later: pay was given for days spent attending the Assembly and for days spent in the theater at the City Dionysia, bascally a religious festival. A third method of making it possible for he magistrates to come from the whole citizen body was to choose nany of them by sortition, or lot. This to the Greeks seemed the emocratic way of choosing magistrates; straight election seemed ligarchic by comparison.

It was a different approach to democracy to watch jealously over he exercise of power by the magistrates and to be sure that their powrs were strictly limited. The development of the popular court was another democratic tendency. The many dicasteries, or divisions of he panel of 6,000 jurors, were able to act as the watchdogs of the *polis* in every field, from judgment on civil and criminal cases to the crutiny of the acts of outgoing officials. The people had full sovreignty. It was a radical democracy because it was not limited in any way and was capable of making even radical changes in the affairs of the *polis*. Its three manifestations, the *Boule,* the Assembly, and the dicasteries were not three branches of government, as are our executive, legislative, and judicial, but were the same sovereign people doing its business now as a whole, now in groups.

Criticism of Democracy: The Old Oligarch

Criticism of the Athenian democracy was not welcome, for freedom to speak about things that really matter is never gracefully tolrated. The Athenians liked to talk about the *parrhesia*, or freedom f speech, that could be enjoyed in Athens. We have seen that Thuydides and others honestly opposed the democratic measures of Pericles, but we have also seen that Thucydides was ostracized. The work of the comic poet Aristophanes is often cited as an example of the freedom with which one could poke fun and criticize in Athens. It is worth noting, however, that despite his obviously conservative sympathies, he does not make direct attacks on or criticisms of the principle of democracy. It has also been remarked that the people in Assembly were always alert to criticisms of democracy.

Nevertheless an adverse judgment on Athenian democracy was offered by a writer of the late fifth century. His name is not known, but he has been happily christened "The Old Oligarch," a nickname that fits him well, for he is a real, hard-shelled opponent of the people. His brief essay opens briskly with the assertion that he has no praise for the constitution of Athens, which gives the poor and the bad pre-eminence over the rich and the good. Then he shrewdly analyzes the constitution from the hostile oligarchic point of view, continually pointing out that it is well designed to cater to the many and to assure the rule of Athens over her allies of the naval league.

He is frankly contemptuous of the people at large; they are untutored, undisciplined, bad. That such people should be allowed to speak in the Assembly or cast votes would be inconceivable in a well-ordered *polis*, where they would be strictly controlled by people of the better sort. The participation of superior people in government obviously benefits the many, however.

Those Athenians who are sent on missions among the allies abuse and injure the better people in the allied *poleis* for the benefit of the many in these *poleis*. Meanwhile, "the good" at Athens sympathize with "the good" among the allies. The Old Oligarch considers the trying of the lawsuits of the allies at Athens another shrewd measure to help democracy, for it enables Athens to help the many and ruin "the good" among the allies. In addition, it brings in money from court dues, from the renting of lodgings and slaves to those who must come to Athens, and from heralds' fees.

He has a penetrating and cynical analysis of the advantages of control of the sea. It suits a democracy, for naval affairs give employment to many, either in the yards or on the ships. It is advantageous to the *polis* as a whole (and here he temporarily drops the antidemocratic note) because those who control the sea have lines of easy communication for themselves and can control the communications of the possible adversaries living on islands or on the coast. Their excellent communications help to free them from the fear of famine

—a real fear for the small independent *polis*. They can wage economic warfare, too, by preventing their adversaries from finding markets for the products they would like to export.

How did oligarchy differ from democracy? We may note that the Old Oligarch would not allow the common man to speak in the Assembly or vote on public affairs. He says plainly that the Athenian populace realizes that under a government of the best people they would soon be reduced to a state of servitude. Presumably he does not mean literal slavery, although the Greek word he uses (*douleuein*) can mean that, but that the many would be completely controlled by the few. What the oligarchs of Athens really did when they saw their opportunity we shall discuss later.

The Boeotian Confederacy, which was founded in 447, offers an interesting oligarchic system to compare to the democracy of Athens. The two systems were in constant contact and competition. There were ten *poleis* in the Confederacy. In each there was a *boule* divided into four parts, one of which was on duty at a time, as were the prytanies of the Athenian *Boule*. All the full citizens were members of the four *boulai* and thus took turns at being in charge of affairs. Apparently one needed property to be a full citizen, and the amount of property was probably the hoplite *census*, the amount of property that would enable a man to equip himself with heavy armor and weapons as an infantryman. The citizens who did not have this amount of property enjoyed the protection of the courts and engaged in all activities other than those of governing. They were expected to fight as light-armed troops.

Our evidence now and then offers us a glimpse of strong democratic sentiments among the many at Thebes and elsewhere in the Confederacy. But the few repressed the many by intimidation or force when necessary. The many were apparently ready at almost any time to betray the whole Confederacy to the Athenians, quite in the Greek tradition of emphasizing the division between the few and the many rather than the patriotism of the whole *polis*, which to us seems obviously more important. The system of the Boeotian Confederacy, which was so elaborate that it must have been the result of conscious theory, was highly successful from its founding in 447 until the Spartans forcibly dissolved it as a consequence of the Peace of Antalcidas in 387 B.C.

CHAPTER

22

THE AGE OF PERICLES:
ART, LITERATURE, AND SCIENCE

THE ARCHITECTURE OF SANCTUARIES

By the time of Pericles, a number of Greek sanctuaries had become very elaborate and impressive. In the beginning, a sanctuary had been nothing more than a place where the power of a god was thought to be manifest. Probably the first step in the cult was to erect an altar to the god and, sometimes, to build a wall around the place. Sometimes a sacred grove was planted. The temple, if there was one, was built later. Early in the sixth century, the idea of building elaborate gateways was conceived and they were constructed at one or two of the sanctuaries, structures that may be thought of as buildings through which the worshipers entered, but with rooms other than the entrance passage. The altar always remained under the open sky.

The sanctuary of Apollo at Delphi contained many buildings. It was on a rather steep hillside in a beautiful situation. One entered at the bottom of the complex and went up the Sacred Way, which had rows of treasuries on either side, small structures that *poleis* had built, most of them in the sixth century, to house their offerings to the god. The Athenian treasury, which can still be seen in fair condition, is thought to have been the first Doric building entirely of marble; it was probably built about 490 B.C. Its appearance is that of a small temple. One can also see the treasury of the little island *polis* of Siphnos, which prospered on its gold and silver mines. This is in the Ionic style, so rarely seen in Greece itself or in the West. It has two caryatids—statues of women that serve as columns, holding up the architrave. There were statues dedicated to the god on either side of the lower part of the Sacred Way. A little farther up, the great temple of Apollo stood on a terrace fortified by a retaining wall at the outer edge and cut into the hillside at the inner edge. At the far end of this terrace was a bowl in the hillside into which the theater was fitted. Still higher, on another artificially widened terrace, was the stadium. If the complex was somewhat littered with dedications in ancient times and the structures were a little crowded, it still must have been a most impressive whole.

The complex of buildings at Olympia was in a flat place where there was no such planning problem as that presented by the hillside at Delphi. Here, too, the buildings had been put up by stages. Nowhere in Greece was there a sanctuary that had been planned from the very beginning as a unit, as I-em-hotep planned and built the mortuary complex of Sakkara for his royal master. Few places can have been as cluttered with statues as Olympia was, for it was the custom to set up statues of the victors in the contests in addition to those dedicated for other reasons. The sanctuary of Apollo at Delos was also very crowded, although some attempt had been made there to arrange the buildings in a definable spatial relation to each other.

The Acropolis of Athens was the most brilliant of all the Greek sanctuaries, and it assumed its final form during the age of Pericles and just after. From the earliest times, the hill had been the citadel of Athens. Its sides are all steep except in one place. The hilltop was thought to be sacred to the goddess Athena, whom this *polis* had always made its favorite and protecting divinity. A great temple to Athena was planned early in the fifth century and was under construction when the Persians came in 480. They burned the scaffolding, but the great substructure of stone was unharmed, as were many stone drums for columns, which had already been brought up the hill.

It was in accordance with Pericles' program of building up the pride and self-consciousness of the Athenians, as well as his program of improving the economic position of the many, to persuade the people that they should use some of the funds of the naval league to finish the temple to Athena, the Parthenon, which had been started fifty years or so before. The conservatives objected that Athens had no right to spend the funds of the league. Pericles argued that the Athenians were giving full value for the money in protection and had a perfect right to spend any surplus left after equipping and supplying the navy. In 447, work was begun on the temple, using funds from the league's treasury, which had been moved from Delos to Athens in 454. The temple was completed in 438. Ictinus deserves to be remembered as the architect. Phidias was responsible for the great chryselephantine statue of the goddess for the chamber of the temple, as he was for the great chryselephantine Zeus of Olympia. It often is said that he was the chief designer of the sculptures, which plainly were executed by a number of men working well together. There is no sound evidence, however, as to who was the designer of the sculptures of the pediments and the friezes of the Parthenon.

The Parthenon is the most important of Doric buildings and has been called the only perfect building ever built. Large for a Greek temple, 101 by 228 feet, it was built throughout of the gleaming white Pentelic marble that came from a mountain not far from Athens, but was expensive in spite of its nearness. We must not think of the temple, however, as being all of snowy whiteness. The Greeks painted their temples as they did their statues. Just as paint could bring out the subtleties of the modeling of statues, so it could bring out the finer points of the sculpture on the metopes, the formal ornament of the triglyphs, or the smaller ornaments above the level of the capitals of the columns. Bronze and gold were also used for parts and ornaments of the roofs, adding both utility and satisfying color.

The sculptures of the Parthenon are the perfection of the style of the fifth century, which had dropped some of the conventions of the sculpture of the century before and had thus become more realistic. On one of the pediments was shown the birth of Athena from the forehead of Zeus; much of this scene is lost. The other pediment showed the great contest between Athena and Poseidon to see whose gifts would win the favor and worship of the Athenians.

The outer frieze is Doric, alternating triglyphs and metopes. On the metopes are carved scenes from the early history of gods and men, wherein the gods struggle with the uncouth monsters who challenged them in earliest times and the men, too, struggle with monsters. The inner frieze is of the Ionic type, a running frieze of continuous figures not interrupted by triglyphs and going around the wall of the cella, or inner building, whereas the Doric frieze was on the outer surface above the columns that go all the way around the building. The inner frieze must have been very difficult to see when it was in place, for it was high above the floor and the viewer could stand only in the fairly narrow space between the row of columns and the wall of the cella, unable to draw back and look up easily. The frieze was a magnificent portrayal of the procession that came up to the Acropolis to give offerings to Athena at the Panathenaic festival celebrating the unification of Attica. There were officials, women and girls with offerings, and young men on horses. Over five hundred feet of frieze was done with the greatest care; there was no formal repetition, but rather a wonderful variety in the figures and their poses. The crowning piece of sculpture was the forty-foot chryselephantine statue of the goddess, which stood in the inner chamber.

It is hard for us to realize how much explicit theorizing the Greeks did and on what a variety of subjects other than the philosophy of which we hear so much. It is certain that a great deal of thought was devoted to the proper proportions of the Doric temple, that there was experimentation in Doric temples against a background of theory, and that a number of books or pamphlets, now lost, were written on the subject of Doric temples. We are told that two men discussed the Parthenon and that one of them was Ictinus himself. From what little we know of the lost theoretical essays on the subject (partly from the book of the Roman Vitruvius on architecture) and from modern study of the remains of the Parthenon and other Doric buildings, we can learn something of the theory and practice of Greek architecture in the Doric order, the order to which most thought was given.

The beautiful marble of the Parthenon lent itself to sharpness of outline and almost necessitated greater subtlety than had yet been attempted, as far as we know. Not only did the columns have the swelling known as *entasis,* which is necessary to keep the columns from looking thinner in the middle, but they also leaned a little. The whole platform on which the temple is built rises from each corner to a high point in the middle. The rise can just be seen if one sights with care along the long side; it amounts to about four inches there. There is also a slight upward bend of the same sort that keeps the architrave from being a straight horizontal. The effect of these and a number of other slight deviations from geometrical rigidity is to give the building a certain life and charm and likewise a certain restfulness to the eye. It is possible, as has been maintained, that some of these slight deviations were due to accident or clumsiness, but it is not likely, because similar ones appear in more than one building and, in addition, passing references in later classical authors show that some were discussed in the lost treatises.

The Acropolis was also given a large and beautiful entrance building, the Propylaea, like those given some other sanctuaries a century before. It was on the one side of the hill that slopes enough to be climbed. The building was irregular and complex. The roadway went through the middle of it, with a sidewalk on either side. Wings projected on each side toward the corners of the hill at that end, and in one wing there was a large room used as a picture gallery. The structure was begun in 437 and was left only partly finished because of the Peloponnesian War.

On one of the corners of the hill, by the end of one wing of the Propylaea, was the dainty little Ionic temple of Nike, or Victory, which apparently was begun not long after the Peloponnesian War started, although it had been planned and the Assembly had authorized it a decade or two before. Athens was almost the only place in Greece that was hospitable to the Ionic order of architecture; the Doric order prevailed elsewhere. We do not know whether the theorists felt any strong discordance between the two orders, but if they did, it did not prevent the Athenians from having not only the temple of Nike on the Acropolis, but also another Ionic temple known as the Erechtheum from the name of a legendary and heroic figure of Athenian history.

The Erechtheum is on the other side of the hill from the Parthenon and on lower ground. It is smaller and of an irregular shape. It balances the Parthenon nicely without challenging it or distracting attention from its effect. The chief feature of the Erechtheum is the Porch of the Maidens, the roof of which is supported by caryatids, beautifully conceived figures of women that serve as columns and carry the weight of the architrave with grace. This building was begun in 421 and finished in 405. Another feature of the Acropolis was the great bronze statue of Athena, Queen of Battle, near the Erechtheum.

It is not surprising that during the long strain of the Peloponnesian War, which filled practically all the rest of the century, the artistic impulse at Athens lost something of its liveliness. Good work was done elsewhere, however, both in the time of Pericles and at the very end of the century.

SOPHOCLES

Sophocles (496–406 B.C.), like the other two masters of Greek tragedy, Aeschylus and Euripides, was an Athenian. He was born to high social position and a comfortable economic condition. It is recorded of him, as of many leading Greeks, that he retained his powers through a long old age. Clearly his tragedies were highly esteemed, for he won twenty-four first prizes. Of the more than a hundred and twenty plays that he wrote, only seven tragedies and one satyr-play survive. He was personally popular in Athens and was elected general once.

Not only did this child of fortune inherit social and economic advantages, a pleasing personality, and one of the great literary talents of all time; it was also given to him to enjoy a life of ninety years during an interesting and a dangerous time. While he was of military age, the Athenian forces were active on many occasions, and Sophocles must have done much more than serve once as general. He survived this military service, and in his sixties he survived the great plague.

In his later years, perhaps he remembered hearing as a six-year-old the news from Marathon. Perhaps he himself played some part at Salamis. He did participate in the great surge of pride and national feeling that followed the Persian Wars. He saw the rise of democracy and of the naval empire of Athens. He was a friend of Pericles and of the historian Herodotus. He must have talked with Socrates many a time. In his earlier career, he was a friend and rival of Aeschylus; in his later career, of Euripides. He saw the rise of the Sophists and the emergence of an increasing individualism.

His plays do not reflect any of these things specifically. In both Aeschylus and Euripides, we find much more reflection of the life and problems of their times than we do in Sophocles. His subject was Man, and he came as close as any writer can to dealing with the problems of human life in a universal manner, not restricted to a certain time or a certain place. The fact is, of course, that this "universal" manner is that of the Western man of modern centuries. In the work of Sophocles, as in much other Greek writing, the system of values and assumptions is highly palatable to the modern Westerner.

Oedipus Rex

Sophocles' play *Oedipus Tyrannus*, "Oedipus the King," is known also as *Oedipus Rex*. The modern knows the background of Oedipus' story so well that he is likely to be surprised by a presentation of the play on the contemporary stage. The Greek audience did not know the background of the story as the well-read modern knows it; quite untrue is the customary modern belief that the average Athenian was a walking handbook of mythology and legend and that the playwrights worked on this assumption. The texts of the plays show clearly that the playwright expected to have to inform his audience about the myth or legend or the version of it or the section of it with which he was dealing. The sophisticated reader or playgoer may derive pleasure from observing with what skill Sophocles imparts the necessary information to his audience a little at a time as it is needed.

The theme of *Oedipus Rex* is one that appears also in Aeschylus, the hereditary curse. The Greeks perceived that sinners do flourish, and they wondered whether there is delayed retribution in the third or fourth generation. Sophocles makes Laius, the father of Oedipus, a quick, decisive, able, but high-tempered and haughty man. His father, the grandfather of Oedipus, had been the same. Oedipus shared these same qualities, and when he and his father met, not knowing each other, their tempers clashed, and Laius died at the hand of his son. It would hardly be necessary to believe in a mysterious hereditary curse in order to predict that in this family there would be great achievements, great crimes, and great disasters.

Laius, king of Thebes, guilty of abduction, had been told by the Oracle that he might expect to have a son who would kill his father and marry his mother. When his son Oedipus was born, he gave him to a shepherd to expose in the hills. But this shepherd gave him to another, who tended the flocks of Polybus, king of Corinth. Polybus and his wife, being childless, raised the baby as their own. When Oedipus was almost a man, someone taunted him with doubtful birth. With his typical quick decisiveness, he went to Delphi, where the Oracle offered him the unattractive prospect of killing his father and marrying his mother. Decisive again, he resolved not to return to Corinth, where he might do so. At a crossroads, he met an elderly stranger with a few servants—his real father. There was a disagreement, tempers flared, and he killed his father and all the servants but one. Going on to Thebes, he found the city terrorized by a monster called the Sphinx, who set a riddle for everyone she met and ate those who could not answer it. The bold and resolute Oedipus succeeded in answering her riddle, whereupon she destroyed herself in chagrin, always the proper thing to do in such circumstances. The grateful Thebans chose him to occupy the vacant throne and gave him the widowed queen, Jocasta, to wife. Oedipus had done both the dreadful things that the Oracle had predicted.

At the beginning of the play, the people of Thebes are asking King Oedipus to help them, for a plague is raging in the city. Oedipus has already sent his wife's brother, Creon, to Delphi. Creon returns with the reply of the Oracle: the murderer of Laius is polluting the land and must be driven out. Oedipus throws himself into the search with his usual energy, pronouncing a dreadful curse on the guilty man. Then the blind prophet Teiresias accuses him of being himself the murderer (the playwright's skill is such that it seems plausible that Oedipus should refuse to reflect seriously on this charge), and we see Oedipus in a rage at the thought that Creon and Teiresias are conspiring against him. His wife, Jocasta, now urges him to disregard oracles, citing as an example of their falsity the oracle given to Laius, which plainly was untrue, because the child had died and a band of robbers slew Laius. At this point, a messenger comes from Corinth to tell Oedipus that Polybus has died and that the Corinthians wish Oedipus as king. Here seems to be another proof that oracles are not to be trusted. The messenger, when the oracle is mentioned, volunteers that Polybus was not the father of Oedipus. He himself had received Oedipus as a small baby from a

Theban shepherd and had carried him to Polybus at Corinth. When the Theban shepherd, summoned to the king's presence, confirms this story, Jocasta rushes from the stage into the palace and hangs herself. Oedipus stays to get all the detail, then follows her into the palace and gouges out his own eyes.

The construction of the play is generally admired. Such awkward questions as why two people threatened with such oracles asked no questions before contracting any marriage do not rise to spoil the appreciation of the play as it is read or seen. Oedipus is a good man whose forceful and decisive way was suited to a king, a man who would have done better in this situation to walk very softly, as Teiresias tried to persuade him, but who was temperamentally unable to do so.

It has been remarked that Sophocles likes to isolate his heroes; that is, he likes to put them into positions in which they must face difficulties without the moral support that one man derives from others. It has also been remarked that he has a habit of "turning the screw" on his heroes; that is, he likes to portray them in circumstances where the difficulties grow greater by stages. Both these observations are true of Oedipus. His royal position isolates him, and his difficulties become greater as he persists in trying to find the murderer of Laius.

Antigone

Both observations about Sophoclean heroes also hold true for *Antigone*. Here, however, there are two chief characters, Oedipus' daughter Antigone and her uncle Creon, the brother of Jocasta. Both Antigone and Creon were isolated as they opposed each other, and both were subjected to increasing pressure. The Creon of this play, incidentally, is of a very different character from the Creon of *Oedipus Rex*. The Greek playwright felt no need to be consistent in such matters.

In this version of the story, Oedipus was succeeded by one of his sons, Eteocles, rather than by Creon, as he was in *Oedipus Rex*. In the matter of plot, too, consistency was not felt to be necessary. Eteocles had exiled his brother Polyneices for plotting against him. Polyneices tried to capture the city, and both brothers died in the fighting. Creon, succeeding to the throne, decreed that Eteocles should be buried and that the body of Polyneices should be cast out, since he had attacked his native city. Antigone gave the body of her less fortunate brother a symbolic burial by throwing a little earth on it, believing that the rite of burial was too sacred to give up, even at the risk of committing treason.

Creon persisted in upholding his decree that anyone who buried Polyneices would suffer the penalty of death, even though Antigone was his niece and engaged to his son. In the end, his stubborn severity involved his whole family in ruin. Creon was a new power on the throne, something like the Zeus of *Prometheus Bound*. He exercised his new authority with a somewhat uneasy and uncertain touch, like Zeus, inclining too much to harshness. Like Zeus, too, he had a difficult problem for the executive, the problem of what to do with a perfectly reckless rebel against his authority.

It is generally hard to show that any play of Sophocles has a single clear-cut abstract thesis. Some critics have asserted that "Antigone" does have such a simple thesis—the superiority of the "higher law" to man-made law. Such an idea is certainly present, and it had much to do with the popularity of the version of the play done by the French playwright Jean Anouilh and first presented during the German occupation of France. But prominent too are the question of the relative importance of the individual and the group, the question of the deportment of those newly in power, and the question of what the government (or the business executive or the head of a family) does when faced with a rebel who is utterly reckless. There is no need to find a single and simple message in these plays.

HERODOTUS AND HISTORY

It is necessary to remind ourselves sometimes that during this most brilliant period of Athenian history there were substantial achievements of every sort made by Greeks from the rest of the Greek world. Many of these men were drawn to live part of their lives in Athens. Others cultivated their talents in a variety of other places.

The rise of prose writing is a noteworthy and interesting feature of the age. The use of verse continued to seem natural in fields where we should not think of employing it, as in the drama (not a single line of Greek drama is written in prose). Prose made its way in the newer fields of activity—in the writing of history, in philosophy (some of which had been written in verse), and in natural science.

During the late sixth and early fifth centuries, there grew up in the Ionian cities of Asia Minor a tradition of writing both the legends and the histories of *poleis* in prose, using the Ionian dialect. We must remember that what we should call legend was the traditional version of great events and was taken seriously. These early attempts at recounting the past were indeed serious work in that they attempted to give accurate versions of what had happened insofar as oral tradition or the very scanty written official records of the cities could serve as sources.

Herodotus, "The Father of History"

Herodotus, a native of Halicarnassus on the coast of southern Asia Minor, was born in 484 B.C. The fact that he was born a Persian subject, knew many Persians and many Greeks who had been among the Persians, and had himself traveled in Persian territory, gave him a breadth of view not possible for every Greek. He had to leave his native city for political reasons and spent a number of years on the island of Samos. Later he was able to return to Halicarnassus, apparently because a practical truce had been made between the aristocracy and the tyrant who ruled for the Persians.

Herodotus was unusually well traveled for his time. He went to Egypt and got some distance up the Nile. He went into the Persian Empire, probably as far as Mesopotamia. He had been in the Black Sea region in ships and knew something of the coastal regions, and, in the other direction, had been to Cyrene. He spent some time in Athens and other places in Greece and was for some time a member of the Athenian colony of Thurii in South Italy. He may have been a merchant or perhaps he only shared the interests of the merchants of his native city; in any case, he noticed many things that would especially interest one who had some connection with trade, the standard or unusual products of a region, the navigability of the rivers, the methods of transporting goods, and the like.

Herodotus' claim to be called the father of history (that is, the first writer of history in the modern style) rests upon the fact that he was the first to write a history larger than a local chronicle and at the same time to do so in a style and with a breadth worthy of his larger theme. He took as his subject the relation between East and West that culminated in the invasion of Greece by Xerxes. Knowing little of the other people who wrote just before him and even during his time, we have no reason to suppose that they were devoid of common sense, industry, and discrimination. Their works, too, had they been preserved, might in some cases seem to us to be respectable historical monographs.

Herodotus' book, in English translation, fills some 700 pages. It has a very carefully planned and elaborate structure, although in so large a work the structure is apparent in its detail only to those who make an effort to see it. Merely to plan and execute a book of this size with so careful a structure was a notable feat, as it would be today, quite without regard to its historical quality. The Homeric poems are comparable feats of planning and execution, and it is likely that Herodotus was helped by familiarity with them.

He begins by dismissing the legends of wrongs done to one another by the people of East and West—the abduction by the Phoenicians of Io, the carrying off of Medea by the Greeks, and so on—as causes of the struggle. Then he starts his serious account with the formation of the kingdom of Lydia, its conquest of the Greek coastal cities of Asia Minor, its fall before the advance of Cyrus the Persian, and the Persian appropriation of the Greek cities. There is a description of the earlier history of Persia, which leads to a description of Egypt, a country of great interest to the Greeks. Persian invasion leads also to an account of the Scythians, the nomads of the territory above the Black Sea.

Thus the historical and geographical and cultural backgrounds of the great struggle are richly presented, with many an interesting incident, tale of character, or detail of wonder as to men's way of life or thought. With the revolt of the Ionian cities he comes to the beginning of the acute phase of the struggle. Then the Persians decide to move upon continental Greece, and the story of their invasion and repulse is told. The first Greek countermoves against the Persians in Asia Minor complete this part of the story. The whole narrative ends with the battle of Sestus in 478 B.C.

Herodotus as Historian

To form a proper judgment on the achievement of Herodotus is in itself an exercise in history and literature well worth some time and trouble. Opinions vary as to the necessity or even the propriety of a strict comparison with the work of Thucydides. Perhaps the most extreme and striking position is the one taken by R. G. Collingwood, who would rank Herodotus higher than Thucydides on the ground that he sought to establish fact without subsuming it under rules and categories of his own devising, as Thucydides did.* If Thucydides is easily the superior of Herodotus in certain respects, as in the understanding of political and military affairs, we must remember both that he had a different training and that he confined himself to a narrower range of facts and ideas.

But such a comparison, often as it is made, is not the most profitable way of approaching the achievement of Herodotus. He was popular in his own day and has given pleasure and instruction to many people since. He is a master storyteller, whether in detail or in the whole effect; the complete story has life and movement, as does the individual page. It is true, however, that the intelligent modern reader sometimes does well to skip certain parts interesting only to those who already know the ancient world rather thoroughly.

Herodotus represents the life and interests of the whole Greek world, not, like many writers, only the narrower Athenian interest. He knows the feelings of those Greeks around the Mediterranean who lived the broader Greek life and constantly rubbed elbows with non-Greeks. His world of the spirit is a wider world than that of Athenian rationalism, for it is full of the older spirit of uncritical piety existing side by side with the newer rationalism. To him we owe many stories of the Delphic Oracle and other religious agencies. In addition facts of geography, commerce, local customs, and systematic anthropology enliven his story of the Greek world and its environs.

His critical sense was well developed. Again and again he presents himself as having been confronted with alternative versions of the facts and shows on what principle he made his choice. When there is no other way of proceeding, he often makes an attempt to reason by

---

* R. G. Collingwood, *The Idea of History,* pp. 30–31.

analogy to the facts. He was a student of monuments of all kinds. He observed closely when he traveled. From the oral sources on which for the most part he had to rely, he extracted a surprising amount of coherent and convincing information.

There are weaknesses in his work to be set against its many strengths. Occasionally he seems to have been persuaded by a tall tale. He dearly loved a story of the marvelous. But with further information, one of his stories occasionally comes to seem less silly. Arion's ride on the dolphin, for instance, seems more plausible since the reliable report in the 1950's of a dolphin that frequented a New Zealand bathing beach and gave rides to many people. He is criticized, too, for the weakness of his analysis of causations as well as for his imperfect understanding of political and military affairs. Further, he is often vague about his chronology. In all these matters, he does not come up to the standard that we like to think that the historian of today sets for himself.

But if we consider the whole process of making the book, we must think of the breadth of his viewpoint, which embraced both Hellenes and non-Hellenes and encompassed an earlier age as well as his own more rationalistic and sophisticated time. We must think of the physical and mental energy involved in the mere mechanical construction of such an edifice of thought, not to mention the wide range of intellectual power required to dominate information gathered mostly from oral informants and covering a huge mass of facts on everything from colonists in Cyrene to nomads in Scythia, from Persian monarchs to tiny Greek democracies.

SCIENCE

Medicine

The study of medicine had reached a high point in Egypt in the seventeenth century before Christ, but continued in later ages with less brilliance. The Greeks, however, as they emerged after 850 B.C. from the period of disturbances, had had a normal mixture of treatment of disease by superstitious means, such as reciting charms, and of attempts to treat and cure the sick by rational means.

In the fifth century, the rational physicians had two chief schools, those of Cnidus and Cos, two islands lying off Caria and not far apart. The school of Cnidus apparently devoted itself to the diagnosis and treatment of individual diseases, a worthy proceeding but ahead of its time, because not enough of the necessary preliminary work had been done. The school of Cos, to which the great name of Hippocrates belongs, gave its attention more to the human body and its ailments in general.

We know little of Hippocrates, although his name is attached to the *Hippocratic Corpus*, the collection of writings by different authors that represents the beginning of scientific medicine as we know it. These authors would probably not regret having retired into an immortality of anonymity, their work well done. *Ars longa, vita brevis* represents a saying of theirs: short as one physician's life is, the art of healing goes on.

The careful observation and recording of cases was the basis of their method. The reports of cases in the *Corpus* are scientific; that is, they describe phenomena exactly and unemotionally. The onset of the disease is described, with such features as fever, coughing, sweating, appearance of the skin, discharges, and then the course of the disease. Many of the cases end with the death of the patient, for they were meant to be scientific reports, not advertisements of wonder cures. Unfortunately, the practice of writing up and collecting reports of cases presently fell into long disuse.

The physician's knowledge of internal anatomy left much to be desired. Even on Cos, a certain amount of theoretical system appeared where knowledge failed, as in the theory of the humors of the body and their relations. Fevers were carefully and subtly observed, but the concomitant phenomenon of the pulse rate seems hardly to have been noticed. Many important diseases—smallpox, measles, scarlet fever, diphtheria, bubonic plague—are not mentioned.

The physicians of the Hippocratic school were aware of the importance of treating the whole man. They recognized the *vis medicatrix naturae*, "the healing force of Nature," and took account of it in their treatment. They also realized that climate can make a difference in matters of health and illness. They were well aware, too, that the psychological condition of the patient is important.

The *Hippocratic Corpus* may have been assembled in the late pre-Christian era out of all the medical writings that the compilers could find. Many authors, schools, and types of treatise are represented. Although the books do not have names attached to them, they plainly were written by many men. The schools of Cos and Cnidus are most prominent, but those of South Italy and Sicily are also represented. Some of the books are introductions to medicine for young students. There are general reference books for practicing physicians, special books, as on the diseases of women, collections of case histories, and books of theory.

Some books of the *Hippocratic Corpus* still make interesting reading. *On the Nature of Man* describes the theory of the four humors of the body, which long was influential. *On Crises* and *On Critical Days* arise from the rigid course taken by malaria, which suggested close observations of courses and rhythms in other diseases. The famous *Airs, Waters, Places* is a brilliant treatise on comparative medical geography, full of sharp observations and shrewd theorizing about the effect of environment on people in health and in sickness. *Prognostic* is another that combines excellent observation with theorizing. Several books consist of case histories, sometimes viewed in relation to some external condition like weather.

Mathematics

Unfortunately our knowledge of Greek mathematics during the age of Pericles is full of serious gaps; we know a number of questions that were raised and sometimes the broad lines of solutions that were attempted, but rarely can we learn the full detail of a solution. The mathematicians of the fifth century raised difficult logical problems; Zeno and Parmenides, for example, raised questions about the nature of space and motion. The geometers of this century did good work in putting together a corpus of geometry. Their attempts to state all geometry systematically and to work up economical and elegant proofs resulted in good progress and the filling in of many gaps in the system.

PHILOSOPHY

The Eleatic School

Parmenides of Elea in Italy was in his prime about 475 B.C., and his first impulse toward philosophy is said to have come from some members of the Pythagorean group. The system that he worked out is much concerned with the idea of being. Parmenides says that only those things that are thinkable exist; what the mind cannot conceive does not exist. The mind cannot conceive nothing, or not-being; therefore not-being does not exist. It follows from this that being does not come into existence, does not cease to exist, is whole, and is motionless. It does not come into being, because there is nothing else for it to come from, and it does not cease to be, because there is nowhere for it to go.

The development of his thought along these lines led to the assertion that all apparent change is a delusion. Logically, all the world is one and unchanging; apparently only our hallucinations change. Such a view seems to outrage common sense, yet it has a certain logicality. Parmenides' pupil Zeno defended it by the method of dialectic that Socrates was soon to manage with such skill. He examines the consequences of the usual pluralistic view and finds severe logical difficulties in what seems to be the view of common sense.

Empedocles

Empedocles of Acragas in Sicily may have been born about 490, for he was in his prime in the middle of the century. His remarkable and striking personality has led to the suggestion that he was the last of a distinguished line of shamans, or medicine men, who claimed to have inspiration in religious matters. He could in fact, have pursued parallel careers as shaman, political figure, and philosopher.

As natural philosopher he suggested that there are four substrates or prime substances—earth, air, fire, and water. They are separate and do not transform themselves into other things. They do mix in varying proportions under the influence of a power that he called love and we should call attraction, then are driven apart by hate, which we should call repulsion. This view leaves him somewhere midway between Parmenides' view that all change is illusion and the view of Heracleitus (discussed in Chapter Sixteen) that change, or flux, is a great reality.

Anaxagoras

Anaxagoras (500—428 B.C.) of Clazomenae, a Greek city of Asia Minor, proposed the view that the seeds of everything are present in everything. It is possible, therefore, for any particle of matter to change into anything. He postulates a mysterious Mind which acts upon Matter to cause the formation of the universe, which then proceeds by itself.

The chief interest in the life and teaching of Anaxagoras lies in the fact that he came from his home in Asia Minor to Athens, apparently at the invitation of Pericles, and was for some thirty years a friend of the great man. He was prosecuted for his religious views, however, for he taught that the heavenly bodies are not gods, but material things. Such theories were very unpopular in fifth-century Athens in spite of the brilliance of her intellectual life. It is probable, too, that the conservatives in the city were glad to embarrass Pericles by the prosecution of his friend the philosopher.

The Atomic Theory of Leucippus and Democritus

Leucippus flourished in the middle of the fifth century. He was concerned most of all with the question of the nature of the primary stuff of the world, a question that had exercised most of his predecessors among the speculative thinkers. His proposal was that the substrate, or primary stuff of the world, is broken up into innumerable bodies too small to be divided further and for that reason called "atoms," which means "undivided."

These atoms can be of different sizes and shapes, but apparently have no other properties. The qualities of things come somehow from the aggregation of atoms. They are uncreated and indestructible and infinite in number. Leucippus insisted upon the fact of empty space, which to Parmenides had seemed supremely impossible. This view allowed a possibility of motion.

His pupil Democritus continued his work in the latter part of the fifth century. He postulated a ceaseless rain of the atoms down through the void, heavier ones sometimes overtaking lighter ones and causing swirls of atoms that resulted in the formation of matter. The process was not at the pleasure of a divinity or a number of divinities. Democritus insisted that strict causal relations were in force and that the whole process was purely mechanical and inevitable. Epicurus the Athenian was to assert later that to be at the mercy of such a vast and inexorable machine was far worse than to be exposed to the whims of the gods. We shall see how Epicurus attempted to circumvent the monstrous machine and to assert the freedom of the will.

Democritus grappled honestly with questions of psychology and epistemology, which cannot always be separated. Epistemology is the science of how we know, the means by which people can have knowledge. Democritus asserted that our senses give us our knowledge of the world around us. Atoms coming to the organs of sense give us impressions, which we learn to deal with. In many ways, his theory of perception and sensation seems modern.

The series of philosophers that begins with Thales and ends with Democritus is known as the pre-Socratic philosophers in recognition of the fact that in the late fifth century, Socrates of Athens gave a new direction to philosophy, although if full justice were done, the Sophists, whom we are about to discuss, would share the credit with Socrates. The philosophic achievement of the pre-Socratics is impressive. They asked many important questions and showed along what lines some answers may be given. They discussed such matters as whether reality is one or many, whether we may perceive it by the senses or by reason or not at all, whether there are realities like the Logos of Heracleitus that are not material but may have an effect on matter, what the nature of the human mind is and what its relation to the body is, and how human values are to be determined.

Their scientific achievement was decidedly less. Although their guesses about astronomy and the earth have provoked some impatience in modern historians of science, they did, however, make beginnings in a number of the fields in which the long and patient collection of facts, aided by experiment if needed, has brought useful results. It may be said that in the early days of philosophy a general speculative curiosity and desire for valid generalizations appeared. Then special fields of thought began to attract men, so that some people became mathematicians or astronomers, although others, such as Zeno and Parmenides, can more properly be regarded as philosophers who did some work in mathematics. Of course, no one then felt that he was definitely labeled, as a man nowadays is labeled a mathematician or a geologist. But by the end of the fifth century, some specialized interest in astronomy, mathematics, medicine, ethics, and psychology had developed.

THE SOPHISTS

Although one would naturally expect the pre-Socratic philosophers to be followed immediately by Socrates, the Sophists must come first, for the earliest of them were nearly a generation ahead of Socrates in giving a new direction to philosophy. They perceived, first, that the philosophers had practically argued themselves to a standstill. Firm knowledge and comprehension of the world had come to seem impossible. Secondly, the Sophists felt that the new freedom of the individual in the less rigid system of the *polis* as opposed to the old rigid system of the clans was the great subject of the time. They therefore turned away from the interests of the former philosophers and devoted themselves to the study of man in society.

This is exactly the line of activity that Socrates is traditionally said to have initiated. One reason for the tradition and the resulting confusion is that the great Plato, Socrates' devoted pupil, in a number of brilliantly effective dialogues so effectively denigrated the Sophists that their achievements were not properly respected until late in the nineteenth century, and even now sole credit is still mistakenly given by implication to Socrates for starting the new trend in philosophy. Another and a better reason is that Socrates, through Plato, exerted great influence on all later systematic philosophy, whereas the most that we can do for the Sophists is to credit them with pioneering work that influenced both Socrates and Plato, as well as others, although it did not lead to any such definite result as Plato's work. How Socrates resembled the Sophists and how he differed from them will be dealt with in Chapters Twenty-five and Thirty-one.

The work of the Sophists had two main aspects. The first was that they attempted to analyze, as the philosophers did, but directed their attention to man and his activities and problems. The second was that they professed to be able, on the basis of their analyses, to teach men how to get along in the world and excel in certain activities, especially in government. They expected to be paid for their teaching. Although many people disapproved of them, many others received and paid for their instruction. The conservative Greek disapproved of advising other men for pay, and he disapproved of any means of getting ahead in the world that might bring forward people or groups who had hitherto been in subordinate positions, as certain to upset things.

The teaching of effective speech was the first activity of the Sophists. Corax of Syracuse made himself a reputation in the 460's as a teacher of convincing oratory. He analyzed successful speeches and claimed to be able to show the difference between the speech that would convince and the one that would not. Gorgias of the town of Leontini in Sicily became famous for his efforts to create a prose full of artifice and ornament comparable to those of poetry.

Protagoras of Abdera, in Thrace, went a step farther and devised and taught methods of making an argument appear stronger than it really is—the sort of thing that is still called "sophistry." He had a habit of offering paired arguments on an interesting question, one for and the other against. This setting up of the arguments on both sides of a question became very popular in Athens and was often presented in the tragedies. Euripides especially was to offer the public some very shrewd paired arguments, for example, those of Jason and Medea in his *Medea*.

Protagoras, like many of the Sophists, refused to subscribe to many of the old values. He is quoted as saying that Man is the measure of all things. If this insistence on putting man and his interests first on the scale of values sometimes offended conservatives, still it led to fresh discoveries about man and his life. Protagoras is said to have been prosecuted and condemned for a book about the gods, presumably a book skeptical in tone.

Like other Sophists, Protagoras was also a student of government. He drew up the constitution for the colony of the Athenians at

Thurii in South Italy in 443 B.C. In the matter of government as in the matter of effective speech, the Sophists played the dual role of analysts who discovered new truths and teachers who imparted a knowledge of how to be successful in the courts or in government. Like the philosophers and scientists, they tried to penetrate the secrets of human activities and discover general laws.

CHAPTER

23

THE PERICLEAN AGE:
ECONOMIC AND SOCIAL LIFE

Although our evidence for the economic and social life of the Greeks is not nearly so rich as that at our disposal for the study of any modern country, it is varied enough and full enough to give us what is probably an adequate and reasonably correct picture. There are, for example, a few scraps of such records as the tribute lists of the Athenian Empire, difficult and tantalizing as they are to interpret in their battered condition, or the fragments of the records of payments to the workmen who worked on the Erechtheum in Athens. There are no ample files of official records. Yet we can learn a great deal by putting together the incidental remarks of writers on various subjects. The comedies of Aristophanes are especially rich in sidelights on Greek life. Archaeological evidence, too, can enlighten us, telling something of the nature and the flow of goods in the Greek world, of houses, clothes, and weapons, of public architecture and the fine arts.

PRODUCTION AND CONSUMPTION

The production of food was the chief business of the entire ancient world from beginning to end. It is probably true that industry never amounted to more than five per cent of the economic activity and that agriculture amounted to ninety-five per cent. We must remember that a great many articles were manufactured on the farm, as indeed they continued to be until comparatively recent times. The farmer built his own simple house (his few iron tools would have to be purchased somehow) and shelters for his animals, fowls, and bees. He made harness or pack saddles for the animals. The wood on the place or perhaps a small deposit of suitable clay provided material for dishes, pails, and other utensils. His olive press he made of wood, perhaps with some stone parts. He either pressed or trampled his grapes, and the containers, like those for the olive oil, were made of clay. The tendency for the subsistence farm to disappear from modern countries of the West makes it all the more necessary to insist upon its former pervasiveness and its dissimilarity to the large modern farm.

Cereals were the most important article of the diet, and barley was generally the chief cereal. Wheat, rye, millet, and spelt were also raised. A variety of vegetables was grown. Oil was pressed from a number of seeds—radish seed, for example, or poppy seed. Meat tended to be expensive and was a rarity on the tables of ordinary people.

The Mediterranean world as the Greeks knew it had widely differing capabilities for the production of food, as it did for the production of other things. The region of the Black Sea was fertile, especially the northern side, which produced cereals and exported them to Athens. The control of this trade route was often threatened, and we see the Athenians making great efforts to keep it open, because they had come to depend on imported cereals. The Greek cities of the Black Sea region, as well as the native peoples, prospered on the trade in cereals and dried fish. Although Thrace and Asia Minor both had excellent soil, we hear little of them as exporters of foodstuffs. Thrace tended to be too little civilized for systematic agriculture directed to export, and Asia Minor was rather too civilized, for it had a denser population than most parts of the ancient world and needed its food to feed itself. Egypt was an exporter of cereals. Her rich land had long been carefully organized by the government so that the surplus could be taken and used as seemed best. In 445 B.C., the Egyptian government was able to send a gift of nearly 50,000 bushels of grain to Athens. Many such gifts are found recorded in the annals of the diplomacy of the ancient world. (In Roman times, too, Egypt was an important exporter of cereals.)

In Greece proper, the soil was somewhat thin for cereals, and especially so for wheat. Athens had early faced this situation and built up a system of export of her products and import of cereals. A number of places even in Greece were somewhat better suited for cereal culture than Attica—the Peloponnesus, the island of Euboea, and Thessaly. These places, however, were fairly well populated and did not rank as exporters.

Greece in the West—southern Italy and Sicily—had flatter and deeper soil and did much better in cereal production. Sicily was to become an important source of supply for the Romans in later times. Southern France was a good country for agriculture and later sent cereals to Rome, although there is no good evidence that any were sent to Greece. The country of the Carthaginians—more or less modern Tunisia—was a good cereal area and was well farmed by native labor under Carthaginian control. Punic cereals may well have been sent to Athens in payment for the Athenian pottery that appears in the remains of Carthage.

Plain oil and plain wine could be procured in many places around the Mediterranean, but then, as now, certain oils and wines were favored far above others. The differences were partly due to fortunate combinations of soils and climates with the strains of trees and vines and partly to superior skill in producing and marketing the oil and wine. The selective breeding of trees and vines as well as of animals was coming to be understood by the fifth century. Some small places, like the island of Chios, became famous for their wine, but production in general must have been of the routine sort.

The olive was eaten green or ripe, as it is now, or was preserved, sometimes by pickling. The best method of preserving it was to make it into oil, which could be stored and used as a food. Until the later invention of soap, olive oil was rubbed on the body, then scraped off, as a method of cleaning. It also was burned for light in simple lamps, often mere dishes with a wick hanging over the edge. These gave a light so slight as to make it possible to find one's way around only a little during the hours of darkness; people tried to do their living during the daylight as much as possible.

The grape, like the olive, could be eaten at once. It could be sundried to make raisins. Best of all, it could be preserved by turning the juice into wine. The preserving of milk in the form of cheese was well understood, and Nature had taught the bees how to put honey away.

The Greeks differed among themselves in their eating habits as they did in many other respects. Naturally the people who lived in a grazing country or a good country for raising pigs ate meat now and then, although for most Greeks meat was a rarity. The meat of sacrifices was generally given to the worshipers after some choice parts had been burned as an offering to the god. There was good eating in general among the Greeks of Sybaris, a wealthy community in southern Italy, which gave its name to the modern sybarite, the devotee of luxurious living. It is said that among them the cook who invented a new dish had the exclusive right to prepare it for a year. Eating was proverbially good in southern Italy and in Sicily and in Thessaly, all places of some fertility. The stern discipline of the Spartans drove them to a plain fare that drew shudders even from Greeks used to the endless fight to gain a living from rocky soils. Probably the *perioeci* of fertile Lacedaemon and even the Helots saw no need to discipline themselves with so cheerless a regime.

The clothing of the Greeks was simple. The basic garment was the *chiton*, a rectangular piece of cloth with a hole for the left arm. It was put on and pinned at the right shoulder and down the right side to form a sleeveless tunic that fell almost to the knee and could be belted at the waist. Women wore longer ones, for the Greek girl or matron, if respectable, was not encouraged to display her physical charms. Another garment, a mantle or cape called the *himation*, was thrown over the *chiton* by those who dressed with any care; to wear it was more or less equivalent to wearing a coat in public in the twentieth century instead of a sweater or windbreaker or merely a shirt. The *himation* was made of very fine wool; for those who dressed carefully, the cut and drape of it were matters of some concern. Trousers seem to have been worn only by the Persians and some people of Gaul; they often seemed odd enough to provoke the mirth of those who saw them on strangers. Many people did not wear shoes at all, and many others wore them only occasionally. Sandals were known, however, and shoes that covered the ankle, and boots. Most people did not wear coverings for their heads. Sailors generally did and blacksmiths, and others who needed protection from a blazing sun, dangerous sparks, or other hazards.

Houses, too, were simple. As far as our scanty information lets us know, they were generally built of adobe, or sun-dried brick. This material is both stronger and more resistant to the weather than one might suppose. A coating of stucco and an overhanging roof do a great deal to protect walls of adobe from rain. The Greek house seems usually to have looked inward to a court rather than outward to the street. It was ordinarily square or rectangular, but many houses were of an irregular shape because the streets were not regularly laid out and the houses therefore stood on irregular plots of land. The house probably had some windows on the street merely to provide light for the rooms on that side, not because anyone wished to look out. The streets were narrow and winding and dirty, so that no one would think of wanting windows to look out of or a porch to overlook the street.

The group of ancient Greek houses most useful for study is found at Olynthus, on the Chalcidic Peninsula. The city, a small one, apparently was built largely in the fifth century. It was to be taken and destroyed by Philip II of Macedonia in 348 B.C. and never inhabited again by any significant number of people, so that there is good reason to believe that most of the things found there belong to the fourth century at the latest.

Olynthus, or the part of it that has been excavated, is unusual in having a regular network of streets and houses of regular shape. The houses generally have from five to seven rooms, two or three of which were on a second floor, the existence of which is proved by the remains of an inner stairway; it must have led to a second floor, because the remains show that the roofs were tiled and pitched and therefore not used as living space. The houses were generally of adobe, although timber must have been somewhat easier to get here, not too far from Macedonia and Thrace, than it was in Greece proper. The floors were often made of packed earth, although the more ambitious houses might have as flooring cobbles, or a sort of cement, or even mosaics of pebbles set in cement. The walls sometimes had a plaster surface over the adobe, and a number of those found were colored.

In some houses at Olynthus, the room used as a kitchen can be distinguished by remains of a hearth and a flue to carry off the smoke. Some houses had a bathroom near the kitchen; hot water had to be carried to the bathroom from wherever it was heated. A number of washbowls on stone stands were found and a number of terracotta bathtubs so made that the bather could sit and put his feet in the lower part. Presumably someone else poured the water over him. It is difficult to distinguish the other rooms of the house according to use, for they probably had little equipment to begin with and that little probably was made of wood, which rarely leaves a trace. Loom weights were found in almost every room of every house. Grain mills and stone mortars were found here and there. A few of the houses had their own cisterns, but water was generally brought in from the fountains of the city, which were supplied by a system of pipes.

The courtyard saw more living, presumably, than any other area of the house. All the rooms opened onto it for light, even those having windows toward the outer side. In a country with a fairly warm sun, it would be possible to live with some comfort in the colder seasons by occasionally taking the chill off the rooms with a brazier of charcoal and spending as much time as possible in the outer air of the courtyard, where the sun could be felt and the winds were somewhat warded off.

Although the three basic products that we have discussed—food, clothing, and houses—must largely have been produced by the users, we have interesting evidence of commercial and professional activity in producing them. Athens imported a great deal of her food, as has been said, and other cities imported some. This plainly implies a large number of commercial farms in many places, although we do not have direct evidence about them. Even within Attica there was commercial production of the fine olive oil that was used in Athens and exported, too.

There must have been much professionalism in the breeding of plants and animals and in the preparation of certain articles of food, especially wine and oil, where skill and proper equipment make a great difference. We have evidence of real professionalism in cooking. A great household might even have a group of specialist cooks—one for meats, one for sauces, one for pastry. The famous cooks even wrote cookbooks.

The first professional in the line of manufacture of clothing was the man who bred sheep to produce better wool. The making of the fabric could involve much skill and equipment. There were towns and whole regions (as in Asia Minor) where there was a tradition of fine work in fabrics for the use of other people. Understandably, many people who could make fine fabrics, and especially those who could design clothes to please exacting patrons, found it profitable to go to Athens or other prosperous cities, such as Corinth. In those centers, we find specialists of many kinds. Some dealt with the production of the fabrics and some with the production of the finished garment. Some specialized in dyeing and some in fulling, the ancient method of cleaning by chemicals and powdered earth and water. There were specialists in shoes, from the tanners, who stank publicly as they continued to do until very recently, to the people who fashioned stout shoes and dainty shoes. The producers of jewelry were in a way a branch of the clothing industry, and there were many of them.

The simplest house could be very simple, and professional production had no part in it. Even now one may see in Greece a shepherd's hut and fold made only of brushwood and some clay to fill it in. The ordinary farmer could build himself an adobe house with only a few pieces of timber to stiffen it here and there. The house of a rich man, however, might well include a fair amount of stone construction, which was expensive, or it might be built entirely of wood, which was regarded as rather ostentatious even for a rich man. We know that there were master builders and carpenters who tended to specialize somewhat and who were equipped with an impressive range of tools for working wood. It was possible, too, to buy fine furniture of wood or wrought iron or partly of ivory.

In the matter of production it is somewhat surprising to realize that the Greeks were not so inventive and ingenious as some of the peoples of the Near East who had flourished earlier. Many Greek craftsmen had fine technique and wonderful ability in design and ornamentation, but they were not strong in the improvement of technical procedures or in the invention of new ones. Even within the general framework of the culture of the time, there was room for advancement. For example, the Greeks might have made improvements in the machinery used for constructing large buildings or in the ovens used for pottery or in the smelters used for metals.

In the matter of consumption, as everywhere in Greek life, there was great variety, and sentimental generalizations are worth little. The Greeks had not heard of the Puritan way of life that Americans tend to associate with the older New England. They were not devoted to plain living (except for the Spartan "Equals") and high thinking. Although the evidence indicates that the majority of them had to be content with very plain living, those who could be comfortable or luxurious apparently were glad to be so. The democratic spirit of Athens acted as a check on ostentatious luxury at times, and this may well have been true in some other cities. On the other hand, ostentatious luxury seems to have been the rule among the well-to-do in Sybaris and many other places in the West. As for high thinking, we have seen that it was a minority who did the glorious high and deep thinking of the Greeks and that they often were mistrusted and opposed by the majority.

LABOR

Although we are somewhat scantily informed about communities of the Greek world other than Athens, we may reasonably believe that a large part of the work—in the house, in the fields, in the shop —was done by people working for themselves. Although the well-to-do family might have a slave to serve in the house, the mistress still had many tasks of her own, and most people could not afford even one domestic.

On the average small farm, slave help was not common, although it seems plain that the larger and more prosperous farms were worked by slaves under slave overseers. If we count all farms, the majority were worked by the owner and his family, and a goodly number had a single slave working with the owner. The free man who hired himself out to another man was a rarity, either on the farm or in the shop. Many shops had only the owner as staff; others had one slave or perhaps two working beside the owner. A factory employing twenty slaves was large, although one is known to have had a hundred and twenty.

There were many gradations of status among those who labored. It may be said that the free man who owned a farm or a shop was at one end of the scale and the slave at the other; in between were such situations as that of the Helots in Sparta or of the Cretan slaves, who had property rights that other slaves did not have. The free man felt the strong constraint of his need to make a living, and the small farmer or shopkeeper may well have worked harder than many slaves. The slave, on the other hand, was not always confined to one spot and made to toil incessantly. The more able and highly trained were offered incentives to increase their productivity. Some even were allowed to live by themselves and work independently, paying their masters a part of what they earned.

The proportion of slaves to free men in the Greek world was small. The farm or shop with several slaves was the exception, even more so the household with more than one slave; and a great number of farms, homes, and shops were without any at all.

The absolute number of slaves in the Greek world cannot be determined or even accurately guessed. For Athens a reasonable calculation, based on evidence from the late fourth century, gives a figure of 20,000 slaves. This would mean that there were three free adults, plus some children, for every slave. It has been suggested that about 10,000 of these were in domestic service and 10,000 divided between the farms and shops of Attica. The *polis* owned a few slaves. It seems reasonable to suppose that other less prosperous and less industrialized cities had a smaller proportion and a smaller number of slaves.

Certain statements of ancient authorities that seem to imply several times this number of slaves are no longer considered worthy of acceptance. Scholars no longer believe, therefore, that Greek civilization was based on slavery. The Greek did not live by the sweat of any such toiling masses. The average man, even if he had a slave, did a fair amount of work himself. He had not lost the secret of going without things that he did not need, however, and his acceptance of a modest material standard of living freed him from much toil.

Apparently the existence of slave labor did not depress the wages or the incomes of free workmen. The free artisans and owners of shops (there is no evidence that there was a class of free hired men on farms or in shops) apparently could not be harmed by slave competition because acquiring or training a skilled slave and giving him adequate incentives to produce was so expensive that the slave's production cost as much as the free man's. The records of the building of the Erechtheum show that the same wages were paid to free men and to slaves for the same work; apparently there was no attempt to make the slave worker take less pay for the same performance. The wage was a drachma a day, a fairly typical wage. The drachma, or six obols, was the monetary unit of ordinary daily use, like the modern shilling or franc. It has been calculated that a man and a wife could barely live on about 200 drachmas a year.

We have no record of complaints from free labor of being injured by slave labor. Among the Romans in later years, such injury did occur: slaves were very cheap then, and large farms or ranches might be formed on which they could work with a minimum of supervision. These conditions also gave rise to slave revolts. We find no evidence of comparable conditions in Greece, nor of slave revolts, nor of hardship caused to free men by the competition of slave labor. There was in general no sense of a class, either slave or free, called "labor."

People became slaves in several ways beside the obvious one of being born to slave mothers. If Greeks fighting against Greeks took captives, they generally got a good ransom for men instead of selling them into slavery. But they usually sold the non-Greeks into slavery. Kidnappers were active on land and sea; they, too, might hold their victims for ransom or sell them into slavery. Some governments actively combatted the kidnappers, and strong maritime powers like Athens, had other reasons, too, for attempting to repress piracy. Any Greek, of any level of society, could fall into slavery as a result of war or kidnapping. Many non-Greek slaves were netted by raids across the border. The chief outside sources of slaves for Greece were Phrygia, Lydia, Caria, Paphlagonia, Thrace, Illyria, and Scythia.

Another source of slaves was the abandonment or sale of infants or young children. It was not illegal in many Greek states to expose (that is to abandon) unwanted babies. A slave dealer might take such a child and raise him. There were risks: if the child had been born a slave, the dealer might lose him on proof of ownership being offered. If he was born a citizen, proof of his citizen birth had the same result. Illness and death took others. A youngster bought from the Thracians, who regularly sold their children, might of course also be lost by illness and death.

The rougher and more intractable slaves were suitable only for hard supervised work in the quarries, or the silver mines of Laurium in Attica. People often bought slaves as investments and leased them out to work at Laurium or elsewhere. Other untrained slaves were used in agriculture or as ordinary domestics. Others were the porters or errand boys, and the females were routine prostitutes.

But many slaves were intelligent and highly trained, some before falling into slavery, others at the expense of dealers or private owners. The better man in agriculture became the overseer. There were posts for superior house servants. A carefully trained girl might become an entertainer or a high-class prostitute. A trained slave might be a shoemaker, a stonecutter, or an accountant for a banker, for example. Yet probably the profit was no greater in owning trained slaves, since their superior productivity was balanced by the higher cost of purchase or training and the necessity of offering them incentives. Very likely there was a great increase in the number of trained industrial slaves during the time of Pericles because of expansion and the fact that citizens were often busy with political and military duties. In such cases, the trained slaves could keep things going in the absence of their masters.

The scanty data available suggest that 200 drachmas, or two minas, was a usual price for a trained slave in the fifth and fourth centuries. Prices ran as high as 300 drachmas for slaves with special qualifications and as low as 50 for children, who were a somewhat risky long-term investment.

The slave was a piece of property; he could be bought, sold, mortgaged, or rented out. The children of slave mothers were slaves. Slaves could not contract legal marriage or own property. Masters could inflict corporal punishment on them; in some places, however, the law did protect them from inhumane treatment. Probably the worst fate for a slave was to be rented out for the hard and unhealthy work in the silver mines of Laurium. Slave workers must have been worked hard and brutally treated in many other places as well.

Yet it must be remembered, on the one hand, that the free man among the Greeks suffered many constraints, some arising from his own lack of ability or his inherited poverty, and some arising from the fact that the free man owed the state many arduous services from which the slave was exempt. On the other hand, humanity and self-interest combined to ameliorate the slave's lot, and local conditions might lead to a modification of unqualified servitude. In Crete, for instance, there was a class of agricultural slaves who could marry and hold property and who had subsidiary rights of inheritance in the land. In Athens, a group of slaves known as "dwellers apart" were encouraged by being allowed to set up their own households and work under their own direction.

Many slaves were allowed to buy their freedom. It is not clear, however, that all of them felt that the effort was worthwhile. One who did was allowed a fictitious ownership of part of his earnings until he could meet the stipulated price. Thus the owner stimulated his slave's production and got back his original investment, making sure that premature death could not cause him loss. The freed slave could still be profitable to his former owner if he worked with facilities belonging to him. At Athens, freed slaves became metics, or resident aliens, a class that was always being strengthened by a steady influx of the able and energetic people who had bought their freedom. Their former slavery did not make of them a special lower class.

Resident Aliens in Greek Communities

Any theory about the causes of the great surge of energy and achievement in Periclean Athens must take into account the fact that Athens, like Sparta and other *poleis*, relied in many ways on the free noncitizens residing within her borders. "Metic" is the customary way of Anglicizing the Greek word *metoikos*, which the Athenians applied to these people. There must have been at least as many metics at Athens as there were Athenian citizens. Although freed slaves became metics, most of the group had come to Athens as free men to better their situation. Other cities, too, had such resident aliens.

Because they were not citizens, there were things the metics could not do and things they could not have. They could not perform any of the civil functions of the citizen, such as holding office, speaking in the Ecclesia, voting, or sitting on juries. They could not perform the functions of the citizen in the court, whether as plaintiff or as defendant, but (at least in earlier times) had to have citizens to represent them. They could not hold land, because the possession of land was connected with citizen status. There was naturally a certain feeling, too, that the noncitizen who devoted himself to trade, if he were allowed to buy land, might be able to get control of a great deal of property that ought to belong to citizens. Metics could marry citizens, but the children (at least after the law of 451) did not have full citizen status.

There were a few things which they were compelled to do. They had to serve in the armed forces, both as hoplites and peltasts, although they were likely to be used in Attica rather than abroad. They were liable to special taxes imposed on them only. They were not subject to the liturgies, or extra duties of the rich, but we know that they sometimes voluntarily made these contributions of money and effort. At the great procession of the Panathenaic festival the metics customarily marched in scarlet gowns.

The thing that they could do and the usual reason for their presence in Athens (or other cities) was to engage in industry and trade of every kind. Further, the metic could be a philosopher (Anaxagoras) or a distinguished writer of speeches for other men to use in the courts (Lysias) or, in the feminine gender, a woman of distinguished personality and cultivation and a professional companion to men (Aspasia, the mistress and then the wife of Pericles). Metics were artists and physicians. Some came from the people whom the Greeks liked to call barbarians, or outsiders. Probably most of them were Greek citizens of one *polis*, but lived and worked in Athens or some other *polis* not their own. But their chief activity was in industry and trade, and it is plain that they were welcome to the good livings made by many of them, for if it had so wished, the citizen body could have reserved for its own members every lucrative occupation. There are scattered pieces of evidence that Athens and other *poleis* definitely invited certain individuals and groups to come as metics.

To remember that Athens and other *poleis*, and also places in Persia and other countries, had many alien Greeks as permanent residents may help us to form a more accurate view of the nature of the *polis*. Greeks had always wandered, to be sure. As early as the ninth century, we find them as mercenaries serving the Egyptian king and others. The resident aliens of the fifth century, however, had left their own *poleis* to live elsewhere permanently, something that we do not expect to find in the ninth century, but typical of the gradual loosening of the tight social bonds of earlier times.

PUBLIC FINANCE

Athens: Income

Athens was in control of a lively commercial empire, and she drew rich profits from her position. After she took the control of the treasury of the Delian League away from the congress of the League in 454 and moved the treasury from Delos to the Acropolis, the Athenian *Boule* was in control of this great fund. Eight thousand talents were brought to the Acropolis in 454; the tribute from the allies in the following years was generally something over 400 talents a year.

We may here remind ourselves that a talent was 60 minas, a mina was 100 drachmas, and the drachma was the ordinary coin corresponding to our quarter or the shilling or the franc. There seems little use in trying to equate the talent with a number of dollars. A drachma was an ordinary day's wage; the talent therefore was 6,000 days' wages. A talent is known to have purchased the hull of a warship in 483, and apparently a few decades later three talents would buy a completely fitted warship. We know that 2,012 talents were spent on the adornment of the Acropolis during one period. The reserve was 6,000 talents when the Peloponnesian War began; at one time it had reached 9,700.

The *Boule* fixed the amount of tribute (after 454) by four-year periods on the basis of the supposed resources of each member state, or ally, or subject, as we may choose to call them. An appeal from this assessment could be made. It would be heard in an Athenian court, as would any case whatsoever arising from the relation of Athens to the allies. The tribute was paid each year in March, at the time of the great festival of Dionysus, and the payment of it formed a part of this festival. In one of the parades, placards were carried to proclaim the assessed value of each ally, thus allowing anyone to make a quick calculation of its tribute. In another part of the parade, jars were carried, a mina of silver in each, to symbolize the state surplus for the preceding year. If any allies failed to pay, they were visited during the summer by Athenian naval units that collected the money. A sixtieth of the tribute, or a mina from each talent, was formally set aside as Athena's share and paid into the treasury of the goddess, which was administered by a board of temple treasurers.

There was income from the empire other than the tribute. Athens profited indirectly from the requirement that all cases at law of persons in the member states must be tried at Athens. Sometimes there were spoils of war from the operations of the empire, and rents came in from some of its properties. The preference or monopoly in trade, which she could insist upon in many areas because of her imperial position, was profitable to Athens as a whole. Her prosperity naturally drew to her the products of the whole world, so that she profited greatly even from the port tax on goods that came to Athens for distribution.

There was no direct tax on the Athenian citizens. The state drew in perhaps 400 talents a year from the lease of the silver mines at Laurium and scattered public lands, from the taxes on metics and the manumission (freeing) of slaves, the tax on the use of the facilities of the port of Peiraeus, and a few other minor taxes. How much was contributed to the state by the rich citizens who performed liturgies is not readily calculable. If a number of men fitted out a trireme apiece for the navy and other men presented the cost of the choruses for the plays and of the choruses that each tribe entered in the singing competition, they must have spent a goodly amount of money for the public good and the public's pleasure.

Athens: Expenditures

During times of peace, Athens' empire yielded a profit, but a difficult war could be very expensive and unprofitable. During peacetime, she would spend to support an active fleet of 60 triremes. The ships had to be steadily replaced, because they neither endured storms and accidents well nor stood up under ordinary service. The shipyards were kept busy replacing some of them every year. About 10,000 Athenian citizens were employed by the state as rowers for eight months or so of every year. The state paid a good many people for official service. Under Pericles, 6,000 dicasts, or jurymen, were paid two obols a day and had their pay raised to three obols a day by Cleon. This, it may be remarked, was a supplementary income rather than a living wage, for three obols was only half a drachma. The 500 members of the *Boule* were paid, as were some 700 other officials. The state also supported a number of slaves, some of them highly expert, like the permanent helpers in the offices of the government. All this establishment could be easily maintained in peacetime. In time of war, however, the extra expense of army and navy caused expenditures to rise far above income. Yet Athens sustained the burden of the Peloponnesian War for a long time in spite of the huge cost of the Sicilian expedition, and she might even have won had not the Persians subsidized a Spartan fleet at the end.

Sparta and Other States

Sparta, unlike Athens, had no income and no reserve at the beginning of the Peloponnesian War. As we have seen, her economy was well organized to keep her independent, somewhat aloof from other people, and out of the stream of modern tendencies, which were largely the result of the exchange of goods and services. Yet she was able to keep troops in the field, some of them mercenaries, and to induce her allies to help her. In times of peace, there was no difficulty in the management of the economic affairs of the Spartan state.

Except for Sparta, we know of no Greek *polis* that intentionally stood apart from the general economic and social tendencies. In part, the average *polis* had a money economy, although the prevalence of subsistence farms allowed much production and exchange of goods without the use of money. We may assume that in a great many *poleis* the rich were expected to make contributions of temples and other public buildings, and to make gifts equivalent to the liturgies at Athens, and, generally, to be the governing class without pay, because they could afford to spend their time in the public service. The average small *polis* did not provide any services for its citizens that required money. Thus, as long as there was a small income from port dues or the rent of public land or a similar source, the small *polis* could easily manage to maintain its government from year to year.

EDUCATION

We shall do better to think of Greek education as a process of teaching the young what society wanted them to know than as a system of schools. Nowadays at all ages and levels, a great deal of educating is done outside of schools. Even more was so done in Greece. Because all Greek societies were more conservative than ours and changed less from generation to generation, there was seldom a succession of new conditions that the young understood and welcomed and to which their elders found it hard to adjust, thus creating constant tension between the generations. Nevertheless, such times did occur in Greece, and the Periclean Age was one of them. Certain new ideas were abroad at this time, even though the age was a conservative one by present standards. To many people the idea of democracy was still radically new. Many new ideas were presented on the tragic stage. The Sophists presented new ideas. None of these new ideas was presented in what we should call a school, although the paid instruction offered by the Sophists was somewhat of this kind.

If we start with the young male Athenian of a rich family, we shall have to count the influence of nurses and other servants among the earliest educational influences, for a certain amount of popular lore and superstition was likely to be transmitted by them. Presently the little boy would go to school, usually under the supervision of a *paidagogos*, a "child-leader" or pedagogue, an elderly and responsible slave. Generally the child went to more than one school, for he must learn something of music from one master and the three R's from another. By the time he began to get his growth, he would also have a master in athletic exercises. None of this instruction was paid for by the state. In the early days, there was objection even to the idea that men had opened schools for profit to which the children of the newly rich might go. The older aristocratic idea was that one managed to have a child taught such things privately and that the new schools opened advantages to people who probably ought not to have advantages. Later we shall find the censors at Rome closing schools of rhetoric on the same principle.

We are poorly informed about the nature of the music that the Greeks performed or heard performed or had taught to their children. We do know that there were differing modes, or scales with differing intervals. The flute and the lyre were popular instruments. We do not know where the line was drawn between the amateur playing suitable for a gentleman and the professional playing more suitable for a slave. Certainly no leading Athenian family could have endured the thought that one of their sons might become a professional musician. On the other hand, not to be able to play at all stamped a man as an oaf. He had to be able to take his turn as the lyre was passed around at a party. Plutarch tells us that Alcibiades refused to play the flute on the ground that a man looked silly while playing it and that his influence was such that flute-playing went out of fashion.

The school that taught the three R's was likely also to introduce the boy to Homer and to some of the lyric poets, as well as Hesiod. There was still no prose literature, and tragedy was to be seen rather than read out of books. Homer, of course, was to be heard in the recitations at the festivals or in performances by entertainers. The average Greek would know long stretches of both *Iliad* and *Odyssey* by heart. Homer's educational influence was that of a compelling picture of life. Life may follow literature, if literature gives what seems to be a compelling and admirable picture of life.

The athletic training took place on an outdoor exercise ground. Such places were meant to provide a combination of manly exercising and passing the time. The older men often went there for sociability. Sometimes the youngsters exercised in armor and with weapons. Their more usual exercises were those of the Olympic and other games—the dash and the longer run, broad-jumping, throwing the discus and the javelin, wrestling, and boxing. The nominal purpose of the exercises was to prepare the citizen for military service by developing his body.

At about fifteen or sixteen, probably, the young Athenian began to have the benefit of having a slightly older man as lover. This practice needs to be made quite clear. It was homosexual love, in the sense that it was love between men—members of the same sex. It does not carry any implication that the older man who initiated the relation was unable to achieve a proper heterosexual life. The word "love" is not ordinarily applied to such a relation today because our idea of the relation between men and women (which would have seemed strange to the Greeks) has made love between men a forbidden word. The emotion that we call love, blended of admiration and sexual attraction, seems to have been genuinely felt in these affairs of Greek men with one another, or those of Greek women, if we may believe Sappho.

The relation between the Greek lover and his male beloved did plainly degenerate at times into an active physical sexual relationship. The Greeks explicitly say so and as explicitly say that this was a most regrettable form of what was usually a lofty and eduational relation. The good that a young man of perhaps twenty-two to twenty-five can do in molding a boy of fifteen to nineteen hardly needs to be described in detail; few influences, either for good or for evil, in the life of a boy can be compared to that of a young man whom he whole-heartedly admires. Such a relation was regarded as a very important and highly approved educational force among the Greeks; its perverted form was just as strongly disapproved.

At the age of eighteen, the young man became liable to two years of military service as a cadet. Little is known exactly about the terms of his service. It is to be presumed that he was given a certain amount of instruction in military matters. It is to be presumed also that there was much comparing of information, misinformation, and attitudes when the group was away from home together on service.

We must remember, too, that the education of the Athenian continued during his manhood. Attendance at the Assembly was a most educational activity, as was attendance at the plays during the festivals. There was constant discussion everywhere that the Greek man went, for he was a great talker, and in the time of Pericles especially there were new ideas in the air that the middle-aged man knew about, even if he was less ready than the young to accept them.

Upper-class women were not always secluded. Although the Athenian girl did not have occupations outside the home and was not schooled as her brother was, it would be a mistake to regard her as living the life of an animal chained in a kennel. Presumably she received more practical education from her mother than the boy did from his father, for the father was in many cases too occupied to take a hand in his son's training. An intelligent Athenian girl brought up by an intelligent mother must have received a good education for the kind of life she was going to live. To the training of her character and the training in her practical duties was added the training that came from some opportunity to watch the public life of Athens, at least in its religious exercises and festivals. If the domestic scene was most of life for her, we need not feel sorry for her or regard her as an unfulfilled person. If she did not receive love as we think of it, we need not think of her as emotionally starved.

The less prosperous classes of society in Athens got a different and livelier kind of education, as the less prosperous classes do everywhere. There were ways of learning the three R's other than going to school, and there were other skills, often shady ones, for which the more prosperous family would not have known how to find a teacher. Naturally the females of the poorer classes were not so much sheltered as the more prosperous, and were more aware of what went on. If the poor man was a citizen, he learned from service with the fleet as a rower or from meetings of the assembly or from the plays or from the endless argument that swirled through the life of the male Athenian. The metic and the slave, too, usually got a more informal sort of education. If the metic was wealthy, however, he might send his son to school, but the youngster would be destined for a career in business, and this he would learn on the job, not in any school. Slaves often received education that would heighten their value, either in handicrafts or in such skills as bookkeeping.

We do not know much about education elsewhere than in Athens. A school for girls was conducted by Sappho in Lesbos. The Spartan system is a good example of a system of education relying little upon formal schooling as we understand it, yet very effective in imparting information, skills, and attitudes. The attitudes of the older people, the exercises, the examples, the rewards, and the punishments were all well calculated to cause the youngster to learn what his elders wished him to learn.

THE AGE OF PERICLES REVIEWED

The Age of Pericles is the first of those few periods in Western history which have so impressed us that we ordinarily use the capital *A* and designate it by the name of some leading person. There was an Age of Augustus in Rome, and in more modern times Elizabeth and Victoria of England and Louis XIV of France lent their names to their times. The student of Greece rarely fails to gain the impression that the time when Pericles was in power deserves to be regarded as a period having definite qualities of its own. This period was extraordinary in the strict sense of the word: it was a time that had something more, something above and beyond the normal and regular course of life and affairs. It will be worth our while to pause to see if it is possible to summarize the qualities of this extraordinary period in a sober and factual way.

In one way, it is easy to define: it was the stretch of about thirty years when Pericles was regularly elected general by his tribe, from 465 B.C., or a year or two later, until his death in 429 from the plague. Perhaps, however, the beginning of this period should be put in 461, when Pericles and Ephialtes together carried through the changes that made Athens more democratic. Although Cleisthenes had moved toward democracy, the Age of Pericles was the time of complete and radical democracy. The period is defined with unusual sharpness at its ending as well as at its beginning, for the combination of the Peloponnesian War and, just at its beginning, the terrible plague and the death of Pericles brought a great change in the life of Athens after 429 B.C. Of course, it is true that many of the tendencies of the Periclean Age continued or first came to full flower in later years. Socrates was formed in this period, as was the historian Thucydides. The activity of the Sophists began in this period. Yet the changes that the war, the plague, and the loss of Pericles wrought in the political and military power of Athens, in the spirit of the Athenian people, and in the spirit of the Athenian government were so great that Athens after the death of Pericles began rapidly to become a different place; an epoch had ended.

From one point of view, the brilliance and the successes of the Athenians in the Age of Pericles may be called one of the great achievements of the *polis*. The historian must, of course, perch far enough above the bustle and the conflict to be able to perceive that there were other and different triumphs for the *polis*—the long, sober, and steady course of Sparta, for example, the brilliance of Corinth, or the humdrum and obscure existence of many tiny *poleis* that did nothing more than attend to their own affairs and allow their citizens, under the law, to lead a quiet life and occasionally attend the great games or the Festival of Dionysus at Athens.

The unity and the energy of the Athenians at this time are a notable phenomenon, and seemed such to their contemporaries. Whatever the Athenians undertook, privately or publicly, they pushed with an energy that knew no bounds. The Athenian manufacturer, the trader, and the Athenians serving in the army or the navy drove hard toward their goals. As a society, they were willing to attempt great things, to run the necessary risks and make the necessary sacrifices. Their goals were not always disinterested; these men were outright imperialists, taking advantage of their former allies, now their subjects, and ready to punish ruthlessly any assertion of independence among them. Their pursuit of their commercial and military interests in other directions was forthright, vigorous, and often brutal.

The members of some modern societies would not approve of the restless energy of the Athenians, for it is the antithesis of the ideal of quietism of these societies. The strenuous life suits the taste of the modern West, however, especially the United States, and we may see in the Athens of the Age of Pericles a remarkable example of a society that was so organized as to seem individually and collectively most energetic. When we attempt to explain how it was done, we are on unsure ground. Certainly we cannot say without further explanation that democracy was the cause. Perhaps the mass of the people felt more enthusiasm for fighting and striving because they could vote in the Assembly. A sense of full participation may have spurred them on. There is no way of proving such a thesis, however, and experience has shown that men can drive hard under the leadership of privileged aristocracies or strong monarchies. It is possible that the personality of Pericles had something to do with the enthusiasm and energy. We know very little about any theory of the collective wisdom of the people current at this time, although Aristotle supports the idea later in his *Politics*. Pericles may well have been a great oral expounder of such a theory, thus arousing great enthusiasm among the many.

This was a period of solid achievement in the arts. The artists of Athens and of Greece in general were working along sound lines and finding ample patronage. Earlier in the century, some of the conventions that had ruled in sculpture had been put aside, giving a freer and more realistic style. There had been a good deal of experiment and discussion about the proper proportions for Doric temples. The general judgment has been that the Greek art of this century and especially of the Age of Pericles remains unsurpassed. We must remember, however, that there are many students of art who object to what they call putting the art of this period in Greece on a pedestal as the only truly classical art and deducing all laws of art from it.

In thought and in literature, the period was extremely lively. The only type of literature in which Athens excelled at this time was the drama; here she had the masters of both tragedy and comedy—Aeschylus, Sophocles, Euripides, Aristophanes, and others. Athens never had a great lyric poet, although the writers of tragedy and comedy could write very fine poetry ("lyrics" to us, but not lyric poetry by the ancient definition) in the choruses of their plays. The only notable prose author, Herodotus of Halicarnassus, was not an Athenian, but he spent much time in Athens, praised her for her part in the Persian wars, was honored by the Athenians, and participated for a time in the Athenian colony of Thurii in Italy. His was the first full-scale history and the first great piece of European prose, in spite of the fact that there were less ambitious efforts before his which have not been preserved. Attic oratory was yet to be developed, as was the philosophy of Plato and others, later to be one of the distinctive productions of Greece of the fourth century. We find, then, when we review the literature of the age of Pericles, that the Athenians were active chiefly in tragedy and comedy. They did not write in many fields.

If we turn our attention to ideas, however, rather than to written or staged productions, we find furious activity, some due to the natives and much to foreigners. The writings of the early philosophers could be had, and their ideas were in the air. The fact that Athens as well as many other *poleis* was still moving out of an earlier age dominated by tradition and fixed codes into a newer age in which authority was losing ground to new rationalized views gave rise to very lively discussions about values that might replace the traditional ones. The most famous figure in this field was to be Socrates, who wrote nothing. The Sophists did more talking than writing. We must suppose that every performance of tragedies similar to those that have been preserved gave rise to lively discussions, which might last even beyond the presentation of the next year's tragedies, for many imply a whole set of problems in values of life and the management of a *polis*. Discussion on the management of a *polis* also arose from those who, without being philosophers or Sophists or anything but citizens with strong opinions about government, set forth their views on whether government should be democratic or aristocratic.

The Athens of this time has been called a men's club. It might also be called a huge discussion group (not long ago the expression would have been "debating society"). The topics most likely to be discussed in the Athens of the Age of Pericles were topics of importance to the thinking of the modern West, which has also been slowly coming out of a traditional society and building up attitudes and values more suitable to a less traditional society, a society based more on rational ideas than on tradition. Both the questions asked by the Greeks and the answers that they gave have often exhilarated Europeans of the last few hundred years as they have gone through the same sort of process that the Greeks experienced. The men of the Age of Pericles seem to be people of our own kind giving a brilliant performance of being rationalists, as we like to think that we are.

CHAPTER

24

THE PELOPONNESIAN WAR

The Peloponnesian War may be said to have lasted from 431 B.C. until the capitulation of Athens in 404, even though technically there was a period of several years of peace after 421. The Thirty Years' Peace of 445 had been intended to make two groups, the Spartan and the Athenian, so nearly equal that neither of them need have undue fear of the other. There is no evidence that the conditions of the fourteen years of peace between 445 and 431 were felt to bear hardly or unfairly on either side. What, then, were the circumstances of the resumption of warfare in the year 431?

THE QUARREL OF CORINTH AND CORCYRA

The quarrel that eventually brought on the conflict started in the western part of Greece. Corinth had founded a colony, Corcyra, on an island off the west coast. Corcyra in turn had sent out a colony, Epidamnus, and the mother city of Corinth had shared in the auspices of the new city, as was often done. Now in Epidamnus the few (the oligarchs) and the many (the democrats) were at swords' points, and the many had got the better of it and exiled a group of the few. The exiled few had enlisted the help of the neighboring

barbarians and were pressing the many hard. The many now appealed
to Corcyra for help and were refused; then they appealed to Corinth
and were accepted, whereupon Corcyra espoused the cause of the
few and decided to take an active part in the siege of Epidamnus.

Corinth and her colony of Corcyra, then, were in active disagreement because a class struggle had come to the fighting point in Epidamnus. Corinth called for volunteers favorable to the many to join
in the defense of Epidamnus. Several small states from western
Greece friendly to her joined her, wishing not only to help the general cause of the many, but also to strengthen Corinthian naval
power in the waters on the way to Italy. In the summer of 435, a
naval battle was decisively won by the Corcyreans, and on that day
they also captured Epidamnus. Corcyra now exploited her victory
by acts of senseless offensiveness and cruelty.

Corinth set to work to build a larger fleet to return to the struggle,
which for her involved important issues of prestige and trade routes.
Corcyra began to cast about for allies. The Spartans would have
approved of her supporting the cause of the few, but they had sensibly and properly urged arbitration on both sides before the battle.
Corinth had refused. The Corcyreans shrewdly turned to Athens,
hoping that other considerations would be more powerful than
Athens' consistent support of the many.

The Corinthians thereupon sent an embassy to urge the Athenians
to refuse, and this momentous issue was debated before the sovereign
people of Athens. Athens could grant Corcyra a defensive alliance
and still be within the terms of the Thirty Years' Peace; an offensive
alliance must be directed against Corinth, a member of the Spartan
Alliance, and would contravene the peace. The Athenians at first
refused Corcyra's request for a treaty, but on the second day, at the
urging of Pericles, they made a defensive alliance with Corcyra.

Pericles must take some responsibility, it seems, for the war that
followed. He had always been a strong advocate of resistance to
Sparta's claims, pretensions, and pressures. That is, he was not above
including in his admirable program a dash of calculated hostility to
another nation as a device to increase his popularity. Such devices
sometimes do not leave a man free to choose the best course, and so
it was with Pericles. It may well be, too, that he considered it a good

idea to move to attach Corcyra to Athens with the thought that an ally on the way to the West might be useful.

In the early autumn of 433, the battle between the Corinthians and the Corcyreans was observed by ten Athenian ships, which came between the combatants when it seemed that all was lost for Corcyra. The Corinthians withdrew when the Athenians told them that they would defend the Corcyreans.

The Athenians had now gained a useful ally in Corcyra, the only naval power in the western waters off Greece and one whose location made it an excellent rallying point for Athenian warships on either peaceful or warlike missions to the West. The Athenians had acted with full knowledge that the move was contrary to the spirit of their treaty with the Spartans. Their professed view was that war would come anyway. The Spartans did not move in retaliation, apparently not intending a war and therefore not proclaiming the inevitability of one. The Corinthians had hoped that the Athenians would not want war and had attempted to argue before them that respect for the Thirty Years' Peace would leave the danger of war remote.

In the next year (432), the Athenians made two more provocative moves. One was to exclude the Megarians (allies of Corinth) from all ports and markets of the Athenian Empire, a deadly blow to a commercial city like Megara. The other was to begin bullying Potidaea, a Corinthian colony in the north near Macedonia, ordering it to tear down its walls on the seaward side, to give hostages to Athens, and to notify the Corinthians that it would no longer receive the yearly magistrates customarily sent to it by its mother city. The Potidaeans appealed to Corinth and Sparta and got a promise that Sparta would invade Attica if Athens attacked Potidaea. The Athenians began a siege of Potidaea late in the summer of 432.

In the early autumn of 432, because the Spartans had made no move, the Corinthians went to them to complain that the Athenians had violated the treaty by their aggression. The Spartans said that they would hear what other peoples had to say about the conduct of the Athenians. At an assembly of the Spartans, complaints against Athens were made by the Corinthians, the Megarians, and others. The assembly was also addressed by some Athenians who had been sent there on other business and who reminded the company of the formidable qualities of Athens. They urged the Spartans to submit

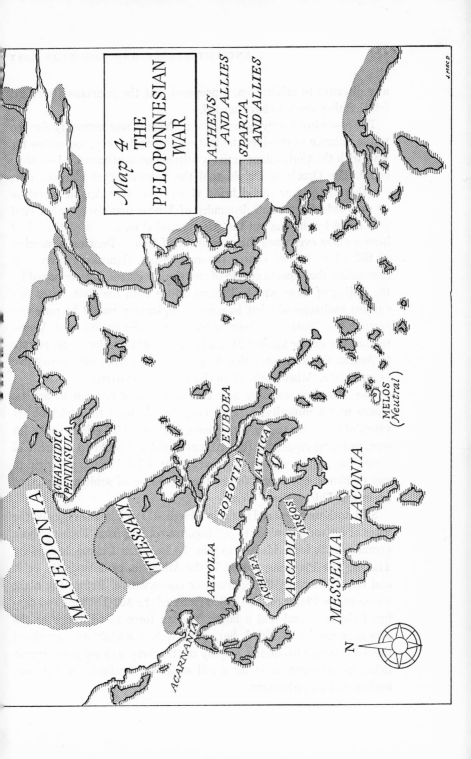

Map 4
THE
PELOPONNESIAN
WAR

ATHENS
AND ALLIES

SPARTA
AND ALLIES

MACEDONIA

CHALCIDIC
PENINSULA

THESSALY

EUBOEA

BOEOTIA

ATTICA

AETOLIA

ACARNANIA

ACHAEA

ARCADIA

ARGOS

MESSENIA

LACONIA

MELOS
(Neutral)

N

any disputes to arbitration, a proposal that the Spartans afterward felt that they ought to have heeded.

The assembly finally voted for war. Now it was necessary for the whole alliance to consider the matter. Presently they, too, voted for war, with the Corinthians actively stirring up sentiment as best they could. The Oracle at Delphi told the Spartans that vigorous prosecution of the war would bring victory and that Apollo would be on their side. Sparta now demanded of Athens that she clear her land of a curse by driving out the Alcmaeonid clan, on whom there had been a curse ever since the conspiracy of Cylon. Pericles, a member of this clan, was of course the real target. Athens countered by demanding that Sparta get rid of two similar curses, both incurred by the killing of those who had taken refuge with the gods. After this curious exchange of what in modern diplomacy would be pure impertinences, Sparta got down to business by demanding that Athens rescind her decree against Megara, leave Potidaea alone, and restore to Aegina the autonomy that had been taken from her twenty-five years before. Athens refused to discuss these matters.

The Athenian assembly now considered their relation to Sparta. There was a minority, a small one, that favored the strict observance of the peace treaty with Sparta made in 445. Pericles spoke for war, insisting especially that Athens could not yield to a threat of force. The answer was sent to Sparta that Athens would not yield to any demands, but would follow the procedure of arbitration agreed on in the Thirty Years' Peace.

Still nothing happened until, in March, 431, a Plataean opened the gates of his town at night to 300 hoplites coming from Thebes, whose errand was to force Plataea to join the Boeotian League, headed by Thebes. The Plataeans moved in the Athenian, or democratic, orbit and the Thebans in the Spartan, or conservative. Before the night was over the Plataeans had killed many of the 300 Thebans and captured the rest, had told a larger Theban force to withdraw or the prisoners would be killed, but, after it had withdrawn, murdered them anyway. This double display of treachery was for some reason taken as sufficient cause for a full scale war by both the Peloponnesians and the Athenians.

THE FIRST STAGE, OR THE ARCHIDAMIAN WAR (431–421 B.C.)

The aim of the Spartan Alliance was to defeat the Athenians in a pitched battle if they could be induced to risk one. If not, they would have to ravage Athenian territory and hope thus to force a battle, because they were not strong enough for any naval offensive. The Athenians adopted the strategy proposed by Pericles of moving the citizens of Attica and their animals inside the city and the Long Walls. Even the woodwork of some of the buildings was moved in, suggesting the prevalence of adobe construction reinforced with wood in farmhouses. The vines and the fruit trees had to be left to be cut down by the invading Spartan army. The reserve hoplites were to guard the walls that surrounded Athens and Peiraeus and connected city and port. The first-line hoplites were to be out with the navy conducting the Athenian offensive, which would strike at Sparta and her allies, now here, now there, making sudden raids on the shore and cutting off trade and food supplies on the sea. Pericles assured the Athenians that if they could find the patience to endure being shut up in Athens while the Spartans ravaged their land and insulted them, they could eventually force the Spartans to end the war by the steady damage that they could inflict on them without ever fighting a great battle on the land. Athens could easily import food or anything else. Some were impatient at this proposal, notably Cleon, who was to be heard from later, but Pericles persuaded the people to endorse it.

In May of 431, the Spartan king Archidamus (from whose name the first part of the war, until 421, is sometimes called "the Archidamian War") led into Attica a mighty army. Although many of the Athenians complained bitterly as the enemy paraded before them and spread destruction through Attica, Pericles, who was in charge, would allow no discussion of an attack. Before the enemy had left Attica, however, the ships of Athens were out carrying the Athenian offensive to many points in the Peloponnesus. Two Corinthian stations in western Greece were captured.

The Plague

In 430, the Peloponnesians again invaded Attica and spread destruction for several weeks. This was the year in which the plague came from the East. Modern physicians have often puzzled over Thucydides' careful description of the symptoms and have tried to identify the disease. Typhus and measles have been thought to be the most plausible suggestions. There may also be merit in the suggestion that germ strains may have changed enough since then so that no disease that we now know is exactly like the plague of ancient times.

The plague raced through the crowded city. Men sickened and, after a few days of misery, died. Some few survived and were immune thereafter. The scanty water supplies were soon infected; prompt and proper disposal of the bodies was impossible. The city and the space between the Long Walls were crowded and uncomfortable enough at best with the country population added to those who normally lived in the city. Now fear stalked everywhere, and for a little while the Athenians degenerated. Extravagant and lawless behavior became common as men awaited a horrible death.

Pericles called his people back to courage, but fear had made them sullen and resentful. They deposed him from his office and fined him. The next year, however, he was re-elected and again put in charge of the war. But in 429 the plague was still there, and in the autumn Pericles died of it. The plague remained until 426.

It has been customary to rate Pericles far more highly than some of the leaders who followed him—Cleon, for instance. These later men deserve to be judged more on their performances and less on their inability to employ the grand manner in their public appearances. All were members of the business class that benefited greatly from the empire. They must have been active in public affairs in many ways even while Pericles was in control. Now their voices were heard in loud and vulgar expressions of opinion in the Assembly; the essence of their policies, however, was generally what Pericles would have advocated.

The Revolt of Mitylene

In the summer of 428, Mitylene, the most important city on the island of Lesbos, revolted from the Athenians, the propertied classes having inspired the move. They asked for help from Sparta; had the Spartans been able to act with promptness, they might have helped Mitylene to break free and might have gained strong recruits for their own side. The Athenians, as usual, did act with promptness; they besieged the city. For a moment we see the relations between the few and the many in more detail than usual. The few were urged by a Spartan adviser to arm the many in order to drive off the Athenian besiegers. But the many, finding themselves armed with real weapons and defensive armor, turned on the few and forced them to surrender the city.

Now a famous debate took place in the Athenian Assembly, the substance of which is reported by the historian Thucydides. Cleon made the incredibly foolish proposal that every adult male in Mitylene—those of the friendly many as well as those of the hostile few —be slaughtered and that the rest of the people be sold into slavery. The resolution was carried and a message sent off to the Athenian commander in Lesbos. But Athens was a radical democracy; that is, what it had done on the spot one day it might undo the next, without serving notice or waiting for committee reports. Next day the Assembly, a little awed by its own vote, heard more discussion, knowing all the while that its message of the day before was on its way to Lesbos.

Diodotus, whose proposal was to be carried this time, argued that the decree of the day before should be repealed because it was unwise. Such severity, he argued, would not prevent further revolts, which to the Greek mind seemed inevitable; it would only embitter and alienate the democratic majority in the cities of the League, the element that favored Athens. Cleon persisted in his belief that exemplary severity was necessary to prevent further trouble. Diodotus managed to have the decree rescinded by a narrow margin, and another ship set out on a spectacular race to overtake the first. The new message arrived just as the Athenian commander in Lesbos was preparing to carry out the first order. The walls of Mitylene were dismantled and its fleet confiscated, for it had been one of the few allies that still had a fleet. The land was parceled out to Athenian settlers for whom the natives had to work. In addition, Cleon persuaded the Athenians to execute a thousand of the leaders of the revolt.

The Mitylenean Debate, as it often is called, has sometimes been taken as an illustration of a hardening of sentiment among the

Athenians as the war went on, especially since Diodotus' arguments for mercy were put on such severely practical grounds. Probably the calculations of the Athenian Empire had all been made on hardheaded and unsentimental grounds; such practical views can hardly have been new.

The unnecessary brutality shown by both sides in the war was, however, something new. Wars in Greece had been conducted on reasonably humane lines up to this time. They were generally settled by pitched battles, which were not followed by pursuit and slaughter of the vanquished. Prisoners ordinarily were not butchered, but were treated with decency until they could be exchanged or ransomed.

At this time, though, there was a notable increase of man's inhumanity to man in the conduct of war. There seems to have been an increase of brutality in the struggles of the few and the many in individual cities, too, although some evidence suggests that these struggles had often been marked by bitterness and cruelty. Perhaps the fact that they involved people more closely connected to each other tended to embitter and degrade them, as often happens. In many cases at this time, the factional struggles in the cities were closely connected with the war. The affairs of Corcyra, Corinth, and Epidamnus before the war, the episode of the Theban attempt on Plataea at the beginning of the war, and the revolt of Mitylene were all episodes of the continual struggle between the few and the many.

The Affair at Corcyra

In 427, Corcyra suffered a factional struggle, which was described in detail by Thucydides and which is notable even among similar contests of the time for the depths to which the participants sank. Corcyra had been on the oligarchic side in the earlier affair of Epidamnus, while Corinth had favored the democrats. Now the democrats were in control in Corcyra, presumably because Athens had assisted them. But the oligarchs, made desperate by the fact that the democrats had imposed confiscatory fines on several of them, attacked the democratic council while it was in session, killed many members, and seized control of the city.

Now a hideous civil war began, punctuated by the intervention of Corinthians and Athenians and a few intervals when the Corcyreans made up their quarrel just enough to conduct naval battles against the Peloponnesian fleet that appeared on the scene, only to resume their domestic warfare with renewed hate and madness. The Athenians were bound by their power politics to favor the democrats; in the end they found themselves standing by while a massacre of the few was perpetrated by the many. Emotions ran so high and cruelty become so riotous that some of the oligarchs were said to have committed suicide rather than trust to the mercies of the democrats when they saw that capture was inevitable. It did not go unnoticed that certain personal projects were advanced in the general confusion; old enmities were liquidated, and sons assisted their fathers to pay their overdue debt to Nature.

Athens Has the Advantage: 428–424 B.C.

During the years between 431 and 428, the Spartans had not succeeded in winning any signal victory over the Athenians. They invaded Attica regularly and made it impossible for any farming to be done there or for the farm folk to feel safe outside the city. But they did not manage to entice the Athenians into a pitched battle. The plague had probably inflicted more loss of life than they could have hoped to do and had for some time damaged Athenian morale; it did not in the long run lessen the Athenian will to victory.

The Athenians had fought their war as a sea power, according to Pericles' plan and advice, with one notable exception. Their energetic general Demosthenes conceived a plan for general land operations in central Greece. He apparently expected to overcome the Aetolians, who lived just north of the Corinthian Gulf in western Greece, and finally to invade and conquer Boeotia in the east. The expected allies refused to co-operate, however, or did so tardily and ineffectively. Furthermore, the Athenian hoplites were at a great disadvantage in the broken country that they were trying to conquer. It was fortunate for the Athenians that this lesson about untried allies and broken terrain was taught to them so thoroughly on a small scale that they did not have to pay for being thus instructed on a large scale. After suffering considerable losses, Demosthenes finally withdrew.

Nevertheless, the Athenians had inflicted considerable damage on the enemy by their continual raids from the sea. They had also established a number of fortified posts in advantageous positions around the periphery of the Peloponnesus. The plague had been a great blow to them, of course, and in addition, they had lost some of their hoplites in the fighting of their raids. It may even be that enough of the hoplite class had perished to change significantly the economic and social composition of the assembly.

In 425, the year after Demosthenes had been given his costly lesson in Aetolia, he blundered into a great success on the west coast of the Peloponnesus, at Pylos. As he lay encamped there with a small force, a superior force of Spartans pounced on him. After the Athenians had defended themselves heroically for two days, a detachment of their fleet came up in the rear of the Spartans and put their ships out of action, leaving 420 Spartan hoplites and the Helots who attended them on the island of Sphacteria, just off shore, where they had based themselves for their attack on the Athenians of Demosthenes.

Nothing could show better than this incident what a terrible figure the well-trained and heavy-armed soldier, especially the Spartan, was in ancient warfare and what weight each of these soldiers carried in the political thinking of the Spartans. The thought of losing these 420 first-line soldiers struck terror into the Spartans. Each man was of great importance, not only for this war, but for the continuing life of Sparta.

The Spartans immediately proposed an armistice; they handed over their whole fleet on condition that the men on Sphacteria be supplied with food. They then sent an embassy to Athens to propose that the two states end the war and make an alliance. It is to be presumed that the predicament of their hoplites and the scanty success of their war to this point were both factors in their willingness to make such an offer. It was made without the concurrence of their allies, a fact that emphasizes their eagerness to have the whole matter at an end.

Possibly Pericles, had he been alive, would have urged acceptance of this offer. It is also possible that he would have done exactly as Cleon did, for Pericles, after all, had been the great leader of expanding Athenian imperialism. Cleon urged the Assembly to demand the surrender of the men on Sphacteria and the cession of a number of key points as a preliminary to serious discussion of peace. The Spartan embassy went home.

On second thought, the Assembly wished that it had been more reasonable. It was proposed that Cleon and someone else be sent to inspect the situation, for the Athenians were maintaining a force of 14,000 to watch the handful of Spartans, so great was their respect for them as fighting men. But Cleon, with his usual violence of tone, insisted that action was what was needed. When he drew the obvious answer that if he thought that the Spartans could be defeated, he ought to go and command the operation, he hesitated, then responded to the jeers of the Assembly by accepting the command, setting sail, fighting a battle, and coming back almost at once with 192 Spartan prisoners, the remnant of the force.

The Athenians now freed themselves from invasion by proclaiming this handful of precious Spartan lives to be hostages who would be lost to Sparta if she invaded Attica. Sparta made repeated offers of peace, which were refused. By the year 424, the Athenians seemed to have prospects of being able to end the war on highly favorable terms.

The Tide Turns: The Peace of Nicias

In that same year, 424, Athens again made the mistake of attempting a major land operation. The democratic element in Thebes conceived the idea of bringing their whole country over to democratic control and asked for Athenian help. An elaborate plan was made for a triple attack on Boeotia, but the local forces that were to cooperate failed as they had failed Demosthenes in Aetolia, and the matter finally came to the only full-scale battle of the war at Delium in southern Boeotia. The Boeotians prevailed, and Athens lost a thousand hoplites who were badly needed in her waning land forces.

The Spartans now sent a force to northern Greece under Brasidas, a commander of quite un-Spartan dash and charm, to raise difficulties for Athens among disaffected allies. After a number of preliminary successes, he captured the city of Amphipolis and gained control of the revenues and ship timber of the region—two welcome additions to Spartan resources. His fair and frank manner also won many friends for Sparta.

The historian Thucydides, who commanded a small fleet based at Thasos, had been summoned but arrived too late to reinforce Amphipolis. The Athenian people in their anger at the loss of the city exiled the unsuccessful admiral. Thus they made him a gift of the leisure in which to gather the material and write his history, at the same time making posterity the gift of a priceless account of these events.

At last, in 423, the two sides were willing to sign a year's truce. But each had a war party with an active man at its head—Brasidas in Sparta and Cleon in Athens. Under their influence, the truce was somewhat less than completely observed. When it ended in 422, Cleon organized a great expedition to go to the north to undo all that Brasidas had done there. The Athenian and Spartan forces met at Amphipolis, and it was the good fortune of both sides that both Brasidas and Cleon fell in the engagement.

Thereafter, peace negotiations began in earnest. Both Athens and Sparta were now willing to settle for the closest possible return to the state of things when the war had started. But here a new element entered. Argos, which had been neutral, seized the opportunity to make demands on Sparta as the price of renewing their treaty of neutrality. Her attitude was in the end to have much to do with the failure of the peace agreement. The Boeotians also were unwilling to make peace on the terms that satisfied Sparta. The effect of all this was that Sparta and Athens drew nearer to each other and made a treaty of mutual support and aid. The peace, concluded in 421, is known as the Peace of Nicias, from the name of the Athenian who was the chief negotiator and of whom we shall soon hear much more.

AN UNEASY PEACE (421–415 B.C.)

Problems of Reorganization

The chief problem of each side after the conclusion of the Peace of Nicias was to bring back into line its disaffected and recalcitrant allies. The difficulties of the Spartans were caused by the ambitions of Argos, which had stayed neutral and escaped the damage of the war, combined with the disgruntlement of the Corinthians and others. For two or three years, a number of ingenious statesmen among these malcontents tried to spin webs of diplomacy that would bind together new combinations to the advantage of their several states and to the disadvantage of Sparta. But too many architects were at work, and not all were seriously trying to build enduring structures. The air was cleared by Sparta's putting a splendid army in the field in 418; it defeated the Argives and their allies without great difficulty and restored all the prestige of Spartan arms.

Athens meanwhile was having great difficulty in reasserting her control over her allies in the north. She refused to return Pylos to Sparta on the ground that Sparta had been bound to restore Amphipolis, which Athens was unable to master. She also flirted with the projects of the Argives for creating a new alliance and even had some troops at the decisive battle in 418. Athens and Sparta themselves remained at peace, however.

Nicias and Alcibiades

Nicias, who gave his name to the peace of 421, was an elderly and wealthy conservative of Athens. He was representative of a good number of men who were not so blindly conservative as to wish for Spartan success and oligarchic government at Athens, but who were cautious and a little old-fashioned. He was a religious man in the old-fashioned style, believing, for example, in omens, a faith that was to cost the Athenians dearly in their coming campaign in Sicily. Yet, even though he was somewhat out of tune with the imperial Athens of his day, he was not a little man or a feeble man.

The historian would be tempted to set the figure of Alcibiades against Nicias for a striking comparison, even if they had not been opponents. Alcibiades took over something of the role of his kinsman Pericles as leader of the popular party and opponent of Sparta, while Nicias was the leading man of the sober conservatives (not of the die-hard oligarchs) and wished to implement his peace with Sparta so that a genuine peace might prevail. Upon Alcibiades every gift had been lavished except one—a healthy personality. He was of noble birth and wealthy. He was vigorous and handsome. All accomplishments came readily to him. He was a man of great charm. He was intelligent and had at his disposal a great fund of resolution and energy that allowed him to do well whatever he wished to do or to play effectively any role that pleased him.

His personality, however, was of a type that some moderns suggest is properly classified as neurotic, a kind of neuroticism often found in our time in connection with a profusion of gifts of circumstance and personality. Alcibiades seemed almost unaware that other people had rights. To satisfy his own convenience or merely his whim, he was capable of treating anyone with disregard or with insolence. He was thoroughly unscrupulous; he could not be trusted to do the kind, the honest, or the pledged thing. The anecdotes in Plutarch's biography of him are well chosen to illustrate his unfortunate traits. They also illustrate the fact that he could direct the overpowering charm of his personality at an individual or at the whole Athenian people and cause forgetfulness of the injuries that he had done and that he obviously would do again whenever it suited him.

There was only one occasion when Nicias and Alcibiades genuinely co-operated. Hyperbolus, who was a man of the people and wished to lead the popular party, tried to set afoot a movement to ostracize Alcibiades. Alcibiades, the wrong person against whom to direct such an attack, made an agreement with Nicias by which the ostracism of Hyperbolus himself was effected. There was a general feeling afterward that something had gone wrong, as there usually was after Alcibiades had done what he wanted at the moment, and the result was that ostracism was never used again.

The Affair of Melos

In 416, the Athenians decided that the island of Melos (better known by its Italian name, since the Venus "di Milo" was found there) must be forced into their alliance. An expedition went there with an invitation to join, which the Melians politely declined, saying that they preferred neutrality. Thucydides reports a discussion of the matter that he represents as having taken place between the Athenian and Melian leaders; it is called "the Melian Dialogue."

This dialogue is of interest because it is an independent work of art, because it shows "the first scientific historian" following the bidding of his strong artistic nature, and because it informs us on an interesting incident of the war. The factors of power politics involved in the situation were clearly set forth to the Melians by the Athenians, who were influenced solely by considerations of power. The dialogue is sometimes taken to illustrate the coarsening and hardening of the Athenian character under the stresses of war, but a coldly factual attitude toward the exercise of power was nothing new at Athens or elsewhere. It might be better to consider the account with the characteristic Western joy in men who, with all their arguments for asserting their freedom beaten down by the enemy towering over them, decided that in defiance of logic and common sense they would nonetheless fight for their independence because it seemed right to them to do so. The Athenians took Melos, killed all the men, and enslaved the women and children.

THE SICILIAN EXPEDITION (415–413 B.C.)

Now the Athenians became involved in the greatest misfortune in all their history. Segesta, an ally in Sicily, asked for a visit from envoys and convinced the men who were sent that she was able to finance an Athenian attack on Selinus, which moved in the Syracusan orbit, and even on Syracuse herself. As the expansive genius of Alcibiades saw it, Athens would be able in the end to dominate Sicily, Carthage, and the Greeks of South Italy. These and the Etruscans were the civilized peoples of the West. No one then was able to foresee what Rome would become.

Alcibiades threw all his influence behind the proposal. Nicias opposed it with his usual cautious conservatism. The Athenian people should be reckoned as an active partner in the decision; they were never mere passive masses dictated to by their leaders. In this case, they were so enthusiastic that when Nicias named a prohibitive number of ships and men as necessary, they promptly voted that number.

Athens had recovered very well during the years that had combined nominal peace and actual maneuvering with hostile intent. Her trade and her tribute brought her a good income. The energy of the Athenian character was still there. The idea of conquering the great powers of the West did not seem fantastic to the masses of the Athenians. If successful, they would have an empire that could guarantee employment and pay to the people and put them beyond fear of the Spartans or, perhaps, in victorious control of them. If the price was likely to be high, they felt able and ready to pay it. If, viewed with the eyes of sixty generations later, the scheme seems one of naked imperialism, it must be remembered that some enterprises of the ancient world that began as plain imperialism ended as guarantors of peace and security for many people. It is possible that this daring enterprise, if successful, would have made life better for many people.

The Affair of the Hermae

In June, 415, the great Athenian armada was ready to set out for Sicily. Almost the night before the fleet was to sail, someone went about the city systematically mutilating the stone statues of the god Hermes that stood in every part of the city. Such a deed of sacrilege shocked and frightened people. An accuser came forward to point out Alcibiades as the leader of a group who had defaced the Hermae during a drunken frolic. To this was added a new charge, that he and his friends had enacted a parody of the Mysteries on another drunken occasion, again a sacrilege, this time against the goddesses Demeter and Persephone, the holy persons of the Mysteries of Eleusis. Alcibiades hotly denied the charges and demanded an immediate trial. But he, with Nicias and Lamachus, was to command the expedition, and this was declared no time for such a trial. So at the June solstice the armada sailed.

Again superstitious fears came to the fore, new accusations were made, and some men fled the country, while others were imprisoned. Finally a respectable citizen, Andocides, finding all the men of his family in prison with him, turned informer and told a story of the affair that led to the execution of four men and the temporary exile of a few others. Those who wished to discredit Alcibiades sent *Salaminia*, one of the state galleys, to bring him home for trial.

Perhaps Alcibiades was not unwilling to dissociate himself from the expedition, which instead of immediately assaulting the Syracusans with all its great force had been allowed to bog down in preparations and trivialities. On the way home he escaped to Sparta.

There he advised the Spartans to send help to Syracuse—help that was to be a prime cause of the Athenian defeat—and to fortify Decelea, a strong point in Attica, so as to hold a paralyzing threat over the Athenians. Sparta thus (in the year 414) committed herself to an invasion of Athenian territory as well as assistance to Athens' enemies, and once again the two powers were openly at war.

Disaster in Sicily

As the Athenians in Sicily soon learned, for the third time in this war they had put too much trust in the allies whom they expected to carry out a major operation in concert with them. The western Greeks were now cool and not very helpful. In the autumn they made a belated attack on Syracuse, which had some success. The Syracusans appealed to Sparta for help. In 414 the Athenians moved on Syracuse again and by summer could feel confident that they had reduced the defenders to real straits of hunger. The arrival of Gylippus in charge of relief forces from Sparta and Corinth was the turning point. Gylippus succeeded in breaking up the blockade of the city and winning some minor engagements. Now Nicias sent home a gloomy letter admitting the sorry state of the affair and asking for reinforcements.

With great effort, the government sent out Demosthenes, a good commander, with reinforcements. He tried to make a decisive attack at once. It failed. He now urged Nicias to give it all up and go home, but Nicias resisted. A far tougher man than he was might have hesitated to return and report to the sovereign people that their great dream of empire in the West had turned into a nightmare. When at last Nicias was convinced, there was an eclipse of the moon (August 27, 413) and both he and the majority of the troops accepted the soothsayers' decree that they ought not to move for twenty-seven days.

This piece of superstitious behavior cost the Athenians dearly. Gylippus and the Syracusans managed to throw up a barrier to contain the Athenian fleet in the great harbor of Syracuse. Nicias and Demosthenes attempted to escape overland with their confused group of soldiers, marines, sailors, rowers from the galleys, and slaves. The gloomy genius of Thucydides is at its best as he tells of the flight, the many swift deaths, the famous imprisonment of the captured Athenians in the quarries of Syracuse, the lingering, painful death of many there, and the sale of the survivors into slavery. This was the worst disaster ever suffered by a Greek armed force or by a Greek state.

THE LAST STAGE OF THE WAR (413–404 B.C.)

The terribly costly defeat of the Sicilian expedition was a turning point in the Peloponnesian War and the fortunes of Athens. Certainly it strengthened the sentiment of both conservatives and moderates that the democratic policy had been too ambitious and not cautious enough. It should be noted, however, that the great energy which was characteristic of the Athenians remained unimpaired. The efforts which they still put forth were the wonder of outsiders.

At this juncture, the Persians decided to take a hand. The Peace of Callias (448 B.C.) had been reaffirmed some ten years before; but in 414 the Athenians had unwisely given aid to a revolt of the Carians from Persia. Perhaps for this reason, perhaps because of the Athenian disaster in Sicily, the Persians decided to regard the treaty as abrogated. They reasserted their claim to tribute from the Greeks of Asia Minor and began to pay naval subsidies to Sparta so that the Spartans could oppose an effective fleet to that of the Athenians in the waters off Asia Minor. The Spartans in return disclaimed the role of protectors of the Asiatic Greeks against the Persians.

The difficulties of Athens in carrying on the war were also increased by the revolt of some of their allies. Thucydides would have us believe that they were ready to revolt at all times out of resentment at Athenian highhandedness and Athenian insistence on democratic constitutions. A careful reading of his own details shows that they do not support his general remarks. The common people everywhere were favorable to Athens, which supported the cause of the many. A large number of the revolts were plainly inspired by the few, as in the case of Mitylene. The few generally hoped for or could count on the support of the Persians or the Spartans. In this last phase of the war, the people who revolted could count on support from both Persia and Sparta.

The Oligarchic Revolution of 411 B.C.

The Sicilian expedition had been essentially the result of a plan of the common people, who had looked forward to benefits for the masses from its success. After its failure, the more conservative and cautious elements in Athens demanded to be heard, and the populace at large may well have been disposed to listen to more sober views. In 413, a newly-created board of ten commissioners was elected; it was intended to be regarded as the highest-ranking board and was to have an important voice in policy.

The conservative, or oligarchic, element must be separated into extremists and moderates. The extremists would have taken away all political rights from the mass of the people. The more moderate element would merely have strengthened the prerogative of the few to lead and direct. All along, the extreme oligarchs had been banded together in clubs that did not call attention to themselves, but actively assisted their members in any situation where union seemed useful, as in campaigns for election.

Not only did the conservatives take heart at the spectacular failure of the democratic policy in Sicily, but they also suddenly received an unexpected offer of assistance from Alcibiades. He had been in Sparta, whither he had fled, and then had gone to Tissaphernes, the Persian satrap in Asia Minor.

In Sparta, Alcibiades, having given the Spartans such an idea of Athenian long-range plans in Sicily and South Italy that they had decided to renew open war against Athens, won their further admiration by playing the Spartan to perfection, living in strenuous simplicity. He had added his own touch by seducing the king's wife and is reported to have said that the bloodline of the royal family would be improved thereby. He found it advisable to change his residence and slipped away from the Spartan fleet, with which he was serving, to Tissaphernes. The Persian grandee was also charmed. The recent Spartan ascetic assumed as the guest of the Persian the role of the devotee of elegance and luxury. Soon a plan suggested itself to his fertile imagination.

He sent a message to the officers of the Athenian fleet at Samos: if an oligarchy were established at Athens, he could get the aid of Tissaphernes for Athens rather than for Sparta, which would give

Athens a new advantage in naval power. The condition that Athens must change over to oligarchic government seemed natural, because the Persians preferred to deal with the more stable governments dominated by the few.

Even to the moderates, the establishment of an oligarchy of some sort seemed preferable to defeat by Sparta. Word of Alcibiades' proposal was sent back from the fleet to Athens, and there the efforts of the conservatives were redoubled. The moderate faction debated the matter and prepared to propose a change to oligarchy. The extremists contrived the murder of a number of democratic leaders, spreading dismay among the people.

A group of the conservatives serving in the fleet had gone to meet Tissaphernes and Alcibiades. But Alcibiades had sensed in the meantime that Tissaphernes was not going to fall in with his plan, and, in order to keep the blame for the failure of the scheme from falling on him, he managed to get the Persian price for co-operation set so high as to be prohibitive. The disappointed envoys prepared to act on their own. Returning to Athens, they obscured their failure with Tissaphernes and proposed to the Assembly that a group be appointed to draw up a new constitution. By implication, it was to be a moderately conservative document.

In June, 411, a meeting was called to hear the report on the new constitution. The meeting was set for Colonus, outside the walls, a spot rather dangerous for a man without armor. The small assembly that met there abolished all existing offices, decreed that there should be no payment made for any public service, and set up a group of four hundred, who were in turn to choose five thousand, all of them men of enough property to furnish themselves with full armor. They were to be the voting public for the balance of the war.

The Four Hundred did not proceed to the nomination of the Five Thousand, as they had been directed to do. They surprised and drove out the regularly elected *Boule* and then murdered or deported whatever democratic leaders remained. They then offered to talk about peace with the Spartans, who received them very cautiously, having some doubts about their powers. The new leaders also sent envoys to the fleet at Samos. But, in the meantime, the men of the fleet had made up their minds that they must represent the democracy of Athens for now. In addition, perhaps because they still thought he had access to Persian money, they had invited Alcibiades to join them, and had elected him general.

Now two governments claimed to be in charge of the Athenian state. Alcibiades made a sensible suggestion that prevented conflict between them: the Four Hundred should proceed at once to the appointment of the Five Thousand and get on with the war.

In the summer of 411, the Five Thousand were appointed—perhaps only half of the men who had property enough to arm themselves fully. Apparently it was intended that others should serve in turn. Although the working of this system is not entirely clear, it seems that there was no pay, that the propertied class monopolized the offices and the council—and thus guided policy—and that the rights of voting in the Assembly and serving on juries (without pay) were open to all. Thus the people could still exercise a final check on policy, but all the initiative lay with the propertied class.

The Five Thousand prosecuted the war energetically. In May of the next year, the Athenians won a naval battle at Cyzicus that caused the Spartans to propose peace. Alcibiades, formally recalled from exile and put in command of the fleet, had won this engagement by his dash and vigor. Many were in favor of peace, but Cleophon, a businessman not unlike Cleon, persuaded the people not to settle for anything less than Spartan capitulation. The government of the Five Thousand was quietly put aside and full democracy restored.

At this point, the Athenian fleet, under the command of Alcibiades, was able to dominate the eastern waters. In 407 he returned to Athens with the fleet and was received by the citizenry with great enthusiasm. The command of all the forces was given him, and in the autumn of that year he sailed back to the east with a strong force, planning to recover all the former Athenian subject cities there that had revolted from the League.

The rest of the war became a drama of futility and folly. Alcibiades fell into disgrace again, this time because a subordinate had disobeyed direct orders and brought about the defeat of a part of the fleet. Knowing his fellow countrymen, Alcibiades retired to a fortress he had established for himself in Chersonesus. The Spartans, having found a good admiral, won some naval engagements. Then the Athenians achieved an impressive victory at Arginusae. But in the rough weather, the men of a dozen disabled ships and a good many men swimming and clinging to wreckage were not picked up. In the midst of deep bitterness of feeling, the people tried the generals in charge as a group, condemned them, and executed them.

Again the Spartans asked for peace and again the people, urged on by Cleophon, decided to press on in the hope of victory. The war ended on a note of pure folly. An Athenian fleet of 180 ships, based at the long, open beach of Aegospotami on the north side of the Dardanelles, was trying to open the strait by defeating a Spartan fleet, based in a harbor on the south shore. Each day the Athenians offered battle to the Spartans, who stayed in their harbor. Late each afternoon the Athenians went back, beached their ships, and scattered to prepare their supper. Alcibiades, whose fortress was in the neighborhood, came and advised the Athenian commanders to move to the protection of the naval base at Sestus, but his suggestion was scorned. Next day, when the Athenians came back and beached their ships, the Spartans swooped down and captured 171 of them. Sparta now ruled the Aegaean.

By late autumn (the year was 405), the Spartans were blockading Athens. After a few weeks starvation began. For a time, Cleophon could inspire the people to defiance, but then the people sent another man, Theramenes, to Sparta to treat. The terms in the end were not unreasonable, and they were gladly accepted, because many were dying of starvation. The Long Walls and the fortifications of Peiraeus were to be demolished, the fleet, except for a small police force, was to be given up, the empire was to be abandoned, exiles were to be recalled, and Athens was to follow Sparta's lead in matters of foreign policy. In April, 404, the Spartans entered the city and the demolition of the Long Walls began.

CHAPTER

25

LATE PERICLEAN THINKERS

Much of the lively intellectual activity of the Periclean Age and the time immediately after it took the form of conversation and debate, lost to us, of course, except for reports of it. Furthermore, only a few of the tragedies and comedies have been preserved entire, although we have references to many others and sometimes quotations of a few lines from them. Also lost are many specialized essays and books, such as, for example, the books of architectural theory that discussed general principles and specific buildings. Other specialized books have survived—on military principles or the interpretation of physiognomy or on dreams—that have not been influential since their own time and offer little to the modern reader. We must remember that the surviving literary works of the Greeks (and the Romans) were not the only books of their time or the only plays, but were a few of the many conceived and executed in an atmosphere of lively competition.

In this chapter we shall consider Socrates, Thucydides, Euripides, and Aristophanes—all Athenians, all formed in the Periclean Age and all active down to the end of the fifth century or a little beyond. It must be emphasized that Socrates wrote nothing. His enormous influence was exercised through conversations and the great charm of a completely developed and honest personality. His conversations are the ones that echo most through other men's writings. Thucydides

441

wrote one book, his account of the Peloponnesian War, which he did not live to complete. His life was that of an Athenian aristocrat, active in government and war and in the intellectual life of the city. He spent some years in exile, as we have seen, and probably profited intellectually by the experience. Euripides wrote a great many tragedies; the twenty-one that we have are perhaps a quarter of his output. We know of him only as a somewhat antisocial Athenian whose life in Athens apart from his playwriting is almost a closed book to us. Although the life of Aristophanes is also little known to us, his comedies show plainly that he was of a conservative temper. Many of his plays, too, are lost, and the many comedies of other Athenians (Eupolis and Cratinus, for example) who were highly regarded have not survived either.

SOCRATES

The conditions that started the Sophists on their characteristic activity also started Socrates on the long career that led at last in the year 399 B.C. to his condemnation for impiety and his death by drinking hemlock. He was an Athenian citizen, born in 469. He learned the trade of stonecutter and worked at it for some years in his early life. At some point, perhaps by the time he had reached the age of thirty, he stopped working at stonecutting and thereafter devoted himself to his life's real work.

That work was to further as much as he could the development of a science of man. Socrates saw correctly, as did the Sophists, that the time had come for careful and systematic study of the conditions by which man really lives. The Sophists were more inclined to study the activities of man, such as oratory and politics; the aim of Socrates was to lay the foundation of a philosophy of human existence.

The rest of Socrates' life was spent in this quest. Unlike many men with a mission or a quest, he did not go to some other place or into retirement. He needed people who would discuss problems with him and whom he could observe. These things he could find in Athens and would have been able to find them there even if Athens had not been the intellectual capital of the world.

In spite of the fact that we know so much about Socrates, it is difficult to be precisely sure what he talked about and what his beliefs were, because he inspired a follower of towering greatness in philosophy—Plato. Socrates appears again and again as the chief character in Plato's philosophical dialogues. We simply cannot be sure how much of what he says there is his own and how much is the later thought of Plato.

We can be sure, however, that the interest of the young man in the inadequate natural science of the earlier philosophers yielded to an interest in man. His questioning of the Athenians and of visitors to Athens, according to Plato and others who heard him, was always on human values, either of the individual or of society as a whole. His chief idea seems to have been that virtue depends on knowledge and that to know the good is to desire it. The most important thing in life, then, is to consider carefully the nature of life and to attempt to learn what the good is.

It may well be that his talk of his *daemon*, or guiding spirit, which occasionally warned him not to do something that he contemplated doing, was a description in the language of his time of the notion that we know as conscience, a sense of values that has become internalized, that is, has become a part of the individual instead of seeming to be enjoined upon him by religion or other outside agencies, so that the command "Thou shalt not—" seems to come from inside rather than from outside.

Socrates had probably been pursuing his quest for about forty years when he was brought to trial in 399 B.C. During that time, he had never left Athens, except on military service in the Peloponnesian War, when he distinguished himself by his calm bravery in battle. He must have had some small property to yield a small income; otherwise he would have been destitute. We must not suppose that he spent all his time accosting people on the streets and asking them for definitions or, indeed, that he spent any great proportion of his time in discussion with unselected companions. He was probably more interested in reflection and in discussions with his friends and with others who promised profit, rather than mere sport, from the time spent.

In the year 423, Aristophanes caricatured Socrates in his comedy, *Clouds*. The main point of the caricature was that Socrates was one of the people who taught the younger generation to argue in an irresponsible and dishonest way—"making the worse cause appear the better"—and not to respect their elders. The play also contains vague references to the study of things "in the heavens and below the earth." Presumably Aristophanes meant to suggest in a veiled way that Socrates was pursuing forbidden studies, for a law of 430 B.C., passed at a time when the people felt that they had just suffered a punishment from Heaven in the form of the great plague, made it actionable not to believe in the existence of the gods or to offer teachings about the things in the heavens—that is, astronomical studies.

Socrates could not have been both the things that Aristophanes suggested—an atheistic Ionian scientist, on the one hand, and a Sophist instructing pupils in oratory, on the other hand. No one did both these things. In fact, Socrates did neither. He had long ago decided that natural science was not useful to him, and he insisted that he taught no one, but only discussed and tried to learn. Probably many of his contemporaries thought of him as a Sophist, however, even though he may be distinguished from them in four ways. First, as was just said, he did not profess to teach. Second, he took no pay from anyone. Third, his interest was in the principles of the good life rather than in the rules for worldly success. Fourth, many of the Sophists are known to have published their writings, but Socrates wrote nothing.

THUCYDIDES AND HISTORY

The historian Thucydides, who lived from about 470 B.C. to about 400, was almost of an age with Socrates, Euripides, and Aristophanes and presumably knew them all. Like the other men, he had grown up in a time when an exhilarating new freedom of thought was being asserted in Athens. His mind had not been formed exactly as theirs had, for he belonged to the class and group that by tradition held the offices and managed the affairs of Athens. He saw political and social questions as one who knows what it is to form a policy and take responsibility for it. He was much impressed with the idea of the Sophists that it was possible to construct a sound body of rules for the conduct of public affairs, thus adding to knowledge of the sort that is handed down within a governing class.

The Writing of His Book

Thucydides tells the reader that he decided when hostilities broke out between the Spartans and the Athenians in 431 to take notes and write the history of a war that was likely to be the greatest war in history. Because he had had the benefit of the Sophists' studies of government, he thought that he could write an account of the conflict that would throw new light on the behavior of groups of men and offer guidance for the future. It would not be merely the entertainment of an hour (a remark meant as a reflection on Herodotus), but a permanent possession. This sober prediction of his own literary immortality has so far been justified.

He does not in general reveal much of himself, however. He took part in the war, as is revealed by his own statement in the fourth book of his history that in 424 he commanded forces operating in Thrace and that he was summoned to the defense of Amphipolis, arriving a little too late to prevent its capture by the Spartans. He was exiled for this failure. It is to be presumed that he spent some of the time of his exile in Sparta and used the opportunity to gather material for his book. It is not known when he returned to Athens. He was able to carry his story only as far as the deposition of the Four Hundred at Athens in favor of the Five Thousand in September 411.

Thucydides as Historian

The traditional opposition between Herodotus the amiable teller of stories and Thucydides the austere scientific historian has been abandoned by serious scholars. Herodotus has come to seem far more than a quaint primitive in the field of history and Thucydides has come to seem no mean artist as well as a fine historian. Although his admirers still sometimes refuse to admit them, Thucydides is also recognized as having some slight weaknesses, the chief of them being that his conservative sympathies sometimes influence his judgments. It is true, too, that he makes mistakes here and there; yet there are a few scholars who believe that everything he says must be correct.

His stature as an artist is considerably greater than used to be allowed. In many parts of the book his narrative Greek prose style is awkward and difficult compared to that of some later authors, for the technique of the elegant and perspicuous complex sentence had not yet been worked out. Thucydides' prose is generally thought to represent the result of the earlier attempts of the Sophists to write effective and elegant Greek. Yet the story moves on straightforwardly and swiftly, and some of his narratives, such as the description of the later stages of the Sicilian Expedition, rise to greatness.

His art is displayed, too, in the selection and reporting of speeches. The fact that he gives what purport to be the speeches of important people in their own words aroused much unnecessary distress among the sober-minded historians of the nineteenth century, who fancied themselves as truly scientific historians and considered this procedure on Thucydides' part unscientific. The modern historical critic prefers to study the apparent purpose and the effect of this technique.

For the historian to present opposing points of view at certain crises is plainly necessary; to present them as formal speeches pretended to be in the exact words of the speaker is not necessary. It is highly effective, however, and the attentive reader of Thucydides may well come to feel that the author is wise to rebel at the self-imposed task of straightforward exposition and analysis and decide to allow himself the pleasure of following his creative imagination for a little while.

The results of this artistic procedure are excellent. The speeches of the Corcyraeans and Corinthians in their attempts to sway the Athenians, the speeches on the policy to be followed at the revolt of Mitylene, and the give and take between the Athenians and the Melians in the so-called Melian Dialogue present the opposing points of view to the reader with a force and weight and nicety of shading that could hardly be achieved in an ordinary statement of conditions and issues. The famous funeral oration of Pericles probably gives us some idea of the style of this famous speaker; it also gives us in the most satisfying detail the picture of the ideal Athenian as a great statesman and leader drew it. This is a useful document for the understanding of the process by which Athens gradually stood forth as different from other Greek cities and became a symbol for Western man.

Thucydides set himself to tell of the war between the Spartans and the Athenians (the name always used now for the book, *The Peloponnesian War*, was applied to it later) as a study of the behavior of people in groups of *polis*-size, and he intended that this study should be useful to later generations. He did not propose a general history, and there is nothing in the book about several aspects of Athenian life, for example, the artistic, that would be found in a modern general history. He digresses once to compare the importance of this war with the importance of the earlier wars of Greece, displaying admirable method in his analysis of the scanty data from earlier times, and a second time to bring the story down from the capture of Sestus in 478 b.c., where Herodotus had stopped, to 431, when the great war began. Otherwise he moves along steadily to the year 411. At times, his faithful reporting of detail wearies the reader. At times, he stops his account of military action to show the attitudes of the conflicting peoples as they bore on the conduct of the war.

Thucydides' highly efficient reporting of fact is objective in tone. Yet it is possible to see that he sometimes subtly shapes his account of the facts so as to imply a judgment of some kind. Although he does not give overt moral judgments, he is decidedly not amoral in tone. The reader may well feel that the historian, like many of his contemporaries, was feeling his way toward valid moral judgments on the affairs of men.

EURIPIDES

Euripides (480–407 b.c.), the last of the three great Athenian writers of tragedy, is another of that company of Athenians who have been dear to the modern Western world because of their rationalistic and individualistic thought. Euripides came to manhood at a time when a number of people were reacting to a new liveliness among the Greeks and a feeling that the ancient and traditional ways were not necessarily above examination. The manner of Aeschylus and Sophocles in conducting such examinations might be described as conservative and gentlemanly. Euripides, like the Sophists and Socrates, dropped the restrictions and reservations of the conservative and the gentleman and worked in an uninhibited and realistic manner.

The Sophists devoted themselves to those analyses that would lead to the development of subjects that could be taught and would be useful for men wishing to get on in the world, such subjects as effective speech and political management. The analysis of Socrates was aimed at basic human values, a whole science of man, as it were. Thucydides applied the Sophists' study of government and man in the mass to the history of the Peloponnesian War and produced the first of the great analytic histories. The same impulse and the same social conditions led Euripides to write plays of frank and realistic questioning.

Euripides first got his plays on the stage in 455 and was still active when he died in 407. He wrote at least eighty-eight plays, but won only five prizes. He was highly popular in the fourth century and thereafter. His great appeal to the Roman Seneca, who wrote adaptations of Greek plays, resulted in a strong Euripidean influence on the early drama of France and England, which used Seneca's plays as one of its chief models.

It was customary to say that Euripides was not a favorite of his own time, despite his subsequent popularity, until recent re-examination of the evidence cast doubt on this assertion. We should remember that the officials who chose the plays must have been somewhat sensitive to public taste; if they repeatedly allowed Euripides to show his work, they must have felt that it would be well received. The plays, as has been said, were in accord with the temper of the times. The form in which they were cast, however, was sometimes unusual. It is possible that the audience enjoyed the plays and that the judges, slightly baffled by certain features of them, did not often wish to award them first prize.

War

War, women, and religion are the favorite subjects of Euripides. *The Trojan Women* is a vivid play that concerns war. It was produced in 415, just after the cruel Athenian capture of Melos and during the preparations for the great expedition against Syracuse. It was the third play of a trilogy, the first two parts of which we know to have been about earlier parts of the story of the Trojan War. In this, the third, the plight of the conquered Trojans and the hollowness of the Greek victory are vividly brought out.

The play has very little plot in the modern sense, and what unity it has comes chiefly from the presence through most of it of Hecuba, or

Hekabe, the widowed queen of Troy. She learns that she is to be the slave of Odysseus, then that her daughter Polyxena has been sacrificed at the tomb of Achilles. Her prophetess daughter, Cassandra, is told that she will be the concubine of Agamemnon, although she was vowed to virgin priestesshood. Andromache, the widow of Hector, is to be the slave of the son of Achilles; her little son is taken from her and cast from the wall, since Odysseus says that it is dangerous to leave a male of the royal blood alive.

After this pitiable series of events Menelaus appears to take Helen from the group of captive women, and a debate ensues of the sort which the Athenians enjoyed. Helen skillfully sets forth the argument that she was the plaything of the gods and is not really guilty of desertion and adultery, whereupon the aged Hecuba leaps into the debate with a passionate argument that Helen must take full responsibility for her own acts. Menelaus promises that Helen shall pay the penalty when she reaches home. At last it is time to go. The remains of Troy have been burned. The Greeks depart to the disasters that the audience knows are awaiting them on the sea.

The play cannot be called an antiwar play or an indictment of war, because there was no such line of thought among the Greeks. Indeed, the possibility of putting an end to war never presented itself to the Greek mind. Aristophanes and the conservatives might oppose the Peloponnesian War as foolish and wasteful, but the people of Athens in general profited directly from imperialism and were willing to wage forthright imperialistic war. In another situation, the conservatives might be the ones to profit from a war. There was no one to argue that this large-scale robbery and murder was wrong in principle, no one who supposed that there was any way of putting an end to it, no one to interpret Euripides' play as a condemnation of war in principle or of the recent and prospective acts of Athenian imperialism in particular.

Women

Medea is the story of a tremendous revenge. It raises again the question, constantly implied in Aeschylus' *Agamemnon*, whether it can be right to repay evil with evil. The audience, which almost inevitably sympathizes with Medea's first impulse of revenge, finally finds itself confronted with deeds of horror, which follow naturally from the beginnings, but with which no one could sympathize. The play also raises questions on the position of women in society.

The story of Medea was an old one, the story of the earliest Greek penetration of the Black Sea, dramatized as the story of Jason and his quest for the golden fleece. He found the fleece in Colchis, at the far end of the Black Sea. The princess Medea, who possessed magic powers, was smitten with his manly charms and helped him to get the fleece from her father, then ran away to Thessaly with him. Jason could not marry a barbarian, of course, but they lived together and had two children.

When Medea used her powers to repay a slighting remark from another young woman, she and Jason were forced to flee from his home in Thessaly and accept the protection of the king of Corinth. The king presently proposed that Jason should marry his daughter, assuming that the barbarian mistress would retire into the background, where she would be adequately provided for. But Medea was not ready to be relegated to limbo. To her this was the basest betrayal, not merely the way of the world.

Euripides was a master of the debate scene and of the persuasive argumentative speech. The debate between Jason and Medea is beautifully done. One amusing touch is Jason's assertion that he has done Medea a great and lasting favor by giving her the opportunity to see Greece. The sympathy of the audience is with the rejected Medea, who now plans to send Jason's intended bride a poisoned robe. The poor little princess tries it on, and her flesh is consumed by the burning of the poison, as is her father's when he tries to help. Then, as a last satisfaction, Medea kills her own two children and carries away their bodies as she flees in the dragon-drawn chariot that she has summoned. Eight hundred years later Saint Augustine, telling in his *Confessions* of his days as a university student in Carthage, speaks of evenings spent in the theater, with a visit to the tavern afterward, and then down the street with his friends, all lustily singing "Medea Flying," by which he means Medea's farewell speech set to music as an aria. *Medea*, translated or adapted, has always been and still is good theater.

To portray so wicked a witch on the stage doubtless seemed unsuitable to the conservatives. Probably also the subject of woman's station, especially a barbarian mistress's, seemed a little ungentlemanly. Yet the motif of the revenge of a woman in such a situation has a poignancy that an ordinary male revenge for an injury could never have.

In *Hippolytus* Euripides portrayed another woman who should have been discussed elsewhere than on the stage, if at all, according to his ancient critics. She was Phaedra, the youthful and beautiful stepmother of the athletic young Hippolytus. The young man, devoted to hunting and riding and outdoor sport in general, was contemptuous of love and its goddess, Aphrodite. The goddess caused his stepmother to fall madly in love with him and callously ruined the lives of the young man, his stepmother, and his father in order to have revenge for the slight to her divinity.

This play, too, has been popular through the ages. The theme of the life that is too devoted to one way of living and neglects other claims is an appealing and important one. Hippolytus is convincingly portrayed as the unsophisticated young man, sure of his own point of view and assertive about its worth. If Phaedra is visited with the pangs of an incestuous passion, she still struggles against it until she is tricked by her old nurse, an earthy-minded groundling, and becomes actively involved in the events that led to the catastrophe and the end of the family's fortunes.

Religion

In plays other than *Hippolytus*, Euripides portrays the gods as something less than entirely admirable beings. He does not deny their existence, however; freedom of speech in Athens did not go that far. In his *Mad Hercules*, he uses one variant of the Hercules story to represent a goddess as filled with petty vindictiveness and cruelty. Hercules, returning from his trip to Hades, finds his wife and children in the grip of the tyrant Lycus, whom he slays on the spot. Then Hera, purely because of her jealousy of him, transforms his rage at the tyrant into a murderous mania that causes him to kill his wife and children. As he returns to his senses and realizes that he has committed a horrible deed against himself and his own family, he is reduced to a pathetic condition of grief and guilt and despair.

His friend, Theseus of Athens, then appears. Theseus pays no attention to Hercules' warnings that he is polluted with blood-guilt or to his protestations that he is not fit to live. In Athenian tragedy, the Athenian always comes off well in such situations. Theseus has no doubt at all as to what is required of him by friendship and common humanity, and the play ends with Athenian humanism triumphant in spirit over the pettiness of the Queen of Heaven.

Euripides' *Bacchae* was the third play of a trilogy that his son produced after his death, presumably the occasion on which one of his plays is said to have won a posthumous first prize. The trilogy was probably written after he left Athens for the court of Archelaus, the culturally-minded king of Macedonia.

The subject of *Bacchae* is the power of Dionysus. This is not a criticism of the gods, nor yet the avowal of a return to religious orthodoxy, as some critics have interpreted it. The portrayal of the peculiar power of Dionysus and the nature of Dionysiac worship made excellent dramatic material. As Euripides viewed it, the god's power and his worship corresponded to basic elements in human nature that are no more open to criticism or approval than is the functioning of the liver, but do make good theater.

Dionysus was the god of the vine and of fertility and of certain irrational urges in human beings difficult to formulate precisely and prosaically. Our irrational joy in beauty and the swelling of sex impulses within us are both Dionysiac, as are occasional acts of irrational cruelty. Sometimes the Dionysiac within us outrages the soberness of our Apollonian, or more ordered side. Indeed, the oracle of the god Apollo encouraged the festivals of Dionysus in order to allow somewhat regulated and periodic expression of the Dionysiac impulses, thus protecting Apollonian orderliness.

The story of the *Bacchae* is fairly simple in its essence. Dionysus came to Thebes to be with his worshippers. Pentheus, the king, opposed the rites and tried to arrest Dionysus, who was in human form, but the god brushed him aside with ease. Then Pentheus was tempted to spy on the women's rites out on the mountains. He was detected by them, and in their religious frenzy they tore him to pieces as they customarily tore to pieces some captured animal as part of the ritual. His own mother carried his head in triumph, fancying in her frenzied condition that it was the head of a mountain lion. The play gives a very strong impression of the inexorable and irresistible power of Dionysus, or of the impulses that he symbolizes.

ARISTOPHANES

Aristophanes lived from about 445 to about 380 B.C. His work has never been so popular in modern times as that of the other men whom we have discussed. His themes lack the universality of the tragedies, and his plays contain a great many local references that obstruct the enjoyment and comprehension of the modern reader.

Nevertheless, he wrote over forty comedies, eleven of which have survived. All except the last one, *Plutus*, are of the type known as Old Comedy. *Plutus* is what is called Middle Comedy, which, by around 300 B.C., led to New Comedy, or what we nowadays would call drawing-room comedy or comedy of manners.

The other ten plays of Aristophanes are the only surviving examples of Old Comedy. They are a curious blend of uproarious slapstick, political and social commentary, personal abuse of individual Athenians, and lovely lyrics. It must be remembered that comedy, like tragedy, grew out of the celebrations of the festivals of Dionysus. We cannot reconstruct all the stages by which comedy grew, but the combination of actors and chorus is much like that of tragedy. The abusive and indecent language that was tossed about at festivals for apotropaic purposes appears in the comedies. The note of hilarity belongs to a joyous festival and reminds us of the drama's origins.

In the typical play of Old Comedy, a character comes forward with a great idea, one full of comic possibilities, but often with overtones of sober sense. For instance, in *Acharnians* (produced in 425), one of the charcoal burners who made up most of the population of the deme Acharnae had the great idea of making a separate personal peace with the Spartans, because there seemed no possibility of a formal ending to the Peloponnesian War. The ending of the war was a favorite subject with Aristophanes, and Athenian freedom of speech made it possible to bring up such a serio-comic proposal to change public policy. The charcoal burner, who was the very type of "the little man," proposed to rise in his wrath, as the little man would always like to do, and conclude a peace between himself and the Spartan state, no matter what the rest of the Athenians did.

Then, in the normal comedy, there is a debate about adopting the great idea. An opponent speaks against it and is heckled. The proponent speaks for it and is heckled. Then there is a vote, and of course the great idea is always adopted. Sometimes, as in *Lysistrata*, the plot goes on to the end very logically. Sometimes a succession of scenes follow, loosely grouped around the great idea and coming to no conclusion that is strictly logical.

Lysistrata (produced in 411) is named for the chief female character, whose great idea was that the women of Athens and the women of Sparta should refuse to have intercourse with their husbands as a means of blackmailing them into concluding the war. The idea was adopted, and the ladies persevered until they had gained their end. The fun is increased by the fact that one or two of the weaker vessels among them have difficulty in standing by their own decision. In perhaps the most amusing part of the play, one of the women teases her husband by pretending that she will yield to his importunities and have intercourse with him then and there. She keeps thinking of one thing and another that is necessary—a blanket, a pillow, a drop of perfume behind the ears—and finally runs away, leaving him in the lurch. The scene is constructed with great skill to extract the last possible laugh from the audience. Yet, with all the fun, the serious idea that the war is a piece of tragic folly is never let drop for long, and at the end there is a rousing and effective lecture on the real bonds that do and should unite the two nations.

The simpler forms of humor have an ample field in which to disport themselves in a comedy with this subject. Aristophanes uses every device that might make people laugh. He has ludicrous situations and subtle plays on words, farcical ideas and slapstick. Through it all run the twin motifs of sex and elimination, the bases of the physiological joke. There is no use in pretending that by some standard Aristophanes is pure-minded. He is indecent in the extreme. Probably not all of his audiences enjoyed his kind of humor; probably most of them did. What is funny may be more funny for being indecent, and the festival was based on the spirit of lusty and energetic life, not out of keeping with his great play with the slang words for the sex organs; he calls attention to the embarrassing condition in which the men found themselves, and at the end he leers and licks his chops at the thought of a reconciliation.

In spite of his broad humor, Aristophanes' repeated proposals that the war should be ended were conservative in spirit. The typical Athenian conservative believed in close co-operation with Sparta; it was the democratic majority who favored the war because it gave them employment and hopes of still wider employment. In *Wasps*, the author's conservative spirit shows itself in a vigorous attack on the jury system, which, like the war, gave employment to many of the democratic majority. It was inevitable that such a conservative should be annoyed at the activities of Socrates and that his annoyance should find expression in *Clouds*, which was produced in 423 B.C.

At his trial in 399 B.C., Socrates protested that many of the jury had had their ideas about him formed and fixed by a comedy of Aristophanes, to whom he refers only as "a comic poet." The great idea in *Clouds* is that a man who was being pressed by the debts his son had incurred in riotous living might go to Socrates' school and become eloquent enough to repel his creditors if they should sue him. Socrates, represented as both an Ionian physical scientist and a Sophist teaching public speaking, is made to combine two careers never joined in one man. The play is not so funny as some of the others; it often has a sour note as well as an unrealistic characterization.

Aristophanes resented Euripides as well as Socrates. He repeatedly criticizes the playwright, and his earnestness is such that often he is not fair. In *Frogs*, produced in 405, shortly after the death of Euripides, the god Dionysus is shown on a trip to Hades to bring him back. It is interesting that Dionysus can be represented as cowardly and effeminate, but more important to us is the question of whether it would not be better to bring back Aeschylus from the dead. There is a great literary contest—what is, in effect, the first written literary criticism. Aeschylus and Euripides are compared at length to determine who could do more to make the citizens better. Euripides is accused of writing on a low literary plane, stooping to sophistical argument, and using immorality. The choice falls upon Aeschylus. In other plays, too, Aristophanes makes opportunities for brief attacks on Euripides.

Aristophanes was a brilliant manager of the economy of both a whole play and of a single scene. He was a master of the technique of squeezing a maximum number of laughs out of a given situation or of raising an isolated guffaw. His conservatism was consistent and sincere, although at times it led him into savage unfairness. Some of his characters and situations are masterpieces of fantasy, and some of the lyrics sung by his choruses are masterpieces of beauty.

CHAPTER

26

AFTER THE GREAT WAR:
GREECE FROM 404 TO 362 B.C.

Because Athens and Sparta have necessarily been so much in the foreground of past chapters, the Spartan triumph in the Peloponnesian War and the end of the Athenian Naval Empire may have come to seem to be events of great and lasting significance in the history of the ancient world. The student of Greek history must at this point attempt to regain his perspective. Outside Greece, the general situation was little changed.

The Persian Empire, which may not have had the real power that it had formerly had under more dynamic and warlike kings, was still the largest and richest political entity. By the judicious employment of their wealth, the Persians had helped the Spartans to become a naval power temporarily and to defeat Athens on the sea, thus bringing about the end of the war and with it the end of the troublesome empire of the Athenians. The Spartans had also been induced to give up their support of the claims of the Asiatic Greeks to freedom, that is, freedom from Persia. The Persians could believe for the moment that their long-range diplomacy had weakened the threat posed by the Greeks of Greece proper to the western possessions of Persia and had made it possible to restore full sovereignty over the Greeks of Asia Minor, the most difficult group in their western possessions.

The Greeks of Sicily must have been relieved at the defeat of Athens. They had repelled the great expedition sent against them, and it was plain that such an attempt could not soon be repeated. Nor was it ever to be. In the century that followed, the Greeks of Sicily, under the leadership of Syracuse, were to prosper greatly and brilliantly.

To the Carthaginians, the defeat of the Athenians may have been a relief. Their empire, with its capital at what is now Tunis, comprised a certain amount of rich farming land in Tunisia, but essentially it was an empire based on control of the western seas and on maritime trade. They had struggled with the Greeks for the control of Sicily. Although they probably were pleased that the Athenians did not succeed in gaining control of Syracuse—and whatever else might have followed—we do find them in diplomatic negotiations with Athens in 406. We do not know what the negotiations were about. Possibly they thought that the Athenians might spare a little strength to join them in putting pressure on Sicily, but not enough strength to make them awkward partners. The Carthaginians, like the Sicilian Greeks, were to prosper in the century that lay ahead, and, in addition, they were to be constantly at odds with the Greeks of Sicily.

To the Spartans, the victory over Athens and her allies brought no great profit, either immediately or in the long run. The Spartans attempted to exercise their influence in a wider sphere than before and in a sphere in which they lacked the necessary experience. In spite of their solid virtues, they did not know how to exercise the hegemony that they now found to be theirs. Their reputation suffered from the unwisdom and the brutality of some of their acts, and their defeat at the hands of Thebes at Leuctra in 371 was to mean the end of their old primacy and influence among the Greeks.

On the other hand, the defeat of the Athenians was a real setback for democracy in the world of the time, because the Athenians had consistently been the champions of the democratic form of government, willing to exert themselves to promote and maintain democracy among their allies. Athens herself, however, was far from being finished as a power among the Greeks. The wartime losses in men and materials were capable of being restored. The sudden rise of the kingdom of Macedon, in northern Greece, under its great king Philip II, was still in the unforeseeable future. Until the rise of Philip and his kingdom, the affairs of Greece were to go on under the shadow of the Persians; but Philip and his greater son, Alexander the Great, were to change the situation radically in both Greece and Persia.

It is a nice question whether the true greatness of Athens, her greatness in the domain of the spirit, received a definitive check in the Peloponnesian War. If she had been able to go on as a great and wealthy imperial city, would she also have advanced to triumphs in her literary, artistic, and intellectual life even greater than those of the fourth century? The question of the relation between these differing activities is a fascinating one, but not one capable of a conclusive answer. We can hardly conjecture what difference it would have made had the war not been fought or had the Athenians not been defeated; but we can say with confidence that the progress of the arts in Athens was neither stopped nor deflected into entirely new directions by the war and its outcome. But let us return to our narrative.

Spartan Management in Greece

The Spartans were as convinced of the superiority of rule by the few as the Athenians were of the superiority of the rule of the many. Naturally they felt that their surest way of exerting control over the former allies of Athens was to reshape local constitutions everywhere so as to place power in the hands of the few, the more wealthy and aristocratic elements who had long had to endure the predominance of the many under Athenian influence. The corollary proposition must have weighed equally heavily with the Spartans: the democratic elements were likely to remain loyal to Athens and to attempt to help her return to power.

It was inevitable that the change should give rise to violence. Lysander, the most influential Spartan at the time, chose governing boards of ten local aristocrats in all the cities formerly allied to Athens. The boards, or decarchies, were charged with devising new aristocratic constitutions and supervising the installation of governments thoroughly in sympathy with Sparta. In the spirit of Greek factional strife, the decarchies confiscated property and put many of the popular leaders to death, relying on the support of small Spartan garrisons under commanders known as harmosts.

As usual, our information is best for affairs in Athens, and there a stirring story played itself out. A group of thirty, rather than ten, was chosen to manage the reorganization. They came to be known simply as "the Thirty." Backed by an unusually strong Spartan garrison, they instituted a reign of terror. The energy of Critias and his uncompromising insistence on complete oligarchic control soon brought him to the leadership of the Thirty. He had once been a follower of Socrates, although he is said to have broken away as soon as he thought that he had learned enough to make him successful in political life. He had been prominent in the oligarchic revolution of the year 411. The moderate aristocratic element was headed by Theramenes, who had also played the role of moderate during the revolution of 411 and who apparently earned the dislike of both the extreme oligarchs and the democratic group by his policy of moderate conservatism.

Critias forthrightly accused many of the prominent democrats of treason and had them executed. Then he moved to a systematic assault on many wealthy men, some of them citizens, some resident aliens, confiscating their wealth. The speech of Lysias, *Against Eratosthenes,* delivered in 399 B.C. and bitterly attacking the man who had had Lysias' brother murdered, gives a vivid description of the cynical way in which the members of the Thirty enriched themselves personally by their misuse of power. It was later estimated that fifteen hundred persons were murdered, with or without a pretense of judicial process. Socrates, in Plato's *Apology,* said that he was ordered by the Thirty to go to Salamis with some others to arrest one Leon, presumably another wealthy victim; the others went and arrested Leon, but Socrates, refusing to involve himself, simply went home.

The extreme group then reduced the list of those with full citizen rights to 3,000, all "politically reliable," instead of allowing full citizen rights to all those whose property allowed them to equip themselves as hoplites, the usual formula for a conservative government. Systematically they eliminated the friends of Theramenes and at last forced Theramenes himself to end his life by drinking hemlock. Hundreds of citizens fled to such friendly nearby cities as Megara.

Thrasybulus, who had played an important part in opposing the oligarchic revolution of 411, escaped to Thebes, which had already begun to be estranged from Sparta. Gathering seventy other bold spirits, he launched a counter movement. The little group found its Sherwood Forest in the half-dismantled fortress of Phyle, in north-eastern Attica near the Theban border. The troops sent against them were unable to take the difficult place by assault, even when it was not properly fortified, and they were prevented by fierce wintry weather from blockading it and starving out the democrats.

By the spring of 403, Thrasybulus had some 700 men, and his forces were growing steadily. He also had a colleague, Anytus, who was to be prominent in the democratic party thereafter and who is best known as one of the accusers of Socrates in 399. Presently the little army made its way down through Attica to Peiraeus and there defeated the enemy forces in a battle that cost the oligarchs the life of their leader, Critias. Faced with his death and with the movement of Thrasybulus and Anytus, the more moderate among the conservatives were able to force the appointment of a new board, this time a board of ten, to head the government, only two of whom had belonged to the Thirty. The rest of the Thirty withdrew to Eleusis, which they had prudently seized before as a possible refuge for themselves.

Yet the Ten were unable to make any agreement with the steadily growing democratic forces at Peiraeus. Finally they appealed to Sparta, and Lysander answered their call. Presumably he would have been able to crush the democratic forces but for the fact that opposition to him at Sparta became so strong as to bring about his removal from command. King Pausanias, who took over the command and the management of this affair, showed a conciliatory spirit, perhaps partly because the more sober element at Sparta realized that she had already lost much of the general popularity and influence that she had enjoyed only a year or two before.

After the Spartan government had heard emissaries from both Athenian factions, it entrusted the settlement to Pausanias and a board of commissioners. The result was that the Athenians of both factions committed themselves to an amnesty, or act of oblivion, late in the year 403. This amnesty, which for Greeks showed truly surprising political wisdom and restraint, provided that all that was past should be forgotten, if not forgiven. The surviving members of the Thirty were allowed to stay in Eleusis as in a separate state. No acts of vengeance for wrongs done under the Thirty were allowed. The Spartans did not interfere in the formation of a new constitution, which naturally was a democratic one. It is perhaps not surprising that the restored democracy took Eleusis in 401, executed the members of the tyrannical government who were captured there, and then again made Eleusis a part of the Athenian state.

The Trial of Socrates

It was probably the strain of recent events that caused the prosecution and condemnation of Socrates in 399 after the Athenians had allowed him to go his way for some forty years. Athens had lost a war, a long, bitter, costly war. She had been convulsed by the terrible rule of the Thirty, with its many murders of innocent people, and by the civil war that had led to the restoration of the democracy.

The ordinary citizen of Athens must have felt that now was a time for Athens to apply all her forces to the task of reconstruction. Those men who represented disruptive forces or were too present reminders of recent events were likely to encounter strong enmity. Socrates was not the only man against whom such feeling was directed in the years just after the restoration of the democracy.

In the corpus of speeches ascribed to the orator Lysias, we find an attack delivered in 399 against the orator Andocides for his impiety. In another speech is a bitter attack on one Agoratus, who had acted as *agent provocateur* for the Thirty. Other speeches, some of this year and some of later years, show that the bitterness engendered by the Thirty lasted long, in spite of the amnesty. As late as 382 a man named Evandros, elected archon, was attacked at his *dokimasia*, or scrutiny, with the charge that he had been an oligarch under the Thirty. To the people of the time some of these trials may well have seemed more important and interesting than that of Socrates.

Socrates was exposed to such bitter feelings partly because the infamous Critias, the worst of the Thirty, had once been a member of his circle. The equally infamous Alcibiades was also thought to have been formed partly by his intimacy with Socrates. Socrates had long but erroneously been regarded as one interested in astronomy and other science and therefore presumed an atheist, although, according to his own version of the matter, he had been much interested in such studies in his earlier years, but had soon abandoned them as unsatisfactory.

But the ordinary citizen might easily feel that Socrates had had an unfortunate connection with the Thirty and that some slight odor of atheism clung to him. He might also feel that Socrates was hindering rather than helping the restoration of Athenian morale and strength. If he made the young men less ready to hear and follow their fathers, he loosened one bond in the state. If he refused to interest himself in the affairs of the *polis* in general and ridiculed the system of choosing officials by lot, he did some harm to unity of feeling.

Socrates' real accuser was Anytus, the prosperous tanner who had been one of the leading figures in the restoration of the democracy and a leader of the democratic party afterward. He persuaded a young poet named Meletus to bring the formal accusation; the principal speech apparently was given by Anytus.

Anytus had done good service for Athens. He had played a man's part in some of the most stirring events of Athenian history — the end of the war, the terror of the Thirty, the adventures of the group that led the resistance and the restoration. We might expect him to plan now for the material and spiritual restoration of Athens and to see himself as its natural leader. We might also expect him to attempt to silence an old man who had not fought in the resistance or the restoration, who attempted to depreciate the importance both of material prosperity and of the sense of unity, who lessened the respect of the young for their elders, and who plainly did not adhere to the simple old-fashioned faith, whatever he believed about the gods.

Anytus may in all fairness be said to represent the man who identifies himself with the group and gives his interest and his enthusiasm to the promotion of common practical ends. Generally, little love is lost between this type and the more individualistic, analytic type of which Socrates is so distinguished an example. Often, too, there is little understanding between them; as in this case, they are hardly able to argue, but can only state their own differing points of view.

The speeches of the accusers have not been preserved. Presumably they emphasized Socrates' taint of atheism and treated him as a Sophist. The need for public unity must have been mentioned. The charge—disbelieving in the gods of the city and holding other ideas of divinity, and demoralizing the youth—probably seemed fairly well proven.

Nor was Socrates' answer preserved. Plato, Xenophon, and several other men wrote their own version of his defense, or *apologia*. Plato's *Apology* probably reproduces much of what Socrates said. It is not, in fact, a very good defense; it is the sort of thing that the detached and analytically-minded man says when charged with not furthering the purposes of a society of men — more a statement of attitude than an answer to charges. The jury voted for conviction, 281 to 220.

Socrates might have saved his life by fleeing into exile before the trial. He might have saved it by afterward proposing a counterpenalty of exile or a fine, as the convicted defendant was allowed to do. Probably everyone expected him to make such a proposal and agree to cease his unacceptable activities. But his attitude now was even more intransigently individualistic and analytic than before: he suggested that he should be rewarded for his services to the state in keeping the Athenians awake and up to the mark and that the reward should be free maintenance at the public expense. Then he added, without enthusiasm, that some of his friends were willing to contribute money for a nominal fine and that he was willing to allow them to pay such a fine for him.

Naturally enough, the jury replied to this defiance by confirming the death sentence originally proposed by Meletus, voting it by an even larger majority. Socrates went to prison, where he would have been forced to drink the hemlock very soon had it not been that no execution could take place until the return of a religious embassy that had been sent to Delos.

During the month that he waited in prison, he had a third opportunity to save his life. Plato's account of the affair in his *Crito* is probably trustworthy because presumably he had to keep close to the known facts. The wealthy Crito, Socrates' friend for many years past, insisted that Socrates allow him to bribe the jailer, as could readily be done, so that Socrates could escape and flee to the protection of friends of Crito in Thessaly. Socrates' refusal, as given by Plato, is a strong affirmation of his loyalty to society, the loyalty that had been questioned at his trial. He refused to harm by disobedience that society whose terms he had accepted; and by implication he affirmed that his past conduct had not harmed society.

It is easy to accuse the Athenians of murdering Socrates because he tried to assert freedom of speech. We must remember, however, that the Athenian state always lived on a more precarious basis than a modern state and that in 399 conditions seemed to the average man to call for a great concerted effort. The trial and condemnation of Socrates stand not as a foul blot on the good name of Athens, but as an example of the difficulty of conducting a human society with justice to all.

The March of the Ten Thousand

Two years before the trial of Socrates, Xenophon the Athenian had accompanied the Greek mercenary troops hired for an attempt on the Persian throne. His account of the expedition not only throws light on the condition of Persia at this time, but presents us with one of the great true stories of adventure as well. Cyrus, the able and charming younger brother of King Artaxerxes, had tried to supplant his brother on the death of their father, Darius II, in 404 B.C. The elder brother had made good his claim to the throne and arrested Cyrus, but the queen mother managed to save her favorite son from punishment and he was allowed to return to his satrapy in Lydia, in Asia Minor.

We hear much in Greek authors about the devotion of the Persians to their sovereigns. Unfortunately, this devotion did not prevail among members of the royal family; Persia had its share, or more, of plots against the reigning monarch by his own family. Cyrus made his preparations carefully, gathered a force of about thirteen thousand Greek mercenaries in addition to his regular troops on the pretext of crushing some unruly mountaineers within his satrapy, and set out to conquer his brother the king.

The title of Xenophon's book, *Anabasis,* means "a journey upcountry from the sea." The expedition started inland toward the unruly region. Xenophon names the Greek captains and brings their characters clearly to life for us. We see the slow progress of the army and a number of such vivid incidents as the futile attempt of Greek cavalrymen to catch wild ostriches. Soon the soldiers realized that they were being led against the king, far from the sea, which to them was a friendly highway and the center of their world. They mutinied, but finally were induced to go on. The narrative leads us into the far country by the banks of the Euphrates where at last the battle took place.

The formidable Greek hoplites easily prevailed over the troops opposed to them, and the victory would have been theirs had not Cyrus dashed forward to attack his brother personally. He was killed, and his local troops at once submitted to the king. Tissaphernes, the satrap in Asia Minor whose guest Alcibiades had been and an old enemy of Cyrus, now advised the king to entice the Greek captains into a conference. They rashly agreed to come, and all were treacherously put to death.

The *Anabasis* records that the remaining Greeks, deprived of their officers, held a meeting in true Greek style and that the proposals of a certain Xenophon, an Athenian (the author, of course), seemed good to them. They elected new officers, of whom Xenophon was one, although he had come on the expedition only as a gentleman adventurer, not as a soldier. Then the ten thousand Greeks marched and fought their way northward to the Black Sea. Xenophon's best picture is that of the long line of troops coming over a ridge and of the great cry, "The sea! the sea!" that went down the line.

It is easy to overestimate the weakness of the Persian Empire as revealed by the exploit of this band of Greek mercenaries. It is true that there were often intrigues over the throne, that the satraps could make war on one another, and that not all the nominally subject peoples could be held to strict obedience. Yet the size and resources of the empire were such that it was not to be shaken by any existing power.

As for the Greeks, the mercenaries of the *Anabasis* were a most unattractive group of ruffians, although historians have not always chosen to call attention to the fact. The latter part of the narrative tells of their adventures as freebooters and mercenaries after their arrival at the coast of the Black Sea. During the rest of this century, such bands of roving soldiers were to be a source of considerable trouble in Greece. The book ends with Xenophon's complacent account of his finally making a real profit out of the expedition by organizing some of his comrades for the kidnapping for ransom of a rich Persian of Asia Minor.

FURTHER WAR WITH PERSIA (400–387 B.C.)

At this point, the relations between the Greeks and the Persians changed radically. After the death of Cyrus, the king promoted Tissaphernes to Cyrus' place as satrap in charge of Asia Minor. He naturally planned reprisals against the Asiatic Greeks, who had supported Cyrus. They appealed to the Spartans for protection. Tissaphernes also asked the Spartans to help him in asserting Persian authority over the Greeks of Asia Minor according to the treaty between Persia and Sparta. The Spartans, appealed to by both sides, repudiated the treaty with the Persians and the ignominious position in which it had placed them in the eyes of all Greeks.

During the winter of 400–399, a Spartan expedition was sent to Asia Minor. The commander raised troops from among the Greeks there and enrolled about six thousand of the men who had made the expedition with Cyrus and were now looking for further military employment. For several years, the Spartan army operated successfully in Asia Minor, helped somewhat by the disinclination of the Persian satraps to co-operate closely. But one of them, Pharnabazus, had the happy idea of raising a large fleet and putting it under the command of the Athenian Conon, who had been among the Persians since his unfortunate defeat by the Spartans in the decisive battle of Aegospotami in 405 B.C. The granting of the money and the building of the fleet was done in the leisurely manner characteristic of the Persians of this time. At last, however, Conon had his fleet, and with it he decisively defeated the Spartans in the naval battle of Cnidus in 394, ending the period of Spartan naval supremacy.

Meanwhile, in 396, troubles at home had forced the recall of the Spartan army from Asia Minor; thereafter there was little real hope of a favorable issue of the war with the Persians. Nevertheless, it was to continue in a desultory way for almost ten years more.

The Spartans were having troubles both at home and with the other Greeks. Those Spartans who could not keep up their economic standing as shown by their contributions to the public messes were reduced to a lower grade of citizenship and known as "the Inferiors." This system was not peculiar to the Spartans, of course; among other Greeks and later among the Romans we find the rule that full citizenship or a certain grade of political competence rests upon the possession of a definite amount of property.

But Spartan contacts with the outside world had affected her semicommunistic system and had caused a considerable number of men to lose their land. Some, at least, of this increasing number of men reduced to the status of Inferior were bitter; and in 397, one of them, named Cinadon, organized an attempt at a social revolution that also included the *perioeci* and the Helots. It was perhaps unfortunate for the larger interests of Sparta that Cinadon talked too freely, was arrested, and under torture revealed the names of all the chief conspirators.

The heavy-handed and arbitrary Spartan manner toward the other Greeks had dissipated the advantages gained by her conduct of the Peloponnesian War. Corinth and Thebes felt that they had had no share in the gains of the war, and other states found the Spartans demanding and unhelpful. In 396, Pharnabazus, the Persian satrap who had devised the idea of fitting out a fleet with Conon in command, sent an agent to Greece with a large sum of money to be spent in encouraging anti-Spartan movements in Argos, Corinth, Thebes, and Athens.

Open hostilities came about in the usual petty way. Thebes seems to have instigated the Locrians to quarrel with the Phocians and then supported them in the quarrel. The Phocians turned to Sparta, who resolved to chastise both Thebans and Locrians. The Athenians responded to the appeal of the Thebans by granting them a perpetual alliance. The Spartans launched a two-pronged invasion of Boeotia, which failed because King Pausanias, in charge of one division, failed to arrive in time at a critical junction point.

Extremely harsh treatment of unsuccessful generals was common among the Greeks. The historian Thucydides was exiled by the Athenians, as we have seen, for just such a failure to arrive in time. On other occasions, the Athenians tried and executed unsuccessful generals. King Pausanias was put on trial for his culpable inefficiency, but managed to escape and spent the rest of his life in exile.

Argos and Corinth now joined Athens and Thebes against Sparta, and further inconclusive warfare followed during the year 394. In that same year, Conon defeated the Spartan fleet at Cnidus, and in 393, he brought his fleet over to control the waters around Greece and raid the coast of the Peloponnesus. He brought, too, further money from the active Pharnabazus with which the Athenians rebuilt the Long Walls and the defenses of Peiraeus. Now that Athens again had a combination of fortified city and fortified naval base, she was able to recover a few of her former island possessions and to take a real part in opposing Sparta.

Although probably in the year 404 the Spartans had thought that it would be a good thing to assume the role of strong leader of all the Greeks, their inept playing of the role had brought them chiefly trouble and distress. Therefore, in 393, their obvious move was to come to terms with the Persians and leave themselves free to deal with the more pressing problems nearer home. The first negotiations broke down. For five more years, small detachments of Spartans in Asia Minor conducted a half-hearted war with the Persians. At the same time, an equally half-hearted and fitful war was conducted on the Greek mainland. Its chief feature was the astonishing successes scored against the heavy-armed Spartan troops by the Athenian Iphicrates and his band of peltasts, or light-armed and mobile troops, foreshadowing a change toward greater flexibility in military methods and the decline of the solid mass of heavy-armed infantry as the most formidable type of military formation. But finally the Spartans were able to catch a large Athenian force at a disadvantage and force an agreement to strive for a general peace.

The Persians, too, were now ready for peace and perceived that they were in a good position to dictate the terms. In 387 the Persian king offered a final formula to Antalcidas, the Spartan representative:

King Artaxerxes regards it as just that the cities in Asia and the islands of Clazomenae and Cyprus should be his, and that the other Greek cities, large and small, be independent, except Lemnos, Imbros, and Scyros, which should belong to the Athenians as formerly. Whatever parties do not accept this peace, I shall fight against them, along with those who are of like mind with me, on land and sea, with ships and money.

In 386 the other Greek states ratified "The King's Peace" or "The Peace of Antalcidas," as it was called. The Thebans claimed the right to sign for all Boeotia, but yielded to a direct threat of force from Sparta.

For the Spartans themselves, it was a great improvement to be freed from war with the Persians and to feel sure that Persia would support whatever they did as guarantors that the Greek states would abide by the terms of the peace. They could overawe any show of resentment among the other Greeks by outright threats of force.

If other Greeks felt bitterness that it was the decree of the Persian king that had brought about the settlement of Greek affairs, the cities of Asia Minor could at least hope for a period of peace in which they might pursue their commercial interests undisturbed. But Thebes had lost the hegemony over Boeotia that she had long been building up, and Athens suffered financially from the precise limit set on any attempts to regain her old influence among the island states.

SPARTAN CONTROL IN GREECE: 387–371 B.C.

Just as the Spartans had interpreted the "freedom of Greece" said to have been won in the Peloponnesian War as an opportunity to advance what they considered to be their own interests, so they now interpreted the autonomy of all the Greek states as guaranteed in the new peace to mean that they should attempt to weaken all the other states to their own advantage. This did not mean commercial advantage or any other tangible advantage. It merely was a policy of breaking up combinations between other states, presumably with the idea of forestalling the rise of possible powerful enemies. It was a completely unconstructive policy.

The Thebans were ordered to give up their claims to preside over all Boeotia. The Corinthians and Argives were compelled to dissolve their alliance, and the Corinthians had to recall their oligarchic exiles. The city of Mantinea, in the Peloponnesus, was forced to dismantle its fortifications and dissolve itself into the five villages that had united a hundred years before to form a city state. The people of Phlius were forced to recall their oligarchic exiles and to accept an oligarchic constitution drafted by the Spartans.

Worse than this, the Spartans broke up a useful league centered at Olynthus, on the Chalcidic peninsula in the north. This league, which had existed for a long time, had ably defended the interests of the Greeks of the region against the kingdom of Macedonia. Now a quarrel over territory led Amyntas, king of Macedonia, to appeal to Sparta. The Spartans could see only that the Olynthian League seemed stronger than they wished any Greek political unit to be, for they lacked the elementary wisdom to see that Macedonia could be an even more formidable enemy to the Greeks and one less easily negotiated with on the usual Greek terms. After four years of war, the Spartans were able in 379 to break up the League and to force its members to enter into treaties with Sparta.

In 382, the Spartans treacherously seized control of Thebes. A Spartan officer passing through with troops designed for the war with the Olynthian League was approached by a member of the oligarchic faction at Thebes, and a plot was formed to seize control of the citadel during a festival. With the help of the Spartan detachment, the oligarchic faction gained control. The "rules" of these struggles between oligarchs and democrats are well illustrated by the fact that at the very beginning of this affair some three hundred of the democrats fled to the protection of Athens. The Spartans sent a garrison to Thebes, and the oligarchs now ruled there as complete sympathizers with Spartan aims.

Control of Boeotia by virtue of control of Thebes was very useful to the Spartan plan of domination of all Greece. With the breaking up of the Olynthian League in 379, Sparta had apparently removed the last serious threat to her own power and the last real focus of democratic sentiment except for Athens. Her control was founded on nothing but force and short-term self-interest. She had deliberately broken up a number of alliances that had been founded on a genuine community of interest between the parties. Spartan domination might have benefited everyone by keeping the peace if it had been exercised with some tact and fairness, but instead it was harsh and unreasonable.

In the winter of 379-378, a conspiracy to recover Thebes was formed by the exiled democrats and the Athenians. The daring agents sent to Thebes succeeded in murdering the chief oligarchs and were at once reinforced by a host of Theban democratic exiles and Athenian volunteers. The Spartans immediately prepared to use force and sent envoys to Athens to foil the Theban plea for Athenian help. The Athenians might well have yielded to Spartan pressure, had not a rash Spartan garrison commander in southern Boeotia made a sudden raid down into Attica to try to seize Peiraeus. The result was that the Athenians decided to co-operate with Thebes and helped to defeat the Spartan attempt to recover control there.

Next the Athenians resolved to organize a full-scale movement against the Spartans and invited all their old allies (except, of course, those given to Persia by the King's Peace) to join in a new naval league whose purpose was to force the Spartans to permit the Greeks to be free and autonomous and in full possession of their own territories. The Athenians offered careful guaranties that they would respect the rights of their allies, and especially that they would not try to acquire property in their states for Athenian settlers, a feature of the old confederacy that had been highly distasteful. The allies were to have a federal council, which was sovereign equally with Athens; Athens, however, was the executive. By the year 377, the Second Athenian Naval Confederacy was a going concern and within three or four years, the number of members apparently rose to about sixty.

The Thebans were fortunate at this time in finding two very able leaders, Epaminondas and Pelopidas. These men resolutely resisted the further attempts of the Spartans to regain control of Boeotia. Their most important move was to reform their army. Henceforth, its core was to be the "Sacred Band" of three hundred hoplites of good family, constituting a permanent and strong regiment that was to be reinforced by the usual militia when necessary. Little by little the Thebans persuaded the other cities of Boeotia to rejoin them and accept their leadership.

The rising power of Thebes so impressed both Sparta and Athens that they soon made moves toward a general peace. There had been desultory warfare between Sparta and the new Athenian Naval Confederacy as well as between Sparta and Thebes. In 371, at the proposal of Athens, the three powers met to establish a lasting peace. As usual, the cardinal point was the freedom and autonomy of all Greek states, in spite of the fact that Athens proposed to continue her new naval league and Sparta to continue the old Peloponnesian League. It was at least proposed that the members of the leagues should join in military or naval operations only on a voluntary basis.

But the Spartans and the Athenians unrealistically proposed that the cities of Boeotia should all sign the new agreement separately, as Sparta had insisted that they should do on the ratification of the King's Peace. Epaminondas, strong in the feeling that Thebes had a new army and a new spirit, insisted that Thebes should represent them. The Spartans, as usual, prepared to implement their demand by force.

Not only did the Thebans have a new army; they had a powerful ally in Jason, the tyrant of Pherae, in Thessaly. This region of Greece, which lay just north of Boeotia, appears so seldom in the full light of Greek history that we know regrettably little of its history. It had few towns. Apparently the nobles, who were organized in the old style of clans and families that had prevailed in the early days of aristocratic domination of Athens, were able to hold the agricultural workers in subjection. Jason appears shortly after 380 as the ruler of Pherae. Shortly thereafter he became *tagus*, or military chief, of all Thessaly. He had joined the new Athenian naval league, but after a short time he withdrew to cultivate the friendship of the Thebans and their league in Boeotia.

During his rise to power, he had been able to find money to hire large numbers of mercenary soldiers. Presently, however, he instituted a new sort of army, a forerunner of that soon to be developed by Philip II of Macedon. He organized and trained a national army of no less than 20,000 hoplites and 8,000 cavalry, supported by large numbers of peltasts. A country that could support an army of this size was indeed a formidable neighbor to the small and divided states of Greece, just as Macedonia was soon to prove formidable. The organization of the country as a whole, however, depended upon the personal abilities of Jason, and when he was assassinated soon after the great trial of strength between Sparta and Thebes in 371, Thessaly lapsed into its former division and ineffectiveness. The character of Macedonia was much like that of Thessaly; the great difference in the history of the two countries in the fourth century was that Macedonia was to be brought to unity and effectiveness by a far greater man, Philip II, who was to be succeeded by his brilliant son, Alexander the Great.

The armies of Sparta and Thebes met at Leuctra, in Boeotia, in the year 371, and the decision went to the Thebans. Epaminondas drew up his army with a very strong concentration of hoplites, led by the Sacred Band, on the left wing to meet the usual Spartan concentration on the right wing. The Spartan right wing, which was relied on to break the line of their opponents, was crushed by the Theban left wing, and the Spartans were forced to withdraw to their entrenched camp.

They lost a thousand men, of whom four hundred were full citizens— a terrible loss in view of the small number of full citizens. When a Spartan relief expedition arrived, they found that Jason of Pherae had arrived on the scene with a strong force. The Thebans wished to push the matter to a conclusion, but Jason prevailed upon them and the Spartans to make a truce.

The battle of Leuctra brought a minor era to its conclusion. It ended the supremacy of Sparta in Greece, as well as the long-established belief that the Spartan army was invincible. Henceforth she was only in the second rank of military powers. Yet if Greece as a whole was benefited by the reduction of Spartan power, the fact that the Peloponnesian League was no longer to serve as a solid federation of many Greek states was, in general, a loss, for in the times ahead a greater unity among the Greeks would have proved useful.

THEBES IN POWER: 371–362 B.C.

The hegemony now briefly exercised by Thebes was unfortunately no better in quality than that which had been exercised by Sparta. Every plan of the Theban leaders was based on the idea that Thebes must be strengthened and other states weakened; no principle of sound leadership can be found in their actions.

The murder of Jason of Pherae and the consequent reduction of the power of Thessaly was advantageous to the Thebans. By the end of the year 370, they had organized a federation of central Greece, which reached from the island of Euboea in the east to Aetolia in the west.

The weakening of Spartan power led to new movements in the Peloponnesus. In many states, the believers in democracy were able to overthrow the oligarchic governments which had long been supported by Sparta. The Mantineans again combined their five villages into the city that Sparta had forced them to dissolve. They also moved to organize a new league of all Arcadia, and many cities accepted. When the group attempted to force Tegea to join, the resultant violence led to Spartan intervention. The Arcadians appealed to Athens for help. In spite of a defensive alliance, the Athenians decided to remain neutral, overlooking the obvious fact that the Arcadians were then certain to appeal to Thebes.

When they did so, Epaminondas responded by leading a large army into the Peloponnesus. He was unable to take Sparta, but devastated a large part of the Spartan territory. Now, with the encouragement of the Thebans, the people of Messenia freed themselves from their long subjection to Sparta, built themselves a capital (the ruins of which can still be seen), and suddenly blossomed forth again as an independent people. But the Athenians, profoundly disturbed by the growth of Theban power, made an alliance with the Spartans and openly ranged themselves against the power of Thebes.

A curious feature of the opposition of the Greek states to one another at this time is their attempt to gain the favor of the Persians. The shadow of the King's Peace still lay across all their moves. The Greeks as a whole felt a certain resentment at Persian dictation, but realistically accepted the fact of Persian power when it seemed to their advantage to do so. Yet the memory of the repulse of the Persian invasion long ago remained with them, and the memory of the expedition of Cyrus and the march of the Ten Thousand, and the memory of the not unsuccessful operations of the Spartans against the Persians just after the Peloponnesian War.

The idea that someday the Greeks might unite in a great imperialistic war against the Persians had been proposed in a speech at the Olympic Games in the year 408 by the Sophist Gorgias, who called on the Greeks to drop their senseless struggles against one another and combine in a great effort against the Persians. About 380 B.C., Isocrates, the leading teacher of oratory at Athens, urged the same arguments in a pamphlet called *Panegyricus* and claimed the primacy in the enterprise for Athens. Philip and his son Alexander were later to make the idea a reality.

For the present, however, the Greeks engaged only in an undignified competition for the endorsement of the Persians. In 367, the King gave his approval to the new Boeotian League and to the independence of Messenia. Pelopidas, the Theban envoy to the Persian court, did not get royal approval of the new Arcadian League, an omission that gave deep offense to the Arcadians.

In the following years, the Thebans found increasing difficulty in managing their relations with the Arcadian League and with their southern neighbors in general. By the year 363, the Arcadian

League was beginning to split, half of it being more inclined to look to Sparta than to Thebes. Athens and Sparta were united in their opposition to Thebes.

Epaminondas felt that force was the only answer to this opposition, and in 362 he led a large army into the Peloponnesus. The opposing armies converged on him as he approached Mantinea, the center of the Arcadian League, which he was determined to reduce, and the battle that ensued was almost a duplicate of the battle of Leuctra. The Theban forces had decidedly the better of the fighting, but Epaminondas was mortally wounded. With his dying breath he advised his countrymen to make peace.

The Boeotian Confederacy continued, but without Epaminondas it could exert no great influence on its neighbors. The brief period of Theban hegemony, like that of Sparta, had brought only further confusion to Greece. The whole period from 404 to 362 B.C. was singularly barren of productive developments in the field of politics.

CHAPTER

27

THE GREEKS OF THE WEST
IN THE FOURTH CENTURY

There was no essential difference between the life of the Greeks in the West and those of Greece proper in the fourth century, although our information about the West is rather less detailed. Like their kinsmen in Greece, they were harmed by struggles with one another that, it would seem, could have been prevented. The Western Greeks also had the Sicilian natives, Carthage, the tribes of Italy, and the Romans to contend with. Like the Greeks elsewhere, the Western Greeks found this century a rather prosperous time in spite of their military and political difficulties. Many of their cities were rich and brilliant, and the drama in particular flourished among them.

If we shift for a moment to the long perspective in history, the Western Greeks had a very important role to play. It was through them that the Romans first became acquainted with the Greek style of civilization. Although the full flood of Hellenism was not to burst upon Rome until the second century B.C., when the Romans campaigned in Greece and Asia Minor and learned to know the achievements of classical Greece, we must not forget that during the fourth and third centuries the Romans were constantly learning about contemporary Greek civilization from the Greeks of South Italy and —especially during the First Punic War, which was largely fought in

Sicily—from the Greeks of Sicily. The Romans might have been disposed to reject the Hellenic style of civilization partly or entirely, as many peoples did reject it. Because the Romans were disposed instead to accept Hellenism and assimilate it, it was probably useful that they began to learn from the Greeks as soon as possible, two centuries before their conquest of Greece.

DIONYSIUS I, TYRANT OF SYRACUSE

Hermocrates of Syracuse, a democrat of conservative cast, guided the Syracusans in their defense against the Athenian attack of 415-413 b.c. His attempt to procure moderate terms for the prisoners was defeated by the extreme democrats, who treated the captives with great harshness. Hermocrates then went to the Aegaean in command of a fleet that was to help the Spartans against the Athenians in that theater of war. While he was gone, the extreme democrats gained control of the government, exiled Hermocrates and his sympathizers of the moderate party in politics, and installed an extreme democracy much like that of Athens. Syracuse is often and justly compared to Athens in her strong fortified position, her power on the sea, and the democratic spirit and the energy and the enterprise of her citizens. She unfortunately lacked (as so many *poleis* did) what the Athenians largely had: ability to avoid bitter factional quarrels.

In 408 b.c., the Carthaginians invaded the Greek part of Sicily for the first time since their great disaster at Himera in 480. Segesta invited them to help her in her continuing quarrel with Selinus, just as she had invited the Athenians in 416. Although Syracuse gave some help to her ally Selinus, the city nevertheless was captured with great loss of life. The Carthaginians then captured Himera and tortured and killed 3,000 prisoners in revenge for the death of their commander there in 480. They retired with a rich booty, leaving garrisons to hold their new territory in Sicily.

During the following winter, Hermocrates, the exile from Syracuse, came back to Sicily with a mercenary force that he had personally recruited, enlisted survivors from Selinus and Himera, and had great success in raids on the Carthaginian garrisons. He petitioned for recall from exile, and when the Syracusans refused him, he tried to enter the city by force. The citizen army killed Hermocrates and most of his men. One of Hermocrates' force who escaped death was the future tyrant Dionysius.

In 406, the Carthaginians came in even greater strength and attacked Acragas, the second city of Sicily. After months of struggle, betrayal, gallantry, and carelessness, the combined Greek forces that had come to help Acragas withdrew, and the Carthaginians took the city and wintered there. In the spring of 405 they destroyed it.

Dionysius had distinguished himself at Acragas. Then, in 405, he spread stories among the Syracusans about the incompetence of their generals, succeeded in getting himself elected as one of a new board of generals, and procured the restoration to citizenship of the other survivors of the moderate group that had been exiled with Hermocrates. In command of some of these returned exiles and of a group of mercenaries, he went to Gela, where he posed as the supporter of the people, confiscated the property of the few, and kept the money to pay his mercenaries. On his return to Syracuse, he had his colleagues on the new board of generals deposed on the ground that they had done nothing for the city while he had been active in her service. Late in 405, the people elected him sole general with full powers. He increased his personal armed force, put his family and close friends into magistracies and military posts, and had the government of Syracuse firmly under his control. He was to be tyrant for thirty-eight years, from 405 to 367.

After Dionysius gained control of the city in 405, he still had the invading Carthaginian army to deal with. His first battle was a defeat, perhaps through his own fault. His Syracusan cavalry would have killed him had he not been protected by his mercenaries. As it was, the cavalry went ahead of him back to Syracuse and stirred up a revolt which he overcame by a lightning march and midnight attack at the head of his mercenaries. Then a stroke of pure good fortune saved him from the advancing Carthaginians. A sudden onset of the plague so reduced their forces that they offered him a treaty that left Syracuse free, although a good part of Sicily was either to be in Carthaginian hands or to pay tribute to Carthage.

His Wars with Carthage

Dionysius almost at once broke certain parts of his treaty with Carthage by extending his power over some of the cities of eastern Sicily that had been recognized as free in the agreement. The Carthaginians had thought of them as allies of a sort, or at least as not friendly to the power of Syracuse. Dionysius drove some of the peoples whom he conquered from their homes, sold some as slaves, and brought some to swell the number of the inhabitants of Syracuse, where labor was needed. The territories that he gained he gave to people whom he wished bound to him by obligations. In this way he created some new communities of Sicels, the original inhabitants of the island, and some of mercenaries imported from Campania.

It has been said that Dionysius was singularly indifferent to all claims of propriety or sentiment. The claims of Greek blood seemed to mean nothing to him. The hoary antiquity of the town of Naxos, the oldest Greek settlement in Italy, did not keep it from being destroyed by him. Probably we should regard this aspect of his activities as part of his system of binding to him as many people as possible. Old ties of sentiment, blood, or common citizenship were of no use to him in maintaining his position. To pardon his fellow citizens who had revolted and whom he could have destroyed was to create an obligation on their part. Early in his reign, he brought back many men who had been exiled during the democratic regime, men whose continued prosperity rested as a result on the existence, at least, of a conservative regime, if not necessarily on the regime of Dionysius. But when he made Syracusan citizens of captives or mercenary soldiers and gave them land, he was beyond doubt creating supporters of his own regime who had everything to lose if he fell. The people whom he settled on the property of conquered cities must also plainly be supporters of his regime, if they were to hold their lands.

His policy of lively trade, as well as his wars undertaken for loot, brought profit to the people of Syracuse in general, for the manufacture of weapons and ships went on constantly and trade in general was good. The magistrates were elected as usual and the assembly met and passed resolutions, but Dionysius was firmly in control, just as the old-time "boss" of some American city might have been. He had the good sense to refrain from direct personal injuries to the citizens. Enough people were eager to assassinate him without his provoking the revenge of an outraged husband or brother or the anger of the relatives of some murdered man. He made a fortress on the island of Ortygia in the harbor and lived there with his mercenaries.

In 398, Dionysius attacked the Carthaginians; the resulting war lasted until 392. The accounts of it are such that we can form some judgment of him as a military man. By ruthless taxation and confiscation he gathered money enough to hire considerable numbers of mercenaries. He is said to have been a forerunner of Philip II of Macedonia and Alexander the Great in that he sometimes campaigned in the winter (a new practice in the ancient world), developed an artillery arm for sieges, and was expert in the co-ordination of all the branches of his forces. Although these assertions are all true, the results that he achieved are not to be compared to those of Philip or of Alexander. Perhaps he was an innovator without being a genius. On the other hand, it is quite possible that his aims were limited, that he wanted much more to keep the Carthaginians as a threat to Syracuse, which would justify his dictatorship, than he wanted to drive them out of Sicily.

In 398 he began the war with the siege of Motya, the Carthaginian coastal fortress at the west end of Sicily. The city was on an island, as many Punic foundations were, and the island had been connected with the mainland by a causeway, which the defenders destroyed. Dionysius built another causeway in order to be able to fight from firm ground rather than from ships. His powerful artillery was thus brought to bear, but the walls of the town were too strong to be breached at once. While this struggle went on, a Punic fleet arrived and entered the harbor, hoping to destroy the Syracusan fleet, which had been beached. But the great catapults that had been battering the town were now turned on the Punic fleet and drove it off with heavy damage. The Carthaginian commander withdrew, leaving Motya to its fate.

The siege was a spectacular affair. Because space on the island was limited, the rich merchants of the island had built their houses upward into soaring towers. The besiegers therefore built wooden towers, and from these they shot at the towers inside with catapults, while the besieged tried to burn the wooden towers of the besiegers. Finally the wall was breached, and the invading army was able to start the task of reducing the city inch by inch. The high houses were the strongest points, and the wooden towers were wheeled inside the walls to deal with them. The Syracusans tried to throw bridges from the towers to the houses, and desperate hand-to-hand struggles took place high in the air. Finally Dionysius, instead of withdrawing for rest, made a sharp attack at night, and the city was taken. Every living person was massacred in repayment for the cold fury with which the Carthaginians had massacred the 3,000 captives from Selinus and Himera a few years before.

Dionysius meanwhile gained control of a number of other cities by bribery or negotiation. The campaign of the first year was thus a real success. In the second year, however, he lost all that he had gained in the first. In Motya he had left a garrison of Sicels, a strange thing for a prudent man to do. The Carthaginians, returning in force, took the city, then abandoned what little was left of it after the struggle and at Lilybaeum, a little south of Motya on the western end of Sicily, founded a great new naval station which was to be their strongest point in Sicily thenceforth. The ineptness with which Dionysius countered their moves in other parts of the island may well leave us in doubt as to whether he had no sense of strategy or felt it advisable for his own purposes to give the Carthaginians some encouragement.

Although Dionysius may have found the hostility of the Carthaginians so useful in maintaining his position in Syracuse that he did not want to discourage them too much, he sometimes was pressed dangerously hard by them. In this war, they drove him back to Syracuse and besieged him there. With great skill and daring he engineered a surprise attack and won a great victory. Then he connived at the escape of the remains of the Punic army. The war was ended by negotiation in the year 392, with Dionysius having made good territorial gains. Twice more, in 383 and in about 368, he engaged in short wars with Carthage. Although we are only poorly informed about them, the general consideration of these wars might well lead to the belief that Dionysius stirred them up, but prosecuted them with less than full vigor.

Dionysius and Italy

Dionysius was shrewd and sensible in his foreign policy toward others than Carthage. His policy aimed at control of the regions of Italy nearest to Sicily and control of certain good harbors in other parts of Italy and in parts of Greece that might yield to his attempts. His consistent friendliness to the Spartans brought him strength when he needed it most; in return, he respected their interests. After making peace with Carthage in 392, he embarked upon the conquest of southern Italy, allying himself with the Lucanians, an Italian people, in order to get the better of the Greek cities in Italy. By about 385, he had gained control of most of Magna Graecia, or "Great Greece," the large region of southern Italy populated by the descendants of Greek colonists. He also took control of the island of Elba from the Etruscans, its iron being its attraction.

His foreign policy also took in the Adriatic Sea and its coasts. To a naval power such as Syracuse, the lands bordering the upper Adriatic offered a field for the sort of exploitation that Greeks had already developed around the Black Sea. Dionysius slowly began to gain control of harbor sites on both sides of the upper Adriatic, on the west coast of Greece and the east coast of Italy. He did good service by suppressing for a while the traditional piracy of the Illyrians, on the west coast of Greece. He was so widely and respectfully known that the Gauls who moved into North Italy about 400 B.C. and sacked Rome in 387 sent an embassy to him offering to make an alliance. Whatever the outcome, we know at least that he had some of these people as mercenaries in the succeeding years.

Dionysius died in 367 B.C., having ruled the *polis* and then the state or empire of Syracuse for thirty-eight years. He had, at the very lowest estimate, shown himself a master of unscrupulous devices by which to gain and hold power over a free people. Often he showed great daring and personal courage. Accounts of him imply that he had considerable administrative ability and was able to surround himself with effective and loyal subordinates. He extended the power of Syracuse over most of Sicily and into Italy, so that, except perhaps for Persia, she was the most powerful state in the world. Presumably the profits of empire were acceptable to the merchant class of Syracuse, in spite of the necessarily heavy taxation. The chief body of the people may not have objected too strongly, for there was work for all and Syracuse did not lose a war during this time. If he was not a military genius, he was at least a reflective and ingenious military man.

The results of all his shrewdness and ingenuity are not, however, impressive. To extend the domain and prosperity of Syracuse he did endless damage in Sicily and Italy, both material and psychological. He offered very little benefit to those whom he conquered. He aroused such hatred among his own people that he lived in constant fear of assassination, and he provoked such hatred among the other Greeks that at the Olympic Games of 388 the great orator Lysias made a speech condemning him, stirring the assembled people to attack his ambassadors and prevent them from offering their sacrifices. He did much to break down useful bonds of feeling between peoples in Italy and Sicily, and he apparently did next to nothing to foster in his own people a sense of unity and co-operation that would be useful in the long run.

Although he cannot be said to have advanced Syracuse culturally as some of the great earlier tyrants had done both in Sicily and in Greece, he showed a very human weakness in fancying himself as a writer of tragedies, which he tried long and unsuccessfully to get produced in Athens. Just before his death, when he had made a treaty with Athens, pressure was put on the officials of the festival of Dionysus to "give him a chorus." Dionysius' work at last had its day in the Theater of Dionysus and was then forgotten.

THE WESTERN GREEKS AFTER DIONYSIUS I

Dionysius I was succeeded in 367 B.C. by his son, Dionysius II, a man of about thirty who had not been trained to govern because his father feared to trust his own son with responsibility. Nevertheless the new tyrant, who assumed the place without any difficulty at his father's death, began to rule in a fairly efficient and rather mild way. His uncle Dion, whom the elder Dionysius had entrusted with power, exerted a strong influence on Dionysius II and was well regarded by the experienced men of the regime.

In 366, Dion persuaded his nephew to invite to the court the noted Athenian philosopher Plato. Dion and Plato had become firm friends during a brief earlier visit by Plato to Syracuse. Plato, who was well known in the Greek world, believed that those who govern should be thoroughly trained in philosophy. Dionysius II, the ruler of the most powerful Greek state of the time, was to study this philosophy. Although Plato probably realized that there would be many difficulties, he could hardly have refused such an invitation to put his theories into practice. Dionysius was amenable and applied himself willingly to the intellectual feast that Plato spread before him.

It was only natural that some of the practical-minded men in the administration of Syracuse began to wonder where this new arrangement would end and to consider the possible effect on the welfare of both the city and themselves. They naturally suspected that Dion intended to push Dionysius gently aside into a life of philosophical retirement. If this were to happen, their own careers might well be harmed, and the men attached to Dion might advance instead. If Dionysius were to remain, his new philosophical principles might well hinder the operation of the military autocracy on which their own careers depended. Therefore, they took steps to strengthen the military establishment and at the same time brought to Dionysius what seemed to be proof of treasonable conduct on Dion's part. Dion was sent into an honorable exile in Italy. Plato stayed on for a little while, but confined himself to the general cultivation of his pupil's mind and avoided any contact with the immediate practical affairs of the regime. He frankly urged the recall of Dion, however, but was refused.

For some years, Dionysius II continued to rule without incident except for more or less normal opposition. Whatever Plato had taught him surely did not bring about a new age in Syracuse. Five years later, in 361, he cordially urged Plato to come again. Plato came and again urged the recall of Dion without success and left after a short and rather cool visit.

In 357, Dion raised a force in Italy and invaded Syracuse. For two years his forces and those of Dionysius struggled, each having periods of ascendancy that were ended by the counterattacks of the other. In spite of the fact that Dion had claimed to come as a liberator, in 355 and 354 he began to seem more and more a tyrant, and he was murdered.

Everywhere in Sicily during this century there was the same sort of factional strife and confusion that Syracuse saw in these three years. The old inner unity of many *poleis* had been broken up, partly by the machinations of Dionysius I. Few men had any experience of moderate, responsible government after the decades of tyranny imposed on many Sicilian *poleis*. Mercenary soldiers were readily available for those who wished to pursue their aims by force. At the same time, the Greek cities of southern Italy were being hard pressed by the Italian tribes, which Dionysius I had encouraged to oppose their Greek neighbors.

In these unhappy circumstances Syracuse sent an appeal for help to Corinth, her mother city, thus setting in motion a train of events very like a fairy story. For some reason, the Corinthians decided to send Timoleon. This respected man had lived mostly in retirement for twenty years after killing his brother, who had tried to make himself tyrant. The strange events of Timoleon's mission to Sicily form one of the most enthusiastic of Plutarch's biographies. Aided by every sort of fortunate chance and coincidence, Timoleon not only restored the health of Syracuse and gave it a sort of democratic government, but also removed the tyrants from other cities of Sicily. He retired in 336 and lived for a few more years as the idol of the Syracusans. At the same time, Dionysius, who had thrown himself on Timoleon's mercy, lived as a private citizen in Timoleon's native Corinth, showing himself at least enough of a philosopher to bear his great fall and the sufferings of his family like a man.

These well-ordered governments in Sicily were not to last long. The *poleis* continued, generation after generation, to struggle with each other and with the Carthaginians until in the third century they came under the power of Rome. A body of Italian mercenaries who called themselves Mamertines, or sons of Mars, made themselves masters of Messana shortly after 290 and harried all eastern Sicily with their raids. The Syracusan Hiero finally had such success in campaigning against them that he gained the position of king of Syracuse about 265. The Carthaginians, seeing the port of Messana, so usefully located on the strait between Sicily and Italy, possibly about to fall into the power of Syracuse, sent a garrison to help and kept the Syracusans from taking it. The Mamertines, made uneasy by the presence of the Carthaginians who had saved them from Syracuse, had the simple idea of calling on the Romans to save them from the Carthaginians.

The decision of the Romans to help the Mamertines is not easy to understand and is much discussed by modern historians of Rome, who find it hard to agree that any plain interest of the Romans was served by helping the Mamertines. The action of the Romans brought on a long war with Carthage (264-241 B.C.), which is known by its Roman name, the First Punic War. Syracuse and some other cities joined the Romans. The long and costly war ended with victory for the Romans and appropriation of Sicily as their first possession outside Italy. The Greek cities that had supported them were left free, while the rest of Sicily was made subject to Rome. In Rome's second war with Carthage (218-201 B.C.), the Syracusans went over to the Carthaginians and forfeited their independence for so doing, since Rome was again the victor.

The Greeks of South Italy

The south Italian Greeks, when they came under Rome's sway, were made members of the Roman federation rather than subjects, the fate of most of the Sicilian Greeks. The conquests of Dionysius I seem to have broken some of the strength of the Greek *poleis* in southern Italy, as had been the case with the *poleis* of Sicily. Two Italian peoples, the Bruttians and the Lucanians, were the Greeks' most dangerous enemies.

The city of Tarentum tried to avoid the domination of the threatening Italian peoples by calling for help from Greece. Sparta was her mother city, and Sparta's king came to her aid with a force of mercenaries, probably in 342 B.C. After three or four years of campaigning against the Italians, he was defeated and killed. A few years later the people of Tarentum again asked for help. This time they brought in Alexander, king of Epirus and uncle of Alexander the Great. The uncle, desirous of equaling the exploits of the nephew, started off well and in a short time had gained control of much of southern Italy. The Tarentines somewhat illogically objected to the strength of this man who was strong enough to deal with their persistent Italian enemies and turned against him. He was finally defeated.

In the end, all the Greeks of South Italy, as well as the Italians who had caused them so much difficulty, were swept into the Roman

net. Slowly the Roman federation had spread southward. The great
Samnite wars of the late 300's and early 200's had ended with victory
for Rome and incorporation of these sturdy people into Rome's
organization. Finally the Tarentines brought on a war with Rome
by attacking a little Roman squadron cruising near Tarentum. Again
they called in a Greek prince, the dashing, generous, able, but incon-
stant Pyrrhus. His erratic behavior, followed by his withdrawal from
the struggle and his return to Greece in 275 B.C., left them helpless
before the Romans. They and all the peoples of lower Italy ended as
members of the Roman federation.

Massilia

The Greeks of Massilia (modern Marseilles) dealt with interesting peoples in Gaul (modern France). Many belonged to the large
group known as the Celts, who were found all over western Europe
and in the British Isles. Occasionally they wandered. For example,
the Gauls who moved into the Po Valley of northern Italy and later
(387 B.C.) sacked Rome were Celts. In the third century, many of
them wandered farther toward the East, and many were absorbed
by the peoples of the Balkans. One detachment wandered into
Greece, was driven back northward, and finally settled in central
Asia Minor. We hear of them there as the Galatians, a name that
comes from the Greek word for Gauls.

The Greeks of Massilia exported Greek wares to the Celts. The
Celts had a flair for the arts, and their workmen transformed the
decorations of Greek objects into exuberant and attractive decorations of their own, which could not be mistaken for Greek work.
The Celts did not develop an urbanized civilization, but they did
develop effective agriculture and a woollen industry. Furthermore,
they kept large parts of Spain, France, the Low Countries, and the
British Isles orderly enough so that their own people or the Massi-
lians or the Etruscans could travel regular trade routes with some
degree of safety.

The merchants of Massilia traded in Spain, went up through Gaul
and as far as northwest Germany, and reached the Celts of the Alps
and northern Italy. The city had earlier been a rival of the Etruscans
both on the sea and in northern Italy and thus had a community of

interest with Rome in their opposition to the Etruscans. When the Romans sent an offering to Apollo of Delphi for their conquest of the Etruscan city of Veii in 396 B.C., they put it in the treasury of Massilia at Delphi. The friendship of Massilia and Rome was to endure and be useful to both until the time of Julius Caesar.

CHAPTER

28

THE RISE OF MACEDONIA

The rise of the kingdom of Macedonia from about 360 to about 330 B.C. was to bring the end of what the Greeks thought of as freedom—that is, freedom to manage their own affairs and to dominate their neighbors if they could. One could say that the system of city states, or *poleis*, had proved its inadequacy. At least, it had proved inadequate to keep the peace and allow all men to pursue their own affairs without interference from others. In this respect, the Greek system seems to have been no more and no less successful than the Sumerian system of city states or the Egyptian system of small principalities during the periods when national unity could not be maintained. The nations of Europe in modern times, although much larger than the Greek polities, have likewise been unable to prevent wars among themselves, wars that in retrospect seem worse than useless.

If we are to strike a balance of achievements for this typically Greek political form, however, we must be sure not to set its real virtues to one side. Our study of the Greeks up to this point has made it plain that many real and permanent advances in civilization were made in the *poleis* and, partly, at least, because of the city state form of organization, which intensified the life of the citizen. We must also remember that although the era of such entirely independent political entities and of endless struggle among them was now to pass away, the other aspects of their culture did not entirely disappear. The lively and intense life of cities continued and became an important part of the combined Greco-Roman civilization, a part that distinguished it from its less advanced neighbors.

EARLIER MACEDONIA

Macedonia's rise under its great king, Philip II, to a position of dominance in Greece is the chief feature of the period before us. The social, economic, and cultural condition of the kingdom at the beginning of his reign was much like that of Thessaly. The people were recognized as akin to the Greeks and therefore eligible to compete in the Olympic Games. City life was little developed. The effective organization of society was by clans and tribes as it had been in Greece proper some time before. The conception of an impersonal government that ruled on a basis of fixed laws was yet to be developed. There was no indigenous artistic or intellectual life. It was natural that in general the Greeks should regard the Macedonians as not quite belonging to the distinctive Greek way of life, but rather to the barbarian way, the way of the "outsiders."

Although we are better informed about the history of Macedonia than about that of Thessaly, we still have only the bare outlines of a history. The first of her strong kings seems to have been Archelaus I, who ruled from 413 to about 400 B.C. He made a great effort to create something like a truly national government, tried to develop a national army, fortified strong points here and there, and began a road system to facilitate military movements. He was an admirer of Greek culture and he invited Greeks—the tragic writers Agathon and Euripides, the painter Zeuxis, the musician and poet Timotheus—to his court.

In one way or another, the Macedonian kings were frequently involved in the affairs of the Greek states. Amyntas II, who ruled from 393 to 370, had invoked the aid of Sparta against the Olynthian League. Later and at different times, he was the ally of Athens, of Jason of Pherae, and of Thebes. During the period of their hegemony, the Thebans concerned themselves somewhat with the affairs of both Thessaly and Macedonia, and from 367 to 365 the young

Philip was kept as a hostage at Thebes in the house of Epaminondas, tutored in Greek philosophy, and apparently allowed the privilege of serious discussions of statecraft with Epaminondas himself.

Philip II Assumes Power

In the year 359, the Macedonian king Perdiccas suffered a crushing defeat at the hands of his western neighbors, the Illyrians, and lost his life. The twenty-three-year-old Philip, who had already been granted some governmental responsibility, was chosen regent for his nephew, the infant son of the dead king. The qualities that were to make him great must already have been well developed, for he managed to dispose of five other members of the family whose ambitions might have been inconsistent with his and for the moment held off the neighboring peoples who were ready to attack the kingdom. A year later he led the Macedonian armies against the Paeonians, then against the Illyrians, and defeated both decisively. After these victories the people made him king instead of merely regent for his small nephew.

Finding himself at the head of a kingdom with a recent history of weakness and disunion, frequent defeat in war by the neighboring tribes, and inadequacy in dealing with the Greek *poleis,* Philip wished to organize Macedonia into a strong and well-functioning national state. He wished to gain the respect of the Greeks, for he had learned to know and admire their ways. There is no evidence that he ever had any imperialistic designs for subduing the states of Greece and compelling them to pay tribute.

Although he had chastised the Paeonians and the Illyrians, the difficulties facing him at the beginning of his reign must have seemed enormous. At home he had to weld an old-fashioned group of tribes and clans into a modern state, a need that Archelaus I had already recognized and tried to meet. The army needed to be improved and the revenues increased. The presence of Olynthus and other Greek cities on Macedonia's eastern flank cut him off from desirable access to the sea and from expansion in that direction. The policies of the Greek states as he had observed them and heard of them were strongly against the development of any new power, so that interference from some quarter might be expected, should he make any progress.

It is not surprising that Philip bent all his energies to developing the internal and external power of his kingdom by fair means or foul. If the latent strength of the kingdom was such that his efforts brought Macedonia to a position where it overshadowed all the states of Greece, we need not therefore accuse him of being a sinister enemy of Greek freedom; rather, he used his sudden authority as a friend of the Greeks.

Philip seems to have begun military reforms even before his rise to the regency. He realized the value of heavy infantry as earlier Macedonians had not. In addition to the cavalry, composed of members of the nobility, he instituted an infantry corps of peasants. Although the smaller units were composed of men from one district, their enrollment in an army that was kept constantly on active duty served to promote a feeling of belonging to a nation. Philip's personal interest in his soldiers and his insistence on rigorous training throughout the twelve months of the year soon created a spirit and an efficiency in the army that made it much superior to the ordinary army of the time.

Philip Moves Outward

In 357, Philip captured Amphipolis, a city in Thrace that Athens regarded as rightfully hers. It had indeed been founded by her, but the sentiment of its citizens was as much pro-Macedonian as pro-Athenian. This conquest gave him a good port on the Aegaean and access to the gold mines of Pangaeus, from which he is said soon to have taken a thousand talents of gold a year. This he used in a splendidly devised new coinage, the first gold coinage in Europe. These fine coins were a means of representing Macedonia as a civilized state, over and above their primary use as money.

Something definite had been gained; but Athens and the Greeks of the northern region had been alarmed. The Olynthians asked for a treaty with Athens, but she would not agree, perhaps because of troubles with her naval confederation. Philip reassured the Olynthians by offering them a treaty. He made himself master of two other towns in the region, Pydna and Potidaea, both of which were dependencies of Athens. The forthrightness of these conquests was somewhat obscured by the fact that he returned without ransom all Athenians captured and that he presented Potidaea to Olynthus.

The Athenians began to realize that Philip could be very troublesome. They had known Macedonia as a rather weak kingdom exposed to raids by its neighbors. Athens made treaties, therefore, with the Paeonians, Illyrians, and Thracians, the people who in the past had given the Macedonians the most trouble, and encouraged them to invade. But Philip retained the initiative. His general, Parmenio, a most valuable right-hand man, defeated the armies of all three neighboring peoples. Philip was now technically at war with Athens, because she had made alliance with his enemies; but the initiative was still his, and for the moment, he preferred to make nothing of the fact.

Mausolus of Caria

Another rising figure caused the Athenians considerable trouble at this time. Mausolus, who ruled Caria, in southern Asia Minor, as Persian satrap, was an ambitious man who during his lifetime gained a great deal of power within the Persian system. In the end, his efforts achieved no more than distinction among satraps, and his name is remembered for little more than the Mausoleum, the great memorial built for him by his widow, Artemisia.

Mausolus, seeing that many of the island members of the Athenian confederacy were dissatisfied with what they regarded as the arbitrary behavior of Athens, encouraged them to revolt. Athens tried to hold them by force. Isocrates, the teacher and political writer, published a pamphlet, *On the Peace*, in which he argued that Athens would be much better advised to give up her confederacy and renounce any sort of domination over other Greeks. Whether Athens was willing or not, she had to let some of the most important members assert their freedom from her league. Mausolus annexed Rhodes and Cos as soon as they were no longer members of the confederacy —the end at which he had been aiming all along.

Further Successes of Philip: The Sacred War

The troubles of Athens with her league had left her little energy to oppose Philip. He was able to consolidate his conquest of Amphipolis and the region of Mt. Pangaeus, just beyond, and then turn his attention to the more general situation. In 356, the year in which Potidaea was captured, Philip's four-horse chariot won at Olympia; he evidently was losing no opportunity to assert the membership of Macedonia in the Greek community. In that year, too, his son Alexander was born. Philip is said to have received the news of the birth of his son, the victory of his horses, and the capture of Potidaea all on the same day. As the story goes, he raised his hands and prayed, "O gods, send me some minor misfortune!"

The so-called Sacred War offered him a chance to present himself and his nation as useful members of the community of Greeks. This was perhaps the most trifling of all the wars of this unhappy period. The Amphictyonic League was an ancient organization around Delphi and in Boeotia, which counted its members by tribes, in the old style, rather than by the cities, which were a recent growth. In the larger sense it controlled the shrine of Delphi, although the city of Delphi managed its everyday affairs.

Because the Thebans could control most of the people of the neighborhood, they were able to count on a majority of the votes of the tribes making up the Amphictyonic League. Around the year 357, they apparently decided to use the League to chastise the people of Phocis, who had withdrawn from the Boeotian League of Thebes immediately after the Theban defeat at Mantinea in 362. The League voted to impose heavy fines on a number of leading citizens of Phocis. The various reasons given by different authors are so vague and contradictory that this move must be regarded as political, although the official reason was sacrilege.

The Phocians were in a very awkward position. They may well have been guilty of nothing but offending the Thebans, for all we can tell, but the Thebans could count on enough force to exact the payment of the fines. The Phocians appealed to the Spartans, who had been fined by the League for their violation of the sacred precinct of Thebes when the city was seized in 382 and had refused to pay. The king of Sparta sent some mercenary soldiers and some money.

Thus encouraged, the Phocians seized Delphi and the temple and fought off a rescue attempt by the nearby Locrians. Having gone this far, they then decided to go the whole way. They levied heavy contributions on the richer citizens of Delphi and hired mercenaries to maintain their position. They sent an appeal to all the Greek states; it is interesting that they seriously quoted the muster roll of the Greeks in Homer's *Iliad* as a proof of old Phocian lordship over Delphi and that the other Greeks (the Spartans, at least, and the Athenians) took this claim seriously.

Naturally, the Amphictyonic League was not to be deterred by a text from Homer. It formally proclaimed a "sacred war" against the violators of Delphi. The Phocians, who had found resolute and skillful leadership for their great moment, at first acquitted themselves well. When presently they suffered a serious reverse, they began openly to "borrow" the treasures of the temple at Delphi. The irreplaceable gifts of many generations were melted down into their original gold, silver, bronze, or iron to make coins or to be fashioned into weapons for this most frivolous of all Greek wars (if it be correct to apply that adjective to any war). Now that there was money, new troops of mercenaries could readily be found, for all over Greece there were men who had lost full citizen rights in their own cities or who were merely restless and glad to make a little money by warfare.

The Phocians made one serious long-range mistake: they used some of the temple money as a gift to Lycophron, the tyrant of Pherae, in Thessaly. The other Thessalians took fright at the thought of such an alliance and appealed to Philip.

Philip had been working away at improving his position in Thrace and weakening the position of Athens, partly by diplomacy, partly by force. The possibility of interfering in the Sacred War was much to his liking. In the year 353, he marched into Thessaly. The Phocian mercenary army was called northward to meet him and defeated him twice. But in the next year, Philip brought a larger army and crushed the Phocians.

The Athenians, who had nominally been at war with Philip since 356, were following these events carefully. They were in nominal alliance with the Phocians, more because both parties were opposed to Thebes than because of the Homeric claims of Phocis. Now it became plain that it was time to act. As Philip prepared to march into central Greece and end the Sacred War by defeating Phocis at home, the Athenians sent a force to the pass of Thermopylae sufficient to block his passage. Philip, who did not believe in doing things the hard way, withdrew for the present. He had been invited to be commander-in-chief of the Thessalians and had taken a most correct step in assisting the Greeks to chastise the Phocian robbers of the treasures of Delphi. These were real practical and psychological advances; he was willing to let the final defeat of the Phocians wait rather than fight with the Athenian force. When, in 347, he did settle the affair of the Phocians, it was done with comparative ease. For the present, however, he withdrew from Greece proper, turned around, and marched across Thrace all the way to the Hellespont, making alliances with the Thracian chiefs and with such Greek cities as Byzantium, which lay along the shores of the waters on which Athens' wheat supply was conveyed.

DEMOSTHENES AGAINST PHILIP

Many of the Athenians remained indifferent to Philip's activities. At least Demosthenes says they did. In three speeches known as *Philippics*, from the name of the king, and in three others known as *Olynthiac Orations*, because they deal with Philip's advance against Olynthus (by the time these speeches were delivered Philip had become an enemy of Olynthus), Demosthenes gives us much detail of his personal campaign against the Macedonian. He scolded, warned, advised, and encouraged the Athenians to wake up and take measures against Philip before it was too late.

Demosthenes, born in 384, was a year or two older than Philip. His father had been a man of some wealth, but he had died when his son was a boy and the guardians whom he left in charge of his son and his property behaved very badly indeed. When Demosthenes came of age, he resolved to prosecute them and recover what he could of his inheritance. It seems probable that his suits against the guardians did recover some part of the property.

Meanwhile he had developed himself as a speaker and a student of the law. He found that he could gain some income by writing speeches for others to use in court. Then, at the unusually young age of thirty, he began to offer himself as a speaker before the Assembly on public affairs. His earliest speeches show a good grasp of issues and a forceful manner.

Now, with Philip's march to the Hellespont in 352, the Athenian lawyer, speaker, and self-appointed adviser of the Assembly realized that his contemporary, the king of Macedonia, was a man to be reckoned with. Both were truly great men. Both had been exercising their own powers as vigorously as they could for many years, Philip in war and other duties of a king ruling a somewhat wild people, Demosthenes in the arts by which the courts or the sovereign assembly of the most civilized people of the time could be moved. Philip was soon to recognize that Demosthenes, too, was a man to be reckoned with, and the careers of the two men were thenceforward involved with each other until the murder of Philip in 336.

Philip ranks as a genius in organization and in the realistic and unscrupulous use of any and every means to gain his ends. No one could have predicted that his kingdom would so quickly overshadow the Greek states; probably Philip himself was somewhat surprised at the power that Macedonia could generate and at the success of his own maneuverings. Demosthenes, on the other hand, ranks as a genius in oratory. Perhaps he was the greatest orator of all time; he might be somewhat surprised that his words still have power to stir the typical Western man.

Both men, politically, were the products of their time. Philip's aims reflect his political background. He was always uncertain to what extent the other Greeks would accept his people or himself as members of the Greek world. He knew that the order of the day was power politics, each state trying to make sure that its own position was secure and each aiming to weaken its most threatening rivals. His moves seem to have been consistently directed to creating a position of strength and safety for his people in such a world. Unlike some others, he sensibly aimed at building good will whenever he could do so. To ascribe to him plans for building a superstate to replace the obsolescent city states would only be reading later history and our own ideas into his purposes.

Demosthenes, too, grew up in a world of power politics. His aims for Athens were much the same as those of Philip for Macedonia: safety lay only in pre-eminence. We must show the same wariness about reading modern ideas into the mind of Demosthenes. He knew nothing of the ideological struggles between twentieth-century democracy and other forms of government; his purpose was not to make the world safe for democracy or to strike a blow against the evils of tyranny. He spoke with ungrudging admiration of Philip's energy and of the desire for glory and achievement that drove him on. There is drama enough, without making the conflict one of modern ideologies, in the long opposition between the king who wished his somewhat crude people to be strong and secure and to gain recognition for it in the family of Greek states, and the greatest orator of the world's most brilliant people who tried by democratic means to spur his fellow citizens to strive as their forefathers had for that same combination of preeminence and security at which Philip was aiming.

Demosthenes' first *Philippic*, probably delivered before the Athenian Assembly in 351, was a call to the people to rouse themselves from their lethargy and perceive how strong a threat to their interests Philip's activities were. The tone of these earlier discussions is simply that of power politics: Philip represents a danger and he is not too strong for us to do something about him. Demosthenes urged the Athenians not to allow Philip the complete exercise of the initiative, but instead to have two modest armies always in readiness to check whatever move he might make.

Philip Moves Against Olynthus

In 352, not long before the probable date of the first *Philippic*, Philip had fallen ill during his campaign in the region of the Hellespont, and until the next year he was not himself. The Athenians, cheered by the news of his illness, gave up an expedition to Thrace intended to protect their interests. In 351, however, Philip began to move against the Olynthian League. There had been a time when the kings of Macedonia found this league a very formidable one, and Philip had so far preserved a correct attitude toward it. But the Olynthians had asked the Athenians for an alliance and had entertained two of the old pretenders to the regency of Macedonia. Philip made proper diplomatic representations to the Olynthians.

In 349, having completed operations to make the western boundary of his kingdom more secure, he gave the Olynthians his full attention. He moved against the cities of the League one by one, and most of them yielded to him without resistance. The Olynthians now implored the assistance of Athens. Again Demosthenes, in his three

Olynthiac Orations, urged the citizens to rouse themselves from their lethargy and boldly oppose Philip.

The Athenians were loath to respond to his urging, even though it was plain that traditional Athenian interests in northern Greece were menaced by Philip's advances. The difficulties of public finance at Athens were one reason. Without the advantages of a flourishing naval league, Athens was not a rich city, and we find much in our sources about the difficulties of finance at this time. The name of the statesman Eubulus is often mentioned in connection with efforts to keep down expenses and preserve financial stability. For example, he was responsible for a prohibition against using the Theoric Fund for any but its stated purpose, that of recompensing the citizens who could not afford to take time off from work to attend the public festivals. And Eubulus seems to have been against any military or naval commitment that could possibly be avoided.

Philip showed his understanding of the difficulties of the Athenians by somehow persuading the cities of Euboea to withdraw from the Athenian naval league. The Athenian attempt to coerce them was unsuccessful, and the league, already much reduced, lost still more members. Demosthenes, whose gaze was steadily fixed on the long-range implications of Philip's actions, called on the Athenians to take a similar long view and make whatever personal and financial sacrifices were necessary. In the first of his speeches on the danger to Olynthus, we see him hinting very warily that the Theoric Fund should be dipped into for military purposes; apparently this was a subject to be approached with great care. In the third speech, however, he openly demands that the Theoric Fund be used.

At last the Athenians agreed to send help to Olynthus, "too little and too late," in the modern phrase. Philip captured the city in 348, destroyed it, and made slaves of its people. He also destroyed a number of other cities in the region and enslaved their inhabitants. Such cruelty was unusual with Philip, in spite of his custom of doing whatever furthered his aims. Sometimes, however, his actions were cruel or deceitful, for (like Julius Caesar later) he carefully studied his problems and solved them variously by clemency, personal charm, or barbarous cruelty, according to his estimate of which would achieve his immediate and long-range purposes.

After Philip's devastating conquest, it was the fate of Olynthus to become one of the great archaeological sites of the twentieth century. Between the two eras the site was never inhabited again on any scale, and archaeological expeditions of the Johns Hopkins University in the 1920's and 1930's, investigating the remains of the city, found it little disturbed since its destruction by Philip. The unusually full publication of the results offers a picture of the life of an ancient city rivaled only by the work done by Yale University scholars for Dura in Mesopotamia, a city of the Roman Empire. The results from Olynthus are especially interesting in relation to the problem of dating certain types of materials, because anything excavated there must date from before 348 B.C., when Philip made good the dire predictions of Demosthenes.

A new figure, some of whose speeches we still possess, now joined Demosthenes in the limelight at Athens. This was Aeschines, who had had experience as a teacher and as an actor. Both as a speaker and as a counselor on public affairs he could rival Demosthenes in every way but one: he remains in the second rank in both fields for lack of the deep conviction and fiery energy that animated the speeches and the public policy of Demosthenes.

In the early 340's, with the backing of Eubulus, Aeschines tried to arouse anti-Macedonian sentiment among the peoples of the Peloponnesus, but without success. Meanwhile, the conduct of the Phocians, who were still at war with the cities of Boeotia, but whose operations had begun to seem more like brigandage than war, gave Philip an opportunity for a new, limited gain. The Thebans appealed to him for assistance against the vicious Phocian raids, while the government of Phocia appealed to the Spartans and Athenians, expecting them to be ready to act against the interests of Thebes. But the troops that Sparta and Athens sent were refused by the commander of the Phocian mercenary forces.

The Peace of Philocrates

The Athenians decided that it was time to end the state of war that had existed since 356, when they had allied themselves with the native chiefs on Macedonia's borders. Aeschines and Demosthenes were both members of the embassy that waited upon Philip at his city of Pella. The discussions, in which Philip treated the envoys with truly royal courtesy, resulted in an agreement to make peace on the sensible basis of the existing situation. Philip, however, insisted on one exception; Phocis was not to be mentioned in the agreement, even though she was an ally of Athens. The embassy returned to Athens and presented its report to the Assembly.

After some debate in which Demosthenes tried to insist on the inclusion of Phocis but in which he was defeated when the envoys sent by Philip to swear the Athenians to the pact refused to accept the change, the Assembly accepted the terms. Then the same group of Athenian envoys went back to Pella to take the king's oath. Demosthenes later insisted that he had tried to make the embassy hurry, fearing that Philip would make new conquests and assert that they formed part of the existing situation. The delegation had indeed moved slowly, and in the meantime Philip had made new conquests in Thrace, somewhat damaging to Athenian interests, but ones that the envoys felt forced to accept. Philip assured them that he had no designs on Phocis, and finally they concluded the matter by accepting his oath. This peace, which was concluded in 346, was known as the Peace of Philocrates from the name of the man who had originally proposed in the Assembly that negotiations be instituted.

The peace was to be the subject of much argument and the cause of many allegations of corruption and treason. Unfortunately, the truth cannot now be sifted out of the welter of charges and countercharges, chiefly exchanged by Demosthenes and Aeschines. The fact may well be that many Athenians regarded the conduct of Philip as neither culpable nor dangerous and, without being bribed, were willing to accept his assertions at face value.

But Philip's next act was highly distressing to the Athenians. He suddenly moved his forces to Thermopylae and accepted the surrender that under the circumstances was the only course open to the Phocian commander. The mercenary soldiers were discharged and allowed to depart. The Phocian government surrendered, having no means of resistance. Philip called the Amphictyonic Council to decide the fate of Phocis, and it was decided that their cities must be dissolved into villages, as Mantinea had been dissolved by the Spartans some time before. A yearly tribute was imposed upon them as restitution to the shrine at Delphi for what they had taken from it, and Philip acquired their votes in the Amphictyonic Council. His pretensions to complete Hellenism were also recognized, at least in these circles, by his being chosen president of the Pythian Games, whose regular celebration at Delphi was about to begin.

The resentment of the Athenians was not allayed by a message from Philip in which he asserted that the Peace of Philocrates had left him free to deal with Phocis as he saw fit. The Assembly, unable to do anything but offer useless insults, was ready to boycott the Pythian Games and refuse Philip's formal request that he be recognized as a member of the Amphictyonic League. But Demosthenes, still trying to preserve the long view, persuaded the Athenians not to make insulting and ineffectual gestures.

Another Athenian whose words we can still read chose to make his views public at this point. Isocrates, the aged teacher and political essayist, published an address to Philip that he had entitled *Philippus*. This student of Greek political matters had been born in 436, five years before the beginning of the Peloponnesian War. Surely no man then living had had so good an opportunity as he to observe the long-term trend of Greek affairs. His attitude at this time was that Philip ought to exert himself to create a *symmachia* (or military alliance) of all the Greek states and then lead a combined expedition against Persia. Philip was not in any sense to be in control of Greece, but merely to preside over the alliance and lead its joint army.

It is interesting to contrast this proposal of a sincere Athenian patriot with the attitude of Demosthenes. Isocrates evidently did not regard Philip as aiming at the conquest of all Greece, and it is clear that he did admire the king's force and ability, for which Demosthenes, too, had shown admiration. Apparently it was still possible for sincere Athenians to feel that a unified purpose under strong leadership was what Greece as a whole most needed.*

---

*But see N. H. Baynes's trenchant Essay VIII in his *Byzantine Studies and Other Essays*; he maintains that the chief purpose of Isocrates, as a man of property, was to induce Philip to enlist the many mercenary soldiers who seemed to menace peace and the security of property throughout Greece, draw them away in a war of imperialistic conquest against the Persians, and then settle them on conquered territory.

Demosthenes against Aeschines

One of the less pleasant sides of Greek life is displayed in the records of the next few years. Demosthenes decided to prosecute Aeschines for treason and the acceptance of bribes during the proceedings that had led to the Peace of Philocrates. Any man who engaged in public life at Athens had to be ready to defend his conduct against accusations of this sort, even when his behavior had been impeccable. It was for this reason that a few decades later the philosopher Epicurus was to recommend complete abstinence from public life, a piece of advice that in the circumstances was far less pusillanimous than it has seemed to many later critics of Epicurus. As men who instituted a prosecution often did, Demosthenes had an associate in the prosecution, Timarchus. Aeschines countered with a slashing suit to disqualify Timarchus from public life on the ground of his immoral life and more specifically on the ground that he had prostituted himself. His able speech *Against Timarchus* makes peculiarly disagreeable reading, but he was successful and inflicted a check on Demosthenes.

The next move was for Hyperides, another associate of Demosthenes, to prosecute Philocrates for treason on the ground that he had instituted the negotiations leading to the peace of 346 that was called by his name. Public resentment at the unfortunate results of the peace was so strong that Philocrates foresaw that he could not possibly defend himself, reasonable as his proposal had been when he made it and when the assembly accepted it. His only course seemed to be to flee into exile.

Demosthenes now reactivated his prosecution of Aeschines. Although he himself had been a member of the embassy, and although he did not have a good case, to judge by his speech and that of Aeschines, both of which we have, he almost succeeded in gaining a conviction.

Philip Triumphs

Meanwhile Philip was rounding out and securing his gains. He managed to gain friends in the Peloponnesus by diplomacy and the use of money, but was obliged to make a show of force from time to time to counter the restlessness of his rude western neighbors.

His main effort, however, was directed toward securing control of Thrace and moving into the Chersonesus. Here he came into conflict with the interest of Athens, which felt that she must maintain her prestige in this neighborhood and safeguard the wheat route from the Black Sea region.

In 341, Demosthenes delivered his third *Philippic*. He called for vigorous action in the Chersonesus and the formation of an alliance against Philip. Although the other Greeks did not respond, the Athenians at last decided to put forth a real effort against the Macedonian. Their power on the sea still made it possible for them to check him here and there, although his land forces were far greater than theirs. In the year 340, Philip's attempts to capture the cities of Perinthus and Byzantium on the wheat route were foiled by Athenian assistance, and in 339, he withdrew from his efforts in that region.

But the Athenians now became involved in a dispute with the Amphictyonic League, a dispute that may have been fostered by Philip's subterranean diplomacy. The League called upon Philip, who promptly marched south. Instead of taking the action that was expected, he suddenly occupied the strong point of Elatea, in Boeotia. From there he sent a message to the Thebans, announcing that he intended to invade Attica and asking for their co-operation.

A messenger arrived at Athens one evening to announce that Philip was at Elatea. Early next morning the Assembly was convened and the herald asked who wished to address the people. After the invitation was repeated, Demosthenes arose to propose an alliance with Thebes and active resistance. An embassy to Thebes managed, in the face of Philip's envoys, to secure the desired alliance.

Surprisingly, the decision by force was delayed until the next summer. Philip called for reinforcements from home and considered his moves carefully. In the summer of 338, the large Macedonian force, some 30,000 men, met an almost equal force of Athenians, Thebans, and mercenaries at Chaeronea in Boeotia. The Macedonians won a decisive victory. Philip was now master of the situation.

Philip's Settlement

As usual, Philip carefully considered what conduct would best advance his interests. Thebes was treated severely ; the captives were sold into slavery, and the other Boeotian cities were declared free of her. The Athenians, who had made preparations for a last-ditch resistance, were surprised to learn that their captives were to be returned without ransom and that Philip had no further warlike intentions toward them. It is to be supposed that he recognized the difficulty of completely reducing a naval power with a strongly forti- fied city and realized the advantages of having such a naval power as an ally. He must also have recognized that Athens was in fact what Isocrates and Demosthenes had proclaimed her to be, the spir- itual leader and center of Greece, and that his purposes would be best served by clemency. He did, however, force her to give up her control over her naval allies.

He now set in circulation the word that he would soon embark on the great war against Persia that had long been discussed in Greece. He also, late in 338, called for the formation of a new Greek league, which came to be known as the League of Corinth, because the convention that formed it met there.

Again the league was in form what the Greeks called a *symmachia*, or military alliance. Philip was to be commander of any military operation, the war against Persia being planned as the first one. Every member was to supply some forces. A congress, called a *synedrion*, was to meet at stated times. Although Philip was not to be a member of the congress, his office as commander-in-chief of the armed forces, added to his prestige and power, obviously gave him sufficient control over the general activities of the league.

This league, the formation of which was the culmination of Philip's long years of military and political action in Greece, was essentially the sort of organization that other influential states had tried to form. It did not represent a mere act of conquest designed to make sure that the economic surplus of the vanquished would be regularly transferred to the victor. It was rather the one method of ensuring the security of the dominant state that had presented itself to the political thought of the Greeks; it was very like the attempts of Athens, Sparta, and Thebes to consolidate their power.

This league was superior to earlier attempts in one respect: Philip did not interfere in the internal organization of the *poleis* as others had done. Athens had tried to promote the democratic form and Sparta the oligarchic form. Philip probably had no strong feeling for either, because he had brought his own country out of disunion to a strong national feeling based on devotion to himself as king. But whatever his reason, he did not insist that changes be made anywhere except at Thebes, which he presented with a sponsored oligarchy, perhaps because he had reason to believe that there he needed a solidly founded party loyal to himself.

Some modern scholars have glorified Philip at the expense of Demosthenes, apparently because their own countries had recently ended periods of weakness by achieving unification, such unification as Greece so sorely needed. Others have glorified Demosthenes at the expense of Philip because Philip seemed to represent a threat to democracy by dictatorial power. The eloquence of Demosthenes has been unfortunate for Philip's reputation. Demosthenes has been able to stir the spirits of Western man by his fight for his democratic nation and by his references to the true greatness of Athens. We can recognize both the greatness of the king who brought his country out of weakness and disunion to become the first true nation of Europe and the greatness of the Athenian orator who still reigns as the master of the spoken word. The aims of both men were the usual aims of the politics of the time. The fact that Philip prevailed is irrelevant to a judgment of their place in history.

The invasion of Persia began in 336. The forces that crossed the Hellespont had persuaded some of the Greek cities of Asia Minor to throw in their lot with the operation. But then came the news of Philip's assassination. The army was withdrawn to await developments. It was soon to be sent into Asia Minor again by Philip's son, Alexander the Great.

CHAPTER

29

ECONOMIC AND SOCIAL LIFE
IN THE FOURTH CENTURY

The fourth century among the Greeks has a reasonable claim to be regarded as a historical period. The fifth was the century of Athenian greatness and can be called a period of history for that reason. And within the fifth century, the Age of Pericles has valid claims to being an epoch. The fourth century as a historical entity may be said to have its beginning in 404 B.C. with the great disaster inflicted on the Athenian Empire by Sparta's victory in the Peloponnesian War and its ending at the death of Alexander the Great, after his brilliant conquest of the Persian Empire. Modern historians feel that another new period, the Hellenistic Age, began after Alexander, and they date it from his death in 323 B.C.

Fourth-century political and military power may not seem to mark a distinct era, but from other points of view, we do seem to have a new period. The historians of art generally will not allow the happiest years of Greek art to extend beyond the fifth century; new tendencies inconsistent with perfect classicism became prominent (they say) in the fourth century. The great period of Attic tragedy was the fifth century; in the fourth there were no great writers working in this field. During the fourth century, Attic comedy changed from the public-minded Old Comedy of Aristophanes and others to the New Comedy, a polished drawing-room comedy concerned with the complications of the private lives of individuals. There is a certain significance in the fact that the young Plato of the late fifth century wrote tragedies and the mature Plato of the first half of the fourth discussed great problems, not in tragedies, but in philosophical essays. The progress of individualism in the fifth (and even more in the fourth) century is shown by the fact that one of the greatest achievements of the men of the fourth century was the construction of four great systems of philosophy, rational and complete systems, by which an individual, a man practically without support from God, clan, or *polis*, could undertake to understand the scheme of things and his place in it, order his life, and find the courage to live it.

It is customary to find a real break in Greek history at the time of Alexander the Great; thus we say that this marks the end of the fourth century as a period. It is true that after Alexander, the Greek world of independent small or middle-sized *poleis* was gone and that the eastern Mediterranean world was dominated by the kingdoms of his successors. Life was different in many ways, most of them caused by the existence of the kingdoms and the increase in individualism. Furthermore, the history of the Greeks before Alexander has a certain unity, interest, and glamor that are not to be found in their later history.

Nevertheless, it would be a mistake to suppose that Greece and the Greeks were unimportant after Alexander's time; indeed, a number of their greatest achievements came then. Many Greeks played important parts in the history of Rome; and the achievements of the Byzantine Empire are Greek achievements. There is a certain temptation to look on the fifth century before Christ as a high point in history that has some biological foundation, as if it were the prime of life of a man, and to see all later Greek history as a slow decadence from that height. More than this, there is a temptation to find in all Greek history after the fifth century signs of decadence to support the notion that some grand design was slowly working itself out. We shall discuss the history of Greece after Alexander and up to the sixth century of our era in connection with the history of Rome, making every effort to avoid unjustified schematization.

COMMERCE

The chief difference between commerce in the fifth century and in the fourth was that Athens could no longer compel the members of her former empire to adopt whatever policy was most advantageous to her. Otherwise, commerce went on much as before. In this field, we are much better informed about the fourth century than the fifth, because we have many detailed discussions of commercial matters in the speeches of the Athenian orators.

Athens remained an important commercial city in spite of her reverse in the Peloponnesian War and the loss of her empire. Although she could no longer compel her allies to bring their cargoes only to Peiraeus, Peiraeus was still centrally located for the trade of the Mediterranean and had not lost its magnificent facilities. Ships could dock in a well-sheltered place. There were warehouse facilities if anyone wanted to use them, although it was more customary to dispose of cargoes at once, either for use in Athens or for shipment to and sale in other places. At this busy port, buyers were readily found. Further, the bankers of Athens (mostly metics) were men of experience in financing business ventures. The Athenian courts gave fair treatment to foreigners; the law itself and the general knowledge of trade among the citizens who sat as jurors naturally reflected the long commercial importance of Athens. Even in the absence of compulsion, it was good business to bring one's cargo to Athens, whether with the idea that the goods were suitable for the city's own needs or with the idea that the cargo might in part be sold to other people to be taken to other ports.

During the first third of the century, the ascendancy of Dionysius I in Syracuse added to the importance of his city and made it a busier port. In spite of the frequent warfare between Dionysius and Carthage, the Carthaginian ships called at Syracuse in times of peace, thus connecting the Greek complex of trade with that of Carthage. Modern finds of Athenian vases at Carthage show that the Carthaginians were in contact with Athens without giving any indication as to how it was done. Perhaps Carthaginian ships called at Peiraeus; it seems less likely that Athenian ships went to Carthage. Possibly Corinthian ships carried Athenian wares, always readily salable, to Syracuse and the Carthaginians got them there. Be that as it may, the Carthaginians remained in control of all the ports of North Africa and southern Spain and continued their policy of policing the western Mediterranean to exclude the ships of other peoples.

Athenian wares were also popular in Etruria, north of Rome. The Etruscan fleet had been destroyed in 474 and Etruscan sea power ended, but the export of Athenian vases that has made the present-day museums of north-central Italy treasure houses of Attic ware continued, presumably balanced by the export of Etruscan iron and bronze and objects made of those two metals. By the fourth century, the Romans were at the head of a little league around Rome and had begun to encroach on the territory of Etruria proper. They still had only rare contact with Greece, however, and were regarded as only one of the groups of less civilized peoples on the periphery of the Greek world.

The ports and maritime cities of the eastern end of the Mediterranean remained much as they had been in the fifth century. Naucratis, the Greek extraterritorial city on one of the branches of the Nile, maintained its prime importance as the port of Egypt until in 332 Alexander the Great founded Alexandria on a fine commercial site. Alexandria at once became the great port of Egypt. Naucratis, however, remained important as an upriver location. The fact that a main road crossed the river here made it important as a place where goods from overseas were distributed through the Delta. In the fifth and fourth centuries, to judge from the archaeological evidence, more Athenian goods were handled at Naucratis than ever before.

It is important to realize how prosperous the Persian Empire was in the fourth century. The Persians in general controlled Asia Minor, Egypt, and the Near and Middle East, the territory in which civilization had first developed and in which, materially at least, it was farthest advanced in the fourth century. Their wise policy of allowing each region to follow its own economic destiny with a minimum of governmental interference and their willingness to make great efforts to keep their subjects secure had given many of their people the best opportunity that they had ever had to develop themselves economically.

In the far eastern part of the Persian realm were rich territories—Bactria, Sogdiana, Margiane—of which we hear little until the great campaign of Alexander in that region. A little to the west of them, the Medes still lived a feudal and tribal life, pasturing cattle in the highlands east of Mesopotamia. Mesopotamia retained all the traditional skill of its long and highly civilized past and prospered on both agriculture and manufacturing. Egypt, too, retained its old organization and skills, as did Palestine and Phoenicia. In the interior of Asia Minor, some regions were mountainous and still primitive; in others, there were fine agricultural regions and old centers of industry. There is every reason to believe that the people of the fourth-century Persian Empire were living what to them seemed a very good life. They had a lively interchange of goods with the Greeks, which passed chiefly through the ports of Phoenicia and Palestine.

Commerce by sea followed a few main routes. The Carthaginians had long ago worked out an ingenious roundabout route for their navigation of the western sea, following prevailing winds and currents. If a ship from Carthage went north in the early summer to Sicily, Sardinia, and Corsica, then she could easily go west to the Punic depots around the lower tip of Spain, calling at the Balearic Islands on the way, and come home in the autumn with favoring winds and currents along the coasts of what are now Algeria and Tunisia in North Africa. On the all-important grain route from the Black Sea to Athens, only one round trip a year was possible, too. The ships that went out in the early summer would have a difficult time making their way against the prevailing northerly winds up past the Chalcidic promontory, along the coast of Thrace, and through the Dardanelles, the Propontis (or Sea of Marmora), and the Bosporus to the Black Sea. On the return trip, however, they would have favoring winds all the way.

The trip from Greece to Egypt and back was another roundabout affair like the Carthaginians' route in the West. If one went south before the prevailing northerlies past Crete to Cyrene on the coast of Africa, he could then make a reasonably easy trip along the coast to Naucratis. On the return voyage, however, he would find it easier to use the winds and currents that would take him up the Phoenician coast to Cyprus and from there make his way across the Aegaean. The route from Corinth to the West was somewhat easier, going as it did through the Gulf of Corinth. Ships from Athens or elsewhere would either transship their cargoes at Corinth or go across the Isthmus on the marine railway. Although most of the ships went to southern Italy and Sicily, others went up the Adriatic Sea to trade in areas where there were good natural products, even though there were few cities and many pirates.

The Athenian orators and other sources give us a certain amount of detailed information about commerce at Athens. The port of Peiraeus was well equipped. Its entrance could be closed. On one side was the navy yard, where there were shops and long sheds to house the warships. On the other side was a long stone quay where the merchant ships tied up. Behind it were five large colonnades where business could be done, whether it was the expediting of goods for Athens or the exchange of goods to be shipped along to other ports. The officials of Athens kept a sharp eye on the scene to see that the peace was kept and the regulations observed. Officials examined and carefully inventoried every incoming cargo; they then collected a tax of 2 per cent. This tax had to be paid even on goods that were in transit. It was a revenue-producing device rather than a protective tariff, something that was unknown in antiquity.

The bankers of Athens were active in serving commerce. They had facilities for storing money left on deposit by their patrons. They could also, through their connections, arrange for payments in other cities without the actual transport of coins. They changed money, an activity that could be as useful as and even more profitable than it is now, because there was not yet a stable and active international money market in which standard relations of currencies could be established.

Athens was more dependent on imports than was any other state of the time. Since the days of Solon, she had been committed to commerce, trade, and satisfaction of some of her basic needs by import. Although Corinth, for example, and Carthage, too, were great trading cities, they had food more readily available than Athens did, and no need of risky sea transport to get it. We are to some extent informed about the measures taken by the Athenians in the fourth century to make sure that their grain supply did not fail. Only a third of any cargo of grain that entered Peiraeus could be forwarded to another port; two-thirds had to remain. No grain could be handled by a citizen or a metic unless it was destined for

Athens. Further, no citizen or metic could finance a cargo of grain destined for any other place. Out of each cargo of grain arriving at Peiraeus, each wholesaler could buy no more than about 75 bushels, so that a corner in grain was impossible.

At times, Athens, like many other cities, found it necessary to appoint commissioners to buy grain wherever they could and bring it to Athens for distribution at normal prices. There are many known instances of supplies of grain being used as gifts in international politics, both at this time and later. Egypt could easily use this method of making political gifts, as could the Sicilians, the Carthaginians, or some of the native dynasts in South Russia. We do not find that the Athenians ever tried to exert governmental control over the production of food in Attica or in any of the cleruchies or other places that they controlled. Such controls had been known in Egypt for over a thousand years and were to be refined by the Ptolemies, the Macedonian dynasty that ruled Egypt during the third, second, and first centuries before Christ. Neither did the Athenians try the device used by the Romans of imperial times, that of organizing one fleet under strict contract to the government to bring grain from North Africa to Rome and another to bring grain from Alexandria to Rome. The Athenians did, however, take great care in controlling the supply of their shipbuilding materials, especially the timber and the pitch. They were able to force the rulers of Macedonia to agree to sell their timber and pitch only to the Athenians, because Athens could control the sea in their area and prevent the export of these commodities elsewhere. Strangely enough, we can find no evidence of public concern in Athens about the volume of exports.

It has been suggested that during the fourth century the peoples to whom the Greeks exported their wares began to be able to produce comparable things for themselves, or at least things with which they were satisfied. The idea rests on archaeological evidence from many places—the Persian Empire, Thrace, the Greek colonies and native cities around the Black Sea, and, in Italy, Etruria and the Greek communities of southern Italy. The comparison of the contents of innumerable finds (and this sort of thing is perhaps the supreme achievement of the scientific archaeologist) and the classification of their contents by origin and periods seems to show that the flow of goods from Greece to all these places slowed down and that the market was partly taken over by goods that betray to the trained eye that they were locally made in imitation of the goods imported from Greece.

SOCIETY IN THE FOURTH CENTURY

Athens

Athens in the late fourth century had perhaps 20,000 adult male citizens, if we can trust the casual remarks of the orators. Assuming two or three other people in the average family, we have a total of about 70,000 free Athenians. The calculation of the numbers in each class is complicated, for it can be based only on stray data given by the orators or by later writers. There was a small group of rather wealthy men at the top, perhaps 300. Conon, the admiral who went over to serve the Persian king, left an estate of 40 talents. A wealthy landowner is known to have left 20 talents. But others in the small rich group had only two or three talents. Men who had nearly one talent were thought to be well-to-do, but not in the top group.

In the year 322 (we are told), there were 9,000 men who owned more than 20 minae, that is, a third of a talent. These men were liable to service as hoplites, and the top 1,000 were required to serve as cavalry. Strangely, this is the same number liable to hoplite service in the revolution of 411 B.C., when the question of who could so serve became important. The thetes were those citizens, 12,000 of them, who owned less than 20 minae. This sum would more or less correspond to the value of a subsistence farm, a place of five or six acres with an adobe house and the usual animals. Probably half the thetes owned such a modest farm. Others owned no land, lived in the city rather than out in Attica, and had little enterprises of some sort, often shops that they handled by themselves or with the help of a single slave.

Our evidence seems to indicate that below the small group of very rich there was a gentle gradation of wealth; a fair part of the population might be regarded as a middle class. The fact that there were a good many small owners of property probably tended to keep down strong opposition between class and class. There was no great mass of Athenian citizens able to regard themselves as shut off from an opportunity to make a living while others had much more than enough. Although Athens had her oligarchic revolutions in 411 and 403, she never had the bitter and reckless class struggles that frequently occurred in the Greek world and about which we hear a great deal elsewhere—at Thebes, for example.

Sparta

Sparta, during the fourth century, produced the curious phenomenon of a rapid shrinkage in the numbers of those who held land that entitled them to be regarded as "Equals," to fight as hoplites, and to take part in the government. This situation resulted from letting the system get out of hand, not from a sharp drop in the birth rate. In 480 B.C., there were 8,000 full citizens; in 371, only 2,000; and a few generations later, only 700. We must suppose, therefore, not that the number of pure-blooded Spartans was dropping at this rate, but that the land was falling into the hands of fewer people.

As we have seen, in the early days of Greece after the Dark Age, it was common to draw careful legislation to prevent men from letting their land slip away because the community was based on a limited number of landowners who were to be the army and the ruling class. It has been suggested that in the fourth century, many Spartans made money as mercenary soldiers and, eager to invest in land, breached the system that connected land and citizen rights, concentrating land in the hands of fewer people (some of them even women) and leaving many pure-blooded Spartans without land and thus without full citizenship.

Many Spartans may well have felt no regret at being excluded from the rigorous life of the first-class male Spartan, even though that life was, in a sense, subsidized. To engage in trade or to take the gold darics of the Persian king and live a companionable, perhaps luxurious life as a soldier in Babylon or Susa, with no one to insist on black soup or visiting one's woman only by stealth, may have seemed far better. In the third century, the kings of Sparta were to make great efforts at land reform and raise a great storm in Sparta and all of Greece, but that story lies outside the scope of this volume.

We have scattered data on population in the fourth century. The general impression has been that men were reluctant to marry, as they had not been before. With the growing sense of individualism, the sense of responsibility to the commonwealth lessened, and one result was less feeling of duty to produce children. We hear of people who refused to marry, and inevitably there are stories of men who found long-term companionship with concubines. There is also evidence that those that did marry tried hard to limit their families. They were thinking of the chances for the individual to live in prosperity and security, and many a man must have felt that in a tightly-organized society he could not afford to have much of a family, because he did not have much property to leave them. The philosopher Aristotle even assumed that the government of a *polis* had to find some way of providing that the population should not exceed a certain number.

All this is a far cry from the fertility rites of earlier people and their concern with increase of human beings as well as of plants and animals. We can easily see that in a small *polis* with limited territory and neighbors all around preventing any expansion, a man might well find it a misfortune to have his marriage too often blessed with offspring. On the other hand, there must have been hundreds of Greek communities in the fourth century where life was not so confined, where there was enough territory to support the people well—with trade opportunities or more land for the energetic man—places where a man might feel that there was room on his farm for three or four strong sons.

MERCENARY SOLDIERS

The mercenary soldier was an important social and economic phenomenon of the fourth century. Long before this time, however, Greeks had hired themselves out as soldiers. The kings of Egypt and their neighbors often hired Greeks (and Carians) from Asia Minor in the seventh and sixth centuries. Psamtik and Amasis especially relied on Greek mercenaries. During the fifth century, there was some employment of mercenaries among the Greeks themselves. It is somewhat surprising, however, that the Spartans hired Arcadian hoplites in the Peloponnesian War. According to our evidence, both the oligarchs and the democrats sought to bolster their forces with a few hundred mercenaries in the struggle of 403, which was brought on by the enormities of the Thirty. The Spartans in their campaigns in Asia Minor against the Persians in the decade after the Peloponnesian War used some mercenaries.

Even before the time when Cyrus gathered the Ten Thousand to march upcountry to try to take his brother's throne, the Persian satraps had learned that the Greek hoplite was superior to the ordinary soldier of the Persian Empire. Many satraps had had Greek bodyguards and some had regular detachments of Greeks in their provincial forces, especially when they thought of fighting one another. At any time after the Peloponnesian War, a force of Greek mercenaries could be recruited without any difficulty other than paying them, whether it was a Greek *polis*, a Persian satrap, or the Great King himself who wished to have an offensive or a defensive force.

Xenophon's *Anabasis* gives us an opportunity to see how Cyrus recruited the Ten Thousand without allowing his brother the king to know what he had in mind. It allows us to see how formidable a force this was in the eyes of the Persians and what a fearsome lot of ruffians it was to the native tyrants and the Greek cities on the Black Sea.

Consideration of such men and of the *condottieri,* or mercenary captains who led them, throws light on the condition of Greece in the fourth century. That so many men from so many *poleis* wished to run the risks of mercenary service for the pay and the possibility of booty shows that life in the *poleis* was less satisfactory than it had been in the fifth century. Possibly money was becoming more important and the possession of cash more desirable. It is plain, however, that we cannot speak of the *polis* as a tightly integrated political and social unit when so many of the citizens were ready to leave home and risk their lives for money in the service of any *polis*, satrap, king, or tyrant who would hire them.

The professionalism of the mercenary soldier and of his captain was another sign of the times. We know something of a handful of Athenians who were successful in organizing and disciplining bands of mercenaries; a notable one was Iphicrates, who developed a formidable corps of peltasts, better armed and far better trained than the light-armed peltasts of earlier times who had skirmished on the flanks of the hoplites or tried to cut off supply trains. His corps was highly trained and subject to stern discipline; even hoplites feared it. The ordinary citizen army could not match such men, all the more so because many *poleis* came to rely on mercenaries and ceased to insist on the old physical and military training of the citizens.

The successful *condottieri* were men of force and independence. Iphicrates succeeded by the ingenuity of his methods and his insistence on training and discipline. Another captain might rely more on personal magnetism and bravery. All could attract and command men. But almost all were more or less indifferent about whom they served and were likely to have estates in foreign parts—often on Persian soil—which they thought of as their ultimate retreat if things went wrong, just as in modern times certain countries have been used as retreats. These were efficient individualists, not men who put an ideal *polis* before their own interests. They found their counterparts in the new tyrants of the fourth century, of whom Dionysius I of Syracuse serves as an example. He, like Iphicrates, was a gifted commander of mercenary troops, as well as a master of ruthless government.

THE LEAGUES

Every possible form of government cropped up at one time or another among the Greeks. No clear pattern of evolution can be discerned, except that in political affairs and life alike there was a growing sophistication and individualism from 800 B.C. onward. No form of government can be said to have established itself as dominant, although monarchy and oligarchy were the most frequent.

We have already observed the working of some Greek leagues. The Peloponnesian League, or "the Spartans and their allies," was a well-conceived and influential organization. The Ionian League of the coastal cities of Asia Minor could not unite its members against the Persian threat. The Hellenic League set up for defense against the Persian invasions of Greece proper served its immediate purpose fairly well. The Delian League, although it started out as a genuine alliance, fell as much or more under the control of Athens as the

Peloponnesian League had under the control of Sparta. The Second Athenian Naval League was never of great importance. The Boeotian League, which lasted from 447 until Sparta forced its dissolution in 386, is interesting as having a constitution that was plainly the work of theorists and a representative body that governed it. The Hellenic League of Philip II had a fair beginning as an alliance to keep the peace at home and fight Persia, but more and more Alexander the Great treated its members as subjects.

A respectable number of attempts at interstate co-operation for limited or extended objectives can be found among this people who have so strong a reputation for not being willing to co-operate with each other. We may add to the number by giving a brief description of four other leagues, our evidence for which lies mainly in the fourth century, groups that did nothing spectacular. The first is the Chalcidic League of the *poleis* of the Chalcidic Peninsula, led by Olynthus, which was near the site of the modern Saloniki. Its situation was such that it was bound to be involved in the affairs of the Greek states and of the kingdom of Macedonia. This was an active confederation, had a real federal government, and was discussing true representative government. As we have seen, the Spartans dissolved it in 379 according to their usual policy. Twenty years later, Philip II and the Athenians competed for an alliance with the League, which had revived and become very prosperous. Philip was the winner. By 349, however, he was ready to swallow the cities of the League, and in 348 he did so. It is regrettable that the *poleis* could not have had further opportunity to develop their advanced ideas of federation and representative government.

In general, we hear very little about the Aetolians, who lived in western Greece just north of the Gulf of Corinth. They did, however, show themselves well organized when the Athenians tried to invade them during the Peloponnesian War, and there is evidence that by the year 367 they were organized into a league. They had a number of small cities that are known by name but not to fame. These cities had set up a central government that could act for the whole group. They called it the *koinon*, which does not mean "league," but something more like "the common organization of the Aetolians." In its functioning, it was a state in the modern sense. The Aetolian state (as we may as well call it) had a representative council. It also had a primary assembly, or assembly of the individual citizens, which met regularly twice a year and could meet more often if necessary.

The Arcadians lived in the north central Peloponnesus. Apparently, they, like the Aetolians, did nothing distinctive, but we must remember that there were many genuine Greeks of whom we know very little. Under pressure from Sparta, the Arcadians formed a league in 370. Its general tone was democratic, it had a council and a primary assembly, as did the Aetolians, and it also had a single chief official, whose title was *strategos*, or general.

The Achaeans, another people of the north central Peloponnesus, also had a league, about which we have a certain amount of rather equivocal and tantalizing information from the fourth, third, and second centuries. It had a council, and, like the others, it had meetings of a primary assembly.

There are differences in terminology in our descriptions of these leagues formed by the less well-known peoples, but unfortunately we cannot be sure what the terms mean in practice. We can be certain, however, that these people had a strong urge to cooperate for the common good (something that is not always granted the Greeks by modern opinion) and that they had some idea of a truly representative government. It is unfortunate that our evidence about the composition and powers of the councils is not fuller and clearer. There is reason to believe that the idea of the superior wisdom of the assembled people impressed the framers of these confederacies as it did some statesmen elsewhere, notably at Athens, and that perhaps earlier moves toward representative government yielded to the idea that a primary assembly wherein the superior wisdom of the whole people could express itself ought to check and ratify the acts of the council. Such a situation, of course, kept the council from acting as a body truly representative of the whole people. No Greek treatise on the theory of co-operation among *poleis* is preserved or mentioned in spite of the plain fact that much thinking was done about the leagues.

THE GROWTH OF INDIVIDUALISM

The growth of individualism, which must be so often mentioned in a history of Greece, deserves a little systematic discussion. Like many other things, individualism can be explained in part by saying what it is not. Those who live in an age of extreme individualism (like the latter part of the twentieth century in the United States) may find it hard to imagine any other kind of existence. The life of the Greeks as we saw them first emerging from the Dark Age, however, allowed very little room for individualism, and is an excellent example of another way of life from ours.

The clans of that early age in fact entirely controlled the lives of their members by their authority. Although the ordinary man must often have been irked by the restraint imposed by the clan, he did not even think of the possibility of the more independent way of life that presently became the rule. If oppressiveness represents one side of such comprehensive authority, the other side is complete support. The members of such a group could expect it to support them with all its power whenever need arose. Loyalties, too, would be almost undivided, for the group, being the only group, could expect complete devotion.

As the *polis* grew, it arrogated to itself functions that had formerly been discharged by the clan: the maintenance of internal order, the management of foreign affairs, and public dealing with the gods. The supervision exercised by the elders of the clan was replaced by that of a council of elders in the *polis*, for example, the Council of the Areopagus at Athens. The withdrawal of general supervisory power from such a council and its replacement by specific statutes may be taken as a sign of a demand for more personal freedom, for a man can be more independent under the reign of definite laws than under a general supervisory body, that is, the ordinary citizen can.

In many places, then, the *polis* took to itself the earlier authority of the clan and the clan's former function of supporting the individual. In many parts of Greece, of course, no great number of *poleis* ever arose, and the social system changed little between the ninth and the fourth centuries. We must not suppose that the supplanting of the clan by the necessarily looser authority of the *polis* meant that social life became like ours. The family was far more tightly organized than it is in the late twentieth century. At Athens, for example, the man who came up for his *dokimasia*, or scrutiny, for membership in the *Boule* had to show that he was scrupulous in his performance of the religious rites of the family and in his maintenance of the family burial place. Parents still maintained real authority. Women had not asserted their individualism. Marriages were arranged for them, and they had no other career. The head of a family was obligated to find husbands for the females as they grew to maturity or when they were widowed, for a woman had to have a male protector. The unmarried head of the family had the choice of marrying the woman himself (a first or second cousin, for example) or finding another man to marry her.

Of course, the world of the fifth century had become much more lively than the world of the ninth or eighth, and it was easier for a young man who wished to go away from home and make a new start far from his *polis* and his family. Even the backwoods Arcadian who had never seen a *polis* could emancipate himself from his clan by going out to live the life of a mercenary soldier, for the recruiting officers often called; but he was rather likely to come back with his pay and his loot, turn them over to the clan, and settle down again.

Not only could a man exchange the close life of the clan for the somewhat freer life of the *polis*, but in the average *polis* of the fifth or fourth century he could choose from a wider range of careers. The choice would still be small by our standards. At least one of a farmer's sons would expect to take over the farm. The son of a small merchant or shopowner would normally follow his father. If a man went out to a colony, he would either farm or be in trade. The church, teaching, and the arts did not offer careers as they do now. Careers in business were few compared to nowadays. We do not hear, then, as we do now, of the man who tries half a dozen different occupations. Still, the range was wider than it had been in the days when one almost had to choose between farming and piracy (or combine them as some did).

Another approach to a study of the growth of individualism is through examination of the varying loyalty of the individual to the group. In the fourth century, Demosthenes complained of the indifference of the Athenians to the public interest, and historians have often supposed that the growth of individualism made them unwilling to tax themselves and fight for their city. Closer examination shows, however, that they were willing to do both. But King Philip could keep pressure on them for long periods, and the Athenian hoplite in modest circumstances was reluctant to go on a lengthy campaign with no pay, thus possibly ruining himself and losing his farm. Earlier campaigns had been very short; those of the fifth century had been paid for; therefore, such sacrifice had not been asked before. As a result, this case will not do as an example of individualism that crippled state policy.

Perhaps the changes in Spartan landholding would serve us better. Whether or not the concentration of Spartan land in the hands of fewer people came about because it was a way of investing the wealth that fortunate individuals had got while serving other governments as mercenaries, the fact remains that the abandonment of the old system of making the land support all the first-class citizens marks a relaxation of the old public spirit and an advance in the willingness of the individual to harm the whole for his private advantage.

The extreme case is the outright traitor, so common in Greek history during the fifth century and after. We must exclude the acts of factions, however often they seem treasonable to us, for they were the actions of opposing groups within the *polis*, not of individuals. The typical Greek traitor betrayed his *polis* to an enemy for money. Typically, his *polis* was a little one; Athens and Sparta were practically free of all but large and equivocal moves against the interest of the *polis*. It is impossible to imagine a man of the ninth century betraying his clan to a hostile group, but the system had changed. The traitor of classical Greece is perhaps the extreme individualist, for he represents the man who deliberately sacrifices the whole group to his own advantage.

We have seen something of the growth of individualism in matters of belief, not only religious belief in the narrowest sense, but also beliefs about the nature of the world and man in general. Much of the best Greek literature reflects this growth and development. By the end of the fourth century, the tendency for the individual to choose for himself his attitudes and beliefs in such matters had probably gone about as far as possible. Parts of Greek society had thus become an "open" society, one in which tradition and prescription in every area of life were replaced by rational investigation and personal decision by the individual. As usual, we cannot overlook the fact that many Greeks had always retained their old attitudes in all such matters. Still others, yielding to the urge to abandon rationalism as too arduous, had moved away from individualism and given themselves to the mystery cults. Even in rationalistic Athens, the old beliefs about the gods were strong enough to support a law dating from the last days of Pericles forbidding the teaching of astronomy on the ground that it represented the heavenly bodies as other than divinities. Socrates was not the only man prosecuted for impiety in 399 B.C.

The growth of the sense of individuality, like the growth of individualism in belief, is reflected in some of the best Greek literature. As we have seen, the characters of Homer have by our standards an imperfect consciousness of themselves. The lyric poets made an advance in the cultivation of the idea of personality, speaking to us with a more modern note. The interest in the individualized self grew in tragedy, until by the end of the fifth century and the beginning of the fourth, it was a matter of prime interest. This element in the plays of Euripides was an important factor in their popularity as revivals during the fourth century. In another area, the orator Lysias demonstrated a wonderfully delicate touch as he portrayed the individual characters of his clients in the speeches that he wrote for them to give in court. Comedy, too, moved on—to the very subtle portrayal of character that we find in the New Comedy. Biography began to be a favorite form, and in historical writing more attention was given to the details of individual character. The tendency is reflected even in art; commissions offered to painters and sculptors came from individuals who wanted representations of themselves, not the gods, and from *poleis* proposing to honor their great men by setting up statues of them.

CHAPTER

30

ART AND LITERATURE
IN THE FOURTH CENTURY

Admiration for the achievements of the Greeks of the fifth century must not keep us from a proper estimate of the achievements of other Greeks in the fourth century and later. The classic combination of form and substance in both fifth-century art and literature is highly satisfying. There are those who regard Greek art of the fifth century as constituting a standard that has not been equaled before or since. Possibly they may be right in one respect: the concentrated attention given to the Doric temple and the tendency to limit its possible variations may be said to have resulted in the perfection of this form, if it can be said that works of art are ever perfect. The Doric temples built during the fourth century or later show some variations in proportion that are less pleasing than the proportions of the fifth century. Establishment of form did not act as a stimulus to the creation of content, as did, for example, the establishment of the sonnet form hundreds of years later, for no such variation of content was possible in a temple.

Excellent work was done in the fourth century, however, and it deserves to be discussed on its own merits, not under the shadow of other times. Admirers of art of other periods—for example, the classic art of Egypt—similarly object to pejorative comparisons with fifth-century Greek art.

ARCHITECTURE AND FINE ART

Architectural Styles

During the fourth century, some fine Ionic structures were built in Asia Minor, the home of this order. The architect Pythius built the temple of Athena in the little town of Priene on the coast and, in addition, wrote a book about it. Detailed modern study of the remains shows that he took great care with the proportions, not only of the ground plan of the building and the relation of vertical and horizontal dimensions at every point, but also of many smaller parts, such as the spacing of the ornaments along the entablature.

Pythius was also one of the two architects of the Mausoleum, the famous tomb of King Mausolus of Caria, who at one time caused the Athenians some embarrassment in their foreign relations. The queen, determined that her husband should be suitably commemorated, held a great festival of laudatory oratory; it is said that all those who delivered encomia of the deceased king were former students of the great Athenian teacher Isocrates (who is discussed later in this chapter).

Pythius with his fellow architect also wrote a book about the Mausoleum, and we probably have some of its material in the description of the building that is found in Vitruvius, the Roman writer on architecture, and in the encyclopedia of Pliny, a Roman who wrote in the first century of our era. Of the building itself nothing remains except some fragments that were reused in later buildings. Many an ancient building was so taken apart and its stones used for other purposes; some were demolished in medieval times merely for the sake of the iron and lead clamps with which the stone blocks were fastened together. We know that the Mausoleum had a high base, about a hundred feet square. On this there was an arrangement of thirty-six Ionic columns, which suggested a temple, and above the columns was a pyramid of twenty-four steps. On a platform at the top of the steps, a hundred and thirty-six feet above the ground, was a sculptured four-horse chariot. The building had three separate friezes and a number of other sculptures, on which four of the most distinguished sculptors of the time are said to have worked. The remains show the tendency of the sculptors of the fourth century to represent figures in vigorous action and with every suggestion of emotion. The best-preserved of these figures are from the frieze depicting the struggle of the Greeks with the Amazons.

An interesting and distinctive form of Greek architecture that has rarely appeared elsewhere was the circular building. *Tholos* is the Greek word for these structures, which had a conical upper part as did the tombs of the Mycenaean Age that are known as tholos-tombs. A few such tombs were constructed after Mycenaean times and into the classical age of Greece. There was a tholos in the agora of Athens, which served as the eating place for the prytany on full-time duty, at which time its meals were supplied by the city. The tholos, too, provoked a book, this one written by the architect Theodorus of Phocaea about the tholos that he built at Delphi. The use of this building in the affairs of the Delphic sanctuary has never been understood, but it is clear from the remains that it was more highly ornamented than buildings usually were, that there was a combination of black and white stones and of Doric and Corinthian capitals, and that it had a double row of columns and a cella, or chamber, in the middle. Another famous tholos was found by excavators in the sanctuary of Asclepius at Epidaurus and another in the sanctuary of Olympia.

Although neither survives, we know of two fourth-century examples of large buildings intended for nonreligious purposes, something very rare among the Greeks. The Thersilion was built for the meetings of the assembly of the Arcadian League in Megalopolis. A large rectangular building, it is especially interesting because the many interior columns that supported the roof were arranged in radiating lines to make it easier to see and hear the speaker. The other building, the naval arsenal at Peiraeus, was a long shed with interior columns that divided it into aisles. We know this building, not from a book or a casual description, but from an inscription that has survived and provided full details of its construction. It was not, in fact, a very well designed building.

In spite of the glorious success of some kinds of Greek buildings, notably the Doric temple, the Greeks did not in general distinguish themselves as architects and builders. Their intense theorizing was exerted in narrow areas. They were not bold or enterprising. They ignored such usable devices as the arch and did not show a great deal of ingenuity in transporting and lifting their materials.

Sculpture

Although the historians of art distinguish subperiods within the fourth century, it will suffice for our purpose to characterize the whole century as a time when sculptors were increasingly realistic and increasingly fond of portraying highly animated subjects. Their work represents almost the opposite of the restraint that we customarily single out as characteristic of the fifth-century art; it may be said that the extreme realism and the somewhat wild action and emotion of the fourth and the following centuries were what the sculptors of the fifth century avoided by restraint. The makers of the archaic sculpture of the sixth century had followed certain conventions that were not realistic, but that gave their work a certain charm. It was the dropping of these conventions, not a great improvement in technical ability, that gave the sculpture of the fifth century its realistic quality—still a restrained realism. In the fourth century, sculptors carried realism much farther.

The Athenian sculptor Praxiteles was active in the middle of the century, by which time the tendency to greater freedom had made itself plain. His Hermes, the work by which he is best known, was one of the many famous statues erected at Olympia. It shows the god, young, graceful, and relaxed, offering a bunch of grapes to the baby god Dionysus. Close examination shows that his figure is realistically constructed, too realistically to please some critics. We must remember, however, that the Greeks painted their statues, and a scheme suggested for this one would stain Hermes' skin a sun-burnt red, leave the child Dionysus white, give Hermes red and gold hair, pick out his eyes and lips and eyebrows as skillful make-up now accents a feminine face, make his sandals golden and the draperies yellow and gold. Such a statue, seen in the bright outdoor sunlight, would be a brilliant piece of artificiality to portray a god rather than mere realism.

The Hermes is one of a group of pieces of Greek art preserved to us by accident. Unfortunately, work in gold or silver was likely to be sold or melted down by those for whom the beautiful had no appeal at all—soldiers, perhaps, who took fine small pieces as loot. Bronze, too, was much in demand as mere metal, mostly during the several simpler ages between the classical Greek and the modern.

Although marble statues could not be used to build other structures, as the dressed stone blocks of buildings were, they could be and were burned down into lime to put on the fields. Many other works of art were carried from their original places by the Romans. Others later were taken to Constantinople. In the eighteenth and nineteenth centuries, a new wave of such polite vandalism enriched the museums of England, France, and Germany.

The Hermes appeared during the great excavations at Olympia carried out in the 1870's by the Germans. Pausanias had described the statue in his guidebook, giving its exact location. The site of Olympia had been shaken by an earthquake soon after the closing of the games at the end of the fourth century, and then the site had been flooded several times. The excavators had to clear away a deep deposit of soil, and the present-day visitor to the site is likely to notice with surprise that around the remains of the temples he can see a vertical wall of dirt many feet high where the excavators cut down into the deposit to free the area of the sanctuary. They looked for the Hermes where Pausanias said that it was, and there it was.

The bronze charioteer of Delphi, now a chief exhibit of the museum there, was part of a complete charioteer and four-horse team and chariot of bronze dedicated at Delphi in the early fifth century to celebrate a victory in the games. Soon afterward a landslide buried the whole combination. Excavators late in the nineteenth century dug up the charioteer and a few fragments of the chariot and the horses. Where is the rest? Presumably someone had already dug up the horses and chariot, which later disappeared, probably melted down for their metal. At least the long ages of burial saved the charioteer for us.

The great bronze statue of Zeus that is now to be seen in the National Museum at Athens was likewise preserved for us in a remarkable way, having been recovered in the 1920's from the sea near Artemisium, at the north tip of Euboea. The statue probably was set up to commemorate the naval victory there in the Persian war. How it got under water we do not know. Perhaps it was being carried off to Rome in a later century. Near it was found a lively little bronze of a jockey in position to ride a plunging horse, but the horse has not been found. Perhaps the strangest of all these cases of survival was that of the Venus of Melos, generally called "di Milo" from the Italian name of the island. This statue was found in its original position in the local gymnasium of Melos, having stood there from ancient times until the early nineteenth century without finding anyone to destroy it or carry it off.

But to return to Praxiteles, who produced a great deal according to the remarks of Greek and Roman authors about him and his works, he was a successful businessman, turning out statues of both bronze and marble. It may well be that many were modeled by him, reproduced a number of times by his assistants, and sold in different places (just as a shop in a small town will guarantee that it has sold no other copy of a dress in town). A number of his figures lean on the stump of a tree or some other support, a characteristic that has suggested that the original form was the bronze, and that the support was designed to provide something aesthetically suitable to brace the leaning figure when it was copied in marble.

The sculptors of the fifth century had already developed several techniques for representing clothing in marble. Sometimes they draped it closely over the figure to reveal the limbs; sometimes they made it fly free; sometimes they simply clothed the figure with it. The Athenian Timotheus, who did some charming work in the fourth century, exemplifies the conservative tendency in his handling of drapery. Other tendencies, however, appear in this century. In the battle frieze of the Mausoleum, for instance, the draperies are part of the vivid motion of the figures. The only manner that we no longer find is the stiff formality of archaic drapery characteristic of the late sixth century.

Scopas, of the island of Paros, was active at the same time as Praxiteles, in the middle of the century. Like Praxiteles he had an active business, and copies may well have been made from his models by his assistants and shipped to different cities. A sculptor and designer of great skill, Scopas tended to specialize in animated figures showing strong emotion. Ancient tradition made him one of the four sculptors of note to whom the queen of Caria entrusted the sculpture on the four sides of the great bottom structure of the Mausoleum. Unfortunately, we do not know to which of the four men the few surviving pieces belong. We may suppose, however, that for some time Scopas and most of his establishment moved to Halicarnassus, the Carian capital, and worked together on this large commission. One commission that we do know that he executed with success was the design of a temple for the city of Tegea, in the Peloponnesus. It was a very pleasing Doric temple, to judge by the remains. The stonework, both the plain blocks and the carving or ornamentation, was most meticulously done, and there was only a modest amount of sculpture. It would be interesting to know whether he was so much of a businessman that he handled the whole contract for the construction of the temple.

Lysippus of Sicyon is another fourth-century Greek said to have organized a shop that turned out a great many statues; one estimate is fifteen hundred, which is probably high. We do not have a single statue that we can be sure is an original from the shop of Lysippus, although there are one or two for which the claim has been made. If any judgment can be made from what are said to be copies of his work, his tendency was to produce quiet, realistic statues suggesting scenes from life. One often ascribed to him is *Apoxyomenos*, a representation of an athlete scraping himself with a *strigil*, a metal object used to scrape off the oil with which he had rubbed himself and with the oil the dirt.

During the fourth century, some unidentified shops in Athens produced beautiful tombstones. In the early years, they were simple low reliefs of rather formal style; but as the century went on, the reliefs became higher. The figures became less formal, more active, and the note of emotion became stronger. Instead of one figure or perhaps two in stiff and formal poses, there are little groups that suggest the poignancy of the eternal parting and almost tell a story of the family relation.

Painting

Our lack of knowledge about Greek painting is tantalizing. It seems, however, that there was a movement toward realism in the fourth century analogous to that in sculpture. We gather from our literary references that late in the fifth century the range of colors was widened and that the use of perspective and chiaroscuro, or strong contrasts of light and shadow, was developed. The painters, like the sculptors, had long before developed the ability to do what they wished in actual representation of a literal kind, as is shown by the story of the contest between Zeuxis and Parrhasius. Zeuxis painted grapes so lifelike that birds flew down to peck them, but Parrhasius painted a curtain so realistic that Zeuxis asked him to draw it back and let his picture be seen.

Apelles of Colophon in Ionia was regarded as the greatest of Greek painters, and the art of painting was thought by ancient critics to have been at its height in the fourth century. We have no works of Apelles to study, however, and almost nothing of anyone else. The great mosaic of Alexander attacking Darius, now in the museum in Naples, is thought to have been copied from a large painting made soon after Alexander's time. Even in the mosaic copy we can feel that we see a striking composition, great technical skill, a good use of color, skill in handling light and shadow, and a lively display of emotion.

Athens and Sicyon (where Lysippus had his sculpture shop) were the centers of painting, we are told. The subjects are said to have been individual figures and groups of gods and men. Some were narrative scenes and some pictorial. There were portraits. Interest in still life as a subject in itself seems hardly to have begun; the same is true of landscapes; the Greeks were more interested in people than in Nature.

ORATORY

In fifth-century Greece, the Sophists had begun the formal study of oratory as part of their program of what we should now call higher studies. The influential Gorgias had sought to create an artistic prose by introducing principles borrowed from the practice of verse, especially those of balance, antithesis, and ornament of all kinds. Others, especially Corax of Syracuse, had studied the most effective arrangement of an argumentative discourse and had laid down the basic structure that is still used: introduction with an attempt to gain the favor of the hearers, narrative of the facts, argument, refutation of the opponent's case, and a conclusion that attempts to clinch one's own case.

Athens was to be the home of the greatest Greek oratory, presumably because conditions there encouraged the development of the art. The late fifth century and the fourth century were the golden age of oratory. The Greek literary critics of later times made a selection of "the ten best orators," which they called the canon of Attic orators, beginning with Antiphon, who died in 411 B.C., and ending with Deinarchus, who was born in 369.

Antiphon employed his skill in the oratorical art in the service of the oligarchic party at Athens (for example, in assisting other oligarchs in court or in assisting oligarchs from the *poleis* of the Athenian Empire in their business in the city) until the opportunity for an oligarchic revolution presented itself in 411. He was convicted of treason at the end of the revolution in spite of a speech in his own defense, which Thucydides rates highly, but which has not been preserved.

The most interesting of his few surviving works is called *Tetralogies*. Three imaginary cases are argued; in each, there are two speeches of the accuser and two of the defendant. In the first case, a citizen, coming home late from a party, was murdered. His slave, who was wounded, named the murderer to the people who found him, then expired. The family of the dead man prosecuted the man who had been named. The four speeches in the case carefully exploit all the probabilities of this difficult and ambiguous set of facts. The assiduous reader of modern mystery stories will find that the line of thought and argument has a curiously familiar ring. Antiphon meant this collection of three cases as a study in the resources open to the practical speaker; it shows what can be done by arguing from probability when the facts are not conclusive.

Lysias, another of the early orators, was a metic. His father, Cephalus, was a wealthy manufacturer and had been persuaded by Pericles to come to Athens from Sicily. The Thirty, in their search for money, murdered the brother of Lysias, and he himself was fortunate to escape. The loss of the family property to the Thirty forced him to take up the career of speech writer for others when the terror was over and he returned to Athens.

The one speech that he himself delivered, his prosecution of Eratosthenes for the murder of his brother, is a vivid picture of the methods of the Thirty. His other speeches were written to the order of men who were involved in legal proceedings. Lysias had great ability in the portrayal of character, and the speeches seem to reflect the man who ordered them—a frank and generous young man, a careful and sober middle-aged man, or whatever was needed. Their language is pure and elegant Attic. Beyond this, they have a charm that is universally recognized and has never been satisfactorily analyzed.

Those speeches of Lysias that have been preserved are useful sources for the situation in Athens just after the fall of the Thirty and the restoration of the democracy. They provide many details about the political events of the time. They show clearly some of the currents of feeling. We learn enough about the prosecutions of the year 399, for instance, to see that the prosecution of Socrates was by no means an isolated event. Many interesting facts about less public matters may also be learned from the speeches. We hear the details of a husband's killing his wife's paramour, whom he caught in his house, learn of the working of a society for mutual aid, hear of the sordid struggle of two middle-aged men over a handsome boy, or are told by a small tradesman why he deserves to have public aid because of his physical handicap.

Isocrates and Higher Education

Isocrates (436–338 B.C.) was more a teacher and essayist than an orator. He frankly admitted that his voice and nerve were not adequate for addressing the Athenian Assembly and the courts. The financial misfortune of his family during the Peloponnesian War forced him to become a writer of speeches for other men to use in court. In 392, he opened his school in Athens, which soon became very successful, and in later years he preferred to forget his speechwriting period. He was a highly successful teacher of what he preferred to call philosophy but we should call forensic and political oratory. He believed that a real education produced a man of broad views who could express himself forcefully in speech or in writing. This was to be the view of the Roman Cicero and, through him, one of the ideals of the more modern West. The school of Isocrates in Athens was a strong influence on the life of the Greek world of the fourth century. Rich young men from Athens itself, from other cities of Greece proper, from the Greek cities of Asia, the Black Sea, Sicily, and southern Italy attended. Many of the minor kings of the regions around the Greek world liked to send their sons to Athens to be educated, as in modern times Oxford has educated many young members of royal families of Asia and Africa, and the natural place in Athens was the school of Isocrates. Plato, too, had a school and would have liked to think that he could train princes better than Isocrates. Presumably, however, the practical-minded young men and their fathers saw more in the oratorical and political studies of Isocrates' school.

The style of Isocrates (of itself and also through its influence on Cicero) was to be the foundation of Western European prose style. Isocrates developed the possibilities of the periodic sentence, the elaborate sentence in which a number of subordinated ideas are grouped around the main idea. He exploited all the possibilities of balance and antithesis. The number of words in one clause was balanced against that in another clause, as was the thought, the construction of the words, and even the sound of the words. Although in reading his work, one often finds that elaboration of form has led to flabbiness of thought, he still is the first exponent of a style that at its best is highly effective in expository and argumentative writing.

Isocrates did not write any theoretical discussion of government, but much about this subject can be gathered from his essays, which he liked to put in the form of orations. He would have made democracy more conservative than it was in his day. He would have replaced the lot with election as a means of choosing officials so that true merit could be recognized. This, he argued, was genuine equality. In a pamphlet entitled *Areopagiticus* (which suggested the title *Areopagitica* to John Milton for a contrary argument on the same subject), he urged that the broad supervisory and judicial powers once possessed by the Council of the Areopagus be restored to it—not a surprising suggestion from a conservative in an age when individualism was rising and many citizens found little force in old rules and ideals. As a trainer of princes, Isocrates took a sympathetic view of monarchy. He wrote one essay on the duties and behavior of a king, and from his other essays remarks could be collected to make a typical manual of "The Mirror of the Prince" type, the kind of essay that we often find among the Romans and later writers, the most famous example being Machiavelli's realistic *The Prince*.

Isocrates was more interested in foreign than in domestic affairs, but again in a practical rather than a theoretical spirit. His chief theme was a common one in his day: the desirability of a combined Greek offensive against the Persians. There are indications that from his point of view this was a conservative idea in that a campaign against Persia would occupy the many restless men who were offering themselves as mercenary soldiers and who were a real danger to conservative interests in Greece. In fact, Greece was ready for a new movement of population overseas, and an imperialistic campaign against Persia, which would use the restless part of the population and then leave it abroad in colonies, was a practical measure.

His *Panegyricus,* which dates from about 380, is in the form of a speech given at the Olympic games (the Greek word means a speech given at a great assembly rather than a speech of laudation). Here he argued that the Greeks should unite under the leadership of Athens to wage war on Persia. His *Philippus,* an open letter to King Philip of Macedonia published in 346, shows a changed point of view; he has given up the hope of any unity proceeding from the Greeks themselves and calls on Philip to unite them by offering to take the lead in a war against Persia. There is no evidence that these urgings had any practical effect.

We know more of his educational opponents than of his political opponents. There were those who thought that this higher education was a waste of time, others who deplored it as alienating the student from life and his fellow men, and others who regarded it as the training of sharp practitioners to plague the citizens in the courts. The word "sophist," used carelessly then as it still is, was the chief pejorative word for both sides. The opponents of Isocrates and of the other teachers of speech and government called them sophists. Plato used all his great literary resources in some of his most effective dialogues to pour ridicule on certain men whom he called sophists; his art was so effective that men still smile contemptuously at his victims. Isocrates, on the other hand, thought of Plato as a sophist, one of the kind teaching mere disputation, and argued that his broad education was better for a man than the narrow arguments of Plato's school. In its own day, the school of Isocrates was far more influential than Plato's. Plato has subsequently outshone him in general opinion, yet the real influence of Isocrates' view of education and of his style has lived on so pervasively that it is taken for granted by the historian rather than given specific acknowledgement.

Demosthenes (384–322 B.C.)

Demosthenes stands first among the orators of Greece and of the world. His political orations show a firm grasp of Greek affairs and great powers of expression and persuasion. He also enjoyed a high reputation as a writer of speeches for clients to deliver in court. He was not first in every aspect of oratory, but if others could surpass him in elegance or charm or resourcefulness in argument, he was admittedly first in the indispensable quality of the orator, the combination of earnestness and energy and power of expression that leads to the persuasion of the hearer.

He seized the opportunity offered him by the times to practice his oratory in the service of the state. He made himself an expert on foreign affairs and opposed the rise of Philip of Macedonia. The *Philippics* and the *Olynthiacs,* his two groups of speeches on this subject, were powerful efforts, but his last pronouncement in this field was the greatest of his orations. In 336, a certain Ctesiphon proposed that Demosthenes be presented by the *polis* with a golden crown for his services to Athens. Aeschines, an old opponent of Demosthenes, thereupon prosecuted Ctesiphon for proposing an illegal decree *(graphe paranomon)* because the crown was to be presented at a different time and in a different place from those set by law and because, as Aeschines claimed, Demosthenes had not in fact benefited the state. For some reason, the trial did not take place until six years later.

Aeschines in his speech made out an excellent case for the irregularity of Ctesiphon's proposal. From the outset, he would have done better to rest his whole case on this aspect of the matter without adding the assertion that Demosthenes had not benefited the state. Demosthenes' reply to him is known either by a Latin title, *De corona,* or an English title, *On the Crown.* It can also properly be called *In Defense of Ctesiphon,* for it was Ctesiphon who was on trial, and Demosthenes' defense of his own political career was offered as the speech of a friend in support of Ctesiphon's own speech of defense.

Demosthenes had no good answer to make to the charge that Ctesiphon had proposed to present the crown under the wrong circumstances. His political activity had indeed failed to stop Philip. Yet, by his characteristic combination of oratorical skill with earnestness and depth of feeling, and by his appeal to the pride of the Athenians in their history and their traditional role as leaders of the Greeks, he won a crushing victory over Aeschines. Aeschines received only a small part of the votes, so few that he suffered the penalty of exile provided for those who prosecuted and could not carry a fifth part of the jury for conviction.

OTHER THOUGHT AND WRITING

In literature the full development of Attic oratory was the great achievement of the fourth century. The Hellenistic Age (the age that followed the death of Alexander the Great in 323 B.C.) produced no orators considered great now or in their own time. The study of oratory did go on, however, especially in the Greek communities of Asia Minor, where the florid and artificial style was developed that is known as the Asianic style. The Attic style was more practical, more designed for persuasion, and much less given to ornaments without function. Romans later studied with the great Hellenistic teachers of oratory, and even at Rome, as we shall find, there could be theoretical disputes about the merit of the Attic and the Asianic styles as applied to Latin oratory.

Tragedy, on the other hand, hardly survived the fifth century. In the fourth century, the most able men preferred to work in other fields. There are no great names from that period, and it was found advisable to allow revivals of the work of the important men of the fifth century, a good sign that tragedy was now an entertainment rather than a vehicle for lively and debatable ideas. The vigorous comedy of the fifth century, generally known as Old Comedy, went through a stage of transition that in the Hellenistic Age issued in an elegant comedy of manners generally known as New Comedy. We shall consider New Comedy, as we do the oratory of the Hellenistic Age, from the point of view of the Romans, who constantly looked to Greek models as they created the Latin literature of Rome.

Philosophy flourished mightily in the fourth century, and all of our next chapter will be devoted to it, especially to philosophy in the sense of complete and reasoned views of the universe and life. For the Greek, philosophy included such lines of thought as mathematics and natural science in general, which we are accustomed to regard as independent subjects.

Xenophon the Athenian (ca. 430–ca. 355 B.C.)

Earlier we described Xenophon's great adventure, his participation in the attempt of Cyrus the Persian to overthrow his brother the king with the help of Greek mercenaries. Xenophon became a great admirer of Agesilaus, the Spartan king who was commanding the troops in Asia at that time. He stayed for some time with Agesilaus, then returned to Sparta with him when he was called home, and took the field with him in 394 at Coronea against his native Athens. Many an Athenian must have sympathized with the conservatism of Sparta and had friends there. Such feelings could be understood; but to fight against Athens was something different, and the Athenians banished him. He lived among the Spartans for many years as a country gentleman.

The writings of Xenophon are those of a man of the second rank in thought and ability to write, yet a man of amiable nature. A surprising number of his books have survived. The *Anabasis*, his story of the great adventure, is a clear and vivid narrative. In the days before he went on the expedition, he was a friend of Socrates and wrote a book about him that tells us much of what people said in criticism of him and what other people said in his defense. The book is not a great one, but it is useful as a frank report of information that we would not otherwise have. He also attempted an *Apology* (defense speech) of Socrates and a *Symposium,* or story of a drinking party at which Socrates had much to say.

Xenophon was a man of many enthusiasms other than his admiration of Socrates and respect for his memory. He wrote an encomium of the Spartan Agesilaus and another on Cyrus, which he called *The Education of Cyrus;* this latter might well be called a historical romance. His essay on the Spartan constitution gives us some valuable information on that subject. He was a great lover of horses and dogs and wrote essays on the outdoor life.

His most serious work was his *Hellenica,* in which he attempted to continue the history of Greece from the point at which Thucydides had left off, 411 B.C., to the defeat of of the Thebans at Mantinea in 362. Although Xenophon did not have the penetration and intensity of Thucydides and was hopelessly biased in favor of Sparta, he may otherwise be called a respectable enough historian.

NATURAL SCIENCE

During the fourth century, mathematics and astronomy made progress in a straightforward and regular manner that led to brilliant work during the Hellenistic Age. Although this period after the death of Alexander the Great in 323 b.c. is more properly discussed in connection with the history of Rome, the early developments made in the fourth century cannot be overlooked.

Until the middle of the fifth century, mathematics was only one of the interests of any man who was advancing knowledge. At about that time, however, there was a strong movement toward differentiation and specialization. Although a few men still tried to work in many fields, within the next few generations most became specialists, so that when we come to the time of Plato we may speak of mathematicians.

Although Plato himself was only an amateur of the art, he had such great enthusiasm that he probably should receive credit for inspiring some very good mathematicians. Mathematics was an important part of the work of his Academy, although we do not have much idea of how it was approached in detail. The figures of mathematics seem to us to have a certain relation to Plato's Forms, or ideal essences, which we shall discuss in the next chapter. The sphere or the triangle or the pyramid of mathematics is perfect, as are the Forms. Although no instrument could be devised, then or now, that would draw or construct those figures with the absolute perfection that belongs to the Forms, the mind may still reach the perfection of those figures, as it may hope to reach the perfection of the Forms. We may see, too, that the discussion of the Academy perhaps helped to make mathematical statements thenceforth more rigorous. It is possible that the participants found that their attempts to conduct rigorous mathematical discussions helped them conduct rigorous discussions on other subjects. One of them, Aristotle, in his characteristically practical way, later invented the science of logic for the direct rather than the indirect testing of the soundness of verbal propositions.

The mathematics of the fourth century consisted in the main of arithmetic and geometry. Algebra was still in the offing. The very first steps were taken in conics, however, and work done on the method of exhaustion in considering volumes was an ancestor of the calculus.

Trigonometry was to come in a few centuries. Much of our information is brief and tantalizingly incomplete, but it is sometimes possible to see in detail what the mathematicians of the fourth century were doing. At the end of this century and the beginning of the third, the great geometrician Euclid was active, from whose work we can learn all that had been accomplished in his field up to his time.

We saw that the Pythagoreans at some earlier time had grasped the idea of irrationals. That is, if two sides of a right triangle each have a length of one, the square of each will be one and the sum of their squares will be two. The square of the hypotenuse, being equal to the sum of the squares of the sides, will be two, and the length of the hypotenuse will therefore be the square root of two, a number that cannot be described in terms of integers and that the Greeks called an irrational number. In the fourth century, further work was done on irrational numbers and lines. Arithmetic and geometry were so extended that it was possible to discuss any proposition with irrational numbers or with irrational lines (lines, that is, whose relation could be expressed only in such an abstract way as to speak of the square root of two) without any awkwardness arising from the fact that the matter was not expressible in terms of integers. This was a step into real mathematics.

The discovery that there are only five regular solids is another characteristic piece of work from this century. Whose work it is is not certain, but the proof is found in Euclid. The five are the pyramid, with four faces, the cube with six, and the polyhedra of eight, twelve, and twenty faces. To discover this fact and construct a proof of it is a nice piece of mathematical work. The other side of the mathematical thought of the age may be illustrated by Plato's reaction to this discovery, which probably was a rather surprising one, since the number of regular polygons is not finite. He decided that some great principle must have been at work to limit the number of the regular polyhedra. Searching for five of something with which to make an analogy, he finally hit upon the four elements proposed by earlier philosophers, plus one to represent the totality of matter. This kind of thinking, which we are tempted to call silly, is likely to occur fairly often in the early stages of a system of thought.

Although specialization had begun, not every mathematician of the fourth century was a specialist. The same man could work out new refinements of the theory of proportions, devise an ingenious solution to the old problem of the duplication of the cube, begin the science of theoretical mechanics, and be highly regarded as a practical statesman. The combination of mathematics and astronomy was a natural one. By the early fourth century, the Greeks had made some observations of the heavenly bodies. Some men had probably had access to the results of Egyptian observations. Possibly some had also learned the results of Babylonian observations, but there is no proof. The great Babylonian astronomer Kidinnu is believed to have discovered the precession of the equinoxes in the fourth century. This theory rests on the fact that over periods of hundreds of years it can readily be observed that the fixed stars seem to have shifted their positions a little. The Babylonians had at their disposal a long series of systematic observations from which this fact was seen. From the apparent shifting of the fixed stars is also deduced the precession of the equinoxes, or the fact that the spring and the autumn come a few seconds earlier each year, because of the same tilting of the earth's axis that makes the fixed stars seem to shift. It was in the third century that the Greek Hipparchus discussed this matter.

To return to the fourth century, the universe was thought to be spherical and finite. The earth was believed to be a planet like the other planets and to rotate eastward on its axis. The great addition of the fourth century was an attempt to explain all the movements of the bodies by a theory of spheres. The theory postulated twenty-seven spheres, all having the same center as the earth. Each heavenly body was fastened to one of these invisible spheres, described only as able to carry the heavenly body around and having no further interest, and each could have its movement influenced also by the action of one or more other concentric spheres. The theory attempted thus to explain all the movements of the planets, which are very complex if observed from the earth. Although the astronomical observations on which the theory was based were incomplete and often inaccurate, it was genuinely scientific, for it attempted to take account of all the known facts and ignore metaphysical considerations. This was the beginning of scientific astronomy, which was to flourish greatly in the next three or four centuries.

The fine medical work of the late fifth century was continued in the fourth and thereafter. A number of the treatises of the *Hippocratic*

Corpus are thought to belong to the fourth century. The son-in-law of Hippocrates and his successor as the head of the school of Cos is thought to have written *On the Nature of Man,* which is our chief source for the theory of the humors of the body, blood, yellow bile, black bile, and phlegm. Probably the collecting of the medical writings that made up the *Hippocratic Corpus* was begun in the fourth century. There were some physicians who began at this time to feel that medicine should take itself very seriously, that medical treatises should be written in the magnificent Attic Greek that had been developed in the late fifth and early fourth centuries, rather than in the dialect used in Cos or Cnidus, and that medicine should take on the high systematic tone of philosophy. Probably these men did some good by comparing and systematizing medical knowledge. In any event, medicine, like mathematics and astronomy, was to make great advances during the Hellenistic Age.

CHAPTER

31

PHILOSOPHY

$\mathbb{A}$lthough the term "pre-Socratic philosophy" is commonly used and understood, we do not say "post-Socratic philosophy." Nevertheless, it should be borne in mind that the greatest achievements of Greek systematic philosophy come not only after Socrates, but also, in large measure, because of Socrates. It was Socrates who saw that philosophy, in the sense of a system for living, had become very necessary. The questionings of the earlier philosophers, of the Sophists, and of the dramatists, combined with the fact that men no longer lived in the tight traditional organization dominated by clan and family, had made it impossible for men in the *poleis* of Greece to live in the old fashion and by the simple old beliefs. Like Adam and Eve, they had lost their innocence and had now to find a set of reasoned beliefs that would serve as a basis for living in a world more complex and less to be taken for granted.

It often is difficult for the modern to understand the importance of philosophy in the lives of many people of the ancient world. For the intelligent man, a philosophy was a necessity, because he was not content to live without some sort of coherent view of the world and man, a view that would make him feel that he was more or less at home in the universe and had a practical set of principles to live by. Perhaps this need is less felt nowadays because many people vaguely assume that natural science explains everything about the universe and that the shocks of life are cushioned in a number of practical ways. The ancient philosophies must be understood as serious guides and aids to living. They performed a real function, which nowadays is often not performed (with unhappy results) or for which recourse is had to self-help books and other stopgap substitutes for a genuine philosophy.

MINOR SOCRATIC CULTS

Surprisingly diverse philosophical views were offered as offspring of Socrates' thought. Although we cannot with any certainty describe the positive doctrines of Socrates, we can be sure that his discussions of basic problems were subtle and stimulating. It is only natural that different people should claim to have been inspired to different views by him.

Cynics and Cyrenaics

Socrates' personality and way of life seem to have been as influential as his thought and discussions on the two disciples who founded the Cynic and the Cyrenaic schools of philosophy. Antisthenes, the founder of the Cynic school, was a mature man when he first met Socrates. He had been a minor Sophist. He was one of those who find it difficult to embrace the amenities, and, in spite of his abilities, he was rough in speech and dress. Furthermore, his abilities did not include depth and subtlety of thought, so that he was inclined to reject those parts of philosophy that he found difficult.

Antisthenes seized on the fact that Socrates had let go all worldly ambition and lived the simple life in order to devote himself to philosophy. This relinquishment of interest in wealth, fame, and family seemed to him the best road to happiness and successful living. When, after the death of Socrates, he returned to his career as a Sophist, the essence of his message was that a man must strip himself of all those things that are subject to the whims and sudden reverses of Fortune. If life has been stripped down to essentials, it is no longer at the mercy of other people or of mischances.

Antisthenes not only renounced wealth and fame, but also argued against ordinary comforts and such institutions as the state, marriage, and conventional courtesy, which are not found in a state of nature but have been devised by men for the ordering of human relations. One must suspect that he was indulging himself in his own boorishness and uncomfortableness in society when he seriously urged that mankind abandon all the proven devices for the living together of numbers of people in an orderly way. If it is possible to construct a serious argument for discarding all such institutions and replacing them by the good impulses of a state of nature, there is no record that Antisthenes offered one.

Apparently it was possible for Antisthenes to make a modest living by promulgating his message, for people were interested in this question of how to live. Although his central theme was how to achieve happiness, he found it necessary to deal with some of the wider philosophical questions that had been raised by Socrates or were being raised by other men, chiefly Plato, after the death of Socrates. The question whether types or classes of things exist was raised by Plato's assertion that there are Forms, as that of justice, which have independent and eternal existence.

It was inevitable that Antisthenes should dismiss all such conceptions as being mere names, with no corresponding reality. In this he was the first notable Nominalist, the first of those who deny any reality to abstractions or principles. Antisthenes went even farther. He denied that it is possible to predicate, that is, he denied that it is possible to say with confidence that man is two-legged or that water is wet. Risky as it is to attribute motives to him, we may guess that this extreme attitude resulted, not from long thought, but from his preoccupation with ethics and his impatience with other aspects of philosophy, as well as from his rather limited ability in dealing with more subtle questions. Any seeker after truth or happiness who insisted on serious handling of the deeper philosophical questions would presumably have left Antisthenes; those to whom his main teachings were acceptable and who, like him, cared little for a complete philosophy, would be satisfied to have such questions cavalierly dismissed.

The Cynic philosophy persisted as a recognizable discipline until the rise of Christianity. Its first hundred years, the fourth century, that is, were its best, for the rise of the Stoic philosophy about 300 B.C. incorporated all the best of Cynic teaching into a better system, and with the best ideas took the best people away from the Cynics.

Aristippus of Cyrene, another follower of Socrates, elaborated another philosophy that purported to represent the essence of Socratic thought. As the somewhat boorish Antisthenes had seized on the simplicity of Socrates' personal life as the essence of Socrates' way, so the elegant aristocrat of the rich and flourishing and pleasure-loving Greek city of Cyrene, situated in a beautiful green section of the North African coast, seized on Socrates' frank enjoyment of worldly pleasures as the key to the happiness of Socrates and the gospel to be proclaimed for the happiness of others. Naturally the two men had had little sympathy with each other when they were together in the company around the living Socrates. Perhaps the best proof of the greatness of Socrates is the fact that his personality and discussions could serve as the basis for two systems like these, both of which attracted followers for some time, and for the far wider and deeper system of Plato.

The arguments of Aristippus about pleasure, which appeared again nearly a hundred years later in the system of Epicurus, started with the naturalness of pleasure. All human experience tells us that good functioning is pleasurable and that bad functioning is either painful or unpleasant. Even human babies and baby animals automatically seek the simple pleasures like food and respond to the warnings of pain that something is wrong. If, then, one is looking for a standard, the rightness of things that are pleasurable has a strong claim, especially since it is supported in so many cases by the painfulness of things that are harmful. Aristippus drew his conclusions straightforwardly and declared that the pleasure of the present moment is the surest guide to conduct, because both past and future pleasures are unreliable as guides. He felt, as did Antisthenes, that there can be little profit in considering the nature of knowledge. He, too, asserted that each man's feelings and pleasures and personality are shut off from other men, so that predication and generalization are impossible.

PLATO (427–347 B.C.)

Historians of philosophy say that all previous philosophical movements are absorbed in Plato and that all later ones spring from him. All previous philosophy, in the proper sense of the word, was Greek and was known to Plato. To absorb it all and take some account of it all in his own system presnted no great difficulty to an exceptionally able man. He could read the speculations of those early philosophers who had dealt with the nature of matter and the world and who had raised the basic questions about the nature of reality and about our apprehension of it. After the death of Socrates, he traveled in South Italy and Sicily, and perhaps in Egypt, and studied the more mathematical type of thought that flourished in these places.

Plato stood in a wonderfully fortunate position for his own fame. A great deal of laborious and difficult work had been done to raise and debate all the basic questions of philosophy. The natural movement of Athenian society had encouraged discussion of all the problems of man and society. Socrates had done much to promote clear definition and to turn attention to the great problem of what kind of reasoned system could replace the traditional and prescribed system that had been adequate before the rise of self-conscious discussion; he had been deeply dissatisfied with views such as that expressed by "Man is the measure of all things" and had believed it worthwhile to search for a more solid basis of belief. The time was ripe for a great attempt to construct a well-rounded philosophy, one that would absorb all that was worthwhile in earlier attempts. It is not surprising that all subsequent philosophy echoes some part of Plato's work or seems indebted to it in some way.

It is impossible to work out the development of Plato's thought with any certainty, because it is impossible to know in what order his works were written. We know from Aristotle, however, that in earlier life he was intimate with Cratylus the Heraclitean. For several years, he was one of the intimates of Socrates. Returning from his travels after the death of Socrates, he gathered a group of friends around him for discussion and in 387 B.C. started a sort of school, known as the Academy, which has been called the first European university. It seems likely that all the chief strains of what we consider his system of thought were present in his mind by the time he organized the Academy, at the age of forty, and probably they had been developed earlier.

One of Plato's first necessities was to establish some firm ground on which to stand, because he had been exposed both to the Heraclitean notion of universal flux and to Socrates' attempts to make correct definitions and win sure knowledge of basic matters. For this purpose, he developed the concept of the Forms. The Greek word is *idea;* Form (with the capital letter) is a better English word for it than the English "idea." The Forms represent the ideal version of qualities, virtues, human relations, and things. There is a Form of justice and a Form of horse. The relation between the Form of tree and the individual tree, for example, is not clearly explained by Plato, yet one can see that if individual trees come and go, there is plainly something preserving the Form of tree, for this does not change from generation to generation. Unlike ideas in our sense, the Forms are not in the minds of men nor are they engendered by the minds of men. They exist from everlasting to everlasting and may be apprehended by men's minds, but only with effort and difficulty. The Forms are the only reality; all else is a somewhat dim version of the Forms. This conception allows the philosopher to recognize the changes of matter that we see while it preserves something that is above and beyond change and can serve as a basis for the rest of the philosophy.

Plato is said to have regarded the *viva voce* discussions of the Academy as the most important part of his work. From time to time, he did publish; it is inconceivable that a literary artist of his stature should have been content not to do so. He cast his works in the dialogue form, except for a few, to which he gave the form of letters, and made Socrates the chief speaker in all but *Laws*.

Cosmology

A theory of the origin and nature of the world is an important part of any philosophy, although in modern times this part of the subject belongs to the offshoot of philosophy known as natural science. *Timaeus,* the dialogue in which Plato dealt with the origin of the world, seems to have come rather late among his published works. In it is found the famous story of the lost continent of Atlantis. The essence of the dialogue is that God (for Plato regularly speaks in monotheistic terms) decided to impose order upon the chaotic mass of matter that existed in the universe and for that purpose constructed a world-soul by using the Forms, which had always existed. When the world-soul had been properly constructed on the best principles, God fashioned the chaotically brawling elements of matter into that fairest of all figures, the sphere, and endowed his new creation with the soul that he had already created. Then he proceeded to the furnishing of this fair habitation with minor divinities, with man, and with the backdrop of the heavens.

Epistemology

The typical ancient philosophy also dealt with epistemology, the question of the nature of knowledge, a subject that nowadays elicits interest more among scientists, who feel that their work borders on the philosophical, than among laymen. It followed from Plato's theory of the nature of the Forms and of matter that the objects apprehended by our senses are not real, but are rather representative of the ceaseless flux and are illusion. The Forms, which are real, are to be perceived by the soul, which has an innate knowledge of them persisting from one incarnation to another. Great effort by the individual is nevertheless necessary; the philosophically trained person may hope for some success in the arduous task of knowing the Forms clearly.

In the beautiful dialogue *Symposium* ("The Drinking Party"), Plato explains the nature of what has come to be called Platonic love. Starting from the ordinary love aroused by a beautiful person (of the same sex, as was customary for men at that time), one rises step by step to a wider and higher love, and at the end one achieves the glorious love of Beauty in her essence, the Form of Beauty, which is the intensification of that experience in ordinary life when we sometimes are awed by some unusually direct experience of beauty. In Plato's scheme, this love is practically synonymous with knowledge. Knowledge may perhaps rise little by little until it achieves the direct perception of the Forms, which is the supreme experience.

The soul of man is immortal. Souls do not perish with the death of bodies, but undergo a thousand-year period of purification. Once in a while some soul has been so defiled with baseness during an incarnation that it cannot be cleansed and is not allowed to return to another incarnation. On the other hand, sometimes a soul has been so uplifted toward virtue that it is allowed release from the cycle of incarnations and is freed for an eternity of the contemplation of the Forms, the highest bliss to which the soul can aspire. *Phaedo* represents Socrates' last discussion, on the immortality of the soul, and gives a touching picture of his drinking the hemlock and his death.

A number of the other dialogues discuss other aspects of the problem of knowledge. It should be remembered, too, that several of Plato's dialogues make almost playful explorations of this and other problems without any pretense of coming to a firm conclusion.

Political Theory: Republic

The ancient philosopher had to offer some theory about the best form of government. In *Politeia*, generally known as *The Republic*, Plato presented a picture of his well-ordered state as a means of writing justice large, so that anyone could read its features and understand what it is. Plato's well-ordered state was plainly not Athens; many features of it were taken from Sparta.

Plato was of aristocratic birth and conservative disposition. The democracy of Athens did not appeal to him as a form of society or as a form of government, and democracy has no place in the state that he constructed as a working model of justice. He believed that at Athens the increase in individualism had gone far beyond the point at which life was so organized as to produce the greatest happiness for the individual or for the whole group. The reforms of Lycurgus in Sparta were regarded by the ancients as a conservative refashioning of a society that had gone too far toward individualism. Plato's plan represents the same attitude; he plans a thoroughgoing revision of society that puts the populace under the direction of a worthy few in order to curb individualism and restore community feeling.

The worthy few—the philosophers—are to be rigorously trained and tested. Philosophy-and-ruling is a career open only to talent. Women are eligible equally with men. The ruling group is not to be weakened by considerations of money or family. Its wants will be supplied and its status assured without any need for wealth. Its children will not inherit the position of the parents. The most able people will be bred like animals and the children raised by the state. Children of nonphilosophers will be carefully examined to find promising candidates for the group of rulers. There are careful prescriptions for the moral and intellectual and physical eduction of the guardian, or philosopher, class, all conservative and static in nature. The education of the less able citizens is designed as the education of those who are to work and obey.

The warrior class is to be composed of those who make some progress in the training for the philosopher class, but are not able to pass the tests for the final stage. The artisan and farmer class will be chosen early from those who show no aptitude for any but the most simple practical training. As the guardian class especially uses the intellect, so the warrior class especially uses its courageous spirit, and the artisan class uses its practical talents. The three classes may be compared to the brain, the heart, and the stomach in man. In state and individual alike, justice consists of a division of functions and each part's performing its own function without wishing or striving to be another part.

The Republic has had enormous influence. Modern states planning to reorganize their societies so as to integrate them more closely have studied the book and used it. Its influence is plainly visible in Orwell's *1984*, a modern satire on contemporary totalitarian movements. If Plato had hoped (as he probably was not foolish enough to do) that his blueprint for a closely integrated and static state would have any immediate practical effect, he was to be disappointed. In a later work, *Laws*, he set forth a grimly practical plan for the creation of a closed society protected against the spread of religious disbelief and other solvents of the bonds that (as it seemed to him) hold society together. The work, which lacks the charm and interest of *Politeia*, suggests a comparison with the creation of the conservative and closed system of Sparta as well as with some twentieth-century attempts to remake society.

Ethics

Every well-rounded philosophy must of course have a system of ethics. If the cardinal problem of philosophy is how men can live well, philosophy must determine what is right in human life and how men can be turned toward right conduct. In minor dialogues, Plato offers discussions of some of the virtues, for example, courage or self-control. In others, he deals with the question whether virtue can be taught. The figure of Socrates is little by little built up in the dialogues into a most appealing picture of the virtuous man. Socrates defending himself before the Athenian people for his attempts to inform himself about right living, Socrates in *Crito* refusing to harm the state by defying its judgment of him by escaping from prison, Socrates in his final hour—these immortal pictures are pictures of the virtuous man. The honesty and elevation of Plato's writing are such that many a man, like the Roman Cicero, has felt that in philosophical questions he preferred to be wrong with Plato than right with others.

Plato's Influence

Plato's thought remained influential in Greece throughout antiquity. The Academy was active until all the universities, or philosophical schools, of Athens were closed by order of the Christian emperor Justinian in A.D. 529. The Aristotelian, Epicurean, and Stoic schools of philosophy, which maintained the other three universities, were all largely indebted to the thought of Plato. The Roman appropriation of Greek thought included the appropriation of philosophy; if more Romans professed themselves Stoics than followers of Plato, they were none the less influenced by Plato to some extent.

Platonic influence upon Christianity was enormous. The idealistic system of Plato was naturally congenial to Christianity, and the able Christian scholars of the third and fourth centuries of our era, laboring to complete the philosophical structure of Christianity, used Plato and Aristotle constantly. The Neoplatonic philosophy, a somewhat mysticized version of Platonism, developed by Plotinus in Rome late in the third century, served for many as a preparation for Christian thought. In the thirteenth century, Aristotle was exalted to the first place in Western thought, but with the Renaissance, Plato again became the favorite Greek philosopher of the West and has remained so.

Plato as Writer

Plato was no less able as writer than as thinker. In his day, Greek prose was just coming to maturity as an instrument of expression. His own contribution to the development of its possibilities was important. Plato's dialogues have many tones and colors, from the playful to the highly serious, from the plain to the gorgeous, from the gracefully charming to the portentously solemn. He portrays effectively a wide range of characters—the many-sided but always attractive Socrates, the blustering and overbearing Sophist, the enthusiastic and ingenuous young follower of Socrates, the honest and troubled old Crito, the courteous discourse of a group of Athenian gentlemen, or the honest sentiment of the jailer who says his farewell to Socrates and goes from the room in tears. Plato's metaphors are many, and some of the extended ones, which may be called allegories, are famous; the allegory of the cave in *The Republic* will serve as an example.

His prose style is so well calculated to further his philosophical purposes that it does not call attention to itself. It is pure Attic, flexible and elegant, with a variety of effective sentence structures. Probably this well-conceived prose has been helpful in forming not only the style of other Greeks but also the style of later men writing in many languages; because it has no mannerisms, its influence is not easily traced. Possibly, for purposes of study, the best example of Plato's style in the service of his thought is *Phaedo*, where he tries to win support and conviction for the cardinal point of the immortality of the soul, connecting it with the emotional theme of the death of Socrates and supporting it with all his art.

ARISTOTLE (384–322 B.C.)

Aristotle was the son of a physician of Stagira, an Ionian colony in Chalcidice. His father had been court physician to the kings of Macedonia. Aristotle went to Athens when he was about eighteen and was enrolled in Plato's Academy, where he stayed for nineteen years. Plato's school was different from a modern university in that a towering intellectual would remain there as a student for such a length of time. When Plato died in 347 B.C., Aristotle was invited by a former student of the Academy, Hermeias, to come to the little principality in Asia Minor of which he was tyrant. Aristotle spent three happy years with Hermeias and other friends of his Academy days; then he accepted the invitation of King Philip of Macedonia (who may well have been a companion of his boyhood at the Macedonian court when his father was physician there) to come to Pella to tutor the thirteen-year-old Alexander. After some years with Alexander, Aristotle returned to Athens in 335 and founded a school that he called the Lyceum, from the name of a gymnasium, or outdoor park and sports ground, where it first began. His school is sometimes known as the Peripatetic School, from the Greek verb meaning "to stroll about," because much of his work was done with a small group who walked about rather than sat. For twelve years he lectured and turned out a great production of philosophical writings. But in 323 Alexander died, and there were threats against Aristotle for his pro-Macedonian views. He withdrew to Chalcis, saying that he would not allow the Athenians to sin again against philosophy, and died in the next year, 322 B.C.

Aristotle's nature and predispositions were very different from Plato's. He was not an aloof aristocrat, as Plato had been. His disposition was always to embrace and examine material things instead of scorning them, to try to understand the working of any organism or system that he saw. But the times were as favorable for his fame as they had been for Plato's. The time was ripe for a man to organize the results of Greek curiosity about things as they are and systems as they are. Aristotle was that man, living at the right time to bring to fruition a great deal of earlier work along this line, as Plato had brought to fruition the earlier work along more abstract lines.

It was inevitable that Aristotle should differ sharply from Plato in a number of matters beside the different direction of his interests. The able disciple of an able man will always have many criticisms and modifications of his master's work to make. During the years of association he will have stored up many observations of areas in which the older man cannot be brought to take an interest, of pet dogmas that the older man does not wish to subject to examination, and perhaps of major or minor unlovelinesses of character.

Aristotle's first task was to work out his independence of Plato in metaphysics. He could not follow Plato's belief that reality is only in the Forms, not in the world with which we are surrounded. He believed that reality is both in the world of individual objects and in the other world of Forms or universals, that the many have as much reality as the One, that the Good is attached to life in this world as well as existing remotely in that other world. His inability and unwillingness to retire with Plato to austere and lonely heights, leaving the fascinating world of every day, still did not keep him from having a large area of agreement with Plato's beliefs. He did believe in universals and abstractions, unwilling as he was to be snobbish about the reality of individuals. He did believe in the Good; he believed in a living God, the supernatural cause of the movements of the physical world.

Had Aristotle been a genius merely of the second order, he would have been only a fine philosopher and encyclopedist: he had a passion for examining, analyzing, and classifying everything in sight. It is his ability to organize his vast body of results into a coherent system that makes him a genius of the first order. He is the first great practitioner of the inductive method.

Cosmology

In the *Physics* and the *Metaphysics*, Aristotle dealt with major problems of cosmology; in spite of modern connotations, the title of the second treatise originally meant only "what comes after *Physics*." He attempts to explain how primeval matter was shaped into the world, the nature of being and becoming, movement, and causes. There is an elaborate discussion of causes as formal, material, efficient, and final. The work of the pre-Socratic philosophers is criticized in detail, and at the end he devotes two of the eleven books to a discussion of Plato's theory of Forms.

His astronomical theories do not show his usual keen originality. He believed that all movements must be circular because he believed that the circle is the best figure for such movements. He had a system of fifty-five spheres, invisible themselves, but each having some heavenly body or several of them fixed in it to be carried around. With this large number of spheres, he felt that he had accounted for the movements of all the visible heavenly bodies.

Logic

It was typical of Aristotle's attitude and interest that he investigated the processes by which judgments and statements are made. His *Categories* classifies the objects of thought. We may regard things under such headings as substance, quality, quantity, relation, place, time, position, state, and so on. He examines the propositions that we can make, trying to determine how we can set them up so that they will not be ambiguous or contain traps and pitfalls. In the *Analytics* he makes his greatest contribution to the subject of logic by developing the theory of the syllogism. The syllogism cannot be called an aid to original thinking; it is rather a means of testing the validity of our statements.

Political Theory

Aristotle is said to have collected the constitutions of one hundred and fifty-eight Greek states in preparation for writing his *Politica*. Presumably not one of these constitutions was written. They must have been described by Aristotle or by his students and collaborators after observation and questioning. We have a large portion of one of these preparatory studies, *The Constitution of Athens*, thanks to its preservation on papyrus in Egypt. It gives an account of the constitutional development of Athens and the form of her constitution.

Politica has generally been translated *Politics*, a slightly misleading title. The book might better be called *Life in a Polis*. Likewise it has been suggested that Aristotle's famous remark "Man is a political animal" should rather be rendered "Man is a creature who lives in a *polis*."

Aristotle and Plato have both been criticized for basing their political theory on life in the *polis* instead of realizing that the *polis* was doomed by the advance of such kingdoms as that of Philip. Such criticism is overschematized. Even the rise of larger kingdoms after the death of Alexander or the spread of the Roman Empire some time later did not remove from the *polis* its significance as a social and political organization.

Politica develops its subject systematically, as is usual with Aristotle's writings, analyzing the *polis* into its parts, villages and households. Evidently the institution of slavery troubled Aristotle somewhat; the discussion is not up to his usual standard and has the unsatisfactory ring of discourses on institutions that are traditional and seem necessary, but are hard to defend.

He has an elaborate discussion of the theoretical schemes of other philosophers and of famous existing commonwealths. Plato's commonwealth comes in for some very sharp criticism. Being of a middle-class rather than an aristocratic temper, he presumably had little sympathy with Plato's idea of reversing recent tendencies by forming an aristocratic, conservative, static society. He would reject the rigid regimentation of the guardian class, with its community of property and denial of normal family life. He discusses the virtues and defects of various kinds of states. Complete democracy and complete oligarchy rank very low. The best kind of state is a mixture of democracy and oligarchy, inclining to the democratic. The Spartan constitution seems to him a successful mixture of types, even though he disapproves of many features of the Spartan way.

The possibility of revolution was always present to the mind of the Greek political thinker, since the history of almost every Greek state was full of revolutions of the many against the few or of the few against the many. Aristotle realistically discusses the relations of the different elements in the several possible kinds of states and points out the probable form that revolution would take in one or another set of circumstances and how to guard against it. Another aspect of his theory is the consideration of the possibility that a political form will degenerate into a worse version of itself, as monarchy can degenerate into tyranny or democracy into mob rule.

Ethics and Other Topics

In *Ethics*, Aristotle discusses the classical virtues of the Greek—courage, wisdom, justice, temperance—and other virtues useful to the member of a *polis*. He specifically gives successful life in the *polis* as the Good to which all these virtues are directed and which makes them worthwhile. In his eyes, every virtue is a mean between two extremes: liberality is between prodigality and meanness; pride is between vanity and undue humility.

His interest in all forms of human life and in the world did not cease when he had considered the usual parts of a systematic philosophy. His *Rhetoric* is a masterly examination of what rhetoric really is, the art of persuasive speech. He examines the mechanics of effective speech and the psychology that must be used in addition if one is to persuade. In *Poetics*, he examines poetry; the construction of tragedy is the topic that has attracted most interest among his readers. In the Renaissance and just afterward, *Poetics* served as a set of rules for the construction of poetry and plays. *Oedipus the King* was Aristotle's favorite play, and he tends to find in it all the virtues possible in a tragedy.

But far more earthy subjects than these could claim his attention. He described many animals and Mediterranean fishes, sometimes so minutely that it seems that he must have dissected specimens, perhaps even with some kind of magnifying glass. Here, as elsewhere, his mind worked systematically, and his observations on animals and fishes and on their proper classifications were the beginning of this branch of natural science.

Aristotle's work was not highly influential in antiquity; perhaps it was too factual and precise to correspond to the temper of the ancient world. Sometimes the Christian Fathers used him in their task of building the philosophical structure of Christianity. In the fourth and fifth centuries of our era, there were a number of learned commentators on his work who helped to make it better known. In the thirteenth century, St. Thomas Aquinas made a fruitful union of the Aristotelian and Christian systems, which for a short time ruled the world of serious thought.

THE EPICUREAN AND STOIC PHILOSOPHIES

The Epicurean and Stoic philosophies are the third and fourth of the four great Greek philosophies. Plato and Aristotle (the first and second), even though they were building up systems for a Greek world that had moved away from the old traditional way of living and needed explicitly formulated views of life and the world to replace the old traditional attitudes, still wrote for men who were members of a *polis*. Their general views, their political views, and their formulations of ethics all reflect the *polis*. Epicurus, for whom the Epicurean philosophy was named, and the outlander Zeno from Cyprus, the founder of the Stoic philosophy, both began their work in Athens just before 300 B.C. Both offered philosophies suitable for men who could in no way rely upon the framework of membership in a *polis* and sometimes perhaps were not even free men.

The Epicurean Philosophy

The son of an Athenian citizen who had gone to Samos, Epicurus seems to have developed his system thoroughly before settling in

Athens in 306 B.C. He did not undertake to teach in Athens, but lived in a large house with a garden suitable for walks and discussions (from which his system is sometimes called "the philosophy of the Garden") and gathered a company of disciples about him. His was the first dogmatic philosophy. He laid down an elementary version of its most important principles to be memorized, then an intermediate version. In the third stage, the learner might consult treatises rather than memorize rules or outlines. Epicurus and his associates and disciples busied themselves with treatises on every aspect of philosophy, with attempts to refute the assertions of the other schools, and with letters to the communities of Epicureans, which soon were found in a number of places in the Greek world. The Epicurean was expected to attempt to make converts. The dogmatic clarity of the philosophy and the warmth of the Epicurean groups combined to win a fair number of people in every generation.

This was a materialistic philosophy. Its cosmology, requiring a world free from the intervention of the gods, whether to help man or to punish him, borrowed the atomic theory of Democritus. The universe was declared to operate on strict principles of causation. The gods do exist, and are superior beings worthy of men's reverence, but they are unconcerned with man and do not interfere with his affairs in any way whatsoever.

Yet a strictly mechanical universe would be worse than capricious gods, for it would be a monstrous, unchangeable, implacable thing. Man must have his free will. So Epicurus postulated what he called a swerve in the atoms ever raining down through the universe. Some atoms, free spirits not entirely adjusted to the group, asserted the freedom of the will for man. It is difficult for us to imagine how the detail of this argument was worked out, since most of Epicurus' writing is lost.

We can see the materialism of this philosophy clearly in its epistemology. Nothing like Plato's Forms exists; one of the elementary rules to be memorized declares that only matter and the void exist. Our senses tell us of the physical world with some reliability. The soul does not play a part in cognition.

The political thought of Epicurus belongs to the new age of larger political units. He saw justice, not as one of Plato's Forms or as the virtue of a well-ordered *polis*, but as a product of man's need to live in peace and quiet, a practical agreement among people to treat each other decently. He urged the avoidance of public life. Such a piece of advice could hardly have been offered a few generations before, and even in his time it may seem pusillanimous, but we must remember how easy it had been in the free *polis* to lose one's life when a competent piece of public service somehow went wrong.

Epicurus' ethical system was earthy and honest. To him wisdom, which had been one of the cardinal virtues for life in the *polis*, meant shrewd and practical common sense. Justice was the universal application of ordinary fair dealing. Not only did he redefine the old virtues in this way; he also added one or two good ones, such as a freedom of speech that would allow a man to correct his friends or associates plainly, but with courtesy.

Friendship held a high place in his thought. It was always more important and necessary in the ancient world than nowadays, for in a less highly organized world, a man had need of definite personal allies. Friendship therefore often took the form more of a formal personal alliance than mere mutual attraction without ulterior motives. The need of such alliances was probably greater in the more individualized society of Epicurus' time than it had been two or three centuries earlier, and, too, the friendship of the Epicureans added a note of warmth and sweetness.

Epicurus began his system of conduct with the primacy of pleasure. Pleasure is to be sought, for it is the concomitant of health and good functioning. He frankly accepted the pleasures of food and sex. Pain, on the other hand, is the sign that something is wrong. But pleasure is not to be unrestrained or dishonorable. From the beginning there were those who called Epicureanism the philosophy of the pigsty. But Epicurus asserted the need for justice and honor in all things; pleasure was not to be sought through injustice or dishonor. He urged the hedonistic calculus, or the careful calculation of pleasure and the avoidance of that overindulgence which suggests the pigsty and detracts from pleasure even to the point of bringing on disgust. His own version of pleasure seems even a little ascetic, for with him the hedonistic calculus could take the form of getting pleasure from extremely simple living, nicely calculated for appreciation of simple things.

One must cultivate the pleasures of the mind, too. *Mens sana in corpore sano* is an Epicurean maxim. He used the Greek word *ataraxia*, or freedom from disturbance. The Epicurean was to cultivate the pleasure of the quiet mind by training himself not to worry uselessly about either past or future, to put away ambition for fame, and to avoid distressing situations. He is even to avoid exposing himself to fortune by entering into marriage and family life. We could hardly be farther from the old spirit of the *polis*.

The Stoic Philosophy

The fourth of the great philosophical schools was founded by a Phoenician from Cyprus, Zeno. At first he had no such place for his teaching as the others had and offered lectures in the great porch, or *Stoa*, at Athens, from which his philosophy came to be called Stoic, or "the philosophy of the Porch." He began his career in Athens a few years after Epicurus.

Although the Stoics were interested most in conduct, it was necessary for their system to be a complete one and offer a general view of life and the world, as did the other philosophies. In their cosmology, there was a story of the formation of the world from unformed stuff, as there was in the others. Their further view, however, was that God is immanent in every part of the world. In their epistemology, the rational soul, or reason, was the source of knowledge. This soul is corporeal and holds the body together and dominates it. The soul has no inherited knowledge, contrary to Plato's view. In the course of time, the school became noted for its close attention to logic and the analysis of propositions as means of drawing nearer to truth.

The Stoic ethics was the cornerstone of the philosophy. True goodness lay in a knowledge of Nature, and this knowledge was to be obtained by reason. "Nature" meant the divinity who is immanent in all of Nature. "Live according to Nature" was their watchword, which could be paraphrased as "Seek to know and follow the will of God." This principle took care of the question of the freedom of the will, too, for true freedom of the will lay in following what was ordained by Nature.

"The Wise Man" was set up as a model of what man should be. He was perfectly virtuous and lived according to reason. The Wise

Man may seem something of a monster to some, for he was wise and virtuous and unruffled, but not inspired by love of his fellow men or mellowed by tolerance. Yet the Stoic ideals of conscience and of duty could and did serve as an inspiration and almost as a religion for many people; in the end, they did much to shape the Western ideal of the gentleman.

The Stoic, then, even if he could not achieve the pitiless perfection of the Wise Man, attempted to order his life by reason. He attempted to keep his conscience clear and do his duty at whatever cost. These were his real goals; other things in life, like wealth or fame or ordinary personal happiness, were specifically classed as indifferent things. His own soul was a fortress, which he could keep his own, where no one and nothing could harm him, and from which he could look on everything else with an indifference that in some cases became real.

The Stoics, like the Epicureans, did not theorize about commonwealths overmuch, in spite of the fact that Zeno in his earlier years had written of an ideal commonwealth inhabited only by Wise Men. The Stoic school in general made up their minds to the fact that they lived in an age when the *polis* was less important politically than large kingdoms were. They drew a conclusion which was just as alien to the spirit of the earlier *polis* as Epicurus' recommendation to avoid political life. They adopted the idea of the brotherhood of man that seems first to have been effectively expressed by Alexander the Great. This was the real contribution made by the political part of their philosophy—to preach that all men are brothers, Greek or barbarian, rich or poor, slave or free. It was a new idea in the world and one that helped to prepare the way for Christianity.

Although there were minor movements in Greek philosophy that flourished temporarily and acquired names of their own (as did the Cynics, for example), the four great schools are most representative of the Greek effort to cope with life by means of reason, an effort that has had great effect in the West, although to other parts of the world it has seemed misguided. They also represent the highwater mark of Greek individualism, for adherence to one of these philosophies meant that a man was attempting as an individual to come to terms with life and the world. The Epicurean and Stoic philosophies, even more than the others, implied that the individual was not relying on traditional values and supports as much as he had in earlier centuries, even though he need not renounce the support of groups and associations and the comfort of acquiescence in tradition. After a few generations, the time was to come when men began to feel uncomfortably exposed in this rational individualism and began to start edging back toward the comfort of more emotional and more communal attitudes and ways of living.

CHAPTER

32

ALEXANDER THE GREAT

The death by assassination of King Philip in 336 B.C. left his son Alexander the king of Macedonia, if he could make good his right to the throne. Alexander, who was twenty years old, had been carefully educated to succeed his father. He had been trained in government and the Macedonian art of war by his father and by his father's able helpers. At the age of sixteen, he commanded one of the armies and crushed a rebellion in Thrace while his father was busy with the siege of Byzantium. At eighteen, he commanded the left wing of his father's army at the meeting with the combined Greek forces at Chaeronea. His polite studies were watched over by tutors whom his father chose, the most noteworthy of them being Aristotle, who was with him for three years, beginning when he was fourteen. Aristotle taught him Greek ways of thought and aroused in him a great love of Greek literature. He introduced him to philosophy and fed his lively curiosity by telling him something of his own practical researches into the world of Nature.

Even as a youth Alexander was very serious-minded and determined to fill his royal position with credit. His sober realization that kings must remain at some social distance even from the nobles is shown by the story that when someone suggested that his speed of foot should be shown in the Olympic Games, he replied that he would enter the games if there were kings for him to race with. He

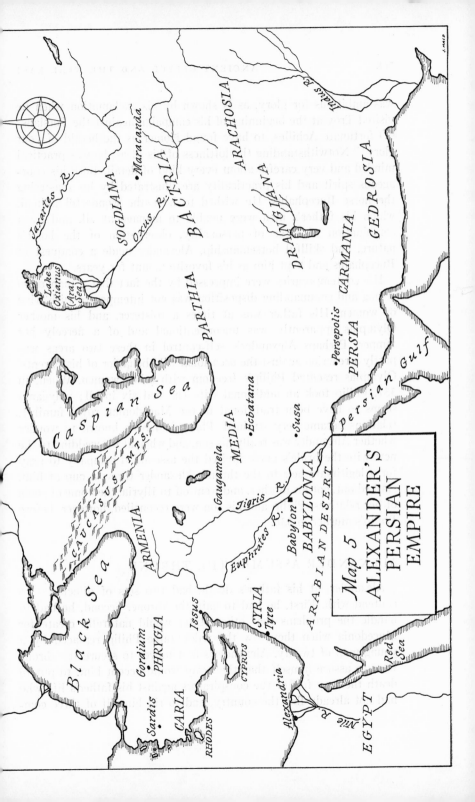

Map 5
ALEXANDER'S
PERSIAN EMPIRE

was ambitious for glory, as is shown by his exclamation when he visited Troy at the beginning of his campaign against the Persians: "O fortunate Achilles, to have found Homer as the herald of your glory!" Notwithstanding the loftiness of his ideas, he was practical minded and very careful about every kind of detail. Both his courageous spirit and his practicality are illustrated by his mastering the horse Bucephalus. He wished to have the wonderful animal, which his father's men were unable to manage at all, and by a combination of force of personality, observation of the horse's nature, and skillful horsemanship, Alexander made a conquest of Bucephalus and kept him as his favorite mount for years.

His contemporaries were impressed by the fact that a man of so strong and commanding disposition was not intemperate with wine or women. His father was at times a roisterer, and his mother Olympias apparently was unconventional and of a fiercely hot temper. Perhaps Alexander's self-control in these two areas was partly a reaction against the occasional wild behavior of his parents. Olympias resented Philip's freedom with other women. When, in 337, Philip took an additional wife (he had six in all; polygamy seems to have been traditional in the Macedonian royal family), relations became very strained. Philip had been known to wonder whether Alexander was really his son, and when at his wedding to the new wife the bride's uncle invited the assembled company to pray for a legitimate heir to the throne, Alexander threw a cup at him, stalked out, got his mother, and went off to Illyria, the home of some of her relatives. Philip and his son were reconciled, however, before Philip's murder in 336.

ALEXANDER ASSUMES THE THRONE

Alexander, at his father's death, had two sets of difficulties to contend with. First, he had to gain the throne. Second, he had to handle the problems that other states would naturally create for Macedonia when they saw the redoubtable Philip replaced by a young man of twenty. Alexander's first moves to secure the throne were to assure himself that the army would accept him, to put to death the very few of the conspirators against his father's life who had not already fled the country, and to rid himself of three competitors for the throne—a pair from another royal house and his cousin Amyntas, the one whom his father had pushed aside as an infant. Alexander's excellent qualities were probably so well known that all the people recognized, as the generals did, that he was the best man for the throne, in addition to his claims as Philip's son.

The second set of difficulties occupied him for two years. First he went to Thessaly, where the anti-Macedonian party had gained control. A swift show of force without actual fighting gained him election as *tagus* of Thessaly, a position Philip had held. Then he swiftly moved southward into Greece, which was grumbling and disaffected, but not ready to unite and fight against him. The members of the League of Corinth sent representatives to Corinth at his call and elected him to the position which his father had had, that of commander of the League's forces for a war against Persia. In years past, Alexander must have assumed that at about this time he would be engaged, with his father, in the war against Persia; his father's death seemed no reason for abandoning the project.

But before he could move against the Persians, he had to deal with the rest of the disturbances caused by Philip's death. The Thracian tribes subject to Macedonia needed to be assured of the firmness of the new king. In the spring of 335, he moved north from Amphipolis and defeated them. Then, with the help of some ships from his ally Byzantium, which had come up the Danube to meet him, he threw a force of men across the river and defeated another tribe that had been preparing to help the Thracian rebels. His western neighbors, the Illyrians, had also decided that the accession of a new and young king offered a good opportunity for an invasion of Macedonia. Alexander made a long and swift march to meet and decisively defeat them.

He had to go down into Greece once more. The democratic exiles from Thebes had regained control of the city from the oligarchy that Philip had installed there and had driven the Macedonian garrison into the citadel. Other Greek states, including Athens, were preparing to help the democrats. Alexander made another lightning march, appeared before Thebes, and called upon the Thebans to honor their oath of allegiance to the League of Corinth. On their refusal, he attacked the city, took it, and destroyed it except for the temples and the house of the poet Pindar. He sold the citizens into slavery and divided the territory of the city among the neighboring cities.

There were no further attempts to try out the temper of the new king of Macedonia. Alexander was able to spend the late autumn of 335 and the winter in preparing for the invasion of Persia. In the spring of 334 he began his campaign.

THE WAR AGAINST PERSIA: ASIA MINOR

The Two Armies

In the spring of 334, Alexander set out for his great adventure in Persia, from which he was not to return. He left Antipater, an elderly and reliable general, in charge of Macedonia with enough troops to overawe the Greeks. Alexander also had hostages from the peoples of Greece in the form of the soldiers and sailors whom they had contributed to the expedition. Philip had sent the reliable general Parmenio into Asia Minor in 336, and the Macedonian forces held a bridgehead on the Asiatic side to which Alexander could cross without difficulty.

In his army there were over 30,000 infantry and over 5,000 cavalry. The flower of the army was the heavy cavalry, the first cavalry force in history to be used as a striking arm rather than for scouting, skirmishing, and pursuit, as cavalry generally had been used. A special section, 2,000 strong and drawn from the best families of Macedonia, was known as the Companions.

The famous Macedonian phalanx consisted of 9,000 men who were known as the Foot-Companions. These men were a specialized kind of hoplite. They were equipped with helmet, breastplate, greaves, and shield, and for offense had short swords and very long spears. The long spears seem to have been especially fearsome to opposing soldiers. The 9,000 were divided into tactical units of 256, or 16 men square. These smaller units were drilled intensively, so that even in the midst of a battle they could change their shape, reverse themselves, or divide to face and fight in two directions. This formidable array of men was sometimes used to "fix" the enemy hoplites, or hold them by its presence so that they did not dare to maneuver or change formation while they were attacked on the wings by the effective Macedonian cavalry. A special body of 3,000 heavy infantry, drawn from the upper classes, was known as the hypaspists.

The League of Corinth contributed 7,000 hoplites, and 5,000 Greek mercenaries had been enrolled. Six thousand light-armed soldiers, of whom 1,000 were Cretan archers, completed the army proper. The League had provided a fleet of 160 ships. There was also a siege corps that could build towers on rollers or on wheels, tall enough to top the ordinary city wall, and catapults that could fire large arrows accurately for 200 yards or throw stones of 50 or 60 pounds for the same distance. This corps could also build pontoon bridges.

Alexander's whole force was engaged on only a few occasions; most of his battles were small ones. Even in the small battles, however, all branches of the army were represented and used in combination. Alexander's dashing manner and glamor have sometimes obscured the fact that he was practical-minded and a master of detail. Not only did he combine his different kinds of soldiers as no one before him had done, except perhaps Dionysius I of Syracuse, but he also insisted on and received excellent performance from his quartermaster's corps and from those at home who enrolled and forwarded his reinforcements.

Alexander's intellectual interests are reflected by his remarkable entourage of noncombatants. A surveying corps recorded the distance of each march and collected data on the geography of each region. The secretarial division kept a running record of the events of each day. Two or three historians apparently were expected to produce at some future time an artistic account of the campaign; no one could know that most future accounts would actually be based chiefly on the private journal of Ptolemy, one of the generals. There was a small group of biologists and botanists, one of whose functions was to send specimens back to Aristotle.

The Persians had no heavy infantry of their own that could match the Greek hoplite or the phalanx of Alexander, although there were perhaps 20,000 Greek hoplites employed by them in various parts of the empire. Their heavy cavalry was plentiful and useful, although man for man and group for group it probably was not so well trained and efficient as the Macedonian. The Persian archers were good.

The chief Persian mistake was that they had not taken the Macedonian threat seriously enough, in spite of the arrival of the first detachment in 336, to gather a major army to oppose it. Another of their mistakes was to reject the recommendation of a high officer that the Persian forces retreat before the Macedonians, removing all supplies, and harry them as they went. Such tactics seemed beneath Persian dignity, even though the Persians must have known how formidable the Macedonian invaders would be.

The Conquest of Asia Minor

The Persians of Asia Minor opposed Alexander at the Granicus River in 334, soon after his landing. They did not have a sufficient force to oppose him properly, and the accounts of the battle sound as if the Persian cavalry massed itself to attempt to cut through to Alexander himself and kill him as a means of getting rid of the moving spirit of the war. They came so near to succeeding that one of the Companions intercepted the slash of the sword aimed at Alexander's head. The Macedonians won the battle, killing many of the Greeks on the Persian side. Two thousand of them were captured, and Alexander sent them as slaves to labor in Macedonia on the ground that they were traitors to the League. He reported the victory as won by the forces of the League under himself as the League's general.

To take the Greek cities subject to the Persians along the coast of Asia Minor was not difficult. The Persians had been governing them by means of Greek tyrants or Greek oligarchies. Alexander announced that he would favor democracy. As the word got around, the democrats in one city after another arose, overthrew the pro-Persian government of the few, and welcomed Alexander. He had almost no fighting to do. When governments of a democratic sort had been set up, some of them tried to purge the population of the conservative element. Alexander found means to convince them that his favoring democracy did not mean that he favored the elimination of the useful conservative element.

His strategy at this point has other interesting elements beside his support of democracy. He showed signs of moving away from the policy of acting as head of the League. For instance, he now began to take into his own service (not that of the League) the Greek mercenaries whom he was able to capture. More striking is his disbanding of his fleet, even while the Persians had an active fleet on the sea and were trying by means of subsidies to raise Greece against him. Alexander's judgment that Greece could not be so raised proved correct. He did not need to fear that the Persian fleet could stop the transportation of his reinforcements across the Hellespont; so tight a blockade was not possible. He knew that he could count on the defection of many units of the Persian fleet that were supplied by the Greek cities of the coast, for when the news got around that their cities had gone over to Alexander and had democratic governments, the rowers of the ships (who were of the people) would simply slip away from the fleet and take the ships home. He looked forward to capturing the remaining bases on the Phoenician coast, which he was in fact able to do in the following year, 332, thus ending the activity of the hostile fleet entirely. His judgment that he himself could get along without a fleet was correct. Further, he was very short of money and could hardly afford to pay for the upkeep of one.

The interior of Asia Minor seemed likely to yield him money. He could hardly demand from the Greek cities of the coast the tribute that they had been used to paying to the Persians. Inland in Asia Minor, however, the natives paid rent to the Persian king for their lands. Alexander moved through the interior, and as he conquered it, sometimes by rather sharp fighting, he put Macedonian officers in as governors and trustworthy men in charge of the collection of the rents.

His long swing through inner Asia Minor brought him to Gordium, the old capital of the Phrygian kings and still an important center of communications. Here, as the story goes, he was shown the chariot of the original king of the Phrygians. On the pole of the chariot was tied a knot that showed no end, and, according to the local story, the man who could untie it was promised rule over all Asia. In spite of its being proverbial that Alexander slashed through the knot with his sword, the other story is rather more in character, that he simply took out the pin that held the pole and slipped the knot off the end of the pole, for his disposition was serious and he had no relish for puzzles and games.

Presently he felt that he had done what he could afford to do in the interior of Asia Minor and came down through the Cilician Gates, a pass at the angle where the southern coast of Asia Minor joins the north-south coast of Syria and Palestine. His purpose was to find the army of the king and fight a decisive battle. King Darius' army was near, but somehow Alexander passed it and left it in his rear. Then, learning at last where it was, he turned back and met it at Issus in October, 333.

The inadequate infantry of the Persians could not stand up to the Macedonians, nor could even their archers, but their Greek mercenaries gave the Macedonians a good fight. Darius himself fled ingloriously as soon as he saw part of his line yield to a charge headed by Alexander. Although Alexander captured the money that the king had brought for the campaign, thereby solving his immediate financial problem, he was not able to capture the person of the king. The Macedonians won the battle and inflicted fairly heavy losses on the Persians. Some of the Greek mercenaries in the Persian service were able to rejoin Darius a little later; another group of 8,000 decided to leave his service and went off to fight for other masters in Egypt and then in Greece.

After the victory, Alexander decided to eat the dinner ready to be served in the luxurious tent of Darius. "So this is being a king," he remarked reflectively; he may well have been genuinely impressed. Presently he heard the weeping of women and was told that the mother, wife, and two daughters of Darius had been captured and were wailing for their lost lord. Alexander sent to tell the royal ladies that Darius was alive and uncaptured. He treated them thereafter with courtesy and consideration.

THE WAR AGAINST PERSIA:
PHOENICIA AND EGYPT

Phoenicia

Apparently the original purpose of the war had been to capture and hold only the rich territory of Asia Minor. Alexander had now done this and had in addition defeated a strong Persian army just outside Asia Minor, at Issus. The defensive operation of merely holding this much territory was uncongenial to his temperament. He turned next to the subjection of the cities of the Phoenician coast, some of which were bases for what remained of the Persian fleet.

A letter from Darius presently reached him in which the Persian king asked for the release of the ladies of his family as a piece of royal courtesy and offered Alexander his friendship and alliance. Alexander sent him in return a statement of the grievances and aims of the League. This, he told Darius, was a war of revenge for Xerxes' invasion of Macedonia and Greece. Both Macedonia and the League had more recent grievances, too, for the Persians had committed many warlike acts against them and had given aid and comfort to their enemies. He also accused the Persians of having caused the murder of his father. He said in conclusion that he regarded himself as king of all Asia (although he did not publicly make this claim and act on it until after the final defeat and subsequent death of Darius) and that Darius must ask him as a vassal for what he might desire.

He went on with his operation in Phoenicia. Although most of the cities submitted to him readily, the siege and capture of Tyre took him seven months. This was the last base available for the Persian fleet, and before the siege was over that fleet had disbanded. The siege of Tyre, which is vividly described in *The Anabasis of Alexander* of Arrian, a later Greek writer, had features reminiscent of the siege of Motya by Dionysius I. Tyre was on an island two miles in circumference and half a mile from the mainland. Alexander undertook the huge task of building a causeway two hundred feet wide out from the mainland, so that the island could be attacked as if from land. The water deepened to eighteen feet near the island. Catapults were set on the causeway as it neared the island, but the Tyrians sent out their ships and destroyed the catapults. Alexander then collected a fleet, partly from other coastal cities that had surrendered to him, sufficient to neutralize the Tyrian fleet. The causeway reached the island, and a spectacular duel took place between the Macedonian offense and the ingenious Tyrian defense. Tyre was captured in July, 332 B.C., after seven months of siege. Most of the inhabitants were sold into slavery.

Ambassadors from Darius came to Alexander while he was busy with the siege of Tyre. The Persian king sought again to make peace and secure a treaty of alliance by offering 10,000 talents, the cession of all territory west of the Euphrates, and a daughter to marry Alexander. Alexander is said to have called a conference of his generals and laid the proposal before them. Parmenio, the most distinguished of them, said that if he were Alexander, he would accept the proposal, to which Alexander replied that if he were Parmenio, he would accept. The story probably is not literally true, but it does represent with plausibility the caution and limited horizon of the older Macedonians and their lack of interest in further possibilities of adventure, gain, and accompanying danger. Alexander replied to Darius that he would not consider any proposals. Actually Darius had not proposed to yield him anything that he had not already conquered except Egypt, which Persia could not dream of holding in any event.

Egypt

After the capture of Tyre, Alexander turned toward Egypt and reached it late in the year 332. The Persian satrap of Egypt yielded at once, for his troops were few and poor compared to the invading army, and the people would plainly be glad to be in Alexander's hands rather than those of the Persians. Alexander's policies in Egypt were a model of well-informed good sense. He first took the trouble to go through all the ceremonies necessary to symbolize his taking of the position of Pharaoh. Then he founded Alexandria, the city that has borne his name ever since. He was to found more than a dozen other Alexandrias when he got to Asia, none of them so successful as this one was. He is said personally to have chosen the excellent site of the Egyptian Alexandria; the new city was in a good position to flourish on trade and to symbolize the new order.

It was highly politic for him to make the long trip to the desert oasis where the famous shrine of the Egyptian god Amun gave oracles that ranked with those of Delphi. Some scholars have conjectured that this was the beginning of a belief on Alexander's part that he had a certain divinity, especially because he is reported to have said that the priest addressed him as son of Amun. The priest was only being correct; he would naturally use that name in speaking to the Pharaoh, who was officially regarded as the son of Amun-Re. As we shall see, Alexander found it politic later, after his complete victory over Darius, to receive the honors, some of them semidivine, traditionally offered to a Persian king. He even sent requests to the Greek states to give honors to him as to a god. All this must not make us suppose that he himself conceived of the idea as anything other than a careful piece of political management.

THE WAR AGAINST PERSIA: VICTORY

The Battle of Gaugamela

After leaving Egypt, Alexander went in pursuit of the main armed forces of the Persians. The battle that finally broke the power of Darius began on the first of October, 331 B.C., at Gaugamela, past the Tigris and in the home territories of Persia. Although the Persians could not form a seasoned army fit to meet Alexander's, they did the best they could by forming a corps of the scythed chariots that they had not used for a long time, hoping that they might thus be able to break the phalanx. Although the battle was in the end a great victory for Alexander, it was not a rout of cowardly Orientals, but a long and bitterly fought affair from which many of the troops of the Persian side withdrew at last in good order and unpursued.

The Persians had chosen a flat place where they thought that the scythed chariots could be used to good advantage. Alexander was willing to meet them on their own ground. The battle was begun by the cavalry, each side sending in more and more for a determined struggle. Then the scythed chariots charged, but Alexander's light-armed men brought down many of the horses as they came, and the heavy infantry, or hypaspists, whom the chariots attacked first, skillfully opened lanes for them and destroyed them as they drove through. The cavalry of the Persian left wing had tended a little more to the left as they struggled with the Greeks, and the other Persians drifted over to give their left more support. Alexander charged the thinner place thus created in their line, and so broke through. Again Darius fled, as he had at Issus.

The battle was far from won, however, for the Persian right wing had pressed the Macedonian left so hard that Parmenio called for help, and Alexander turned back from the pursuit to help him. A large group of the Persian cavalry had also broken through the Macedonian line as part of it moved forward to charge the Persian line. Finally they were driven off, and the left under Parmenio was able to drive off the Persians who had pressed it so hard. Alexander was off again in pursuit of Darius and those with him. After it became dark, Alexander and his men rested until midnight, then went on until in the early hours of morning light they reached Arbela, more than 60 miles away, where they gave up the pursuit. Darius' 2,000 Greek mercenaries had retired from the field in good order, as had the bulk of the forces of both the right and the left of the Persian army. The victory was nevertheless decisive; the Persians did not attempt to put another major army in the field against Alexander.

The Persian Capitals

Alexander marched southward for over two hundred miles, then crossed the Tigris westward into Mesopotamia and went over to Babylon, on the Euphrates. Here the commander of the Persian right wing at Gaugamela came out to surrender to him. Alexander made him governor of this district, the first Persian to be appointed to an administrative position, although Egyptians had been left at the head of the administrative system of their country. The Persian was to have two Macedonian associates in charge of the army and finance, however. The people of Babylon welcomed Alexander, who gave the inhabitants the right to follow all their native customs.

The army then moved southward into Persis, the original territory of the Persians, where the troops of the local satraps put up the resistance that duty required. Alexander was able to suppress it without great difficulty. He took the royal cities of Susa, Pasargadae, and Persepolis. Again he chose Persians as civil administrators of districts based on the former Persian satrapies, giving them Macedonian colleagues to handle the military and financial tasks. He deliberately burned the palace of Persepolis, the original royal city of the Persians, not as a crude act of vandalism, but as a symbol of the end of Persian power.

In the royal treasuries of the three cities Alexander found gold and silver coin and bullion worth about 180,000 talents, as well as gold and silver plate and purple dye. He put a large part of the coin and bullion into circulation, largely by the method of making lavish gifts to his officers and soldiers. It is impossible today to assign a value in dollars to the royal treasure. It is also impossible to know how much other gold and silver was in circulation at the time. We do know that subsistence farming and home manufacture were so common that the number of wants supplied by the payment of money was far less than it is now. The effect of putting so much new precious metal into circulation must therefore have been great. Our evidence, scanty as it is, suggests that there was a general rise in the level of prices.

Darius was still at liberty in Ecbatana, the old capital of the Medes. In March, 330, Alexander started northward from Persepolis. At his approach, Darius fled eastward to Bactria, allowing Alexander to occupy Ecbatana without a struggle. Here Alexander dismissed the troops that the League of Corinth had sent for the expedition. They could re-enlist if they wished, but in the forces of the King of Macedonia, Egypt, and Persia, not the expeditionary force of the League of Corinth. This gesture made it plain that Alexander felt that the panhellenic war of revenge on the Persians was over.

At this time, too, he began to wear Persian dress on some occasions. Presumably he was revolving in his mind methods of bringing the Greeks and Persians together as one and thought it advisable sometimes to adopt the behavior of a Persian as a reinforcement to his careful appropriation of the symbolism that belonged to the kingship of Persia. The Macedonian officers were not pleased, for they could not see beyond the simple idea of conquering the Persians and lording it over their rich country.

In the middle of the summer, Alexander, hearing that Darius was collecting a new army in Bactria, decided to forestall him. He moved swiftly eastward and presently heard that the satraps of the East had foresworn their allegiance to Darius and made him a captive. Alexander took a small force and raced after them. At his approach, they stabbed Darius and fled, so that Alexander captured only his body. He was saved embarrassment by not having to deal with Darius living. Now the only hindrance to his claiming to hold the throne of Persia in the fullest sense was that he had not marched through the eastern territories.

ALEXANDER IN THE EAST

Resentment of his Policies

Most of Alexander's high officers were men of noble blood and some could even claim royal blood. Naturally they liked the old

Macedonian idea that the king was the chief among peers and resented the clear signs that Alexander proposed to stand alone above all other men. They might have admitted that this attitude was best for a Persian king, but they found difficulty in understanding Alexander's growing intention of ruling Persia as one responsible for the welfare of all his subjects. A tangible point of difference of opinion was his attempt to introduce among them the Persian custom of *proskynesis*, or prostrating one's self before the king. Among the Persians it was only a sign of deep respect, but among the Greeks a man prostrated himself only before a god. Some Macedonians merely laughed at the idea; others resisted and argued. Although Alexander agreed to confine this custom to Asiatics, he was deeply annoyed that he could not gain the co-operation of his high officers in this matter.

He was to have worse troubles with his officers. Philotas, son of Parmenio, commanded the Companion cavalry. In the autumn of 330, a conspiracy against the life of Alexander was reported to him. He said nothing and took no action. The news of the conspiracy came to Alexander by another route, and he crushed it. Philotas and two others were tried for treason in the old-fashioned way, before the army. Philotas was found guilty and executed, and the other two were acquitted. Alexander then bowed to the hard necessity of government and sent swift messengers to kill Parmenio, the father of Philotas, who had been left in charge of the troops in Persia, for by the code of the time the death of his son left Parmenio no alternative to rebellion.

Eastward in Samarcand came another incident in 328 that was less dangerous but dramatically illustrative of the tensions. Probably all the company had drunk too much of the strong native wine. Cleitus, a dear friend of Alexander, the man who had saved him from the sword of the leading Persian at the battle of the Granicus River, fell to taunting him during the evening, comparing his present attitudes to those of his father Philip and reminding him that the Macedonians from whom he was now withdrawing himself had by their strength and valor brought him to his exalted position. In spite of Alexander's attempts at self-control and the attempts of others to quiet Cleitus, the matter proceeded to the point where Alexander killed his friend with a javelin. For three days he was beside himself with remorse and raged up and down his tent without eating.

Meanwhile, his expedition fought its way slowly through a part of the Persian Empire that refused to accept the decision of Gaugamela. Bactria and Sogdiana were rich territories, fertile and mostly well watered. Alexander saw the northern part of modern Iran, northern Afghanistan, and the southern part of the Soviet republics of Turkmen, Uzbek, and Tadzhik. Much of the years 329 and 328 was spent in fighting in this region.

By now he was regularly using Asiatics in his army. This move was in accord with his political strategy of co-operation between the Greeks and the local peoples, although he also needed even more men than his steady reinforcements from home could supply, for many were lost in the fighting and many were needed for garrisons, new cities, and military colonies. For political reasons, too, he married a beautiful Bactrian girl named Roxane. Rather than the *poleis* of the Greek type that he had founded in the more pacific parts of the Persian realm, he founded military colonies in this region. They were composed of men still capable of active fighting. Although they had fortified centers and land enough to support the men, they did not have the complete civil and religious organization of the *poleis*.

India

Alexander apparently believed that India, just beyond the Indus River, was on the edge of the eastern ocean and that he could complete his conquest of that part of the world by going only a little farther. In 326 he reached the Indus. There he was greeted by Taxiles, the king of a large region thereabout, with whom he made a treaty of peace and alliance. Then he marched still farther eastward to the Hydaspes River, on the other side of which was the rich kingdom ruled by Porus. Against Porus, Alexander fought what proved to be the most difficult of all his battles, especially because of the enemy's use of elephants. He left both Taxiles and Porus in charge of their respective kingdoms, demanding only a nominal acknowledgment of his suzerainty.

The troops marched another hundred miles to another river, and then their patience came to an end. They had willingly followed Alexander through incredible difficulties and over incredible distances, not troubling themselves overmuch about those considerations that had made their officers uneasy. Now they were shaken by their battle with Porus and by the thought that there might be more elephants to meet. Beside, the land of India seemed to stretch out indefinitely. They refused to go farther.

Alexander was bitterly disappointed. He had counted on reaching the eastern ocean and having a fleet built by the shipwrights he had brought with him, so that the army could go back by water. He planned to build ports on the shore of that far sea for trade with Persia and with Greece. He shut himself up in his tent and sulked a monumental sulk like that of Achilles, but the men had already walked 11,000 miles and they did not care whether the ocean was to be seen from the next hilltop. Alexander gave in.

Back to Babylon

Back at the Hydaspes River, on the edge of Porus' kingdom, Alexander had a fleet of ships built. Late in the year 326, the army started down along the banks of the river, while many men and the supplies traveled in the ships on the river. In the summer of 325, they reached its mouth, where Alexander founded a city as part of the system of trade. Then the fleet set out to go up the Persian Gulf, while the army marched along the shore. In the spring of 324, Alexander was at Susa.

On his return, he found that a number of his friends had betrayed his confidence by flagrant misbehavior in their official posts. They were put to death. He abolished the Persian coinage and decreed that all his empire should follow the Attic system of coinage. He married one of the daughters of Darius and persuaded eighty of his officers to marry noble Median and Persian women. Many of the common soldiers had already contracted marriages with native women. Furthermore, Alexander had earlier ordered that a group of 30,000 native youths should learn Greek and be trained in the Macedonian fashion for military service; they were now enrolled in the army.

When he proposed to send home 10,000 veterans, all his old soldiers mutinied. Alexander discharged them all, saying that he would use a Persian army if he was to be abandoned far from home by his Macedonians. A great reconciliation scene followed. He then organized a huge banquet both for his officers and for leading men of every sort from the new empire. Nine thousand persons took part in a libation, or ceremony of pouring out a little wine in honor of the gods before drinking. All had drawn their wine from a huge mixing bowl, and Alexander prayed that he might unite them all as if he had mixed all their lives like the wine. This action of Alexander's is generally taken to be the first expression of the idea of the brotherhood of man, an idea which has made only modest and irregular progress in the years since.

In 323, Alexander went to Babylon and settled down to hard work on his many plans for his empire, but he was not to be able to watch over the empire and try to govern it in accordance with his own ideas or even try to work for their general acceptance. He died of a fever in June, 323 B.C.

On his deathbed, he would say only that he left his empire to the best man. His legal heirs were his feeble-minded half-brother and his posthumous son by Roxane, both of whom were brushed aside in the struggle for the succession and, after a short time, murdered.

For forty years after Alexander's death, the strong men struggled over the control of the lands of the eastern Mediterranean. By 280 B.C., three great kingdoms were firmly established: that founded by Antigonus in Macedonia, that founded by Seleucus in Asia, and that founded by Ptolemy in Egypt. The balance of power among the three was such that they endured without great changes of territory until they all were conquered by the Romans in the second and first centuries before Christ. The process was completed when in 30 B.C. the Roman Octavian, soon to be known as Caesar Augustus, captured Cleopatra, Queen of Egypt, a descendant of Ptolemy, and took her kingdom. Thus, the history of the eastern Mediterranean lands after 323 B.C. may appropriately be related in connection with the history of the Roman Republic.

BIBLIOGRAPHY

This bibliography is not intended to be in any sense complete or even well balanced. The books have been chosen because they should be interesting and useful to the ordinary reader and are likely to be readily available either in the library or the bookshop. The less expensive editions, generally paperbacks, are marked with an asterisk (*). It is regrettable that there are not several books of the sort chosen here to be cited for every chapter. The reader who wishes to go more deeply into some point will find specialized and more technical bibliographies in many of the books listed here.

I GENERAL WORKS

The Cambridge Ancient History. 12 vols. Cambridge, Cambridge University Press, 1923–39.
  The best ancient history. In 1961 separate fascicles began to appear of a new edition of the first two volumes, which depend largely on archaeology and have partly become obsolete because of the advance of archaeological knowledge.

McDermott, W. C., and Caldwell, W. E. *Readings in the History of the Ancient World.* New York, Holt, Rinehart and Winston, 1951.

The Oxford Classical Dictionary. Oxford, Oxford University Press, 1949. Has informative short articles.

Van der Hayden, A. A. M., and Scullard, H. H. *Atlas of the Classical World.* London, Nelson, 1960.
  An unusually interesting and informative text accompanies the many maps and charts.
The reader interested in archaeology will find many interesting articles in two popular journals of archaeology, *Antiquity* and *Archaeology*. Technical reports of recent discoveries appear in *The American Journal of Archaeology*.

II THE NEAR EAST AND EGYPT

Albright, William F. *The Archaeology of Palestine.** Penguin Books.
  A scholarly and interesting account, especially of the basis of dating events in Palestine by archaeology.

———. *From the Stone Age to Christianity,** Garden City, Doubleday, 1957.

Aldred, Cyril. *The Egyptians.* New York, Praeger, 1961.
  A general account for the reading public.

Bevan, E. R., and Singer, Charles. *The Legacy of Israel*. New York, Oxford, 1929.
A collection of essays by different hands covering several aspects of the legacy of ancient Israel to the modern world.

Bibby, Geoffrey. *Four Thousand Years Ago*. New York, Knopf, 1962.
An imaginative reconstruction of the life of man in the second millennium before Christ. It is especially interesting and useful because it attempts to show what life may have been like in such places as China, Scandinavia, and southern Africa on the basis of the archaeological evidence.

―――. *The Testament of the Spade*. New York, Knopf, 1956.
A sound and interesting account of the great men and the methods of the rise of archaeology in the nineteenth century written by a good practicing archaeologist.

Ceram, C. W. *Gods, Graves, and Scholars*. New York, Knopf, 1951.
A popular account of the great archaeological discoveries.

Chiera, Edward. *They Wrote on Clay*.* Chicago, University of Chicago Press, 1938.
An interesting and authoritative account of the method of writing on clay tablets and the things that were written.

Childe, V. Gordon. *Man Makes Himself*.* Mentor Books.
One of the best accounts of very early man.

Cottrell, Leonard. *Lost Cities*. New York, Rinehart, 1957.
An account of some of the great archaeological discoveries.

Edwards, I. E. S. *The Pyramids of Egypt*.* Penguin Books.
An interesting description of lesser-known pyramids as well as the greater ones.

Finegan, Jack. *Light from the Ancient Past*. Princeton, Princeton University Press, 1959.
Probably the most useful single book for the comprehension of the archaeological basis of the history of the Near East and Egypt.

Forbes, Robert J. *Man, the Maker: A History of Technology and Engineering*. New York, Abelard Schuman, 1958.

Frankfort, Henri. *The Art and Architecture of the Ancient Orient*. Penguin Books.
Authoritative and beautifully illustrated.

―――. *Before Philosophy*.* Penguin Books.
A stimulating discussion of early thought and belief (entitled in the original edition *The Intellectual Adventure of Ancient Man*).

Frazer, James G. *The Golden Bough*.* Edited by Theodore Gaster. Doubleday Anchor Books.
A classic of anthropology condensed and modernized by a deep and lively scholar.

Glanville, S. R. K. (ed.). *The Legacy of Egypt.* Oxford, Clarendon, 1942.
A collection of informative essays by different scholars.

Gordon, Cyrus. *Before the Bible.* Evanston and London, Harper and Row, 1963.
Careful and detailed description of the early period in the Near East by a scholar working in the field.

———. *Hammurapi's Code.** New York, Holt, Rinehart, and Winston, 1960.
A brief, interesting, and sound description of the code.

Gurney, O. R. *The Hittites.** Penguin Books.
A thorough account of the Hittites.

Hayes, William C. *The Scepter of Egypt.* 2 vols. New York, Harper and the Metropolitan Museum, 1953, 1959.
The most useful single work on Egypt. The scholarly and interesting account of Egypt is connected with the great collection in the Metropolitan Museum by many illustrations and references to them in the text.

Kees, Hermann. *Ancient Egypt: A Cultural Topography.* Edited by T. G. H. James. Chicago, University of Chicago Press, 1961.
A great deal of significant and interesting information about Egypt is given in connection with various places in Egypt.

Kramer, Samuel N. *History Begins at Sumer.** Doubleday Anchor Books.

———. *The Sumerians: Their History, Culture, and Character.* Chicago, University of Chicago Press, 1963.
The first of Kramer's books is popular in tone, giving an interesting and informative list of "firsts" to be credited to the Sumerians. The second book is a serious and thorough treatment of Sumerian civilization.

Moscati, Sabatino. *Ancient Semitic Civilizations.** New York, G. P. Putnam's Sons (Capricorn Books), 1960.
An interesting discussion of the chief Semitic peoples of antiquity, including the Arabs and Ethiopians.

Oesterley, W. O. E., and Robinson, T. H. *A History of Israel.* 2 vols. Oxford, Clarendon, 1932.
Detailed and sober.

Olmstead, Albert T. *History of Assyria.* New York, Scribner, 1923.

———. *History of the Persian Empire.** Chicago, University of Chicago Press, 1948.
These books are useful and interesting and are based on a scholarly knowledge of the original source materials.

Orlinksy, Harry. *Ancient Israel.* Ithaca, Cornell University Press, 1954.
A concise, interesting, and scholarly account of ancient Israel.

Pritchard, James B. (ed.). *Ancient Near Eastern Texts Relating to the Old Testament.* Princeton, Princeton University Press, 1950; rev. ed., 1955.
A large collection of documents of all kinds and of great interest, translated by the best scholars.

Rowley, H. H. (ed.). *The Old Testament and Modern Study.** Oxford Paperbacks.
Scholarly discussions of the results of biblical scholarship which will interest the serious reader.

Singer, Charles J. (ed.). *A History of Technology.* 5 vols. Oxford, Clarendon, 1954–58.

Steindorff, Geo., and Seele, K. *When Egypt Ruled the East.* Chicago, University of Chicago Press, 1957.

Wilson, John A. *The Burden of Egypt.* Chicago, University of Chicago Press, 1951.
An unusually interesting and useful book that discusses many problems of Egyptian history and aspects of Egyptian life (available in Phoenix paperback edition under the title *The Culture of Egypt*).*

Woolley, Charles Leonard. *Digging up the Past.* London, Benn, 1954.

———. *Excavations at Ur.* New York, Barnes and Noble, 1955.
Lively reports and discussions by the great excavator of Sumerian sites.

Zeuner, F. E. *Dating the Past.* 4th edition. London, Methuen, 1958.
An authoritative book that contains much of interest for serious readers. Every known method of dating is discussed.

III GREECE

Barker, Ernest (ed.). *The European Inheritance.* Vol. I. Oxford, 1954.
Has summary articles on prehistory and Near Eastern, Greek, and Roman history, interestingly written by able scholars.

———. *Greek Political Theory.* London, Methuen, 1918.
A standard book by a specialist in political thought (republished in paperback, New York, Barnes and Noble, 1960).

Bieber, Margarete, *The History of the Greek and Roman Theater.* Princeton, Princeton University Press, 1960.
The second edition of a standard work.

Blegen, Carl W. *Troy.* 3 vols. Princeton, Princeton University Press, 1950–53.
The detailed report of a great modern excavation.

Bonner, Robert J. *Aspects of Athenian Democracy.* Berkeley, University of California Press, 1933.

Bowra, Cecil M. *The Greek Experience.* Cleveland and New York, The World Publishing Co., 1957.
The reflections on Greece of a distinguished British classicist.

Bulfinch, Thomas. *Mythology of Greece and Rome.** New York, Collier Books, 1962.
This pleasant book has been a favorite for several generations under its original title, *The Age of Fable.*

Burn, Andrew R. *The Lyric Age of Greece.* New York, St Martin's, 1960.
A description of Greece from 700 to 500 B.C. that treats the Greeks all over
the Mediterranean rather than concentrating on a few notable places.

———. *The World of Hesiod.* New York, Dutton, 1937.
The Greek world from 900 to 700 B.C.

Dinsmoor, W. B. *Architecture of Ancient Greece.* London and New York,
Batsford, 1950.

Dodds, E. R. *The Greeks and the Irrational.** Boston, Beacon Press, 1957.
(Originally published by the University of California Press, 1951.)
This book has done great service in explaining one side of the Greek character and in correcting sentimental ideas of the Greeks as disembodied intel-
lects. It is not easy, but repays study.

Ferguson, William S. *Greek Imperialism.* Boston, Houghton Mifflin, 1913.

Finley, Moses (ed.). *Slavery in Classical Antiquity.* Cambridge, Heffer, 1960.
A collection of reprints of scholarly articles on slavery; very useful in correcting long-held and wrong ideas.

———. *The World of Odysseus.* New York, Viking, 1954.
A pleasant but penetrating sociological analysis of the world of Odysseus.

Freeman, Kathleen. *Greek City States.* New York, Norton [n.d.]
An account of what is known about some of the lesser *poleis.*

Fuller, B. A. G. *A History of Philosophy.* 3rd edition. New York, Holt, 1955.
A useful account of Greek philosophy; the author takes great pains to make
Greek philosophy intelligible in modern terms.

Glotz, G. *Ancient Greece at Work.* New York, Knopf, 1926.

———. *The Greek City and Its Institutions.* New York, Knopf, 1930.

Graham, James Walter, *The Palaces of Crete.* Princeton, Princeton University
Press, 1962.
An analysis of minor as well as major palaces, with many interesting side-
lights on ancient Crete.

Guthrie, W. K. C. *The Greek Philosophers: From Thales to Aristotle.* London,
Methuen, 1950.

Hammond, Nicholas G. L. *A History of Greece to 322 B.C.* Oxford, Clarendon,
1959.

Harsh, Philip W. *A Handbook of Classical Drama.* Palo Alto, Stanford University Press, 1944.
Full of detailed information of every sort about Greek and Roman drama.

Huxley, G. L. *Early Sparta.* Cambridge, Harvard University Press, 1962.
A good discussion of the puzzling problems of the history of Sparta.

Janson, Horst W. *Key Monuments of the History of Art.* New York, Prentice-
Hall, 1959.

————. *The Picture History of Painting.* New York, Abrams, 1957.

Jones, Arnold H. M. *Athenian Democracy.* Oxford, Blackwell, 1957.
Practical and informative essays on Athenian life and government.

Lawrence, A. W. *Greek Architecture.* Penguin Books.

Livingstone, R. W. *The Legacy of Greece.* Oxford, Clarendon, 1924.
Useful and interesting essays on many aspects of Greek life.

Lord, Albert B. *The Singer of Tales.* Cambridge, Harvard University Press, 1960.
An account of the modern illiterate bard and his methods, with the application of these investigations to Homeric problems, by the leading scholar in this field.

MacKendrick, Paul. *The Greek Stones Speak.* New York, St Martin's, 1962.
An account of some of the most important archaeological investigations and their meaning in Greek history.

Michell, H. H. *Sparta.* Cambridge, University Press, 1952.
A study of some of the striking features of Spartan life as well as a general description.

Mongait, A. L. *Archaeology in the USSR.** Pelican Books.
Gives an interesting account of the investigations of Russian scholars into the archaeology of the very early and the mediaeval periods of their country as well as that of the Greek and Roman periods.

Mylonas, G. E. *Ancient Mycenae.* Princeton, Princeton University Press, 1957.

Neugebauer, O. *The Exact Sciences in Antiquity.* Providence, Brown University Press, 1957.
A difficult but stimulating study of some aspects of very early science.

Parke, H. W. *Greek Mercenary Soldiers.* Oxford, Clarendon, 1933.

————, and Wormell, D. E. W. *The Delphic Oracle.* Oxford, Blackwell, 1956.
A detailed scholarly study.

Pendlebury, J. D. S. *The Archaeology of Crete.* London, Methuen, 1939.

Richter, Gisela, M. A. *The Sculpture and Sculptors of the Greeks.* New Haven, Yale University Press, 1929.

Robertson, D. S. *Greek and Roman Architecture.* New York, Cambridge University Press, 1945.

Rose, H. J. *Handbook of Greek Literature.** Everyman Library.

Seltman, Charles. *Approach to Greek Art.** New York, Dutton, 1960.
Fresh and stimulating.

————. *Greek Coins.* London, Methuen, 1933.

Snell, Bruno. *The Discovery of the Mind.** New York, Harper, 1960.
A study of the growth of self-consciousness among the Greeks; very modern
in the questions it asks and the techniques it uses to answer them.

Starr, Chester G. *The Origins of Greek Civilization.* New York, Knopf, 1961.
A useful detailed study of the emergence of the Greeks from their Dark Age.

Swindler, Mary H. *Ancient Painting.* New Haven, Yale University Press, 1929.

Tarn, W. W. *Alexander the Great.* 2 vols. Cambridge, Cambridge University
Press, 1948.

Wace, A. J. B., and Stubbings, F. A. (eds.). *A Companion to Homer.* New York,
St Martin's, 1962.
Essays by competent scholars on every aspect of the study of Homer.

Woodhead, A. G. *The Greeks in the West.* London, Thames and Hudson, 1962.
A good summary account with interesting illustrations.

Zimmern, Alfred. *The Greek Commonwealth.* 5th edition. Oxford, Clarendon,
1931.
An excellent attempt to make Greek life intelligible in modern terms (with
a new edition in The Modern Library and a paper edition in the Galaxy
Books of the Oxford University Press).

INDEX

GREEKS

PHOENICIANS

GREEK AND PHOENICIA